A Dictionary-Catalog
of Modern British
Composers

**Recent Titles in
the Music Reference Collection**

Library Resources for Singers, Coaches, and Accompanists: An Annotated
Bibliography
Ruthann Boles McTyre

A Bibliographical Guide to Spanish Music for the Violin and Viola, 1900–1997
Laura Klugherz

Anton Rubinstein: An Annotated Catalog of Piano Works and Biography
Larry Sitsky

An Index to African-American Spirituals for the Solo Voice
Kathleen A. Abromeit, compiler

Sinatra: An Annotated Bibliography, 1939–1998
Leonard Mustazza

Opera Singers in Recital, Concert, and Feature Film
Sharon G. Almquist, compiler

Appraisals of Original Wind Music: A Survey and Guide
David Lindsey Clark

Popular Singers of the Twentieth Century: A Bibliography of Biographical Materials
Robert H. Cowden

The Printed Elvis: The Complete Guide to Books about the King
Steven Opdyke

One Handed: A Guide to Piano Music for One Hand
Donald L. Patterson, compiler

Brainard's Biographies of American Musicians
E. Douglas Bomberger, editor

The Mozart-Da Ponte Operas: An Annotated Bibliography
Mary Du Mont

A Dictionary-Catalog of Modern British Composers

A–C

Alan Poulton

Foreword by Vernon Handley

Music Reference Collection, Number 82

Greenwood Press
Westport, Connecticut • London

Library of Congress Cataloging-in-Publication Data

Poulton, Alan J.
 A dictionary-catalog of modern British composers / Alan Poulton ; foreword by
Vernon Handley.
  p. cm.—(Music reference collection, ISSN 0736–7740 ; no. 82)
  Includes bibliographical references and indexes.
  ISBN 0–313–31623–6 (set : alk. paper)—ISBN 0–313–28711–2 (v. 1 : alk. paper)
  —ISBN 0–313–28712–0 (v. 2 : alk. paper)—ISBN 0–313–28713–9 (v. 3 : alk. paper)
  1. Composers—Great Britain—Bibliography. I. Title. II. Series.
ML120.G7P68 2000
016.78′092′241—dc21   00–026439

British Library Cataloguing in Publication Data is available.

Library of Congress Catalog Card Number: 00–026439
ISBN: 0–313–31623–6 (set)
ISBN: 0–313–28711–2 (v. 1)
ISBN: 0–313–28712–0 (v. 2)
ISBN: 0–313–28713–9 (v. 3)
ISSN: 0736–7740

First published in 2000

Greenwood Press, 88 Post Road West, Westport, CT 06881
An imprint of Greenwood Publishing Group, Inc.
www.greenwood.com

Printed in the United States of America

The paper used in this book complies with the
Permanent Paper Standard issued by the National
Information Standards Organization (Z39.48–1984).

10 9 8 7 6 5 4 3 2 1

Copyright Acknowledgements

The editor and publisher gratefully acknowledge permission for use of the following material:

Hugo Cole, *Malcolm Arnold: An Introduction to His Music*. London: Faber Music, 1989. Reprinted by permission of the publisher.

Peter Dickinson, *The Music of Lennox Berkeley*. London: Thames Publishing, 1989. Reprinted by permission of Thames Publishing.

Arthur Bliss, *As I Remember*. London: Faber, 1970; rev. ed.: Thames Publishing, 1991. Reprinted by permission of Thames Publishing.

Lewis Foreman, *Arthur Bliss: Catalogue of the Complete Works*. Sevenoaks: Novello, 1980; supplement: 1982. Reprinted by permission of the author.

John Evans, Philip Reed and Paul Wilson, *A Britten Source Book*. Aldeburgh: The Britten-Pears Library, 1987. Reprinted by permission of the Britten-Pears Library.

For Mary Rose, Stephen, Michael, Julian and David

Contents

x   Contents

Foreword

A well-known foreign conductor was recording a great classical symphony with a British orchestra in London. The sessions (preceded by generous rehearsal times and three public concerts) were going badly. The conductor berated the orchestra, the producer and the engineer. The atmosphere was leaden. Towards the end of the sessions the maestro realised that he was to blame and tried to make amends by being jolly and pretending to show interest in his recording team. "What are you doing next?" he asked the engineer. "We're going up to Birmingham to record some Elgar and Vaughan Williams" was his reply. "Fascinating," said the conductor, "Tell me, did either of them write anything that is worth recording?"

This dreadful story is an extreme example of the general attitudes abroad to British music. Whilst acknowledging our excellence as practitioners, people from cultures not a million miles away cheerfully state their ignorance of our composers. In Finland or Australia, it is taken for granted that a good proportion of concert programmes will be native music, much of it commissioned. A Finnish conductor will expect to conduct a fair amount of the music of his own country, and that goes for a German conductor, or a French, or a Russian. A British conductor will expect to conduct the music of all the above countries, and more. Foreigners simply do not know of the existence of a number of British composers.

Alan Poulton's magnum opus seeks to change this situation, especially if the work finds its way, as it should, into every music library in the world. Even for a British musician who plays and advocates the playing of his native music, the book will regularly amaze. For me it contains a powerful reminder that music of the twentieth century is subject to the influence of fashion, and that composers who seemed to be making a considerable impression twenty or thirty years ago are often forgotten today. For chamber musicians, teachers and virtuoso soloists it is a gold mine, for the author's selection of information about each work, where information is available, is enough to invite further investigation.

The period covered is an excitingly rich one in the history of British musical composition. Page after page one is intrigued, and eventually worried by one's own patchy knowledge of the huge output of this country's composers. The timeliness of Alan Poulton's epic endeavour is just. As we struggle through a period when commercialism further narrows the repertoire, his glorious list both humbles and inspires.

Vernon Handley

Introduction

It all started with Bush - Alan that is. In 1979 Ronald Stevenson had suggested a symposium to celebrate the composer's forthcoming eightieth birthday in 1980 and I'd volunteered to provide a complete list of works. Little did I know that my researches for the symposium would be the catalyst for complete chronological listings of over fifty other British composers filling three volumes and amounting to nearly 750,000 words.

But how do you start researching a composer's output about whom you know very little apart from a basic, and often incomplete, work list in **Grove V** or **VI,** and plumbing the depths of the **Gramophone Classical Catalogue** for first recordings? Most publishers tend to list only those works they publish and composers like Alan Bush, and many others of his generation, had a multiplicity of publishers. So the best place is probably with the man (or woman) himself (herself) and the immediate circle of family and close friends.

In Alan Bush's case he was an immensely methodical man with a voluminous library and archive. He had compiled a chronological list of works both with and without opus numbers (not all composers do this and several have assigned the same opus number to two different works to add to the confusion!) and, most helpfully, a series of scrapbooks and folders containing press cuttings, photographs and programmes of significant premieres and other performances, mostly arranged and filed in chronological sequence. Researching Bush was therefore (comparatively) simple and the results of my researches were published as an Appendix to the Bravura Studies symposium for the composer's eightieth birthday entitled **Time Remembered** (Pub. Kidderminster, 1980).

However during several visits to the Bush household in Radlett, Hertfordshire, the British Music Information Centre in London, as well as various festival and orchestral offices, together with a long series of letters and telephone calls to performing artists, it was clear that many other lesser-known British composers were also busily at work during this period. Simultaneously there was the establishment of the Society (Committee) for the Promotion of New Music, the founding of the Cheltenham and Aldeburgh Festivals after the Second World War and a considerable number of British premieres at the Henry Wood Promenade Concerts during this "golden age" of British music-making particularly between 1940 and 1970. Newly emerging composers were making headlines with some regularity across the pages of the British musical press - Searle, Lutyens, Chagrin, Seiber, ApIvor and Daniel Jones as well as more familiar and better documented composers such as Berkeley, Bliss, Howells and Rubbra.

Further Bravura studies followed in which I catalogued the complete works of both Alan Rawsthorne and William Alwyn, the latter in collaboration with Stewart Craggs (whose own researches on British composers, particularly William Walton and

Arthur Bliss, were invaluable and whose encouragement for me to "keep going" has been inspirational). These, as well as a commission from Faber Music to produce a complete catalogue of the music of Malcolm Arnold (London, 1986) reinforced my belief that a Dictionary of Modern British Composers on similar lines to the pioneering Kenneth Thompson **A Dictionary of Twentieth Century Composers (1911-1971)** (Faber & Faber, London, 1973) was long overdue.

I planned that the scope of each composer entry was to provide a complete chronological listing of each work including year of composition (and date of completion where known), dedicatee, commissioning/funding sources, performance information (e.g. duration, instrumentation, publication data), music history (first, first concert, first broadcast, first British, European, American and other regional premieres where available, to include names of performing artists, groups, orchestras, conductors), original manuscript location where known, and a selective bibliography. I also proposed to list concert music separately from documentary and/or feature films as well as from other incidental music (for radio, television and stage), with arrangements and various appendices shown last. An alphabetical title index for each composer would be listed separately at the end of each volume and an addendum covering any amendments, corrections or additions to all three volumes would be printed at the conclusion of the third volume.

I started out with the intention of covering composers whose birth dates were within the period 1893 to 1923, i.e. from Arthur Benjamin to Don Banks, and for the work to be published in 1993. Sufficient progress was made in the decade between 1982 and 1991 to approach various publishers with a proposal for a three-volume Dictionary arranged chronologically. In the Spring of 1992 Greenwood Press agreed to proceed, with the proviso that the catalogue of works of each composer should be supplemented by a list of first/significant recordings. As a consequence of fulfilling this requirement and the addition of a further twenty-four composers (extending the period now covered from 1891 to 1923 and arranged alphabetically) the final draft was not completed until December 1998. Several of the "younger" composers included in the short list of fifty-four are still actively composing to this day (November 1999) - among them are Richard Arnell, John Gardner, Iain Hamilton and Ian Parrott, and I have continued to update theirs and the other individual catalogues as more works are announced (or discovered) and/or have been given first performances either in the concert hall or broadcasting studios.

Finally the Dictionary should be regarded as a living document, potentially ever-changing in the scope and refinement of its knowledge base. Enthusiasts of British music are encouraged to assist the compiler and publishers in "filling the gaps" so that coverage can be even more comprehensive in the future. However, there comes a time when the author must cry "Enough - no more" and lay down his pen with a heartfelt sigh and consign the "unfinished" work to the publisher, with a debt of gratitude to the many who have contributed their particular piece of this fascinatingly complex, if frustratingly uneven, musical collage.

Alan Poulton
Guildford, November 1999

Acknowledgements: Personal Notes about the Composers

1. **JOHN ADDISON (1920-1998)**
   Having taken several years to track him down in America, I was delighted to receive a list of works, including comprehensive coverage of his considerable film and television scores which form the bulk of his entry. I was later able to telephone him when he made occasional visits to the UK when he would expand on his later compositions. In December 1998 while proofreading the catalogue of his works, I received the sad news of his death at his home in Vermont.

2. **WILLIAM ALWYN (1905-1985)**
   The chronological listing is based on the catalogue of works co-authored by Stewart Craggs and myself in 1984 (Bravura Publications) with additional material provided by Anne Surfling of the William Alwyn Foundation who hold many of the original manuscripts.

3. **DENIS APIVOR (1916 -)**
   I first contacted the composer to write an essay on Alan Rawsthorne for a three volume symposium I was planning (Bravura Publications, Kidderminster, 1984). Later he sent me a comprehensive list of works with opus numbers and we have regularly corresponded over the last ten to fifteen years with updated information. Further input has also been provided by Alastair Chisholm and David C. F. Wright, and from the list of original manuscripts held by the British Library.

4. **RICHARD ARNELL (1917 -)**
   Several years ago Tony provided me with a basic listing of his works (with opus numbers) including juvenilia/student works. However much of his early American period is still to be documented in full and in later years he has begun a new opus numbering system! (His latest work, a **Symphony for Nelson Mandela**, is in preparation). Thanks also to David C. F. Wright for putting us back in touch after a long absence and to the British Library for their list of Arnell original manuscripts.

5. **MALCOLM ARNOLD (1921 -)**
   I am grateful to Martin Kingsbury of Faber Music for their permission to produce an updated version of my catalogue of works first published by them in 1986 in celebration of the composer's sixty-fifth birthday. I must also acknowledge the kind assistance of both Susan Bamert and Leslie East at Novello, the Royal College of Music Library who sent me details of their Arnold manuscript collection and to Stewart Craggs for information on several recently-unearthed manuscripts, details of which are contained in his bio-bibliography of Malcolm Arnold published by Greenwood Press.

6.   **DON BANKS (1923 - 1980)**
Information on this composer was difficult to come by until I received a letter from Valerie Banks, the composer's widow, enclosing a list of compositions. My thanks are also due to Vicki Jones (Australian Music Centre) for performance and bibliographical details, to Prue Neidorf (National Library of Australia, Canberra) for details of their manuscript holdings, and, in particular to Sheila O'Connor of the Australian High Commission in London who put us all in touch.

7.   **STANLEY BATE (1911 - 1959)**
The majority of this catalogue is based on the researches and input of two Bate enthusiasts - Tony Hodges (Royal Northern College of Music Library) and Michael Barlow. Their efforts to bring alive this "shadowy" figure in British music is gratefully acknowledged.

8.   **ARTHUR BENJAMIN (1893 - 1960)**
Despite several failed attempts in the early eighties to track down the composer's friend Jack Henderson, I've still been able to compile a reasonably detailed list of works from a multitude of sources, most notably from fellow Benjamin devotee, Rob Barnett of the British Music Society. Thanks also to the British Library for supplying a list of the original manuscripts held by them.

9.   **LENNOX BERKELEY (1903 - 1989)**
Stewart Craggs and I had planned a complete Berkeley catalogue as long ago as 1980 and I recall visiting the composer to talk about our plans. Since then Peter Dickinson's book has been published by Thames (London, 1988) and this, together with the Chester/Berkeley catalogue of works has formed the basis for my own chronological listing. My thanks to John Bishop at Thames Publishing for permission to do so. Additional information has been kindly provided by Stewart Craggs, Peter Dickinson, Christopher Headington, Joan Redding and Rosamunde Strode. I am also grateful to the staff at Chester Music over the years - among them Robin Boyle, Rosemary Johnson, Sheila MacCrindle, Rhiannon Mathias and Jane Williams. Thanks also to Chris Banks at the British Library who sent me the list of original manuscripts placed on loan by Lady Berkeley in September 1990.

10.   **ARTHUR BLISS (1891 - 1975)**
The basis for this dictionary entry is the excellent catalogue of works compiled by Kenneth Thompson and published in the **Musical Times** in August 1966 (rev. August 1971). Additions and amendments to the original Thompson catalogue have been generously provided by Stewart Craggs, Giles Easterbrook and Lewis Foreman. Thanks are also due to John Bishop at Thames Publishing for permission to use data from their (revised) Bliss autobiography **As I Remember** (London, 1989) and to Richard Andrewes of Cambridge University Library for sending me a list of their Bliss Archive Collection with the kind permission of the syndics of the University.

11.   **BENJAMIN BRITTEN (1913 - 1976)**
It was only a few weeks before the final draft of this, the largest entry in the Dictionary, was completed that I learned of the plans of The Britten-Pears Library to produce their own comprehensive list of published works (**A Catalogue of the Published Works** ed. Paul Banks, Pub. Aldeburgh, 1999). This would effectively update the joint Boosey & Hawkes/Faber Music catalogue of 1973 (rev. 1978) as well as other lists compiled by, among others, Eric Walter White, Michael Kennedy, Peter Evans, Donald Mitchell and Hans Keller, all of which I had used as a basis for my Dictionary entry. Following discussions with Paul Banks and

Jenny Doctor, it was clear that my chronological listing would be a complementary study to their own and I am therefore most grateful to The Britten-Pears Library for permission to use material from their 1999 catalogue and to draw on material concerning the incidental music and recordings contained in their **Britten Source Book** (Pub. Aldeburgh, 1987). Much detailed information on first performances has been supplied by Philip Reed, Paul Banks, Pam Wheeler, Paul Wilson, Anne Surfling, Judith le Grove and Elizabeth Gibson and, in particular, Jenny Doctor. Thanks also to David Allenby of Boosey & Hawkes and to Tim Brooke of Faber Music in providing additional information and filling gaps in this highly complex catalogue of works.

12. **ALAN BUSH (1900 - 1995)**
     This entry is a re-formatted version of the list of works provided as an appendix to **Time Remembered**, an eightieth birthday symposium edited by Ronald Stevenson and published by Bravura in 1980. My thanks are also due to Chris Banks at the British Library for details of their manuscript holdings which has enabled me to update much of the original information, including the later opus numbers.

13. **GEOFFREY BUSH (1920 - 1998)**
     In compiling this Dictionary entry the composer and I had corresponded for several years and we updated the listings as more works were written, various first performances took place and new recordings issued. Geoffrey always took a keen interest on how work was progressing on the catalogue, and one of my regrets is that he never lived to see it in print.

14. **FRANCIS CHAGRIN (1905 - 1972)**
     This was one of the first catalogues I completed following several visits to the composer's house in North London where I sampled the hospitality of Nicholas Chagrin and his family to whom I am most grateful. Chagrin's output was enormous - his scores of film and incidental music occupied several feet of floor space both horizontally and vertically (fortunately much of it is now housed at the British Library). Nevertheless he kept a typewritten list of works and a series of notebooks, which assisted enormously in identifying performance and broadcast dates and venues. I must also acknowledge the work of Jonathan Tichler, who compiled an invaluable *Music and Tape Catalogue* in April 1976.

15. **ARNOLD COOKE (1906 -   )**
     I first corresponded with Arnold Cooke when he was living in Kent and, using the Novello brochure as a starting point, sent him a provisional listing to work on. His letters of thanks and and encouragement were much appreciated at that time, and I was later grateful to Julie Earnshaw (the composer's niece), Eric Wetherell (whose British Music Society Monograph, 1996, was most timely) and the Rev. Peter Marr for providing additional information on this composer's output, whose ninetieth birthday was celebrated in 1996.

16. **CHRISTIAN DARNTON (1905 - 1981)**
     I first came across the name of Christian Darnton when I was researching for the Alan Bush symposium during 1979-80. I later made contact with his widow, Vera, who was living in Hove, Sussex, and was to learn from Denis ApIvor that Darnton's considerable manuscript collection was housed at the British Library. It was clear that Darnton should be a further candidate for the Dictionary, and I was fortunate to engage the services of Andrew Plant in Peterborough who has compiled a very detailed chronological catalogue of a composer who was the exact contemporary of Rawsthorne, Lambert and Tippett.

17. **HOWARD FERGUSON (1908 - 1999)**
Compiling a list of Ferguson's compositions was relatively simple - his output is small: his last work for the concert hall is dated 1958, though he celebrated his ninetieth birthday in 1998. I am grateful to Thames Publishing for permission to use their 1989 symposium on the composer (ed. Alan Ridout) as the basis for the Dictionary entry, and to Howard Ferguson himself for his encouraging flurry of postcards over the years. (Sadly, he died in November 1999, a few days after his ninety-first birthday).

18. **GERALD FINZI (1901 - 56)**
I am grateful to Peter Ward-Jones of the Bodleian Library in Oxford for details of their manuscript holdings, to Timothy Day of the National Sound Archive for discographical input, and to Stephen Banfield whose book on Finzi (Faber & Faber, 1997) helped to fill several gaps in my own chronological listing.

19. **BENJAMIN FRANKEL (1906 - 1973)**
I have been corresponding with the composer's stepson, Dimitri Kennaway, for over a decade now and he has been the main provider of much-needed information on the unpublished works, film and television scores and the wealth of new recordings (particularly from CPO) which have emerged in the last few years. I must also acknowledge the help given to me by the British Library (who now hold most of the original manuscripts), the Benjamin Frankel Society, the composer Buxton Orr and the staff at Novello whose brochure on the composer was the starting point for this entry.

20. **PETER RACINE FRICKER (1920 - 1990)**
The composer sent me his own comprehensive list of works only a few months before his death in February 1990. Apart from the addition of various recording and biographical details, the catalogue is published virtually as received from his home in Santa Barbara, California in October 1989.

21. **JOHN GARDNER (1917 -)**
The composer himself has been the main provider of this Dictionary entry. Gardner's methodical approach to assigning opus numbers is a model of consistency and we have exchanged a long series of letters and postcards over the years as his output continues to increase unabated.

22. **ROBERTO GERHARD (1896 - 1970)**
The London Sinfonietta brochure of 1973, which included David Atherton's comprehensive catalogue of works, has formed the basis for this entry, together with discographical information provided by Timothy Day at the National Sound Archive and a list of the manuscript holdings/catalogue of works kindly provided by Richard Andrewes and with the permission of the Syndics of the Cambridge University Library.

23. **RUTH GIPPS (1921 - 1999)**
"Wid" was an exact contemporary of Malcolm Arnold - they both studied at the Royal College of Music in London and I first met her at the Barbican in London in 1983 when she was conducting an early piece of Malcolm's entitled **Larch Trees**. We since corresponded over the years, building up a chronological list of her music now numbering over 100 compositions. As we go to press I was saddened to hear of her death in Eastbourne on 23 Februry 1999 following a stroke.

24. **EUGENE GOOSSENS (1893 - 1962)**
In compiling this list of compositions I must acknowledge the work of Andrew Guyatt whose own Goossens catalogue and discography was the starting point. Later amendments and additions to Andrew's catalogue have been kindly

provided by Pamela Main who also holds many of the original manuscripts and much archive material relating to the composer's American and Australian periods. Thanks also to Carole Rosen, author of **The Goossens: A Musical Century** (Pub. London, André Deutsch, 1993) for permission to use material from her book concerning various performance dates and venues.

25. **PATRICK HADLEY (1899 - 1973)**
Andrew Plant has been largely responsible for seeing this catalogue of works through to publication and I must also acknowledge the assistance of Andrew Bennett of the Pendlebury Library, Cambridge for details of their manuscript holdings. Thanks also to Lewis Foreman of Triad Press for permission to use information from their Walter Todd's study **Patrick Hadley: A Memoir** (Rickmansworth, 1974), to John Bishop of Thames Publishing for similar data from Eric Wetherell's book **Paddy: The Life and Music of Patrick Hadley** (London, 1997). Thanks also to Matthew Mellor and Dr. James Gibson for additional information on Hadley's small but concentrated output.

26. **IAIN HAMILTON (1922 -)**
My thanks to the composer for keeping me updated over the years both on new works/premieres and on new recordings. Thanks also to Robert Hahn of Universal Edition for publishing data and to the National Sound Archive for discographical information.

27. **HERBERT HOWELLS (1892 - 1983)**
I am most grateful both to Paul Andrews for providing much of the information both on Howells's considerable output and on the various locations of the manuscripts and to Thames Publishing for permission to use data from Christopher Palmer's centenary study of the composer (London, 1992). Thanks also to the National Sound Archive whose own published discography of the composer's music was invaluable in enabling me to identify the multiplicity of first recordings.

28. **GORDON JACOB (1895 - 1984)**
Cataloguing one of the most prolific composers with a wide range of publishers would have been almost impossible without the assistance of Margaret Hyatt (Jacob) who provided me with a voluminous series of computer print-outs detailing performances, broadcasts, manuscript dates and such like, as well as hand written notes, all of which provided the basis for this long Dictionary entry. It has been supplemented by additional information from Eric Wetherell's centenary biography of Gordon Jacob (Pub. London, 1995) with the kind permission of Thames Publishing. Thanks also to Tim Reynish at the Royal Northern College of Music who allowed me access to the complete catalogue of Gordon Jacob's wind band music.

29. **DANIEL JONES (1912 - 1993)**
Several years ago the composer sent me a provisional work list plus biographical and recording data which enabled me to build up a chronological listing. Malcolm Binney and Giles Easterbrook were later to add more information to my database but I believe there is much still 'below the surface'.

30. **CONSTANT LAMBERT (1905 - 1951)**
I am grateful to Thames Publishing for permission to use their Richard Shead revised study on the composer (Pub. London, 1973) as the basis for this chronological listing. Also to Isabel Lambert for encouragement to press on with my work: incidentally, it was while visiting her studios in deepest Essex that I came across the original piano score of the **Tiresias** ballet! Thanks also to Sally

Broadhurst and Simon Wright at Oxford University Press for information on publication dates and other manuscript locations.

31.   **WALTER LEIGH (1905 - 1942)**

Having tracked down the original manuscripts to the British Library and made contact with both Andrew Leigh and Veronica (Leigh) Jacobs, I was most grateful to Ken Dance for his kind assistance in providing much needed performance and recording data to supplement my sketchy first draft.

32.   **GEORGE LLOYD (1913 - 1998)**

This was the first composer website I ever visited - and though websites can be constantly refreshed, my long series of correspondence with the composer were always by "Royal Mail". He was not always very forthcoming about early works and there may be buried treasure somewhere. In the meantime I must thank Lewis Foreman for checking through my catalogue of works, Gareth Jones of Albany Records for discographical information and F. M. Ellis of the John Foster Black Dyke Mills Band for some useful performance history.

33.   **ELISABETH LUTYENS (1906 - 1983)**

I was researching Lutyens's considerable output at much the same time as Susie Harries, whose biography of the composer, **A Pilgrim Soul**, was published by Michael Joseph in 1989. As a result we pooled our information (discovering simultaneously the occasional muddled opus numbering system which the composer adopted early on!) and I've continued to update the catalogue with various additions to the discography. Thanks are also due to Glyn Perrin (musical executor of the Lutyens estate), the British Library for sending me their complete list of original manuscripts and to Kim Sommerscheid of Universal Edition for essential publication details.

34.   **ELIZABETH MACONCHY (1907 - 1994)**

Having compiled an initial Maconchy work-list with the assistance of the composer's publisher I was both surprised and delighted to receive a copy of Jenny Doctor's comprehensive catalogue of Maconchy's music which supercedes mine. I am most grateful to her for permission to reproduce her list as the definitive Dictionary entry. (N.B. This list is Jenny Doctor's copyright.)

35.   **E. J. MOERAN (1894 - 1950)**

Geoffrey Self (author of **The Music of E. J. Moeran**, Toccata Press, 1986) kindly provided me with a basic chronological listing. This, together with data from Lionel Hill's personal recollections, **Lonely Waters** (Pub. Thames, 1985) and the early Stephen Wild study (Pub. Triad Press, 1974) enabled me to make a start on compiling data on this somewhat elusive composer. Thanks for permissions from the above publishers and to Rob Barnett and Geoffrey Self for useful discographical information.

36.   **HERBERT MURRILL (1909 - 1952)**

I am most grateful to Michael Barlow who, through his contact with the composer's daughter, Carolyn Evans, generously provided the fruits of his own researches on this composer which form the basis for this Dictionary entry.

37.   **ANDRZEJ PANUFNIK (1914 - 1991)**

The appendix in the composer's autobiography, **Composing Myself** (Pub. Methuen, London, 1987) provided a useful starting point for my researches and I'm grateful to David Higham Associates for permission to extract pertinent information on performance dates and venues to build up the catalogue of works. The data was supplemented by publication details from Boosey & Hawkes, a list of the Panufnik manuscript collection provided by the British Library, and various broadcast details from Alan Hall, Music Producer at the BBC.

38.   **IAN PARROTT (1916 -)**
The composer himself is largely responsible for this Dictionary entry and we have corresponded intermittently over the years to supplement and amend data as new works are composed and performed, expanding our knowledge on this composer's considerable output now approaching 200 works.

39.   **PRIAULX RAINIER (1903 - 1986)**
I was fortunate to be able to make contact with Miss Rainier in the year or so before she died. She was able to furnish me with details of several early works and their performers as well as instrumentation/duration data. Later, through the executor of her estate, Desmond Winfield, I made contact with Herbert van der Spuy of Cape Town University, who generously loaned me a copy of his thesis which included a list of Rainier's music and details of a number of South African premieres.

40.   **ALAN RAWSTHORNE (1905 - 1971)**
This chronological listing is a re-formatted version of the one I compiled as part of the three volume Alan Rawsthorne Symposium (Bravura, Kidderminster, 1984). Further updates, particularly on first recordings and rediscovered works, have been kindly provided by various members of the Alan Rawsthorne Society, namely John McCabe, Anthony Hodges and John Belcher, and from Helen Thompson at OUP, the composer's main publisher.

41.   **FRANZ REIZENSTEIN (1911 - 1968)**
I first made contact with the composer's widow, Margaret, in the early eighties and following several visits and telephone calls to her North London home, she was able to provide me with a complete list of manuscripts (including much interesting juvenilia), Performing Right Society printouts, publisher brochures and other data which has enabled me to produce this reasonably complete chronological catalogue of works.

42.   **EDMUND RUBBRA (1901 - 1986)**
I am grateful to Lewis Foreman of the Triad Press for permission to use information from his pioneering symposium on the composer (Pub. Rickmansworth, 1977) and to Ralph Grover, author of the invaluable Scolar Press/Ashgate book on the composer (Pub. Aldershot, 1993), for much additional information and advice. My starting point for this entry, however, was the Lengnick catalogue of works (Pub. South Croydon, June 1971), the substantial British Library listings of original manuscripts and the comprehensive discography published by the National Sound Archive which enabled me to identify the many first recordings.

43.   **HUMPHREY SEARLE (1915 - 1982)**
I first corresponded with the composer during 1981-82 when I was planning a series of personal reminiscences to be included in the Rawsthorne symposium mentioned earlier. Humphrey Searle kindly provided one of the essays and later, when I presented a copy of the book to his widow, Fiona, I mentioned that I intended to compile a list of his works for inclusion in the Dictionary. Fiona generously loaned me not only the typescript of Humphrey's then unpublished autobiography, but also a complete list of his works. This formed the basis of the entry supplemented by discographical data and additions/amendments provided by two Searle enthusiasts, Howard Davies (the film and incidental music) and David C. F. Wright (the concert works). My thanks also to Arthur Searle

(no relation!) at the British Library for sending me details of their substantial Humphrey Searle manuscript collection.

44.   **MATYAS SEIBER (1905 - 1960)**
I am most grateful to Mrs. Lilla Seiber for her kind hospitality and patience while visiting her Caterham (Surrey) home to read through her husband's notebooks, papers and scrapbooks, which enabled me to build up a well documented catalogue of his considerable output. Thanks once again are due to Arthur Searle at the British Library for sending me a complete listing of their Seiber manuscripts, to Jeremy Hamilton and Hugh Wood for further information and advice, and Paul Andrews for help in identifying some of the early song material.

45.   **ROBERT SIMPSON (1921 - 1998)**
I first contacted Robert and Angela Simpson just as they were moving to Ireland in February 1986. Despite the bad timing I was nevertheless delighted to receive the composer's computer print-out of his music. I was later to supplement this basic data with details of the Simpson manuscripts held at the Royal Holloway College, Egham, Surrey (kindly supplied by Lionel Pike). Thanks also to members of the Robert Simpson Society (Jim Pattison, John Brooks, Brian Duke and Douglas Gordon) and to Martin Anderson, Raymond Clarke and Graham Melville-Mason for other Simpson memories. Finally my thanks to Philip Maund of Rosehill Music for useful performance data.

46.   **BERNARD STEVENS (1916 - 1983)**
Though I had corresponded with the composer during the early eighties, I regretted not having the chance to meet him, particularly as he generously sacrificed time from composition and teaching to write two fine essays (for Bravura Publications) on the choral music of both Alan Rawsthorne and Alan Bush on which subject he was the acknowledged expert. I had wanted to thank him personally but it was not to be - however I was later to meet his widow, Bertha, at a concert in Thaxted church and we began a long series of correspondence during which I built up, with Bertha's help, a reasonably comprehensive catalogue of works, initially based on the Bernard Stevens Trust catalogue and the list of manuscript holdings housed at the British Library. Thanks also to Kahn & Averill for permission to use data from their symposium on the composer (Pub: London, 1989).

47.   **PHYLLIS TATE (1911 - 1987)**
It was Alan Frank who suggested I should include his wife, Phyllis Tate, among my list of fifty composers (he also suggested Peter Warlock and E. J. Moeran!). Following a note in the musical press I was fortunate to receive a letter from Natalie Gray, who had chosen the music of Phyllis Tate as the subject for her thesis at the Colchester Institute of Higher Education. The majority of this entry is therefore the result of her splendid research work, re-formatted to conform to the Dictionary "style". My sincere thanks, therefore, to Miss Gray - also to Sally Broadhurst at OUP for the loan of scores and the provision of other essential publishing data.

48.   **MICHAEL TIPPETT (1905 - 1998)**
The basis for this entry was the catalogue of works in **Tippett: The Composer and his Music**, Ian Kemp (Pub. London, 1984), with the kind permission of Faber & Faber Ltd., together with the many brochures produced by Schott. These, combined with the British Library listings of Tippett manuscripts, both Alan Woolgar's and the National Sound Archive's published discographies, Gordon Theil's bio-bibliography (Greenwood Press) together with further data provided

by Peter Owens and Nicholas Wright, have enabled me to produce a particularly well-documented entry.

49. **WILLIAM WALTON (1902 - 1983)**

The name of Stewart Craggs is now synonymous with this composer, and I'm grateful both to Dr. Craggs and Walton's publishers, OUP, for permission to use his thematic catalogue (Pub. Oxford, 1977, 2nd ed. 1990) as the lynchpin for the chronological listing. My own Bravura discography of Walton's music was published in 1979 and this has provided the basis for details of first recordings. Since then, however, there has been much activity with the Chandos recordings of the complete works and news from OUP of a complete Walton edition, which will add substantially to our knowledge and awareness of this well-documented composer. My thanks also to OUP for permission to quote from Michael Kennedy's book **Portrait of Walton** published in 1989, and to the following OUP staff who have provided much useful publication data - Karen Cooper, Helen Thompson and Valerie Williams.

50. **PETER WARLOCK (1894 - 1930)**

Once again I must thank Andrew Plant for compiling the comprehensive catalogue of works which has been supplemented by Anthony Ingle's discography (with Malcolm Walker's later amendments and additions). Thanks also to the following who assisted in various ways - Judith Barnes (British Library), John Bishop, David Cox, Malcolm Rudland, Neil Somerville (BBC Written Archives) and Fred Tomlinson.

51. **GRACE WILLIAMS (1906 - 1977)**

My thanks to Lengnick/Complete Music Ltd., incorporating the University College Cardiff Press, for permission to use the catalogue of works compiled by Malcolm Boyd in his study of the music of Grace Williams (Cardiff, 1980) as the basis for this entry. Thanks also to A. J. Heward Rees, formerly at the Welsh Music Information Centre, Helen Thompson at OUP and especially to the composer's sister, Marion Glyn Evans, for further details on early works and performances.

52. **PETER WISHART (1921 - 1984)**

The composer's friend and librettist, Don Roberts, has kindly provided much of the data which makes up this well documented entry on a composer who was an exact contemporary of Robert Simpson.

53. **WILLIAM WORDSWORTH (1908 - 1988)**

I first contacted 'Bill' in the early eighties and through a series of correspondences was able to compile a reasonably comprehensive chronological listing, together with further data provided by, among others, John Dodd and Rhona Ritchie.

54. **DAVID WYNNE (1900 - 1983)**

Richard Elfyn Jones's study of the composer (Pub. Cardiff, 1979) formed the basis for my own chronological catalogue and I'm grateful, once again, to Sally Willison at Lengnick/Complete Music Ltd. for permission to do so. Thanks are also due to David C. F. Wright for information and advice on the composer, and to the soprano, Janet Price, for additional performance dates and venues.

Having obtained a basic catalogue of works for each composer, it was then necessary to go about the task of obtaining performance information (e.g. durations, instrumentation and publication data), music history (e.g. performance premieres), first recordings and bibliography. I must now acknowledge the assistance of many publishers and recording companies; festival, orchestral and concert hall administrators; libraries,

colleges and other educational establishments; choral and chamber music groups; as well
as soloists and private individuals who have enabled me to build up a "picture" of each
composer and his (or her) output.

Among these are:

(i) Publishers - Boosey & Hawkes (David Allenby, Robert Cowan, Jane Scherbaum, Felicity Williams); Bosworth (Howard C. Friend); Chester Music (Jane Williams, Catherine Long); Faber Music (Martin Kingsbury, Tim Brooke); Forsyth Bros. (Ian Taylor); Lengnick (Sally Willison); OUP (Helen Leiper, Helen Thompson); Peters Ed. (Maria Johnson); Roberton (Kenneth Roberton); Schott (Sally Groves); Stainer & Bell (Antony Kearns); Studio Music (Sandra Williams); UMP (Jane Williams); Warner Chappell (Caroline Underwood); Weinberger (Sean Gray) and Yorke Ed. (Rodney Slatford).

(ii) Record companies - Chandos (Dawn Ovens, Steven John); Collins Classics (Kate Jones); Hyperion (Celia Ballantyne, Richard Howard); Lyrita (Richard Itter); Meridian (John Shuttleworth); Phoenix (Robert Matthew Walker); Redcliffe (Francis Routh) and Unicorn Kanchana (Jane Ward).

(iii) Festival and Concert Hall Administrators - Bromsgrove Festival (C. V. Darley); Cheltenham Festival (Kim Sargeant, Jeremy Tyndall); Lichfield Festival (Paul Spicer); The Old Vic (Karen Taylor); Royal Opera House, Covent Garden (Francesca Franchi); Stroud Festival (Maurice Broadbent); Wigmore Hall (Robert Richardson) and Youth and Music (Alan Fluck).

(iv) Orchestral/Band Administrators - BBC Philharmonic Orchestra (Roger Turner); BBC Scottish Symphony Orchestra (Christopher Dale); BBC Symphony Orchestra (Ruth Potter); Bournemouth Symphony Orchestra (Marion Aston); City of Birmingham Symphony Orchestra (Beresford King-Smith); English Chamber Orchestra (Tony Woodhouse); Guildford Philharmonic Orchestra (Kathleen Atkins); London Sinfonietta (Ann Richards) and the National Youth Brass Band of Scotland (E. J. B. Catto).

(v) Libraries/Societies/Educational Establishments - BBC Music Library (Hilary Dodds, Kathy Hill, Michael White); BBC Television Library (Martin Cotton); Bristol University Theatre Collection (Christopher Robinson); British Library (Arthur Searle, Chris Banks); British Music Information Centre (Roger Wright, Tom Morgan, Matthew Greenall); British Music Society (Rob Barnett, Brian B. Daubney, John Talbot); Britten-Pears Library (Philip Reed, Jenny Doctor, Pam Wheeler, Paul Wilson); British Film Institute (Pat Perilli); Dean Close School, Cheltenham (C. G. Sherratt); National Sound Archive (Timothy Day); Performing Right Society (Lesley Bray); Royal Northern College of Music (Anthony Hodges, Timothy Reynish); Shakespeare Birthday Trust (Marion Pringle); Welsh Music Information Centre (A. J. Heward Rees).

(vi) Individuals - Richard Adeney, John Amis, Lady Evelyn Barbirolli, John Bishop, Nicholas Braithwaite, David Brown, Michael Bryant, Michael Bush, Toni Calam, Stewart Craggs, David Cummings, Eiluned Davies, Howard Davies, Anthony Day, Richard Deering, Peter Dickinson, Georgina Dobrée, Jack Doherty, Carl Dolmetsch, John Fisher, Dr. Watson Forbes, Lewis Foreman, Virginia Fortescue, Hannah Francis, Sarah Francis, Margaret Good, Don Goodsell, Michael Graubart, Sidney Griller, Andrew Guyatt, Alan Hacker, Sir Edward Heath, Lionel Hill, Paul Hindmarsh, Annetta Hoffnung, Kathleen Isaac, Philip Jones, Iris Lemare, Stephen Lloyd, Ann Macnaghten, Philip Maher, Diana McVeagh, Gareth Morris, Gillian Newson, William Pleeth, Robert Ponsonby, Janet Price, James Reid-Baxter,

Catherine Roma, Lyndon Rust, Peggie Sampson, Jorgen Schaarwächter, Phyllis Sellick, Robert Sherlaw-Johnson, Tricia Staple, Kathryn Stott, John Turner, Ian Wallace, William Waterhouse, Sir David Willcocks and David C. F. Wright.

I also owe a debt of gratitude both to George Hall and the staff at the BBC's Music Presentation Department who provided much detailed information on first broadcast performances and other vital data, as well as to Malcolm Walker, the former editor of **Gramophone** who kindly checked and advised on the accuracy of many first recordings. Thanks also to Alastair Mitchell for allowing me to see an advance proof copy of his pioneering **A Chronicle of First Musical Performances Broadcast in the United Kingdom (1923-1996)** to be published by Ashgate (Aldershot).

Finally, three further acknowledgements. First, my thanks to Pat Curren, who word -processed this entire work, hampered both by my appalling handwriting and the jealous attention of her two cats, Porgy and Bess. Secondly to my editorial team at Greenwood Press over the last nine years, namely Marilyn Brownstein, Alicia Merrett and, latterly, Pamela St. Clair and Frank Saunders who have seen the work through to its conclusion - my thanks to them for their patience and stamina in overcoming what seemed to be insurmountable problems and challenges. Lastly my sincere thanks and good wishes to Vernon (Tod) Handley, a conductor of international renown and a staunch advocate of the British musical tradition, whose encouraging prefatory essay to these three volumes has been much appreciated.

Composer Productivity:
An Analytical Approach

Having compiled a complete set of chronological listings of fifty-four British composers it was then a relatively simple task to calculate not only the productivity of each composer by decade (Table 1) but also to analyse their total output by genre (Tables 2 and 3) and to summarise the number of first performances at the principal music festivals/concert series (Table 4 and Appendix).

In the case of composer productivity one can calculate their Total Compositional Duration (TCD) as a figure expressed in minutes. In the case of John Addison, for instance, he composed a total of 169 individual works (N.B. the number of compositions is shown in a **bold** font style) lasting 2432 minutes (his TCD). By further analysing the output in each decade of a composer's total creative life one can also build up a picture of the peaks and troughs of his output. Compare, for instance, William Alwyn's output between the ages of 31 and 40 (154 works with a total duration of 1689 minutes) with the 9 works (duration: 246 minutes) composed between the ages of 61 and 70 .

In calculating the final TCD some averaging of the incidental and film music has been necessary; a timing of 10 minutes has been applied throughout this analysis for each piece of incidental music and 20 minutes for each film, whether documentary or feature. N.B. Arrangements are included as part of the TCD for each composer but unfinished/missing works are not; the latter, however, are referenced in the genre tables.

A word of explanation on the definitions of genre in Table 2. Concert music includes all orchestral symphonies, concertos, overtures and occasional pieces.Theatre music is defined as opera, ballet and music-theatre pieces but does not include incidental music for the stage which is shown in a separate column. Choral and vocal music includes both accompanied or unaccompanied works. Keyboard also includes organ, harpsichord and clavichord works.

Table 3 expands some of the genre into subsections. Thus, some of the Concert works are divided into symphonies and concertos and Theatre works are divided into opera and ballet. Oratorio is defined as a major choral work with orchestral/chamber ensemble accompaniment. Song cycles with any acompanying forces are included if a minimum of eight songs are set. Piano sonatinas are not included in the Piano Sonata subsection. Incomplete works are shown with an *, withdrawn works with a **(w)**, missing works with an **(m)** and destroyed works with a **(d)**.

Festival/concert series first performances in Tables 4 and 5 include world premieres as well as various regional first performances (e.g. British, American and so on).

It is now possible to establish the ten most productive British composers (within the time span of this Dictionary) and to compare their TCDs with those of past masters such as Beethoven, Wagner, Tchaikovsky and Bartok, the results of which are set out below. The "past masters" TCDs have been drawn from an earlier survey of composer productivity published in *Classical Music* magazine on 29 April 1978.

Pos.	Composer	TCD
-- 1.	BEETHOVEN	7200
1. 2.	**BRITTEN**	6493
2. 3.	**ALWYN**	5375
3. 4.	**LUTYENS**	5267
-- 5.	VERDI	5220
-- 6.	DVORAK	4740
-- 7.	TCHAIKOVSKY	4560
4. 8.	**ARNOLD**	4348
-- 9.	SCHUMANN	4320
-- 10.	BRAHMS	4260
5. 11.	**JACOB**	4258
-- 12.	STRAUSS (RICHARD)	4020
-- 13.	WAGNER	3660
6. 14.	**HAMILTON**	3546
-- 15.	MENDELSSOHN	3420
7. 16.	**SEARLE**	3082
8. 17.	**ARNELL**	3053
9. 18.	**BUSH (ALAN)**	3021
10.19.	**CHAGRIN**	2934
-- 20.	BARTOK	2880

In summary, Britten's output places him top of the British listings (and a close second to Beethoven) by virtue of the phenomenal number of works composed before the age of 20. Many of the remaining "Top Ten" British composers have been prolific in the field of film and incidental music (e.g.William Alwyn , Elisabeth Lutyens, Malcolm Arnold, Humphrey Searle, Richard Arnell and Francis Chagrin), and this is reflected in some very high outputs in particular decades. The others, Gordon Jacob, Iain Hamilton and Alan Bush, have consistently composed a high output of works over a long composing career in a wide variety of genres.

TABLE 1

Composer	11-20	21-30	31-40	41-50	51-60	61-70	71-80	81-90+	undated	arrs.	Tot./TCD
Addison	- / -	10/142	52/863	39/572	35/445	28/308	5/42	- / -	- / -	(1)/60	169/2432
Alwyn	10/208	45/532	154/1689	96/1513	46/817	9/246	7/225	- / -	- / -	(21)/145	367/5375
Aplvor	2/18	8/164	19/463	14/412	22/537	19/324	18/258	- / -	- / -	(11)/135	102/2311
Arnell	6/50	63/937	40/667	34/463	36/406	21/249	22/221	- / -	- / -	(3)/60	222/3053
Arnold	15/81	81/957	122/1992	58/698	20/315	18/245	- / -	- / -	- / -	(10)/60	314/4348
Banks	- / -	8/120	64/706	43/585	11/130	- / -	- / -	- / -	- / -	- / -	126/1541
Bate	3/200	38/567	46/669	18/349	- / -	- / -	- / -	- / -	4/20	- / -	109/1865
Benjamin	2/27	14/175	13/242	38/410	32/467	12/273	- / -	- / -	6/55	(7)/65	117/1714
Berkeley	- / -	33/287	36/463	40/627	39/528	34/408	22/221	- / -	6/27	- / -	210/2561
Bliss	5/35	25/214	30/326	21/307	21/411	33/463	40/271	12/118	- / -	(9)/128	187/2273
Britten	168/1435	121/1620	35/1230	38/802	22/677	9/115	- / -	- / -	- / -	(59)/624	393/6493
Bush(A)	3/35	19/249	19/288	33/549	27/451	21/557	27/306	30/353	7/23	(70)/210	186/3021
Bush(G)	3/22	25/315	18/293	23/241	11/159	15/259	10/70	- / -	- / -	(16)/163	105/1522
Chagrin	- / -	53/266	93/708	114/1122	70/585	20/193	- / -	- / -	- / -	(7)/60	350/2934
Cooke	3/40	15/222	16/228	22/496	37/468	25/401	21/322	8/83	- / -	- / -	147/2240
Darnton	33/281	41/473	28/317	16/261	- / -	2/45	1/20	- / -	16/115	(2)/30	137/1542
Ferguson	3/18	7/86	5/87	11/122	- / -	- / -	- / -	- / -	- / -	(7)/60	26/373
Finzi	15/65	27/275	8/108	12/151	10/123	- / -	- / -	- / -	- / -	(4)/23	72/742
Frankel	1/3	15/196	43/523	73/1170	29/537	12/303	- / -	- / -	2/6	(1)/3	175/2738
Fricker	- / -	31/355	57/685	41/399	33/330	21/301	- / -	- / -	- / -	(1)/10	183/2080
Gardner	4/38	9/99	37/519	63/624	52/755	37/349	60/465	- / -	- / -	- / -	262/2849
Gerhard	1/10	8/73	14/153	16/459	28/368	46/575	4/94	- / -	- / -	(24)/250	117/1962
Gipps	33/303	29/419	19/210	5/69	3/65	14/145	5/40	- / -	- / -	- / -	108/1251
Goossens	8/98	42/446	23/416	8/140	7/187	5/58	- / -	- / -	2/6	(25)/320	95/1671
Hadley	- / -	21/91	12/104	8/63	14/140	- / -	- / -	- / -	4/12	(60)/633	59/1043
Hamilton	- / -	19/346	35/429	24/527	30/1190	21/616	12/438	- / -	- / -	-	141/3546
Howells	11/121	90/705	83/428	35/402	22/167	21/219	35/278	15/77	11/60	(6)/35	323/2492

TABLE 1 (continued)

Composer	11-20	21-30	31-40	41-50	51-60	61-70	71-80	81-90	undated	arrs	Tot./TCD
Jacob	8/66	41/290	60/444	55/518	55/750	79/761	68/707	83/722	9/43	(42)/623	458/4258
Jones	-/-	7/89	18/464	12/384	16/316	18/284	8/150	1/20	44/695	(5)/62	134/2014
Lambert	11/174	15/254	8/128	3/86	-/-	-/-	-/-	-/-	-/-	(30)/569	37/1211
Leigh	6/33	32/587	31/308	-/-	-/-	-/-	-/-	-/-	15/70	-/-	84/998
Lloyd	4/88	3/288	5/281	4/127	12/295	8/264	13/285	5/105	-/-	-/-	54/1733
Lutyens	1/8	11/142	43/378	121/1291	96/1291	77/1268	53/631	-/-	45/158	(9)/100	447/5267
Maconchy	14/85	30/333	30/268	28/338	34/336	34/526	32/407	1/2	6/42	-/-	209/2337
Moeran	2/6	29/237	34/214	15/222	7/100	-/-	-/-	-/-	2/8	(16)/96	89/883
Murrill	11/118	37/333	16/88	5/32	-/-	-/-	-/-	-/-	26/100	(27)/285	95/956
Panufnik	8/71	12/177	17/217	9/153	12/203	16/264	8/142	-/-	-/-	(3)/30	82/1257
Parrott	9/77	39/347	29/415	36/321	28/183	17/221	19/136	-/-	-/-	(12)/60	177/1760
Rainier	1/10	4/23	8/78	10/107	6/92	9/153	6/108	-/-	-/-	(3)/25	44/596
Rawsthorne	3/15	24/264	43/406	43/618	31/411	13/179	-/-	-/-	-/-	(10)/50	157/1943
Reizenstein	33/193	30/292	15/269	37/553	13/187	-/-	-/-	-/-	-/-	(23)/260	128/1754
Rubbra	7/63	34/188	32/514	22/263	40/446	29/289	20/196	5/34	2/10	(2)/30	191/2033
Searle	20/132	20/247	33/334	83/1018	50/673	17/338	-/-	-/-	9/90	(18)/250	232/3082
Seiber	14/140	22/209	50/488	62/882	47/561	-/-	-/-	-/-	-/-	(64)/500	195/2780
Simpson	-/-	3/66	7/148	6/132	16/468	27/676	1/25	-/-	-/-	(1)/60	60/1575
Stevens	2/20	16/173	29/355	15/200	12/135	8/109	-/-	-/-	3/10	(13)/115	85/1117
Tate	-/-	16/178	20/191	33/416	46/551	28/318	2/60	-/-	4/21	(9)/48	149/1783
Tippett	-/-	18/285	15/274	15/332	17/355	8/291	8/247	6/198	-/-	(6)/240	87/2222
Walton	14/188	12/153	23/366	12/181	29/479	9/36	5/25	-/-	-/-	(7)/85	104/1513
Warlock	21/53	97/411	38/108	-/-	-/-	-/-	-/-	-/-	4/8	(220)/1939	160/2519
Williams	2/13	20/172	9/130	27/296	22/245	15/194	-/-	-/-	8/30	(50)/305	103/1385
Wishart	2/27	18/252	30/505	36/528	18/468	-/-	-/-	-/-	-/-	(11)/200	104/1980
Wordsworth	-/-	10/148	26/494	32/523	27/320	20/253	12/144	-/-	-/-	-/-	127/1882
Wynne	-/-	-/-	2/47	14/229	25/420	30/432	8/239	-/-	8/46	-/-	87/1413

TABLE 2

Composer	Concert	Choral	Vocal	Chamber	Keyboard	Theatre	Film	Incidental	Total
Addison	15	1	2	15	–	1	71	64	169
Alwyn	50	3	13	53	27	5	169	46	367
Apivor	20	11	17	32	11	–	–	–	102
Arnell	50	10	15	62	31	15	29	10	222
Arnold	85	12	6	57	15	8	113	18	314
Banks	12	5	6	28	2	–	52	21	126
Bate	28	–	12	15	28	11	5	10	109
Benjamin	23	14	12	21	18	7	22	–	117
Berkeley	39	43	28	40	33	7	6	14	210
Bliss	39	29	29	40	18	6	9	17	187
Britten	42	68	66	63	67	18	29	40	393
Bush (A)	35	46	11	41	33	10	2	8	186
Bush (G)	20	31	24	9	14	5	1	1	105
Chagrin	66	3	54	40	20	2	125	40	350
Cooke	24	11	17	66	20	3	1	5	147
Darnton	35	3	10	24	42	3	13	7	137
Ferguson	5	3	5	8	3	1	–	1	26
Finzi	13	25	27	4	2	–	–	1	72
Frankel	29	5	7	25	9	2	88	10	175
Fricker	37	20	24	49	36	1	7	9	183
Gardner	29	136	15	35	28	9	2	8	262
Gerhard	18	2	19	19	3	6	11	39	117
Gipps	24	7	13	45	4	2	–	13	108
Goossens	22	2	16	29	14	3	5	4	95
Hadley	5	25	21	3	–	–	–	–	59
Hamilton	37	20	13	37	18	13	2	1	141
Howells	26	149	61	21	63	1	–	2	323

TABLE 2 (continued)

Composer	Concert	Choral	Vocal	Chamber	Keyboard	Theatre	Film	Incidental	Total
Jacob	128	83	48	139	25	4	9	22	458
Jones	58	14	1	28	21	2	-	10	134
Lambert	11	3	2	-	9	7	2	3	37
Leigh	7	2	20	8	8	2	21	16	84
Lloyd	33	6	-	5	7	3	-	-	54
Lutyens	39	39	72	81	29	14	101	72	447
Maconchy	39	43	42	57	15	11	-	2	209
Moeran	14	19	31	11	12	-	-	2	89
Murrill	4	13	25	16	20	4	3	10	95
Panufnik	40	12	6	11	6	1	6	-	82
Parrott	39	25	16	56	31	5	3	2	177
Rainier	8	4	8	15	6	-	3	-	44
Rawsthorne	31	11	25	30	10	1	27	22	157
Reizenstein	13	2	5	45	39	3	10	11	128
Rubbra	26	65	40	33	20	1	-	6	191
Searle	38	13	22	32	15	7	40	65	232
Seiber	18	18	24	34	10	3	52	36	195
Simpson	22	2	-	28	6	-	-	2	60
Stevens	17	16	6	16	25	1	3	1	85
Tate	11	62	30	30	6	10	-	-	149
Tippett	23	18	7	17	9	8	-	5	87
Walton	23	22	6	17	5	4	14	13	104
Warlock	3	28	123	-	3	2	-	1	160
Williams	24	19	30	12	3	3	4	8	103
Wishart	18	24	21	15	12	5	-	9	104
Wordsworth	27	23	19	37	8	1	-	12	127
Wynne	19	15	7	32	12	2	-	-	87

TABLE 3

Composer	Symphony	Concerto	Ballet	Opera	Oratorio	Song Cycle	Str. Quartet	Piano Sonata
Addison	—	5	1	—	—	—	—	—
Alwyn	5	7	1	4	1	5	16	2
Aplvor	5	9	7	4	5	3	3	—
Arnell	6	9	4	11	2	4	9	1
Arnold	9	19	5(+1*)	3(+2*)	4	2	2	1
Banks	—	2	—	—	2	2	1	—
Bate	4	17	8	3	—	3	4	4
Benjamin	1	6	2	5	—	2	2	—
Berkeley	4	12	3	4(+1*)	6	4	3	1
Bliss	1	6	4	2	8	6	4	1
Britten	1(+1*)	10	2(+1*)	16	14	22	8	9(+3m)
Bush(A)	4	7	2	8	2	5	2	3
Bush(G)	2	6	—	5(+1d)	4	13	1	2
Chagrin	2	3	2	—	—	—	—	1
Cooke	6	8	1	2	2	6	5	6
Darnton	3(+1*)	6(+1*)	1	1	2	1	4	2
Ferguson	(1m)	1	1	—	2	—	—	1
Finzi	—	5	—	—	6	9	—	—
Frankel	8(+1*)	3	1	1(+1*)	1	2	5	—
Fricker	5	11	1	—	5	4	3	1
Gardner	3	4	2	6	18	5	3	2(+1m)
Gerhard	5(+1*)	3	5	1	2	5	2	—
Gipps	5	8	2	—	4	—	1	—
Goossens	2	5	1	2(+1*)	1	2	2	—
Hadley	—	—	—	—	6	—	1	—
Hamilton	4	10	1	8	15	6	4	3
Howells	—	6	1	—	10	5	1(+2m)	—

TABLE 3 (continued)

Composer	Symphony	Concerto	Ballet	Opera	Oratorio	Song Cycle	Str.Quartet	Piano Sonata
Jacob	2	30	3	1	10	4	2(+1*)	2
Jones	12	6	–	2	5	1	14	2
Lambert	–	2	7	1	2	1	–	1
Leigh	–	1	–	2	–	–	1	–
Lloyd	12	7	–	3	3	–	–	–
Lutyens	–	5	4	10	8	18	13	(1)
Maconchy	2(+2w)	13	3	8	6	3	13	–
Moeran	1(+1*)	3	–	–	2	5	2	–
Murrill	–	2(+1*)	3	1	–	1	1	–
Panufnik	10(+2d)	6	1	–	4	–	3	(1)
Parrott	5	6	1	4(+1*)	5	3	5	–
Rainier	–	4	–	–	1(+1*)	4	2	–
Rawsthorne	3	9	1	(2*)	5	7	5	4
Reizenstein	(1*)	5	1	2	2	1	1	–
Rubbra	11(+1*)	6	(1*)	1	6	3	4	1
Searle	5(+5*)	6	3	4	4	2	2	1
Seiber	–	4	1	2	4	2	3	–
Simpson	11	4	–	–	–	–	16	1
Stevens	2	4	–	1(+1*)	3	1	2	1
Tate	–	3	–	10	7	8	2	–
Tippett	5	3	2	6	4	5	7	5
Walton	2(+1*)	4	2	2	3	3	2	–
Warlock	–	–	1	(1m)	–	3	–	–
Williams	2	6(+1*)	1(+1m)	1	4	3	–	1
Wishart	2	5(+1*)	–	5	9	6	3(+1*)	1
Wordsworth	8	4	–	1	4	1	6	1
Wynne	3	5	–	2(+1*)	5	5	5	4

TABLE 4

Composer	Pr	Ch	Ald.	M/L	Iscm	Cpnm	Edn	3Ch.	Cdf.	P.L	Dart.	Red	CoL	Swn.	Fnm.	Bth	Eist	Lee
Addison	1	2	—	2	1	—	2	—	—	—	—	—	—	—	1	—	-	—
Alwyn	8	4	4	1	—	—	—	—	—	—	—	—	—	—	1	1	—	—
Apivor	2	1	—	3	—	1	1	—	—	1	—	4	—	—	—	—	—	—
Arnell	1	7	—	—	—	—	1	1	—	—	—	—	—	—	—	1	—	—
Arnold	10	8	3	1	—	8	1	—	1	1	1	—	—	—	2	1	—	—
Banks	1	3	—	—	2	—	1	—	—	—	—	—	—	—	2	—	—	—
Bate	1	1	—	1	1	1	—	—	—	—	—	—	—	—	—	—	—	—
Benjamin	5	4	—	1	—	1	1	—	—	—	—	1	—	—	1	1	—	1
Berkeley	17	10	9	1	3	—	—	2	1	2	1	—	2	—	—	—	—	—
Bliss	12	5	2	1	3	—	2	3	—	—	—	—	—	—	—	—	—	1
Britten	21	3	99	8	6	1	1	—	3	—	1	—	3	—	—	1	—	4
Bush (A)	10	3	—	4	2	—	—	1	—	—	2	—	—	—	—	—	—	—
Bush (G)	2	4	—	—	—	—	—	1	—	—	—	—	—	—	—	—	—	—
Chagrin	1	—	—	—	—	3	1	—	—	—	—	—	—	—	—	—	—	—
Cooke	7	3	1	4	—	—	—	—	3	—	—	—	1	—	—	1	—	—
Darnton	—	—	—	4	1	—	—	—	—	—	—	—	—	—	—	—	—	—
Ferguson	—	—	—	3	—	—	—	3	—	—	—	—	—	—	—	—	—	—
Finzi	2	2	—	11	—	—	—	4	—	—	—	—	—	—	—	—	—	—
Frankel	2	6	—	—	2	2	1	1	2	4	2	3	—	—	—	—	—	—
Fricker	5	14	3	1	2	2	1	1	2	—	1	1	—	—	2	1	—	1
Gardner	2	4	3	—	—	—	1	—	—	—	3	—	—	—	—	—	—	—
Gerhard	10	2	1	3	8	—	1	1	2	1	—	—	—	—	2	—	—	—
Gipps	1	—	—	—	—	—	—	—	—	—	—	—	1	—	—	—	—	—
Goossens	12	—	—	—	—	—	—	1	—	—	—	—	—	—	—	—	—	—
Hadley	3	—	—	—	—	—	—	2	—	—	—	—	—	—	—	—	—	—
Hamilton	13	7	—	—	1	2	6	—	—	2	2	—	—	—	1	1	—	—
Howells	6	1	—	—	—	—	—	7	—	—	—	—	—	—	1	—	—	—

TABLE 4 (continued)

Name	Pr	Ch	Ald	M/L	Iscm	Cpnm	Edn	3Ch	Cdf	P.L	Dart.	Red	CoL	Swn	Fnm	Bth	Eist	Lee
Jacob	11	2	—	3	—	—	—	1	—	—	—	—	—	—	—	—	—	—
Jones	5	2	—	2	—	2	—	—	—	—	—	—	—	8	—	—	3	—
Lambert	7	—	—	—	—	—	—	—	—	—	—	—	—	—	—	—	—	—
Leigh	—	—	—	1	1	—	—	—	—	—	—	—	—	—	—	—	—	—
Lloyd	1	1	—	—	—	—	—	1	—	—	—	2	—	—	—	1	—	—
Lutyens	9	5	—	15	4	2	—	—	—	5	4	—	—	—	—	—	—	—
Mac'chy	8	5	3	18	3	—	—	1	—	3	—	—	1	—	—	1	—	—
Moeran	9	—	—	1	—	—	—	—	—	—	—	—	—	—	—	—	—	—
Murrill	1	—	—	—	—	—	—	—	—	—	—	1	1	—	1	—	—	—
Panufnik	5	—	2	—	2	1	—	—	—	—	—	—	—	—	—	—	—	—
Parrott	—	2	—	—	—	—	—	—	—	—	2	—	—	3	—	—	2	—
Rainier	4	1	5	1	—	—	1	—	2	1	—	4	—	—	—	—	—	—
Rawst'ne	9	8	—	5	3	—	4	—	1	1	—	—	—	—	1	—	—	—
Rei'stein	1	1	—	1	—	1	—	1	—	—	—	—	—	—	—	—	—	—
Rubbra	5	7	3	2	2	—	4	—	2	—	—	—	1	—	1	—	—	—
Searle	4	5	3	—	6	1	—	—	2	—	—	—	—	—	—	1	—	—
Seiber	1	2	1	1	—	—	—	—	1	—	—	—	—	—	—	—	—	—
Simpson	—	6	—	1	—	—	—	—	1	1	—	—	—	—	—	—	—	1
Stevens	1	4	—	2	1	1	—	—	3	—	—	—	—	—	—	—	—	—
Tate	—	4	—	3	—	—	3	—	—	—	—	—	—	—	1	—	—	1
Tippett	10	3	3	1	5	—	3	—	—	—	1	—	—	—	—	3	—	2
Walton	12	—	7	—	—	—	1	—	—	—	—	—	4	1	—	1	—	—
Warlock	1	—	—	—	—	—	—	—	1	—	—	—	—	—	—	—	—	—
Williams	2	1	—	6	—	—	1	—	1	—	—	—	—	2	—	—	2	—
Wishart	—	1	—	1	—	—	—	—	—	—	—	—	—	—	—	—	—	—
Word'th	—	7	—	2	—	—	2	—	—	—	—	—	—	—	—	—	—	—
Wynne	—	1	—	2	—	11	—	—	7	—	—	—	—	1	1	—	4	—
TOTAL	262	162	149	118	59	40	36	31	28	22	20	16	15	15	14	14	11	10

TABLE 5

Alwyn - Norwich (1)

ApIvor - Brighton (2)

Arnell - Wearmouth (1)

Arnold - Bromsgrove (1), King's Lynn (1), Leicester (1), Newcastle (1), St.Pancras (1)

Banks - Adelaide (1), Bromsgrove (2), English Bach (1), Perth (1)

Bate - Eastbourne (1), Guildford (1)

Berkeley - Canterbury (1), Chichester (1), King's Lynn (1), North Wales (1), Norwich (1), Stroud (2), Windsor (1)

Bliss - Bournemouth (2), Cambridge (1), Coventry (1), Norwich (1), Salzburg (1), St.Ives (1)

Britten - Adelaide (4), Amsterdam (2), Berlin (1), Caramoor (3), Chester (1), Coventry (1), Drottningholm (1), Florence (2), Holland (4), Norwich (1), Prague (1), Salzburg (1), Scheveningen (2), Stratford(Can.)(2), Tanglewood (4), Venice (2)

Bush(G) - Brighton (1)

Chagrin - Nottingham (1), St. Pancras (1)

Cooke - Huddersfield (1), Malvern (1)

Ferguson - Belfast (2)

Frankel - St. Ives (1), Stroud (1), York (1)

Fricker - Liverpool (1), Venice (2)

Gardner - Bracknell (1), Chichester (1), Harrogate (1), Leith Hill (1)

Gerhard - Camden (1), Florence (1), Guildford (1)

Gipps - Brighton (1)

Goossens - Berkshire (1), Bournemouth (2), Lucerne (1)

Hadley - Cambridge (3), King's Lynn (2), Norwich (2), St.Bees (1)

Hamilton - Arundel (1), Camden (1)

Howells - Cork (1), Eastbourne (1), Leith Hill (1)

Jacob - Cambridge (1), Eastbourne (1), Harrogate (1), Hastings (1), St.Bees (1), York (2)

Jones - Bromsgrove (1), Fishguard (2), Guildford (1), Llandaff (3), North Wales (1), St.David's (2)

Lambert - Bromsgrove (1)

Lloyd - Beaford (1), Brighton (1), Eastbourne (1), St.Bart's (2)

TABLE 5 (continued)

Lutyens - Berlin (1), Bracknell (2), Camden (1), Exeter (1), Hampstead (1), Harrogate (1), Leicester (1), Malton (1), Spitalfields (1), Tilford Bach (1), Wexford (1), York (3)

Maconchy - Camden (1),Chelmsford (1), Chester (1), Cork (2), Cricklade (1), Dorchester (1), Huddersfield (1), King's Lynn (1), Norwich (1), Southern Cathedrals (1), Thaxted (1)

Moeran - Norwich (2)

Murrill - Malvern (1)

Panufnik - North Wales (1), Warsaw (11)

Parrott - Bromsgrove (3), Harrogate (2), North Wales (2), Tenby (1)

Rawsthorne - Cambridge (1)

Rubbra - Cork (2), Llandaff (1), Malvern (1), Stroud (1), Tilford Bach (2)

Searle - Aspen (3), Berlin (1), Cork (3)

Seiber - Venice (1)

Simpson - Cork (1), Malvern (5), Nottingham (1)

Stevens - Cambridge (1), Tilford Bach (3)

Tate - Ashington (1), Burton (1), Camden (1), Hampstead (5), Newcastle (1), North Wales (1), St.Pancras (1), York (1)

Tippett - Adelaide (3), Aspen (4), Brighton (1), CBC Toronto (5) , King's Lynn (1), La Rochelle (1), Lichfield (1), Perth (4), Royaumont (1), Salzburg (1), St.Ives (1)

Walton - Adelaide (2), Aspen (1), Cork (1), English Bach (3), Perth (1)

Williams - Llandaff (2), North Wales (1), St.David's (1)

Wishart - Birmingham (2)

Wordsworth - Guildford (1)

Wynne - Anglesey (1), Caerphilly (2), Llandaff (1), Lower Machen (1), North Wales (1)

Abbreviations

Dictionary entries - a brief explanation:

(1938) date of composition - this usually means date of completion. Where a work has taken several years to write the span of composition is shown viz. (1936-38). Where a score has an exact date of completion this is shown separately.

[...........] Song/movement titles always shown in square brackets.

Dur: Duration of work shown in minutes (')(') and seconds (")("). This is the <u>average</u> of the various timings given and is generally within +/- 10%. Shorter works may be shown timed to the nearest 15 seconds.

Instr: Chamber music group/ensemble shown in full (capital initial letters). Orchestral scoring is abbreviated e.g. 2/2/2/2 - 4/3/3/1 - timp. perc. hp. str. means 2 flutes, 2 oboes, 2 clarinets, 2 bassoons, 4 horns, 3 trumpets, 3 trombones, 1 tuba, timpani, percussion (number of players shown in brackets) harp and strings (first and second violins, violas, cellos and double basses.

f.p. See list of abbreviations (Part 2) for full explanation.

f.rec. First/significant recording. Where there is an early (78 r.p.m./LP) issue then a subsequent first stereo and/or CD recording may also be shown. See also list of abbreviations (Part 1).

Pub: Original publisher and date of publication shown first (subsequent changes in publisher names shown second).

MS Location Original manuscript location where traced - see list of abbreviations (Part 3).

[B] and/or [D] Bibliography section only; these indicate more detailed bibliographies and/or discographies which are included in, mainly, book-length studies.

1.   Instrumentation/General

Al.	Alto
Al.Fl./al. fl.	Alto Flute
Al.Sax.	Alto Saxophone
arr.	arranged
Bar.	Baritone
Bs.Cl./bs.cl.	Bass Clarinet
BD	Bass Drum
Bs.	Bass
Bs.Fl./bs.fl.	Bass Flute
Bs.Gtr./bs.gtr.	Bass Guitar
Bsn./bsn.	Bassoon
c.	circa
Ca./ca.	Cor Anglais
Cbsn./cbsn.	Contra Bassoon
Cel./cel.	Celeste
Cimb./cimb.	Cimbalom
Cl./cl.	Clarinet
Con.	Contralto
cond.	Conducted by
Cnt./cnt.	Cornet
Cpte.	Complete
Cym.	Cymbal
Db./db.	Double Bass
Dur.	Duration
Ed./ed.	Edited by
elec.gtr.	Electric Guitar
exc.(s)	excerpt(s)
Fl./fl.	Flute
Flgl.Hn.	Flugelhorn
Gtr./gtr.	Guitar
Harm.	Harmonium
Hmn./hmn.	Harmonica
Hn./hn.	Horn
Hp./hp.	Harp
H(h)pschd.	Harpsichord
Instr.	Instrumentation
Mar./mar.	Marimba
M/S	Mezzo Soprano
Narr.	Narrator
ND	No Date
Ob./ob.	Oboe
Orch.	Orchestrated
Org./org.	Organ
Perc./perc.	Percussion
Picc./picc.	Piccolo
Pno./pno.	Piano
poss./prob.	possibly/probably
Pub./pub.	Published
q.v.	which see (Latin)

Rec.	Recorder/Reciter
rec.	recorded on
rev.	revised
Sax./sax.	Saxophone
SD	Side Drum
str.	string(s)
Tba./tba.	Tuba
Tbn./tbn.	Trombone
Ten.Sax.	Tenor Saxophone
Ten./ten.	Tenor
Timp./timp.	Timpani
Trans./trans.	Transcribed/translated
Treb.	Treble
Treb.Rec.	Treble Recorder
Va.d'am.	Viola d'amore
Va.da gam.	Viola da Gamba
Va./va.	Viola
Vc./vc.	Violincello
Vn./vn.	Violin
Xyl./xyl.	Xylophone
es	electronic stereo
MC	cassette
CD	compact disc
m	mono
V	video
L	Laser

2.   Music history

f.Afr.p.	first African performance
f.Am.p.	first American performance
f.amat.p.	first amateur performance
f.Austr.p.	first Australian performance
f.Brit.p.	first British performance
f.broad.p.	first broadcast performance
f.Can.p.	first Canadian performance
f.conc.p.	first concert performance
f.doc.p .	first documented performance
f.Eng.p.	first English performance
f.Eur.p.	first European performance
f.Ind.p.	first Indian performance
f.Jap.p.	first Japanese performance
f.Lon.p.	first London performance
f.mod.p.	first modern performance
f.N.Am.p.	first North American performance
f.NZ. p.	first New Zealand performance
f.p.	first performance
f.Pol.p.	first Polish performance
f.priv.p.	first private performance
f.prof.p.	first professional performance

f.pub.p.	first public performance
f.Russ.p.	first Russian performance
f.SA.p.	first South African performance
f.S.Am.p.	first South American performance
f.Scot.p.	first Scottish performance
f.Sp.p.	first Spanish performance
f.st.p.	first stage performance
f.tel.p.	first televised performance
f.trans.	first transmission

3.   Manuscript Location

AG	Ann Griffiths
AH	Annetta Hoffnung
BBC	BBC Music Library
BBCB	BBC, Belfast
BBCC	BBC, Cardiff
BBCTV	BBC Television Library
B&H	Boosey & Hawkes
BIFA	Barber Institute of Fine Arts Library (Birmingham)
BL	British Library
BLO	Bodleian Library, Oxford
BML	Berkeley Music Library (USA)
BO	Buxton Orr
BPA	Bamboo Pipe Association
BPL	Britten-Pears Library (Aldeburgh)
BrHr	Breitkopf & Hartel
BUL	Birmingham University Library
BYU	Brigham Young University (USA)
CBSO	City of Birmingham Symphony Orchestra Library
CCC	Clare College, Cambridge
CCO	Christ Church College, Oxford
CDMG	Centre de Documentacio Musical de la Generalitat (Barcelona)
CE	Carolyn Evans (daughter of Herbert Murrill)
CPL	Cheltenham Public Library
CUL	Cambridge University Library
DT	Delius Trust
EH	Edward Heath
EO'C	Eileen O'Casey
ET	Ernest Tomlinson
FFC	Farnham Festival Committee
FG	Frederick Grinke
FMC	Fitzwilliam Museum, Cambridge
GD	George Dannatt
GG	Gordon Green
GLC	Greater London Council
GPL	Gloucester Public Library
GS	Geoffrey Self
HB	Howard Brakespear
HM	Hilary McNamara

JA	John Amis
JB	James Blades
JUL	Jewish University Library (Jerusalem)
LHU	Lehigh University (USA)
LOC	Library of Congress (USA)
LPO	London Philharmonic Orchestra Library
MBF	Musicians' Benevolent Fund
MCL	Morley College Library
MG	Margaret Good
MH	Margaret Hyatt (Jacob)
MP	Mary Peppin (c/o Edward Williams)
MR	Mark Raphael
MRZ	Margaret Reizenstein
MS	Merete Soderhjelm
NC	Nicholas Chagrin
NCC	Nottingham City Council
NLA	National Library of Australia (Canberra)
NLS	National Library of Scotland
NLWA	National Library of Wales (Aberystwyth)
NOV	Novello
NWU	Northwestern University (Evanston, Illinois, USA)
NYBBS	National Youth Brass Band of Scotland (E.J.B. Catto)
NYO	National Youth Orchestra Library
NYPL	New York Public Library
OUP	Oxford University Press
PLC	Pendlebury Library, Cambridge
PM	Pamela Main
PML	Pierpont Music Library (New York)
PS	Paul Sacher
RAA	Royal Academy of Arts
RAB	Royal Artillery Band Library
RAM	Royal Academy of Music Library
RCM	Royal College of Music Library
RH	Ruth Harte
RHC	Royal Holloway College
RL	Royal Library
RMSM	Royal Military School of Music Library (Kneller Hall)
RNCM	Royal Northern College of Music Library
ROHCG	Royal Opera House, Covent Garden
RP	Ruth Pizer
RS	Rodney Slatford
RSA	Royal Scottish Academy
RSC	Royal Shakespeare Centre Library (Stratford upon Avon)
S&B	Stainer & Bell
SCH	Schott
SH	Susie Harries
SHO	St Hilda's College, Oxford
SJC	St John's College, Cambridge
SW	Susana Walton
TC	Tebbutt Collection

TUL	Texas University Library (Austin)
UCT	University of Capetown (South Africa)
VAL	Institut d'Estudis Vallencs, Valls (Spain)
VB	Valerie Banks
VCA	Victoria College of Arts (Melbourne)
WAF	William Alwyn Foundation
WAS	Wishart Archive (Somerset)
WBA	Warner Brothers America
WF	Watson Forbes
WMIC	Welsh Music Information Centre
WW	William Waterhouse
WWM	William Walton Museum (Ischia)
YUL	Yale University Library

4.   Festivals/Concert Series

Ald.	Aldeburgh
Bth.	Bath
Cdf.	Cardiff
Ch.	Cheltenham
CoL	City of London
Cpnm	Committee (Society) for the Promotion of New Music
Dart.	Dartington
Edn.	Edinburgh
Eist.	Eistedfodd
Fnm.	Farnham
Iscm	International Society for Contemporary Music
Lee	Leeds
M/L	Macnaghten/Lemare Concerts
P.L.	Park Lane Concerts
Pr.	Promenade Concerts
Red.	Redcliffe Concerts
Swn.	Swansea
3Ch.	Three Choirs

COMPOSER CATALOGUES

John Addison
(1920–1998)

Three Terpsichorean Studies for orchestra (1948)
Dur: 17'
Instr: 2/2/2/2 - 4/2/3/(1) - timp. perc. str.
f.p.   Royal College of Music First Orchestra/Richard Austin - Royal College of Music, London, 24 March 1949
f.broad.p. BBC Scottish Orchestra/Ian Whyte - 1950
f.pub.p. Scottish National Orchestra/Walter Susskind - Edinburgh, 1951
Pub: Joseph Williams; Stainer & Bell

Variations for piano and orchestra (1948 rev. 1949)
Dur: 12'
Instr: 2/2/2/2 - 4/2/3/0 - timp. perc. str.
f.p.   Margaret Kitchin - BBC broadcast, 1960

Sextet for woodwind (1949)
Dedicated to Frederick Thurston, Addison's teacher at the Royal College of Music.
Dur: 21'
Instr: Fl. Ob. Ca. Cl. BCl. Bsn.
f.p.   Royal College of Music Chamber Ensemble/Frederick Thurston - Royal College of Music, London, 13 July 1949
f.pub.p. Chamber Ensemble - HMV Studios, London, 1950 (a Prom Circle recital)
f.Eur.p. Chamber Ensemble - Frankfurt, 25 June 1951 (ISCM Festival)
f.Brit.broad.p. Virtuoso Chamber Ensemble - BBC Third Programme, 9 June 1955 (there had also been a 1950 broadcast from Paris)

Three Part Songs for men's chorus (1949)
[1. Song of Bethsabe (George Peele) 2. Grenadier (A. E. Housman) 3. Old Roger (Anon.)]
Pub: Joseph Williams; Galliard

Concerto for trumpet, string orchestra and percussion (1949)
Dur: 18'

f.p.   David Mason/New London Orchestra/Alec Sherman - Hampton Court, July
            1950 (Serenade Concert)
f.broad.p. David Mason/City of Birmingham Symphony Orchestra/George Weldon -
            8 December 1950
f.Am.p.   cond. Robert Nagel - Hunter College Assembly Hall, New York, 1953 (and at
            New York Town Hall)
f.p.   (as a ballet `Cyclasm') Princes Theatre London, September 1953
Choreography: Walter Gore
f.rec.   Leon Rapier/Louisville Orchestra/Jorge Mester - *Louisville (USA) LS 695,
            RCA GL 25018*
Pub: Joseph Williams, 1951 (arr. trumpet and piano); Schirmer (USA)

Trio for flute, oboe and piano (1949)
Dur: 14'
f.p.   Geoffrey Gilbert (Fl.)/John Wolfe (Ob.)/Norman Franklin (Pno.) -
            BBC Third Programme, 11 April 1950 (the first work of Addison's to be
            broadcast)
f.conc.p.   Dubois Trio - Croydon, Surrey, April 1950 (lunch hour concert)
f.Lon.p.   Sylvan Trio - Institute of Contemporary Arts, 1953.
Pub: Augener, 1952; Schirmer (USA)

Trio for oboe, clarinet and bassoon (1950)
Dur: 13'
f.p.   Melos Ensemble - Mercury Theatre, London, 1952
Pub: Augener; Galliard

Overture: Heroum Filii (1951)
Commissioned by Wellington College where the composer was educated and whose
motto is `Heroum Filii' or `The Sons of Heroes'
Dur: 9'
Instr: 2/2/2/2 - 2/2/0/0 - perc. str.
f.p.   London Symphony Orchestra/John Addison - Wellington College, 1951
f.Lon.p.   New London Orchestra/Alec Sherman - Victoria & Albert Museum, 1951
f.broad.p. Leighton Lucas Orchestra/Leighton Lucas - Third Programme, 1952
Pub: Joseph Williams; Stainer & Bell

Divertimento for brass quartet (1952)
[1. Fanfare 2. Valse 3. Scherzo 4. Lullaby 5. Gallop]
Dur: 8'30"
Instr: 2 Tpt. Hn. Tbn.
f.p.   Philip Jones Brass Quartet, Leighton House, London, 1952
f.broad.p. above artists - Third Programme, 8 January 1953
f.rec.   above artists - *Argo ZRG 813*
Pub: Joseph Williams, 1954; Galliard

Carte Blanche - ballet (1953)
Commissioned by Sadler's Wells Theatre Ballet
Dur: c.22'
Instr: 2/2/2/2+cbsn. - 4/2/2/0 - perc. hp. cel. pno. str.

f.p.   Sadler's Wells Theatre Ballet cond. John Lanchberry - Edinburgh, 10
            September 1953 (Edinburgh Festival)
Choreography: Walter Gore
f.Lon.p.   above artists - Sadler's Wells Theatre, 1953
f.S.A.p.   Sadler's Wells Theatre Ballet, 1953 (on tour)
f.Can.p.   CBC broadcast, 1956
f.Eur.p.   (as the ballet 'Cat's Cradle') International Ballet of the Marquis de Cuevas
            cond. John Addison - Theatre des Champs Elysées, Paris, 1958
Choreography: John Cranko
Designer: Desmond Heeley
Principals: Rosella Hightower, Jacqueline Morean, Serge Golovie
Suite from the above
[1. Prelude and Waltz 2. Bagatelle 3. Scherzo and Bacchanale
 4. Interlude 5. Romanza and Postlude]
Dur: 16'
Instr: 2/2/2/3(2) - 4/2/2/0 - timp. perc. hp. (pno./cel) str.
f.p.   BBC Midland Orchestra/Gilbert Vinter - BBC, 15 November 1954
f.conc.p.   BBC Symphony Orchestra/John Addison - Royal Albert Hall, London,
            11 August 1956 (Promenade Concert)
f.rec.   Pro Arte Orchestra/John Addison - *Pye Golden Guinea GGC 4048 (m), GSGC
            14048; EMI CDM7 64718-2 (CD)*
Pub: OUP
(Sir Thomas Beecham conducted the suite at a Royal Philharmonic Society Concert in
the Royal Festival Hall on 8 November 1959 - the work had been specially selected
from a list submitted to Beecham by the Composers' Guild)

Scherzo for orchestra (1954)
Written for the London Schools Orchestra
f.p.   London Schools Orchestra/Dr. Leslie Russell - Royal Festival Hall, London,
            1956

Concert Overture (1955)
Dur: 8'
Instr: 2/2/2/2 - 4/2/3/1 - timp. perc. hp. str.
f.p.   City of Birmingham Orchestra/Rudolf Schwarz - Birmingham, 1956
Pub: Schirmer (USA)

Sinfonietta (1956)
Commissioned by the National Youth Orchestra of Great Britain
Dur: 12'30"
Instr: 2/2/2/2 - 4/3/3/1 - timp. perc.(2) hp. str.
f.p.   National Youth Orchestra of Great Britain/Jean Martinon - Royal Festival
            Hall, London, 11 April 1956
Pub: OUP

Inventions (Variations) for oboe and piano (1956-57)
[1. Prologue 2. Rhapsody 3. Caprice 4. Waltz 5. Finale with Epilogue]
Written for Evelyn Rothwell
Dur: 13'

f.p.   Evelyn Rothwell (Ob.)/Wilfrid Parry (Pno.) - BBC, 24 June 1958
f.conc.p.   above artists - Arts Council Drawing Room, London, 1958 (Macnaghten
            Concert)
Pub: OUP, 1959; 1973

Serenade (Sextet) for wind quintet and harp (1956-57)

[1. Invention 2. Intermezzo 3. Toccata 4. Elegy 5. Passacaglia al Minuetto
6. Finale]
Commissioned by the BBC and dedicated to the composer's father.
Dur: 18'30"
Instr: Fl. Ob. Cl. Bsn. Hn. Hp.
f.p.   Virtuoso Chamber Ensemble - Edward Walker (Fl.), Leon Goossens
            (Ob.), Sidney Fell (Cl.), Ronald Waller (Bsn.), John Burden (Hn.), Osian Ellis
            (Hp.) - Cheltenham Town Hall, 15 July 1957 (Cheltenham Festival)
f.Am.p.   Philadelphia Woodwind Quintet - New York, 1968 (and by the American
            Harp Society)
f.Lon.p.   London Wind Quintet - Purcell Room, January 1973
f.rec.   Toronto Woodwind Quintet - *CBC (Canada) SM 186*
Pub: OUP, 1958

Conversation Piece for piano and orchestra (1958)

Commissioned by the BBC for the 1958 Light Music Festival
Instr: 2/2/2/2 - 4/2/3/0 - timp. perc. hp. str.
f.p.   Semprini/BBC Concert Orchestra/Stanford Robinson - Royal Festival Hall,
            London, 1958 (BBC Light Music Festival)
Pub: OUP

Concertino for piano and orchestra (1958)

Commissioned by the Festival of Schools Music
Instr: 2/1/2/2 - 4/3/3/1 - timp. perc.(3) str.
f.p.   Philip Jenkins/Schools Festival Orchestra/Malcolm Arnold - Royal Albert
            Hall, London, 1958
f.broad.p. Wilfrid Parry/BBC Northern Orchestra/Stanford Robinson - 1961
Pub: OUP

Wellington Suite, for two horns, piano and orchestra (1959)

Written to celebrate the centenary of Wellington College where Addison had been a
pupil.
Dur: 16'
Instr: 0/0/0/0 - 0/0/0/0 - timp. perc. str.
f.p.   G. Mallock (Hn.)/B. Preston (Hn.)/Courtney Kenny (Pno.)/Wellington College
            Orchestra/John Addison, Wellington College, summer 1959
f.Am.p.   San Raphael Chamber Orchestra/Hugo Rinaldi - California, 1962
Pub: OUP

Concertante for oboe, clarinet, horn and orchestra (1959)

Commissioned by the BBC
Instr: 2/0/0/2 - 2/2/3/0 - timp. perc. str.

f.p.   Roger Lord (Ob.)/Gervase de Peyer (Cl.)/Barry Tuckwell (Hn.)/ London
            Symphony Orchestra/John Addison - Cheltenham Town Hall, 13 July 1959
            (Cheltenham Festival)
Pub: OUP

Partita for string orchestra (1961)
Dur: 16'
f.p.   Hirsch Chamber Players/Leonard Hirsch - Conway Hall, London, 1961
f.broad.p. above artists - 13 November 1961
f.NZ.p.   cond. John Hopkins, 1963
Pub: OUP/CML, 1973

Apples and Water - song for voice and guitar (1965)
[Words: Robert Graves]
Commissioned by Jupiter Recordings for `The Jupiter Book of Contemporary Ballads'.
f.p.   Patricia Kern (Sop.)/Desmond Dupré (Gtr.) - (and issued on *Jupiter LP JUR
            0A10*)

Display for orchestra (1969)
Commissioned by Mrs. W. O. Manning for the 1969 Farnham Festival
Instr: 2/2/2/1 - 2/2/2/0 - timp. perc.(2) str.
f.p.   Combined orchestras of Tiffins School and Farnham Grammar School/ Denis
            Bloodworth - Parish Church, Farnham, Surrey, 16 May 1969 (Farnham
            Festival)
Pub: OUP

Bagatelle for flute and piano (1969)
Commissioned by OUP
Pub: OUP (Modern Flute Music)

Overture from the film 'Sleuth' (1972)

Conversation Piece ('The Man we shall Marry') for two sopranos, harpsichord, chamber organ and harp (1974)
[Words: Caryl Brahms]
Dur: 3'
f.p.   Elizabeth Leigh-Harwood (Sop.)/Lisa Gray (Sop.)/Leslie Pearson
            (Org./Hpschd.)/John Marston (Hp.) - Wigmore Hall, London, 4 April 1974
            (`Music Now and Then')

Illyrian Lullaby for guitar and piano (1976)
Pub: OUP, 1976 (in `Easy Modern Guitar Music')

Celebration for two oboes, bassoon and harpsichord (1989)
[1. Midsummer's Eve (Fairies) 2. Hallow'een 3. St. Valentine's Day Waltz
 4. Twelfth Night (Lord of Misrule)]
Commissioned by South West Arts for Sheba Sound
Dur: 9'30"
f.p.   Sheba Sound - Town Hall, Chipping Sodbury, Oxon. 3 October 1989

Four Miniatures for four bassoons (1990)
[1. Air 2. Scherzo 3. Waltz 4. March]
Pub: Emerson

Divertimento for wind quintet (1990)
Commissioned by the Mladi Quintet of Los Angeles
Dur: 10'
Instr: Fl. Ob. Cl. Bsn. Hn.
f.p.   Mladi Quintet - Los Angeles, USA, 19 May 1990
Pub: OUP (New York), 1993

Five Dialogues for flute and clarinet (1991)
Commissioned by Emerson Edition
Dur: 7'30"
Pub: Emerson, 1993

Harlequin* for soprano saxophone and piano (1992)
Commissioned by Steven Stusek
Dur.   4'
f.p.   Steven Stusek (Sax.)/Michael Arnowitt (Pno.) - Park McCullogh House, North
            Bennington, Vermont, USA, July 1992
Pub: Emerson, 1993
(*originally entitled `Rondo Giocoso, Harlequin and Columbine')

Bagatelles for brass quintet (1993)
Dur: 9'30"
Instr: 2 Tpt. Hn. Tbn. Tba.
Pub: OUP (New York), 1994

Concertino for orchestra (1993)
Commissioned by the Sage City Orchestra
Dur: 12'45"
Instr: 2/1/2/1 - 4/2/3/1 - timp. perc.(2) pno. str.
f.p.   Sage City Orchestra/John Addison - Sage City, Vermont, USA, 3 October
            1993

Serenade for viola and piano (1993)
Commissioned by Bennington College, Vermont
Dur: 7'
f.p.   Jacob Glick (Va.)/Veronica Jacobs (Pno.) - Bennington College, Vermont,
            USA, 13 October 1993

ARRANGEMENTS

Polly - ballad opera by John Gay arr. (1953)
Commissioned by the BBC.
Instr: 1/1/1/1 - 1/0/0/0 - timp. hp. str.
f.p.   English Opera Group Chorus and Orchestra/Norman Del Mar - BBC
            broadcast, 28 December 1953
Principals: April Cantelo, Alexander Young, Norman Lumsden, Trevor Anthony

FILM MUSIC

(i) Documentary Films

Operation Hurricane - for Ministry of Supply (1953)
Awarded a Diploma of Merit at the Seventh International Edinburgh Film
Festival in 1953.

The Queen's Colours (1953)

**Tonight in Britain - Associated British Pathé for British Travel and
Holidays Association (1954)**

Highways of Tomorrow (1955)

The Concert (1973)
Director: Julian Chagrin

(ii) Feature Films

Brighton Rock - Associated British (1946)
Director: John Boulting
Song arrangement only - main score by Hans May

The Guinea Pig (1948)
School song and dance music only - main score by John Wooldridge

Seven Days to Noon - London Films (1950)
Director: John Boulting

Pool of London - Ealing (1951)
Director: Basil Dearden
f.rec. (exc.) *Citadel CT-0F1-1* (The Golden Age of British Film Music)

High Treason - GFD/Conqueror (1951)
Director: Roy Boulting

Brandy for the Parson - Group Three (1951)
Director: John Eldridge

f.conc.p.   (exc.) BBC Concert Orchestra/Carl Davis - BBC Radio 3, 28
             March 1995 (`Music for the British Movies' - Fairest Isle Series)

The Hour of Thirteen - MGM (1952)
Director: Harold French

Time Bomb - MGM (1952)
US Title: Terror on a Train
Director: Ted Tetzlaff

The Red Beret - Warwick (1953)
US Title: Paratrooper
Director: Terence Young

The Man Between - London Films (1953)
Director: Carol Reed
f.conc.p.   (exc.) BBC Concert Orchestra/Carl Davis - BBC Radio 3, 28
             March 1995 (`Music for the British Movies' - Fairest Isle Series)
f.recs.   (excs.) *London (USA) 1389 and 1487*
             (exc. Theme) Orchestra/Ron Goodwin - *EMI CDGO 2059 (CD)*
             complete film (V)

The Maggie - Ealing (1954)
US Title: High and Dry
Director: Alexander Mackendrick

The Black Knight - Warwick (1954)
Director: Tony Garnett

The End of the Road - Group Three (1954)
US Title: Man and Boy
Director: Wolf Rilla

Make Me an Offer - Group Three (1954)
Director: Cyril Frankel
f.rec.   complete film (V)

One Good Turn - GFD/Two Cities (1954)
Director: John Paddy Carstairs
f.rec.   complete film (V)

That Lady - TCF/Atlanta (1954)
Director: Terence Young

Touch and Go - Ealing (1955)
U.S. Title: The Light Touch
Director: Michael Truman
f.recs.   (exc.) *Citadel CT-0F1-1* (The Golden Age of British Film Music)
            complete film (V)

Josephine and Men - Charter (1955)
Director: Roy Boulting

The Cockleshell Heroes - Columbia/Warwick (1955)
Director: José Ferrer
f.rec.   (excs.) *London (USA) 1443*
                  complete film (V)

It's Great to be Young - AB Pathé/Marble Arch (1955)
Director: Cyril Frankel
(Scherzo only - main score by Ray Martin)

Private's Progress - British Lion/Charter (1956)
Director: John Boulting
f.rec.   complete film (V)

Reach for the Sky - Rank/Pinnacle (1956)
Director: Lewis Gilbert
f.recs.   (excs.) *HMV 8265 (45) Parlophone 4198 (45)*
                  (Main Theme) Geoff Love Orchestra - *Music for Pleasure HR
                  8140(MC), CC211(CD)*
                  complete film (V)

Three Men in a Boat - Romulus (1956)
Director: Ken Annakin
f.rec.   complete film (V)

The Shiralee - Ealing (1957)
Director: Leslie Norman

Lucky Jim - British Lion/Charter (1957)
Director: John Boulting
f.rec.   complete film (V)

Barnacle Bill - Ealing (1957)
US Title: All at Sea
Director: Charles Frend

I was Monty's Double - ABP/Maxwell Setton (1958)
US Title: Hell, Heaven and Hoboken
Director: John Guillermin
f.rec.   complete film (V)
Exc.   `March' arr. orchestra
Dur: 3'
Instr: 2/1/2/1 - 2/2/3/0 - timp. perc. hp. str.
Pub: Chappell, 1958

Carlton-Browne of the Foreign Office - British Lion/Charter (1958)
US Title: Man in a Cocked Hat

Director: Roy Boulting
f.rec.   complete film (V)

School for Scoundrels - ABP/Guardsman (1959)
Director: Robert Hamer
f.rec.   complete film (V)

Look Back in Anger - ABP/Woodfall (1959)
Director: Tony Richardson
f.rec.   complete film (V)

The Entertainer - British Lion (1959)
Director: Tony Richardson
f.rec.   complete film (V)

A French Mistress - British Lion/Charter (1960)
Director: Roy Boulting
f.rec.   (excs.) *London (USA) 3238/231*

His and Hers - Eros (1960)
Director: Brian Desmond Hurst

A Taste of Honey - British Lion (1961)
Director: Tony Richardson
f.recs.   (soundtrack) - *United Artists (USA) UAL 3249 (m), UAS 6249*
            complete film (V)

Go to Blazes - ABP (1961)
Director: Michael Truman
f.rec.   complete film (V)

The Loneliness of the Long-Distance Runner - British Lion (1962)
Director: Tony Richardson
f.recs.   *(soundtrack) Warner Bros. S 1548*
            complete film (V) (L)

Tom Jones - UA/Woodfall (1963)
Director: Tony Richardson
f.recs.   (soundtrack) cond. John Addison - *United Artists (USA) UAL 4113
            (m), UAS 5113, MCA 39068 (and MC)*
            complete film (V) (L)

The Girl in the Headlines - Bryanston/Viewfinder (1963)
US Title: The Model Murder Case
Director: Michael Truman

Girl with Green Eyes - UA/Woodfall (1963)
Director: Desmond Davis
f.rec.   complete film (V)

The Peaches (1963)
Director: Michael Gill

Guns at Batasi - Twentieth Century Fox (1964)
Director: John Guillermin
f.rec.   complete film (V)

The Uncle - Play Pix (1964)
Director: Desmond Davis

The Amorous Adventures of Moll Flanders - Paramount/ Winchester (1965)
Director: Terence Young
f.recs.   (soundtrack) cond. John Addison - *RCA Victor (USA) LOC 1113*
               complete film (V)

I was happy here - Partisan (1965)
US Title: Time Lost and Time Remembered
Director: Desmond Davis

The Loved One - MGM/Filmways (1965)
Director: Tony Richardson

A Fine Madness - Warner Seven Arts (1966)
Director: Irvin Kershner
f.rec.   complete film (V)

Torn Curtain - Universal (1966)
Director: Alfred Hitchcock
f.recs. (soundtrack) cond. John Addison - *Decca (USA) DL 9155; Varese Sarabande (USA) VSD 5296 (CD) (and MC)*
               (Main Title) Prague City Philharmonic Orchestra/Paul Bateman - *Silva Screen FILMCD 159 (CD)*
               complete film (V) (L) (S)

The Honey Pot - UA/Famous Artists (1966)
Director: Joseph L. Mankiewicz
f.recs. (soundtrack) cond. John Addison - *United Artists (USA) UAL 4159 (m), UAS 5 519; MCA 25106 (and MC)*
               complete film (V)

Smashing Time - Paramount (1967)
Director: Desmond Davis
f.rec.   (soundtrack) - *EMI SSL 10224*

The Charge of the Light Brigade - UA/Woodfall (1968)
Director: Tony Richardson
f.recs.   (soundtrack) cond. John Addison - *United Artists (USA) UAS 5177*
               complete film (V)

Two Times Two - Warner/Norbud (1969)
US Title: Start the Revolution Without Me
Director: Bud Yorkin
f.rec.   complete film (V)

Country Dance - MGM/Keep-Windward (1969)
US Title: Brotherly Love
Director: J. Lee Thompson

Mr. Forbush and the Penguins - EMI (1971)
Director: Roy Boulting

Sleuth - Palomar (1972)
Director: Joseph L. Mankiewicz
f.recs.   (soundtrack) - *CBS S 70127, Columbia (USA) S 32154*
             complete film (V) (L)
Exc.   Overture - see concert music

Luther - American Express (1973)
Director: Guy Green
f.rec.   complete film (V)

Dead Cert (1974)
Director: Tony Richardson

Ride a Wild Pony (1975)

Joseph Andrews - UA/Woodfall (1976)
Director: Tony Richardson
f.rec.   (soundtrack) - *Tony Thomas Productions (USA) TT-JA-2*

The Seven-per-cent Solution - Universal (1976)
Director: Herbert Ross
f.recs.   (soundtrack) - *Citadel (USA) CT-JA-1*
             (theme) cond. Lanny Meyers - Vanguard VSD 5692 (CD)
             complete film (V)

The Scarlet Buccaneer - Universal (1976)
US Title: Swashbuckler
Director: James Goldstone
f.recs.   (soundtrack) - *MCA Records (USA) MCA 2096*
             complete film (V) (L)

A Bridge Too Far - United Artists (1977)
Director: Richard Attenborough
f.recs.   (soundtrack) - *United Artists (USA) LA 762 H*
             (complete) - *RYKO RCD 10746(CD)*
             complete film (V) (L)

(Exc.March) City of Birmingham Symphony Orchestra/Marcus
Dods - *HMV Greensleeve ED 290109-1*
(Exc. Overture) Prague City Philharmonic Orchestra/Paul Bateman
- *Silva Screen FILMCD 151 (CD)*
Excs. [1. The Dutch tragedy 2. Theme]
Band of the Parachute Regiment/Capt. Ian McElligott - *Bandleader
BNA 5126(CD)*

The Pilot - Summit/New Line (1979)
Director   Cliff Robertson

Highpoint (1980)

Strange Invaders - EMI (1983)
Director: Michael Laughlin
f.rec.   complete film (V) (L)

Grace Quigley - Cannon/Northbrook (1984)
US Title: The Ultimate Solution of Grace Quigley
Director: Anthony Harvey
f.rec.   complete film (V)

Codename: Emerald - NBC/MGM-UA (1985)
Director: Jonathan Sanger
f.rec.   complete film (V)

INCIDENTAL MUSIC

a)   **Television**

Steps into Ballet - BBC (1955)
f.p.   Children's programme, 29 December 1955
Music played by: Melos Ensemble
Producer: Naomi Capon

Sambo and the Snow Mountain - BBC (1961)
Producer: Margaret Dale

The Orchestra - BBC Series (1964)

Detective - BBC Series (1964)

The Search for Ulysees - CBS Special (1965)
Director: Martin Carr

Hamlet - NBC/ATV (1970)
[Shakespeare]

Director: Peter Wood
Principal: Richard Chamberlain
f.p.   17 November 1970 (in USA), August 1971 (UK)
f.rec.   *RCA VDM 119-2 (V)*

Trial by Wilderness - Anglia (1973)

The Way of the World - Thames Series (1973)

Back of Beyond - BBC (1974)
Director: Desmond Davis
Principal: Rachel Roberts

Grady - NBC series (1975)
Producer: Bud Yorkin

Black Beauty - NBC Mini-series (1977)
Producer: Peter Fischer

The Bastard - Universal Mini-series (1978)
UK Title: The Kent Chronicles
Director: Lee H. Katzin

Centennial - NBC Mini-series (1978)
Director: Virgil Vogel and others

A Death in Canaan (1978)
Director: Tony Richardson

The Eddie Capra Mysteries - NBC series (1978)
Producer: John Wilder

Pearl - ABC Mini-series (1978)

The French Atlantic Affair - ABC Mini-series (1979)

Like Normal People - ABC (1979)
Director: Harvey Hart

Love's Savage Fury - ABC (1979)
Director: Joseph Hardy

Power Man - ABC pilot (1979)
Director: John Llewellyn Moxey

Nero Wolfe - series (1980-81)
Director: Frank D. Gilroy and others

Mistress of Paradise (1981)
Director: Peter Medak

Charles and Diana: A Royal Love Story (1982)
Director: James Goldstone

Eleanor, First Lady of the World (1982)
Director: John Erman

T. J. Hooker (1982)

I was a Mail Order Bride (1982)
Director: Marvin J. Chomsky

The Devlin Connection - series (1982)

Ellis Island - Mini-series (1984)

Murder She Wrote - theme and pilot (1984)

Dead Man's Folly (1985)
Director: Clive Donner

Thirteen at Dinner (1985)
Director: Lou Antonio

Bigger than a Bread Box (1986)

Something In Common (1986)

Mr. Boogedy (1986)
Director: Oz Scott

Bride of Boogedy (1987)
Director: Oz Scott

Amazing Stories (1987)
[1. The Greibble 2. The Pumpkin Competition]
Producer: Stephen Spielberg

Strange Voices (1987)
Director: Arthur Allan Seidelmann

Beryl Markham: A Shadow on the Sun - Mini-series (1988)
Director: Tony Richardson

The Phantom of the Opera - Mini-series (1989)
Director: Tony Richardson
f.rec.   Soundtrack - *Colossal (USA) XCD 1004 (CD)*

Deadly Price of Paradise (ND)

Firefighter - Series (ND)
Producer: Greg Simms

b)   **Stage**

Cranks - review (1955)
[John Cranko]
Winner of an Evening Standard Award
f.p.   New Watergate Theatre, London, 19 December 1955 (later transferred
            to Duchess & St. Martins, and Lyric, Hammersmith)
Music conducted by: Anthony Bowles
Director: John Cranko
Designer: John Piper
Principals: Annie Ross, Anthony Newley, Hugh Bryant and
            Gilbert Vernon
f.Am.p. Bijou Theatre, Broadway, New York, 26 November 1956
f.rec.   original cast - *HMV CLP 1082 (m)*
Pub: Chappell, 1956 (vocal score)

The Entertainer (1957)
[John Osborne]
f.p.   Royal Court Theatre, London, 10 April 1957 (later transferred to the
            Palace Theatre)
Director: Tony Richardson
Designer: Alan Tagg
Principals: Laurence Olivier, Richard Pasco, Dorothy Tutin

The Chairs (1957)
[Ionesco trans. Donald Watson]
f.p.   Royal Court Theatre, London, 14 May 1957
Director: Tony Richardson
Designer: Jocelyn Herbert
Principals: Joan Plowright, George Devine

The Apollo de Belac (1957)
[Jean Giraudoux trans. Ronald Duncan]
f.p.   Royal Court Theatre, London, 14 May 1957
Director: Tony Richardson
Designer: Carl Toms
Principals: Alan Bates, John Osborne, Richard Pasco, Heather Sears

Keep your Hair on - musical comedy (1958)
[John Cranko]
f.p.   Apollo Theatre, London, 13 February 1958.
Music conducted by: Anthony Bowles
Director: John Cranko

Scenery and Costumes: Tony Armstrong-Jones and Desmond Heeley.
Principals: Betty Marsden, Eric Mörk, Rachel Roberts and Barbara Windsor.
Excs. published separately -
[1. I do, I do, I do, 2. Misfit, 3. One Day - but When?
 4. Crocodile Tears]
Pub: Francis, Day & Hunter, 1958

Luther (1961)
[John Osborne]
f.p.   Royal Court Theatre, London, 27 July 1961 (after provincial tour)
Director: Tony Richardson
Designer: Jocelyn Hebert
Principals: Albert Finney, Julian Glover, George Devine, Bill Owen
f.Eur.p.   Theatre des Nations, Paris
f.Am.p.   Broadway, New York (starring Albert Finney)

Plays for England (1962)
[John Osborne 1. Blood of the Bambergs, 2. Under Plain Cover]
f.p.   Royal Court Theatre, London, 19 July 1962
Directors: John Dexter and Jonathan Miller
Designer: Alan Tagg
Principals: Alan Bennett, Anton Rodgers, Avril Elgar

A Midsummer Night's Dream (1962)
[Shakespeare]
f.p.   Royal Court Theatre, London, 24 January 1962
Director: Tony Richardson
Designer: Jocelyn Herbert
Principals: Nicol Williamson, Rita Tushingham, Lynn Redgrave,
Ronnie Barker

Semi-Detached (1962)
[David Turner]
f.p.   Saville Theatre, London, 5 December 1962
Director: Tony Richardson
Designer: London Sainthill
Principals: Laurence Olivier, Mona Washbourne, James Bolam

The Broken Heart (1962)
[John Ford]
f.p.   Chichester Festival, 1962
Director: Laurence Olivier

The Workhouse Donkey (1963)
[John Arden]
f.p.   Chichester Festival, 1963
Director: Stuart Burge
Principals: Frank Finlay
(the play was later broadcast, with music conducted by Michael Moores)

Hamlet (1963)

[Shakespeare]
f.p.   National Theatre, London, 22 October 1963 (the opening production)
Director: Laurence Olivier
Principals: Peter O'Toole

The Seagull (1964)

[Anton Chekhov]
f.p.   Royal Court Theatre, London, 12 March 1964
Director: Tony Richardson
Designer: Jocelyn Herbert
Principals: Peggy Ashcroft, Peter Finch, Vanessa Redgrave

St. Joan of the Stockyards (1964)

[Berthold Brecht]
f.p.   Royal Court Theatre, London, 11 June 1964
Director: Tony Richardson
Designer: Jocelyn Herbert
Principals: Alec Guinness, Siobhan McKenna, Rachel Kempson

Listen to the Mocking Bird (1964)

[John Weir and Claude Cockburn]
f.p.   The Playhouse, Nottingham
Director: John Neville

A Patriot for Me (1965)

[John Osborne]
f.p.   Royal Court Theatre, London, 30 June 1965
Director: Anthony Page
Designer: Jocelyn Herbert
Principals: Sebastian Shaw, Maximilian Schnell, George Devine

The Amazons - musical (1971)

[David Heneker]
f.p.   Nottingham Playhouse, 7 April 1971
Music conducted by: Denys Rawson
Director: Philip Wiseman
Choreography: Irving Davies
Scenery and costumes: Robin Archer and Michael Stennett

Popkiss - musical (1972)

[Michael Ashton]
f.p.   Cambridge Arts Theatre, 16 May 1971
Music conducted by: Raymond Bishop
Director: Richard Cottrell
Choreography: Malcolm Clare and David Drew
Scenery: Robin Archer
Principals: Daniel Massey, Patricia Hodge, John Standing, Joan Sanderson
f.Lon.p. Globe Theatre, 22 August 1971

Director: Michael Ashton

I, Claudius (1972)
[Robert Graves]
f.p.   Queens Theatre, London, July 1972
Director: Tony Richardson

Twelfth Night (1973)
[Shakespeare]
f.p.   Arts Theatre, Cambridge

Antony and Cleopatra (1973)
[Shakespeare]
f.p.   South Bank Theatre, London
Director: Tony Richardson

Bloomsbury (1974)
[Peter Luke]
f.p.   Phoenix Theatre, London
Director: Richard Cottrell

Antony and Cleopatra (1987)
[Shakespeare]
f.p. Los Angeles Theatre Centre
Director: Tony Richardson

MS LOCATION

The majority of the film scores are located at Brigham Young University Library, Utah.
(BYU)

2

William Alwyn
(1905–1985)

Sparkling Cascade for solo piccolo (1913)

The Fairy Fiddler - opera for soloists, chorus and orchestra (1917 rev. 1927-29)
[Words: Elizabeth Shane]
Dedication: `To Peter'
Dur: 90'
Excs.
(i)Derybeg Fair - overture for orchestra (1922 rev. 1925)
Score dated: Haslemere, 9 March 1925
Dur: 7'
(ii)Prologue (1922 rev. London, 9 September 1929)
Dur: 6'30"

Ad Infinitum - tone poem for orchestra (1920s)
Dur: 10'

String Quartet No. 1 in B flat minor (1922)
Score dated: Northampton, 17 November 1922

Peter Pan - Suite for small orchestra (1923)
Score dated: Northampton, 29 November 1923
Dur: 23'
f.p.   Queen's Hall Orchestra/Sir Henry Wood - Queen's Hall, London, 1923

String Quartet No. 2 (c.1923-24)

Five Little Pieces for string quartet (1924)
[1. Winter morning 2. A marching tune 3. Peter Puck 4. The Fairy Fiddler
 5. Hurdy Gurdy]
Score dated: Northampton, 23 February 1924

April Morn - Four little pieces for piano (c.1924-26)
[1. The Lost Lamb 2. April Showers 3. Bluebells* 4. Violets**]
Dedication: 'To Peter'
Pub: Associated Board, 1924, 1925*, 1926**

String Quartet No. 3 in F (1925)
Score dated: Northampton, 19 April 1925
Dedication: 'To Peter'

Prelude for orchestra (1925)
Score dated: London, 29 August 1925
Dedication: 'To Peter'
f.p.   Royal Academy of Music, London, cond. Sir Henry Wood

String Quartet No. 4 in C (c.1925-27)
Dur: 12'

String Quartet No. 5 in A minor (c.1925-27)
[1. Prelude 2. Passacaglia 3. Rondo 4. Retrospect]

Blackdown - tone poem for orchestra (c.1926)
Dur: 7'
f.p.   Guildford Symphony Orchestra/Claud Powell - St. Nicholas Hall, Guildford,
            Surrey, 23 November 1926

Haze of Noon - for piano (1926)
Dedication: 'To Peter'
Dur: 3'
Pub: OUP, 1926 (Oxford Piano Series, ed. A. Forbes Milne)

Two Irish pieces for piano (1926)
[1. From the Countryside 2. Paddy the Fiddler]
Dedication: 'To Peter'
Pub: OUP, 1926

Fancy Free - Four pieces for piano (1927)
[1. Sunday Morning 2. Snowdrops 3. Twilight 4. Happy-Go-Lucky]
Dedication: 'To Peter'
Pub: OUP, 1927 (Oxford Piano Series, ed. A. Forbes Milne)

String Quartet No. 6 in E minor (1927)
Score dated: London, 2 October 1927
Dedicated to John McEwen
Dur: 30'

Five Preludes for orchestra (1927)
Dedication: 'To my dear Peter' - the score is dated London, 25 March 1927
Dur: 8'
Instr: 2/2/2/2 - 4/2/3/1 - hp. str.

f.p.   Henry Wood Symphony Orchestra/Sir Henry Wood - Queen's Hall, London,
            22 September 1927 (Promenade Concert)

Three Children's Songs for unison voices and piano (1927)
[Words: Alec M. Smith 1. My Garden 2. Teddy and Me 3. Bed Time]
Pub: Curwen, 1927

Phantasy Trio (1928)
Score dated: London, 14 April 1928
Dedication: `To Peter'
Dur: 15'
Instr: Vn. Va. Vc.

Bhairvi 'Renunciations' - Dervish Song arr. string quartet (1929)
Score dated: London, 27 March 1929

String Quartet No. 7 in A major (1929)
Score dated: London, December 1929
Dur: 30'

On Milton Hill - tone poem for flute, oboe and piano (1930s)
Dur: 7'

Short Suite for oboe (1930s)
[1. Siciliano 2. March 3. Interlude 4. Jig]

Sonatina for oboe and piano (1930s)
Dur: 15'

Sonatina for violin and piano (1930s)
Dur: 12'

Songs of Experience - Four songs for voice and piano (1930s)
[Words: William Blake 1. The Lily 2. A Poison Tree 3. Ah, Sunflower!
 4. My Pretty Rose-tree]

Three Pieces - Suite for string quartet (1930s)
Dur: 10'

Ballade for viola and piano (1930s)
Dur: 10'

The Wind and the Rain - for piano (1930s)

Piano Concerto No. 1 (1930)
Dedicated to Clifford Curzon - the score is dated, London, August/September 1930
Dur: 17'
Instr: 3/3/3/2 - 4/2/3/1 - timp. perc. hp. str.

f.p.   Clifford Curzon/Bournemouth Municipal Orchestra/William Alwyn - Winter
            Gardens, Bournemouth, 30 December 1931
f.Lon.p.   Vivian Langrish/London Symphony Orchestra/Warwick Braithwaite - Royal
            Academy of Music, 5 December 1934 (RCM Patron's Fund Concert)
f.rec.   Howard Shelley/London Symphony Orchestra/Richard Hickox - *Chandos
            CHAN 9155(CD)*

Songs of Innocence - Twelve Songs for voice and piano* (1930-32)
[Words: William Blake 1. Piping down the valley wild 2. The Blossom
 3. The Little Lamb 4. Spring 5. The Echoing Green 6. Nurse's Song
 7.* The Divine Image (voice and string quartet) 8. The Little Black Boy
 9. Infant Joy 10. Laughing Song 11. The Little Boy Lost
 12. The Little Boy Found]
Score dated June 1930 to 20 May 1931 - the final song to be completed was No. 8 written
on board the R.M.S. Otranto and dated 2 June 1932

Odd Moments - suite for piano (1930-32)
[1. All Forlorn* 2. Chattering*** 3. Light-foot 4. On the Heath**]
Pub: Associated Board, 1930, 1932*, 1933**, 1935***
            (No. 3 only) as No. 1 of Two Pieces for Piano 1937

Contes Barbares: Homage to Paul Gauguin - for piano (1930-33)
[1. Auti te pape - Woman at the River 2. Le Vivo (Danse Tahitienne)
 3. Mano Tapapau - She dreams of Returning 4. Dance Fragment
 5. Nevermore 6. Te Atau - The Gods]
f.p.   Clifford Curzon, 3 March 1940

Two Intermezzi for piano (1931)
Dedicated to Vivian Langrish
f.p.   Vivian Langrish

Three Easy pieces for flute and piano (1931)
Pub: Joseph Williams, 1931 (also arr. violin and piano, ed. Spencer Dyke, 1932)

String Quartet No. 8 in D minor (1931)
Score dated: London, 3 April 1931

Four Songs for voice and piano (1931)
[1. Cuckoo (Gerard Manley Hopkins)
 2. Heaven Music (Gerard Manley Hopkins)
 3. Lament of the tall tree (William Alwyn) 4. Wood magic (William Alwyn)]
Score dated: 1 June 1931 and London, 12 December 1931

String Quartet No. 9 in C (1931)
Score dated: London, 22 August 1931
Dur: 12'

String Quartet No. 10 'En Voyage' (1932)
[1. Departure 2. Sea birds 3. The lonely waters 4. Trade winds]

Score dated: R.M.S. Rangitiki, Pacific Ocean, December 1932
Dedication: `To the Ship'
Dur: 16'15"
f.p.   (probably) on board R.M.S. Rangitiki, 1932/33

Serenade for orchestra (1932)
[1. Prelude 2. Bacchanale 3. Air 4. Finale]
Score dated: Queensland, Australia, July/August 1932
Dur: 15'

Aphrodite in Aulis (after George Moore) - Eclogue for small orchestra (1932)
Dur: 8'
Instr: 1/0/0/0 - 2/0/0/0 - str.

One Thousand and One Nights - Five Songs for voice, flute, cor anglais and cello (1932)
[1. Splendour 2. The Slave's Song 3. Fragment 4. Song of the Indian lute
5. Epilogue]
Dedicated to Allen C. Lewis - the score is dated, Sydney, August/September 1932

Hunter's Moon - suite for piano (1932-33)
[1. Midsummer Magic 2. The Darkening Wood 3. Ride by Night*]
Dedication: `To Jonathan'
Pub: Associated Board, 1932, 1933*

Pomegranates - song for voice and piano (1933)
[Words: Roy Campbell]
Dedicated to Lesley Duff - the score is dated, London, March 1933
Dur: 10'

String Quartet No. 11 in B minor (1933)
Score dated: Tatsfield and London, April/May 1933
Dedication: `For my wife'
Dur: 25'

By the Farmyard Gate - Four pieces for piano (1934)
[1. The Duck Pond 2. A Ride on Dobbin 3. Sheep in the Paddock
4. Swinging on the Gate]
Dur: 3'30"
Pub: Joseph Williams, 1934

Oboe Sonata (1934)
Dedication: `For Helen Gaskell'
Dur: 13'30"
f.p.   Helen Gaskell (Ob.)
f.rec.   Nicholas Daniel (Ob.)/Julius Drake (Pno.) - *Chandos CHAN 9197(CD)*
Pub: Boosey & Hawkes,1996

Cricketty Mill - for piano (1935)
Score dated London, March 1935

String Quartet No. 12 'Fantasia' (1935)
Score dated: London, July 1935
Dedication: `To Alan Bush' (q.v.)
Dur: 12'
f.p.   Stratton Quartet - Mercury Theatre, London, 11 January 1937 (Lemare
            Concert)

Wooden Walls - suite for piano (1935)
[1. Riding at Anchor 2. Poor Jack 3. Powder Monkey 4. Heading for Harbour]
Pub: Forsyth Brothers, 1935

French Suite (1935)
[1. Fanfare 2. Rondeau 3. Gavotte 4. Two interwoven tunes (Les Matelots de
l'Isle de Cythère and Les Sept Saints) 5. Two Minuets 6. Air de Chasse]
Dedication: `For Gordon Walker and the Lyra Quartet'
Dur: 13'
Instr: Fl. Vn. Va. Hp.
f.p.   Lyra Quartet, 13 April 1941 (BBC Overseas Service)

English Overture - The Innumerable Dance (1935)
Dur: 10'
f.p.   BBC Symphony Orchestra/Aylmer Buesst - BBC Studios, London,
            8 December 1935

Suite for school orchestra (1935)
Dur: 17'

The Orchard - Six pieces for piano (1935-36)
[1. Peach bloom*** 2. A Rest in the Shade***
3. The Pear Tree is laden with fruit** 4. A Windfall of Apples*
5. The Cherry Orchard*** 6. Ripe Plums***]
Pub: Associated Board, 1935, 1939*, 1946**, 1949***

King of the Mists - Ballet (1935-36)
[Scenario: W.B. Yeats]
Dur: 20'
f.p.   Abbey Theatre, Dublin
Choreography: Ninette de Valois

The Marriage of Heaven and Hell - an oratorio (1935-36)
[Words: William Blake]
Dur: 120'
Instr: 3/3/3/3 - 4/3/3/0 - perc. org. hp. str. (and quartet of soloists and double chorus)

Midsummer Night - suite for piano (1936)
[1. The Trysting Oak 2. There Sleeps Titania 3. Faery Lands Forlorn 4. The Piper's Fancy]
Pub: Forsyth Brothers, 1936

Green Hills - for piano (1936)
Dedicated to Hugh Anson
Dur: 2'15"
Pub: OUP, 1936, Braydeston Press, 1979

String Quartet No. 13 (1936)
Score dated: London, October/November 1936
Dur: 18'

Four pieces for violin and piano (1936)
[1. One Sunday Morning 2. Along the Road 3. A Happy Evening
4. When the wind blows]
Pub: (Nos. 1 and 2) Associated Board, 1936

Tragic Interlude (Overture) for small orchestra (1936)
Dur: 10'
Instr: 0/0/0/0 - 2/0/0/0 - timp. str.
f.p.   City of London Sinfonia/Richard Hickox - a recording for Chandos and issued
            on *CHAN 9065 (CD)*

Scenes from Old London - Five Pieces for piano (1936)
[1. The steeple clock 2. Gossip in the market place 3. The street singer
4. The lavender seller 5. Post Haste]
Score dated: London, August 1936
Pub: (No. 5) as No. 2 of Two Pieces for Piano - Associated Board, 1937

Mountain Scenes - suite for cello and piano (1937)
[1. In the Canoe 2. Emerald Lake 3. On the Trail]
Dur: 6'
Pub: Schott, 1937 (Schott's Selected Scenes No. 7)

Three Pieces for flute, clarinet, violin, cello and piano (1937)
[1. Overture 2. Nocturne 3. March]
Dur: 9'

Harvest Home - suite for piano (1938)
[1. The Village Band 2. The Tinker's Tune 3. Harvest Moon
4. The Church Bells Ring]
Dur: 7'
Pub: Banks (York), 1938

From Town and Countryside - suite for piano (1938)
[1. The Shepherd's Song 2. A Ride on the Motor Bus 3. A Seat in the Park
4. The Shade of the Woods 5. The Soldiers March Past 6. The Farm Cart

7. The Organ Grinder 8. The Road Mender]
Pub: Chappell, 1938

Violin Concerto (1938)
f.p.   (a `war-time' version for violin and piano) Frederick Grinke (Vn.)/ Clifford
            Curzon (Pno.) - 3 March 1940
f.rec.   Lydia Mordkovitch/London Symphony Orchestra/Richard Hickox - *Chandos
            CHAN 9187(CD)*

Novelette for string quartet (1938-39)
Dur: 2'15"
Pub: OUP, 1940 (Oxford String Quartet Series)

Movement for string trio (1939)
Dedicated to the Philharmonic Trio
Dur: 8'
f.p.   Philharmonic Trio

Sonata quasi Fantasia (Sonata Impromptu) for violin and viola (1939)
[1. Prelude 2. Theme and Variations 3. Finale alla Capriccio]
Dur: 12'
f.p.   Frederick Grinke (Vn.)/Watson Forbes (Va.) - 3 March 1940
f.rec.   Leland Chen (Vn.)/Clare MacFarlane (Va.) - *Chandos CHAN 9197(CD)*

Rhapsody for piano quartet (1939)
Dedicated to the London Piano Quartet
Dur: 12'
Instr: Vn. Va. Vc. Pno.
f.p.   London Piano Quartet
f.rec.   David Willison (Pno.)/members of the Quartet of London - *Chandos ABRD
            1153 (and MC), CHAN 8440(CD)*
Pub: OUP, 1942; Lengnick, 1985

Pastoral fantasia for viola and string orchestra (1939)*
Dur: 11'40"
f.p.   (`War-time' version with piano acc.) Watson Forbes (Va.)/Clifford Curzon
            (Pno.) - 3 March 1940
f.p.   (orch. version) Watson Forbes/BBC Symphony Orchestra/Sir Adrian Boult -
            Corn Exchange, Bedford, 3 November 1941 (broadcast by the BBC)
f.Austr.p. Max Gilbert/Boyd Neel Orchestra/Boyd Neel - Adelaide Conservatorium of
            Music c. July 1947
f.rec.   Stephen Trees/City of London Sinfonia/Richard Hickox - *Chandos CHAN
            9065 (CD)*
(* the score was lost for over fifty years so the Chandos recording was the work's first
modern performance)

Suite for small orchestra (1939)
[1. Overture 2. Pastoral 3. Nocturne 4. March]
Dur: 10'15"

Night Thoughts for piano (1939)
Dedicated to Peter Latham
Pub: OUP, 1940

Divertimento for solo flute (1940)
[1. Introduction and fughetta 2. Variations on a ground 3. Gavotte and musette
 4. Finale alla gigue]
Dur: 9'
f.p.   René LeRoy - McMillan Theatre, Columbia University, New York,
            19 May 1941 (ISCM Festival)
f.Brit.p.   John Francis - Wigmore Hall, London, 17 October 1942 (Boosey & Hawkes
            Concert)
f.Eur.p.   G. Tassinari - Milan, 28 June 1950
f.rec.   Christopher Hyde-Smith - *Lyrita SRCS 61, Musical Heritage Society (USA)*
            MHS 1742T
Pub: Boosey & Hawkes, 1943

Overture to a Masque (1940)
Dur: 9'
f.p.   (projected, but cancelled because of the war) London Symphony Orchestra/Sir
            Henry Wood - Queen's Hall, London, 24 September 1940 (Promenade
            Concert)
f.rec.   London Symphony Orchestra/Richard Hickox - *Chandos CHAN 9093 (CD)*

Down by the Riverside for piano (1940)
Dur: 3'15"

Short Suite No. 1 for viola and piano (1941)
[1. Prelude 2. Dance 3. Aria 4. Finale]
The score is dated January 1941
Dur: 9'

Land of our Birth - song for baritone, chorus and orchestra (1941)
[Words: Gordon Boshel]
Dur: 4'

March from the film 'They Flew Alone' (1942)
f.p.   BBC Northern Orchestra/Muir Mathieson - BBC, 7 July 1943

National Fire Service March from the film 'Fires were started' (1942)
f.p.   BBC Northern Orchestra/Muir Mathieson - BBC, 13 August 1943

More Air Force - March for military band (1943)
f.p.   Central Band of the Royal Air Force - BBC, 29 April 1943

The Fraternity of Fellows - March for military band (1943)
Commissioned by the BBC for a programme in their Latin-American (Brazil) Service

March of Liberation from the film 'Tunisian Victory' (1943)

f.p.   BBC Northern Orchestra/Muir Mathieson - BBC, 13 August 1943

Women of Empire - March for military band (1943)

Commissioned by the BBC

Concert Suite from the film 'Desert Victory' (1943)

[1. Prelude - El Alamein/Holding the Line 2. The Eighth Army in Training
3. Preparing for battle 4. The calm before the storm 5. The Advance begins
6. Rommel in full retreat/The attack from the Air 7. March - Desert Victory]
Dur: 10'
Instr: 2/1/2/1 - 2/2/3/0 - perc. str.
f.p.   (complete) BBC Northern Orchestra/Muir Mathieson - BBC, 13 August 1943
            (the March had been recorded earlier on 19 July 1943)
f.rec.   (March only) Orchestra/Sidney Torch - *Columbia DX 1241/2 (78)*
March also arr. for military band by W. J. Duthoit
f.rec.   Band of the Grenadier Guards/Lt. F. Harris - *Columbia DB 2140 (78)*

Concerto Grosso No. 1 in B flat (1943)

Commissioned by the BBC and dedicated 'To George Stratton and my friends in the
L.S.O.'
Dur: 11'
Instr: 1/1/0/0 - 2/1/0/0 - perc. str. (and solo violin)
f.p.   BBC Symphony Orchestra/Clarence Raybould - BBC Studio, Bedford,
            18 November 1943
f.rec.   City of London Sinfonia/Richard Hickox - *Chandos CHAN 8866 (CD)*
Pub: Lengnick, 1952

March from the film 'The Way Ahead' (1944)

f.p.   BBC Northern Orchestra/Muir Mathieson - BBC
f.rec.   Orchestra/Sidney Torch - *Columbia DX 1241/2 (78)*
Pub: Chappell, 1944 (arr. for piano by the composer)

Short Suite No. 2 for viola and piano (1944)

Written for Watson Forbes (who edited the viola part)
Dur: 8'25"
f.p.   Watson Forbes (Va.)/Alan Richardson (Pno.) - BBC, 1944
f.conc.p.   above artists - Bath Chamber Music Club, March 1946

Suite for oboe and harp (1944-45)

[1. Minuet 2. Valse Miniature 3. Jig]
Dedicated to Léon and Sidonie Goossens
Dur: 5'
f.p.   Léon Goossens (Ob.)/Sidonie Goossens (Hp.) - BBC broadcast,
            11 November 1945
f.rec.   members of the Haffner Wind Ensemble of London - *Chandos CHAN
            9152(CD)*

Concerto for oboe, harp and string orchestra (1944-45)
Dur: 18'
f.p.   Evelyn Rothwell/London Symphony Orchestra/Basil Cameron - Royal Albert
            Hall, London, 12 August 1949 (Promenade Concert)
f.rec.   Nicholas Daniel/City of London Sinfonia/Richard Hickox - *Chandos CHAN*
            8866(CD)
Pub: Lengnick, 1951 (arr. oboe and piano by the composer)

Prelude and Fugue for piano formed on an Indian scale (1945)

The Cherry Tree - carol for voice and harp (1945)
[Words: Trad.]
Dur: 7'30"

Calypso Music from the film 'The Rake's Progress' (1945)
f.rec.   London Symphony Orchestra/Muir Mathieson - *Decca K.1544 (78), London*
            (USA) T 5054 (78); Ariel (USA) CBF 13(m); EMI CDGO 2059(CD)

Men of Gloucester - Overture in the form of a serenade for wordless chorus and
orchestra (1946)
Dedication: `A tribute to Gustav Holst and Ralph Vaughan Williams, English
Musicians'
Dur: 7'
Instr: 2/1/0/0 - 2/1/0/0 - pno. str.
f.p.   London Symphony Orchestra/Muir Mathieson - Bourton-on-the-Water,
            Gloucestershire, June 1946

Suite of Scottish Dances arranged for orchestra (1946)
[1. The Indian Queen 2. A Trip to Italy 3. Colonel Thornton's Strathspey
 4. Reel - `The Perth-shire Hunt'  5. Reel - `Loch Earn' 6. Carleton House
 7. Miss Ann Carnegie's Hornpipe]
Dedicated to Muir Mathieson
Dur: 7'
Instr: 2/1/2/1 - 2/1/1/0 - timp. perc. str.
f.p.   BBC Scottish Orchestra/Guy Warrack
f.rec.   Royal Ballet Sinfonia/Gavin Sutherland - *ASV WHL 2113(CD)*

Three Songs for high voice and piano (1946)
[Words: Louis MacNeice
 1. The Streets of Laredo (variations on a Cowboy tune) 2. Slum Song 3. Carol]
Dedication `For Hedli' (Hedli Anderson, wife of Louis MacNeice)
f.p.   Hedli Anderson (Sop.)/Norman Franklin (Pno.) - Wigmore Hall, London, 17
            November 1946
Pub: OUP, 1948, 1952
No. 2 arr. for small orchestra by H. Carruthers
Instr: 1/1/2/1/ - 0/0/2/0 - timp. hp. str.

Sonata alla Toccata for piano (1946)
Score dated, London, June 1946

Dur: 12'30"
f.p.   Denis Matthews - Cheltenham Town Hall, 7 June 1953 (Cheltenham Festival)
f.rec.   Sheila Randell - *Lyrita RCS 16(m)*
Pub: Lengnick, 1951

Suite 'Manchester' for orchestra - from the film 'A City Speaks' (1947)
[1. Prelude 2. March 3. Interlude 4. Scherzo 5. Finale]
Dur: 14'
Instr: 3/3/2/2 - 4/3/3/1 - timp. perc. hp. str.
f.p.   Hallé Orchestra/Sir John Barbirolli - King's Hall, Belle Vue, Manchester, 30
          November 1947

Theme from the film 'Odd Man Out' (1947)
f.rec.   Paul Weston and his Orchestra - *Philips BBL 7085(m)*

Suite from the film 'Odd Man Out' arr. by Christopher Palmer (1947)
[1. Prelude 2. Police Chase 3. Delirium and Lullaby 4. Nemesis (Finale)]
f.rec.   London Symphony Orchestra/Richard Hickox - *Chandos ABTD 1606(MC),
          CHAN 9243(CD), (exc.) CHAN 7008(CD)*

Three Winter Poems for string quartet (1948)
[1. Winter Landscape 2. Frozen Waters 3. Snow Shower (Serenade)]
Dedicated to John B. McEwen - the score is dated 13 April 1948
Dur: 7'30"

Suite from the film 'The Fallen Idol' arr. by Christopher Palmer (1948)
[1. Overture 2. Prelude and Opening Scene 3. Love Scene (Part 1) 4. Love Scene (Part
2) 5. Hide and Seek (Scherzo) 6. Panic 7. Finale 8. Coda (End Titles)]
f.rec.   London Symphony Orchestra/Richard Hickox - *Chandos ABTD 1606(MC),
          CHAN 9243(CD)*

Sonata for flute and piano (1948)
Dur: 10'
f.p.   Gareth Morris (Fl.)/Ernest Lush (Pno.) - BBC broadcast, 6 November 1948
f.rec.   Kate Hill (Fl.)/Julius Drake (Pno.) - *Chandos CHAN 9197(CD)*

Concerto Grosso No. 2 in G for string orchestra (1948)
Dedication `For Muir' (Muir Mathieson)
Dur: 15'
f.p.   London Symphony Orchestra/Sir Malcolm Sargent - 7 May 1950
f.rec.   London Philharmonic Orchestra/William Alwyn - *Lyrita SRCS 108, SRCD
          230(CD)*
Pub: Boosey & Hawkes, 1951

Symphony No. 1 in D (1949)
Dedicated to Sir John Barbirolli
Dur: 45' (rev. version 35')
Instr: 3/3/2/2 - 4/3/3/1 - timp. perc. hp. str.

f.p.	Hallé Orchestra/Sir John Barbirolli - Cheltenham Town Hall, 6 July 1950 (Cheltenham Festival)
f.Lon.p.	London Symphony Orchestra/Sir John Barbirolli - Royal Festival Hall, 22 February 1953
f.rec.	London Philharmonic Orchestra/William Alwyn - *Lyrita SRCS 86, SRCD 227(CD); Musical Heritage Society (USA) HNH 4040*
Pub:	Lengnick, 1952

Suite from the film 'History of Mr. Polly' arranged by Christopher Palmer (1948)

[1. Prelude 2. Wedding and Funeral 3. Fire (Murder Arsonical) 4. Christabel
5. Punting Scene (The Ferry) 6. Utopian Sunset (Finale)]

f.rec.	London Symphony Orchestra/Richard Hickox - *ABTD 1606(MC), CHAN 9243(CD)*

Theme from the film 'The Cure for Love' (1950)

f.rec.	Sidney Crook (Pno.)/London Symphony Orchestra/Muir Mathieson - *HMV B 9879(78)*

Suite for clarinet, violin and piano 'Music for Three Players' (1950)

Dedicated to the Claviano Trio - the score is dated London, November 1950

Dur:	12'
f.p.	Claviano Trio
f.rec.	members of the Haffner Wind Ensemble of London - *Chandos CHAN 9152(CD)*
Pub:	Boosey & Hawkes, 1996 (as 'Conversations')

Festival March for orchestra (1950)

Commissioned by the Arts Council of Great Britain for the 1951 Festival of Britain.

Dur:	6'30"
Instr:	3/2/2/2 - 4/3/3/1 - timp. perc. hp. str.
f.p.	London Symphony Orchestra/Sir Malcolm Sargent - Royal Festival Hall, London, 20 May 1951
f.rec.	London Philharmonic Orchestra/William Alwyn - *Lyrita SRCS 99, SRCD 229(CD)*
Pub:	Lengnick, 1951

arr. for brass band by Denis Wright (1951)

f.p.	Massed bands (Black Dyke Mills, Cory Workmen's Silver, Fairey Aviation, Morris Motors, Munn and Felton's Scottish CWS) cond. Dr. Denis Wright - Royal Albert Hall, London, 12 May 1951 (National Brass Band Club Concert)
Pub:	Chappell, 1951

arr. for military band by W.J. Duthoit

Pub:	Chappell, 1951

Trio for flute, cello and piano (1951)

Dedicated to René LeRoy, Jacques Fevrier and Roger Alberi - the score is dated London, May/June 1951

Dur:	15'
f.p.	René LeRoy (Fl.)/Roger Alberi (Vc.)/Jacques Fevrier (Pno.)

f.rec.   members of the Haffner Wind Ensemble of London - *Chandos CHAN 9152(CD)*

Symphonic Prelude: The Magic Island (1952)
Commissioned by the Hallé Orchestra - the score is dated, London, 20 March 1952
Dur: 10'
Instr: 3/3/2/2 - 4/3/3/1 - timp. perc. cel. hp. str.
f.p.   Hallé Orchestra/Sir John Barbirolli - Free Trade Hall, Manchester,
       25 March 1953
f.Lon.p.   London Symphony Orchestra/Hugo Rignold - Royal Festival Hall,
       20 March 1955
f.rec.   London Philharmonic Orchestra/William Alwyn - *Lyrita SRCS 63, SRCD 229(CD); Musical Heritage Society (USA) MHS 3300T*
Pub: Lengnick, 1953

Nine Children's Piano Pieces (1952)
[1. The Trees are heavy with snow 2. The Village Bellringers
 3. What the Mill Wheel told me 4. Hunting Scene 5. The Sun is setting
 6. The Sea is angry 7. Bicycle Ride 8. Water Lilies 9. Cinderella]
Pub: Lengnick, 1952 (`Five by Ten' series ed. Alec Rowley)

The Heated Minutes - song for high voice and piano (c. 1952)
[Words: Louis MacNeice]

'Pirate Capers' - overture from the film 'The Crimson Pirate' (1952)
Dur: 7'30"
f.rec.   *Silva Screen FILMCD 188(CD)*

String Quartet No. 1 in D minor (1953)
Score dated, London, November 1953
Dur: 25'
f.p.   New London Quartet - Recital Room, Royal Festival Hall, London,
       1 May 1954
f.broad.p.   Hirsch String Quartet - 23 September 1955
f.rec.   Gabrieli Quartet - *Unicorn UNS 241*
Pub: Lengnick 1955

Symphony No. 2 (1953)
Dur: 27'30"
Instr: 3/2/2/2 - 4/3/3/1 - timp. perc. hp. str.
f.p.   Hallé Orchestra/Sir John Barbirolli - Free Trade Hall, Manchester,
       14 October 1953
f.Lon.p.   BBC Symphony Orchestra/Sir John Barbirolli - Royal Festival Hall,
       3 February 1954
f.rec.   London Philharmonic Orchestra/William Alwyn - *Lyrita SRCS 85, SRCD 228(CD); HNH (USA) HNH 4020; Musical Heritage Society (USA) MHS 3644W*
Pub: Lengnick, 1954

Lyra Angelica - concerto for harp and string orchestra (1953-54)
The score is dated 6 January 1954
Dur: 25'
f.p.   Sidonie Goossens/BBC Symphony Orchestra/Sir Malcolm Sargent -
            Royal Albert Hall, London, 24 July 1954 (Promenade Concert)
f.rec.   Osian Ellis/London Philharmonic Orchestra/William Alwyn - *Lyrita SRCS*
            108, SRCD 230(CD)
Pub: Lengnick, 1955

Autumn Legend for cor anglais and string orchestra (1954)
The score is dated, Thornhill, Cowes, I.O.W., November 1954
Dur: 11'
f.p.   Roger Winfield/Hallé Orchestra/Sir John Barbirolli - Cheltenham Town Hall,
            22 July 1955 (Cheltenham Festival)
f.Lon.p.   above artists - Royal Albert Hall, 2 September 1955 (Promenade Concert)
f.rec.   Geoffrey Browne/London Philharmonic Orchestra/William Alwyn - *Lyrita*
            SRCS 108, SRCD 230(CD)
Pub: Lengnick, 1956

Prologue for narrator and orchestra (1954)
[Words: Christopher Hassall]
Commissioned by and written for the Inaugural Concert of the Bournemouth Symphony
Orchestra, renamed and reconstituted after sixty one years of service to British music.
f.p.   Christopher Hassall (Narr.)/Bournemouth Symphony Orchestra/
            Sir Charles Groves - Winter Gardens, Bournemouth, 7 October 1954

Farewell Companions - a ballad opera for soli, chorus and orchestra (1954-55)
[Words: H.A.L. Craig (based on the life of the Irish patriot, Robert Emmet)]
Commissioned by the BBC
Instr: 2/2/2/2 - 4/2/3/0 - timp. perc. hp. str.
f.p.   BBC Chorus/Sinfonia of London/Muir Mathieson - BBC Third Programme,
            August 1955
Repetiteur:Douglas Gamley
Principals: Thomas Hemsley, Marion Studholme, Inia Te Waita, Denis Quilley
Producer: Douglas Cleverdon

Crépuscule for harp (1955)
Dedicated to Sidonie Goossens
Dur: 3'
f.p.   Sidonie Goossens - BBC broadcast, 25 December 1955
f.rec.   Ieuan Jones - *Chandos CHAN 9197(CD)*
Pub: Lengnick, 1956

The Moor of Venice - Dramatic Overture for brass band (1956)
Commissioned by the BBC Light Programme
Dur: 9'
f.p.   Scottish All Star Band/Scottish CWS Band/Foden's Motor Works
            Band/William Alwyn - Usher Hall, Edinburgh, 26 May 1956
f.recs.   Foden's Motor Works Band/Derek Garside - *Decca SB 341 (and MC)*

Williams Fairey Band/James Gourley - *Chandos CHAN 4547(CD)*
Pub: Besson, 1957

Theme from the film 'Smiley' (1956)
f.rec.   Shirley Abicair/Reginald Owen and his Orchestra - *Parlophone R 4197 (78), GEP 8612 (45)*

Symphony No. 3 (1956)
Commissioned by the BBC and dedicated to Richard Howgill - the score is dated London, 11 June 1956
Dur: 31'
Instr: 3/2/2/2 - 4/3/3/1 - timp. perc. cel. hp. str.
f.p.   BBC Symphony Orchestra/Sir Thomas Beecham* - Royal Festival Hall, London, 10 October 1956
f.rec.   London Philharmonic Orchestra/William Alwyn - *Lyrita SRCS 63, SRCD 228(CD); Musical Heritage Society (USA) 3300T*
Pub: Lengnick, 1957
(*Beecham was called in as a late replacement for Sir John Barbirolli who had been taken ill.)

Fantasy - Waltzes for piano (1956-57)
Dedicated to Richard Farrell
Dur: 31'
f.p.   (complete) Richard Farrell - BBC broadcast, 2 June 1957 (Farrell had previously played some of the waltzes in New Zealand)
f.rec.   Sheila Randell - *Lyrita RCS 16(m)*
Pub: Lengnick, 1956

Six Elizabethan Dances for orchestra (1956-57)
Commissioned by the BBC for the Light Music Festival of 1957 and dedicated to Bernard de Nevers
Dur: 16'
Instr: 2/2/2/2 - 4/3/3/0 - timp. perc. cel. hp. str.
f.p.   BBC Concert Orchestra/William Alwyn - Royal Festival Hall, London, 6 July 1957
f.rec.   (Nos. 1, 2, 4 and 5) London Symphony Orchestra/William Alwyn - *Lyrita SRCS 57, SRCD 229(CD); Musical Heritage Society (USA) MHS 1672F*
f.rec.   (complete) London Symphony Orchestra/Richard Hickox - *Chandos CHAN 8902(CD)*
Pub: Lengnick, 1958

Fanfare for a Joyful Occasion (1958)
Written for the Nottingham Youth Orchestra and dedicated to James Blades
Dur: 4'
Instr: 0/0/0/0 - 4/3/3/1 - timp. perc.
f.p.   Nottingham Youth Orchestra
f.rec.   Locke Consort of Brass/James Stobart - *Unicorn RHS 349*
Pub: OUP, 1964

Twelve Preludes for piano (1958)
Score dated 21 April - 13 June 1958
Dur: 24'
f.p.   Cor de Groot (Pno.) - BBC broadcast, 26 June 1959
f.rec.   John Ogdon - *Chandos ABRD 1125 (and MC), CHAN 8399(CD)*
Pub: Lengnick, 1959

String Trio (1959)
Commissioned by the South-Western Arts Association and dedicated to the Oromonte
Trio
Dur: 17'
f.p.   Oromonte Trio - Falmouth Arts Centre, Cornwall, 23 October 1960
f.broad.p. Oromonte Trio - 24 October 1960
f.rec.   members of the Gabrieli Quartet - *Unicorn UNS 241*
Pub: Lengnick, 1963

Symphony No. 4 (1959)
Dur: 36'
Instr: 2/2/2/2 - 4/3/2/1 - timp. str.
f.p.   Hallé Orchestra/Sir John Barbirolli - Royal Albert Hall, London,
            26 August 1959 (Promenade Concert)
f.rec.   London Philharmonic Orchestra/William Alwyn - *Lyrita SRCS 76, SRCD
            227(CD); Musical Heritage Society (USA) MHS 3574H*
Pub: Lengnick, 1960

Overture: Derby Day (1959-60)
Commissioned by the BBC
Dur: 6'30"
Instr: 3/2/2/2 - 4/3/2/1 - timp. perc. str.
f.p.   BBC Symphony Orchestra/Sir Malcolm Sargent - Royal Albert Hall, London,
            8 September 1960 (Promenade Concert)
f.rec.   London Philharmonic Orchestra/William Alwyn - *Lyrita SRCS 95, SRCD
            229(CD)*
Pub: Lengnick, 1962

Piano Concerto No. 2 (1960)
Originally written for Cor de Groot during the 1960 series of Promenade Concerts, but
cancelled because of his illness
Dur: 35' (rev. version 20')
Instr: 2/2/2/2 - 4/3/3/0 - timp. perc. str.
f.rec.   Howard Shelley/London Symphony Orchestra/Richard Hickox - *Chandos
            CHAN 9196(CD)*

Movements for piano (Sonata No. 2) (1961)
Dedicated to Doreen Carwithen (the composer's wife)
Dur: 15'45"
f.p.   Terence Beckles - BBC broadcast, 23 February 1963
Pub: Chester, 1962

Sonata for clarinet and piano (1962)
Dedicated to Anthony Friese-Greene
Dur: 11'30"
f.p.   Thea King (Cl.)/Celia Arieli (Pno.) - Leighton House, London,
           3 November 1962
f.rec.   John Denman (Cl.)/Paula Fan (Pno.) - *Concert Artists FED4-TC-043 (MC)*
Pub: Boosey & Hawkes, 1963

Fanfare of Welcome (1964)
Written for the opening of the Congress of the Confédération Internationale de Sociétiés
d'Auteurs et Compositeurs
Dur: 30"
f.p.   Trumpeters of the Royal Military School of Music/Colonel Basil H. Brown -
           The Guildhall, London, 15 June 1964

Concerto Grosso No. 3 - Tribute to Sir Henry Wood (1964)
Commissioned by the BBC on the twentieth anniversary of the death of Sir Henry Wood
Dedication: `A Tribute to the "ever-living" memory of Sir Henry Wood'
Dur: 15'
Instr: 3/2/2/2 - 4/3/3/1 - hp. str.
f.p.   BBC Symphony Orchestra/William Alwyn - Royal Albert Hall, London,
           19 August 1964 (Promenade Concert)
f.rec.   City of London Sinfonia/Richard Hickox - *Chandos CHAN 8866(CD)*
Pub: Lengnick, 1964

Twelve Diversions for the five fingers (1964)
[1. Prelude 2. Crépuscule 3. Chimes 4. Siesta 5. Anvil Tune
 6. Berceuse (Cradle Song) 7. Rondel 8. Scherzetto 9. Nocturne (Night Song)
 10. Aquarium 11. Valse Triste 12. Russian Dance]
Pub: Keith Prowse, 1964

Juan or The Libertine - opera in Four Acts (1965-71)
[Words freely adapted by the composer, from John Elroy Flecker's play `Don Juan'.
Other sources include Byron's `Don Juan' (Canto 2), Molière's `Don Juan ou la festin de
Pierre', and the final chorus `Chorus Mysticus' of Goethe's `Faust' (Part 2)]
Dur: 120'
Instr: 3/2 + ca./2 + bcl/2 - 4/3/3/1 - timp. perc. hp. str.

Homage March for trombone quartet (1968)
Written for the link-up of ADAM with the University of Rochester, New York
f.p.   St. Stephen Trombone Ensemble - The French Institute, London,
           17 October 1968

Moto perpetuo for recorders (1970)
Dedicated to R.B. Coles and the Nene Consort
f.p.   Nene Consort, Northampton, 27 March 1971

Sinfonietta for string orchestra (1970)
Commissioned by the Cheltenham Festival with funds provided by the Arts Council of
Great Britain and dedicated to Mosco Carner
Dur: 23'
f.p.   Hurwitz Chamber Orchestra*/Adrian Sunshine - Town Hall, Cheltenham, 4
            July 1970 (Cheltenham Festival)
f.rec.   London Philharmonic Orchestra/William Alwyn - *Lyrita SRCS 85, SRCD*
            229(CD); HNH (USA) HNH 4020; Musical Heritage Society (USA) MHS
            3644W
Pub: Lengnick, 1974
(* the work was originally intended for the strings of the San Francisco Symphony
Orchestra who were due to tour England in 1970)

`Mirages' - song cycle for baritone and piano (1970)
[Words: William Alwyn
 1. Undine 2. Aquarium 3. The Honeysuckle 4. The Metronome
 5. Portrait in a Mirror 6. Paradise]
Dedicated to David Willison
Dur: 25'
f.p.   Benjamin Luxon (Bar.)/David Willison (Pno.) - The Maltings, Snape, 9 June
            1974 (Aldeburgh Festival)
f.broad.p. above artists - Radio 3, 6 October 1974
f.Lon.p.   Peter Allanson (Bar.)/Stephen Betteridge (Pno.) - British Music
            Information Centre, 25 May 1982
f.p.   (as a ballet): Another Dance Group - Oval House, London, 29 May 1975
Choreography: Sue Little
f.rec.   Benjamin Luxon (Bar.)/David Willison (Pno.) - *Lyrita SRCS 61; Musical*
            Heritage Society (USA) MHS 1742T
Pub: Lengnick, 1977

Naiades: `Fantasy Sonata' for flute and harp (1971)
Dedicated to Christopher Hyde-Smith and Marisa Robles
Dur: 13'
f.p.   Christopher Hyde-Smith (Fl.)/Marisa Robles (Hp.) - at the home of
            William Rees-Mogg, Stone Easton, 29 May 1971 (Bath Festival)
f.broad.p. above artists - Radio 3, 8 October 1971
f.Lon.p.   above artists - RSA Soirée, John Adam Street, 22 March 1972
f.rec.   above artists - *Lyrita SRCS 61; Musical Heritage Society (USA) MHS 1742T*
Pub: Boosey & Hawkes, 1973; Lengnick, 1986

Symphony No. 5 (Hydriotaphia)* (1972-73)
Commissioned by the Arts Council of Great Britain for the Norfolk and Norwich
Triennial Festival of 1973 and dedicated `to the immortal memory of Sir Thomas Browne
(1605-1682), citizen of Norwich, physician, philosopher and incomparable master of
English prose'
Dur: 15'
Instr: 3/3/2/2 - 4/3/3/1 - timp. perc. hp. str.
f.p.   Royal Philharmonic Orchestra/William Alwyn - St. Andrews Hall, Norwich,
            27 October 1973 (Norfolk and Norwich Festival)

f.Lon.p.   BBC Symphony Orchestra/Gennadi Rozhdestvensky - Royal Festival Hall, 16
            April 1980
f.rec.   London Philharmonic Orchestra/William Alwyn - *Lyrita SRCS 76, SRCD
            228(CD); Musical Heritage Society (USA) MHS 3574H*
Pub: Lengnick, 1973
(* The title refers to the great elegy of Sir Thomas Browne published in 1658 entitled
'Hydriotaphia : Urn Burial or a Discourse of the Sepulchral Urns lately found in Norfolk')

Six Nocturnes - song cycle for baritone and piano (1973)
[Words: Michael Armstrong 1. Everything is now 2. Summer rain 3. Visitation
4. Summer Night 5. Circle 6. Response]
Dedicated to Benjamin Luxon - the score is dated 4 May 1973
Dur: 17'
f.p.   Benjamin Luxon (Bar.)/David Willison (Pno.) - Saville Club Convivium,
            London, 13 November 1975
f.broad.p. above artists - Pebble Mill Studios, Birmingham, 5 December 1975

String Quartet No. 2 (Spring Waters) (1975)
Commissioned by the Norfolk and Norwich Music Club and dedicated 'To RW' (Reg
Williamson). The score is dated 11 September 1975
Dur: 23'
f.priv.p.   Gabrieli String Quartet - Blackfriars Hall, Norwich, 29 May 1976
f.pub.p.   above artists - The Maltings, Snape, 5 June 1976 (Aldeburgh Festival)
f.broad.p. above artists - Radio 3, 30 August 1977
f.Lon.p.   Quartet of London - Wigmore Hall, 23 November 1983
f.rec.   Quartet of London - *Chandos ABRD 1063 (and MC), CHAN 9219(CD)*
Pub: Lengnick, 1979

Miss Julie - opera in 2 Acts (1977)
[After the play by August Strinberg - words by the composer]
Dur: 117'
Instr: 2+picc./2+ca./2/2 - 4/3/3/0 - timp. perc. bells. xyl. cel.
            hp. str.
f.p.   BBC Concert Orchestra/Vilem Tausky - BBC Radio 3, 16 July 1977 (recorded
            in Brent Town Hall, 17 February 1977)
Producer: Elaine Padmore
Repetiteur: Alexa Maxwell
Principals: Jill Gomez, Benjamin Luxon, Della Jones, Anthony Rolfe-Johnson
f.st.p.   Britten Sinfonia/Nicholas Cleobury - Theatre Royal, Norwich, 15 October
            1997 (Norfolk and Norwich Festival)
Producers: Benjamin Luxon and Peter Wilson
Designer: Andrew Leigh
Principals: Judith Howarth, Karl Daymond, Fiona Kimm, Ian Caley
f.rec.   above (BBC) artists - *Lyrita SRCS 121/2, SRCD 2218(CD)*

A Leave-Taking - song cycle for tenor and piano (1977)
[Words: John Leicester Warren, Lord de Tabley (1835-95)
1. The Pilgrim Cranes 2. Daffodils 3. The Ocean Wood 4. Fortune's Wheel
5. Study of a Spider 6. The Two Old Kings 7. A Leave-Taking]

Dedicated to Anthony Rolfe-Johnson - the score is dated June, July/September 1977
Dur: 21'30"
f.p.   Anthony Rolfe-Johnson (Ten.)/David Willison (Pno.) - Blythburgh Church,
            Suffolk, 10 June 1979 (Aldeburgh Festival)
f.broad.p. above artists - Radio 3, 15 November 1979
f.rec.   Anthony Rolfe-Johnson (Ten.)/Graham Johnson (Pno.) - *Chandos ABRD 1117*
            (and MC), CHAN 9220(CD)
Pub: Lengnick, 1984

Invocations - song cycle for soprano and piano (1977)
[Words: Michael Armstrong
 1. Through the Centuries 2. Holding the Night 3. Separation 4. Spring Rain
 6. Invocation to the Queen of Moonlight 7. Our Magic Horse]
Dedicated to Jill Gomez - the score is dated 12 December 1977
Dur: 25'
f.p.   Jill Gomez (Sop.)/John Constable (Pno.) - BBC Radio 3, 18 December 1979
f.rec.   above artists - *Chandos ABRD 1117 (and MC), CHAN 9220(CD)*
Pub: Lengnick

Concerto for flute and eight wind instruments (1980)
Dedicated to the English Chamber Orchestra Wind Ensemble - the score is dated 23 June
1980
Dur: 16'
f.p.   English Chamber Orchestra Wind Ensemble - Concert Hall, BBC
            Broadcasting House, 27 September 1984
f.broad.p. above performance - Radio 3, 27 February 1985
f.rec.   Haffner Wind Ensemble of London/Nicholas Daniel - *Chandos CHAN*
            9152(CD)

Seascapes - Four songs for soprano, treble recorder and piano (1980)
[Words: Michael Armstrong
 1. Dawn at Sea 2. Sea-mist 3. Song of the Drowned Man 4. Black Gulls]
Commissioned by John Turner with funds provided by North West Arts and dedicated to
John Turner - the score is dated 24 December 1980
Dur: 12'
f.p.   Honor Sheppard (Sop.)/John Turner (Rec.)/Alan Cuckston (Pno.) - Whitworth
            Art Gallery, University of Manchester, 14 October 1982
Pub: Forsyth (Manchester), 1985

Chaconne for Tom: for descant recorder and piano (1982)
Written in celebration of Thomas Pitfield's 80th birthday and inscribed for John Turner to
play
Dur: 7'
f.priv.p.   John Turner (Rec.)/Stephen Reynolds (Pno.) - Eddisbury Hall,
            Macclesfield, Cheshire, 30 April 1983
f.pub.p.   above artists, All Saint's Church, Altrincham, Cheshire, 6 May 1983
Pub: Forsyth (Manchester), 1983 (in `A Birthday Album for Thomas Pitfield')

String Quartet No. 3 (1984)
Dedicated to the memory of Sir Cecil Parrott
Dur: 26'
f.p.   Quartet of London - Blythburgh Parish Church, 13 June 1985 (Aldeburgh
              Festival)
f.Lon.p.   above artists - Purcell Room, 19 September 1985
f.rec.   above artists - *Chandos ABRD 1153 (and MC), CHAN 8440(CD)*
Pub: Lengnick

FILM MUSIC

(i) Documentary Films

The Future's in the Air* - Strand (1937)
Director: Alexander Shaw
Commentator: Ivan Scott
Music played by: London Symphony Orchestra/William Alwyn - (recorded at
the Gaumont-British Film Studios, Lime Grove)
(* Raymond Bennell wrote the original score but the recording failed after
Bennell had gone overseas, so Paul Rotha approached William Alwyn who
composed a new score which was so successful he was then offered other film
work.)

Air Outpost - Strand for Imperial Airways (1937)
Directors: John Taylor and Ralph Keene

Lifeboats - Strand (1937)
Director: Not traced

Conquest of the Air - Film Productions (1937)
Director: Alexander Shaw

**Bath: Strand for Travel and Industrial Development Association of Great
Britain (1937)**
Director: Alexander Shaw

The Birth of the Year - Strand Zoological Films (1938)
Director: Evelyn Spice

Monkey into Man - Strand Zoological Films (1938)
Co-directors: Stanley Hawes, Evelyn Spice and Donald Alexander

The Zoo and You - Strand Zoological Films (1938)
Director: Ruby Grierson

Zoo Babies - Strand Zoological Films (1938)
Director: Evelyn Spice

Whipsnade Freedom (Free to Roam) - Strand Zoological Films (1938)
Director: Paul Burnford

Mites and Monsters - Strand Zoological Films (1938)
Director: Donald Alexander

Behind the Scenes - Strand Zoological Films (1938)
Director: Evelyn Spice

Fingers and Thumbs - Strand Zoological Films (1938)
Director: Evelyn Spice

New Worlds for Old - Realist for the British Commercial Gas Association (1938)
Directors: Frank Sainsbury and Paul Rotha

These Children are Safe - Strand for Travel and Industrial Development Association of Great Britain (1939)
Director: Alexander Shaw

Wings over the Empire - Strand (1939)
Director: Stuart Legg

Roads Across Britain - Realist (1939)
Director: Sidney Cole

Trinity House (S.O.S.) - Merton Park for C.O.I. (1940)
Directors: John Eldridge/Martin Curtis

The New Britain - Strand (1940)
Director: Ralph Keene
Music conducted by: Muir Mathieson

The Big City - Strand (1940)
Director: Ralph Bond
Music conducted by: Muir Mathieson

Wealth from Coal - Realist (1940)
Director: Edgar Anstey

Steel goes to Sea - Merton Park (1940)
Director: John Curthoys

W.V.S. - Verity (1940)
Director: Louise Birt

Architects of England - Strand for the British Council (1941)
Director: John Eldridge

Salute to Farmers - Publicity Films (1941)
Director: Montgomery Tully

Playtime - Raylton Pictures for the British Council (1941)
Director: S. Raymond Elton

(Film on) Evacuation - Realist for C.O.I. (1941)
Director: Not traced

Night Watch - Strand (1941)
Director: Donald Taylor

The English Inn - Verity Films (1941)
Director: Muriel Baker

H.M.S. Minelayer - Verity Films (1941)
Director: Henry Cass

An African in London - Strand (1941)
Director: George Pearson

Women in Industry - Verity (1941)
Director: Not traced

The Harvest shall come - Realist for ICI (1941)
Director: Max Anderson

Border Weave - Turner Film Production for the British Council (1941)
Director: J.L. Curthoys

Western Isles - Merton Park (1941)
Director: Terence Bishop

Wales - Green Mountain, Black Mountain - Strand (1941)
Director: John Eldridge
Music conducted by: Muir Mathieson

The Countrywomen - Seven League (1942)
Director: John Page

Life Begins Again - Rotha Films (1942)
Director: Donald Alexander

The Crown of the Year - Greenpark (1942)
Director: Ralph Keene
Music played by: London Symphony Orchestra

British News - British Council Film Unit (1942)
Director: Not traced

Queen Cotton - Merton Park (1942)
Director: Cecil Musk

Man of Science - Turner Film Productions (1942)
Director: Not traced

Rat Destruction - Rotha Films (1942)
Director: Budge Cooper

Spring on the Farm - Greenpark (1942)
Director: Ralph Keene

Winter on the Farm - Greenpark (1942)
Director: Ralph Keen

The Battle for Freedom - (1942)
Director: Alan Osbiston

Fires were started - Crown Film Unit (1942)
US Title: I was a Fireman
Director: Humphrey Jennings
Music played by: BBC Northern Orchestra/Muir Mathieson (recorded at
Pinewood Recording Theatre)

World of Plenty - Paul Rotha Productions for C.O.I. (1943)
Director: Paul Rotha

Citizens of Tomorrow (A Start in Life) - Realist (1943)
Director: Brian Smith

A Letter from Ulster - Crown Film Unit (1943)
Director: Brian Desmond Hurst

Africa Freed - Army Film Unit (1943)
Director: Hugh Stewart
(this film was not released - the American authorities objecting to the fact that
the film did not sufficiently emphasise the contribution of their forces to the
victory in North Africa. See below.)

There's a Future in it - Strand (1943)
Directors: Leslie Fenton, Phil Regal
Music conducted by: Muir Mathieson

A.B.C.A. magazine series - Army Film Unit (1943)
Director: Ronald Riley

**Desert Victory - Army Film and Photographic & RAF Production Film
Units (1943)**
Director: Roy Boulting

Music played by: London Symphony Orchestra/Muir Mathieson (recorded at Pinewood)
Pub: Chappell, 1963 (March only arr. piano by the composer)

Tunisian Victory - British and American Services Film Units (1943)
Written in collaboration with Dimitri Tiomkin - a revised version of **Africa Freed** q.v.
Co-directors: Roy Boulting, Frank Capra, John Huston and Anthony Veiller
Music played by: London Symphony Orchestra/Muir Mathieson

Lift your head, comrade (1943)
Director: Michael Hankinson

The Royal Mile, Edinburgh (1943)
Director: Terry Bishop

Summer on the Farm - Greenpark (1944)
Director: Ralph Keene

A Welcome to Britain - Strand for C.O.I./American Army (1944)
Directors: Anthony Asquith and Burgess Meredith

French Town - September 1944 - Realist (1944)
Director: Alexander Shaw

Atlantic Trawler - Realist (1944)
Director: Frank Sainsbury

Your Children's Eyes - Realist for the C.O.I./Departments of Child Health and Council for Health Education (1944)
Director: Alexander Strasser

Your Children's Ears - Realist for the C.O.I./Departments of Child Health and Council for Health Education (1944)
Director: Albert Pearl

Your Children's Teeth - Realist for the C.O.I./Departments of Child Health and Council for Health Education (1944)
Director: Jane Massey

Accident Service (They Live Again) - Gaumont British Instructional (1944)
Director: A. Reginald Dobson

Our Country - Strand for C.O.I. (1944)
Director: John Eldridge
Music conducted by: Muir Mathieson
Verse commentary written by Dylan Thomas

Soldier, Sailor - Realist for C.O.I./War Office (1944)
Director: Alexander Shaw
Music conducted by: Muir Mathieson

The Grassy Shires (Midland Shires) - Verity/Greenpark (1944)
Director: Ralph Keene

The Gen - RAF Newsreel (1944-45)
Director: Not traced
Music played by: RAF Symphony Orchestra/Muir Mathieson

Today and Tomorrow - World Wide for C.O.I. (1945)
Director: Robin Carruthers
Music conducted by: Muir Mathieson

Total War in Britain - Films of Fact for C.O.I. (1945)
Directors: Paul Rotha and Michael Orrom

The True Glory - British and American Service Film Units (1945)
Co-directors: Carol Reed and Garson Kanin
Pub: Chappell, 1945 (exc. March for piano arr. by Chris Langdon)

Worker and Warfront (magazine series Nos. 1-18) - Films of Fact for C.O.I. (1945-47)
Director: Paul Rotha (and others)

Peace Thanksgiving (1945)
Director: N. Walker (Denham)

Penicillin - Realist (1945)
Directors: Alexander Shaw, Kay Mander

Trade Unions - Verity (1945)
Director: Not traced

Employment Exchange - Avons Kinematograph Section (1945)
Director: Not traced

Proud City - Greenpark for Ministry of Information (1945)
Director: Ralph Keene

A Modern Miracle - Strand (1945)
Director: Desmond Dickinson

Country Town (1945)
Director: Julian Wintle

Land of Promise - Rotha Films for the Gas Industry (1945)
Director: Paul Rotha

Each for All (1946)
Director: Montgomery Tully

Home and School - Crown Film Unit for C.O.I./Ministry of Education (1946)
Director: Gerry Bryant

Approach to Science (1947)
Director: Bill Mason

Three Dawns to Sydney - Greenpark for BOAC (1947)
Written in collaboration with Eric Rogers
Director: John Eldridge
Music played by: London Philharmonic Orchestra/John Hollingsworth

A City Speaks - Films of Fact for Manchester City Corporation (1947)
Directors: Francis Gysin and Paul Rotha
Music played by: Hallé Orchestra/Sir John Barbirolli

Your Children and You - Realist for C.O.I./Ministry of Health and Central Council for Health Education (1948)
Director: Brian Smith

Your Children's Sleep - Realist for C.O.I./Ministry of Health and Central Council for Health Education (1948)
Director: Jane Massey

One Man's Story - Horizon for C.O.I./Foreign Office (1948)
Directors: Maxwell Munden and Dennis Shand

Daybreak in Udi - Crown Film Unit (1949)
Award Winner from the American Academy of Motion Pictures and Best Specialised Film Award from the British Film Academy, both in 1949.
Director: Terry Bishop
Music played by: London Philharmonic Orchestra/John Hollingsworth

Under One Roof (1949)
Director: Lewis Gilbert

Potato Blight - Realist (1950)
Director: Not traced

Royal River - International Realist for the BFI (1951)
US Title: Distant Thames
Director: Brian Smith

Festival in London - Crown Film Unit for C.O.I./Commonwealth Realtions Office (1951)
Director: Philip Leacock

Royal Heritage - Wessex Productions for London Films International (1952)
Director: Diana Pine

Alliance for Peace - for Supreme Headquarters, Allied Powers, Europe (1952)
Director: Not traced

Powered Flight - the Story of the Century - Shell Film Unit for Shell Petroleum (1954)
Written in collaboration with Malcolm Arnold
Director: Stuart Legg
Music conducted by: Malcolm Arnold

(ii) Feature Films

Penn of Pennsylvania - British National (1941)
US Title: The Courageous Mr. Penn
Director: Lance Comfort
Music conducted by: Muir Mathieson
f.rec.   complete film (V)

They Flew Alone - Imperator/RKO (1941)
US Title: Wings and the Woman
Director: Herbert Wilcox
Music played by: London Symphony Orchestra/Muir Mathieson

Squadron Leader X - RKO (1942)
Director: Lance Comfort
Music played by: London Symphony Orchestra/Muir Mathieson

Escape to Danger - RKO (1943)
Director: Lance Comfort
Music played by: London Symphony Orchestra/Muir Mathieson

On Approval - GFD/Independent (1943)
Director: Clive Brook
Music conducted by: Muir Mathieson
f.rec.   complete film (V)

The Way Ahead - GFD/Two Cities (1944)
US Title: Immortal Battalion
Director: Carol Reed
Music played by: London Symphony Orchestra/Muir Mathieson (recorded at Denham)
f.rec.   complete film (V)

Medal for the General - British National (1944)
Director: Maurice Elvey

Great Day - RKO-British (1945)
Director: Lance Comfort
Music conducted by: Muir Mathieson
f.rec.   complete film (V)

The Rake's Progress - GFD/Individual (1945)
US Title: Notorious Gentleman
Director: Sidney Gilliat
Music played by: National Symphony Orchestra/Muir Mathieson

I see a Dark Stranger - GFD/Individual (1945)
US Title: The Adventuress
Director: Frank Launder
Music played by: London Symphony Orchestra/Muir Mathieson
f.rec.   complete film (V)

Green for Danger - Rank/Individual (1946)
Director: Sidney Gilliat
Music played by: London Symphony Orchestra/Muir Mathieson
f.rec.   complete film (V)

Odd Man Out - GFD/Two Cities (1947)
US Title: Gang War
Director: Carol Reed
Music played by: London Symphony Orchestra/Muir Mathieson
f.rec.   complete film (V) (L)

Take my Life - GFD/Cineguild (1947)
Director: Ronald Neame
Music played by: London Symphony Orchestra/Muir Mathieson

Captain Boycott - GFD/Individual (1947)
Director: Frank Launder
Music played by: London Philharmonic Orchestra/Muir Mathieson

The October Man - GFD/Two Cities (1947)
Director: Roy Baker
Music played by: London Symphony Orchestra/Muir Mathieson
f.rec.   complete film (V)

Escape - TCF (1948)
Director: Joseph Mankiewicz
Music played by: Philharmonia Orchestra/Muir Mathieson

So Evil my Love - Paramount British (1948)
Written in collaboration with Victor Young
Director: Lewis Allen
Music played by: Philharmonia Orchestra/Muir Mathieson

The Winslow Boy - British Lion/London Films (1948)
Director: Anthony Asquith
Music played by: London Film Symphony Orchestra/Hubert Clifford
f.rec.   complete film (V)

The Fallen Idol - London Films (1948)
US Title: The Lost Illusion
Director: Carol Reed
Music played by: London Film Symphony Orchestra/Hubert Clifford
f.rec.   complete film (V) (L)

The History of Mr. Polly - GFD/Two Cities (1949)
Director: Anthony Pelissier
Music played by: Royal Philharmonic Orchestra/Muir Mathieson

The Rocking Horse Winner - Rank/Two Cities (1949)
Director: Anthony Pelissier
Music played by: Royal Philharmonic Orchestra/Muir Mathieson
f.rec.   complete film (V)

The Cure for Love - London Films (1949)
Director: Robert Donat
Music played by: London Symphony Orchestra/Muir Mathieson

The Golden Salamander - GFD/Pinewood (GFD) (1949)
Director: Ronald Neame
Music played by: London Symphony Orchestra/Muir Mathieson

Madeleine - GFD/Cineguild (1949)
Director: David Lean
Music played by: Royal Pilharmonic Orchestra/Muir Mathieson
f.rec.   complete film (V)

Morning Departure - Rank/Jay-Lewis (1950)
Written in collaboration with Gordon Jacob q.v.
US Title: Operation Disaster
Director: Roy Baker

State Secret - British Lion/London Films (1950)
US Title: The Great Manhunt
Director: Sidney Gilliat
Music played by: Royal Philharmonic Orchestra/Muir Mathieson

The Magnet - Ealing (1950)
Director: Charles Frend
Music played by: Philharmonia Orchestra/Ernest Irving

No Resting Place - Rotha Films (1950)
Director: Paul Rotha

The Mudlark - TCF (1950)
Director: Jean Negulesco
Music conducted by: Muir Mathieson

Night Without Stars - GFD/Europa (1951)
Director: Anthony Pelissier
Music played by: London Symphony Orchestra/Muir Mathieson

The Magic Box - Festival Films (1951)
Director: John Boulting
Music conducted by: Muir Mathieson
f.rec.   complete film (V)

The House in the Square - TCF (1951)
US Title: I'll Never Forget You
Director: Roy Baker
Music conducted by: Muir Mathieson

Lady Godiva Rides Again - British Lion/London Films (1951)
Director: Frank Launder
Music conducted by: Muir Mathieson

Saturday Island - Coronado (1951)
US Title: Island of Desire
Director: Stuart Heisler

The Card - Rank/British Film Makers (1952)
US Title: The Promoter
Director: Ronald Neame
Music played by: London Symphony Orchestra/Muir Mathieson
f.rec.   complete film (V)

Mandy - Ealing (1952)
US Title: The Crash of Silence
Director: Alexander Mackendrick
Music played by: Philharmonia Orchestra/Ernest Irving
f.rec.   complete film (V)

The Crimson Pirate - Warner/Norma (1952)
Director: Robert Siodmak
Music played by: London Symphony Orchestra/Muir Mathieson
f.rec.   complete film (V) (L)

The Long Memory - Rank/Europa (1953)
Director: Robert Hamer
Music conducted by: Muir Mathieson

Malta Story - GFD/British Film Makers (1953)
Director: Brian Desmond Hurs

Music played by: London Symphony Orchestra/Muir Mathieson
f.rec.   complete film (V)

The Master of Ballantrae - Warner Bros. (1953)
Director: William Keighley
Music conducted by: Muir Mathieson
f.rec.   complete film (V) (L)

Personal Affair - Rank/Two Cities (1953)
Director: Anthony Pelissier
Music conducted by: Muir Mathieson

The Million Pound Note - GFD/Group Films (1954)
US Title: Man with a Million
Director: Ronald Neame
Music conducted by: Muir Mathieson

The Rainbow Jacket - Ealing (1954)
Director: Basil Dearden
Music played by: Philharmonia Orchestra/Dock Mathieson

The Seekers - GFD/Fanfare (1954)
US Title: Land of Fury
Director: Ken Annakin
Music played by: Philharmonia Orchestra/Muir Mathieson
f.rec.   complete film (V)

Svengali - Alderdale/Renown (1954)
Director: Noel Langley
Music played by: Royal Philharmonic Orchestra/Muir Mathieson with
Elizabeth Schwarzkopf (Sop.)
f.rec.   complete film (V)

Bedevilled - MGM (1955)
Director: Mitchell Leisen
Music conducted by: Muir Mathieson

The Ship that died of Shame - Ealing (1955)
US Title: P.T. Raiders
Director: Basil Dearden
Music played by: London Symphony Orchestra/Dock Mathieson
f.rec.   complete film (V)

Geordie - British Lion/Argonaut (1955)
US Title: Wee Georgie
Director: Frank Launder
Music played by: London Symphony Orchestra/Muir Mathieson

The Black Tent - Rank (1956)
Director: Brian Desmond Hurst
Music played by: London Symphony Orchestra/Muir Mathieson
f.rec.   complete film (V)

Safari - Warwick (1956)
Director: Terence Young
Music played by: Royal Philharmonic Orchestra/Muir Mathieson

Smiley - TCF/London Films (1956)
Director: Anthony Kimmins
Music played by: Sinfonia of London/Muir Mathieson

Odongo* - Warwick/Columbia (1956)
Director: John Gilling
(* Alwyn's contribution was the song `Safari blues')

Zarak - Warwick/Columbia (1957)
Director: Terence Young
Music played by: Sinfonia of London/Muir Mathieson

Fortune is a Woman - Columbia (1957)
US Title: She Played with Fire
Director: Sidney Gilliat
Music played by: Royal Philharmonic Orchestra/Muir Mathieson

The Smallest Show on Earth - British Lion (1957)
US Title: Big Time Operators
Director: Basil Dearden
Music played by: Sinfonia of London/Muir Mathieson

Manuela - British Lion/Ivan Foxwell (1957)
US Title: Stowaway Girl
Director: Guy Hamilton
Music played by: Sinfonia of London/Muir Mathieson

I Accuse! - MGM (1957)
Director: José Ferrer
Music played by: Sinfonia of London/Muir Mathieson

The Silent Enemy - Romulus (1957)
Director: William Fairchild
f.rec.   complete film (V)

Carve her Name with Pride - Rank/Keyboard (1958)
Director: Lewis Gilbert
Music played by: Sinfonia of London/Muir Mathieson
f.rec.   complete film (V)

A Night to Remember - Rank (1958)
Director: Roy Baker
Music played by: Sinfonia of London/Muir Mathieson
f.rec.   complete film (V)

Shake Hands with the Devil - United Artists/Troy/Pennebaker (1959)
Director: Michael Anderson
Music played by: Sinfonia of London/Muir Mathieson
f.recs. (soundtrack) - *United Artists (USA) UAL 4043(m), UAS 5043*
        complete film (V)

The Killers of Kilimanjaro - Warwick (1959)
US Title: Adamson of Africa
Director: Richard Thorpe
Music played by: Sinfonia of London/Muir Mathieson

Third Man on the Mountain - Walt Disney (1959)
Director: Ken Annakin
Music played by: Sinfonia of London/Muir Mathieson
f.rec.   complete film (V)

Devil's Bait - Rank/Independent Artists (1959)
Director: Peter Graham Scott
Music played by: Sinfonia of London/Muir Mathieson

The Professionals - Independent Artists (1960)
Director: Don Sharp
Music played by: Sinfonia of London/Muir Mathieson

The Swiss Family Robinson - Walt Disney (1961)
Director: Ken Annakin
Music played by: Sinfonia of London/Muir Mathieson
f.recs. (soundtrack) - *Vista (USA) 3309 and 3319 (excs.)*
        complete film (V)

The Naked Edge - United Artists (1961)
Director: Michael Anderson
Music played by: Sinfonia of London/ Muir Mathieson
f.rec.   complete film (V)

Night of the Eagle - Independent Artists (1962)
US Title: Burn Witch, Burn
Director: Sidney Hayers
Music conducted by: Muir Mathieson

Life for Ruth - Rank/Allied Film Makers (1962)
US Title: Condemned to Life
Director: Basil Dearden
Music conducted by: Muir Mathieson

Fever Pitch (1962)
Director: Not traced

In Search of the Castaways - Walt Disney (1962)
Director: Robert Stevenson
Music played by: Sinfonia of London/Muir Mathieson
f.rec.   (soundtrack excs.) - *Decca DFE 8512 (45)*

The Running Man - Columbia/Peet (1963)
Director: Carol Reed
Music played by: Sinfonia of London/Muir Mathieson

INCIDENTAL MUSIC

(a) Radio

Commandos (1942)
f.broad.p.   17 October 1942

Britain to America (1942)
[Written and produced by D.G. Bridson]
Instr: 2/2/2/2 - 4/2/3/1 - timp. perc. hp. str.
Music played by: Alexandra Choir/London Symphony Orchestra/Muir Mathieson
f.broad.p.   (USA) 26 July 1942
f.Brit.broad.p. Home Service, 14 August 1942

Translantic Call - People to People (1943)

Made in Britain (1943)
[A contribution to Worker's Gala Night - produced by Leonard Cottrell]
Instr: 5 0/0/0/0 - 2/2/2/0 - hp. str.
Music played by: London Symphony Orchestra/Muir Mathieson
f.broad.p.   Home Service and Forces Programmes, 1 June 1943

Four Years at War (1943)
[Written by Louis MacNeice and produced by Laurence Gilliam]
Instr: 1/1/2/1 - 2/2/2/0 - perc. str.
Music played by: London Symphony Orchestra/Muir Mathieson
f.broad.p.   Home Service, 3 September 1943

Pulse of Britain (c. 1944)
Instr: 2+picc./2/2/2 - 4/2/3/0 - timp. perc. hp. str.

The Spirit of '76 (1944)
[Written and produced by D.G. Bridson]
Instr: 2/2/2/1 - 4/2/3/0 - timp. perc. xyl. str. (and male voice chorus)
Music played by: London Symphony Orchestra/Muir Mathieson

f.broad.p. Home Service, 4 July 1944

The Chimes (1944)
[Charles Dickens, adapted for broadcasting by Joan Littlewood and produced by D.G. Bridson]
Instr: 1/1/1/1 - 2/0/0/0 - timp. perc. glock. vib. hp. pno. str.(with chorus)
Music conducted by: Walter Goehr
f.broad.p. Home Service, 30 December 1944

Britain's our Doorstep (1944-45)
[Written and produced by Leonard Cottrell]
Instr: 1/1/3+3sax./1 - 2/3/2/0 - timp. perc. pno. str.
Music played by: London Symphony Orchestra/Muir Mathieson
f.broad.p. Home Service, 12 January 1945

Their Finest Hour: The People of Britain (1945)
[Written and produced by Leonard Cottrell]
Instr: 1/1+ca./1/0 - 2/1/0/0 - timp. perc. str.
Music conducted by: Muir Mathieson
f.broad.p. Home Service, 17 May 1945 (pre-recorded 13 May 1945)

London Victorious (1945)
[Written and produced by Louis MacNeice]
Instr: 2 Hn. Perc. Ten.
Music played by: Norman del Mar (Hn.), Neil Sanders (Hn.), James Blades (Perc.), Jan van der Gucht (Ten.), cond. William Alwyn
f.broad.p. Home Service, 18 May 1945

Transatlantic Flight (1945)
Instr: 2+picc./1/2/1 - 2/2/0/0 - timp. perc. str.

Ex-Corporal Wilf (1945)
[Written and produced by D.G. Bridson]
Instr: Fl. Perc.
Music played by: James Blades (Perc.), Arthur Cleghorn (Fl.), cond. William Alwyn
f.broad.p. Light Programme, 31 October 1945 (pre-recorded, 29 October 1945)

Armagh: City set on a Hill (1945)
[Written by W.R. Rodgers and produced by Louis MacNeice]
Instr: Fl. Hp. Vn. Ten. (and chorus)
Live music played by William Alwyn (Fl.), who also directed: Aileen MacArdle (Hp.)/Thomas Turkington (Vn.)/Hugo Stirling (Ten.)
f.broad.p. Northern Ireland Home Service, 15 November 1945

Wherever you may be - Christmas feature (1945)
[Arranged and produced by Laurence Gilliam and Leonard Cottrell]
Instr: 2/2/2/2 - 4/3/3/1 - timp. perc.(2) hp. str.

Music played by: London Symphony Orchestra/Muir Mathieson
f.broad.p. Home Service and Light Programme, 25 December 1945

Threshold of the New (1945)
[Written and produced by Louis MacNeice]
Music played by: BBC Chorus/Leslie Woodgate
f.broad.p. Home Service, 31 December 1945

Nalinakanti (Indian folk tune) - Features production (1946)
Instr: picc./1/1/0 - 0/0/0/0 - hp. str. (2/1/1/1)
Music played by: Welbeck Small Orchestra/Hubert Clifford (recorded 21 March 1946)

Flying Visit - Features production (1946)
Instr: 1/1/1/1 - 2/2/0/0 - perc. str.

Man from Belsen (1946)
[Written and produced by Leonard Cottrell]
Instr: Perc.
Percussive effects played by: James Blades and Henry Taylor
f.broad.p. Home Service, 12 April 1946

The Careerist - a psycho-morality play of modern life (1946)
[Written and produced by Louis MacNeice]
Instr: Fl. Ten.
Music performed by: William Alwyn (Fl.)/Jan van der Gucht (Ten.) (pre--recorded 18 October 1946)
f.broad.p. Third Programme, 22 October 1946

Home Again - Christmas feature (1946)
[Arranged and produced by Laurence Gilliam and Leonard Cottrell]
Instr: 2/2/2/2 - 4/3/3/1 - timp. perc. xyl. hp. str.
Music played by: London Symphony Orchestra/Muir Mathieson
f.broad.p. Home Service and Light Programme, 25 December 1946

The Hare - Features production (1947)
Instr: 0/0/0/0 - 2/0/0/0 - str.
Music recorded: 18 February 1947

The Pharoah Akhnaton (1947)
[Written and produced by Leonard Cottrell]
Instr: 3/3/0/0 - 4/3/0/0 - perc. hp. str. (0/1/1/1)
Music played by: BBC Men's Chorus/London Symphony Orchestra/ Muir Mathieson
f.broad.p. Third Programme, 6 July 1947

The Moon in the Yellow River (1947)
[Written and produced by Denis Johnston]
Instr: voice and piano

Song performed by Cyril Cusack with Arthur Dulay (Pno.)
f.broad.p.   Home Service, 14 July 1947

Christmas Journey - Christmas feature (1950)
[Produced by Laurence Gilliam and Leonard Cottrell]
Instr: 2/2/2/2 - 4/3/3/0 - timp. perc. hp. str.
Music played by: London Symphony Orchestra/Muir Mathieson (recorded 18 December 1950)
f.broad.p.   Home Service and Light Programme, 25 December 1950

The Gifts of Christmas - Christmas feature (1951)
[Produced by Laurence Gilliam and R.D. Smith]
Instr: 2/2/2/2 - 4/3/3/0 - timp. cel. hp. str.
Music played by: London Symphony Orchestra/Muir Mathieson (recorded 17 December 1951)
f.broad.p.   Home Service and Light Programme, 25 December 1951

The Queen's Inheritance - Christmas Day Programme (1952)
[Produced by Laurence Gilliam and Alan Burgess]
Instr: 2/2/2/2 - 4/3/3/0 - timp. perc. hp. str.
Music played by: London Symphony Orchestra/John Hollingsworth (recorded 17 December 1952)
f.broad.p.   Home Service and Light Programme, 25 December 1952

Long Live the Queen - Coronation Programme (1953)
[Produced by Laurence Gilliam and Alan Burgess]
Instr: 2+picc./2/2/2 - 4/3/3/0 - timp. perc. cel. hp. str.
Music played by: London Symphony Orchestra/Muir Mathieson (recorded 28 May 1953)
f.broad.p.   Home Service, 2 June 1953

Coronation Day Across the World (1953)
[Produced by Laurence Gilliam and Michael Barsley]
Music played by: London Symphony Orchestra/Muir Mathieson (recorded 28 May 1953)
f.broad.p.   Home Service, 2 June 1953

The Mouth of God: The tragedy of Girolamo Savonarola (1957-58)
[Written by H.A.L. Craig and produced by Douglas Cleverdon]
Music performed by four boys from Highgate School Choir (recorded 8 February 1958)
f.broad.p.   Third Programme, 11 February 1958

The Seekers - Christmas feature (1958)
[Produced by Laurence Gilliam and Alan Burgess]
Instr: 2/2/2/2 - 4/3/3/1 - timp. perc. str.
Music played by: BBC Concert Orchestra/Muir Mathieson (recorded 3 December 1958)
f.broad.p.   Home Service and Light Programme, 25 December 1958

Music for Lovers (ND)
Instr: 1/1/1/1 - 4/1/0/0 - perc. hp. str.

Moorland Music (ND)
Instr: 2/2/2/2 - 4/2/3/1 - timp. perc. hp. str.

(b) Television

Colonel March of Scotland Yard - theme music (1953)
[Sapphire Productions - in 26 episodes]

Henry Moore: Sculptor (1954)
[Written and produced by John Read]
First transmission: BBC Television, 30 April 1951 (music recorded 20 April 1951)

Black on White (1954)
Directed by John Read
Music played by: William Alwyn (Pno.) (recorded 21 September 1954)
First transmission: BBC Television, 28 November 1954

War in the Air (1954-55)
[Written and produced by John Elliot]
Alwyn contributed music to two of the 15 BBC TV films:-
(i)   Fifty North:
        Instr: 2/2/2/2 - 4/3/3/0 - timp. perc. str.
        Music played by: London Symphony Orchestra/Muir
        Mathieson (recorded 23 September 1954)
        First transmission: BBC Television, 22 November 1954
(ii)   Eastern Victory:
        Music played by: London Symphony Orchestra/Muir
        Mathieson (recorded 5 January 1955)
        First transmission: BBC Television, 31 January 1955

The Empty Sleeve (1961)
Instr: Solo Vn.
First transmission: Associated Rediffusion Television c. 1961

Drawn from Life (1961)
First transmitted: Granada Television, 9 October 1961

(c) Stage

Sweeney Agonistes (1935)
[Words: T.S. Eliot]
f.p.   Westminster Theatre, London, 1 October 1935
Producer: Rupert Doone

Japanese Noh Play (1935-36)

Queen of Sheba (1935-36)

The Sleeping Beauty (1935-36)
[Words: T.E. Ellis]

Spanish Scene (1935-36)

Harlequin's Child (1937)
Dur: 30'
Instr: Fl. Vc.

Shut the Window Please! - mime (1938)
Dur: 12'
Instr: Pno.

ARRANGEMENTS

(i) Other Composers

Two Bach arrangements for cello and piano (1936)
[1. Air in F major 2. Sleepers, Wake!]
Dur: 4'
Pub: OUP, 1936

Tchaikovsky: `Album for the Young' - arr. for instrumental quintet (1937)
[1. Overture 2. Nocturne 3. March]
Dur: 10'
Instr: Fl. Cl. Vn. Vc. Pno.

Bach: Siciliano - trio arranged for flute, violin and piano (1938)
Dur: 2'

Handel: Bourée - trio arranged for flute, violin and piano (1938)
Dur: 1'30"

John McEwen: March of the Little Folk* arr. (1938)
(* From Nugae: 7 Bagatelles for strings, 1912)

Tchaikovsky: `Album for the Young' - arr. for instrumental quintet (1938)
[1. Polka 2. Folk Song 3. Old French Melody 4. Landler
 5. The Nurse's Tale 6. The New Doll 7. Waltz]
Dur: 12'
Instr: Fl. Cl. Vn. Vc. Pno.

Prelude and Fugue for string orchestra (1939)
[1. Fugue for five instruments - Beethoven Op. 137 - freely transcribed for
string orchestra. 2. Dedicatory Prelude to the above]
Dur: 4'50"

f.p.   Orchestra/Nicholas Choveaux - Church of St. Bartholomew, West
           Smithfield, London, late 1946

(ii) Traditional Tunes

Seven Irish Tunes - suite for string quartet (1923)
[1. The Little Red Lark 2. Air 3. The Maiden Ray
4. The Ewe with the Crooked Horn 5. The Gentle Maiden
6. Jig 7. Who'll buy my Besoms?]
Score dated, Northampton, 10 August - 21 September 1923
Dur: 15'
f.p.   Jean Pougnet Quartet

The Boys of Wexford - Irish Air arr. for violin and piano (c.1927)
Dur: 3'
Pub: Associated Board, 1927

Two Folk Tunes - arr. for cello and piano (c.1929)
[1. Meditation on a Norwegian folk song fragment
2. Who'll buy my Besoms? (Irish folk tune used by permission of the Irish Literacy Society)]
Dedicated to Douglas Cameron
f.rec.   Watson Forbes (Va.)/Maria Korchinska (Hp.) - *Decca K.941/3 (78)*
Pub: OUP, 1936

Four Folk Tunes - suite for cello quartet (1930s)
Dur: 10'

From Ireland - Seven Traditional Tunes for piano (c.1931)
[1. The Gobby 2. The Dove 3. Lady Gordon's Minuet
4. Blackbirds and Thrushes 5. The Lullaby
6. Lord Robert and Fair Ellen 7. Cousin Frog went out]
Pub: Keith Prowse, 1931

Eight Irish Folk Tunes - suite for flute, violin, viola and harp (c.1934)
Dedication: For Gordon Walker
Dur: 10'
f.p.   Lyra Quartet - Gordon Walker (Fl.), Jean Pougnet (Vn.), Anthony
           Collins (Va.), John Cockerill (Hp.) - BBC, 26 March 1934

Three Negro Spirituals - arr. for cello and piano* (1935)
[1. I'll hear the trumpet sound
2. Didn't my Lord deliver Daniel? 3. I'm travelling to the grave]
Dur: 4'30"

also arr. for viola and piano by Watson Forbes
f.rec.   Watson Forbes (Vc.)/Etiennette de Chaulieu (Pno.) - *Decca M 577
           (78)*

Three Negro Spirituals - arr. for violin, cello and piano (c.1935)
[1. Rise brothers rise 2. Save me 3. The Fountain]

Three Negro Spirituals arr. piano (c.1935)
[1. I'm troubled in mind 2. Air
3. I've just come from the fountain]

Seven Irish Tunes - suite for small orchestra (1936)
[1. The Little Red Lark 2. Country Tune 3. The Maiden Ray
4. Reel 5. The Gentle Maiden 6. The Sign 7. Jig]
f.p.   BBC Midland Light Orchestra, Birmingham - 1937/38

Two Russian Folk Tunes - arr. for flute quartet (1937)
Dur: 5'

Two Irish Folk Songs - arr. for cello quartet (1938)
[1. The song my love is dead 2. A wee bag]
Dur: 7'

Two Irish pieces - arr. for string quartet (1939)
[1. Idyll 2. The spinning wheel]
Dur: 5'30"

Irish Suite for string quartet (1939-40)
[1. As through the woods I chanced to roam
2. The little cuckoo of Ard Patrick 3. A Lament
4. Lower Ormond 5. The fair nurse's song
6. The piper's finish]

The Londonderry Air - arr. for instrumental quintet (1941)
Dur: 3'20"
Instr: Fl. Cl. Vn. Vc. Pno.

MS LOCATION

Majority of MS are held by the Alwyn Archive (**AA**) at the Britten-Pears Library. Other locations are:

BBC   Songs of Experience (1930s), The Cherry Tree (1945),
Farewell Companions (1954-55), Miss Julie (1977),
and many radio feature scores - Britain to America (1942),
Made in Britain (1943), Four Years at War (1943),
Pulse of Britain (c.1944), The Spirit of '76 (1974),
The Chimes (1944), Britain's our Doorstep (1944-45),
The People of Britain (1945), Transatlantic Flight (1945),
City set on a Hill (1945), Wherever you may be ((1945),
Nalina Kanti (1946), Flying Visit (1946), Home Again (1946),
The Hare (1947), The Pharoah Akhnaton (1947),
The Moon in the Yellow River (1947), Christmas Journey (1950),

The Gifts of Christmas (1951), The Queen's Inheritance (1952),
Long Live the Queen (1953), The Seekers (1958).

BBCTV   War in the Air (1954-55)

WF   Three Negro Spirituals arr. (1935)
Short Suite No. 2 (1944)

FG   Violin Concerto (1938)

RH   Two Intermezzi (1931), Crickety Mill (1935)

RAM   Piano Concerto No. 1 (1936), Aphrodite in Aulis (1932)
Pastorale Fantasia (1939), Prelude and Fugue (1945)

TC   Three Winter Poems (1948)

BIBLIOGRAPHY

Alwyn, William   **The technique of film music.** Focal Press, 1957

Anon.   **William Alwyn.** Miklos Rozsa Society, Vol. 8, No. 3, Summer
1980

Craggs, Stewart and
Alan Poulton   **William Alwyn: A catalogue of his music.** Hindhead: Bravura
Publications, 1985 [B] [D]

Culot, Hubert   **William Alwyn: A Memorial Tribute.** Journal of the British
Music Society, Vol. 7, October 1985

Culot, Hubert   **William Alwyn: A recent discography.** British Music Society
Newsletter No. 29, March 1986

Hold, Trevor   **Senior British Composers - 9. The Music of William Alwyn.**
Composer, No. 43, Spring 1972 and No. 44, Summer 1972

Routh, Francis   **William Alwyn** in his `Contemporary British Music'. London:
Macdonald, 1972

Denis ApIvor
(1916–)

Four Chaucer Songs for baritone and string quartet Op. 1 (1936)
Dedicated to the memory of Bernard Van Dieren (1887-1936)
[1. The Man in Black 2. Rosamounde 3. Mercilés Beauté 4. Alceste]
Dur: 9'

Alas Parting - Five songs for high voice and string quartet* Op. 2 (1936-37)
[1. Alas Parting (Henry VIII) 2. As the holly groweth green (Henry VIII)
 3. Brown is my love (Anon 16th cent.)
 4. In a glorious garden green (Anon 16th cent.)
 5. Ah! my heart, what ayleth thee? (Thomas Wyatt)]
Dur: 9'
(*for piano version, see Op. 3)

Twenty Songs for voice and piano Op. 3 (1935-40)
[1. Quho is at my window, quho? (Scottish Wedderburn Book) (1939)
  2. There is no rose of swych vertu (Anon 13th cent.) (1937)
  3. My Song is in Sighing (Richard Rolle of Hampole) (1937)
  4. Be merry (Anon 15th cent.) (1935) 5. Lully Lullay (Anon) (1939)
  6. Blow, Northerne Wynd (Anon 13th cent.) (1938)
  7. If ever I marry (Anon 16th cent.) (1937)
  8. Farra-Diddle-Dyno (Anon 16th cent.) (1938)
  9. Mercilés Beauté (Chaucer) (see also Op. 1 No. 3) (1937)
 10. Alas Parting (Henry VIII) (from Op.2) (1936-37)
 11. As the holly groweth green (Henry VIII) (from Op2.) (1936)
 12. Brown is my love (Anon 16th cent.) (from Op. 2) (1936)
 13. In a glorious garden green (Anon 16th cent.) (from Op.2) (1936)
 14. Ah! my heart, what ayleth thee? (Thomas Wyatt) (from Op.2) (1936)
 15. Cakes and ale (Anon 16th cent.) (1938)
 16. Sailing Homeward (Chan-Fang-Sheng, trans. Arthur Waley)
 17. Tarantella (Hilaire Belloc)
 18. The Carrion Crow (Thomas Lovell Beddoes)
 19. This gentle day (Anon. 16th Cent.) (c.1938)
 20. Fear no more the heat o' the sun (Shakespeare) (originally from Op. 6)]

f.p.   (Nos. 5, 6 and 9 only) Frederick Fuller (Bar.)/L. Isaacs (Pno.) - St. Martin's
            School of Art, London, 1946 (SPNM Concert)
f.p.   (No. 17) Astra Desmond (Sop.)/Gerald Moore (Pno.) - Wigmore Hall,
            London, 1948
f.p.   (No. 11) Wills Morgan (Ten.)/Richard Black (Pno.) - British Music
            Information Centre, London, January 1996

Nocturne for string orchestra - 'Fantasia on a song of Diego Pisador'
Op. 4 (1938)
[Si la noche hace escura (If the night is so dark, why do you not come my love?) (6th
cent.)]
Dur: 10'

The Hollow Men - for baritone solo, male voice chorus and orchestra Op.5 (1939 rev. 1949)
[Words: T.S. Eliot]
Dur: 16'
Instr: 2/0/1/2 - 2 sax/3/3/0 - pno. perc.(3) str.
f.p.   Redvers Llewellyn (Bar.)/BBC Male Voice Choir/London Symphony
            Orchestra/Constant Lambert - BBC Broadcasting House, London,
            21 February 1950 (LCMC Concert)
Pub: OUP, 1951

Four Songs for voice and piano Op. 6 (1940-45)
[1. A heart tae break (Scottish)
 2. Venetian Boat Song - Sospira cuor (Frederick William Rolfe, the self-
styled Baron Corvo)
 3. To a Greek Marble (Richard Aldington) 4. Flos Lunae (Ernest Dowson)]
Dur: 10'30"
f.p.   (Nos. 1 and 3 only) Astra Desmond (Sop.)/Gerald Moore (Pno.) -
            Wigmore Hall, London, 1948
f.p.   (No. 4) Moira Harries (Sop.)/Richard Black (Pno.) - British Music Information
            Centre, London, January 1996
No. 2 also arr. for voice and guitar.

Concertante for clarinet, piano and percussion Op. 7 (1945)
Written for and dedicated to Frederick Thurston - this work won the Edwin Evans Prize
in 1951.
Dur: 23'
f.p.   Frederick Thurston (Cl.)/Kyla Greenbaum (Pno.)/James and Thomas Blades
            (Perc.) cond. Denis ApIvor - BBC Third Programme, 27 January 1948
f.conc.p.   above artists - RBA Galleries, London, 24 April 1951 (LCMC Concert)

also arr. for clarinet and orchestra Op. 7a (1949)
Instr: hp. pno. (cel.) perc. str.

Six Songs of Federico Garcia Lorca for high voice and piano* Op. 8 (1945-46)
[1. La guitarra (The guitar)
 2. La nina del bello rostro (The girl with the beautiful face)
 3. Cancion de jinete (The rider's song) 4. Pueblo (Village)
 5. Virgen con marinaque (Virgin in a crinoline)
 6. Raiz amarga (The bitter root)]
Dur: 16'30"
f.p.   Frederick Fuller (Bar.)/Daniel Kelly (Pno.) - Wigmore Hall, London,
            April 1947
f.broad.p. Trefor Jones (Ten.)/Clifton Helliwell (Pno.), 23 January 1951
Pub: Berben Milano, 1972 (* version for voice and guitar)

Violin Sonata Op. 9 (1946 rev. 1951-52)
Dur: 17'
f.p.   Antonio Brosa (Vn.)/Kyla Greenbaum (Pno.) - Wigmore Hall, London, 1947
            (LCMC Concert)
f.conc.p.   (rev. version) Leonard Dight (Vn.)/Eiluned Davies (Pno.) - Swansea Music
            Club, 23 February 1952
f.broad.p. (rev. version) Leonard Dight (Vn.)/Eiluned Davies (Pno.) - BBC Wales,
            2 May 1952

Estella Marina for SATB Chorus and organ (or string orchestra) Op.10 (1946)
[Words: Pierre de Corbian (13th cent.) trans. Dr. Aston Cambridge)]
Dur: 10'
f.p.   St. Columba's Episcopal Choir and Orchestra cond. Alastair Chisholm -
            Church of Mary, Star of the Sea, Largs, Ayrshire, 17 June 1983

Inventions on an interval for piano (1947 rev. 1981))

Here we go round - Children's songs Op. 11 (1948-49)
[1. Carillon (Lavender's Blue) 2. The Fiddler's Wife
 3. Cuckoo Song (W. Brightly Rands) 4. Three Brothers from Spain
 5. O my Kitten, a Kitten 6. Song of the Jellicles (T.S. Eliot)]
Dur: 7'
f.p.   (No. 6 only) Astra Desmond (Sop.)/Gerald Moore (Pno.) - Wigmore Hall,
            London, 1948

She stoops to Conquer - Opera buffa in 3 Acts Op. 12 (1942-47 rev. 1952)
[Libretto: Denis ApIvor based on Oliver Goldsmith's play]
Dur: c.120'
Instr: 2/2/2/2 - 4/2/3/1 - hpschd. timp. perc. str.

Five Songs from the opera:
[1. Ah, memory, thou fond deceiver (contralto) 2. Drinking Song (baritone)
 3. Bagpipe Song (baritone) 4. When lovely woman stoops to folly (soprano)
 5. Ah me, when shall I marry me? (soprano)]
Dur: 8'

Piano Concerto Op. 13 (1948 rev. 1954)

Dur: 25'
Instr: 2/2/2/2 - 4/2/3/1 - hp. timp. perc.(2) cel. str.
f.p   Eiluned Davies/BBC Welsh Orchestra/Mansel Thomas - BBC Cardiff,
             12 October 1950
f.conc.p.   Patrick Piggott/London Philharmonic Orchestra/Basil Cameron - Royal Albert
             Hall, London, 15 September 1958 (Promenade Concert)

Seven Pieces for piano Op. 14 (1950)

[1. Prelude and Study 2. Invention 3. Dance: Tempo di valse
4. Nocturne 5. Tarantella 6. Marche Funebre 7. Finale (Toccata)]
Dur: 17'45"
f.p.   (Nos. 4 & 7 only) Virginia Fortescue - Wigmore Hall, London, 30 April 1950
f.p.   (complete) Eiluned Davies - Arts Council Drawing Room, London, 29 January
             1952 (Macnaghten Concert)
f.broad.p.   Eiluned Davies, 30 April 1957
Nos. 2, 4, 6 and 7 were later arr. for organ as part of **Five Pieces Op.92** q.v.

Landscapes for tenor and six instruments Op. 15 (1950)

[Words: T.S. Eliot: Introduction - 1. Children's voices in the orchard.
2. Virginia 3. Usk 4. Rannoch, by Glencoe 5. Cape Ann]
Dur: 12'
Instr: Fl. Cl. Hn. Vn. Va. Vc.
f.p.   Wilfred Brown (Ten.)/Virtuoso Ensemble/Denis ApIvor - Recital Room
             Royal Festival Hall, London, 2 July 1953 (ICA Coronation Concert
             Season)
f.broad.p.   above artists (recorded 23 November 1954)

Concerto No. 1 for violin and 15 instruments Op. 16 (1950)

Dur: 17'
Instr: 1/1/1/1 - 1/1/1/0 - pno. hp. xyl. timp. perc.(2) 2db.
f.p.   Alan Loveday/London Classical Orchestra/Trevor Harvey - Maida Vale
             Studios London, 25 March 1952 (LCMC Concert, in association with the
             BBC)

Bouvard et Pécuchet - Overture Op. 17 (1950)

(see also **Op. 49**)

The Goodman of Paris `Le Ménagier de Paris' - Ballet in 1 Act Op. 18 (1951)

[Scenario by the composer based on the story from the medieval treatise trans. Eileen
Power.]
Dur: 20'
Instr: 2/1/2/2 - 2/2/0/0 - timp. perc. str. (+ piano obligato)
f.p.   Walter Gore Ballet Company - Princes Theatre, London, 1953
Choreography: Andrée Howard

Piano Concertino from the ballet Op. 18a

See also **Seven Pianoforte Pieces Op. 85** (1990)

A Mirror for Witches - Ballet in 1 Act Op. 19 (1951)*
[Scenario by Andrée Howard based on the Salem Delusion, the subject of the novel by Esther Forbes.]
Commissioned by the Royal Ballet
Dur: 45'
Instr: 3/3/3+sax./3 - 4/3/3/1 - hp. pno/cel. timp. perc.(2) str.
f.p.   Sadler's Wells Ballet Company/Orchestra of the Royal Opera House, Covent
           Garden/Robert Irving - Royal Opera House, Covent Garden, London,
           4 March 1952
Choreography: Andrée Howard
Decor: Norman Adams and Andrée Howard
Principals: Julia Farron, Anne Heaton, Philip Chatfield and John Hart
(* This ballet was the last collaboration arranged by Constant Lambert in his capacity as Artistic Director - the music is dedicated to his memory.)

Symphonic Suite from the above Op. 19a (1954)
[1. Introduction and fire music 2. Dramatic scena: Introduction and Pas de deux 3. Forest music]
Commissioned by the BBC for the Promenade Concerts.
Dur: 25'
f.p.   BBC Symphony Orchestra/John Hollingsworth - Royal Albert Hall, London,
           13 September 1954 (Promenade Concert)
f.broad.p   BBC Northern Orchestra/John Hopkins - 19 October 1955

La belle dame sans merci (1951-53)
Television ballet. MS in piano score only

Te Deum for SATB chorus and organ Op. 20 (1951)
Dur: 15'

Aquarelles for piano Op. 21 (1951)
[1. Adagio 2. Moderato con moto 3. Molto vivace]
MS destroyed

Symphony No. 1 Op. 22 (1952-53)
Dur: 21'
Instr: 3/3/3/3 - 4/3/3/1 - timp. pno. hp. perc.(2) str.

Blood Wedding - Ballet in 1 Act Op. 23 (1953)
[Scenario by the composer and Alfred Rodrigues, based on the play `Bodas de Sangre' by Federico Garcia Lorca.]
Commissioned by the Royal Ballet
Dur: 30'
Instr: 2/2/2/3 - 4/2/3/1 - timp. pno. hp. perc.(2) str.
f.p.   Sadler's Wells Theatre Ballet/Theatre Orchestra/John Lanchberry - Sadler's
           Wells Theatre, London 5 June 1953
Choreography: Alfred Rodrigues
Decor: Isabel Lambert
Principals: David Poole, Elaine Fifield, Pirmin Trecu

f.Am.p.   American Ballet Theatre, New York, 6 May 1957
f.Eur.p.   Royal Danish Ballet, Copenhagen, 31 January 1960

Four Songs of Thomas Lovell Beddoes for tenor and piano Op. 24 (1954)
[1. The heart's ease 2. A ho, A ho, love's horn doth blow.
3. How many times do I love thee, dear 4. To sea! To sea!]
Dur: 11'30"
f.p.   Wilfred Brown (Ten.)/Eiluned Davies (Pno.) - Arts Council Drawing Room, London, 1 November 1954 (Macnaghten Concert)
f.broad.p. Wilfred Brown (Ten.)/Clifton Helliwell (Pno.) - 24 June 1959

Thamar and Amnon for soloists, chorus and orchestra Op. 25 (1953-54)
[Words: Federico Garcia Lorca, from the `Romancero Gitano' trans. Denis ApIvor.]
Dur: 20'
Instr: 3/3/3/3 - 4/3/3/1 - timp. pno. hp. perc.(2) str.
f.p.   Magda Laszlo (Sop.)/Raymond Nilsson (Ten.)/Francis Loring (Bar.)/ BBC Chorus/Royal Philharmonic Orchestra/Sir Eugene Goossens - Maida Vale Studios, London, 3 January 1956 (ICA Music Section Concert in association with theBBC)

Concertino for guitar and orchestra Op. 26 (1954)
Written for Julian Bream
Dur: 19'
Instr: 2/1/2/2 - 2/2/0/0 - pno. hp. timp. perc. str.
f.p.   Julian Bream/BBC Scottish Orchestra/Berthold Goldschmidt - BBC Glasgow, 11 February 1958
f.conc.p. James Woodrow/RNCM Chamber Orchestra/Richard Deakin - Royal Northern College of Music, Manchester, 9 March 1984
Pub: Schott, 1962 (arr. for guitar and piano)

Saudades (Nostalgia) - Ballet in 1 Act Op. 27 (1955)
[Scenario by the composer and Alfred Rodrigues based on a Portugese legend]
Commissioned by the Royal Ballet
Dur: 30'
Instr: 2/2/2/2 - 4/2/2/0 - hp. pno. timp. perc.(2) str.
f.p.   Sadler's Wells Theatre Ballet/Theatre Orchestra/John Lanchberry - Royal Court Theatre, Liverpool, 13 October 1955
Choreography: Alfred Rodrigues
Decor: Norman Adams
Principals: Donald MacLeary, Maureen Bruce, Margaret Hill
f.Lon.p.   cond. John Lanchberry - Sadler's Wells Theatre, 1956.

Yerma - Opera in 3 Acts Op. 28 (1955-59)
[Libretto: Montagu Slater and Denis ApIvor, based on the play by Federico Garcia Lorca.]
Commissioned by the Sadler's Wells Opera Trust
Dur: 158'
Instr: 2/2/2/2 - 4/2/3/1 - hp. pno. cel. timp. perc.(2) str.

f.conc.p.   BBC Chorus/BBC Symphony Orchestra/Sir Eugene Goossens - Camden
            Theatre, London, 21 November 1961 (with Joan Hammond in the title role)
This opera has not been staged.

Variations for solo guitar Op. 29 (1958)
Commissioned by and dedicated to Julian Bream
Dur: 10'
f.p.   Isabel Smith - Wigmore Hall, London, 1968 (Park Lane Concerts)
Pub: Schott, 1960

Seven Pieces for piano Op. 30 (1960)
Dur: 6'
f.p.   Eiluned Davies - BBC 20 June 1965
f.conc.p.   Malcolm Binns - Arts Council Drawing Room, London, 29 January 1965
            (Macnaghten Concert)

Wind Quintet Op. 31 (1960)
Dur: 6'
Instr: Fl. Ob. Cl. Bsn. Hn.
f.p.   Virtuoso Wind Quintet - Edward Walker (Fl.), Léon Goossens (Ob.), Sidney
            Fell(Cl.), Ronald Waller (Bsn.), John Burden (Hn.) cond. Norman del Mar -
            BBC, 8 July 1962 (rec. 20 December 1961)
f.conc.p.   above artists - Wigmore Hall, London, 19 April 1967 (Pollitzer
            Trust Concert)

Cantata: 'Dylan Thomas' for 4 soloists, speaker, small chorus and chamber orchestra Op.32 (1960-61)
[Words: Dylan Thomas `Altarwise by owl light' - a collection of 10 sonnets.]
Dur: 20'
Instr: 1/1/2/1 - 1/1/1/0 - cel. pno. gtr. mand. perc.(3) str.
(The cantata is designed to take advantage of radio medium with specially recorded echo
effects on tape.)

Orchestral Variations: Overtones (Paul Klee Pieces I*) Op. 33 (1962)
[1. Dance with veil. 2. Dance of the sad child.
3. Fragment of a ballet for Aeolian harp. 4. Animals at full moon.
5. Gentle drumroll. 6. Sun and moon flowers. 7. Departure of the ships.
8. The twittering machine. 9. Uncomposed objects in space.]
Dur: 20'
Instr: 2/2/3/1 - 1/1/2/1 - cel. pno. hp. vib. xyl. mand. gtr. perc.(3) str.
f.p.   Philharmonia Orchestra/Bryan Balkwill - BBC Radio 3, 29 December 1967
            (Music in Our Time series)
(* May be also performed as a `mixed media' piece with back projections of the 9 Klee
paintings.)

Five Mutations for cello and piano Op. 34 (1962)
Dur: 10'

f.p.   Christopher van Kampen (Vc.)/Malcolm Binns (Pno.) - Wigmore Hall,
             London, 19 April 1967 (Pollitzer Trust Concert)
f.broad.p. Christopher van Kampen/Martin Jones - 14 April 1971

Animalcules - 12 short pieces for piano Op. 35 (1963)
Dur: 11'
f.p.   Malcolm Binns - Wigmore Hall, London, 19 April 1967 (Pollitzer Trust
             Concert)

Symphony No. 2 Op. 36 (1963)
Dur: 14'
Instr: 1/1/1/1 - 1/1/2/1 - hp. pno. gtr. mand. timp. perc. str.
f.p.   BBC Welsh Orchestra/John Carewe - BBC Cardiff, 5 January 1970

String Quartet No. 1 Op. 37 (1964)
Dur: 12'
f.p.   Amici String Quartet - Wigmore Hall, London, 19 April 1967 (Pollitzer Trust
             Concert)

Chorales (The Secret Sea) - Cantata for baritone, chorus and orchestra Op.38 (1964)
[Words: Hugo Manning]
Dur: 17'
Instr: 2/2/2/2 - 3/2/2/1 - timp. perc.(2) hp. str.

Crystals (Concert Miniscule) for six players Op. 39 (1964)
Dur: 10'
Instr: Hammond organ, amplified guitar, marimba, perc.(2) db.
f.p.   Virtuoso Ensemble/Norman del Mar - Wigmore Hall, London, 19 April 1967
             (Pollitzer Trust Concert)

Ubu Roi (King Ubu) - Opera in 3 Acts Op. 40 (1965-66)
[Libretto: Denis Aplvor based on the play by Alfred Jarry.]
Dur: c.110'
Instr: 2/1/3+alto sax./0 - 2/2/2/1 - pno. acc. timp. perc.(2) str.

Trio-Harp, Piano, Piano-Harp* Op. 41 (1966)
Dur: 8'
Instr: percussionist* (playing only the inside of the upright piano strings with
             fingers and beaters)
f.p   John Marson (Hp.)/Susan Bradshaw (Pno.)/John Tilbury (Pno.Hp.) - BBC,
             19 April 1967 (Composer's Portrait Series)

Corporal Jan - Ballet in 1 Act Op. 42 (1968)
Commissioned by BBC Television
Dur: 40'
Instr: 4/0/0/0 - 0/2/2/0 - pno. acc. org. `piano-harp', perc.(4) str.
f.p.   English Chamber Orchestra/Norman del Mar - BBC Television, 1968

Choreography: Peter Wright

Triple Concerto* for string trio and string orchestra Op. 43 (1967)
Commissioned by the Cheltenham Festival
Dur: 18'
Instr: str. (8/7/6/5/4)
f.p.   Delmer Trio - Galina Solodchin (Vn.), John Underwood (Va.), Joy Hall
            (Vc.)/London Philharmonic Orchestra/Igor Buketoff - Cheltenham Town
            Hall, 10 July 1968 (Cheltenham Festival)
(* Original title "String Abstract")

Ten String Design - Duo for violin and guitar Op. 44 (1968)
[Antiphony - Monody and Resonances - Diaphony]
Dur: 13'

The Lyre Playing Idol* for piano Op. 45 (1968)
[Introduction: Playing the Dawn; Playing the Wind (Toccata 1);
 Playing the Rain (Toccata 2); Playing the Thunder (Toccata 3);
 Playing the Night (Nocturne)]
Dur: 13'
f.p.   Eiluned Davies - BBC Radio 3, 14 April 1977
f.conc.p.   Penelope Roskell - British Music Information Centre, London, 21 May 1985
f.Can.p.   Gordon Rumson - Calgary, Alberta, November 1997
(* Based on the idea of the lyre-playing god in the Cycladic sculptures of Athens
Museum.)

Tarot* - Variations for chamber orchestra Op. 46 (1968-69)
Dur: 30'
Instr: 2/1/2+alto sax./1 - 1/1/1/0 - vib. xyl. perc.(3) hp. pno. str.
(* Based on the `Greater Arcana' of the Tarot Pack - designed to be played either as pure
music or as music with back projection and dancing.)

Neumes* - Variations for orchestra Op. 47 (1969)
Dur: 15'
Instr: 2/2/3+sax./2 - 2/2/2/1 - hp. cel. pno. piano-harp' perc.(3) str.
f.p.   BBC Symphony Orchestra/Norman del Mar - BBC Maida Vale Studios,
            17 November 1973
f.broad.p. above performance -14 October 1974
(* Based on the inflexional idea of the `neume', an early musical notation)

Discanti for solo guitar Op. 48 (1970)
Written for the Italian guitarist Angelo Gilardino
Dur: 10'
f.p.   Julian Byzantine - Purcell Room, Royal Festival Hall, London, 1 December
            1971 (Redcliffe Concerts)
Pub: Bèrben, (Ancona) 1971

Bouvard et Pécuchet - Opera buffa in 3 Acts Op. 49 (1971-74)
[Libretto: Denis ApIvor based on the novel by Gustave Flaubert.]
Dur: 175'
Instr: 2/2/3+sax./2 - 3/2/2/1 - hp. hpschd. pno. gtr. mand. perc.(3) str.

Orchestral Suite from above (1986)
[1. `Little Preludes and Entr'actes']
Dur: 12'

Orgelberg - (Paul Klee Pieces 2) for organ Op. 50 (1971)
[1. Town with watch towers. 2. Lagoon City. 3. Flagged Tower (Night piece) 4.
Monument in fertile country.]
Commissioned by the Redcliffe Concerts for the Festival Hall organ.
Dur: 12'
f.p.   Christopher Bowers Broadbent - Royal Festival Hall, London, 18 June 1972
             (Redcliffe Concerts)
f.broad.p.   above performance, 22 April 1974

**El Silencio Ondulando* (The Trembling Silence) for guitar and chamber orchestra
Op.51 (1972)**
Dur: 14'
Instr: 1/ca./1+bcl./0 - 1/0/0/0 - hp. `piano-harp', perc.(3) str.
f.conc.p.   James Woodrow/RNCM Ensemble - Royal Northern College of Music,
             Manchester, February 1983
(* Based on a short poem from the `Cante Jondo' of Federico Garcia Lorca)

Exotic's Theatre - (Paul Klee Pieces 3) for chamber ensemble Op. 52 (1972)
Commissioned by the Redcliffe Concerts
Dur: 20'
Instr: Fl. Cl. Tpt. Tbn. perc.(2) Hohner pianet (or Hammond organ) Vn. Vc. Db.
f.p.   Redcliffe Ensemble/Russell Harris - Queen Elizabeth Hall, London,
             26 March 1975 (Redcliffe Concerts)

Saeta* for guitar Op. 53 (1972)
Dur: 5'
f.p.   Nigel Morgan - East Anglia, 1976
Pub: Bèrben, (Ancona) 1975
(* Based on the poem in the Cante Jondo of Federico Garcia Lorca and the idea of the
`saeta', the arrow of song thrown up in the procession of the saint during `fiesta')

**Resonance of the Southern Flora (Paul Klee Pieces 4) - Poem for orchestra Op. 54
(1972)**
Dur: 19'
Instr: 4/4/4+sax./3 - 6/4/3/1 - hp. pno. `piano-harp' acc. mand. gtr.
             perc.(8) str. + concert organ and (wordless) SATB chorus

Psycho Pieces (Paul Klee Pieces 5) for clarinet and piano* Op. 55 (1973)
[1. Warning - Flight from oneself.
 2. Fear of becoming double - Attack by those coming after.

3. Downwards - Fall. 4. Pathos. 5. Successful Incantation.
6. The Way Out at Last.]
Dur: 12'30"
f.p.   Thea King (Cl.)/Susan Bradshaw (Pno.) - BBC Radio 3, 27 May 1975
* also arr. for violin, cello and piano (1984)

Fern Hill for tenor and eleven instruments* Op. 56 (1973)
[Words: Dylan Thomas]
Commissioned by the Redcliffe Concerts with funds provided by the Arts Council of
Great Britain.
Dur: 10'
Instr: 2/1+ca/1/0 - 1/0/0/0 - pno. Vn. Vn. Va. Vc.
f.p.   Philip Langridge (Ten.)/Redcliffe Ensemble/Edwin Roxburgh - Queen
           Elizabeth Hall, London, 8 December 1976 (Redcliffe Concerts)
(* may also be sung unaccompanied.)

Seven Studies for solo wind Op. 57 (1974)
Dur: 2'- 5' each
Instr: Fl. Ob. Cl. Bsn. Hn. Tpt. Tbn.
f.p.   (No. 7 only) Martin Harvey (Tbn.) - British Music Information Centre,
           London, 6 May 1986

Vox Populi - 14 Songs, unaccompanied or with piano accompaniment Op. 58 (1974-75)
[Words from Faber Book of Popular Verse: 1. Hush-a-ba burdie (Scottish)
 2. The Pretty Ploughboy (English) 3. Hollin, green hollin (English)
 4. Maw bonnie lad (Newcastle) 5. Of everykune tree (English)
 6. False Luve (Scottish) 7. Jonny cam tae our toun (Scottish)
 8. My feddih and I tegither (Scottish) 9. Kiss'd yest'r e'en (Scottish)
 10. The Well-Wake (early English) 11. This ean night (Yorkshire dirge)
 12. Merry Ways for to gone (English, 15th cent.)
 13. Cider through a straw (American) 14. Birmingham Jail (American)]
Dur: 25'30"
f.p.   (No. 4 only) Moira Harries (Sop.)/Richard Black (Pno.) - British Music
           Information Centre, London, January 1996
           (Nos. 2 and 11) Sarah Poole (Sop.)/Andrew Zelinsky (Pno.) - Purcell Room,
           London, 11 February 1996 ("Constant Lambert and Friends" Concert)
Nos. 1 and 4 also arr. voice and guitar.

Triptych - Three Carols for chorus and organ Op. 59 (1975)
[1. In Bethlehem, that fair city (Anon, Medieval, from the opera **Bouvard et Pécuchet**
     Op. 49)
 2. Quho is at my window, quho (Scottish Wedderburn Book; from Op. 3 No. 1)
 3. Merry ways for to gone (English, 15th cent; from **Vox Populi** Op. 58 No. 12)]
Dur: 6'25"
f.p   .   Largs Academy Senior Choir, with Derek Fry (organ) cond. Alastair Chisholm
           Clark Memorial Church, Largs, Ayrshire, 2 December 1980

Clarinet Quintet Op. 60 (1975)
Dur: 16'
Instr: Cl. Vn. Vn. Va. Vc.
f.p.   Thea King (Cl.)/Allegri String Quartet - BBC Radio 3, 13 March 1979

Violin Concerto (No.2) Op. 61 (1975)
Dur: 24'
Instr: 2/2/2/2 - 2/2/2/0 - gtr. mand. hp. perc.(2) str.

Liaison - duo for guitar and keyboard* Op. 62 (1976)
Dur: 7'30"
f.conc.p. Nigel Morgan (Gtr.)/James Gray (Kybrd.) - Leighton House, London, 1977
(* the composer specifies a Hohner pianet)

String Quartet No. 2 Op. 63 (1976)
Dur: 25'

Cello Concerto Op. 64 (1976-77)
Dur: 23'
Instr: 2/2/2/2 - 3/2/3/0 - pno. hp. perc.(3) str.
f.p.   Raphael Wallfisch/BBC Welsh Symphony Orchestra/Owain Arwel Hughes -
           BBC Cardiff, Radio 3, 10 January 1982

Chant Eolien- duo for oboe and piano Op. 65 (1977)
Dur: 7'30"
f.p.   Anne Tabor (Ob.)/Peter Copley (Pno.) - Lewes, Sussex, 15 October 1996
           (Musicians of All Saints Concert)

Glide the Dark Door Wide - Ballet in 1 Act Op. 66 (1977-78)
[Scenario: Janet Randell, based on an ancient Sumerian fertility myth, 2000 BC]
Dur: 30'
Instr: 2/2/2/1 - 2/2/1/0 - hpschd. perc.(2) str.
Alt.Instr: 2/ca./0/0 - 0/0/0/0 - hpschd. timp. perc.(2)

Symphony No. 3 Op. 67 (1978-79)
Dur: 25'
Instr: 2/2/2/2 - 4/2/3/1 - hp. pno. timp. perc.(2) str. (8/7/6/5/4)

Bats - Song for high voice and 3 instruments Op. 68 (1979)
[Words: George Macbeth]
Dur: 6'30"
Instr: Picc. Vn. Piano-harp

Serenade for solo guitar Op. 69 (1980)
Dur: 6'30"

Fantasy Concertante for horn and orchestra Op. 70 (1980)
Dur: 22'

Instr: 2/1/2/1 - 0/2/2/0 - hp. timp. perc. str.
f.p   Frank Lloyd/BBC Scottish Orchestra/Nicholas Kraemar - BBC,
          19 December 1983

Duo Concertante for horn and piano Op. 71 (1981)
Dur: 20'
f.p.   Michael Thompson (Hn.)/Catherine DuBois (Pno.) - BBC Radio 3,
          January 1984

Ten Pieces for solo guitar Op. 72 (1981)
Dur: 20'
Pub: Musical New Services in association with the `Guitar' magazine (as "An
          introduction to serial composition for guitarists"), Bridport, Dorset, 1983

Six Divertimenti for solo bassoon Op. 73 (1983)
Dedicated to Sylvia Morteaux
Dur: 9'

Seven Songs for choir and orchestra (or organ) Op. 74 (1935-75 compiled 1984)
[Part I - 1. My song is in sighing (Richard Rolle) (from Op. 3 No. 3)
 2. There is no rose of swych vertu (Anon 13th cent.) (from Op. 3 No. 2)
 3. Lully Lullay (Anon) (from Op. 3 No. 5)
 4. Be Merry (Anon 15th cent.) (from Op. 3 No. 4)
 Part II - 5. In Bethlehem that fair city (Anon) (from the opera, **Bouvard et
 Pécuchet** Op. 49 - see also Op. 59)
 6. Quho is at my window, quho (Scottish Wedderburn Book) (from Op. 3 No. 1
 - see also Op. 59) 7. Merry Ways for to gone (English 15th cent.) (from **Vox Populi** Op.
 58 No.12   - see also Op. 59)]
Dur: 16'
Instr: 1/2/1/1 - 2/2/1/0 - timp. str.

Sonatina for solo guitar Op. 75 (1983)
Dur: 11'30"
f.p.   James Woodrow - Royal Northern College of Music, Manchester,
          12 May 1984

Love's Season - 14 Songs for high voice and piano* - to poems by Ernest Dowson Op.76 (1983)
[1. Villanelle (Prologue) 2. Lady April. 3. A broken lute. 4. The Devil's Dance.
5. Song of a Winter's day. 6. April Love. 7. Aspiration. 8. The Heart's Country.
9. Spleen. 10. In Spring. 11. The Wood. 12. The Twilight of the Heart. 13. The night is
now at hand.   14. Parting (Epilogue)]
Dur: 40'
f.p.   (No. 1 only) Wills Morgan (Ten.)/Richard Black (Pno.) - British Music
          Information Centre, London, January 1996
* Alt. version for voice and string quartet or string orchestra (2/2/2/2/1)
f.p.   (excs.) Neil Jenkins (Ten.)/Orchestra of the Musicians of All Saints/ Jonathan
          Grieves-Smith - Lewes, Sussex, Autumn 1996

Vista for double wind quintet Op. 77 (1983)
Commissioned by Morley College for their anniversary.
Dur: 23'
f.p.   Morley Wind Ensemble/Lawrence Leonard - Morley College, London,
          1 June 1984

Nocturne for solo guitar Op. 78 (1984)
Dur: 5'30"
f.p.   Helen Sanderson - Brighton, May 1995 (Brighton Festival)

Cinquefoil - trio for flute, viola and guitar Op. 79 (1984)
Dur: 15'

Melisma for solo recorder Op. 80 (1984)
Dur: 9'15"
f.p.   John Turner - Cannington International Guitar Summer School,
          6 August 1985
Pub: Forsyth Bros. (Manchester), 1985 (in 'Pieces for Solo Recorder', Vol. 2)

Symphony No. 4 Op. 81 (1985)
Dur: 25'
Instr: 2/2/2/2 - 4/2/2/0 - pno. perc.(3) str. (8/7/6/5/4)

**Majestatis dei Ultra Stellas for SATB chorus and keyboard (or small orchestra) Op.
82 (1986)**
[Setting of Psalm 8 adapted by the composer]
Dur: 7'
Instr: 2/1/1/1 - 2/2/0/0 - timp. perc. hp. pno. str.

Trodden Leaves - song for high voice and piano Op.83 (1987-88)
[Words: Susan Rapoport]
Dur: 2'30"

String Quartet No. 3 Op.84 (1989)
[1. Quantum 2. Residum 3. Plenum]
Dur: 23'

Seven Pianoforte Pieces from `Le Ménagier de Paris', Op.85 (1990)
Dur: 18'
(re-arranged from the original ballet of 1951)

Seven Pianoforte Pieces (two sets) Op.86 (1990-91)
[Set I - Four Pieces Set II - Danzas (Three Pieces)]
Dur: 6' (Set I) 3'35" (Set II)
f.p.   (Set II) Geoffrey Burford - British Music Information Centre, Stratford Place,
          London, 28 July 1999

Symphony No. 5 Op.87 (1991)
Dur: 24'

Instr: 2/2/2/2 - 2/2/2/0 - perc.(2) hp. pno./hpschd. gtr., elec.bs.gtr., str.

Pieces of Five* for solo alto-saxophone Op.88 (1992)
Dur: 15'
f.p.   Tony Sions - Chapel Royal, Brighton, 1994 (Brighton Festival)
(* The score is prefaced `The five colours make a man's eyes blind. The five notes make his ears deaf.' - Lao Tsu, 500BC.)

Sonatina sopra on 'Quia amore Langueo'* for alto saxophone and piano Op.89 (1992)
Dur: 15'
(*Based on a melodic fragment from the mediæval refrain.)

Sonatina sopra 'Fayre love let us gan play'* for viola and piano Op.90 (1992)
Dur: 13'
(* From the same literary source as Op.89.)

Preludes and Postludes in three books for organ Op.91 (1992)
Dur: c.30'
(*The composer notes that `each book can be played as a continuous piece or in sections, as preludes and postludes. The style is influenced by Spanish Renaissance organ music.')

Five Pieces for organ Op.92 (1992)
[1. Adagietto (from Op.88) 2. Invention (from **Seven Pieces for piano** Op.14 No. 2) 3. Toccata (Op.14 No. 7) 4. Nocturne (Op.14 No. 4) 5. Solemn March (Op.14 No. 6)]
Dur: 16'

In the Landscape of Spring* - septet Op.93 (1993)
Commissioned by the University of Cape Town in celebration of the centenary of Warlock's birth.
Dur: 20'
Instr: Fl./Picc. Ob./Ca. Hn. Vn. Vn. Va. Vc.
f.p.   Instrumental Ensemble cond. Dr. Barry Smith - University of Cape Town, South Africa, 8 April 1994 (Peter Warlock Memorial Concert)
(*Based on the aphorisms of two 7th century Ch'an masters.)

Four Elegiac Sonnets for unaccompanied SATB soloists (or small chorus) Op.94 (1993)
[Words: Hilaire Belloc. 1. Rise up and do begin the days adorning 2. O my companion, O my daughter sleep. 3. The Winter Moon has such a quiet ear.
4. We will not whisper, we have found the place of silence.]
Dur: 14'

Five Eliot Songs for voice, (optional) recorder* and piano Op.95 (1994-95)
[1. Eyes that last I saw in tears 2. The wind sprang up at four o'clock
 3. Lines to a Persian Cat* 4. Lines to a Yorkshire Terrier*
 5. Lines to a Duck in the Park*]
No. 1 dedicated to the memory of Peter Warlock in his centenary year.

f.p.   (No. 1) Katherine Laurie Jones (Sop.)/Alastair Chisholm (Pno.) -
            Cathedral of the Isles, Millport, August 1994.
f.Can.p.   (No. 1) Katie Partridge (Sop.)/Gordon Rumson (Pno.) - Calgary, Alberta,
            7 June 1997
f.p.   (Nos. 3 and 4) Tracey Chadwell (Sop.)/John Turner (Rec.)/Keith Swallow
            (Pno.)- Clarence House, Thaxted, Essex, 11 September 1994 (Alan
            Rawsthorne Society Concert)
f.p.   (No. 5) Alison Wells (Sop.)/John Turner (Rec.)/John Wilson (Pno.) -
            Downing College, Cambridge, 7 September 1996 (Alan Rawsthorne Society
            Concert)
No. 1 later arr. for voice and seven instruments (1995)*
(* As No. 4 of a set of `Four Songs by British Composers' - see arrs.)

Homage to St. Cecilia: A Decoration in Brass Op.96 (1994)
Commissioned for the St. Cecilia's Day Service from Brighton Composers.
Dur: 2'45"
Instr: 2 Tpt. 2 Tbn.
f.p.   Brass Ensemble - St. Martin's Church, Brighton, 20 November 1994.

Lady of Silences, for SATB (chorus), harp, cymbals and piano-harp Op.97 (1994)
[Words: T. S. Eliot]
Dur: 8'30"

Canzona delle lettere amorose (Mediæval love-letters) for soprano, baritone,
saxophone and bass (electric) guitar Op.98 (1994)
[Mediæval text in French, Latin and English]
Alt.Instr:Oboe or clarinet/viola (for sax.), string cello or double bass (for bs. gtr).

Sonetto: Dammi oggi tuoi fior, O Primavera (Give me this day your flowers O
Spring) - song for high voice and two guitars Op. 99 (1994)
[Words: Vincenzo de Simone]
Dur: 5'

Lamentaciones - Five Songs for high voice and piano Op. 100 (1996)
[Words: Federico Garcia Lorca from `Poema del Cante Jondo'
 1. Lamentación de la muerte 2. Cuando yo me muera 3. Conjuro
 4. El desierto 5. La merte de la Petenera]
f.p.   (No. 1 only) Wills Morgan (Ten.)/Richard Black (Pno.) - Chapel Royal,
            Brighton Autumn 1996 (80th birthday concert)

ARRANGEMENTS

Busoni: Fantasia Contrappuntistica - arr. for orchestra (1940 rev. 1946 and 1977)
Dur: 30'
Instr: 2/2/2/3 - 4/3/3/1 - hp. pno. timp. perc.(2) str. (8/7/6/5/4)
f.p.   BBC Symphony Orchestra/Clarence Raybould - 1952

Veneziana - Ballet in 1 Act (c. 1953)
Music from the operas of Gaetano Donizetti, selected and orchestrated by Denis ApIvor
Commissioned by the Royal Ballet
Dur: 30'
Instr: 3/3/2/3 - 4/3/3/1 - timp. perc.(2) cel. str.
f.p.   Royal Ballet Company/Orchestra of the Royal Opera House, Covent
            Garden/John Hollingsworth - Royal Opera House, Covent Garden, London,
            9 April 1953
Choreography: Andrée Howard
Decor: Sophie Fedorovitch
Principals: Violetta Elvin, Ray Powell, Desmond Doyle

Bernard van Dieren: Three Songs arr. for high voice and chamber ensemble (or orchestra)
1. Balow (Anon 16th cent.)
Dur: 8'30"
Instr: 1/1/2/1 - 2/0/0/0 - str. quintet (str.)
2. Voici les lieux charmants (Nicholas Despreaux)
Dur: 4'
Instr: 1/1/1+sax./1 - 1/0/0/0 - hp. str. quintet (str.)
3. Les roses étaient toutes rouges (Verlaine)
Dur: 5'
Instr: 1/1/1/1 - 1/0/0/0 - str. quintet (str.)

Bernard van Dieren: Song from 'The Cenci' and Rapsodia arr. for tenor and string quartet
[Levana - de Quincey]
Dur: 10'

Warlock: Saudades - Three Songs arr. for high voice and string quartet
[1. Along the stream. 2. Take, O take those lips away.
 3. They told me Heracleitus]
Dur: 6'

Bizet: Michaela's Love Song from 'Carmen' arr. for solo guitar
Dur: 5'

Satie: Gymnopèdie arr. for solo guitar
Dur: 2'15"

Three French lute songs arr. for voice and guitar
[1. Quel espoir de guarir (Guedron) 2. Heureux qui se peut pleindre (Guedron)
 3. Pavane: Belle qui tiens ma vie (Arbeau)]
Dur: 15'

So praiss me as ye think causs quhy - arr. for voice and guitars (1985)
[Anon: Scottish - 16th cent.]
Dur: 4'

Mozart: Deh vieni alla finestra from 'Don Giovanni' arr. for voice and guitar (1985)
Dur: 2'

'A Flower Held' - Four Songs by British composers arr. for high voice and instrumental septet (1994)
[1. Alan Rawsthorne: Infant Joy (William Blake)
2. Christian Darnton: Les Trois Amis (Claire Hallis)
3. Peter Warlock: Take, O take those lips away (Shakespeare)
4. Denis ApIvor: Eyes that last I saw in tears (T. S. Eliot)]
Instr: Fl. Cl. Hn. Hp. Vn. Va. Vc.

MS LOCATION

Majority of MS are held by the British Library **BL**

Other locations are:

B&H Fantasia contrappuntistica (1940 rev. 1977)

TUL Chorales (1964)

BBC Mirror for Witches -Suite (1954)

BIBLIOGRAPHY

ApIvor, Denis **Contemporary Music - the British scene.** The Critic 1946.

ApIvor, Denis **Bernard van Dieren**. Music Survey. Vol. 3, No. 4. 1951.

ApIvor, Denis **Bernard van Dieren**. Composer No. 59. Winter 1976/77.

ApIvor, Denis **Bernard van Dieren**. Composer No. 90. Spring 1987.

ApIvor, Denis **Christian Darnton**. Composer No. 74. Winter 1981/82.

ApIvor, Denis **Personal Recollections** in `Alan Rawsthorne - Biographical Essays' ed.
          Alan Poulton. Kidderminster: Bravura Publications, 1984.
Routh, Francis
          Denis ApIvor in his `Contemporary British Music'. London: Macdonald,
          1972.
Rumson, Gordon
          Denis ApIvor - a brief biography. British Music Society Newsletter No.
          79, September 1998.

4

Richard Arnell
(1917–)

Classical Variations in C for string orchestra Op.1 (1939)
[Theme in Fugato - 1. Chorale 2. Canzona 3. Minuet 4. Alla breve
5. Intermezzo 6. Scherzo]
Dur: 12'
f.p.   WQXR Radio Station, New York, 31 December 1941 (the first professional
          broadcast of his music)
f.Can.p. C.B.C. Vancouver Chamber Orchestra/Richard Arnell - Vancouver,
          April 1959
Pub: Schott; AMP (USA); Chester (UK)

Overture: The New Age Op.2 (1939)
Dur: 8'
Instr: 3/2/2/2 - 4/3/3/1 - timp. str.
f.p.   New York Philharmonic Orchestra/Leon Barzin - Carnegie Hall, New York,
          13 January 1941
Pub: Hinrichsen

Three Childhood Impressions - part songs for SATB chorus Op.3 (1939)
Pub: Boston Music Pub.

String Quartet No. 1* Op.4 (1939)
f.p.   Galimir Quartet - New York Public Library, 1940
Pub: Broadbent & Dunn
(*there are 3 earlier string quartets. See Juvenilia and student works)

Divertimento No. 1 for piano and chamber orchestra Op.5 (1939)
Dur: 17'
Instr: 1/1/2/1 - 2/0/0/0 - str.
Pub: Hinrichsen

Handel: Suite No. 4 in E minor arr. oboe and piano Op.5 No. 1 (1939)

Overture: `1940' Op.6 (1939)

**Bach: Prelude and Fugue from the `48' arr. oboe, clarinet and bassoon
Op.6 No. 1 (1939)**

Divertimento No. 2 for chamber orchestra Op.7 (1940)
Dur: 20'
Instr: 1/1/1/1 - 2/0/0/0 - str.
f.Eur.p.   Haydn Orchestra/Harry Newstone - Conway Hall, London,
            15 February 1951
Pub: Hinrichsen

Siciliana and Furiante for piano Op.8 (1940)
f.Brit.p.   Kyla Greenbaum - BBC, 19 September 1947
Pub: Music Press (USA) c.1947; Theodore Presser (USA)

Concerto in one movement for violin and orchestra Op.9 (1940)
Dur: 20'
Instr: 2/2/2/2 - 4/3/3/1 - timp. str.
f.p.   Harold Kohon/National Orchestral Association/Leon Barzin - Carnegie Hall,
            New York, 22 April 1946
f.Brit.p.   Jean Pougnet/BBC Northern Orchestra/Charles Groves - BBC,
            16 September 1947
f.Brit.conc.p. Harold Kohon/Royal Philharmonic Orchestra/Richard Arnell -
            Royal Festival Hall, London, 27 January 1954
Pub: Schott
also arr. by the composer for violin and piano Op.9a
Pub: Schott, 1952

Prelude and Double Fugato for flute quartet Op.10 (1940)

Violin Sonata No. 1 Op.11* (1940)
(* originally allocated to the film 'Farm Front' q.v.)

(Two)Concert Suites from the film 'The Land' Op.12 Nos.1 and 2 (1941)

Sinfonia quasi Variazione Op.13 (1941)
Dur: 17'
Instr: 2+picc./2/2/2 - 4/3/3/1 - timp. perc. str.
f.p.   New York City Symphony Orchestra/Sir Thomas Beecham - Carnegie Hall,
            New York, 15 March 1942
f.broad.p. Royal Philharmonic Orchestra/Sir Thomas Beecham - 21 June 1947
            (this was Arnell's first work to be broadcast in Britain)
f.Brit.conc.p. London Symphony Orchestra/Richard Arnell - Gloucester
            Cathedral, September 1953 (Three Choirs Festival)
Pub: AMP (USA); Chester (UK)

String Quartet No. 2 Op.14 (1941)
f.p.   New Jersey, USA.
f.Brit.p.   Martin String Quartet - BBC, 19 September 1947
f.Brit.conc.p. New London Quartet - Cheltenham Town Hall, 14 July 1952

(Cheltenham Festival)
Pub: Broadbent & Dunn

Secular Cantata for chorus and orchestra Op.15 (1941)
[Words: Swinburne]

Four Serious Pieces for cello and piano Op.16 (1941)
[1. Prelude 2. Toccata 3. Intermezzo 4. Recitative and Scherzo]
f.p.   Florence Hooton (Vc.)/Ross Pratt (Pno.) - Royal Festival Hall, London,
             February 1954
f.broad.p.   above artists -18 October 195(4?)
Pub: Hinrichsen, 1958

Fantasia for orchestra Op.17 (1941)
Dur: 14'
Instr: 3/2/2/3 - 4/3/3/1 - timp. str.
Pub: Hinrichsen

Sonata for chamber orchestra Op.18 (1941)
Dur: 8'
Instr: 1/1/1/1 - 2/0/0/0 - str.
Pub: Schott; Music Press (USA), 1947; Theodore Presser (USA)

Classical Sonata No. 1 for organ Op.19 (1942)
[1. Ricercare 2. Alla breve 3. Fughetta]
Dur: 9'
Pub: Hinrichsen, 1961

Prelude and Presto for piano Op.20 (1942)

Organ Sonata No. 2 Op.21 (1942)
[1. Aria 2. Chorale 3. Chaconne]
f.p.   E. Power Biggs (?)
f.Brit.p.   Arnold Richardson - All Souls', Langham Place, London, 1951
             (Festival of Britain Concert given by the Organ Music Society)
Pub: Hinrichsen, 1957
also arr. for piano, 4 hands, Op.21a

The Force that through the Green Fuse Drives the Flowers - song for soprano and piano Op.22 (1942)
[Words: Dylan Thomas]

Passacaglia for solo violin Op. 23 (1942)
Dur: 7'
f.p.   Harold Kohon - New York
f.Brit.p.   Max Salpeter - BBC, 11 July 1950
Pub: Hinrichsen, 1960 (ed. Harold Kohon)
also arr. for solo viola by G. Gloubitz Op.23a

Twenty-two Variations on an original theme for piano Op.24 (1943)
f.p.   1943 (Canadian Broadcasting System)
f.Brit.p.   Kyla Greenbaum - BBC, 19 September 1947
Pub: Belwyn Mills, 1948

Piano Quartet Op.25 (1942-43 rev. 1945, 1976)
Dur: 27'
f.p.   Helicon Piano Quartet - British Music Information Centre, London,
            29 July 1997

Chamber Cantata for tenor, flute and string trio Op.26 (1943)
[Words: Plato]
Dur: 8'
Pub: Hinrichsen

Symphonic Suite - six episodes for orchestra Op.27 (1943)

Study, Fugue and Fantasia for piano Op.28 (1943)

Two Songs for voice and piano Op.29 (1943)
[1. Reach with your whiter hands to me (James Herrick)
 2. Never seek to tell thy love (William Blake)]

Partita for solo viola Op. 30 (1943)
Dur: 8'
Pub: Hinrichsen, 1961

Symphony No. 1 Op.31 (1943)
Dedicated to Sir Thomas Beecham
Dur: 26'
Instr: 1/1/1/1 - 2/0/0/0 - str.
f.p.   Canadian Broadcasting System Symphony Orchestra/Bernard Herrmann -
            CBS broadcast, 19 January 1944
f.conc.p.   cond. Sir Thomas Beecham, 15 March 1944
f.Brit.p.   London Classical Orchestra/Harry Newstone - Chelsea Town Hall,
            London, 23 January 1951
Pub: Hinrichsen

Piano Sonata No. 1 Op.32 (1943)
Pub: Hinrichsen

Symphony No. 2 Op.33 (1944)
Dur: 25'
Instr: 2/2/2/2 - 4/3/3/1 - timp. str.
f.p.   BBC Philharmonic Orchestra/Edward Downes - BBC Radio 3,
            26 September 1988
Pub: Hinrichsen

Baroque Prelude and Fantasia for organ Op.34 (1944)

Sonata No. 1 for solo cello Op.35 (1944)
(no longer extant - see Op.48)

The War God - Cantata for soprano, chorus and orchestra Op.36 (1944)
[Words: Sir Stephen Spender]
Commissioned by the Columbia Broadcasting Corporation
f.p.   cond. Bernard Herrmann - New York, 1945
also arr. by the composer for soprano, chorus and organ Op.36a
f.conc.p.   Joyce Millward (Sop.)/ London Choral Society/Herbert Dawson (Org.)/John
            Tobin - St. Margaret's, Westminster, London, 20 March 1952
(see also rev. version Op.155)

Canzona and Capriccio for violin and string orchestra Op.37 (1945)
Dur: 7'
Pub: Schott; Music Press (USA); Theodore Presser (USA)

Oboe Quintet Op.38 (1945)

Red is the Womb - song for tenor and piano Op.39 (1945)

Symphony No. 3 Op.40 (1944-45)
Dedicated `to the political courage of the British people.'
Dur: 47' (rev.) 60' (original)
Instr: 3/2/2/3 - 4/3/3/1 - timp. perc. str.
f.p.   BBC Northern Orchestra/Norman del Mar - BBC, 16 April 1952
f.conc.p.   (rev. version) Hallé Orchestra/Sir John Barbirolli - Cheltenham
            Town Hall, 9 June 1953 (Cheltenham Festival)
Pub: Hinrichsen

String Quartet No 3 in E flat Op.41 (1945)
Dur: 19´30˝
f.p.   Blech Quartet - Cheltenham Town Hall, 30 June 1949 (Cheltenham Festival)
f.broad.p. above artists - 4 November 1949
Pub: Broadbent & Dunn

Fugal Flourish for organ Op.42 (1945)
Pub: Hinrichsen, 1961

Ceremonial and Flourish for brass Op.43 (1946)
Written to celebrate the visit of Sir Winston Churchill to Columbia University in 1946
Dur: 26'
Instr: 3/2/2/3 - 4/3/3/1 - timp. perc. str.
f.p.   Columbia University, 1946
f.Am.conc.p. Houston Symphony Orchestra/Leopold Stokowski - Houston,
            18 March 1957
f.rec.   Locke Brass Consort - *Koch 37202-2(CD)*
Pub: AMP (USA); Chester (UK)

Piano Concerto Op.44 (1946)

Dur: 27′
f.p.   Vera Brodsky/Canadian Broadcasting System Symphony Orchestra/ Bernard
           Herrmann - CBS broadcast, 29 January 1947
f.Am.p.   Moura Lympany/New York Philharmonic Orchestra/Leon Barzin - Carnegie
           Hall, New York, 1948
f.Brit.broad.p.Ross Pratt/Royal Philharmonic Orchestra/Royalton Kisch -
           13 May 1950
f.Brit.conc.p. Ross Pratt/Royal Philharmonic Orchestra/Richard Arnell -
           Royal Festival Hall, London, 3 March 1954
also arr. by the composer for two pianos Op.44a
Pub: Schott

Cassation for woodwind quintet Op.45 (1946)

Score dated - New York, 29 June 1946
Instr: Fl. Ob. Cl. Bsn. Hn.
f.Brit.p. Virtuoso Ensemble - BBC, 9 January 1959

The Black Mountain - Prelude for orchestra Op.46 (1946)

Dur: 5′
Instr: 3/2/2/2 - 4/3/3/1 - timp. perc. str.
f.Brit.p. National Youth Orchestra/Hugo Rignold - Leeds, 4 January 1953
           (Sixth anniversary concert)
Pub: Hinrichsen

Trio for violin, cello and piano Op.47 (1946)

Dur: 22′30″
f.p.   at an S.P.N.M. Concert with Richard Arnell (Pno.)
f.broad.p. Rubbra-Gruenberg-Pleeth Trio - 19 September 1951
Pub: Hinrichsen

Sonata No. 2 `Suite' for solo cello Op.48 (1947)

Dur: 10′
Pub: Hinrichsen, 1960

Punch and the Child - ballet Op.49 (1947)

Commissioned by the Ballet Society of New York
Dur: 20′
Instr: 2/2/3/2 - 4/2/3/1 - timp. perc. str.
f.p.   New York City Ballet, November 1947
Choreography: Fred Danielli
Decor: Horace Arminstead

Suite from the ballet Op.49a (1947)

f.p.   Royal Philharmonic Orchestra/Sir Thomas Beecham - Royal Albert Hall,
           London, 15 May 1951 (Royal Philharmonic Society Concert)
f.rec.   above artists - Columbia *LX 1391/3(78), Sony SMK 46683(CD), SBK 62748
           (CD and MC)*
Choreography: Kenneth MacMillan

Pub: Hinrichsen
also arr. by the composer for piano Op.49a

Abstract Forms - suite for string orchestra Op.50 (1947)
Dur: 15'
f.p.   Boyd Neel String Orchestra/Boyd Neel - Bath, 2 June 1951 (Bath Festival)
f.broad.p. above artists - 22 July 1953
Pub: Hinrichsen

Concerto for harpsichord and chamber orchestra Op.51 (1947)
Dur: 15'
Instr: 1/1/1/1 - 2/0/0/0 - str.
Pub: Hinrichsen
also arr. for piano and chamber orchestra Op.51a

Symphony No. 4 Op.52 (1948)
Dedicated to Leon Barzin
Dur: 27'
Instr: 3/2/2/2 - 4/3/3/1 - timp. str.
f.p.   BBC Northern Orchestra/Charles Groves - BBC, 29 November 1948
f.Am.p.   New York Philharmonic Orchestra/Leon Barzin - Carnegie Hall,
            New York, 1949
f.conc.p.   Hallé Orchestra/Sir John Barbirolli - Cheltenham Town Hall,
            29 June 1949 (Cheltenham Festival)
f.Lon.p.   Royal Philharmonic Orchestra/Sir Thomas Beecham - Royal Festival
            Hall, 5 March 1953
Pub: Hinrichsen

Recitative and Aria for piano Op.53 (1948)
Pub: Schott, 1951

Sonata da camera for violin, viola da gamba and harpsichord Op.54 (1948)

Violin Sonata No. 2 Op.55 (1948)
Dedicated to Jean Pougnet
Dur: 14'30"
f.p.   Maria Lidka (Vn.)/Margaret Kitchin (Pno.) - Lausanne, Switzerland,
            February 1950
f.Brit.p.   Jean Pougnet (Vn.)/Wilfrid Parry (Pno.) - BBC, 26 February 1950
Pub: Schott, 1950

Caligula - incidental music Op.56 (1949)

Blech: Serenade for ten wind instruments and double bass Op.57 (1949)
Dur: 16'
f.Brit.p.   Wind Music Society - Chelsea Town Hall, London, 12 May 1958
f.rec.   London Baroque Ensemble/Karl Haas - *Pye Golden Guinea GGC 4040(m),
            GSGC 14040; GSGC 7054 (and MC)*
Pub: Hinrichsen

also arr. by the composer for piano, 4 hands Op.57a

Andante and Allegro for flute and piano Op.58 No.1 (1949)
Dur: 2'45"
Pub: Schott, 1950

Allegro for trumpet and piano Op.58 No.2 (1949)
Pub: Schott, 1952

Ode to the West Wind for soprano and orchestra Op.59 (1950)
[Words: Shelley]
Written for Emily Hooke
f.p.   Jennifer Vyvyan/Royal Philharmonic Orchestra/Sir Thomas Beecham -
          Royal Festival Hall, London, 23 February 1955 (Royal Philharmonic Society
          Concert)
also arr. by the composer for soprano and piano Op.59a

String Quintet Op.60 (1950)
Instr: Vn. Vn. Va. Va. Vc.
f.p.   Blech Quartet/Kenneth Essex (Va.) - Cheltenham Town Hall, 6 July 1950
          (Cheltenham Festival)
Pub: Broadbent & Dunn

Sonatina for piano, 4 hands Op.61 (1950)
f.p.   Helen Pyke/Paul Hamburger - RBA Galleries, London, 26 October 1950
Pub: Peer Southern (USA) 1960; Elkin

String Quartet No. 4 Op.62 (1950)
Dur: 9'45"
f.p.   New London Quartet - Cheltenham Town Hall, 14 July 1952
          (Cheltenham Festival)
f.broad.p. above artists - 27 April 1953
Pub: Broadbent & Dunn

Harlequin in April - ballet Op.63 (1951)
Commissioned by Sadler's Wells Theatre Ballet (for the junior Company) with funds
provided by the Arts Council for the Festival of Britain, and suggested by T. S. Eliot's
'The Waste Land'
f.p.   Sadler's Wells Theatre Ballet Orchestra/Richard Arnell - Sadler's Wells
          Theatre, London, 8 May 1951
Choreography: John Cranko
Decor: John Piper
Principals: Stanley Holden, David Blair

Suite from the ballet Op.63b (1951)
Dur: 25'
Instr: 2/1/2/1 - 4/2/2/0 - timp. perc. str.
f.p.   Royal Philharmonic Orchestra/Richard Arnell - Royal Albert Hall, London,
          5 September 1959 (Promenade Concert)

Pub: Hinrichsen

Overture (Trio) for flute, cello and piano Op.64 (1951)
Dur: 5'
Pub: Hinrichsen

Suite from the film `The Dagenham Story' Op.65 (1952)
Dur: 16'
Instr: 3/2/2/2 - 4/3/3/1 - timp. perc. pno. str.
f.p.   (exc. `Assembly March') National Youth Orchestra/Hugo Rignold - Leeds,
            4 January 1953 (Sixth Anniversary concert)
f.p.   (complete) Helsinki State Orchestra/Edward Renton - 1954
Pub: Hinrichsen

Impromptu for piano Op.66 (1952)
Pub: Peer Southern (USA), 1960

Lord Byron - Symphonic Portrait Op.67 (1952)
[1. Prelude 2. Newstead 3. Augusta 4. Success and Disgrace 5. Voyage
 6. Serenade 7. Battles 8. Epilogue]
Commissioned by Sir Thomas Beecham, the work's dedicatee, for the Royal
Philharmonic Orchestra
Dur: 20'
Instr: 3/3/3/3 - 4/3/3/1 - timp. perc. cel. str.
f.p.   Royal Philharmonic Orchestra/Sir Thomas Beecham - Royal Festival Hall,
            London, 19 November 1952 (Royal Philharmonic Society Concert)
f.broad.p. BBC Symphony Orchestra/Sir Thomas Beecham - 25 November 1953
Pub: Hinrichsen

The Great Detective* - ballet Op.68 (1953)
Commissioned by the Sadler's Wells Theatre Ballet with funds provided by the Arts
Council of Great Britain.
Dur: 25'
Instr: 2/2/2/2 - 4/2/2/0 - timp. perc. str.
f.p.   Sadler's Wells Theatre Ballet Orchestra/Richard Arnell - Sadler's Wells
            Theatre, London, 21 January 1953
Choreography: Margaret Dale
Decor: Bryan Robb
(* Scenario based on Sherlock Holmes)

Suite from the ballet Op. 68a
Dur: 15'
f.Can.p.   C.B.C. Vancouver Chamber Orchestra/Richard Arnell - Vancouver,
            April 1959
f.rec.   Pro Arte Orchestra/Richard Arnell - *Pye Golden Guinea GGC 4048(m), GSGC
            14048; EMI CDM7 64718-2 (CD)*
Pub: Hinrichsen

The Grenadiers - variations for brass Op.69 (1953)

Concerto Capriccioso for violin and small orchestra Op.70 (1953)
Dur: 19'
Instr: 2/1/2/1 - 2/2/2/0 - perc. str.
f.p.   Jack Kessler/C.B.C. Vancouver Chamber Orchestra/Richard Arnell -
           Vancouver, April 1959
also arr. by the composer for violin and piano Op.70a

Andantino for organ Op.71 (1954)

Music for harp with string trio Op.72 No. 1 (1954)
also arr. for solo harp Op.72 No. 2
also arr. for harp, flute, violin and viola Op.72a

Suite in D for two pianos Op.73 (1955)
Dur: 10´
Pub: Hinrichsen

Love in Transit - opera in one Act Op.74 (1955)
[Libretto: Hal Burton]
f.p.   BBC Television
f.conc.p. London, 27 February 1958

Fox Variations* for piano Op.75 (1955)
[1.Prelude 2. Chorale 3. Staccato 4. Nocturne 5. Courante
6. Note-spinning 7. Theme 8. Farewell]
Dedicated to Mr. and Mrs. Uffa Fox and written for their wedding.
f.p.   Peter Wallfisch - 6 February 1960
Pub: Belwyn Mills, 1958
(* the theme is the traditional tune "Oh dear, what can the matter be?")

Variations on an American Theme, for violin and piano Op.76 (1955)
f.broad.p. Lionel Bentley (Vn.)/Wilfrid Parry (Pno.), 7 December 1962
Pub: Lengnick, 1958; Elkin

Symphony No. 5 'The Gorilla' Op.77 (1955-57)
Score completed 26 June 1957
Dur: 27'
Instr: 3/3/3/3 - 4/3/3/1 - timp. perc. str.
f.Lon.p.   Royal Philharmonic Orchestra/Richard Arnell - Odeon, Swiss
           Cottage, 22 March 1966
?f.broad.p. BBC Northern Symphony Orchestra/John Carewe - 1 July 1977
Pub: Lengnick; Elkin

Landscapes and Figures for orchestra Op.78 (1955)
[1. The City 2. The Plains 3. Gargoyle 4. The Quarry 5. Flower Piece
6. Self Portrait 7. Heirloom 8. Apotheosis]
Commissioned for the Edinburgh Festival and dedicated to Sir Thomas Beecham
Dur: 16'30"
Instr: 3/2/2/3 - 4/3/3/1 - timp. perc. pno. str.

f.p.   Royal Philharmonic Orchestra/Sir Thomas Beecham - 1956 (Edinburgh
            Festival)
f.Lon.p.   above artists - Royal Festival Hall, 24 November 1956
Pub: Hinrichsen

Thoughts and Second Thoughts - for piano, 4 hands Op.79 (1955)

Four Songs of Minous Op.80 (1955)

The Angels - ballet Op.81 (1956)
Written for the Royal Ballet for performance by the junior company
Dur: 30'
Instr: 2/1/2/1 - 2/2/2/0 - timp. perc. hp. cel. str.
f.p.   Junior company of the Royal Ballet cond. Richard Arnell - Royal Opera
            House, Covent Garden, London, 26 December 1957
Choreography: John Cranko
Scenery: Desmond Heeley
Principals: Patricia Cox, Yvonne Lakier, Anne Heaton, Donald Britton,
            Donald MacLeary and Johaar Mosaval
also arr. by the composer for piano solo Op.81a
Exc. `Roundelay' Op.81aa

Music for horns Op.82 (1956)
[1. Statement 2. Answer 3. Slow March 4. Scherzo 5. Return 6. Allegretto
 7. Solo 8. Second Solo 9. Chant]
Dur: 15'
Pub: Hinrichsen, 1965

Moonflowers (`Love in a Cave') - opera Op.83a (1956)
[Libretto: Richard Arnell]
f.p.   Kent, 23 July 1959
originally arr. by the composer for piano solo Op.83

Four in D for piano Op.84 (1956)
Pub: Hinrichsen, 1961

A Lifeboat Song Op.84a (1956)

The Petrified Princess - puppet operetta Op.85 (1957-59)
[Libretto: Bryan Guinness]
Commissioned by the BBC
f.p.   Virtuoso Ensemble/Richard Arnell - BBC Television, 5 May 1959
Principals:Dorothy Dorow, Trevor Anthony, Raimund Herincx

Clarinet Pieces for clarinet and piano Op.86 (1957)
Dur: 9'30"
Pub: Hinrichsen

'Impressions - Robert Flaherty' for orchestra Op.87 (1958)

John Anthony Gifford, for flute, violin and piano Op. 88 (1960)

Shadow of a Pale Horse - music for television Op.88 No.1 (1959)

Chorale Variation on 'Ein Feste Burg' for organ Op.89 (1960)
Pub: Hinrichsen, 1961
Exc. 'Prelude' Op.89a

Divertimento Concertante for cello and string orchestra Op.90 (1961)

Six Guitar Pieces Op.91 (1960)
Pub: Peer Southern (USA), 1968

The Magic Tree - music for television Op.92 (1960)

Sally Truro - opera Op.92 No.1 (1961)
[Libretto: Richard Arnell]

Brass Quintet 'Poor Wayfaring Stranger' Op.93 (1961)

Midsummer Sun - music for television Op.93 No.1 (1961)

Wales - a Miner's Song for male voices and piano Op.94 (1961)

The General Strike - music for television Op.95 (1961)

Summer is Coming, for soprano, mezzo-soprano and piano Op.96 (1961)

Six Pieces for harpsichord   Op.97 (1961)
[1. Exposition 2. Vivace 3. Aria 4. Siciliana 5. Voluntary and Researches
 6. Invention]
Dur: 15'
Pub: Hinrichsen

Pensum Latinum for unaccompanied women's chorus Op.98 (1962)
Dur: 8'

String Quartet No. 5 Op.99 (1962)
Dur: 16'
Pub: Broadbent & Dunn

You, Love and I ('Counting the Beats') song for tenor and piano Op.100 (1963)
[Words: Robert Graves]
Commissioned by Patric Dickinson for the 1963 Festival of Poetry - Lennox Berkeley
(q.v.), Nicholas Maw and Humphrey Searle (q.v.) were also asked to contribute their own
setting of the poem.
Dur: 5'
f.p.   Gerald English (Ten.)/John Constable (Pno.) - Royal Court Theâtre, London,
            16 July 1963

Pub: Hinrichsen

Musica Pacifica for orchestra Op.101 (1963)
Dur: 10'
Instr: 3/3/3/3 - 4/3/3/1 - timp. perc. glock. hp. str.
Pub: Hinrichsen

Larghetto and Furiante for piano Op.102 (1963)

Inventions for treble instruments Op.103 (1963)

Three Related Pieces for organ Op.104 (1963)

Adam: Giselle - ballet arr. Op.104 No.2 (1964)

Adagio for cello and piano Op.105 (1965)

Festival Flourish for brass Op.106 No.1 (1965)

A Flourish for the Salvation Army, for ceremonial trumpets, brass band and organ Op.106 No.2 (1965)

Quintet 'The Gambian' - Prelude and Variations for treble recorder and string quartet Op.107 (1965)
Instr: Rec. Vn. Vn. Va. Vc.
f.p.   Carl Dolmetsch (Rec.)/Martin String Quartet - Wigmore Hall, London, 10 February 1966

'Clarinet and Piano 107' Op.108 (1966)

Seven Love Poems - song cycle Op.109 (1967)

Sections - Concerto for piano and orchestra Op.110 (1967)
Commissioned by the Royal Philharmonic Orchestra in celebration of their 21st anniversary.
Dur: 35'
Instr: 3/2/2/2 - 4/3/3/1 - timp. perc. str.
f.p.   John Ogdon/Royal Philharmonic Orchestra/Richard Arnell - Fairfield Hall, Croydon, 16 September 1967
Pub: Hinrichsen

Concerto Minima for double wind quintet Op.111 (1968)

The Food of Love - overture Op.112 (1968)
Dur: 12'
Instr: 2/2/2/2 - 4/2/2/0 - timp. perc. str.
Pub: Hinrichsen

Wind Symphony Op.113 (1968)

(N.B. renamed and renumbered as Op.114)

My Lady Greensleeves (A British Worthy) for wind band Op.114 (1968)
Dur: 15'
Instr: 3/3/3/3 - 4/3/3/1 - timp. perc. cel.
f.p.   Hofstra College, Hempstead, New York, 27 April 1969
Pub: Peer Southern (USA)

Stedmans Grandsire Doubles for brass band Op.115 (1968)

Combat Zone (a visit to a War Museum) - mixed media piece Op.116 (1969)
[Words: Louis Cox]
f.p.   Hofstra College, Hempstead, New York, 27 April 1969

Songs of Gambia - variations for recorder and string quartet Op.117 (1969)

The Town Crier (Concord Boy) for narrator and orchestra Op.118 (1970)
Commissioned by the Pro Arte Orchestra of Hofstra University
f.p.   Pro Arte Orchestra of Hofstra University - Carnegie Hall, New York,
            March 1970

Nocturne: Prague, August 20, 1968 - mixed media piece Op.119 (1970)
[Words: Ralph Gustafson]
Commissioned by Bishop's College, Quebec
f.p.   Montreal, March 1970

Cretaceous Intermission - song cycle Op.120 (1971)
f.p.   Lavinia Lascelles (Sop.)/Antony Saunders (Pno.) - Wigmore Hall, London,
            30 April 1971

Zero Growth - film Op.121 (1971)

I think of all soft limbs - mixed media piece* for narrator, tape, organ and percussion Op.122 (1971)
[Words: Ralph Gustafson]
Commissioned by the Canadian Broadcasting Corporation
f.p.   Montreal, Winter 1971 (* in association with Tristram Cary)

Quiet Tension - library music Op.123a (1972)

Achievement - library music Op.123b (1972)

Trinity Fanfare - the 100 notes for brass ensemble Op.124 (1972)

Thirteen Pages Plus One, for clarinet and harpsichord Op.125 (1972)

Prelude and Boxes for solo clarinet Op.125a (1972)

Codes for chorus and orchestra Op.126 (1973)

Astronaut one - mixed media piece Op.127 (1973)
[Words: Edward Lucie Smith]
Commissioned by Ceolfrith Arts, Sunderland
f.p.   Wearmouth Thirteen Hundred Festival, November 1973

Regal Garland - arrangement Op.127a (1973)

Stained Glass - film Op.128 (1974)

Four Minutes for Four People for string trio (sic.) Op.129 (1974)

Lifeboat Voluntary for organ Op.130 (1974)
Written for the R.N.L.I.

J(ennifer) and R(obert) = W(edding) for piano, 4 hands Op.131 (1975)

'Ring Bells - Happy New Year' for piano Op.132a (1976)

'Ring Bells - Happy Jubilee' for piano Op.132b (1977)

'Call-Short Music' - Concerto for harp and orchestra Op.133 (1979)
f.p.   London Philharmonic Orchestra - Royal Festival Hall, London,
              28 January 1979

Op.134 (1980)
Not used/listed

Wedding Piece for organ Op.135 (1980)

The Antagonist - film Op.136 (1980)

Op.137 (1980)
Not used/listed

Alpha Omega - arrangement for soloists, chorus, orchestra and narrator Op.138 (1980)
f.p.   Helen Walker/Keith Lewis/St. Michael's Singers/Young Musicians
              Symphony Orchestra/James Blair - Coventry Cathedral, 13 November 1980

Dilemma - film Op.139 (1980)

Chickens Never Walk Backwards - film Op.140 (1981)

Improvisations for Jessie, for piano Op.141 (1983)

Doctor in the Sky - film Op.142 (1983)

Toulouse Lautrec - film Op.143 (1984)

We are Many - film Op.144 (1984)

Words and Sounds Op.145 (1984)
Written under the pseudonym Ynot L'heur

R. V. W.'s almanac for four clarinets Op.146 (1984)
Commissioned by the Ebony Quartet
f.p.   Ebony Quartet - Purcell Room, London, 12 October 1984

Bach Mantra Op.147 - unfinished (1984)

Op.148
Not used/listed

'Happy Birthday Michael Scott' Op.149 No.1 (1985)
(words and sounds)

'Happy Birthday Hazel Morfey' Op.149 No.2 (1985)
(words and sounds)

Six Lawrence Poems for narrator, soprano and brass band Op.150 (1985)
Commissioned by East Midlands Arts.
f.p.   Richard Baker (Narr.)/Rosemary Whaley (Sop.)/Desford Colliery Dowty
           Band/Howard Snell - Nottingham, 24 September 1985 (D. H. Lawrence
           Centenary Festival)

Computer Animation for Television Op.151 (1986)

'Non-Event for an Event' - mixed media piece Op.152 (1986)

Masters of Animation - film Op.153 (1986)

Ode to Beecham for narrator and orchestra Op.154 (1986)
[Words: Richard Arnell]
Commissioned by the Royal Philharmonic Orchestra for their 40th anniversary.
f.p.   Bruce Montague/Royal Philharmonic Orchestra/Arthur Davison - Fairfield
           Hall, Croydon, Surrey, 24 September 1986

**War God II - revised version for narrator, soprano, brass, percussion, synthesisers,
chorus and tape Op.155 (1987)**
[Words: Sir Stephen Spender]
Co-wrote with David Hewson
f.p.   Richard Arnell/Miriam Bowen/Michael Kibblewhite/David Hewson -
           St.John's, Smith Square, London, 14 March 1987

**'Event 35/70 - 24 hours in TT Scale' for piano, tape and narrator
Op.156 (1988)**
[Words: Richard Arnell]

Written in honour of the 250th anniversary of the Royal Society of Musicians - Co-wrote with David Hewson

Light of the World - film Op.157 (1988)

Shortest Symphony* for orchestra Op.158 (1988)
(* one page!)

Gesualdo - text for music theatre work Op.159a (1988)
[Words: Richard Arnell]

Con Amore - text for women's chorus and piano Op.160a (1989)
[Words: Richard Arnell]
Commissioned by East Midlands Arts for the Cantamus Girls' Choir.

Symphony X, for orchestra, tape and keyboard Op.161 (1990)

Sadness for John Ogdon for piano Op.162 (1990)

Accompanied Fugato and Chorale for Virgil, for piano Op.163 (1990)

Call - revised version for harp and orchestra Op.164a (1990)

Divertimento No. 1 - revised version Op.165a (1990)

Not Wanted on Voyage - mixed media piece Op.166 (1991)
[Words: Richard Arnell]
Co-wrote with David Hewson

Music for Michaela, for treble recorder and electronics Op.167 (1991)

Three for Three, for flute, cello and piano Op.168 (1991)
Commissioned by the YH Arts Commission

Treble Music for recorder Op.169
Written at the request of John Turner

String Quartet No. 6 Op.170 (1990-92)
[1. Statement 2. Look Back 3. Dance 4. Duo 5. Accompanied Cadenza 6. Restatement]
Commissioned by the Cheltenham Festival - the score is dated 22 May 1992
f.p.   Maggini Quartet - Pittville Pump Room, Cheltenham, 5 July 1992
            (Cheltenham Festival)
Pub: Broadbent & Dunn

Symphony No. 6 'The Anvil' Op.171 (1992-94)
Written with the financial assistance of the Arts Council of Great Britain.
f.p.   BBC Philharmonic Orchestra/Adrian Leaper - Radio 3, 9 January 1995
            (rec. April 1994)

Xanadu, for soprano, chorus, percussion and piano (1992-93)
[Words: Coleridge `Kubla Khan']
f.p.   Ely Cathedral, 1993

(N.B.)   Arnell has recently adopted a new numbering system whereby **Symphony No.
6** is now **Op. 179** - the following works reflect this change.)

Fanfare for a Lifeboat Op. 180 (1994)
Written for the Royal National Lifeboat Institute (R.N.L.I.) for a launching at Aldeburgh.

Last Song, for soprano and piano Op. 181 (1996)
Commissioned by Ian Bruce-Jones.
f.p.   Yvonne Roberts (Sop.)/Maurice Ridge (Pno.) - Jubilee Hall, Aldeburgh, April
            1997 (80th Birthday concert).
f.Lon.p.   above artists - British Music Information Centre, Stratford Place,
            25 November 1997

Five Emily Songs, for soprano and piano Op. 182 (1996)
[Words: Emily Dickinson]
Commissioned by Ian Bruce-Jones.
f.p.   Yvonne Roberts (Sop.)/Maurice Ridge (Pno.) - Jubilee Hall, Aldeburgh,
            April 1997 (80th Birthday concert).
f.Lon.p.   above artists - British Music Information Centre, Stratford Place,
            25 November 1997

The Hoffman Cantata, for baritone and piano Op. 183 (1996)
[Words: Ralph Gustafson]
Commissioned by Donald Hoffman (USA)

Fanfare for Trinity College of Music, for brass band Op. 184 (1997)
Commissioned by Trinity College of Music, London.

JUVENILIA AND STUDENT WORKS

Air in G minor (1934)

String Trio No. 1 (1936)

String Quartet No. 1 (1937)

String Quartet No. 2 (1937)

Overture (1937)

String Trio No. 2 (1937)

Concerto for violin and orchestra (1938)
(First performed by students at the Royal College of Music, London, in 1938 and
re-written in 1940 as his Op. 9 q.v.)

String Quartet No. 3 (1938)

Sinfonia Concertante for violin, viola and chamber orchestra (1938)

Intermezzo for oboe quartet (1938)

Sinfonia (1938)

Cello Pieces for cello and piano (1939)

Symphony for string orchestra (1939)

Piano Pieces (1939)

FILM MUSIC

(i)   **Documentary Films**

Farm Front Op.11 - U.S. Department of Agriculture (1941)
Director: Robert Flaherty

The Land Op.12 - U.S. Department of Agriculture (1941)
Director: Robert Flaherty

The Dagenham Story Op.65 - Gerard Holdsworth Productions (1952)
An advertising production for the Ford Motor Company where the music was composed first and the film sequences added later.
Producer: Gerard Holdsworth
Music played by: London Symphony Orchestra

The Scheme Op.101 - James Archibald Productions for Duke of Edinburgh's Award Scheme (1963)
Producer: James Archibald

Flying Machine Op.102 No.1 (1963)

Topsail Schooner (Sir Winston Churchill) Op.108 - Gerard Holdsworth Productions (1966)
Producer: Gerard Holdsworth

Bequest to a Village Op.115 - Gerard Holdsworth Productions for R.N.L.I. (1969)
Producer: Gerard Holdsworth

Rain Folly - US Conservancy Board, Maine (1969)

Zero Growth Op.121 - London Film School, Animation Department (1971)

Director: Richard Arnell
Animation: Pierre Gandry

One in Five Op.121 No. 1 - ACT Films for TGWU (1971)
Director: Ralph Bond

Second Best Op.122 No. 1 - Capricorn Productions (1971)
With electronic music by Lawrence Casserly

War to the Last Itch Op.126 - CRM Scientific Productions (1973)
With electronic music by David Hewson
Director: Alistair MacEwan

Knockdown and Kill - CRM Scientific Productions (1974)
With electronic music by David Hewson
Director: Alistair MacEwan

Stained Glass Op.128 - London Film School (1974)
With electronic music by Lawrence Casserly
Director: Jeremy Hogarth

Wires over the Border Op.128 No. 2 - John Shearman for British Transport Films (1974)
Director: David Lochner
Music performed by: Sticky George Group
f.rec.   soundtrack - *FAME Video TV8 (V)*

Rothko and the Tate - Richard Arnell (c.1975)
Director: Peter Day

The Poetry of Vision - R.O.S.C. Op.132 No. 2 (1979)

Doctor in the Sky Op.142 (1983)
Co-wrote with David Hewson

Toulouse Lautrec - John Halas Op.143 (1984)
Co-wrote with David Hewson

Masters of Animation Op.153 (1986)
Co-wrote with David Hewson

The Light of the World - John Halas Op.157 (1988)
Co-wrote with David Hewson

(ii)   Feature Films

Der Besuch (The Visit) Op.102 - Twentieth Century Fox (1963)
Additional music written for British release - the original score was provided
by Hans-Martin Majewski

Director: Bernhard Wicki

The Third Secret Op.104 - Twentieth Century Fox/Hubris (1963)
Director: Charles Crichton

The Man Outside Op.109 - London International (1967)
Director: Sam Gallu

The Black Panther - Impics Op.132 (1977)
Director: Ian Merrick

The Antagonist Op.136 (1980)

Dilemma Op.139 - John Halas (1980)
Co-wrote with David Hewson

Chickens Never Walk Backwards Op.140 (1981)

We are Many Op.144 (1984)

INCIDENTAL MUSIC

(a) **Radio**

They call them Leathernecks Op.32 No.1 (1944)

The Proof of the Pudding   Op.62 No.1 (1950)

(b) **Television**

Wanted - commercial Op.64 No.1 (1952)

Shadow of a Pale Horse Op.88 No.1 - Granada Production (1959)

The Magic Tree - puppet play Op.92 (1960)

Midsummer Sun Op.93 No.1 (1961)

The General Strike Op.95 - Granada Production (1961)
Producer: Jeremy Isaacs

Hospitaliday - vocal jingle Op.115 No.1 (1969)

Computer Animation Op.151 Nos. 1 and 2 (1986)
Co-wrote with David Hewson

(c) Stage

> **Caligula Op.56 (1949)**
> [Alfred Camus]

ARRANGEMENTS

N.B. These are listed in the main body of the catalogue. See Op. 5 No. 1 (Handel), Op. 6 No. 1 (Bach), Op. 104 No. 2 (Adam)

MS LOCATION

BL   String Quartet No. 1 (1939), String Quartet No. 2 (1941),
String Quartet No. 3 (1945), String Quartet No. 4 (1950),
String Quartet No. 5 (dyeline) (1962), String Quartet No. 6 (1990-92)
Symphony No. 4 (1947), Symphony No. 5 (1957),
Symphony No. 6 (1994), Harlequin in April (1951), Lord Byron (1951),
Concerto Capricioso (1954), Love in Transit (1954),
Counting the Beats (1963), Astronaut One (1973).

BIBLIOGRAPHY

Arnell, Richard   **John Ireland 1879-1962** Tempo, Spring/Summer 1962

Arnell, Richard   **Arnold Cooke - a Birthday conversation**
Composer No. 24, Summer 1967

Arnell, Richard   **Composing for animation film** Composer, 1981

Arnell, Richard   **16 Years in the Electronic Maze** Composer, 1984

Dawney, Michael   **Richard Arnell at 75** Journal of the British Music Society, Vol. 14, 1992.

Patrick, Jonathan   **Richard Arnell - list of works** 1985 rev. February 1991

Wright, David C.F.   **Richard Arnell - a personal tribute** British Music Society Newsletter No. 78, June 1998.

5

Malcolm Arnold
(1921–)

Haile Selassie - March for piano (1936)

Theme and Three Variations (1937)
[Theme - Var.I (Fugato) Var.II (Bouree) Var.III (Marcia Funebre)]
Score dated 20 January 1937
Instr: not specified

Allegro in E minor for piano (1937)
Score dated 13 February 1937
Dur: 40"
f.rec.   Benjamin Frith - *Koch 3-7162-2(CD)*

Three Piano Pieces (1937)
[1. Prelude 2. Air 3. Gigue]
Score dated 15 February 1937
Dur: 3'30"
f.rec.   Benjamin Frith - *Koch 3-7162-2(CD)*

Serenade in G for piano (1937)
Score dated 3 October 1937
Dur: 2'15"
f.rec.   Benjamin Frith - *Koch 3-7162-2(CD)*

Kensington Gardens - song cycle for medium voice and piano (1938)
[Words: Humbert Wolfe 1. Night 2. Tulip 3. Noon 4. Daffodil 5. Lupin
6. Hawthorn Tree 7. The Rose 8. Laburnum 9. The Chestnut and the Beech Tree]
Score dated 24 April - 24 July 1938
Dur: 7'30"

Grand Fantasia* for flute, trumpet and piano (c.1938)
f.p.   probably Richard Adeney (Fl.)/Malcolm Arnold(Tpt.)/Betty Coleman(Pno.)
(the piece is inscribed as "Opus 973", 'composed by A.Youngman')

Day Dreams for piano (1938)
Score dated 3 October 1938
Dur: 3'30"
f.rec.   Benjamin Frith - *Koch 3-7162-2(CD)*

Suite Bourgeoise - miniature trio (c. 1939)
[1. Prelude 2. Tango (Elaine) 3. Dance (censored!) 4. Ballad 5. Valse]
Dur: 13'
Instr: Fl. Tpt. Pno.
f.p.   Richard Adeney (Fl.)/Malcolm Arnold (Tpt.)/Betty Coleman (Pno.) -
            Cornwall, summer 1939

Two Part Songs (1939)
[Words: Ernest Dowson 1. Spleen
 2. Vitae Summa Brevis Spem Nos Uetat Incohare Longam]
Score dated 24 September 1939
Dur: 1'45"

Sonata for flute and piano* (1940 rev. 1942)
Score dated 12 November 1942
Dur: 8'30"
f.p.   Richard Adeney (Fl.)/Malcolm Arnold (Pno.) - Northampton Town Hall, 1940
f.mod.p.   Richard Adeney (Fl.) with student pianist at the Royal Academy of Music,
            London, c. spring 1985
f.rec.   Colin Chambers (Fl.)/Janice Warren (Pno.) - *private cassette (rec. 1984)*
(* an experiment in serial technique - the Sonata bears the title "Sonate poor (sic) flute by
A. Youngman")

Overture for wind octet (arr. for piano duet) (1940)
later arr. for string orchestra by P.Wood (1993)

Trio for flute, trumpet and cello (c. 1940)
Dur: 2'
f.priv.p.   Richard Adeney* (Fl.)/Malcolm Arnold (Tpt.)/Miss Adeney (Vc.) - Royal
            College of Music, London, c. 1940
(* Adeney recalls it being "a little rumba")

Phantasy for String Quartet* (1941)
Dur: 12'
Score dated: London 6-17 June 1941
f.p.   Allegri Quartet - Purcell Room, London, 21 March 1996
(* originally entitled 'Vita Abundans', this work won second prize in the W.W. Cobbett
competition: the winner that year was Ruth Gipps, for whom Arnold later composed the
Variations for Orchestra Op. 122 q.v.)

Two Sketches for oboe and piano (1941)
Score dated 28 August 1941

Two Piano Pieces (1941)
Score dated 3 October 1941
Dur: 2'30˝
f.rec.   Benjamin Frith - *Koch 3-7162-2(CD)*

Piano Sonata in B minor (1942)
Dur: 10'
f.p.   Richard Deering - British Music Information Centre, London, 15 May 1984
f.broad.p. Richard Deering - BBC World Service, 3 August 1984
f.rec.   Benjamin Frith - *Koch 3-7162-2 (CD)*
Pub: Roberton, 1984
later arr. for saxophone and string orchestra by David Ellis as 'Saxophone
Concerto'(1994)
f.p.   Gerard McChrystal/Milton Keynes City Orchestra/Hilary Davan Wetton -
            Stantonbury Campus Theatre, Milton Keynes, 10 February 1996
Pub: Roberton (also arr. for saxophone and piano)

Divertimento No. 1 for orchestra Op.1 (1942)
Dur: 10'30"
Instr: 3/2/2/2 - 4/3/3/1 - timp. perc.(2) str.
f.p.   London Symphony Orchestra/Benjamin Frankel - Guildhall School of Music,
            London, 29 May 1945 (CPNM Concert)

Wind Quintet Op.2 (1942)
Written for the London Philharmonic Wind Quintet
Dur: 13'
Instr: Fl. Ob. Cl. Hn. Bsn.
f.p.   London Philharmonic Orchestra Wind Quintet - Richard Adeney (Fl.)/
            Michael Dobson (Ob.)/John Lucas (Cl.)/Charles Gregory (Hn.)/ George
            Alexandra (Bsn.) - Trinity College of Music, London, 7 June 1943 (CPNM
            Concert)
f.pub.p.   above artists - Harpenden, Herts. summer 1943
f.broad.p. above artists - BBC European Service, late 1943

Three Piano Pieces (1943)
Score dated London, 6 May 1943
[1. Prelude 2. Romance 3. Lament]
Dur: 7'30˝
f.p.   Yonty Solomon - Purcell Room, London, 11 April 1996
f.rec.   Benjamin Frith - *Koch 3-7162-2(CD)*

Larch Trees* - Tone poem for orchestra Op.3 (1943)
Score dated London, 20 June 1943
Dur: 11'15"
Instr: 2/2/2/2 - 4/0/0/0 - str.
f.p.   London Philharmonic Orchestra/Malcolm Arnold - Royal Albert Hall,
            London, 1 October 1943 (CPNM Concert)
f.broad.p. Northern Sinfonia/Christopher Seaman - Radio 3, 7 December 1984

f.mod.p.   London Repertoire Orchestra/Ruth Gipps - Guildhall School of Music and
Drama, Barbican, London, 26 February 1984

f. rec.   London Musici/Mark Stephenson - *Conifer MCFC 211 (MC), CDCF 211
(CD), 75605 51211-2(CD)*

Pub: Faber, 1985

(* Hugo Cole in his book **Malcolm Arnold: an Introduction to his Music,** Faber Music,
1989, tells us that "the impulse to write it sprang direct from Arnold's delight in a glade of
larch trees he discovered on a Yorkshire holiday.")

Three Shanties* for Wind Quintet Op.4 (1943)

Written for the London Philharmonic Wind Quintet to play on their wartime tours

Dur: 6'30"

Instr: Fl. Ob. Cl. Hn. Bsn

f.p.   London Philharmonic Orchestra Wind Quintet (see Op.2) - Filton Aerodrome,
Bristol, c.August 1943 (lunchtime recital)

f.recs.   London Wind Quintet - *Argo RG 326(m)/ZRG 5326; Decca SPA 396, KCSP
396 (MC)*

Nash Ensemble - *Hyperion A 66173 (and MC/CD)*

Pub: Paterson, 1952; Carl Fischer (New York), 1967

(* the Quintet features the tunes `What shall we do with the drunken sailor?', `Johnny
come down to Hilo' and `Boney was a warrior' to humorous effect)

Beckus the Dandipratt* - Comedy Overture for orchestra Op.5 (1943)

Dur: 8'30"

Instr: 2+picc./2/2/2 - 4/2 + cnt./3/1 - timp. perc. str.

f.p.   BBC Scottish Orchestra/Ian Whyte - BBC Third Programme,
29 November 1946

f.conc.p.   London Philharmonic Orchestra/Eduard van Beinum - Royal Opera House,
Covent Garden, 16 November 1947

f.Am.p.   University of Illinois Symphony Orchestra/Rafael Kubelik - University
Auditorium, Illinois, 29 March 1952

f.recs.   London Philharmonic Orchestra*/Eduard van Benium - *Decca K 1844 (78)*;
London (USA) T 5231 (78) (* with Malcolm Arnold as first trumpet and Denis
Egan on cornet)

Royal Philharmonic Orchestra/Malcolm Arnold - *Philips NBL 5021 (m), NBE
11038 (45m); Epic (USA) LC 3422 (m)*

Bournemouth Symphony Orchestra/Malcolm Arnold - *HMV ASD 3823 (and
MC); HMV Greensleeve ESD 107780-1 (and MC)*

London Philharmonic Orchestra/Malcolm Arnold - *Reference RR-48 (and CD)*

Pub: Lengnick, 1948

(* the composer has explained the title as trying "to express in music the spirit and the
reckless attitude of the complete urchin")

Trio for flute, viola and bassoon Op.6 (1943)

Written for members of the London Philharmonic Orchestra

Dur: 12'30"

f.p.   Richard Adeney (Fl.)/Wrayburn Glasspool (Va.)/George Alexandra (Bsn.) -
Fyvie Hall, London, 18 January 1944 (CPNM Recital)

f.broad.p.   William Bennett (Fl.)/Kenneth Essex (Va.)/Gwydion Brooke (Bsn.) -

10 January 1965
f.rec.   Judith Pearce (Fl.)/Roger Chase (Va.)/Brian Wightman (Bsn) - *Hyperion A 66172 (and MC/CD)*
Pub: Paterson, 1954

Quintet Op.7 (1944)
Written for members of the London Philharmonic Orchestra
Dur: 13'30" (rev. 7'30")
Instr: Fl. Vn. Va. Hn. Bsn.
f.p.   Richard Adeney (Fl.)/Albert Chasey (Vn.)/Wrayburn Glasspool (Va.)/ Charles Gregory (Hn.)/George Alexandra (Bsn.) - London, 21 December 1944 (National Gallery Concert)
f.p.   (rev. version) Geoffrey Gilbert (Fl.)/Granville Jones (Vn.) Frederick Riddle (Va.)/Alan Civil (Hn.) Gwydion Brooke (Bsn.) - Maida Vale Studios, London, 8 March 1960 (BBC Invitation Concert)
f.broad.p. (rev. version) Wigmore Ensemble - 8 December 1960
f.rec.   Judith Pearce (Fl.)/Marcia Crayford (Vn.)/Roger Chase (Va.)/John Pigneguy (Hn.)/Brian Wightman (Bsn.) - *Hyperion A 66173 (and MC/CD)*
Pub: Paterson, 1960 (rev. version)

Two songs for voice and piano Op.8 (1944)
[1. Neglected (Mei Sheng translated Arthur Waley)
 2. Morning Noon (Maurice Carpenter)]
Dur: 5'
f.p.   Joyce Newton (M/S)/Mabel Lovering (Pno.) - Salle Erard, London, 25 February 1947 (CPNM Recital)
f.mod.p.   Georgina Anne Colwell (Sop.)/Nigel Foster (Pno.) - St. Mary's Church, Alverstoke, Hampshire, 2 March 1996

Variations on a Ukrainian Folk Song, for piano Op.9 (1944)
Dedicated to John Kuchmy, a Ukrainian violinist in the London Philharmonic Orchestra, at whose suggestion the variations were written - the theme was later transformed into the popular song "Yes, my darling daughter".
Dur: 15'
f.p.   Edith Vogel - Salle Erard, London, 19 November 1946 (CPNM Recital)
f.broad.p. Edna Iles (rec. September 1977)
f.rec.   Benjamin Frith - *Koch 3-7162-2 (CD)*
Pub: Lengnick, 1948
Later arr. for string orchestra by Roger Steptoe
f.p.   Budapest String Orchestra - St. Andrew's Hall, Norwich, 13 October 1993 (Norfolk and Norwich Festival)
Pub: Lengnick, 1993

Duo for flute and viola Op.10 (1945)
Score dated Ewhurst, Surrey, 18 March 1945
Dur: 13'
f.p.   John Francis (Fl.)/Bernard Davies (Va.) - Salle Erard, London, 3 December 1946 (CPNM Recital)
f.rec.   Judith Pearce (Fl.)/Roger Chase (Va.) - *Hyperion A66173 (and MC/CD)*

Pub: Faber, 1985

Concerto No. 1 for horn and orchestra Op.11 (1945)
Dedicated to Charles Gregory, the first horn of the London Philharmonic - the score is dated London, 9 June 1945

Dur: 22'
Instr: 2+picc./2/2/2 - 0/0/0/0 - timp. str.
f.p.   Charles Gregory/London Philharmonic Orchestra/Ernest Ansermet - Royal
            Opera House, Covent Garden, London, 8 December 1946
f.broad.p. Alan Civil/BBC Midland Light Orchestra/Gilbert Vintner - c.1949/50
f.rec.   Richard Watkins/London Musici/Mark Stephenson - *Conifer MCFC 228(MC),*
            CDCF 228 (CD), 75605 51228-2(CD)
Pub: Lengnick, 1947 (2nd movement arr. horn and piano by the composer)

Symphonic Suite for orchestra Op.12 (1945)
Written in memory of the composer's brother, Philip, who was killed in the Second World War

Dur: 15'
Instr: 2 + picc./2/2/2 - 4/3/3/1 - timp. perc.(2) str.
(N.B. material from the first movement was later incorporated into the **Little Suite No. 1 Op. 53** q.v.)

Prelude for piano (1945)
Dur: 2'45"
Score dated London, 18 December 1945
f.rec.   Benjamin Frith - *Koch 3-7612-2(CD)*

Symphony for string orchestra Op.13 (1946)
Written for the Riddick String Orchestra*

Dur: 20'
f.p.   Riddick String Orchestra/Kathleen Riddick - Kensington Town Hall, London,
            29 April 1947
f.broad.p. Jacques Orchestra/Reginald Jacques - Third Programme, 21 January 1948
f.rec.   BBC Concert Orchestra/Vernon Handley - *Conifer 75605 51298-2(CD)*
Pub: Lengnick, 1947
(* in which orchestra Arnold's first wife, Sheila Nicholson, played violin)

Festival Overture for orchestra Op.14 (1946)
Written for Philip Pfaff, a former organist of St. Matthew's Church in Northampton, who had taught Arnold in the early thirties. (See also **Laudate Dominum Op. 25**)

Dur: 6'
Instr: 2/2/2/2 - 2/2/0/0 - timp. str.
f.p.   Ipswich Symphony Orchestra/Philip Pfaff - Ipswich Town Hall c. 1946

Sonata No.1 for violin and piano Op.15 (1947)
Score dated London, 3 March 1947
Dur: 15'
f.p.   Nona Liddell (Vn.)/Daphne Ibbott (Pno.) - Arts Council Drawing Room,
            London, 2 October 1951 (CPNM Recital)

f.rec.   Marcia Crayford (Vn.)/Ian Brown (Pno.) - *Hyperion A 66171 (and MC/CD)*
Pub: Lengnick, 1948

Children's Suite for piano Op.16 (1947)
[1. Prelude 2. Carol 3. Shepherd's Lament 4. Trumpet Tune 5. Blue Tune
6. Folk Song]
Dur: 5'
f.rec.   Benjamin Frith - *Koch 3-7162-2 (CD)*
Pub: Lengnick, 1948
arr. for recorder quartet by Dennis Bloodworth
Pub: Lengnick, 1993 (as 'Miniature Suite')

Sonata for viola and piano Op.17 (1947)
Dedicated to Frederick Riddle - the score is dated London, 30 March 1947
Dur: 13'
f.p.   Frederick Riddle (Va.)/pianist unknown - BBC Latin American Service, 1948
f.Brit.broad.p. Watson Forbes (Va.)/Alan Richardson (Pno.) - Third Programme,
            22 November 1949
f.rec.   Roger Chase (Va.)/Ian Brown (Pno.) - *Hyperion A 66171 (and MC/CD)*
Pub: Lengnick, 1948

Two Bagatelles for piano Op.18 (1947)
Score dated London, 29 September 1947
Dur: 4'45″
f.p.   Richard Deering - British Music Information Centre, London, 15 May 1984
f.rec.   Benjamin Frith - *Koch 3-7162-2 (CD)*
Pub: Paterson, 1988

Sonatina for flute and piano Op.19 (1948)
Dedicated to Richard Adeney - the score is dated London, 5 February 1948
Dur: 8'
f.p.   Richard Adeney (Fl.)/pianist unknown c.1948
f.broad.p. Richard Adeney (Fl.)/Frederick Stone (Pno.) - Third Programme,
            20 October 1952
f.rec.   Judith Pearce (Fl.)/Ian Brown (Pno.) - *Hyperion A 66172 (and MC/CD)*
Pub: Lengnick, 1948
Exc. 'Blues' arr. for flute and string orchestra by Christopher Palmer

'To Youth' - Suite for orchestra* (1948)
[1. Prelude 2. Pastoral 3. March]
Written for Ruth Railton and the National Youth Orchestra of Great Britain for their
inaugural concert
Dur: 9'30"
Instr: 2/2/2/2 - 4/3/3/1 - timp. perc.(2) str.
f.p.   National Youth Orchestra of Great Britain/Reginald Jacques - The Pavilion,
            Bath, 21 April 1948
Pub: Paterson, 1956 (*as **Little Suite No. 1 Op.53** q.v.)

Concerto No. 1 for clarinet and string orchestra Op.20 (1948)

Dedicated to Frederick Thurston - the score is dated London, 15 February 1948

Dur: 16'30"

f.p.   Frederick Thurston/Jacques Orchestra/Reginald Jacques - Usher Hall,
            Edinburgh, 29 August 1949 (Edinburgh Festival)

f.Am.p.   Benny Goodman/California Chamber Symphony Orchestra/Hendi Temianka -
            Royce Hall, University of California, Los Angeles, 2 October 1967

f.recs.   Janet Hilton/Bournemouth Sinfonietta/Norman del Mar - *EMI EL 270264-1
            (and MC), CDM7 63491-2 (CD), Eminence CD-EMX 2271 (CD)*
            Michael Collins/ London Musici/Mark Stephenson - *Conifer 74321
            15004-2(CD)*

Pub: Lengnick, 1952 (also arr. for clarinet and piano)

The Smoke* - Overture for orchestra Op.21 (1948)

Dedicated to Rudolf Schwarz and the Bournemouth Municipal Orchestra - the score is
dated London, 19 July 1948

Dur: 7'

Instr: 2+picc./2/2/2 - 4/3/3/1 - timp. perc.(3) hp. str.

f.p.   Bournemouth Municipal Orchestra/Rudolf Schwarz - Royal Albert Hall,
            London, 24 October 1948

f.rec.   London Philharmonic Orchestra/Malcolm Arnold - *Reference RR-48 (and CD)*

Pub: Lengnick, 1948

(* 'The Smoke' is a Cockney term for London)

Symphony No.1 Op.22 (1949)

Score dated London, 16 February 1949

Dur: 28'30"

Instr: 2 + picc/2/2/2 - 4/3/3/1 - timp. perc. hp. str.

f.p.   Hallé Orchestra/Malcolm Arnold - Cheltenham Town Hall, 6 July 1951
            (Cheltenham Festival)

f.Lon.p. London Philharmonic Orchestra/Malcolm Arnold - Royal Festival Hall,
            16 November 1951

f.rec.   Bournemouth Symphony Orchestra/Malcolm Arnold - *HMV ASD 3823 (and
            MC); EMI CDM7 64044-2 (CD)*

Pub: Lengnick, 1952

String Quartet No.1 Op.23 (1949)

Score dated London, 19 August 1949

Dur: 18'45"

f.p.   New London String Quartet - BBC Third Programme, 13 November 1950

f.conc.p. New London String Quartet - Institute of Contemporary Arts, London,
            26 October 1951

f.rec.   McCapra Quartet - *Chandos CHAN 9112 (CD)*

Pub: Lengnick, 1951

Henri Christophe* - unfinished Opera in four Acts (1949)

[Libretto: Joe Mendoza]

Commissioned by The Arts Council of Great Britain for the Festival of Britain

Instr: 3/2/2/2 - 4/3/3/1 - timp. perc.(2) hp. str. (+ four soloists)

(* the true story of the negro general who became the first King of Haiti, the western half of the island of San Domingo in the Caribbean)

Divertimento No.2 for orchestra Op.24 (1950)
[1. Fanfare 2. Tango 3. Chaconne]
Written for the National Youth Orchestra of Great Britain for their first European tour.

Dur:	9'
Instr:	2+picc./2/2/2 - 4/3/3/1 - timp. perc.(2) hp. str.
f.p.	National Youth Orchestra of Great Britain/Malcolm Arnold - The Dome, Brighton, 19 April 1950
f.Eur.p.	above artists - Palais de Chaillot, Paris, 21 April 1950 (and repeated in the Salle Pleyel on 22 April)
f.broad.p.	above artists - Third Programme, 28 August 1950
f.Lon.p.	National Youth Orchestra of Great Britain/Hugo Rignold - Royal Albert Hall, 10 August 1957 (Promenade Concert)
f.rec.	Leicestershire Schools Symphony Orchestra/Eric Pinkett - *Pye Golden Guinea GGC(m)/GSGC 14103*
Pub:	Paterson, 1961 (As **Op.75** q.v.)

Psalm CL 'Laudate Dominum' for SATB chorus and organ Op.25 (1950)
Commissioned by and dedicated to "The Rev. Canon Walter Hussey, the Choir and Organist of St. Matthew's Church, Northampton" - the score is dated
6 April 1950

Dur:	7'
f.p.	St. Matthew's Church Choir, with Philip Pfaff (organ) - St. Matthew's Church, Northampton, 1950
f.doc.Lon.p.	Royal Academy of Music Chamber Choir - Marylebone Parish Church, 20 June 1996 (British and Americal Film Music Festival)
Pub:	Lengnick, 1950

Serenade for small orchestra Op.26 (1950)
Written for the Hampton Court Serenade Concerts - the score is dated 8 May 1950

Dur:	13'30"
Instr:	2/2/2/2 - 2/2/0/0 - timp. str.
f.p.	New London Orchestra/Alec Sherman - The Orangery, Hampton Court, 4 June 1950 (Serenade Concert)
f.recs.	Bournemouth Sinfonietta/Ronald Thomas - *HMV ASD 3868 (and MC)* London Musici/Mark Stephenson - *Conifer MCFC 211(MC), CDCF 211(CD), 75605 51211-2(CD)*
Pub:	Lengnick, 1950

English Dances for orchestra (Set 1) Op.27 (1950)
Dedicated to Bernard de Nevers, Arnold's publisher, whose idea it was to produce a set equal in popularity to the Dvorak **Slavonic Dances** - the score is dated London, 5 December 1950

Dur:	8'
Instr:	2+picc./2/2/2 - 4/3/3/1 - timp. perc.(2) cel. hp. str.
f.p.	London Philharmonic Orchestra/Sir Adrian Boult - Central Hall, East Ham, London, 14 April 1951

f.broad.p. BBC Northern Orchestra/Charles Groves - Home Service, 15 September 1951
f.recs.   London Philharmonic Orchestra/Sir Adrian Boult - *Decca LW 5166(m), Ace of Clubs ACL 113(m), Eclipse ECS 646(m); London (USA) LD 9178 (m), LLP 1335(m); London 425 661-2 (CD)*
            London Philharmonic Orchestra/Malcolm Arnold - *Lyrita SRCS 109, SRCD 201 (CD)*
            (No. 3) Philharmonia Orchestra/Malcolm Arnold - *Columbia SED 5529; EMI CDM7 64044-2 (CD) (and MC)*
Pub: Lengnick, 1951
also arr. for piano duet by Franz Reizenstein
Pub: Lengnick, 1958
also arr. for wind band by Maurice Johnstone
f.recs.   Cornell University Wind Ensemble - *Cornell (USA) CUWE 27*
            Dallas Wind Symphony/Jerry Junkin - *Reference RR-66(CD)*
Pub: Lengnick, 1965
also arr. for military band
f.rec.   (2 dances only) Royal Marines Band/Capt. W. W. Shillito - *Decca SB 703*
also arr. for brass band by Ray Farr (1985)
f.p.   Grimethorpe Colliery Band/Elgar Howarth - 1 February 1993
f.rec.   above artists - *Conifer MCFC 222 (MC), CDCF 222 (CD), 76506 16848-2(CD)*
Pub: Lengnick, 1993

Sonatina for oboe and piano Op.28 (1951)

Written for Léon Goossens, the score is dated London, 3 January 1951
Dur: 7'30"
f.p.   Léon Goossens (Ob.)/John Wilson (Pno.) - Northern College of Music, Manchester, 15 January 1952
f.recs.   Vladimir Kurlin (Ob.)/M. Karandashova (Pno.) - *Melodiya (USSR) D.026527/8 (m)*
            Gareth Hulse (Ob.)/Ian Brown (Pno.) - *Hyperion A 66172 (and MC/CD)*
Pub: Lengnick, 1951
later arr. for oboe and string orchestra by Roger Steptoe (1993)
f.p.   Nicholas Daniel/City of London Sinfonia/Christopher Robinson, Bromsgrove, Worcestershire, 7 May 1994 (Bromsgrove Festival)
f.rec.   Nicholas Daniel/Bournemouth Symphony Orchestra/Vernon Handley - *Conifer 75605 51273-2(CD)*
Pub: Lengnick, 1992 (as 'Concertino for oboe and strings' Op.28a)

Up at the Villa - unfinished Opera in one Act* (1951)

[Libretto: Joe Mendoza after Robert Browning]
(* Preliminary sketches only - later discarded)

Sonatina for clarinet and piano Op.29 (1951)

Score dated London, 18 January 1951
Dur: 7'45"
f.p.   Colin Davis (Cl.)/Geoffrey Corbett (Pno.) - RBA Galleries, London, 20 March 1951
f.recs.   Jack Brymer (Cl.)/David Lloyd (Pno.) - *Discourses ABK 16*

Michael Collins (Cl.)/Ian Brown (Pno.) - *Hyperion A 66172 (and MC/CD)*
Pub: Lengnick, 1951
later arr. for clarinet and string orchestra by Roger Steptoe
f.p.   Emma Johnson/East of England Orchestra - Leicester, 5 June 1993 (Leicester
            Festival)
Pub: Lengnick, 1992 (as `Concertino for clarinet and strings' Op.29a)

Symphonic Study (`Machines'*) for brass, percussion and strings Op.30 (1951)
Score dated 14 February 1951
Dur: 6'
Instr: 0/0/0/0 - 4/3/3/1 - timp. perc.(2) str.
f.p.   BBC Scottish Symphony Orchestra/Sir Charles Groves - Henry Wood Hall,
            Glasgow, 5 October 1984
f.broad.p. above performance - Radio 3, 16 October 1984
Pub: Faber, 1984
(* a re-working of the film music `Report on Steel' q.v.)

A Sussex Overture for orchestra Op.31* (1951)
Commissioned by the Festival of Brighton and dedicated to Herbert Menges and the
Southern Philharmonic Orchestra - the score is dated London, 15 March 1951
Dur: 8'30"
Instr: 2+picc/2/2/2 - 4/3/3/1 - timp. perc. str.
f.p.   Southern Philharmonic Orchestra/Herbert Menges - The Dome, Brighton,
            29 July 1951 (N.B. the work was revived at the 1985 Brighton Festival.)
f.rec.   London Philharmonic Orchestra/Malcolm Arnold - *Reference RR-48 (and CD)*
Pub: Lengnick, 1951
(* the composer comments that `the music is an attempt to express the feeling of
exhilaration that comes over one when walking on the downs or by the sea in Sussex.')

Concerto for piano duet and string orchestra Op.32 (1951)
Written at the suggestion of Mosco Carner and dedicated to Helen Pyke (Dr. Carner's
wife) and Paul Hamburger - the score is dated London, 15 May 1951
Dur: 21'30"
f.p.   Helen Pyke/Paul Hamburger/Goldsbrough Orchestra/Mosco Carner - BBC
            Third Programme, 17 August 1951
f.conc.p.   Helen Pyke/Paul Hamburger/Bournemouth Municipal Orchestra/ Charles
            Groves - Winter Gardens, Bournemouth, June 1953
f.Lon.p.   Helen Pyke/Paul Hamburger/London Symphony Orchestra/Basil Cameron -
            Royal Albert Hall, 31 July 1953 (Promenade Concert)
f.rec.   David Nettle/Richard Markham/London Musici/Mark Stephenson - *Conifer
            MCFC 228(MC), CDCF 228 (CD), 75605 51228-2 (CD)*
Pub: Lengnick, 1951 (piano score)

English Dances for orchestra (Set 2) Op.33 (1951)
Dedicated to Bernard de Nevers, Arnold's publisher (See also **Op.27**) - the score is dated
London, 26 June 1951
Dur: 9'
Instr: 3/2/2/2 - 4/3/3/1 - timp. perc. cel. hp. str.

f.p.   BBC Symphony Orchestra/Sir Malcolm Sargent - Royal Albert Hall, London,
          5 August 1952 (Promenade Concert)

f.recs.   London Philharmonic Orchestra/Sir Adrian Boult - *Decca LW 5166(m), Ace of
          Clubs ACL 113(m), Eclipse ECS 646(m); London (USA) LD 9178 (m), LLP
          1335(m); London 425 661-2 (CD)*
          London Philharmonic Orchestra/Malcolm Arnold - *Lyrita SRCS 109, SRCD
          201 (CD)*
          (No. 1) Philharmonia Orchestra/Malcolm Arnold - *Columbia SED 5529; EMI
          CDM7 64044-2 (CD) (and MC)*

Pub: Lengnick, 1951
also arr. for piano duet by Franz Reizenstein
Pub: Lengnick, 1958
also arr. for brass band by Ray Farr (1985)
f.p.   Grimethorpe Colliery Band/Elgar Howarth - 1 February 1993
f.rec.   above artists - *Conifer MCFC 222 (MC), CDCF 222 (CD), 76506
          16848-2(CD)*
Pub: Lengnick, 1993

The Dancing Master - Opera in one Act Op.34 (1952)

[Libretto: Joe Mendoza based on a play by William Wycherley]
Score dated London, 18 May 1952
Dur: 68'
Instr: 1+picc./2/2/2 - 4/3/3/1 - timp. perc (2). cel. hp. str.
f.p.   (piano version*) cond. Lucy Reynolds - Barnes Music Club, Kitson Hall,
          Barnes, 1 March 1962 (as a double bill with Anthony Collins's **Catherine
          Parr**)
Producer: Leigh Howard
Choreography: Herald Braune
Decor: Jane Pearson-Gee and David Kentish
Principals: Guelda Cunningham, Margaret Lindsay, Donald Franke and Fergus
          O'Kelly.
f.prof.p. (piano version) cond. Marcus Dods (a tape exists of this performance)
Pub: Paterson
(*N.B. unperformed in the orchestral version)

Two Ceremonial Psalms for unaccompanied SSA boys' chorus Op.35 (1952)

[1. O come, let us sing unto the Lord (Psalm 95) 2. Make a joyful noise unto the Lord
(Psalm 100)]
Written for Ann Mendoza (the sister of Joe Mendoza, librettist of **The Dancing Master**)
Dur: 5'
f.p.   Roehampton Choir - Marble Arch Synagogue, London, January 1952 (at Ann
          Mendoza's wedding to Philip Goldesgeyme)
f.doc.pub.p. Royal Academy of Music Chamber Choir - Marylebone Parish
          Church, London, 20 June 1996 (British and American Film Music Festival)
f.rec.   (No. 1 only) Rye Singers Choir/Leslie Brownbill - *MSR MSRS 1429*
Pub: Paterson, 1952

Eight Children's Piano Pieces Op.36 (1952)

[1. Tired Bagpipers 2. Two Sad Hands 3. Across the Plains 4. Strolling Tune

5. Dancing Tune 6. Giants 7. The Duke goes a-hunting 8. The Buccaneer]
Dur: 9´45″
f.rec.   Benjamin Frith - *Koch 3-7162-2 (CD)*
Pub: Lengnick, 1952 (in the series `Five by Ten' ed. Alex Rowley)
later arr. for orchestra as 'Children's Suite' by Dennis Bloodworth (1995)
Instr: 2/2/2/2 - 4/3/3/1 - timp. perc. str.

Divertimento for wind trio Op.37 (1952)
Dur: 8'45"
Instr: Fl. Ob. Cl.
f.p.   Richard Adeney (Fl.), Sidney Sutcliffe (Ob.) and Stephen Waters (Cl.) -
            Mercury Theatre, Notting Hill Gate, London, c.1953 (Macnaghten Concert)
f.recs.   A. Korneyev (Fl.)/A. Zaionts (Ob.)/V. Tupikin (Cl.) - *Melodiya (USSR) SM
            02641 2*
            Judith Pearce (Fl.)/Gareth Hulse (Ob.)/Michael Collins (Cl.) - *Hyperion
            A66173 (and MC/CD)*
Pub: Paterson, 1952

The Sound Barrier* - Rhapsody for orchestra Op.38 (1952)
Score dated London, 31 May 1952
Dur: 7'30"
Instr: 2+picc/2/2/2 - 4/3/3/1 - timp. perc.(2) hp. cel. str.
f.p.   Royal Philharmonic Orchestra/Malcolm Arnold - 24 March 1953
f.broad.p. Ulster Orchestra/Yannis Daras - BBC Radio 3, 23 May 1984
f.recs.   Royal Philharmonic Orchestra/Malcolm Arnold - *Columbia SED 5542 (45m),
            Ariel (USA) CBF 13; EMI CDGO 2059(CD), CDM5 66120-2(CD)*
            Royal Philharmonic Orchestra/Kenneth Alwyn - *Cloud Nine CNS 5446(CD)*
Pub: Paterson, 1952
also arr. for wind band
f.p.   Chicago, USA, 20 December 1995
f.Brit..p. European Wind Band/Rodney Parker - The Anvil, Basingstoke, 10 February
            1996
Pub: Novello, 1996
(* derived from the film music q.v.)

Concerto for oboe and string orchestra Op.39 (1952)
Commissioned by and dedicated to Léon Goossens - the score is dated London,
17 August 1952
Dur: 15'
f.p.   Léon Goossens/Boyd Neel Orchestra/Boyd Neel - Royal Festival Hall,
            London, 26 June 1953
f.broad.p. Léon Goossens/Boyd Neel Orchestra/Anthony Collins - Third Programme,
            10 January 1954
f.rec.   Gordon Hunt/Bournemouth Sinfonietta/Norman del Mar - *EMI EL 270264-1
            (and MC); CDM7 63491-2 (CD), Eminence CD-EMX 2271(CD)*
Pub: Paterson, 1952, 1957 (arr. for oboe and piano)

Symphony No.2 Op.40 (1953)

Commissioned by the Winter Gardens Society, Bournemouth and dedicated to Charles Groves and the Bournemouth Municipal Orchestra in celebration of their Diamond Jubilee - the score is dated London, 9 February 1953

Dur:	30'
Instr:	2+picc./2/2/2 + cbsn. - 4/3/3/1 - timp. perc. hp. str.
f.p.	Bournemouth Municipal Orchestra/Charles Groves - Winter Gardens, Bournemouth, 25 May 1953
f.broad.p.	BBC Scottish Orchestra/Alexander Gibson - BBC Third Programme, 9 February 1954
f.Eur.p.	L'Orchestre Symphonique du Conservatoire de Grenoble/Eric-Paul Stekel - Grenoble, France, 4 March 1954
f.Can.p.	CBC Symphony Orchestra/John Avison - Vancouver, 26 April 1954
f.Lon.p.	London Philharmonic Orchestra/Malcolm Arnold - Royal Festival Hall, 3 June 1954
f.Am.p.	Chicago Symphony Orchestra/Fritz Reiner - Civic Opera House, Chicago, 13 December 1956
f.SA.p.	Cape Town Orchestra/Anthony Collins - City Hall, Cape Town, 25 April 1957
f.Austr.p.	Sydney Symphony Orchestra/Sir Bernard Heinze - Town Hall, Sydney, 10 February 1963
f.recs.	Royal Philharmonic Orchestra/Malcolm Arnold - *Philips NBL 5021 (m); Epic (USA) LC 3422 (m)*
	Bournemouth Symphony Orchestra/Sir Charles Groves - *HMV ASD 3353 (and MC); HMV Greensleeve ED 29046-1 (and MC); EMI CDC7 49513-2 (CD), CDM7 63368-2 (CD)*
Pub:	Paterson, 1953

'Katherine, Walking and Running' for two violins (1952)

Written for Katherine (Arnold), aged four, to play with a school friend

Dur:	40"

Sonatina for recorder* and piano Op.41 (1953)

[1. Cantilena 2. Chaconne 3. Rondo]
Written for and dedicated to Philip Rodgers, the blind recorder player - the score is dated 16 February 1953

Dur:	7'45"
f.p.	Philip Rodgers (Rec.)/Albert Hardie (Pno.) - BBC Home Service, 14 July 1953
f.rec.	(Fl. version) Judith Pearce (Fl.)/Ian Brown (Pno.) - *Hyperion A 66172 (and MC/CD)*
Pub:	Paterson, 1953 (*or flute or oboe)

Homage to the Queen - Ballet Op.42 (1952)

Commissioned by the Sadler's Wells Ballet Company in honour of the Coronation of Her Majesty Queen Elizabeth II. (Humphrey Searle was initially approached but declined as he felt he could not complete the project on schedule. Despite a number of film commitments, Arnold was still able to deliver the finished score in a matter of weeks.)
[1. Prelude and Opening Scene 2. `Earth'  3. `Water' 4. `Fire'  5. `Air' 6. Finale]

Dur:	40'
Instr:	2+picc./2/2/2 - 4/3/3/1 - timp. perc.(2) cel. hp. str.

f.p.   Orchestra of the Royal Opera House, Covent Garden, cond. Robert Irving -
Royal Opera House, Covent Garden, London, 2 June 1953 (Coronation Night)

Choreography: Frederick Ashton

Scenery and costumes: Oliver Messel

Principals: Nadia Nerina, Violetta Elvin, Beryl Grey, Margot Fonteyn

f.Am.p.   Metropolitan Opera House, New York, 18 September 1957

f.rec.   Philharmonia Orchestra/Robert Irving - *HMV CLP 1011(m); Victor (USA) LM 2037(m); EMI CDM5 66120-2(CD)*

Pub: Paterson

Ballet Suite Op.42a (1953)

[1. `Air': Man's Variation 2. Pas de deux 3. Finale]

Dur: 17'

Instr: 2+picc./2/2/2 - 4/3/3/1 - timp. perc.(2) cel. hp. str.

f.p.   London Philharmonic Orchestra/Malcolm Arnold - New Theatre, Northampton, 19 July 1953

f.broad.p. BBC Northern Symphony Orchestra/Stanford Robinson - BBC Light Programme, 13 May 1957

Pub: Paterson, 1954

Ballet Suite (Finale) also arr. for military band by Lt. Col. Sir F. Vivian Dunn

f.rec.   Royal Marines Band/Lt. Col. Sir F. Vivian Dunn - *Columbia Studio 2 TWO 285 (and MC); EMI Note NTS 123 (and MC)*

also arr. for wind band by H.Kondo

f.rec.   Japan Band Festival 93 - *Sony (Jap.) SRCR 9421(CD)*

Suite also arr. for piano solo

[1. `Earth': Girl's Variation  2. `Water' 3. `The Spirit of Fire'
4. `The Queen of the Air' 5. Pas de deux 6. Homage March]

Dur: 9'

f.rec.   Pauline Martin - *Koch 3-7266-2(CD)*

Pub: Paterson, 1954

Sonata No.2 for violin and piano Op.43 (1953)

Commissioned by Suzanne Rozsa and Paul Hamburger

Dur: 9'

f.p.   Suzanne Rozsa (Vn.)/Paul Hamburger (Pno.) - Recital Room, Royal Festival Hall, London, 21 October 1953

f.recs.   Marcia Crayford (Vn.)/Ian Brown (Pno.) - *Hyperion A 66171 (and MC/CD)*
Ruggiero Ricci (Vn.)/Rebecca Pennies (Pno.) - *One Eleven (USA) URS 91060 (CD)*

Pub: Paterson, 1953

Flourish for a 21st birthday Op.44 (1953)

Dedicated to "Sir Adrian Boult and the London Philharmonic Orchestra in celebration of the 21st anniversary of the founding of the orchestra"

Dur: 3'

Instr: 0/0/0/0 - 4/3 + 2 cnt./3/1 - timp. perc.(3)

f.p.   London Philharmonic Orchestra/Sir Adrian Boult - Royal Albert Hall, London, 7 October 1953

Pub: Studio Music, 1986

also arr. for brass band by Philip Sparke
Pub: Studio Music, 1987

Concerto No. 1 for flute and string orchestra Op.45 (1954)

Written for and dedicated to Richard Adeney (see also **Op.111**) - the score is dated
London, 3 February 1954

Dur: 12'30"
f.p.   Richard Adeney/Boyd Neel Orchestra/John Hollingsworth - Victoria & Albert
            Museum, London, 11 April 1954
f.broad.p. Richard Adeney/London Chamber Orchestra/Anthony Bernard - BBC Third
            Programme, 3 September 1954
f.recs.   John Solum/Philharmonia Orchestra/Neville Dilkes - *HMV ASD 3487 (and
            MC); EMI CDM7 63491-2 (CD)*
            Richard Adeney/Bournemouth Sinfonietta/Ronald Thomas - *HMV ASD 3868
            (and MC); EMI Eminence CD-EMX 2271(CD)*
Pub: Paterson, 1954 (also arr. flute and piano)

Concerto for harmonica and orchestra Op.46 (1954)

[1. Grazioso 2. Chaconne 3. Tarantella (incorporating a Neapolitan air)]
Commissioned by the BBC for their Diamond Jubilee season of Promenade Concerts, the
Concerto was written for and dedicated to Larry Adler - the score is dated 26 June 1954

Dur: 9'
Instr: 0/0/0/0 - 4/3/3/1 - timp. perc.(2) str.
f.p.   Larry Adler/BBC Symphony Orchestra/Malcolm Arnold - Royal Albert Hall,
            London, 14 August 1954 (Promenade Concert)
f.rec.   Larry Adler/Royal Philharmonic Orchestra/Morton Gould - *RCA SB 6786, GL
            42747 (and MC); Victor (USA) LSC 3078*
Pub: Paterson, 1954

Concerto for organ and orchestra Op.47 (1954)

Written for Denis Vaughan and specially composed for the organ of the Royal Festival
Hall

Dur: 12'30"
Instr: 0/0/0/0 - 0/3/0/0 - timp. str.
f.p.   Denis Vaughan/London Symphony Orchestra/Leslie Woodgate - Royal
            Festival Hall, London, 11 December 1954 (Robert Mayer Concert)
f.broad.p. Hugh McLean/London Philharmonic Orchestra/Sir Adrian Boult - Third
            Programme, 17 February 1957 (rec. 21 November 1955)
f.rec.   Hugh McLean/CBC Vancouver Orchestra/John Avison - *CBC (Canada) SM
            129*
Pub: Paterson, 1954

Sinfonietta No.1 for chamber orchestra Op.48 (1954)

Dedicated to the Boyd Neel Orchestra

Dur: 12'
Instr: 0/2/0/0 - 2/0/0/0 - str.
f.p.   Boyd Neel Orchestra/Anthony Collins - Albert Hall, Nottingham,
            3 December 1954
f.Lon.p.   Boyd Neel Orchestra/Anthony Collins - Royal Festival Hall, 7 March 1955

f.Brit.broad.p. Francis Chagrin Ensemble/Francis Chagrin - BBC Home Service,
            11 April 1957 (first broadcast on French Radio)
f.recs.   English Chamber Orchestra/Malcolm Arnold - BBC *Radio Classics 15656*
            91817(CD) (recorded 'live' in the Pittville Pump Room, Cheltenham, 14 July
            1973 during the Cheltenham Festival)
            Northern Sinfonia/Boris Brott - *Mace (USA) MCS 9068*
            Philharmonia Orchestra/Neville Dilkes - *HMV ASD 3487 (and MC)*
Pub: Paterson, 1955

Rinaldo and Armida - Ballet Op.49 (1954)

Written for the Sadler's Wells Ballet Company, the score is dated 31 December 1954
Dur: 23'
Instr: 2+picc./2/2/2 - 4/3/3/1 - timp. perc.(2) cel. hp. str.
f.p.   Orchestra of the Royal Opera House, Covent Garden cond. Malcolm Arnold -
            Royal Opera House, Covent Garden, London, 6 January 1955
Choreography: Frederick Ashton
Scenery and costumes: Peter Rue
Principals: Michael Somes, Svetlana Beriosova, Julia Farron
f.Am.p.   Sadler's Wells Ballet - New York , 20 September 1955
f.broad.p. BBC Northern Orchestra/Malcolm Arnold - 6 November 1971
Pub: Faber, 1984
Exc.   Introduction and Pas-de-deux
Dur: 9'
f.conc.p.   BBC Concert Orchestra/Barry Wordsworth - Queen Elizabeth Hall, London,
            26 October 1991 (70th Birthday Concert)
Pub: Faber, 1984

Serenade for guitar and string orchestra Op.50 (1955)

Written for and dedicated to Julian Bream
Dur: 5'30"
f.p.   Julian Bream/Richmond Community Centre String Orchestra*/ Malcolm
            Arnold - Richmond Community Centre Hall, Richmond, Surrey,
            Summer 1955
f.Lon.p.   Julian Bream/Kalmar Chamber Orchestra/Leonard Friedman - Wigmore Hall,
            11 June 1956
f.broad.p. John Williams/BBC Concert Orchestra/John Carewe - Light Programme,
            18 July 1964
f.rec.   John Williams/English Chamber Orchestra/Sir Charles Groves - *CBS 76634*
            (and MC); Columbia (USA) M 35172
Pub: Paterson, 1955 (also arr. guitar and piano, 1977)
(* Arnold's first wife, Sheila, was leader of the orchestra)

Tam O'Shanter* - Overture for orchestra Op.51 (1955)

Dedicated to Michael Diack (Arnold's publisher and amateur horn player) - the score is
dated 2 March 1955
Dur: 7'30"
Instr: 2+picc./2/2/2 - 4/3/3/1 - timp. perc.(2) str.
f.p.   Royal Philharmonic Orchestra/Malcolm Arnold - Royal Albert Hall, London,
            16 August 1955 (Promenade Concert)

f.Scot.p.   Scottish National Orchestra/Alexander Gibson - Usher Hall, Edinburgh,
             23 March 1956 (the performance was encored)
f.Am.p.   cond. Sir John Barbirolli - January 1959 (during a tour of many of the major
             American cities)
f.recs.   Royal Philharmonic Orchestra/John Hollingsworth - *Philips NBL 5021 (m),
             NBE 11038 (45m), SBF 117; Epic (USA) LC 3422 (m)*
             Philharmonia Orchestra/Malcolm Arnold - *Columbia SED 5529 (m); EMI
             CDM7 64044-2 (CD) (and MC); HMV Classics 5 72480-2(CD)*
Pub: Paterson, 1955
also arr. for wind band by John Paynter
f.rec.   Dallas Wind Symphony/Jerry Junkin - *Reference RR-66(CD)*
Pub: Carl Fischer (New York)
(* the Overture takes its name from the work that inspired it, the narrative poem by
Robert Burns, the introduction to which is printed on the cover of the score.)

Fanfare for a Festival, for brass and percussion (1955)
Written for the Hastings Festival
Dur: 2'
Instr: 4 Hn. 3 Tpt. Cnt. 3 Tbn. Tba. Timp. Perc.(3)
f.rec.   Band of the Royal Military School of Music, Kneller Hall/Lt.Col. Duncan
             Beat - *Polyphonic CPRM 111D (MC)*
Pub: Studio Music, 1986
also arr. for brass band by Philip Sparke
Pub: Studio Music, 1986

John Clare Cantata for SATB chorus and piano duet Op.52 (1955)
[1. Winter Snow Storm 2. March 3. Spring 4. Summer 5. Autumn 6. Epilogue]
Dur: 11'
Commissioned by William Glock for the 1955 Dartington Summer School of Music
f.p.   Summer School Choir/Viola Tunnard and Martin Penny (piano duet) cond.
             John Clements - Dartington Hall, Totnes, South Devon, 5 August 1955
             (Dartington Summer School Concert)
f.broad.p.   BBC Chorus/Viola Tunnard and Martin Penny (piano duet) cond. Alexander
             Gibson - BBC Third Programme, 16 April 1956
Pub: Paterson, 1956

Little Suite No.1 for orchestra Op.53 (1955)
[1. Prelude 2. Dance 3. March]
Originally written for the National Youth Orchestra of Great Britain and entitled `To
Youth' Suite (q.v.), it was revised with a change of central movement title from `Pastoral'
to `Dance'
Dur: 9'30"
Instr: 2/2/2/2 - 4/3/3/1 - timp. perc.(2) str.
f.p.   (rev. version) Schools' Music Association Orchestra/Malcolm Arnold - Royal
             Albert Hall, London, April 1955 (Schools' Music Association Concert)
f.recs.   (March only) Pro Arte Orchestra/Gilbert Vinter - *HMV CLP 1836 (m), CSD
             1588; World Record Club ST978; Capitol (USA) P(m)/SP 8642;
             EMI CDGB 50 (CD)*

(complete) City of London Sinfonia/Richard Hickox - *Chandos CHAN 9509(CD)*
Pub: Paterson, 1956
Exc. March Op.53a arr. for military band by Peter Sumner (c.1963)
Dur: 2'30"
f.rec.   Band of H.M. Royal Marines/Lt. Col. Sir F. Vivian Dunn - *HMV CLP 1684 (m), CSD 1515; Starline SRS 5112; Executive EXE 59 (MC)*
Pub: Paterson/Carl Fisher (New York), 1965

Piano Trio Op.54 (1956)

Dedicated to Pauline Howgill, the founder of the St. Cecilia Trio
Dur: 12'30"
Instr: Vn. Vc. Pno.
f.p.   St. Cecilia Trio - Sylvia Cleaver (Vn.)/Norman Jones (Vc.)/Pauline Howgill (Pno.)- International Music Association, London, 30 April 1956
f.broad.p.   above artists - BBC Home Service, 7 September 1956
f.recs.   Arthur Tabachnik (Vn.)/Shirley Evans (Vc.)/Hilda Freund (Pno.) - *Concert Disc (USA) M.1234 (m), CS 234; Everest (USA) SDBR 4234*
Marcia Crayford (Vn.)/Christopher van Kampen (Vc.)/Ian Brown (Pno.) - *Hyperion A 66171 (and MC/CD)*
Pub: Paterson, 1956

Song of Praise for unison voices and piano (or orchestra) Op.55 (1956)

[Words: John Clare]
Commissioned by Ruth Railton for the Jubilee of Wycombe Abbey School
Dur: 4'
Instr: 1/1/1/1 - 2/2/2/0 - timp. perc. org. str.
Alt.Instr: pno. str.
f.p.   Pupils of Wycombe Abbey School/Ruth Railton - Wycombe Abbey, 1956
Pub: Paterson, 1956

Solitaire - Ballet (1956)

Written for the Sadler's Wells Ballet Company, the music comprises the earlier sets of English Dances (in a new order) and two newly-composed dances - Sarabande and Polka.
Dur: 25'30"
Instr: 2+picc./2/2/2 - 4/2/2/0 - timp. perc.(2) cel. hp. str.
f.p.   Sadler's Wells Theatre Orchestra cond. John Lanchberry - Sadler's Wells Theatre, London, 7 June 1956
Choreography: Kenneth MacMillan
Scenery: Desmond Heeley
Principals: Margaret Hill, Donald McLeary, Brenda Bolton, Donald Britton
f.Am.p.   Sadler's Wells Ballet- New York, 17 September 1957
f.Eur.p.   Stuttgart Ballet, 1960
f.recs.   (Sarabande and Polka) Bournemouth Symphony Orchestra/Malcolm Arnold - *HMV ASD 3823 (and MC); HMV Greensleeve ESD 107780-1 (and MC); EMI CDM7 64044-2 (CD) (and MC)*
London Philharmonic Orchestra/Malcolm Arnold - *Lyrita SRCS 109, SRCD 201 (CD)*
Pub: Lengnick, 1956

Exc.   Sarabande and Polka arr. for piano solo
Dur: 8'30"
Pub: Paterson, 1959
Exc.   Sarabande and Polka arr. for wind band
Pub: Paterson/Carl Fischer (New York)
Exc.   Sarabande and Polka arr. for brass band by Ray Farr

Fanfare for a Royal Occasion (1956)
Written for the opening of the 1956 St. Cecilia's Day Concert
Dur: 1'30"
Instr: 3 Tpt. 3 Tbn.
f.p.   Trumpeters of the Royal Military School of Music, Kneller Hall/Lt. Col.
        David McBain - Royal Festival Hall, London, 19 November 1956 (St. Cecilia's
        Day Concert on behalf of the Musicians' Benevolent Fund - this concert was
        also televised and attended by Her Majesty Queen Elizabeth the Queen
        Mother)
f.rec. Band of the Royal Military School of Music, Kneller Hall/Lt.Col. Duncan
        Beat - *Polyphonic CPRM 111D (MC)*
Pub: Studio Music, 1986 (as No. 4 of `Four Fanfares')

The Open Window - Opera in one Act Op.56 (1956)
[Libretto: Sidney Gilliat based on a short story by H. H. Munro (Saki)]
Commissioned by BBC Television
Dur: 30'
Instr: Fl. Cl. Bsn. Hn. Hp. Perc. Vn.(2) Va. Vc. Db.
f.p.   BBC Television production, 14 December 1956
Music played by: English Opera Group Orchestra/Lionel Salter
Producer: George R. Fox
Designer: Richard Wilmot
Principals: John Carolan, June Bronhill, Flora Nielsen, Niven Miller
f.st.p.   Lincoln Opera Group/Lionel Barnby - Horton-cum-Beckering Country
        Theatre, Lincolnshire, April 1958

A Grand, Grand (Festival) Overture for orchestra Op.57 (1956)
Written for the Hoffnung Music Festival - the score is dated 19 October 1956 and bears a
dedication to President Hoover
Dur: 8'
Instr: 2+picc./2/2/2 - 4/3/3/1 - timp. perc.(2) org. str. (+ 3 vacuum cleaners, 1 floor
        polisher and 4 rifles)
f.p.   Morley College Symphony Orchestra/Malcolm Arnold with Dennis Brain
        (organ) - Royal Festival Hall, London, 13 November 1956 (Hoffnung Music
        Festival)
f.Austr.p. Sydney Symphony Orchestra/Edmund Kurtz - John Farnsworth Hall, Perth,
        Spring 1959
f.recs.   Morley College Symphony Orchestra/Malcolm Arnold - *Columbia 33CX 1406
        (m); HMV Set SLS 870 (m), SLS 5069 (m); Angel (USA) 35500 (m), S-37028;
        EMI CMS7 63302-2(CD)*
        Royal Philharmonic Orchestra/Malcolm Arnold - *Columbia SED 5542 (45m);
        EMI CDM7 64718-2 (CD); HMV Classics 5 72480-2(CD)*

Pub: Paterson, 1956
also arr. for symphonic wind band by Keith Wilson
Pub: Paterson/Carl Fischer (New York), 1983
also arr. for military band by Rodney Bashford
Instr: (muted cornets substitute for the floor polisher in this arrangement!)
also arr. for brass band by Ray Farr (1985)

Concerto No.2 for horn and string orchestra Op.58 (1956)

Written for and dedicated to Dennis Brain - the score is dated 15 December 1956
Dur: 13'30"
f.p.   Dennis Brain/Hallé Orchestra/Malcolm Arnold - Cheltenham Town Hall,
            17 July 1957 (Cheltenham Festival)
f.broad.p. Barry Tuckwell/BBC Scottish Orchestra/Bryden Thomson - 17 October 1966
f.Lon.p.   Alan Civil/BBC Symphony Orchestra/Malcolm Arnold - Royal Albert Hall,
            8 August 1970 (Promenade Concert)
f.recs.   Alan Civil/English Chamber Orchestra/Malcolm Arnold - *BBC Radio Classics*
            15656 91817(CD) (recorded at the Bishopsgate Institute, London,
            13 March 1969)
            Alan Civil/Bournemouth Sinfonietta/Norman del Mar - *EMI EL 270264-1*
            (and MC), CDM7 63491-2 (CD), Eminence CD-EMX 2271(CD)
Pub: Paterson, 1956 (also arr. for horn and piano)

Four Scottish Dances for orchestra Op.59 (1957)

[1. Strathspey 2. Reel (a tune attributed to Robert Burns) 3. Hebridean (Waltz) 4.
Highland Fling]
Commissioned by the BBC for their Light Music Festival to whom the work is dedicated
Dur: 8'30"
Instr: 1+picc./2/2/2 - 4/2/3/0 - timp. perc. hp. str.
f.p.   BBC Concert Orchestra/Malcolm Arnold - Royal Festival Hall, London,
            8 June 1957 (BBC Light Music Festival)
f.Scot.p.   Scottish National Orchestra/Alexander Gibson - c.1958
f.p.   (as the ballet `Flowers of the Forest') Sadler's Wells Royal Ballet, London,
            1986 (and on a tour of the USA the same year)
Choreography: David Bintley
f.recs.   Philharmonia Orchestra/Robert Irving - *HMV CLP 1172 (m); Bluebird (USA)*
            LBC 1078 (m); Capitol (USA) G 7105 (m); EMI CDM5 66120-2(CD); HMV
            Classics 5 72480-2(CD)
            London Philharmonic Orchestra/Malcolm Arnold - *Everest LPBR 6021 (m),*
            SDBR 3021, EVC 9001(CD); World Record Club T(m)/ST 99; Desto (USA)
            DC 6448; Phoenix PHCD 102 (CD)
            London Philharmonic Orchestra/Malcolm Arnold - *Lyrita SRCS 109, SRCD*
            201 (CD)
Pub: Paterson, 1957
also arr. for symphonic wind band by John Paynter, President of the National Band
Association of America
f.recs.   Interlochen High School Symphonic Band/George C. Wilson - *Golden Crest*
            (USA) GC 403 (m)
            Dallas Wind Symphony/Jerry Junkin - *Reference RR-66(CD)*
Pub: Paterson/Carl Fischer (New York)

also arr. for military band
f.rec.   (exc.) Band of the Royal Scots Guards - *EMI Note NTS 162, Bandleader BNA 5038(CD)*
also arr. for brass band by Ray Farr (1984)
f.p.   Manger Brass Band/Michael Antrobus - Usher Hall, Edinburgh, 6 May 1984
f.recs.   Band of the Royal Military School of Music, Kneller Hall/Lt. Col. Basil H. Brown - *HMV CLP 1730 (m), CSD 1538*
        Grimethorpe Colliery Band/Elgar Howarth - *Conifer MCFC 222 (MC), CDCF 222 (CD), 76506 16848-2(CD)*
Pub: Paterson, 1984
Exc.   (No. 3) arr. for piano solo by Stephen Duro
        Pub: Chester, 1997 (in 'Contemporary Classics' No. 1)

H.R.H. The Duke of Cambridge* - March for military band Op.60 (1957)
Written to celebrate the centenary of The Royal Military School of Music, Kneller Hall and dedicated to Lt. Col. David McBain
Dur: 3'30"
f.p.   Band of The Royal Military School of Music, Kneller Hall/Rodney Bashford - Kneller Hall, Twickenham, 28 June 1957 (at a garden party attended by both Her Majesty the Queen and the composer)
f.broad.p. Band of the Grenadier Guards/Major Rodney Bashford - 9 September 1968
f.recs.   Band of the Royal Military School of Music, Kneller Hall/Lt. Col. Basil H. Brown - *HMV CLP 1730 (m), CSD 1538*
        Kneller Hall All-Star Band/Rodney Bashford - *Bandleader BNA 5109(CD)*
Pub: Paterson/Carl Fischer (New York), 1957
also arr. for symphonic wind band
f.rec.   Dallas Wind Symphony/Jerry Junkin - *Reference RR-66(CD)*
(* Commander in Chief of the British Army who founded Kneller Hall in 1857 and who is said to have taken his title from the public house at the Hall's main gates.)

Oboe Quartet* Op.61 (1957)
Written for and dedicated to Léon Goossens on the occasion of his sixtieth birthday - the score is dated 2 April 1957
Dur: 12'45"
Instr: Ob. Vn. Va. Vc.
f.p.   Léon Goossens/Carter String Trio - Mary Carter (Vn.), Anatole Mines (Va.), Eileen McCarthy (Vc.) - Cambridge University Music School, 2 May 1957
f.broad.p. above artists - BBC Third Programme, 18 June 1958
f.rec.   Gareth Hulse (Ob.)/Marcia Crayford (Vn.)/Roger Chase (Va.)/ Christopher van Kampen (Vc.) - *Hyperion A 66173 (and MC/CD)*
Pub: Faber, 1966; Emerson
(* originally entitled 'Serenade for Oboe Quartet')

Toy Symphony Op.62 (1957)
Dedicated to the Musicians' Benevolent Fund - the score is dated 25 July 1957
Dur: 9'30"
Instr: Pno. Vn. Vn. Va. Vc. (+ 12 toy wind and percussion instruments)
f.p.   Soloists/Amici String Quartet/Joseph Cooper (Pno.) cond. Malcolm Arnold - Savoy Hotel, London, 28 November 1957 (St. Cecilia Festival Dinner)

f.broad.p. members of the BBC Scottish Orchestra/Colin Davis* - 1 April 1958
Pub: Paterson, 1958
(* who seven years earlier had premiered the **Clarinet Sonatina Op. 29** q.v.)

Symphony No.3 Op.63 (1957)
Commissioned by and dedicated to the Royal Liverpool Philharmonic Society
Dur: 32'30"
Instr: 2+picc./2/2/2 - 4/3/3/1 - timp. str.
f.p.   Royal Liverpool Philharmonic Orchestra/John Pritchard - Royal Festival Hall,
            London, 2 December 1957
f.broad.p. above artists - Home Service, 25 April 1958
f.(Liverpool) p. above artists - Philharmonic Hall, 10 December 1957
f.rec.   London Philharmonic Orchestra/Malcolm Arnold - *Everest LPBR 6021 (m),*
            SDBR 3021, EVC 9001 (CD); World Record Club T(m)/ST 99; Desto (USA)
            DC 6448; Phoenix PHCD 102 (CD)
Pub: Paterson, 1958

Commonwealth Christmas Overture for orchestra Op.64 (1957)
Commissioned by the BBC for the 1959 "Christmas Round the World" programme
celebrating the 25th anniversary of the first Christmas broadcast by a British monarch
(King George V in 1932) - the score is dated London, 17 November 1957
Dur: 14'30"
Instr: 2+picc./2/2/2 - 4/3/3/1 - timp. perc.(4) cel. hp. str. (+ 3 guitars, marimba and
            Afro-Cuban percussion group)
f.p.   BBC Symphony Orchestra/Rudolf Schwarz - BBC, 25 December 1957
f.conc.p.   London Symphony Orchestra/Alexander Gibson - date unknown
f.rec.   London Philharmonic Orchestra/Malcolm Arnold - *Reference RR-48 (and CD)*
Pub: Lengnick, 1991

Richmond Fanfare for brass (1957)
Originally commissioned by the BBC as part of the **Royal Prologue** music q.v.
Dur: 36"
Instr: 3 Tpt. 3 Tbn.
f.conc.p.   Fanfare trumpeters of the Royal Military School of Music, Kneller
            Hall/Rodney Bashford - Richmond, Surrey, Christmas 1957
f.broad.p. above artists - 2 April 1962
Pub: Studio Music, 1986 (as No. 2 of `Four Fanfares')

Sinfonietta No.2 for chamber orchestra Op.65 (1958)
Written for the 21st anniversary of the Jacques Orchestra and dedicated to Reginald
Jacques - the score is dated 26 May 1958
Dur: 12'30"
Instr: 2/0/0/0 - 2/0/0/0 - str.
f.p.   Jacques Orchestra/Reginald Jacques - Victoria and Albert Museum, London,
            15 June 1958
f.broad.p. above artists - BBC Home Service, 15 July 1959
f.rec.   Philharmonia Orchestra/Neville Dilkes - *HMV ASD 3487 (and MC)*
Pub: Paterson, 1958

United Nations for 4 military bands, organ and orchestra (1958)
Commissioned for the 1958 Hoffnung Interplanetary Music Festival
Dur: 13'
Instr: picc.+2/2/2/2 - 4/3/3/1 - timp. perc.(3) str.
f.p.   Band of the Royal Military School of Music, Kneller Hall/Morley College
            Symphony Orchestra/Malcolm Arnold - Royal Festival Hall, London, 21
            November 1958 (Hoffnung Interplanetary Music Festival)
f.rec.   Band of the Royal Military School of Music/Morley College Symphony
            Orchestra/Malcolm Arnold - *Columbia 33CX 1617 (m); World Record Club
            T(m)/ST 701; HMV Set SLS 870 (m), SLS 5069 (m); Angel (USA) 35500 (m),
            S-37028; EMI CMS7 63302-2(CD)*

Five William Blake Songs for contralto and string orchestra Op.66 (1959)
[1. O Holy Virgin! Clad in purest white
 2. Memory hither come and tune your merry notes
 3. How sweet I roam'd from field to field   4. My silks and fine array
 5. Thou Fair-hair'd angel of the evening]
Written for Pamela Bowden
Dur: 13'30"
f.p.   Pamela Bowden/Richmond Community Centre String Orchestra/ Malcolm
            Arnold - Richmond Community Centre Hall, Richmond, Surrey,
            26 March 1959
f.Lon.p.   Pamela Bowden/Jacques Orchestra/Reginald Jacques - Victoria and Albert
            Museum, 12 July 1959
f.broad.p. Pamela Bowden/BBC Northern Orchestra/Malcolm Arnold - Third
            Programme, 28 January 1966 (Manchester Midday Prom Concert)
f.rec.   above (first broadcast) performance - *BBC Radio Classics 15656 91817(CD)*
Pub: British & Continental Music Agency, 1966 (also arr. voice and piano);
            Studio Music)

Four Pieces for chamber ensemble (1959)
[1. Prelude 2. Waltz 3. Chorale 4. Carillon]
Written for the Arnold family to play as practice pieces
Instr: 3 Vn. Rec.

Concerto for guitar and chamber ensemble (or orchestra) Op.67 (1959)
Commissioned by and dedicted to Julian Bream (the second movement is dedicated to the
memory of Django Reinhardt)
Dur: 21'30"
Instr: Fl. Cl. Hn. Vn. Va. Vc. Db.
Alt.Instr: 1/0/1/0 - 1/0/0/0 - str.
f.p.   Julian Bream/Melos Ensemble/Malcolm Arnold - BBC Third Programme,
            18 June 1959
f.conc.p.   Julian Bream/Melos Ensemble/Malcolm Arnold - Jubilee Hall, Aldeburgh,
            25 June 1959 (Aldeburgh Festival)
f.Lon.p.   Julian Bream/Melos Ensemble/Malcolm Arnold - Victoria and Albert
            Museum, 6 March 1960

f.recs.   Julian Bream/Melos Ensemble/Malcolm Arnold - *RCA RB 16252 (m), SB 6826, GL 13883 (and MC), 09026 61583-2 (CD set), 09026 61598-2(CD); RCA (USA) LM (m)/LSC 2487, AGL 13883*
             Julian Bream/City of Birmingham Symphony Orchestra/Simon Rattle - *EMI CDC7 54661-2 (CD)*
Pub: Paterson, 1961 (also arr. guitar and piano)

Kingston Fanfare for brass (1959)
Dur: 0'30"
Instr: 3 Tpt. 3 Tbn.
Pub: Studio Music, 1986 (as No. 1 of `Four Fanfares')

Sweeney Todd - Ballet Op.68 (1959)
Written for the Royal Ballet Company - the score is dated London, 5 November 1959
Dur: 23'
Instr: 1+picc./1/2/1 - 2/2/2/0 - timp. perc. pno. cel. hp. str.
f.p.   Royal Ballet Orchestra cond. John Lanchberry - Shakespeare Memorial Theatre, Stratford-upon-Avon, 10 December 1959
Choreography: John Cranko
Designer: Alix Stone
Principals: Donald Britton, Elizabeth Anderton, Desmond Doyle
f.Lon.p.   above artists, Royal Opera House, Covent Garden, 16 August 1960
Pub: Faber, 1984
Concert Suite Op.68a from the above arr. by David Ellis (1984)
Dur: 20'
f.p.   University Chamber Orchestra/Christopher Austin - Bristol University, 19 June 1990
f.broad.p. BBC Concert Orchestra/Malcolm Arnold - Radio 3, 6 November 1991
f.rec.   Royal Philharmonic Orchestra/Vernon Handley - *Conifer CDCF 224 (CD), 74321 16847-2(CD)*
Pub: Faber, 1989

Song of Simeon - Nativity Masque for mimers, soloists, SATB chorus and orchestra Op.69 (1959)
[Words: Christopher Hassall 1. Prelude 2. The Place of the Annunciation 3. The Inn at Bethlehem 4. Susana's Dance 5. Shepherd's Song 6. Arak's Scene 7. Processional Hymn 8. Outside the Temple]
Written for a charity matinee in aid of refugee children - the score is dated London, 5 December 1959
Dur: 29'30"
Instr: 0/0/0/0 - 0/3/3/1 - timp. perc.(2) cel. hp. str.
Alt.Instr: Recorders, piano duet, timp. perc. str.
f.p.   Nicholas Chagrin/Imogen Hassall/St. Martin's Singers and Concert Orchestra/Malcolm Arnold - Drury Lane Theatre, London, 5 January 1960 (concert given under the auspices of the Vicar of St. Martin-in-the Fields)
Producer: Colin Graham
Choreography: John Cranko
Designer: Annena Stubbs

f.conc.p.   Ambrosian Singers/English Chamber Orchestra/Malcolm Arnold - BBC
             broadcast (from Walthamstow Town Hall), 12 January 1967
Principals: Ann Dowdall, Christopher Keyte, Forbes Robinson, Jean Allister, Ian
             Partridge (in the title role)
f.rec.   above (BBC) performance - *BBC Radio Classics 15656 91817(CD)*
Pub: OUP, 1960; Faber, 1986 (vocal score)
Exc. from above:
(i)   The Pilgrim Caravan arr. unaccompanied SATB chorus
             Dur: 3'
             Pub: OUP, 1960; Faber, 1986
(ii)   The Pilgrim Caravan arr. unison voices (with optional descant) and
             orchestra
             Instr: 2/2/2/2 - 2/3/3/0 - timp. perc.(2) pno. str.
             Alt.Instr: pno. str.
             Pub: OUP, 1960; Faber, 1986

March - 'Overseas' for military band Op.70 (1960)

Commissioned by the Central Office of Information for the 1960 British Trade Fair in
New York
Dur: 2'30"
f.p.   New York, 1960
f.rec.   Dallas Wind Symphony/Jerry Junkin - *Reference RR-66(CD)*
Pub: Paterson/Carl Fischer (New York), 1960

Symphony No.4 Op.71 (1960)

Commissioned by the BBC - the score is dated London, 13 July 1960
Dur: 36'
Instr: 2+picc./2/2/2 + cbsn.- 4/3/3/1 - timp. perc.(3) cel. hp. str.
f.p.   BBC Symphony Orchestra/Malcolm Arnold - Royal Festival Hall, London,
             2 November 1960
f.recs.   above (first) performance - *Aries (USA) LP 1622* (pirate recording)
             London Philharmonic Orchestra/Malcolm Arnold - *Lyrita SRCD 200 (CD)*
Pub: Paterson, 1960

Carnival of Animals for orchestra Op.72 (1960)

[1. The Giraffe 2. Sheep 3. Cows 4. Mice 5. Jumbo* 6. Chiroptera (Bats)]
Commissioned for the Hoffnung Memorial Concert
Dur: 8'30"
Instr: 2+picc./2/2/2 - 4/3/3/1 - timp. perc.(2) str.
f.p.   Morley College Symphony Orchestra/Malcolm Arnold - Royal Festival Hall,
             London, 31 October 1960 (Hoffnung Memorial Concert)
f.rec.   Royal Philharmonic Orchestra/Vernon Handley - *Conifer CDCF 240 (CD),
             75605 51240-2(CD)*
Pub: Zomba Music
(* here the composer 'borrows' the famous pizzicato movement from **Sylvia** by Delibes!)

A Hoffnung Fanfare (1960)

Written for the Hoffnung Memorial Concert
Instr: 36 trumpets in 3 groups of 12

f.p.   Trumpeters of the Royal Military School of Music, Kneller Hall - Royal
            Festival Hall, London, 31 October 1960 (Hoffnung Memorial Concert)

Brass Quintet No. 1 Op.73 (1961)
Written for and dedicated to the New York Brass Quintet - the score is dated 23 January
1961
Dur: 13'
Instr: 2 Tpt. Hn. Tbn. Tba.
f.p.   New York Brass Quintet - New York, 1961
f.Brit.p.   Francis Chagrin Ensemble - London, 17 March 1962 (St. Pancras Festival)
f.recs.   Hallé Brass Consort - *Pye Golden Guinea GGC (m)/GSGC 14114*
            Philip Jones Brass Ensemble - *London 430069-2(CD)*
Pub: Paterson, 1961

Fanfare for the Farnham Festival (1961)
Written for the inaugural Farnham Festival (the composer's gift)
Dur: c.2'
Instr: 5Hn. 6Tpt. 5Tbn. Tba. Cym. Timp.
f.p.   Brass of Tiffin's School, Kingston upon Thames and Farnham Grammar
            School/Dennis Bloodworth - Farnham Parish Church, Farnham, Surrey,
            8 May 1961 (Farnham Festival)

Symphony No.5 Op.74 (1961)
Commissioned by the Cheltenham Festival Society* - the score is dated Richmond, 7
May 1961
Dur: 33'
Instr: 2+picc./2/2/2 - 4/3/3/1 - timp. perc.(2) cel. hp. str.
f.p.   Hallé Orchestra/Malcolm Arnold - Cheltenham Town Hall, 3 July 1961
            (Cheltenham Festival)
f.broad.p. BBC Northern Symphony Orchestra/Malcolm Arnold - BBC Music
            Programme, 1 May 1967
f.Lon.p.   New Philharmonia Orchestra/Malcolm Arnold - Royal Festival Hall,
            16 December 1971
f.rec.   City of Birmingham Symphony Orchestra/Malcolm Arnold - *HMV ASD 2878
            (and MC); HMV Greensleeve ED 290461-1 (and MC); EMI CDC7 49513-2
            (CD), CDM7 63368-2 (CD)*
Pub: Paterson, 1961
Exc.   'Slow Movement Theme' arr. for piano solo by Stephen Duro
Pub: Chester 1997 (in 'Contemporary Classics' No. 2)
Exc.   2nd movement arr. for symphonic wind band
f.rec   Bunkyo University Ensemble Band/Seiji Sagawa - *Sony (Jap.)*
(* the composer comments in a programme note that 'After the first performance of my
Fourth Symphony there were so many things I felt needed to be said musically that I am
more than grateful for the opportunity given me by the Cheltenham Festival Society to
attempt to say these things.')

Divertimento No.2* for orchestra Op.75 (1961)
[1. Fanfare 2. Nocturne 3. Chaconne]
Dur: 9'

Instr: 2+picc./2/2/2 - 4/3/3/1 - timp. perc.(2) hp. str.
f.p.   Royal Liverpool Philharmonic Orchestra/Lawrence Leonard - Leeds Town
            Hall, 24 October 1961 (Rostrum Concert)
f.Lon.p.   Royal Philharmonic Orchestra/Kenneth V. Jones - Royal Festival Hall,
            26 March 1962
f.rec.   Leicestershire Schools Symphony Orchestra/Eric Pinkett - *Pye Golden Guinea
            GGC (m)/GSGC 14103*
Pub: Paterson, 1961
(* A complete re-write of the 1950 **Divertimento No.2** and a change of central movement
title from 'Tango' to 'Nocturne')

Grand Concerto Gastronomique for eater, waiter, food and large orchestra Op.76 (1961)

[1. Prologue - Oysters 2. Soup - Brown Windsor 3. Roast Beef 4. Cheese
5. Peach Melba 6. Coffee, Brandy, Epilogue]
Written for the Hoffnung Astronautical Music Festival
Dur: 20'
Instr: 2+picc./2/2/2 - 4/3/3/1 - timp. perc.(2) hp. str.
f.p.   Henry Sherek (eater)/Tutte Lemkow (waiter)/Morley College Symphony
            Orchestra/Malcolm Arnold - Royal Festival Hall, London, 28 November 1961
            (Hoffnung Astronautical Music Festival)

Leonora No.4 (Beethoven - Strasser) Overture for large orchestra (1961)

Written for the Hoffnung Astronautical Music Festival
Dur: 9'30"
Instr: 2+picc./2/2/2 - 4/2/3/1 - timp. perc.(2) str. (+ off-stage trumpets and street
            band)
f.p.   Morley College Symphony Orchestra/Norman del Mar - Royal Festival Hall,
            London, 28 November 1961 (Hoffnung Astronautical Music Festival)
f.recs.   Morley College Symphony Orchestra/Norman del Mar - *Columbia 33CX 1785
            (m), SAX 2433; HMV set SLS 870 (m), SLS 5069 (m); Angel (USA) 3-37028
            (m); EMI CMS7 63302-2 (CD)*
            Philharmonia Orchestra/Michael Massey - *Decca 444 921-2DF2(CD)*

Concerto for two violins and string orchestra Op.77 (1962)

Written for Yehudi Menuhin and his pupil Alberto Lysy - the score is dated 25 April
1962*
Dur: 16'30"
f.p.   Yehudi Menuhin/Albert Lysy/Bath Festival Orchestra/Malcolm Arnold -
            Guildhall, Bath, 24 June 1962 (Bath Festival)
f.Lon.p.   Yehudi Menuhin/Robert Masters/Bath Festival Orchestra/Malcolm Arnold -
            Victoria & Albert Museum, 17 June 1964
f.broad.p. Alfredo Campoli/Derek Collier/London Symphony Orchestra/ Malcolm
            Arnold - BBC Music Programme, 28 December 1965 ('Composer's Portrait'
            series)
f.Am.p.   Paul King/Peter McHugh/Louisville Orchestra/Jorge Mester - Louisville,
            Kentucky, c.1974

f.recs.   Alan Loveday/Frances Mason/London Philharmonic Orchestra/ Malcolm
            Arnold - *BBC Radio Classics 15656 91817 (CD)* (recorded `live' at a
            Promenade Concert, Royal Albert Hall, London, 5 August 1966)
            Paul Kling/Peter McHugh/Louisville Orchestra/Jorge Mester - *Louisville*
            (USA) LS 731; RCA GL 25018
            Kenneth Sillito/Lyn Fletcher/London Musici/Mark Stephenson - *Conifer*
            MCFC 172 (MC), CDCF 172 (CD), 74321 15004-2(CD)
            Albert Lysy/Sophia Reuter/Camerata Lysy/Yehudi Menuhin - *Dinemec*
            Classics DCCD 001(CD)
Pub: Faber, 1966 (also arr. for violin and piano by Elspeth Roseberry)
(* N.B. The score was begun in India while the composer was working on his researches
for the film score **Nine Hours to Rama** q.v.)

Little Suite No.2 for orchestra Op.78 (1962)
[1. Overture 2. Ballad 3. Dance]
Commissioned by Elphicks of Farnham for the 1963 Farnham Festival
Dur: 10'
Instr: 2/2/2/2 - 4/3/3/1 - timp. perc.(3) str.
f.p.   Combined Orchestras of Farnham Grammar School and Tiffin School/ Dennis
            Bloodworth - Farnham Parish Church, Surrey, 13 May 1963 (Farnham
            Festival)
f.Lon.p.   London Junior and Senior Orchestras/Oliver Broome - Royal Festival Hall,
            25 May 1964
f.recs.   Atlantic Symphony Orchestra/Kenneth Elloway - *CBC (Canada) SM 215*
            City of London Sinfonia/Richard Hickox - *Chandos CHAN 9509(CD)*
Pub: Paterson, 1963

The Peacock in the Zoo for unison voices and piano (1963)
[Words: Katherine Arnold*]
Dur: 2'
Pub: Paterson, 1963
(* the composer's daughter and eldest of his three children, see also **Symphony No. 7**
Op.113)

Electra - Ballet in One Act Op.79 (1963)
Commissioned by the Royal Ballet Company - the score is dated Thursley, 13 March
1963
Dur: 25'
Instr: 2+picc./2/2/2 - 4/3/3/1 - timp. perc.(3) hp. str.
f.p.   Orchestra of the Royal Opera House, Covent Garden, cond. John Lanchberry -
            Royal Opera House, Covent Garden, London, 26 March 1963
Choreography: Robert Helpmann
Decor: Arthur Boyd
Principals: Nadia Nerina, David Blair, Monica Mason, Derek Rencher
f.Austr.p. Australian Ballet Company, Adelaide, 14 March 1966

Little Suite No.1 for brass band Op.80 (1963)
[1. Prelude 2. Siciliano 3. Rondo]

Commissioned by the Scottish Amateur Music Association for the National Youth Brass Band of Scotland

Dur: 10'

f.p.   National Youth Brass Band of Scotland/Bryden Thomson - High School for Girls, Aberdeen, July 1963

f.broad.p. Hanwell Brass Band/Eric Bravington - 30 November 1965

f.recs.   National Youth Brass Band of Great Britain/Geoffrey Brand - *Pye GGL (m)/GSGL 10428; World Record Club T(m)/ST 391*

            Grimethorpe Colliery Band/Elgar Howarth - *Conifer 76506 16848-2(CD)*

Pub: Paterson, 1965; Studio Music

also arr. for symphonic wind band by John Paynter

f.rec.   Dallas Wind Symphony/Jerry Junkin - *Reference RR-66(CD)*

Pub: Paterson/Carl Fischer (New York), (as `Prelude, Siciliano and Rondo')

also arr. for military band by Dennis Bloodworth

Pub: Molenaar (Holland)

Water Music for wind and percussion Op.82 (1964)

Commissioned by the National Trust in celebration of the opening of the Stratford Canal (the composer was made a life member of the Trust soon after-wards)

Dur: 10'

Instr: 2+picc./2/2 + EbCl./2/ - 4/3/3/1 - perc.(2)

f.p.   Ensemble*/Brian Priestman - Stratford-upon-Avon, 11 July 1964 (after a performance of Shakespeare's **Henry V**)

f.conc.p. Royal Northern College of Music Wind Ensemble/Clark Rundell - Royal Northern College of Music, Manchester, 3 November 1984 (BASWBE Conference)

f.rec.   Dallas Wind Symphony/Jerry Junkin - *Reference RR-66(CD)*

also arr. for orchestra as Op.82b (1964)

Instr: 2+picc./2/2/2 - 4/3/3/1 - timp. perc.(2) str.

f.p.   Hallé Orchestra/Lawrence Leonard - Free Trade Hall, Manchester, 21 March 1965

f.rec.   BBC Concert Orchestra/Vernon Handley - *Conifer 75605 51298-2(CD)*

Pub: Paterson, 1965

(* played by musicians on a barge moored in the middle of the River Avon at the point where the Stratford Canal enters the river behind the Shakespeare Memorial Theatre)

A Sunshine Overture for orchestra Op.83 (1964)

Written at the request of Beryl Grey for a Gala Concert in aid of the Sunshine Home for Blind Babies

Dur: 2'

Instr: 2/2/2/2 - 2/2/1/0 - perc. str.

f.p.   Sunshine Gala Orchestra/Dudley Simpson - Palace Theatre, London, 14 July 1964

Five Pieces for violin and piano Op.84 (1964)

[1. Prelude 2. Aubade (based on an Indian raga) 3. Waltz

4. Ballad (derived from the Arioso in the ballet **Rinaldo and Armida** q.v.)

5. Moto perpetuo (dedicated to Charlie Parker)]

Written for Yehudi Menuhin to use on his American tour as `encore' pieces - the score is
dated Thursley (Surrey), 8 August 1964
Dur: 9'
f.p.   Yehudi Menuhin (Vn.)/Ivor Newton (Pno.) - Bamburgh Castle,
            Northumberland, 24 July 1965
f.broad.p. Derek Collier (Vn.)/Ernest Lush (Pno.) - BBC Home Service, 29 January 1966
f.recs.   Stephen Levine (Vn.)/Peter Lawson (Pno.) - *Auracle AUC 1002*
            Marcia Crayford (Vn.)/Ian Brown (Pno.) - *Hyperion A 66171 (and MC/CD)*
            Ruggiero Ricci (Vn./Rebecca Pennies (Pno.) - *One Eleven (USA) URS 93040
            (CD)*
Pub: Paterson, 1965

Sinfonietta No.3 for chamber orchestra Op.81 (1964)
Score dated Thursley, 1 September 1964
Dur: 14'30"
Instr: 1/2/0/2 - 2/0/0/0 - str.
f.p.   New Philharmonia Orchestra/Malcolm Arnold - Fairfield Hall, Croydon,
            Surrey, 30 January 1965
f.broad.p. BBC Concert Orchestra/Malcolm Arnold - BBC Music Programme,
            10 October 1967
f.rec.   Bournemouth Sinfonietta/Ronald Thomas - *HMV ASD 3868 (and MC)*
Pub: Paterson, 1964

Duo for two cellos Op.85 (1965)
Commissioned by Novello for a teaching book, the score is dated 5 January 1965
Dur: 5'
f.rec.   Christopher van Kempen/Moray Welsh - *Hyperion A 66171 (and MC/CD)*
Pub: Novello, 1971 (in `Playing the Cello' by Hugo Cole and Anna Shuttleworth)
also arr. for two violas by Alison Milne
Pub: Novello, 1986

Fantasies for solo wind instruments
Arnold was commissioned by the City of Birmingham Symphony Orchestra to write a
series of 5 Fantasies for the Birmingham International Wind Competition in 1966. The
names of the individual class winners are, therefore, credited with the first performance
of each Fantasy

Fantasy for bassoon Op.86 (1965)
Dur: 4'30"
f.p.   Frantisek Herman - Birmingham Town Hall, May 1966
f.recs.   Otto Eiffert - *Gasparo (USA) GS 103*
            Brian Wightman - *Hyperion A 66172 (and MC/CD)*
Pub: Faber, 1966

Fantasy for clarinet Op.87 (1966)
Dur: 4'30"
f.p.   Aurelian-Octav Popa - Birmingham Town Hall, May 1966
f.rec.   Michael Collins - *Hyperion A 66172 (and MC/CD)*
Pub: Faber, 1966

Fantasy for horn Op.88 (1966)

Dur: 4'30"
f.p.   Ferenc Tarjani - Birmingham Town Hall, May 1966
f.broad.p. Alan Civil - BBC Music Programme, 11 October 1967
f.recs.   Lowell Greer - *Coronet (USA) 3100*
           John Pigneguy - *Hyperion A 66172 (and MC/CD)*
Pub: Faber, 1966

Fantasy for flute Op.89 (1966)

Dur: 4'30"
f.p.   James Galway - Birmingham Town Hall, May 1966
f.Lon.p.   Elizabeth Dean - Bethnal Green, 1967 (Society for Modern Music Concert)
f.rec.   Judith Pearce - *Hyperion A 66172 (and MC/CD)*
Pub: Faber, 1966

Fantasy for oboe Op.90 (1966)

Dur: 4'30"
f.p.   Maurice Bourgue - Birmingham Town Hall, May 1966
f.rec.   Gareth Hulse - *Hyperion A 66172 (and MC/CD)*
Pub: Faber, 1966

Four Cornish Dances for orchestra Op.91 (1966)

Dedicated to the composer's second wife, Isobel - the score is dated St. Merryn,
Cornwall, 26 May 1966
Dur: 10'
Instr: 2+picc./2/2/2 - 4/3/3/1 - timp. perc.(2) hp. str.
f.p.   London Philharmonic Orchestra/Malcolm Arnold - Royal Albert Hall,
           London, 13 August 1966 (Promenade Concert)
f.recs.   above (first) performance - *BBC Radio Classics 15656 91817(CD)*
           City of Birmingham Symphony Orchestra/Malcolm Arnold - *HMV ASD 2878
           (and MC); ESD 107780-1 (and MC)*
           London Philharmonic Orchestra/Malcolm Arnold - *Lyrita SRCS 109, SRCD
           201 (CD)*
Pub: Faber, 1968
also arr. by the composer with additional parts for brass band (1968)
Score dated 29 January 1968
f.p.   Penzance Orchestral Society/Cornwall Symphony Orchestra/St. Dennis Silver
           Band/St. Agnes Silver Band/Malcolm Arnold - Truro Cathedral, Cornwall, 16
           March 1968
also arr. for concert band by Thad Marciniak (c.1968)
Pub: Faber, 1968 and G. Schirmer (New York), 1975
also arr. for brass band by Ray Farr (1985)
f.p.   Grimethorpe Colliery Band/Elgar Howarth
f.Lon.p.   Williams Fairey and Yorkshire Imperial Brass Bands/Geoffrey Brand -
           Kenwood Lakeside, 28 April 1996
f.rec.   Grimethorpe Colliery Band/Elgar Howarth - *Conifer MCFC 222(MC), CDCF
           222(CD), 76506 16848-2(CD)*
Pub: Faber, 1985; Studio Music

**Theme and Variation - for Severn Bridge Variations on a Welsh Folk Song 'Braint'
for orchestra - composite work* (1966)**
Written to commemorate the first birthday of the BBC Training Orchestra on its first visit
to Wales and of the opening of the first Severn Bridge
Dur: 19'30" (complete work)
Instr: 3/2+ca./2+bcl./0 - 4/3/3/1 - timp. perc.(2) hp. str.
f.p.   BBC Training Orchestra/Sir Adrian Boult - Brangwyn Hall, Swansea,
           11 January 1967
f.Lon.p.   BBC Welsh Symphony Orchestra/Boris Brott - Royal Albert Hall,
           20 July 1976 (Promenade Concert)
(* the other contributors were Alun Hoddinott, Nicholas Maw, Daniel Jones,
 Grace Williams and Michael Tippett, an equitable split of three Welsh and three
English composers!)

Jolly Old Friar, for unison voices and piano (1966)
[Words: Frank Richards]
f.p.   BBC Radio Three announcers - Comic Relief Day, 1991
Pub: Cassell, 1966 (Greyfriar's School Annual)

The Turtle Drum* - a children's play for television Op.92 (1967)
[Libretto: Ian Serraillieu 1. The Turtle Drum 2. Go back where you belong
 3. Round of Welcome 4. Divertissement of the Deep 5. The Four Seasons
 6. Sayonara Song]
Commissioned by BBC Television for their opening programme of a series entitled
`Making Music'
Dur: 50'
Instr: Fl./Picc. Tpt. Gtr.(s) Perc. Db.
f.p.   James Blades and pupils of the David Livingstone Primary School -
           BBC Television, 26 April 1967
Producer: John Hosier
Director: Moyra Gambleton
Pub: OUP, 1968; Faber
(* originally entitled `Kaisoo the Fisherboy')

Little Suite No.2 for brass band Op.93 (1967)
[1. Round 2. Cavatina 3. Galop]
Commissioned by the Cornwall Youth Band
Dur: 8'45"
f.p.   Cornwall Youth Band/Malcolm Arnold - Cornwall, 26 March 1967
f.broad.p. Brighouse & Rastrick/Carlton Main Frickley Colliery and Grimethorpe
           Colliery Institute Bands/Malcolm Arnold - Radio 3, 19 August 1968
f.recs.   Black Dyke Mills Band/Geoffrey Brand - *Paxton LPT (m)/SLPT 1028*
           Grimethorpe Colliery Band/Elgar Howarth - *Conifer MCFC 222(MC), CDCF
           222(CD), 76506 16848-2(CD)*
Pub: Henrees Music, 1967; Studio Music
also arr. for military band by Jan Singerling
f.rec.   Dallas Wind Symphony/Jerry Junkin - *Reference RR-66(CD)*
Pub: Molenaar (Holland), 1967

The Padstow Lifeboat - March for brass band Op.94 (1967)
Written to celebrate the launching of the new lifeboat near to the Trevose Head
lighthouse whose foghorn `D' features throughout the piece
Dur: 4'30"
f.p.   Black Dyke Mills and BMC Concert Bands/Malcolm Arnold - Royal Festival
            Hall, London, 10 June 1967 (BBC International Festival of Light Music)
f.broad.p. BMC Concert Band/Harry Mortimer - 11 December 1967
f.(Cornish) p. St.Dennis Silver Band/Malcolm Arnold - Padstow, 19 July 1968
            (on the occasion of the visit of Princess Marina to name the new lifeboat)
f.recs.   BMC Concert Band/Harry Mortimer - *HMV (m)/CSD 3650; Starline SRS
            5105; Studio 2 TWOX 1048 (and MC)*
            Grimethorpe Colliery Band/Malcolm Arnold - *Conifer MCFC 222 (MC),
            CDCF 222(CD), 76506 16848-2(CD)*
Pub: Henrees Music, 1967; Studio Music
also arr. for military band by Ray Woodfield
f.recs.   Royal Marines Band/Capt. W. W. Shillito - *Decca SB 701*
            Dallas Wind Symphony/Jerry Junkin - *Reference RR-66(CD)*
Pub: Henrees Music, 1967

Symphony No.6* Op.95 (1967)
Score dated St. Merryn, Cornwall, 28 July 1967
Dur: 26'
Instr: 2+picc./2/2/2 - 4/3/3/1 - timp. perc.(3) hp. str.
f.p.   BBC Northern Symphony Orchestra/Malcolm Arnold - City Hall, Sheffield,
            28 June 1968
f.Lon.p.   Royal Philharmonic Orchestra/Malcolm Arnold - Royal Albert Hall,
            24 September 1969
f.rec.   Royal Philharmonic Orchestra/Vernon Handley - *Conifer CDCF 224 (CD),
            74321 16847-2(CD)*
Pub: Faber, 1974
(* The only symphony not to have been commissioned, the work also bears no dedication.
However, the first movement pays homage to Charlie Parker, the great alto saxophonist
of the Bebop era, and the slow movement has been described by the composer as `a
lament for a pop style which will be dead before this symphony is performed.')

Trevelyan: Suite for Ten Instruments Op.96 (1967)
[1. Palindrome 2. Nocturne 3. Apotheosis]
Written for the opening of Trevelyan College*, University of Durham, by Lord Butler -
the score is dated St. Merryn, Cornwall, 13 October 1967
Dur: 8'
Instr: 3Fl. 2Ob. 2Cl. 2Hn. Vc. (or 2Bsn.)
f.p.   University of Durham Ensemble/Malcolm Arnold - Trevelyan College,
            University of Durham, 12 March 1968
f.rec.   above performance (private reel-to-reel tape)
Pub: Faber, 1970; Emerson, 1979
(* Arnold's daughter Katherine was at that time an Undergraduate at the College)

Peterloo* - Overture for orchestra Op.97 (1967)
Commissioned by the Trades Union Congress for the 100th anniversary of its first

meeting in Manchester in June 1868 - the score is dated St. Merryn, Cornwall, 31
October 1967

Dur: 9'45"

Instr: 2+picc./2/2/2 - 4/3/3/1 - timp. perc.(4) hp. str.

f.p.   Royal Philharmonic Orchestra/Malcolm Arnold - Royal Festival Hall, London,
            7 June 1968

f.recs.   BBC Symphony Orchestra/Malcolm Arnold - *BBC Radio Classics 15656
            91817(CD)* (recorded `live' at a Promenade Concert, Royal Albert Hall,
            London, 3 August 1968)
            City of Birmingham Symphony Orchestra/Malcolm Arnold - *HMV ASD 2878
            (and MC), ESD 107780-1 (and MC); EMI CDC7 49513-2 (CD), CDM7
            63368-2 (CD); HMV Classics 5 72480-2(CD)*

Pub: Faber, 1979

also arr. for wind band by Charles Sayre (1979)

f.rec.   Japan Band Festival 93 - *Sony (Jap.) SRCR 9421(CD)*

Pub: Studio Music/Hal Leonard

(* a reference to the infamous massacre which took place at St. Peter's Fields, Manchester
on 16 August 1819 - the new Bridgewater Hall is built on the site of the massacre and
where Arnold's overture was played at a Royal Gala Concert by the Hallé Orchestra
conducted by Kent Nagano on 4 December 1996 celebrating both the composer's 75th
birthday and the opening of the new hall.)

This Christmas Night for unaccompanied SATB chorus (1967)

[Words: Mary Wilson*]

Written at the invitation of the Daily Telegraph

Dur: 2'

Pub: Faber, 1968

(* wife of the then Prime Minister, Harold Wilson)

A Salute to Thomas Merritt for two brass bands and orchestra Op.98 (1967)

Written to celebrate the 60th anniversary of the death of the Cornish composer, Thomas
Merritt - the score is dated St. Merryn, Cornwall, 24 December 1967

Dur: 5'

Instr: 2+picc./2/2/2 - 4/3/3/1 - timp. perc.(4) hp. str.

f.p.   Penzance Orchestral Society/Cornwall Symphony Orchestra/St. Dennis Silver
            Band/St. Agnes Silver Band/Malcolm Arnold - Truro Cathedral, Cornwall,
            16 March 1968

f.broad.p. above performance - Radio 3, 17 April 1968

f.rec.   above performance - *Hassell HASLP 938/9 (limited edition)*

Hong Kong Anniversary Overture for orchestra Op.99 (1968)

Written for the 21st birthday of the Hong Kong Philharmonic Society - the score is dated
St. Merryn, Cornwall, 15 July 1968

Dur: 4'

Instr: 2/2/2/2 - 4/2/3/0 - timp. perc. str.

f.p.   Hong Kong Philharmonic Orchestra/Arrigo Foa - City Hall, Hong Kong,
            8 December 1968

f.Brit.conc.p. Orchestra of the Light Music Society/Malcolm Arnold - Royal
            Festival Hall, London, 17 December 1970 (South Bank `Pops' Concert)

f.broad.p.   BBC Northern Symphony Orchestra/Malcolm Arnold - c.1971
f.recs.   BBC Northern Symphony Orchestra/Malcolm Arnold - *Aries (USA) LP 1622*
             (pirate recording)
             BBC Concert Orchestra/Vernon Handley - *Conifer 75605 51298-2(CD)*
Pub: Central Music Library, 1974; Faber, 1989 (as `Anniversary Overture')

Savile Centenary Fanfare for two trumpets (1968)
Written in celebration of the Savile Club centenary
Dur: c.1'
f.p.   Trumpeters of the Brigade of Guards - Savile Club Ballroom, London,
          30 October 1968

St. Endellion Ringers - Canon for voices (1968)
Written for the St. Endellion Festival for performance in the church of St. Endellion
(Endelienta), a few miles inland from Port Isaac in Cornwall.
Dur: 30"

Fantasy for trumpet Op.100 (1969)
Dedicated to Ernest Hall, Arnold's teacher at the Royal College of Music
Dur: 4'
f.rec.   Bret Jackson - *Summit (USA) DCD 153(CD)*
Pub: Faber, 1969

Fantasy for trombone Op.101 (1969)
Dur: 4'
f.rec.   John Iveson - *Argo ZRG 851*
Pub: Faber, 1969

Fantasy for tuba Op.102 (1969)
Dur: 4'
f.rec.   John Fletcher - *Two Ten 001*
Pub: Faber, 1969

The Song of Accounting Periods for high voice and piano Op.103 (1969)
[Words from the 1965 Finance Act]
Commissioned John Godber and John Gould for a touring recital programme `The
Invisible Backwards Facing Grocer'
Dur: 2'45"
f.p.   John Godber (Ten.)/John Gould (Pno.) - Manchester University Theatre,
          17 April 1969
f.Lon.p. above artists - Purcell Room, 4 May 1969

Concerto for two pianos (3 hands) and orchestra Op.104 (1969)
Commissioned by the BBC and dedicated "To Phyllis and Cyril with affection and
admiration" - the score is dated 12 June 1969
Dur: 12'30"
Instr: 2+picc./2/2/2 - 4/3/3/1 - timp. perc.(2) hp. str.
Alt.Instr: 2/2/2/2 - 2/2/1/1 - timp. perc. hp. str.

f.p.   Phyllis Sellick/Cyril Smith/BBC Symphony Orchestra/Malcolm Arnold -
            Royal Albert Hall, London, 16 August 1969 (Promenade Concert - the finale
            was encored)
f.recs.   above (first) performance - *BBC Radio Classics 15656 91817(CD)*
            Phyllis Sellick/Cyril Smith/City of Birmingham Symphony Orches-
            tra/Malcolm Arnold - *HMV ASD 2612; HMV Greensleeve ESD 7065 (and
            MC); EMI CDM7 64044-2(CD) (and MC); HMV Classics 5 72480-2(CD)*
            David Nettle/Richard Markham/Royal Philharmonic Orchestra/Vernon
            Handley - *Conifer 75605 51240-2(CD)*
Pub: Faber, 1969
also arr. for two pianos (4 hands) and orchestra by Julian Elloway
Instr: 2/2/2/2 - 2/2/1/1 - timp. perc. hp. str.
Pub: Faber, 1990

Concerto for 28 players Op.105 (1970)
Commissioned by the Stuyvesant Foundation and written specially for the English
Chamber Orchestra - the score is dated St. Merryn, Cornwall, 2 April 1970
Dur: 22'
Instr: 1/2/0/1 - 2/0/0/0 - str. (6/6/4/4/2)
f.p.   English Chamber Orchestra/Malcolm Arnold - Queen Elizabeth Hall, London,
            25 April 1970
f.rec.   London Musici/Mark Stephenson - *Conifer MCFC 211 (MC), CDCF 211
            (CD), 75605 51211-2(CD)*
Pub: Faber, 1970

Fanfare for Louis for two trumpets (or two cornets) (1970)
Written for `Louis Armstrong's 70th birthday with admiration and gratitude'
Dur: 1'30"
f.p.   Elgar Howarth and Stanley Woods - Queen Elizabeth Hall, London, 4 July
            1970 (Louis Armstrong 70th Birthday Concert sponsored by `Melody Maker')
f.recs.   above artists - *Polydor 2460 123*
            members of the Dallas Wind Symphony (4 trumpets)/Jerry Junkin - *Reference
            RR-66(CD)*
Pub: Studio Music, 1986

Fantasy for audience and orchestra* Op.106 (1970)
Commissioned by the BBC for performance at the `Last Night of the Proms'
Dur: 13'30"
Instr: 2+picc./2/2/2 - 4/3/3/1 - timp. perc.(3) hp. organ str.
f.p.   BBC Symphony Orchestra/Colin Davis - Royal Albert Hall, London,
            12 September 1970 (Promenade Concert)
(* the work includes a traditional hornpipe in 5/4 time and begins with the tune `On the
road to Freedom, we shall not be moved')

Fantasy for guitar Op.107 (1970)
[Prelude - Scherzo - Arietta - Fughetta - Arietta - March - Postlude]
Written for and dedicated to Julian Bream
Dur: 10'
f.p.   Julian Bream - Queen Elizabeth Hall, London, 16 May 1971

f.broad.p.   Julian Bream - Radio 3, 5 May 1975
Pub: Faber, 1971 (ed. Julian Bream)

Concerto for viola* and chamber orchestra Op.108 (1971)

Commissioned by Northern Arts and dedicated to the Northern Sinfonia and Roger Best (their principal viola) - the score is dated St. Merryn, Cornwall, 2 March 1971

Dur: 20'
Instr: 1/2/2/2 - 2/0/0/0 - str.
f.p.   Roger Best/Northern Sinfonia/Malcolm Arnold - Carlisle Market Hall,
              13 October 1971 (Newcastle Festival)
f.Lon.p.   above artists - Queen Elizabeth Hall, 15 October 1971
f.broad.p.   above artists - BBC Radio 3, 3 May 1972 (rec. 18 October 1971)
f.recs.   above (first broadcast) performance - *BBC Radio Classics 15656 91817(CD)*
              Rivka Golani/London Musici/Mark Stephenson - *Conifer MCFC 211 (MC),
              CDCF 211 (CD), 75605 51211-2(CD)*
Pub: Faber, 1980 (also arr. viola and piano)

(* as early as 1959 Arnold had intimated to Roy Plomley on Desert Island Discs that he was writing a viola concerto for William Primrose!)

Fanfare for one, eighty years young - for solo trumpet (1971)

Commissioned by the Council and Chairman of the Composer's Guild in celebration of the eightieth birthday of their President, Sir Arthur Bliss and to whom the Fanfare is dedicated 'with admiration, respect and affection'. Among the other British composers who provided musical birthday greetings were William Alwyn, Lennox Berkeley, Benjamin Britten, Alan Bush, Geoffrey Bush, Arnold Cooke, Elizabeth Maconchy, Edmund Rubbra, Humphrey Searle and Grace Williams.

Popular Birthday for orchestra - composite work (1972)

Commissioned by André Previn and the London Symphony Orchestra and written "for the seventieth birthday of Sir William Walton* O.M., with homage and every expression of friendship" - the other composers were Richard Rodney Bennett, Thea Musgrave, Robert Simpson, Nicholas Maw and Peter Maxwell Davies.

Dur: 1'
Instr: 1+2 picc./2/2/2 - 4/3/3/1 - timp. perc.(2) hp. str.
f.p.   London Symphony Orchestra/Malcolm Arnold - Royal Festival Hall, London,
              28 March 1972 (Walton's 70th Birthday Concert)
f.rec.   London Philharmonic Orchestra/Jan Latham-Koenig - *Chandos ABTD 1602
              (MC), CHAN 9148 (CD)*
also arr. for chamber ensemble
Instr: Fl. Pno. Perc.(2) Vn. Vn. Va. Vc.
f.p.   Nash Ensemble/Marcus Dods - BBC2 Television, 29 March 1972 ('Walton at
              70')

(* the work contains a quotation from Walton's `Popular Song' from **Facade**)

Song of Freedom* for SA chorus and brass band Op.109 (1972)

[1. Prelude (Maureen Parr, Nina Truzka, Susan Selwyn*)
 2. Hymn (Vivienne McClean)
 3. Intermezzo (Diana Henry, Caroline Richardson)
 4. Postlude (John Michael Thompson, Maureen Parr)]

Dur: 19'
Commissioned by and dedicated to the National School Brass Band Association
(NSBBA) in celebration of their 21st anniversary.
f.p.   Netteswell School Band and Choir/Malcolm Arnold - Harlow Sports Centre,
            12 May 1973
f.Lon.p.   Harrow Schools' Girls' Choir/GUS (Footwear) Band/Geoffrey Brand - Royal
            Albert Hall, 6 October 1973 (National Brass Band Championships of Great
            Britain Festival Concert)
f.rec.   above (London) artists - *Decca Sound of Brass SB 313*
Pub: Henrees Music, 1972; Studio Music (vocal score)
(* The words were chosen by the composer from poems on freedom written by children
as part of a nationwide competition sponsored by NSBBA)

The Fair Field Overture for orchestra Op.110 (1972)
Commissioned by Croydon Arts Festival for the tenth anniversary of the opening of the
Fairfield Hall* and dedicated to `William Walton with the greatest esteem and affection' -
the score is dated Dublin, 2 October 1972
Dur: 7'30"
Instr: 2+picc./3/3/3 - 4/3/3/1 - timp. perc.(2) str.
f.p.   Royal Philharmonic Orchestra/Malcolm Arnold - Fairfield Hall, Croydon,
            Surrey, 27 April 1973
f.broad.p. BBC Symphony Orchestra/Malcolm Arnold - BBC Radio 3, 16 March 1977
            (rec. 10 April 1976)
f.recs.   above (first broadcast) performance - *BBC Radio Classics 15656 91817(CD)*
            London Philharmonic Orchestra/Malcolm Arnold - *Reference RR-48 (and CD)*
Pub: Faber/Central Music Library, 1973
(* The Fairfield Halls were built on the site of the old Fair Field in Croydon - the
composer writes that "in [this] overture .... I have attempted to create the atmosphere of a
pastoral fair **field**, with overtones of a **funfair** field, by means of one long theme heard in
various guises [following] the historical events that have taken place [there].")

Concerto No. 2 for flute and chamber orchestra Op.111 (1972)
Written for and dedicated to Richard Adeney - the score is dated Dublin, 8 December
1972
Dur: 14'
Instr: 0/2/0/0 - 2/0/0/0 - str.
f.p.   Richard Adeney/English Chamber Orchestra/Kenneth Sillito - The Maltings,
            Snape, 28 June 1973 (Aldeburgh Festival)
f.Lon.p.   Richard Adeney/English Chamber Orchestra/Wilfried Boettcher - Queen
            Elizabeth Hall, 1 October 1973
f.recs.   John Solum/Philharmonia Orchestra/Neville Dilkes - *HMV ASD 3487 (and
            MC); EMI CDM7 63491-2 (CD)*
            Richard Adeney/Bournemouth Sinfonia/Ronald Thomas - *HMV ASD 3868
            (and MC); EMI Eminence CD-EMX 2271(CD)*
Pub: Faber, 1973 (also arr. flute and piano, 1978)

A Flourish for orchestra Op.112 (1973)
Written to celebrate the 500th anniversary of the Charter of the City of Bristol - the score
is dated Dublin, 11 January 1973

Dur: 3'30"
Instr: 2+picc./2/2/2 - 4/3/3/1 - timp. perc.(3) str.
f.p.   Bournemouth Symphony Orchestra/Rudolph Schwarz - Colston Hall, Bristol,
            26 September 1973
f.Lon.p.   BBC Concert Orchestra/Barry Wordsworth - Queen Elizabeth Hall,
            26 October 1991 (70th Birthday Concert)
f.rec.   BBC Concert Orchestra/Vernon Handley - *Conifer 75605 51298-2(CD)*
Pub: Faber, 1973

Symphony No.7 Op.113 (1973)
[1. Katherine 2. Robert 3. Edward]
Commissioned by the New Philharmonia Trust and dedicated to Arnold's children (each
of the three movements is a musical portrait) - the score is dated Dublin, 9 September
1973
Dur: 45'
Instr: 2+picc.2/2/2+cbsn. - 4/3/3/1 - timp. perc.(3) hp. str.
f.p.   New Philharmonia Orchestra/Malcolm Arnold - Royal Festival Hall, London,
            5 May 1974
f.broad.p. BBC Symphony Orchestra/Malcolm Arnold - Radio 3, 16 March 1977
f.rec.   Royal Philharmonic Orchestra/Vernon Handley - *Conifer MCFC 177 (MC),
            CDCF 177 (CD), 74321 15005-2(CD)*
Pub: Faber, 1974

Fantasy for brass band Op.114a (1973)
[Prelude - Dance - Elegy - Scherzo - Postlude]
Written as the test piece for the 1974 National Brass Band Championships and dedicated
to Tony Giles
Dur: 10'
f.p.   Cory Band/Major H. A. Kenney - Royal Albert Hall, London, 5 October 1974
            (National Brass Band Championships)
f.broad.p. above performance - Radio 3, 21 October 1974 (the composer's 53rd birthday)
f.recs.   above artists - *Decca Sound of Brass SB 319*
            Grimethorpe Colliery Band/Elgar Howarth - *Conifer 76506 16848-2(CD)*
Pub: Henrees Music, 1974; Studio Music

Two John Donne Songs for tenor and piano Op.114b (1974)
[1. The Good-Morrow 2. Woman's Constancy]
Dur: 6'
Dedication: `for Niamh' - the score is dated Dublin, 15 February 1974
f.p.   Ian Partridge (Ten.)/Jennifer Partridge (Pno.) - Bristol University,
            23 June 1977
f.broad.p. above performance - Radio 3, 20 October 1977
f.Lon.p.   above artists - Purcell Room, 28 March 1996
f.rec.   Gavin Cuthbertson (Ten.)/Audrey Hyland (Pno.) - *British Music Society
            Environs ENV 021 (MC)*
Pub: Roberton, 1977

Concerto No.2 for clarinet and chamber orchestra Op.115 (1974)
Written for and dedicated to Benny Goodman `with admiration and affection' - the third

movement is subtitled `The Pre-Goodman Rag' - the score is dated Dublin, 24 April 1974

Dur:	17'30"
Instr:	1+picc./2/0/2 - 2/0/0/0 - timp. perc. str.
f.p.	Benny Goodman/Denver Symphony Orchestra/Brian Priestman - Red Rocks, Denver, Colorado, USA, 17 August 1974 (Red Rocks Music Festival)
f.Brit.p.	Benny Goodman/Park Lane Music Players/Malcolm Arnold - St. John's, Smith Square, London, 11 October 1976 (at a gala concert to support St. John's and the Park Lane Group given in the presence of Princess Margaret)
f.Jap.p.	Kokubunji Philharmonic Orchestra/Seiji Sagawa - Tokyo, 24 November 1996
f.rec.	above (first) performance - *Classic Record Library (USA) 30-5550*
	Michael Collins*/London Musici/Mark Stephenson - *Conifer MCFC 228 (MC), CDCF 228 (CD), 75605 51228-2(CD)*
Pub:	Faber, 1981 (also arr. for clarinet and piano)
	(*with a specially composed cadenza for the first movement by Richard Rodney Bennett - the cadenza was first heard at the `Last Night of the Proms' in September 1993, again played by Michael Collins)

Fantasy on a theme of John Field* for piano and orchestra Op.116 (1975)

Dedicated to John Lill - the score is dated Dublin, 17 March 1975

Dur:	20'
Instr:	2+picc./2/2/2 - 4/3/3/1 - timp. perc.(2) hp. str.
f.p.	John Lill/Royal Philharmonic Orchestra/Lawrence Foster - Royal Festival Hall, London, 26 May 1977
f.broad.p.	Martin Roscoe/BBC Philharmonic Orchestra/Edward Downes - Radio 3, 21 October 1986 (65th Birthday Concert)
f.rec.	John Lill/Royal Philharmonic Orchestra/Vernon Handley - *Conifer CDCF 224 (CD), 74321 16847-2(CD)*
Pub:	Faber, 1975

(* from the `Nocturne in C major' for solo piano)

Railway Fanfare for 6 trumpets (1975)

Commissioned by the British Railways Board in celebration of the 150th anniversary of railways in Britain - the score is dated Dublin, 7 May 1975

Dur:	1'30"
f.p.	at the London Parks Exhibition of Stevenson's `Rocket' in 1975
Pub:	Studio Music, 1986 (as No. 3 of `Four Fanfares')

Fantasy for harp Op.117 (1975)

Dedicated to Osian Ellis

Dur:	11'
f.p.	Osian Ellis - Law Society Hall, London, 27 January 1976
f.broad.p.	Osian Ellis - Radio 3, 8 May 1978 (rec. 11 October 1977)
f.rec.	above (first broadcast) performance - *BBC Radio Classics 15656 91817(CD)*
Pub:	Faber, 1978 (ed. Osian Ellis)

String Quartet No.2 Op.118 (1975)

Dedicated to Hugh Maguire* who was then the first violin in the Allegri Quartet - the score is dated Dublin, 12 August 1975

Dur:	29'

f.p.   Allegri String Quartet - Hugh Maguire (Vn.), David Roth (Vn.), Patrick
            Ireland (Va.), Bruno Schrecker (Vc.) - Dublin Castle, 9 June 1976
f.Brit.p.   Allegri String Quartet - The Maltings, Snape, 12 June 1976 (Aldeburgh
            Festival)
f.broad.p. above (Aldeburgh) performance - Radio 3, 25 January 1980
f.rec.   McCapra Quartet - *Chandos CHAN 9112 (CD)*
Pub: Faber, 1976
(* Maguire, a native of Ireland and, like Arnold, a Dublin resident, is given the
opportunity to display his skills as a Celidh fiddler in the quartet's second movement.)

The Three Musketeers* - incomplete sketches for a ballet (1976)
Written for the Australian Ballet Company
(* one of the dances was used as part of the slow movement of the **Flute Sonata Op. 121**
q.v.)

The Return of Odysseus - Cantata for SATB chorus and orchestra Op.119 (1976)
[Words: Patric Dickinson]
Commissioned by the Schools' Music Association - the score is dated Dublin,
30 March 1976
Dur: 30'
Instr: 2/2/2/2 - 4/3/3/1 - timp. perc.(2) hp. str.
f.p.   Schools' Music Association Choirs/Orchestra of the Royal College of
            Music/Sir David Willcocks - Royal Albert Hall, London, 24 April 1977
Pub: Faber, 1976 (vocal score)

Philharmonic Concerto for orchestra Op.120 (1976)
[1. Intrada 2. Aria 3. Chacony]
Commissioned by the Commercial Union Assurance Company for the London
Philharmonic Orchestra's bi-centennial tour of the USA in 1976 sponsored by Columbia
Artists Management - the score is dated Dublin, 23 May 1976
Dur: 15'
Instr: 2+picc./2+ca./2/2+cbsn. - 4/3/3/1 - timp. perc.(3) hp. str.
f.p.   London Philharmonic Orchestra/Bernard Haitink - Royal Festival Hall,
            London, 31 October 1976
f.Am.p.   above artists - Chicago, 7 November 1976 (N.B. the first New York
            performance took place in Carnegie Hall on 22 November 1976)
f.rec.   BBC Concert Orchestra/Vernon Handley - *Conifer 75605 51298-2(CD)*
Pub: Faber, 1976

Sonata for flute and piano Op.121 (1977)
[I. Allegro II. Andantino III. Maestro con molto]
Commissioned by the Welsh Arts Council and dedicated to James Galway - the score is
dated Dun Loaghaire, 22 January 1977
Dur: 14'
f.p.   James Galway (Fl.)/Anthony Goldstone (Pno.) - New Hall, Cardiff,
            19 March 1977 (Cardiff Festival)
f.broad.p. Richard Adeney (Fl.)/David Johns (Pno.) - Radio 3, 19 October 1981
f.rec.   Judith Pearce (Fl.)/Ian Brown (Pno.) - *Hyperion 66173 (and MC/CD)*
Pub: Faber, 1980

Variations for orchestra on a theme* of Ruth Gipps Op.122 (1977)
Score dated: Dun Laoghaire, 22 June 1977
Dur: 13'
Instr: 1+picc./2/2/2 - 2/2/0/0/ - timp. str.
f.p.   Chanticleer Orchestra/Ruth Gipps - Queen Elizabeth Hall, London,
            22 February 1978
f.rec.   City of London Sinfonia/Richard Hickox - *Chandos CHAN 9509(CD)*
Pub: Faber, 1978
(* from her **Coronation March** of 1953)

Symphony for brass instruments Op.123 (1978)
Written for the Philip Jones Brass Ensemble and dedicated to Philip Jones on his fiftieth
birthday - the score is dated London, 9 March 1978
Dur: 30'
Instr: 4 Tpt. 4Hn. 4 Tbn. Tba.
f.p.   Philip Jones Brass Ensemble/Howard Snell - Cheltenham Town Hall,
            8 July 1979 (Cheltenham Festival)
f.broad.p. above performance - Radio 3, 20 October 1979
f.Lon.p.   Philip Jones Brass Ensemble/Howard Snell - Queen Elizabeth Hall,
            16 March 1980
f.rec.   above artists - *Argo ZRG 906 (and MC); London 430 369-2 (CD)*
Pub: Faber, 1978

Symphony No.8 Op.124 (1978)
Commissioned by the Rustan K. Kermani Foundation in memory of Rustan K. Kermani*
- the score is dated London, 11 November 1978
Dur: 25'
Instr: 2+picc./2/2/2 - 4/3/3/1 - timp. perc.(2) hp. str.
f.p.   Albany Symphony Orchestra/Julius Hegyi - Troy Savings Bank, Music Hall,
            Albany, New York, USA, 5 May 1979
f.Brit.p.   BBC Northern Symphony Orchestra/Sir Charles Groves - Royal Northern
            College of Music, Manchester, 2 October 1981
f.Lon.p.   Young Musicians' Symphony Orchestra/James Blair - St. Johns Smith Square,
            26 November 1982
f.rec.   Royal Philharmonic Orchestra/Vernon Handley - *Conifer MCFC 177 (MC),
            CDCF 177 (CD), 74321 15005-2(CD)*
Pub: Faber, 1981
(* Edmund Rubbra's **Sinfonietta** for strings and George Lloyd's **Eleventh** and **Twelfth**
Symphonies have also been commissioned by this American Foundation q.v.)

Concerto for trumpet and orchestra Op.125 (1982)
Commissioned by the Arts Council of Great Britain in celebration of the 100th
anniversary of the founding of the Royal College of Music in 1883 and written for John
Wilbraham
Dur: 8'
Instr: 2/2/2/2 - 4/2/3/1 - timp. perc.(2) hp. str.
f.p.   John Wallace/Royal College of Music Great Gala Orchestra/Sir Alexander
            Gibson - Royal Albert Hall, London, 30 January 1983

f.rec.   John Wallace/Bournemouth Sinfonietta/Norman del Mar - *EMI EL 270264-1*
          (and MC); CDM7 63491-2 (CD), Eminence CD-EMX 2271(CD)
Pub: Faber, 1982 (also arr. for trumpet and piano)

Four Irish Dances for orchestra Op.126 (1986)

Dedicated to Donald Mitchell, the then Chairman of Faber Music - the score is dated 18
June 1986
Dur: 11'
Instr: 2+picc./2/2/2 - 4/3/3/1 - timp. perc.(2) hp. str.
f.p.   London Philharmonic Orchestra/Malcolm Arnold - Lyrita recording studios
           (see below)
f.pub.p.   Wren Orchestra/Malcolm Arnold - Leeds Castle, Kent, 10 October 1987
           (Leeds Castle Festival)
f.Lon.p.   Wren Orchestra/Malcolm Arnold - Kenwood Bowl, 18 June 1988
f.broad.p. Ulster Orchestra/Simon Jolly - Radio 3, 19 May 1990
f.p.   (as a ballet) Washington Ballet Company - Washington D.C., USA,
           5 February 1996
Choreography: Tom Pimble
f.recs.   Philharmonia Orchestra/Bryden Thomson - *Chandos ABTD 1482 (MC)*,
           CHAN 8867 (CD)
           London Philharmonic Orchestra/Malcolm Arnold - *Lyrita SRCD 201 (CD)*
Pub: Faber, 1986

Fantasy for descant recorder Op.127 (1986)

Commissioned by Wingfield Arts and Music, and dedicated to Michala Petri - the score is
dated 9 June 1986
Dur: 11'
f.p.   Michala Petri - St. Michael's Church, Beccles, 11 July 1987
f.Lon.p.   Catherine Sing - Royal College of Music, 13 May 1992
f.rec.   Michala Petri - *RCA RD 87946 (and CD)*
Pub: Faber, 1986

Symphony No. 9 Op. 128 (1986)

Written for the BBC Philharmonic Orchestra and dedicated to Anthony John Day - the
score is dated 12 August - 5 September 1986
Dur: 52'30"
Instr: 2+picc./2/2/2 - 4/3/3/1 - timp. perc.(2) hp. str.
f.p.   (last movement only) BBC Concert Orchestra/Malcolm Arnold - BBC
           Television, October 1991 (an 'Omnibus' documentary celebrating the
           composer's seventieth birthday and directed by Kriss Rusmanis)*
f.p.   (complete) BBC Philharmonic Orchestra/Sir Charles Groves - Studio 7, BBC
           Manchester, 20 January 1992 (invitation concert for the Friends of the BBC
           Philharmonic Orchestra)
f.Lon.p.   London Festival Orchestra/Ross Pople - Royal Festival Hall, 19 October 1996
           (75th Birthday Concert)
f.Am.p.   Susquehanna Symphony Orchestra/Sheldon Blair - Maryland, 11 March 2000
f.rec.   National Symphony Orchestra of Ireland/Andrew Penny - *Naxos 8.*
           553540(CD) (including an interview between composer and conductor)
Pub: Novello

(* this BBC Music and Arts Production `Malcolm Arnold at 70' was presented by the director at the Royal Academy of Music, London on 18 June 1996 as part of the British and American Film Music Festival)

Three Fantasies for piano Op. 129 (1987)
Dedicated to Eileen Gilroy
Dur: 4´15″
f.rec.   Benjamin Frith - *Koch 3-7162-2(CD)*

Fantasy for cello Op.130 (1987)
Commissioned by and dedicated to Julian Lloyd Webber
Dur: 16'
f.p.   Julian Lloyd Webber - Wigmore Hall, London, 13 December 1987
f.rec.   above artist - *ASV DCA 592 (and MC/CD)*
Pub: Faber, 1988

Little Suite No. 3 for brass band Op. 131 (1987)
Commissioned by Keith Wilson and dedicated to the Brass Band of University College, Salford (previously the Salford College of Technology)
Dur: 10'
f.p.   University College of Salford Brass Band/Roy Newsome - Maxwell Hall, University College, Salford, 4 November 1987(L.S.Lowry Centenary Festival Concert)
Pub: Studio Music, 1988

Brass Quintet No. 2 Op.132 (1987)
Commissioned by the Fine Arts Brass Ensemble with funds provided by the British Reserve Insurance Co. Ltd.
Dur: 8'
Instr: 2 Tpt. Hn. Tbn. Tba.
f.p.   Fine Arts Brass Ensemble - Pittville Pump Room, Cheltenham, 11 July 1988 (Cheltenham Festival)
f.Eur.p.   above artists - Bremen Radio, Germany, 9 October 1988
f.Lon.p.   above artists - Wigmore Hall, 23 January 1989
f.tel.p.   above artists - Central Television, 7 February 1989 (a documentary in the "Contrasts" series directed by Terry Bryan)
Pub: Faber, 1988

Concerto for recorder and chamber orchestra Op.133 (1988)
Commissioned by the English Sinfonia with funds provided by Eastern Arts Association and dedicated to Michala Petri.
Dur: 14'
Instr: 0/2/0/0 - 2/0/0/0 - str.
f.p.   Michala Petri/English Sinfonia/Steuart Bedford - Wingfield College, Thaxted, Essex, 3 June 1988
f.broad.p. Michala Petri/Scottish Chamber Orchestra/Jaime Laredo - Radio 3, 3 March 1990
f.rec.   Michala Petri/English Chamber Orchestra/Okko Kamu - *RCA Red Seal 09026 62543-2(CD), 74321 48020-2(CD)*

Pub: Faber, 1992

Serenade for tenor and string orchestra ('Contrasts') Op. 134 (1988)
[1. Hermit Hoar in Solemn Cell (Samuel Johnson) 2. Then tell me, what is the material world? (William Blake) 3. Saint Jerome in his Study kept a great big cat (Anon) 4. To this world farewell (Chikamatsu Monzaemon) 5. Answer July, where is the bee ....? (Emily Dickinson)
Words chosen by Robert Tear for whom it was written 'with affection and admiration' and in celebration of Tear's 50th birthday - the work is dedicated to Anthony John Day
Dur: 9'
f.p.   Robert Tear/City of London Sinfonia/Richard Hickox - St. Andrew's Hall, Norwich, 11 April 1989
Pub: Novello, 1989

Divertimento (Duo) for two B flat clarinets Op. 135 (1988)
f.rec.   Linda Merrick(playing both parts) - *Serendipity SERCD 0220(CD)*

Concerto for cello and orchestra ('Shakespearean') Op. 136 (1988)
Commissioned by the Royal Philharmonic Society with funds provided by Greater London Arts and dedicated to Julian Lloyd Webber.
Dur: 25'
Instr: 2+picc./2/2/2 - 4/3/3/1 - timp. perc. str.
f.p.   Julian Lloyd Webber/Royal Philharmonic Orchestra/Vernon Handley - Royal Festival Hall, London, 9 March 1989
Pub: Novello, 1989

Wind Octet Op. 137 (1988)
Commissioned by the Manchester Camerata Wind Soloists with financial assistance from North West Arts and dedicated to Janet Hilton.
Dur: 15'
Instr: 2Ob. 2Cl. 2Bsn. 2Hn.
f.p.   Manchester Camerata Wind Soloists/Janet Hilton - Royal Northern College of Music, Manchester, 17 February 1990
f.Lon.p.   above artists - Wigmore Hall, 15 March 1990
f.broad.p. above artists - Radio 3, 15 April 1991
Pub: Novello, 1989

Four Welsh Dances for orchestra Op.138 (1988)
Commissioned by the Hallé Concerts Society with funds provided by Bass North Ltd., and dedicated to Emrys Lloyd-Roberts.
Dur: 10'
Instr: 2+picc./2/2/2 - 4/3/3/1 - timp. perc.(2) hp. str.
f.p.   Hallé Orchestra/Owain Arwel Hughes - Free Trade Hall, Manchester, 19 June 1989
f.rec.   Queensland Philharmonic Orchestra/Andrew Penny - *Naxos 8.553526(CD)*
Pub: Novello, 1989

Flourish for a Battle, for wind band Op. 139 (1989)
Commissioned by the Royal Air Force Benevolent Fund and dedicated to the RAF

Benevolent Fund's 50th anniversary of the Battle of Britain Appeal.

Dur: 10'

f.p.   Royal Air Force Band/Wing Cdr. Barrie Hingley - Royal Festival Hall,
            London, 6 April 1990 (at a concert marking the fiftieth anniversary of the
            Battle of Britain, given in the presence of Her Majesty the Queen and HRH
            the Duke of Edinburgh)

Pub: Novello, 1990

Theme and Variations: Fantasy for recorder and string quartet Op. 140 (1990)

Commissioned for Michala Petri by the Carnegie Hall Corporation in honour of the
Carnegie Hall's Centennial Season and dedicated to Michala Petri.

Dur: 20'

f.p.   Michala Petri/Cavani String Quartet - Weill Recital Hall, Carnegie Hall, New
            York, 15 March 1991

f.Brit.p.   Evelyn Nallen/Lindsay String Quartet - Music Department, Manchester
            University, 15 November 1991

f.Lon.p.   Michala Petri/members of the Academy of St. Martin in the Fields - Barbican
            Hall, London, 11 March 1992

Pub: Novello, 1991

also arr. for recorder and string orchestra by Giles Easterbrook (as Op. 140a)

f.p.   Michala Petri/Guildhall String Ensemble/Robert Salter - Royal Hall,
            Harrogate, Yorkshire, 6 August 1991 (Harrogate Festival)

Pub: Novello

Robert Kett* Overture for orchestra Op. 141 (1990)

Commissioned by the Education Department of the Norfolk County Council.

Dur: 8'

Instr: 2+picc./2/2/2 - 4/3/3/1 - timp. perc.(4) str.

f.p.   Norfolk Youth Orchestra/Simon Halsey - St. Andrew's Hall, Norwich,
            25 July 1990 (Kings Lynn Festival)

f.Lon.p.   Norwich Students' Orchestra - Royal Festival Hall, 13 July 1996

Pub: Novello, 1990

(* Robert Kett, a local tanner and Norfolk landowner, was the leader of the 16th century
rebellion which first blockaded, then took possession of Norwich, in protest against their
eviction from the common land. Kett's Oak, from where the insurgents began their march
to Norwich in 1549, can still be seen near Wymondham [the composer's former home].)

A Manx* Suite for orchestra (Little Suite No. 3) Op. 142 (1990)

Commissioned by Alan Pickard, Music Adviser, Isle of Man Department of Education for
the Manx Youth Orchestra under the patronage of the Isle of Man Bank Ltd. in
celebration of the Bank's 125th anniversary.

Dur: 10'

Instr: 2+picc./2/2/2 + cbsn. - 4/3/3/1 - timp. perc.(2) hp. str.

f.p.   Manx Youth Orchestra/Malcolm Arnold - Villa Marina, Douglas, Isle of Man,
            8 December 1990.

f.rec.   City of London Sinfonia/Richard Hickox - *Chandos CHAN 9509(CD)*

Pub: Novello, 1990

(* A number of Manx tunes are incorporated in the score.)

FILM MUSIC

(i) Documentary Films

Avalanche Patrol - Swiss Avalanche Patrol (1947)
Director: Jack Swain
Music played by: London Symphony Orchestra/John Hollingsworth

Seven R.A.F. Flashes - Cavalier Films (1947)
Music played by: Orchestra/John Hollingsworth

**Charting the Seas - Realist for the Central Office of Information/
Admiralty (1948)**
Director: Harold Lowenstein
Music played by: Orchestra/John Hollingsworth

Two R.A.F. Flashes - Cavalier Films (1948)
Music played by: Orchestra/John Hollingsworth

Gates of Power - Anglo-Scottish Films (1948)
Alt. Title: Stairway to the Sea
Director: Anthony Squires
Music played by: Orchestra/James Walker

Report on Steel - Data Films for the Central Office of Information (1948)
Director: Michael Orrom
Music played by: Orchestra/John Hollingsworth

Mining Review - Data Films for the Central Office of Information (1948)
Director: Michael Orrom
Music played by: Orchestra/Malcolm Arnold

Metropolitan Water Board - World Wide Films (1948)
Alt.Title: Hydrography
Music played by: Orchestra/John Hollingsworth

**Hawick - Queen of the Border - Crown Film Unit for the Central Office of
Information/Board of Trade (1948)**
Music played by: Orchestra/John Hollingsworth

Women in our time - This Modern Age* (1948)
Music played by: London Symphony Orchestra/Muir Mathieson
(*this was the first of many `This Modern Age' productions for which Arnold
provided the music - it is probable that Muir Mathieson conducted them all.)

Cotton - Lancashire's Time for Adventure - This Modern Age (1948)

The Struggle for Oil - This Modern Age (1948)

E.V.Ws. - Data Films for the Central Office of Information (1949)
Director: Michael Orrom
Music played by: Orchestra/John Hollingsworth

This Farming Business - Green Park (1949)
Music played by: Orchestra/John Hollingsworth

The Frasers of Cabot Cove - Green Park (1949)
Alt. title: An Island Story
Director: Humphrey Swingler
Music played by: Orchestra/John Hollingsworth

Drums for a Holiday - Anglo-Scottish Films (1949)
Director: A. R. Taylor
Music played by: Orchestra/James Walker

Terra Incognita - Verity (1949)
Music played by: Orchestra/Malcolm Arnold

The Beautiful County of Ayr - Anglo-Scottish Films (1949)
Music played by: Orchestra/James Walker

Fight for a Fuller Life - This Modern Age (1949)

Trieste: Problem City - This Modern Age (1949)

Dollars and Sense - Crown Film Unit (1949)
Director: Diana Pine
Music played by: Orchestra/John Hollingsworth

When you went away - This Modern Age (1949)

Science in the Orchestra - Realist for the Central Office of Information/Ministry of Education (1950)
This series of three films won First Prize in the Music Section of the Venice International Film Festival in 1951 - they were designed as the scientific counterpart of the 1946 film **Instruments of the orchestra** where the music was provided by Benjamin Britten q.v.
Director: Alex Strasser
Music played by: Orchestra/Muir Mathieson

Oil Review No.5 - Green Park (1950)
Music played by: Orchestra/John Hollingsworth

Fifty Acres - Green Park (1950)
Director: Peter Plaskitt
Music played by: Orchestra/John Hollingsworth

Airways - John Harvel (1950)
Music played by: Orchestra/John Hollingsworth

The Riddle of Japan - This Modern Age (1950)

Where Britain Stands - This Modern Age (1950)

This is Britain - Crown Film Unit for the Central Office of Information/Board of Trade (1950)
Music played by: Orchestra/John Hollingsworth

Let go For'ard - Esso Film Unit for Esso Petroleum (1950)
Music played by: Orchestra/Malcolm Arnold

Alien Orders - Crown Film Unit for the Central Office of Information (1950)
Alt. Title: Malaya
Music played by: Orchestra/John Hollingsworth

Power for All - Wessex Films (1950)
Directors: Graham Wallace and Anthony Squires
Music played by: Orchestra/Malcolm Arnold

Man and Machines - Wessex Films (1950)
Music played by: Orchestra/Malcolm Arnold

The Local Newspaper - Crown Film Unit for Central Office of Information/Foreign, Commonwealth Relations and Colonial Offices (1952)
Music played by: Orchestra/John Hollingsworth

Channel Islands - British Transport Films for British Transport Commission (1952)
Director: Michael Orrom
Music played by: Orchestra/Malcolm Arnold

The Island - Data Films (1952)
Alt. title: Kent Oil Refinery
Directors: Peter Pickering and John Ingram
Music played by: Orchestra/John Hollingsworth

Gilbert and Sullivan - London Films (1953)
Music played by: Orchestra/Sir Malcolm Sargent

Powered Flight: the story of the Century - Shell Film Unit for Shell Petroleum (1953)
Documentary based on original research for the Royal Aeronautical Society by Adrian de Potier
Editor: Ralph Sheldon

Music played by: Orchestra/Malcolm Arnold

Devil on Horseback* - Group Three (1953)
Director: Cyril Frankel
Music played by: Orchestra/Malcolm Arnold
(* The story of Lester Piggot)

The Royal Tour: New Zealand - Associated British Pathé (1954)
Music played by: Orchestra/Muir Mathieson

Welcome the Queen - Associated British Pathé (1954)
Music played by: Orchestra/Muir Mathieson

Roses Tattoo - Anglo-Scottish Pictures (1956)
Music played by: Orchestra/James Walker

Coupe des Alpes - Shell Film Unit for Shell Petroleum (1958)
Director: John Armstrong
Music played by: Orchestra/Malcolm Arnold

North Sea Strike - Gerald Holdsworth Productions (1967)
Director: Don Kelly
Music played by: Orchestra/Malcolm Arnold

(ii) Feature Films

Badger's Green - Highbury Films (1948)
Director: John Irwin
Music played by: Orchestra/Muir Mathieson

Britannia Mews - TCF (1949)
US Title: The Forbidden Street
Director: Jean Negulesco
Music played by: Royal Philharmonic Orchestra/Muir Mathieson

Your Witness - Warner (1949)
US Title: Eye Witness
Director: Robert Montgomery
Music played by: Orchestra/John Hollingsworth

Julius Caesar - Parthian (1949)
Music played by: Philharmonia Orchestra/Malcolm Arnold

Antony and Cleopatra - Parthian (1949)
Music played by: Philharmonia Orchestra/Malcolm Arnold

Up for the Cup* - A.B. & D. Limited (1950)
Director: Jack Raymond

(* Percival Mackay composed most of the music but Malcolm Arnold scored several of the longer sequences)

No Highway - Fox (1950)
US Title: No Highway in the Sky
Director: Henry Koster
Music played by: Orchestra/Marcus Dods

Home to Danger - Lance Comfort (1950)
Director: Terence Fisher
Music played by: Orchestra/Muir Mathieson

Wings of Danger - Exclusive-Lappett (1950)
Director: Terence Fisher
Music played by: London Philharmonic Orchestra/Malcolm Arnold

Home at Seven - London Films (1950)
US Title: Murder on Monday
Director: Ralph Richardson
Music played by: Orchestra/Muir Mathieson

Stolen Face - Exclusive Films (1952)
Director: Terence Fisher
Music played by: Orchestra/Malcolm Arnold

The Holly and the Ivy - London Films (1952)
Director: George More O'Ferrall
Music played by: Royal Philharmonic Orchestra/Muir Mathieson
Excs later arr. for orchestra by Christopher Palmer (see **The Holly and the Ivy Suite**)

The Sound Barrier - London Films (1952)
US Title: Breaking the Sound Barrier
Director: David Lean
Music played by: Royal Philharmonic Orchestra/Muir Mathieson
f.rec.   complete film (V)

Curtain Up - Constellation (1952)
Director: Ralph Smart
Music played by: Orchestra/Muir Mathieson

The Ringer - London Films (1952)
Alt. title: Gaunt Stranger
Director: Guy Hamilton
Music played by: Orchestra/Muir Mathieson

It Started in Paradise - British Film Makers (1952)
Director: Compton Bennett
Music played by: Orchestra/Muir Mathieson with Diana Decker

Exc.   Song: `Young Love - A Question of We'
[Words: Marghanita Laski]
Pub: Paterson, 1952

Four Sided Triangle - Exclusive Films (1952)
Director: Terence Fisher
Music played by: Royal Philharmonic Orchestra/Muir Mathieson

Invitation to the Dance* - MGM (1952)
Written in collaboration with Jacques Ibert
Director and Choreographer: Gene Kelly
Music played by: Orchestra/John Hollingsworth
(* The music was not used. André Previn provided the score when the film
was released.)

The Captain's Paradise (1953)
Director: Anthony Kimmins
Music played by: Orchestra/Muir Mathieson
f.recs.   (exc.) *MGM (USA) SE 4271*
             complete film (V)

Albert R.N. - Dial (1953)
US Title: Break to Freedom
Director: Lewis Gilbert
Music played by: Orchestra/Philip Martel

You Know What Sailors are - Julian Wintle (1953)
Director: Ken Annakin
Music played by: Orchestra/Muir Mathieson
Exc.   Scherzetto arr. for clarinet and orchestra by Christopher Palmer
f.rec.   Thea King (Cl.)/English Chamber Orchestra/Barry Wordsworth -
         Hyperion CDA 66634 (CD)

Hobson's Choice - London Films (1953)
Director: David Lean
Music played by: Royal Philharmonic Orchestra/Muir Mathieson
f.rec.   complete film - *TEVP video cassette TXE 90 0203*
Excs. (i)   Souvenir Selection for piano solo arr. by Tony Fones
       (ii   Hobson's Choice - Theme
       (iii)   The Willie Mossop Theme [Words: Ginette Bozec]
       Pub: Paterson, 1954
Suite from the film arr. for orchestra by Christopher Palmer
[1. Overture and Shoe Ballet 2. Willie and Maggie 3. Wedding Night
 4. Finale]
Dur: 17'
Instr: 2/2/2/2 - 4/2/2/1 - timp. perc.(3) pno.(cel.) hp. str.
f.p.   Royal College of Music Sinfonietta/Neil Thomson - Royal College of
        Music, London, 3 July 1996

f.rec.   London Symphony Orchestra/Richard Hickox - *Chandos ABTD 1600 (MC), CHAN 9100 (CD)*
Pub: Novello
Suite also arr. for brass band by Robin Dewhurst
f.p.   Salford University Brass Band/David King - Peel Hall, Salford University, 8 November 1996
Suite also arr. for piano trio by Leslie Hogan
f.rec.   St. Clair Trio (Detroit) - Emmanuelle Boisvert (Vn.), Marcy Chanteaux (Vc.), Pauline Martin (Pno.) - *Koch 3-7266-2(CD)*

The Sleeping Tiger - Insignia (1954)
Director: Joseph Losey
Music played by: Orchestra/Muir Mathieson

The Beautiful Stranger - Maxwell Setton/John R. Sloan (1954)
US Title: Twist of Fate
Director: David Miller
Music played by: Orchestra/Malcolm Arnold

The Belles of St. Trinian's - London Films (1954)
Director: Frank Launder
Music played by: Orchestra/Malcolm Arnold
f.rec.   complete film (V)
Suite 'Exploits for Orchestra' arr. by Christopher Palmer
Dur: 8'
Instr: 2/12/1 - 0/2/1/1 - perc.(4) pno. str.
Pub: Novello

The Sea shall not have them - Daniel M. Angel (1954)
Director: Lewis Gilbert
Music played by: Orchestra/Muir Mathieson
f.rec.   complete film (V)

The Constant Husband - London Films (1954)
Director: Sidney Gilliat
Music played by: London Philharmonic Orchestra/Muir Mathieson

A Prize of Gold - Warwick (1954)
Director: Mark Robson
Music played by: Orchestra/Muir Mathieson

The Night my Number came up - Ealing (1955)
Director: Leslie Norman
Music played by: London Symphony Orchestra/Muir Mathieson

I am a Camera - Romulus (1955)
Director: Henry Cornelius
Music played by: Orchestra/Muir Mathieson
f.rec.   complete film - *CBS/Fox video cassette* (V)

Value for Money - Group Films (1955)
Director: Ken Annakin
Music played by: Orchestra/Muir Mathieson

The Deep Blue Sea - London Films (1955)
Director: Anatole Litvak
Music played by: Orchestra/Muir Mathieson

The Woman for Joe - Rank (1955)
Director: George More O'Ferrall
Music played by: Orchestra/Muir Mathieson

1984 - Holliday (1955)
Director: Michael Anderson
Music played by: London Symphony Orchestra/Louis Levy
f.rec.   complete film (V)

Port Afrique - David E. Rose (1956)
Director: Rudolph Maté
Music played by: Orchestra/Muir Mathieson

Trapeze - Hecht-Lancaster (1956)
Director: Carol Reed
Music played by: Orchestra/Muir Mathieson
f.recs. soundtrack - *Columbia (USA) CL 870 (m); (excs.) Philips PB 626 (78)*
        complete film (V)

A Hill in Korea - Wessex (1956)
US title: Hell in Korea
Director: Julian Amyes
Music played by: Orchestra/Muir Mathieson

Wicked as They Come - Film Locations (1956)
US title: Portrait in Smoke
Director: Ken Hughes
Music played by: Sinfonia of London/Muir Mathieson

The Barretts of Wimpole Street* (1956)
(*Arnold provided the original score and conducted his own music for this
film. However, Bronislau Kaper's music was eventually used when the film
was released.)

Tiger in the Smoke - Rank (1956)
Director: Roy Baker
Music played by: Orchestra/Malcolm Arnold

Island in the Sun - Twentieth Century Fox (1957)
Director: Robert Rossen
Music played by: Royal Philharmonic Orchestra/Malcolm Arnold

f.recs. (theme) Geoff Hughes Orchestra - *Reader's Digest (set) RDM 23125*
complete film (V)
Exc.   Themes arr. piano solo by Cecil Bolton
Pub: Robbins Music, 1957

Blue Murder at St. Trinian's - Vale (1957)
Director: Frank Launder
Music played by: Orchestra/Malcolm Arnold

The Bridge on the River Kwai - Horizon (1957)
Arnold was awarded a Hollywood Oscar for best music score in 1957 (among
the other nominations were Hugo Friedhofer for `An Affair to Remember' and
Johnny Green for `Raintree Country')
Director: David Lean
Music played by: Royal Philharmonic Orchestra/Malcolm Arnold
f.recs. soundtrack - *Columbia (USA) CL 1100 (m), CS 9426; Philips BBE
12194 (45m), Silva Screen VSD 5213 (CD); Legacy/
Columbia CK 66131-2(CD)*
complete film (V)
Excs.
   (i)   River Kwai Album
          ·Pub: Columbia Pictures Music, New York and Campbell Connelly,
          London, 1958
   (ii)   River Kwai March arr. for piano solo by Robert C. Haring
          Pub: Columbia/Campbell Connelly, 1957
   (iii) River Kwai March arr. for orchestra by G. Green
          Pub: Campbell Connelly
   (iv) River Kwai March arr. for military band by Gilbert Vinter
          Pub: Campbell Connelly
   (v)   River Kwai Patrol arr. for military band by R. Berry

Suite from the film arr. for orchestra by Christopher Palmer
[1. Prelude: The Prison Camp 2. Colonel Bogey (Kenneth Alford)
 3. The Jungle Trek 4. Sunset 5. Finale: The River Kwai March]
Commissioned by the BBC in honour of Arnold's 70th birthday
Dur: 24´
Instr: 3/3/3+E flat cl./2+cbsn. - 4/3/3/1 - timp. perc.(6) pno.(2) hp.(2). str.
f.p.   BBC Concert Orchestra/Barry Wordsworth - Queen Elizabeth Hall,
        London, 26 October 1991 (70th Birthday Concert)
f.Eur.p.National Symphony Orchestra of Ireland - National Concert
        Hall, Dublin, 8 July 1994
f.rec. London Symphony Orchestra/Richard Hickox - *Chandos ABTD 1600
        (MC), CHAN 9100 (CD)*
Pub: Novello

Dunkirk - Ealing (1957)
Director: Leslie Norman
Music played by: Sinfonia of London/Muir Mathieson

The Key - Open Road (1958)
Director: Carol Reed
Music played by: Orchestra/Malcolm Arnold
f.recs. soundtrack - *Columbia (USA) CL 1185 (m)*
        complete film (V)

The Roots of Heaven - Twentieth Century Fox (1958)
Director: John Huston
Music played by: Orchestra/Malcolm Arnold
f.rec.   soundtrack - *Fox (USA) M.3005 (m), S.3005*
Exc.   Overture
Dur: 5′15″
f.conc.p. BBC Concert Orchestra/Carl Davis - Radio 3, 21 March 1995
        ('Fairest Isle' concert series)
f.rec.   Royal Ballet Sinfonia/Gavin Sutherland - ASV WHL 2113(CD)

The Inn of the Sixth Happiness - Twentieth Century Fox (1958)
The film score won an Ivor Novello award
Director: Mark Robson
Music played by: Royal Philharmonic Orchestra/Malcolm Arnold
f.recs. soundtrack - *Fox (USA) M.3011 (m), S.3011; Vega (France)*
        45P 138 (m)
        complete film (V)
Excs.
    (i)   Title Song [Words: Paul Francis Webster]
             Pub: B. Feldman, 1958
    (ii)   Title Song [Swedish Text: Gosta Rybrant]
             Pub: Reuter and Reuter Forlass AB, Stockholm, 1958
    (iii)   Theme arr. for piano solo
             Pub: B. Feldman, 1958
    (iv)   This Old Man (arr. by Cecil Sharp)
             Pub: B. Feldman, 1958
    (v)   This Old Man [Swedish Text: Ninita]
             Pub: Reuter and Reuter Forlass AB, Stockholm, 1958
    (vi)   This Old Man arr. for orchestra
             Pub: B. Feldman, 1958
    (vii)   Children's March arr. for military band
             f.rec. Band of the Grenadier Guards/Lt. Col. Rodney Bashford -
             London (USA) PS 434
    (viii)   Selection arr. for brass band by Edrich Siebert
             Dur: 6'
             Pub: B. Feldman, 1958; Studio Music
Suite from the film arr. for orchestra by Christopher Palmer (c.1993)
[1. The London Prelude 2. Romantic Interlude
 3. Happy Ending (Mountain Crossing - The Children)]
Dur: 14'
Instr: 3/2/3/2 - 4/3/3/1 - timp. perc.(4) pno.(cel.) hp.(2) str.
f.p.   Hampshire County Youth Orchestra - Bryanston School, Blandford,
         Dorset, 11 April 1993

f.prof.p. Bournemouth Symphony Orchestra/Richard Hickox - Wessex
        Hall, Poole, Dorset, 18 September 1993
f.Lon.p. Royal Academy of Music Sinfonia/Ron Goodwin - Duke's
        Hall, Royal Academy of Music, 18 June 1996 (British and American
        Film Music Festival)
f.rec.   London Symphony Orchestra/Richard Hickox - *Chandos ABTD 1600
        (MC), CHAN 9100 (CD)*
Pub: EMI/Novello

The Boy and the Bridge - Xanadu (1959)
Director: Kevin McClory
Music played by: Orchestra/Malcolm Arnold

Solomon and Sheba* - United Artists (1959)
Director: King Vidor
f.recs. soundtrack - *United Artists (USA) UAL 4051 (m), UAS 5051*
        complete film (V) (L)
(* though Mario Nascimbene is credited with the entire score, Malcolm
Arnold wrote the 'Funeral Music' sequence)

Suddenly Last Summer - Horizon (1959)
Director: Joseph L. Mankiewicz
Music played by: Orchestra/Buxton Orr (who collaborated on the score)
f.rec.   complete film (V)

The Angry Silence - Beaver (1960)
Director: Guy Green
Music played by: Orchestra/Malcolm Arnold
f.rec.   complete film (V)

Tunes of Glory - Knightsbridge (1960)
Director: Ronald Neame
Music played by: Orchestra/Malcolm Arnold
f.recs. soundtrack - *United Artists (USA) UAL 4086 (m), UAS 5086*
        complete film (V)
Excs.(i) The Black Bear arr. for piano solo
        Pub: United Artists Music, 1960
    (ii)Tunes of Glory theme [Words: Mel Mandel and Norman Sachs]
        Pub: United Artists Music, London and New York, 1961

The Pure Hell of St. Trinian's - Vale (1960)
Director: Frank Launder
Music played by: Orchestra/Malcolm Arnold

No Love for Johnnie - Five Star (1960)
Director: Ralph Thomas
Music played by: Orchestra/Malcolm Arnold
f.rec.   complete film (V)
Exc.   Theme [Words: Leslie Bricusse]

f.rec.   Gerry Beckles/Johnny Douglas Orchestra - *Oriole 45CB 1606 (45m)*
Pub: Film Music Publishing, 1961

Whistle down the Wind - Allied Film Makers/Beaver (1961)
Director: Bryan Forbes
Music played by: Orchestra/Malcolm Arnold
f.rec.   complete film - *Rank Video Library cassette 0053C*
Excs.
-   (i)   Theme arr. for piano solo
            Pub: Henrees Music, 1961
-   (ii)   Theme arr. for orchestra by Johnny Arthie
            f.rec. The Wayfarers - *Decca F.11370 (45m)*
            Pub: B. Feldman
-   (iii)   March 'We Three Kings of Orient are' arr. piano and orchestra
            (1962)
            Pub: Henrees Music, 1962

Suite from the film arr. for small orchestra by Christopher Palmer (c.1993)
[1. Prelude (Theme) 2. The Three Kings 3. Finale]
Dur: 9'
Instr: 2/1/2/0 - 2/0/0/0 - perc.(2) pno.(cel.) hp. gtr. str.
f.p.   Perth Youth Orchestra - City Hall, Perth, Scotland, 11 April 1993
f.prof.p. London Symphony Orchestra/Richard Hickox - Barbican Hall,
          London, 16 December 1993
f.rec.   London Symphony Orchestra/Richard Hickox - *Chandos ABTD 1600*
          (MC), CHAN 9100 (CD)
Pub: Novello

On the Fiddle - Anglo-Amalgamated (1961)
US title: Operation Snafu (Situation Normal All Fouled Up)
Director: Cyril Frankel
Music played by: Orchestra/Malcolm Arnold
Exc.   Theme arr. for piano solo
Pub: Henrees Music, 1961

The Inspector - Twentieth Century Fox (1962)
US title: Lisa
Director: Philip Dunne
Music played by: Orchestra/Malcolm Arnold
Excs.
-   (i)   Lisa's theme arr. for piano solo
            Pub: Henrees Music, 1962
-   (ii)   Theme arr. for orchestra by K. Papworth
            f.rec. The Wayfarers - *Decca F.11473 (45M)*
            Pub: Henrees Music

The Lion - Twentieth Century Fox (1962)
Director: Jack Cardiff
Music played by: Orchestra/Malcolm Arnold
f.rec.   soundtrack - *London (USA) M.76001; Decca DFE 8507 (45)*

Exc.   Theme arr. for piano solo
Pub: Henrees Music, 1962

Nine Hours to Rama - Twentieth Century Fox/Red Lion (1962)
Director: Mark Robson
Music played by: Orchestra/Malcolm Arnold
f.rec.   soundtrack - *London (USA) M.76002; Decca LK(m)/SKL 4527*
Exc.   Theme arr. for piano solo
Pub: Henrees Music, 1963

Tamahine - Associated British Pictures (1963)
Director: Philip Leacock
Music played by: Orchestra/Malcolm Arnold
Exc.   Theme
Pub: Harms Witmark,, 1963
Exc.   Royal Fireworks Music
f.conc.p. Royal Northern College of Music Wind Ensemble/Clark Rundell -
        RNCM, Manchester, 3 November 1984 (BASWBE Conference)

The Chalk Garden - Quota Rentals (1963)
Director: Ronald Neame
Music played by: Orchestra/Malcolm Arnold
f.rec.   complete film (V)
Exc.   Madrigal [Words: Mark David]
Pub: Henrees Music, 1964
f.recs. The Wayfarers - *Decca F.12339 (45m)*
        Andy Williams/Robert Mersey Orchestra - *CBS BPG 62372*

The Thin Red Line - ACE (1964)
Director: Andrew Marton
Music played by: Orchestra/Malcolm Arnold

The Heroes of Telemark - Benton (1966)
Director: Anthony Mann
Music played by: Orchestra/Malcolm Arnold
f.recs. soundtrack - *Mainstream (USA) 56064 (m), S.6064*
        complete film - *Rank Video Library Cassette 0068C (V)*
Excs.   Anna (Love Theme) and Main Title arr. for piano solo
Pub: Screen Gems - Columbia Pictures Music, New York, 1966

Sky West and Crooked - John Mills (1966)
US title: Gypsy Girl
Director: John Mills
Music played by: Orchestra/Malcolm Arnold
f.rec.   complete film - *Rank Video Library cassette (V)*
Exc.   Theme arr. for piano solo
f.rec.   The Wayfarers - *Decca F.12339 (45m), DFE 8655*
Pub: Henrees Music, 1966

The Great St. Trinian's Train Robbery - Frank Launder and Sidney Gilliat (1966)
Directors: Frank Launder and Sidney Gilliat
Music played by: Orchestra/Malcolm Arnold
f.rec.   complete film (V)

Africa Texas Style - Vantors (1966)
US Title: Cowboy in Africa
Director: Andrew Marton
Music played by: Orchestra/Malcolm Arnold
f.rec.   complete film - *Guild Home video cassette (V)*

The Reckoning - Ronald Shedlo (1969)
Alt. Title: A Matter of Honour
Director: Jack Gold
Music played by: Orchestra/Malcolm Arnold
Exc: Souvenir Selection arr. for piano solo
Pub: Screen Gems - Columbia Pictures Music, 1969

The Battle of Britain* - United Artists (1969)
Director: Guy Hamilton
Music played by: Orchestra/Malcolm Arnold and William Walton (for the March)
f.rec.   soundtrack - *United Artists UAS 29019, United Artists ((USA)*
         UAS 5201; Sunset SLS 50407 (and MC)
         complete film (V)
(* Arnold assisted in the orchestration of several sections and was responsible for re-scoring and expanding Walton's original soundtrack when more music was required by the film company - this included the famous "Battle in the Air" sequence.)

David Copperfield - Omnibus/Biography (1969)
Director: Delbert Mann
Music played by: Orchestra/Malcolm Arnold
f.rec.   soundtrack - *GRT (USA) 10008; Label `X' (USA) 10-1601*

The Wildcats of St. Trinian's* - Wildcat Films (1980)
Director: Frank Launder
f.rec.   complete film - *Enterprise Home video cassette 016 (V)*
(* using music composed for earlier St. Trinian's films q.v.)

INCIDENTAL MUSIC

(a)   Radio

Candlemas Night - a fantastic comedy (1955)
[Ernest Reynolds]
Dur: 1'45"

Instr: Picc. 2 Fl. Tpt. Timp. Perc. Hp. Cel.
Music played by: Chamber Ensemble/Lionel Salter (recorded 18 November 1955)
f.p. BBC Third Programme, 25 December 1955
Producer: Frederick Bradnum
Principals: Vivienne Bennett, Gordon Davies, Freda Jackson, Hamilton Dyce

For Mr. Pye an Island (1957)
[Mervyn Peake (based on incidents from his novel 'Mr. Pye')]
Dur: 60'
Instr: 2 Fl. Cl. Bcl. Tpt. Perc. Hp. Pno. Cel. Db.
Music played by: Chamber Ensemble/Malcolm Arnold
f.p. BBC Home Service, 10 July 1957
Producer: Francis Dillon
Principals: Oliver Burt, Betty Hardy

(b) Television

War in the Air - BBC series (1954)
[1. The Fated Sky (8 November 1954)
 2. Maximum Export (29 November 1954)
 3. Operation Overlord (10 January 1955)]
Written and produced by John Elliot
Instr: 2/1/2/1 - 4/3/3/1 - timp. perc. str.
Music played by: London Symphony Orchestra/Muir Mathieson
Series director: Philip Doreté

Fanfare - ABC titles (1956)
Written for the launch of the ABC Television Network
Dur: 1'30"
Music played by: Orchestra/Muir Mathieson

Royal Prologue - BBC (1957)
[Christopher Hassall]
Commissioned by the BBC
Dur: 31'
Instr: 1/1/2/0 - 1/2/1/0 - timp. perc. hp. pno. str.
Music played by: Trumpeters of the Royal Military School of Music/Royal Philharmonic Orchestra/Malcolm Arnold, with Sir William McKie (organ)
f. trans. 25 December 1957
Producer: Rex Moorfoot

Concert Piece for percussion (1958)
Originally written for BBC Television and dedicated to James Blades - the score is dated 1 June 1958
Dur: 4'30"
Instr: Pno. Timp.(3) Perc.(3)
Pub: Faber, 1984

later arr. for concert use by James Blades as:
Concert Piece for percussion and piano (1961)
f.p. James Blades (Perc.)/Joan Goossens (Pno.) - Grendon Hall, Northants,
     16 December 1961
f.broad.p.above artists - BBC Music Programme, 30 December 1966
f.rec. above artists - *Discourses ABK 13*
Pub: Faber, 1984

Music for You - signature tune for BBC Series (1958)
Dur: 2'30"
Instr: 2 + picc./2/2/2 + cbsn. - 4/3/3/1 - timp. perc. hp. str.
f. trans. 22 March 1959

Parasol - BBC musical (1960)
[Book and Lyrics by Caryl Brahms and Ned Sherrin based on the 'Anatol'
dialogues by Arthur Schnitzler]
Commissioned for BBC Television by Eric Maschwitz, Head of Television
Light Entertainment
Dur: 75'
Music played by: Eric Robinson Orchestra/Marcus Dods
Musical numbers staged by: Alfred Rodrigues
f. trans. 20 March 1960 (pre-recorded 18 March 1960)
Producer: Ned Sherrin
Designer: Clifford Hatts
Costumes: Angela Flanders
Principals: William Hutt, Hy Hazell, Pip Hinton, Peter Sallis, Irene Hamilton,
Moira Redmond
Pub: Feldman, 1961 (vocal selections)

Espionage - ATV series (1963)
f. trans. 5 October 1963
Executive Producer: Herbert Hirschman

Gala Performance - signature tune for BBC series (1963)
Dur: 1'30
Instr: 2/2/2/2 - 4/2/3/1 - timp. perc.(2) hp. gtr. str.
f. trans. - 19 November 1963 (pre-recorded 27 October 1963)
Music played by: Orchestra/Malcolm Arnold

Theme for 'Players' (1965)
Written for John Player Tobacco as an TV advertising theme - it was not used
Dur: 45"
later revised for whistler and piano as:
`Thême pour mon Amis' (1984)
Written at the request of John Amis for performance on the BBC Television
programme `My Music'
Dur: 70"
f.p.   John Amis (whistler)/Steve Race (Pno.) - BBC2 Television, 19
        December 1985 (`My Music' Christmas Programme)

f.rec.   John Amis (whistler)/Penelope Thwaites (Pno.) - *Nimbus NI 5342(CD)*

The First Lady - opening and closing titles for BBC series (1968)
Dur: 2'
Instr: 0/0/0/0 - 0/3/3/1 - perc.(2) cel. hp.(2) + SATB chorus
f. trans. 7 April 1968
Series Producer: David E. Rose

Hard Times - ITV theme music* (1977)
[Charles Dickens]
Instr: 3 Fl. Ca. 2 Hn. 3 Tpt. 3 Tbn. Timp. Perc.
Music played by: Ensemble/Marcus Dods
f.trans. Granada Television, 25 October 1977
(* an arrangement by Marcus Dods of the `Cavatina' from the **Little Suite for brass band Op.93**)

(c) Stage

Music for a Pageant - composite work (1947)
[Scenario: Montagu Slater]
Written to mark the centenary of the Communist Manifesto - Arnold's contribution was a `Factory Scene' in two parts. Among the other composers were Christian Darnton and Bernard Stevens (q.v.).

Purple Dust (1953)
[Sean O'Casey]
Instr: Fl. Hp. Perc. Vn. Vn. Va. Vc.
f.p. Theatre Royal, Glasgow, April 1953
f.Lon.p. Lyceum Theatre, May 1953
Producer: Sam Wanamaker
Principals: Siobhan McKenna, Miles Malleson, Walter Hudd

The Tempest (1954)
[Shakespeare]
Score dated London, 6 April 1954
Instr: Ob. Cl. Tpt. Tbn. Perc. Hp. Timp. Glock. Cel.(Vib)
f.p. Old Vic Theatre, London, 13 April 1954
Music played by: Old Vic Theatre Orchestra/Christopher Whelan
Producer: Robert Helpmann
Costumes and decor: Leslie Hurry
Principals: Michael Hordern, Claire Bloom, Richard Burton, Robert Hardy

Excs.   Three Songs for unison voices and piano
[1. Come unto these yellow sands 2. Full Fathom Five thy
 Father lies 3. Where the bee sucks]
f.conc.p. Choir of Old Buckenham Hall/Gordon Pullin - Old
            Buckenham Hall, Suffolk, 25 May 1996
Pub: Paterson, 1959

Paddy's Nightmare - revue number (1954)
Written for the Laurier Lister entertainment `Joyce Grenfell Requests the Pleasure'
Instr: Cl./Sax. Tpt. Drums Pno. Vn. Va. Vc. Db.
f.Lon.p.* Paddy Stone with the Fortune Theatre Orchestra cond.William Blezard - Fortune Theatre, 2 June 1954
Choreography: Paddy Stone
Decor: Joan and David de Bethel and Peter Rice
(* there had been a pre-London provincial tour taking in Cambridge, Folkstone, Dublin and Bath)

Electra (1955)
[Sophocles trans. E. F. Watling]
Instr: Fl. Perc.
Music played by: Christopher Hyde-Smith (Fl.) and James Wolfenden (Perc.)
f.p. Borough Polytechnic Players - Edric Hall, Borough Polytechnic,
      London, 7 December 1955
Producers: Thomas Vaughan and Donald Bisset
Principals: Thomas Vaughan, Monica Evans, Margaret Davies

ARRANGEMENTS

Three short pieces arr. for solo clarinet (c.1938)
[1. Pardon me pretty baby 2. Georgia 3. I ain't got nobody]

Two Pieces arr. for trumpet, horn and trombone (1943)
[1. Motet: Marie Assumptio 2. Machaut: Double Hoquet]
f.p.   Malcolm Arnold (Tpt.), Dennis Brain (Hn.), George Maxted (Tbn.) - St.
           Peter's Church, Eaton Square, London, 15 August 1943
f.broad.p. cond. Constant Lambert - Third Programme, 1 February 1949

Only a Little Box of Soldiers - music hall song arr. for voice and piano (1948)
[Words: Fred Leigh]

Albeniz: Tango in D from `Espana' Op.165 No.2 arr. orchestra (1953)
Instr: 2/2/2/2 - 4/2/3/0 - timp. perc. hp. str.

Purcell: On the brow of Richmond Hill arr. contralto and string orchestra (1959)
[Words: Tom Durfey]
Written for Pamela Bowden
f.p.   Pamela Bowden/Richmond Community Centre String Orchestra/ Malcolm
           Arnold - Richmond Community Centre Hall, Surrey, 26 March 1959

Christmas Carols arr. guitar, baritone, SATB chorus, brass band and orchestra (1960)
Written for Save the Children Fund
[1. The First Nowell 2. Away in a Manger 3. Good King Wenceslas]
Instr: (max.) 2/2/2/2 - 4/2/3/1 - timp. perc.(2) pno. cel. hp. str.

f.p.   St. Martin-in-the-Fields, Drury Lane, London, 19 December 1960
later arr. for orchestra by Christopher Palmer (see **The Holly and the Ivy Suite**)

Thomas Merritt: Coronation March* arr. for brass band (1967)
Score dated St. Merryn, Cornwall, 17 December 1967
Dur: 5'
f.p.   St. Dennis Silver Band/St. Agnes Silver Band/Malcolm Arnold - Truro
            Cathedral, 16 March 1968
Pub: Henrees Music, 1968; Studio Music
(* composed in 1901 to celebrate the Coronation of H. M. King Edward VII)

Thomas Merritt: Anthems and Carols arr. SATB chorus, brass bands and orchestra (1968)
[1. Carol: `Awake with Joy, Salute the Morn' 2. Carol: `Send out The Light'
3. Anthem: `The Eyes of all wait for Thee' 4. Anthem: `Awake up my glory']
Score dated St. Merryn, Cornwall, 12-17 January 1968
Instr: (max.) 2+picc./2/2/2 - 4/3/3/1 - timp. perc.(3) hp. str.
f.p.   Mixed choirs/Penzance Orchestral Society/Cornwall Symphony Orchestra/St.
            Agnes Silver Band/St. Dennis Silver Band/Malcolm Arnold - Truro Cathedral,
            16 March 1968
f.broad.p. (No. 4) above performance - Radio 3, 17 April 1968

Walton: String Quartet arr. of fourth movement for string orchestra (1971)
f.p.   Academy of St. Martin-in-the-Fields/Neville Marriner - Australia, 2 March
            1972 (Perth Festival)
f.rec.   above artists - *Argo ZRG 711*
Pub: OUP, 1973 (as `Sonata for String Orchestra')

The Holly and the Ivy* - Suite arr. for orchestra by Christopher Palmer (c.1991)
Dur: 6'
Instr: 3/2/2/2 - 4/3/3/1 - timp. per :.(3) pno. cel. hp. str.
f.p.   London Symphony Orchestra/Richard Hickox - Barbican Hall, London, 21
            December 1991
f.rec.   Royal Philharmonic Orchestra/John Scott - *RPO Records CDRPO 7021 (CD)
            (and MC)*
Pub: Novello
(* Subtitled `A Fantasy on Christmas Carols', the music is derived from the soundtrack of
the feature film **The Holly and the Ivy** as well as the carol arrangements Arnold made
for the `Save the Children Fund' in 1960.)

MS LOCATION

The majority of the manuscripts are now held by the Royal College of Music, London
(RCM)
Other locations are:

BL   Symphony No. 2 (1953)
LPO   Flourish for a 21st Birthday (1953). Fanfare for a Festival (1955)

NLS	Tam O'Shanter (1955)
BBC	Fanfare for a Royal Occasion (1956), Commonwealth Christmas Overture (1957), Fantasy Op.106 (1970), Popular Birthday (1972), War in the Air (1954), Candlemas Night (1955), Royal Prologue (1957), Music for You (1959), Parasol (1960), The Turtle Drum (1967), The First Lady (1968)
AH	Horn Concerto No. 2 (1956), A Hoffnung Fanfare (1960), Leonora No. 4 (1961)
RMSM	HRH the Duke of Cambridge (1957), Kingston Fanfare (1959)
JB	Concert Piece (1958)
ROHCG	Rinaldo and Armida (1954), Sweeney Todd (1959)
FFC	Fanfare for a Festival (1961)
CPL	Symphony No. 5 (1961)
NYBBS	Little Suite No. 1 for brass band (1963)
CBSO	Wind Fantasies (1965)
EO'C	Purple Dust (1953)

BIBLIOGRAPHY

Arnold, Malcolm   **Film Music.** Recorded Sound, April 1965

Arnold, Malcolm   **My Early Life.** Music and Musicians, October 1986

Budd, Vincent   **Malcolm Arnold and Jon Lord.** British Music Society Newsletter
            No. 76, December 1997

Burton-Page, Piers   **Arnold at 70.** Musical Times, October 1991

Burton-Page, Piers   **Philharmonic Concerto.** London: Methuen, 1994 [B]

Cole, Hugo   **Malcolm Arnold at 60.** Music and Musicians, October 1981

Cole, Hugo   **Malcolm Arnold: An Introduction to his Music.**
            London: Faber Music, 1989

Craggs, Stewart R.   **Malcolm Arnold: A Bio-Bibliography.** Connecticut: Greenwood
            Press, 1998 [B] [D]

Crankshaw, Geoffrey **Malcolm Arnold at 70.** Musical Opinion, February 1992

Day, Anthony   **Music Master.** The Lady, 15 October 1996

Dunnett, R.   **Malcolm Arnold:Freeman of Northampton.** Musical Opinion,
            March 1990

Fawkes, R.   **Heights and Depths.** Classical Music, 19 October 1991

Goddard, Scott   **Malcolm Arnold.** Canon, April 1962

Goodall, Philip   **Malcolm Arnold Discography.**The Malcolm Arnold Society, February 1999

Greenfield, Edward   **Norfolk Notes.** The Guardian, 7 July 1989

Jolly, James (ed.)   **Arnold at 75 - a birthday tribute to Sir Malcolm Arnold.** General Gramophone Publications, 1996 [D]

Mellor, David   **What about Arnold?** The Spectator, 7 December 1991

Mitchell, Donald   **Malcolm Arnold.** Musical Times, August 1955

Palmer, Christopher   **Malcolm Arnold.** Gramophone, October 1991

Poulton, Alan   **The Music of Malcolm Arnold: A Catalogue.** London: Faber Music, 1986 [B] [D]

Preston, R.   **Light and Shade.** Music and Musicians, April 1989

Ritchie, C.   **A Filmography/Discography of Malcolm Arnold.** Soundtrack No.26, 1986 (with an interview in No.27, 1987)

Schafer, Murray   **Malcolm Arnold** in his 'British Composers in Interview' London Faber & Faber, 1963

Snook, P.   **Peevish Puck of British Music.** Fanfare, Vol.10 No.2, 1986

Stasiak, Christopher   **The Symphonies of Malcolm Arnold.** Tempo No. 161/2, June/September 1987

Stewart, A   **Malcolm Arnold.** Music Teacher, June 1989

Swallow, J.   **Malcolm Arnold at 70.** Instrument No.46, October 1991

Thompson, Kenneth   **Malcolm Arnold.** BASBWE Journal No.3, Autumn 1984

Various   **Tributes** in 65th birthday programme, October 1986

Waugh, A.   **Faithful in his fashion.** Sunday Telegraph Magazine, 17 September 1995

Widdicombe, Gillian   **Arnold at 50.** Financial Times, 18 October 1971

6

Don Banks
(1923–1980)

Trio for flute, violin and cello (1948)

Fantasia (1949)

Duo* for violin and cello (1951-52)
[1. Invention 2. Theme and Variation 3. Finale]
f.p.   members of the English Chamber Music Players - RBA Galleries, London,
           26 February 1952 (LCMC Concert)
f.Eur.p.   Salzburg, 23 June 1952 (ISCM Festival)
f.broad.p. Jan Sedivka (Vn.)/Sela Trau (Vc.) - 4 December 1957
(* Edwin Evans Memorial Prize-Winning work)

Divertimento for flute and string trio (1951-52 rev. 1960)
[1. Pastorale 2. Rondo]
Instr: Fl. Vn. Va. Vc.
f.p.   ICA, London, 29 February 1952
f.broad.p. Wigmore Ensemble - 25 April 1955

Violin Sonata (1951-52)
Dedicated to Matyas Seiber
Dur: 15'
f.p.   Maria Lidka (Vn.)/Margaret Kitchin (Pno.) - Holst Room, Morley College,
           London, 15 February 1953
f.Eur.p.   Haifa, 7 June 1954 (ISCM Festival)
f.rec.   Robert Cooper (Vn.)/Clemens Leske (Pno.) - *Australian Broadcasting
           Corporation O/N 40526*
Pub: Schott, 1954

Four Pieces for orchestra (1953)
Dur: 14'
Instr: 2/2/3/3 - 4/2/3/1 - perc.(2) hp. cel. str.
f.p.   London Philharmonic Orchestra/Sir Adrian Boult - BBC, Third Programme,
           1 June 1954 (ICA/BBC Concert)

f.rec.   Melbourne Symphony Orchestra/Willem van Otterloo - *Australian Broadcasting Corporation RRCS 124A*
Pub: Schott

Five North Country Folk Songs for high voice and piano (1953-54)
[1. Buy Broom Buzzems 2. My Bonny Lad 3. King Arthur's Servants
4. Bonny at Morn 5. O, The Bonny Fisher Lad]
Written for Sophie Wyss
Dur: 8'45"
f.p.   Sophie Wyss (Sop.)/Douglas Gamley (Pno.) - Australia House, London, 19 November 1953
f.broad.p. Sophie Wyss (Sop.)/Clifton Helliwell (Pno.) - 26 April 1954
Pub: Schott, 1957
Later arr. for high voice and string orchestra (1954)
f.p.   Sophie Wyss (Sop.)/Concert Artists String Orchestra/Arthur Dennington - Wigmore Hall, London, 15 September 1954
Pub: Schott

Psalm 70 for soprano and chamber orchestra (1953)

Three Studies for cello and piano (1954)
Written for the Australian cellist, Nelson Cooke
Dur: 7'
f.p.   Nelson Cooke (Vc.)/Colin Kingsley (Pno.) - Recital Room, Royal Festival Hall, London, 10 March 1954
f.broad.p. Christopher Bunting (Vc.)/Peter Wallfisch (Pno.) - 4 January 1956
f.Eur.p. Rome, 12 June 1959 (ISCM Festival)
Pub: Schott, 1954

Three North Country Folk Songs for high voice and piano (1955)
[1. Wrap Up 2. The Oak and the Ash 3. Adam Buckham O]

Pezzo Dramatico for piano (1956)
Written for and dedicated to Margaret Kitchin
Dur: 6'30"
f.p.   Margaret Kitchin - Berne, Switzerland, 1956
Pub: Schott, 1956 (in album of Contemporary British Piano Music)

Episode for chamber ensemble (1958)
Dedicated to `Maestro Scherchen'
Instr: Fl. Cl. Bcl. Vn. Va. Vc. Pno. Perc.

Sonata da camera for chamber ensemble (1961)
Commissioned by the BBC for the 1961 Cheltenham Festival and composed in memory of Banks's teacher, Matyas Seiber (q.v.)
Dur: 15'
Instr:*   Fl. Cl. Bcl. Vn. Va. Vc. Pno. Perc.
f.p.   Virtuoso Ensemble/John Carewe - Cheltenham Town Hall, 6 July 1961 (Cheltenham Festival)

f.rec.   members of the Western Australia Symphony Orchestra/Thomas Mayer -
            Australian Broadcasting Corporation RRCS 385
Pub: Schott
(* the same instrumental ensemble as used in Seiber's `Three Fragments from a Portrait
of the Artist as a Young Man')

Horn Trio (1961-62)
Commissioned by Lord Harewood and the Edinburgh Festival Society
Dur: 15'
Instr: Hn. Vn. Pno.
f.p.   Barry Tuckwell (Hn.)/Brendon Langbein (Vn.)/Maureen Jones (Pno.) -
            Edinburgh, 31 August 1962 (Edinburgh Festival)
f.broad.p. members of the Melos Ensemble - 5 May 1964
f.rec.   Barry Tuckwell (Hn.)/Brendon Langbein (Vn)/Maureen Jones (Pno.) - *Argo
            ZRG 5475*
Pub: Schott, 1962

Elizabethan Miniatures - transcriptions of anonymous Elizabethan melodies (1961)
Dur: 8'
Instr: Fl. Va. da gamba Lute Str.
Alt.Instr: Fl. Vc. Hp. (Gtr.) Str.
f.p.   Sinfonia of London/Douglas Gamley
f.rec.   above artists - *HMV CLP 1571(m), CSD 1444*
Pub: Schott

Equation I for jazz group and chamber ensemble (1963-64)
Commissioned by the Bromsgrove Festival, 1969 and dedicated to Keith and Jill Humble.
Instr: (a) Tpt. Ten.Sax. Gtr. Db. Drums Perc. (b) Vn. Va. Vc. Hp. Perc.
f.p.   John Patrick Jazz Ensemble/John Bradbury String Trio/Ann Griffiths (Hp.) -
            College of Further Education, Bromsgrove, Worcs. 20 April 1969
            (Bromsgrove Festival)
f.broad.p. John Patrick Orchestra/John Patrick - BBC, 18 November 1969
f.Lon.p.   London Contemporary Chamber Players/Roger Norrington - Purcell Room,
            3 December 1973

Three Episodes for flute and piano (1964)
Written for the Australian flautist, Douglas Whittaker
Dur: 10'
f.p.   Douglas Whittaker (Fl.)/Don Banks (Pno.) - Wigmore Hall, London,
            25 October 1965
Pub: Schott, 1967

Divisions for orchestra (1964-65)
Commissioned by the John Feeney Trust
Dur: 16'
Instr: 3/3/3/3 - 4/3/3/1 - timp. perc.(2) str.
f.p.   City of Birmingham Symphony Orchestra/Sir Adrian Boult, Cheltenham
            Town Hall, 12 July 1965 (Cheltenham Festival)

f.rec.   Queensland Symphony Orchestra/Patrick Thomas - *Australian Broadcasting Corporation AC 1008*
Pub: Schott, 1965

Concerto for horn and orchestra (1965)
Commissioned by the Peter Stuyvesant Foundation for the London Symphony Orchestra and specially written for Barry Tuckwell
Dur: 18'
Instr: 3/3/3/3 - 3/3/3/1 - timp. perc.(3) hp. pno. cel. str.
f.p.   Barry Tuckwell/London Symphony Orchestra/Colin Davis - Royal Festival Hall, London, 27 February 1966
f.rec.   Barry Tuckwell/New Philharmonia Orchestra/Norman Del Mar - *Argo ZRG 726*
Pub: Schott, 1968

Settings from Roget for female jazz singer and jazz quartet (1966)
Commissioned by Lord Dynevor for Cleo Laine and John Dankworth
Dur: 12'
Instr: Alto Sax. Pno. Drums Db.
f.p.   Cleo Laine/John Dankworth Quartet - 16 September 1966
f.Lon.p.   Jazz Ensemble/Howard Rees - Purcell Room, 19 December 1969
f.rec.   Cleo Lane/John Dankworth Quartet - *Fontana STL 5483*
Pub: Schott, 1966

Assemblies for orchestra (1966)
Commissioned by and dedicated to the University of Melbourne Conservatorium of Music
Dur: 14'
Instr: 2/2/2/2 - 4/3/3/1 - timp. perc.(3) pno. hp. str.
f.p.   University of Melbourne Conservatorium of Music Orchestra - Melbourne, Australia, 3 December 1966
f.broad.p. Australian Youth Orchestra/John Hopkins - 31 December 1970
f.rec.   Sydney Symphony Orchestra/John Hopkins - *Australian Broadcasting Corporation AC1001*
Pub: Schott, 1966

Sequence for solo cello (1967)
Commissioned by the 66 Group, Cardiff
Dur: 10'
f.p.   George Isaac - Newport, Monmouthshire, 30 November 1967
f.broad.p. Jennifer Ward-Clarke - 9 March 1969
f.recs.   George Isaacs - *Argo ZRG 695*
            Christian Woitowicz - *Australian Broadcasting Corporation AC 1010*
Pub: Schott,1969

Concerto for violin and orchestra (1967-68)
Commissioned by the BBC and dedicated to Wolfgang Marschner
Dur: 25'
Instr: 3/3/3/3 - 4/3/3/1 - timp. perc.(3) hp. pno. (cel.) str.

f.p.   Wolfgang Marschner/BBC Symphony Orchestra/Norman Del Mar - Royal
           Albert Hall, London, 12 August 1968 (Promenade Concert)
f.rec.   Yfrah Neaman/Royal Philharmonic Orchestra/Norman Del Mar -
           Argo ZRG 726
           Leonard Dommett/Melbourne Symphony Orchestra/Patrick Thomas -
           Australian Broadcasting Corporation WRD5/5264
Pub: Schott, 1968, 1973

Tirade: Triptych for mezzo-soprano, piano, harp and percussion (1968)

[Words: Peter Porter]
Written for Keith Humble and his Centre de la Musique
f.p.   Josephine Nendick/Ensemble of the American Centre, Paris/Keith Humble -
           Paris, 16 February 1968
f.broad.p. above artists - 20 September 1968
f.recs.   Marilyn Richardson/Chamber Ensemble - *World Record Club (Australia)*
           record number untraced
           Marilyn Richardson/Chamber Ensemble - *Australian Broadcasting*
           Corporation, record number untraced
Pub: Schott, 1968

Prologue (Prelude), Night Piece and Blues for Two - for clarinet and piano (1968)

f.rec.   Nigel Westlake (Cl.)/David Bollard (Pno.) - *Tall Poppies TP004 (CD)*
Pub: Schott, 1970

Equation II for jazz group and chamber ensemble (1969)

Dedicated to Keith and Jill Humble - the score is dated 8 March 1969.
Instr: a) Tpts. Ten.Sax. Gtr. Db. Drums Perc. (b) Vn. Va. Vc. Hp.
f.p.   John Patrick Jazz Ensemble/John Bradbury String Trio/Ann Griffiths (Hp.) -
           College of Further Education, Bromsgrove, Worcs. 20 April 1969
           (Bromsgrove Festival)
f.broad.p. John Patrick Orchestra/John Patrick - BBC, 18 November 1969
f.Lon.p. London Contemporary Chamber Players/Roger Norrington - Purcell Room,
           3 December 1973
Pub: Schott

Findings Keepings for SATB chorus and instrumental ensemble (1969)

[1. Tomorrow is 2. Injury to Insured
 3. Of 91 men leaving an underground station]
Instr: Db. Elec.Gtr. Drums
f.p.   BBC Chorus/Beller Bell (Elec.Gtr.)/Don Lawson (Drums)/Alan G. Melville -
           BBC, 3 March 1969
Pub: Novello, 1968

Dramatic Music for youth orchestra (1969)

Commissioned by Watney Mann Limited for the 1969 Farnham Festival and dedicated to
the Cheltenham Young People's Orchestra
f.p.   Cheltenham Young People's Orchestra/Michael Burbage - Farnham Grammar
           School Hall, Farnham, Surrey, 10 May 1969 (Farnham Festival)

f.rec.   Queensland Symphony Orchestra/Patrick Thomas - *Australian Broadcasting Corporation AC 1008*

Pub: Schott, 1969

Intersections for electronic sounds and orchestra (1969)

Commissioned by the Triad Trust for Arthur Davison's Children's Concerts

f.p.   London Philharmonic Orchestra/Arthur Davison - January 1970

Pub: Schott, 1970

Fanfare and National Anthem arr. for orchestra (1969-70)

Commissioned by the Australian Music Association for their celebration concert, 1970

f.p.   Royal Philharmonic Orchestra/Charles Mackerras - Royal Festival Hall, London, 13 April 1970

Pub: Schott, 1970

Meeting Place for chamber orchestra, jazz group and two synthesisers (1970)

Commissioned by the London Sinfonietta with the financial support of the Calouste Gulbenkian Foundation

Instr: Six woodwind, Hn. 2 Tpt. Tbn. Perc.(2) String Quintet + Flugel Hn. Tbn. 3 Sax. Rhythm section

f.p.   London Sinfonietta/David Atherton - Queen Elizabeth Hall, London, 15 June 1970

Pub: Schott, 1970

Music for wind band (1971)

Commissioned by the Farnham Festival

f.p.   Farnborough Grammar School Wind Band/Peter Mound - Farnham, Surrey, 13 May 1971 (Farnham Festival)

Pub: Schott, 1971

Nexus for symphony orchestra and jazz quintet (1971)

Commissioned by the Kassel Staatstheater

f.p.   John Dankworth Quintet/Kassel Staatstheater Orchestra - Kassel, 8 April 1971

f.Brit.p.   John Dankworth Quintet/Royal Philharmonic Orchestra/Arthur Davison - Fairfield Hall, Croydon, 27 November 1971

f.rec.   Don Burrows Group/Sydney Symphony Orchestra/John Hopkins - *Australian Broadcasting Corporation RRCS 1465*

Pub: Schott

Commentary for piano and two-track tape (1971)

Commissioned by the English Bach Festival for Paul Crossley

f.p.   Paul Crossley - Oxford, 22 April 1971 (English Bach Festival)

f.Lon.p.   Paul Crossley - St. John's Smith Square, 6 May 1971

Pub: Schott

Three Short Songs for female jazz singer and jazz quartet (1971)

[1. Love is a sickness (Samuel Daniel) 2. Sospira (Anon.)
3. Enjoy thy April now (Samuel Daniel)]

Commissioned by the Cheltenham Festival in association with the Arts Council of Great Britain

Instr: Alto Sax. Pno. Drums Db.
f.p.   Cleo Laine with John Dankworth (Alto Sax.), John Taylor (Pno.), Chris
            Karen (Drums), Ken Baldock (Db.) - Cheltenham Town Hall, 9 July 1971
            (Cheltenham Festival)
Pub: Schott, 1971

Limbo - cantata for three voices, eight instruments and two-track tape (1971)
Commissioned for the John Bishop Memorial Award by the Adelaide Advertiser and University of Adelaide

f.p.   Adelaide Arts Festival - March 1972
f.Brit.p.   Rosemary Hardy (Sop.)/Ian Thompson (Ten.)/Antony Ransome
            (Bs./Bar.)/London Contemporary Chamber Players/Roger Norrington - Purcell
            Room, London, 3 December 1973
Pub: Schott, 1971
Exc. Aria arr. for mezzo-soprano, chamber ensemble and tape (1972)
Instr: Hn. Cl. Vc.
Pub: Schott (also arr. for voice and piano)

Four Pieces for string quartet (1971)
Commissioned by the Music Department, University College of Wales, Cardiff

f.p.   Cardiff University Ensemble - National Museum of Wales, Cardiff,
            10 October 1972 (1?)
f.broad.p. Sydney String Quartet - Harry Curby (Vn.), Dorel Tincu (Vn.), Alexandru
            Todicescu (Va.), Nathan Waks (Vc.) - 6 July 1978
Pub: Schott

Walkabout for children's voices and percussion (1972)
Dedicated "to Gillian Bonham and the Students of Melrose High School, Canberra."

Equation III for chamber ensemble, jazz quartet and sound synthesisers (1972)
Instr: Cl. Hn. Vc. Gtr. Db. Drums Perc.
Pub: Schott

Shadows of Space: 4 track electronic music tape (1972)

Take Eight (Equation IV) for string quartet and jazz quartet (1973)
Commissioned by the Fellowship of Australian Composers with the assistance of the Music Board of the Australian Council for the Arts

Instr: Vn. Vn. Va. Vc. Cl./Sax. Perc. Gtr. Db. Drums
f.p.   Carl Pini Quartet/Don Burrows Quartet - Opera House Music Room, Sydney
            Opera House, Australia, 1 November 1973
Pub: Schott, 1973

Prospects for orchestra (1973-74)
Commissioned by the Australian Broadcasting Commission and the Music Board of the Australian Council for the Arts to mark the opening of the Sydney Opera House

f.p.   Sydney Symphony Orchestra/Willem van Otterloo - Sydney Opera House

f.Brit.p.   above artists - Royal Albert Hall, London, 12 September 1974 (Promenade
             Concert)
f.rec.   Sydney Symphony Orchestra/Willem van Otterloo - *RCA (Australia) record
             number untraced*
Pub: Schott, 1974

String Quartet (1975)
Commissioned by Musica Viva for the Austral Quartet with assistance from the
Australian Council for the Arts
Dur: 20'
f.p.   Austral Quartet - Seymour Centre, Sydney, Australia, 17 October 1975
f.Brit.p.   above artists - Australia House, London, 2 December 1975
Pub: Chester

Carillon: electronic music stereo tape (1975)

4/5/7 - graphic piece for student performers (1976)

Trio (1976)

Benedictus for voices, jazz quartet, five synthesisers, Fender electric piano and tape (1976)

Trilogy for orchestra (1977)
Commissioned by the Adult Education Authority of Tasmania with assistance from the
Music Board of the Australian Council for the Arts
Dur: 26'
Instr: 2/2/2/2 - 4/2/3/0 - timp. perc.(2) pno. hp. str.
f.p.   Tasmanian Symphony Orchestra/Vanco Cavdars - ABC Odeon Theatre,
             Hobart, Tasmania, 18 April 1977
Pub: Chester, 1984

One for Murray - for solo clarinet (1977)
Written for Murray Khoun

4 x 2 x 1* for clarinet and stereo tape (1977-78)
f.broad.p. Murray Khoun, 29 March 1979
(* or Four pieces for two clarinets and one player)

Magician's Castle for stereo tape - computer music (1977)

An Australian Entertainment* (1979)
Commissioned for the King's Singers for their 1979 Australian tour by Musica Viva
Australia with assistance from the Music Board of the Australian Council for the Arts
Dur: 14'
f.p.   King's Singers - Concert Hall, Perth, Australia, 18 April 1979 (Perth Festival)
(* described by the composer as `a kind of potted history' of life in Australia)

Form X - a graphic score for 2 to 10 players (1979)

FILM MUSIC

(i) Documentary Films

> **Alpine Roundabout - Cyril Jenkins (1957)**
> Director: Cyril Jenkins
>
> **Your Petrol Today - Halas & Batchelor for Esso (1958)**
> Director: Ronald Stark
>
> **Professor's Paradise - Cyril Jenkins (1959)**
> Director: Cyril Jenkins
>
> **Kerosene - World Wide Pictures for Shell (1960)**
> Director: P. Hopkinson
>
> **I am a Passenger - Associated British Pathe (1960)**
> Director: Terry Ashwood
>
> **May Wedding - Associated British Pathe (1960)**
> Director: Terry Ashwood
>
> **Michali of Skiathos - Greenpark (1960)**
> Co-wrote with Theodorakis
>
> **Alpine Artists - Cyril Jenkins (1960)**
> Director: Cyril Jenkins
>
> **The Transistor Story - Greenpark (1961)**
>
> **Freedom to Die - Greenpark (1961)**
> Director: Francis Searle
>
> **Postman's Holiday - Cyril Jenkins (1961)**
> Director: Cyril Jenkins
>
> **The Cattle Carters - Greenpark (1961)**
> Director: Derek Williams
> Theme sung by Frank Ifield
>
> **Belgian Assignment - Cyril Jenkins   (1961)**
> Director: Cyril Jenkins
>
> **Commonwealth Story - Halas & Batchelor   (1962)**
>
> **Midnight Sun - Cyril Jenkins (1962)**
> Director: Cyril Jenkins

The Diamond People - World Wide Pictures (1963)
Director: Don Kelly

With General Cargo - World Wide Pictures (1963)
Director: Don Kelly

Britain Today - World Wide Pictures (1964)
Director: Don Kelly

The Prince in the Heather - Holdsworth Productions (1965)
Director: Patrick Filmer-Sankey

Island Boy - Cyril Jenkins (1966)
Director: Cyril Jenkins

The Small Propellor - BP Trading (1966)
Director: John Spencer

Abu Dhabi - World Wide Pictures (1967)
Director: Julian Spiro

(ii) Feature Films

Murder at Site 3 - Eternal (1958)
Director: Francis Searle

The Price of Silence - Eternal (1959)
Director: Geoff Tully

The Treasure of San Teresa * - Associated British Pictures (1959)
Director: Alvin Rakoff
(*Halliwell credits Philip Martell with the music)

Jackpot - Eternal (1960)
Director: Montgomery Tully

The Third Alibi - Eternal (1961)
Director: Montgomery Tully
Theme sung by Cleo Laine

Captain Clegg - Hammer/Universal (1961)
U.S. Title: Night Creatures
Director: Peter Graham Scott

Petticoat Pirates - Associated British Pictures (1963)
Director: David Macdonald
f.rec.   complete film (V)

The Punch and Judy Man - Associated British Pictures (1963)
Co-wrote with Derek Scott
Director: Jeremy Summers
f.rec.   complete film (V)

The Evil of Frankenstein - Hammer/Universal (1963)
Director: Freddie Francis
f.rec.   complete film (V) (L)

Crooks in Cloisters - Associated British Pictures (1963)
Director: Jeremy Summers

Nightmare - Hammer (1963)
Director: Freddie Francis

Hysteria - Hammer/MGM (1964)
Director: Freddie Francis

The Brigand of Kandahar - Hammer (1964)
Director: John Gilling

Rasputin, the Mad Monk - Hammer (1965)
Director: Don Sharp

The Reptiles - Hammer (1966)
Director: John Gilling
f.rec.   complete film (V)

The House at the End of the World - Alta Vista (1966)
Director: Daniel Haler

The Mummy's Shroud - Hammer (1966)
Director: John Gilling

The Frozen Dead - Goldstar (1967)
Director: Herbert J. Leder

Torture Garden - Screen Gems/Columbia (1970)
Co-wrote with James Bernard
Director: Freddie Francis
f.rec.   complete film (V) (L)

(iii)   Animated (Cartoon) films

(a) General Distribution

Posterman - Guild Animation for Shell (1957)

Best Seller - Halas & Batchelor for Shell (1958)
Directors: John Halas and George Singer

The Paying Bay - Halas & Batchelor for Shell (1958)
Director: Gerald Potterton

Follow that Car - Halas & Batchelor for Shell (1959)
Directors: John Halas and George Potterton

Dam the Delta - Halas & Batchelor for the Dutch Government (1960)
Director: Joy Batchelor

Road Safety - Halas & Batchelor for the Central Office of Information (1960)
Director: Joy Batchelor

Colombo Plan - Halas & Batchelor for the Central Office of Information (1961)
Director: Joy Batchelor

(b) Cinema Advertising

Silvikrin - Halas & Batchelor (1957)

Marks & Spencer - Greenpark (1958)

Orion - Halas & Batchelor (1959)

Forhan's Toothpaste - Halas & Batchelor (1960)

INCIDENTAL MUSIC

(a) Radio

Advertising Jingles - Radio Luxembourg (1956)

Hancock's Half Hour - BBC series (1956)
[Ray Galton and Alan Simpson]

The Man who could work Miracles - BBC play (1956)
[H.G.Wells]

(b) Television

(i) Series

The Flying Doctor (39 episodes) - ABC Television (1958-59)

Foo-Foo - Halas & Batchelor (1959-60)

Snip and Snap - Halas & Batchelor (1960)

Habatales -   Halas & Batchelor (1962)

Dimension of Fear (6 episodes) - ABC Television (1962)

Silent Evidence (6 episodes) - BBC Television (1962)

A Boy at War (12 episodes) - Yorkshire Television (1969)

(ii) Plays

Reg Dixon Comedy Series - ATV London (1958)

Saturday Spectacular - ATV London (1958-59)

Cynara - Associated Rediffusion (1959)

Comedy Playhouse (4 episodes) - BBC TV (1962-63)

(iii) Titles

Armchair Theatre - Halas & Batchelor for Associated
Rediffusion (1965)

Scottish Television (ND)

(iv) Commercials (1957-70)
(Composed between for various advertising agencies including J.
Walter Thompson, Doyle and Dane Bernback).

(c) Stage

Dick Whittington - pantomime (1956)
Producer: Emilie Littler

Cinderella - pantomime (1957)
Producer: Emilie Littler

Royal Command Performance (1957)
Written for Geraldo and his orchestra to perform at the London Palladium

Nymphs & Satires - revue (1965)
f.p. New Apollo Theatre, London

(d) Supermarkets

Branston - series of jingles (1957)

(e) Record Library Music (1958-67)
(Many composed for Boosey & Hawkes, Charles Brull and Conroy Records)

MS LOCATION

Majority of MS are located at National Library of Australia, Canberra - **NLA**

Other locations are:

VB   Violin Sonata (1951-52), Five North Country Folk Songs arr. (1953-54), Pezzo Dramatico (1956), Horn Trio (1960-62), Elizabethan Miniatures (1961), Three Episodes (1964), Sequence (1967), Prologue, Night Piece and Blues for Trio (1968), An Australian Entertainment (1979)

BIBLIOGRAPHY

Banks, Don   **Learning with Films** in 'Twenty British Composers' ed. Peter Dickinson. London: Chester Music, 1975

Banks, Don   **The Musician at Work** in 'The Creative Artist at Work' ed. Warren J. Lett. McGraw-Hill Book Company, 1975

Banks, Don   **In Memoriam Matyas Seiber**. Musical Times, September 1970

Banks, Don   **Converging Streams**. Musical Times, June 1970

Callaway, Frank ed.   **Don Banks** in 'Australian compositions in the Twentieth Century', Melbourne: OUP, 1978

Callaway, Frank   **Don Banks - Australian Composer**. AJME No. 11, October 1972

Covell, Roger   **Don Banks** in his 'Australian Music'. Melbourne: Sun Books, 1967

Mann, William   **The Music of Don Banks**. Musical Times, Vol. 59, 1968

McCredie, Andrew   **Don Banks** in 'Catalogue: 46 Australian Composers and selected works'. Australian Government Survey (CAAC), 1969

Murdoch, James   **Don Banks in Australia**. Music Now, Vol. 1, No. 3, 1970.

Murdoch, James   **Don Banks** in his 'Australian Contemporary Composers'. Macmillan, 1972.

Routh, Francis   **Don Banks** in his 'Contemporary British Music'. London: Macdonald, 1972.

7

Stanley Bate
(1911–1959)

Op. Nos. 1-3 and **5-8** not used (may have been allocated to some of the following works)

The Forest Enchanted - opera (1928)
f.p.   Tamaritan Quartette/Stanley Bate - Plymouth

All for the Queen - opera in 3 Acts (1929-30)
[Libretto: Stanley Bate]
f.p.   cond. Stanley Bate - Globe Theatre, Royal Marines Barracks, Plymouth,
              30 November 1931
Producer: W. G. Lennox

Three Winter Pieces for piano Op.4 (early 1930s)
[1. Jack Frost (dedicated to Hazel) 2. Told by the Fireside (To Aileen*)
 3. Snowflakes (To Peggy**)]
Pub: Parker and Smith, Plymouth
(* Aileen Mills, who sang in both of the early operas
 ** Peggy Glanville-Hicks, who later became Bate's first wife)

(2) String Quartet(s) (1933)
With one of these quartets Bate won the W. W. Cobbett Prize at the Royal College of
Music

Symphony No. 1 in E flat (c.1934)
f.p.   Royal College of Music, London, 1936 (Patron's Fund Concert)
(MS later destroyed)

Piano Concerto (c.1934)
f.p.   Stanley Bate(?) - Royal College of Music, London, December 1934 (Patron's
              Fund Concert)

Eros in Piccadilly - ballet (1935)

Overture for orchestra (1936)
f.p.   Royal College of Music, London, 1936 (Patron's Fund Concert)

Two Preludes for chamber orchestra (1936)
f.p.   Chamber Orchestra/Iris Lemare - Ballet Club (Mercury) Theatre, London,
            22 February 1937 (Lemare Concert)

Suite for string orchestra (c.1936)

Piano Concerto No. 1 (1936)
(MS later destroyed)

String Quartet No. 1 (1936)

Goyescas - ballet (1937)
Exc. Goya Dances from the above arr. string quartet and piano

Violin Concerto No. 1 (1936 orch. 1937)
Instr: 2/2/2/2 - 4/2/3/1 - timp. str.

Wind Quintet (c.1936-37)

Piano Sonata (1937)
Score dated 15-18 September 1937

Sonata for flute and piano Op.11 (1937)
Score dated 23 September 1937
Dur: 8'30"
f.p.   probably Marcel Moyse (Fl.)/Louis Moyse (Pno.)
            (recorded in 1938 on two 10" 78rpm discs sponsored by the publishers
            Editions de L'Oiseau Lyre)
Pub: Oiseau-Lyre

Trio for flute, cello and piano Op.9 (1938)
Dur: 7'

Op. 10 (not used)

Sonatina for treble recorder (or flute) and piano Op.12 (1938)
Dedicated to Manuel Jacobs
Dur: 7'
f.p.   Carl Dolmetsch (Rec.)/Joseph Saxby (Pno.) - London, St. John's Wood,
            17 June 1939 (LCMC concert at the home of Sir Robert Mayer)
Pub: Schott

Six Pieces for an infant prodigy for piano Op.13 (c.1938)
Dur: 4'
Pub: Mercury

Four Songs of A. E. Housman for voice and piano Op.51 (1938)

Op. Nos. 14-18 (not used)

Piano Sonatina No. 1 Op.19 No. 1 (c.1939)
Dedicated to Dorothy Jukes
Pub: AMP

Piano Sonatina No. 2 Op.19 No. 2 (c.1941)
Dedicated to Ivy Froome
Pub: AMP

Symphony No. 2 Op.20 (1937-39)
Dur: 30′
Instr: 3/2/2/2 - 4/3/3/1 - perc. str.
Pub: AMP

Concertino for piano and chamber (small) orchestra Op.21 (1937)
Commissioned by the Eastbourne Festival - the score is dated 17 December 1937
Dur: 11′
Instr: 1/2/2/1 - 2/1/0/0 - timp. perc. str.
f.p.   Stanley Bate/Eastbourne Municipal Orchestra/Kneale Kelly - Eastbourne,
          Sussex, 8 February 1938 (Eastbourne Festival)
f.broad.p. Stanley Bate/BBC Symphony Orchestra/Nadia Boulanger - 4 November 1938
Pub: Lengnick

Sinfonietta No. 1 Op.22 (1938)
Dur: 17′30″
Instr: 2/2/2/2 - 4/2/2/0 - perc. str.
f.p.*   California Youth Orchestra/Willem van den Burg - Mills College, Berkeley,
          California, 2 August 1942 (ISCM Festival)
f.Brit.p. BBC Scottish Orchestra/John Hopkins - BBC, 8 January 1952
Pub: Lengnick
(* the work received its first professional performance in Boston and New York
conducted by Serge Koussevitsky)

Seven Pieces for piano (1938)
Dedicated to Surica Maejito
Pub: Schott

Five Pieces for string quartet Op.23 (c.1937)
[1. Moderato 2. Ostinato 3. Romanza 4. Valse 5. Chant]
Dur: 8′

Concertante for piano and string orchestra Op.24 (1936 orch. 1938)
Dur: 24′
f.p.   Lloyd Powell/Riddick String Orchestra/Kathleen Riddick - Aeolian Hall,
          London, 5 June, 1939

f.Austr.p.   Stanley Bate/Sydney Symphony Orchestra/Percy Code - National Programme
             broadcast, 16 November 1940
f.N.Am.p.   Stanley Bate/New York Philharmonic Orchestra/Bruno Walter -
             Carnegie Hall, New York, 30 January 1943
f.S.Am.p.   Stanley Bate/Orquestra Sinfonica do Brazil/Eugen Szenkar -
             Municipal, Rio de Janeiro, 1945
Pub: Schott

Romance (Romanza) and Toccata for piano Op.25 (1941)
Dur: 5′
f.p.   Gyorgy Paxman

Perseus - ballet Op.26 (1939)
Dur: 20′
Instr: Fl. Pno. Vn. Vn. Va. Vc. Db. (or piano solo)
f.p.   Les Trois Arts Ballet Company cond. Emanuel Yourovsky - Lyric Theatre,
             London, 18 November 1939
Choreography: John Regan
Decor: Toni del Renzio
Later arr. as a ballet suite
Instr: 2/2/2/2 - 2/2/2/0 - timp. perc. str.
Pub: Schott

Cap over Mill - ballet Op.27 (1939)
Commissioned by the Arts Theatre Group
Instr: 2 pianos
f.p.   Ballet Rambert - Arts Theatre, London, 8 February 1940
Choreography: Walter Gore
Decor: Nadia Benois
later arr. as a ballet suite
Dur: 12′

Piano Concerto No. 2 in C major Op.28 (1940)
Commissioned by Sir Henry Wood for performance at the 1940 Promenade Concerts
(prevented by the Blitz) and dedicated to Nadia Boulanger and later to the composer's
first wife, Peggy Glanville-Hicks
Dur: 21′
Instr: 2/2/2/2 - 4/3/3/1 - timp. str.
f.p.   Stanley Bate/New York Philharmonic Orchestra/Sir Thomas Beecham -
             Carnegie Hall, New York, 8 February 1942
f.S.Am.p.   Stanley Bate/Orquestra Sinfonico do Brazil/Eugen Szenkar - Municipal,
             Rio de Janeiro, Brazil, 1945
f.Brit.p.   Stanley Bate/Bournemouth Municipal Orchestra/Rudolf Schwarz -
             Bournemouth, 14 December 1950
f.broad.p. Stanley Bate/BBC Symphony Orchestra/Stanford Robinson - Third
             Programme, 1958
Pub: Lengnick

Symphony No. 3 Op.29 (1940)
Dedicated to Sir John Barbirolli
Dur: 28′
Instr: 3/2/2/2 - 4/3/3/1 - perc. str.
f.p.   Hallé Orchestra/Sir John Barbirolli - Cheltenham Town Hall, 14 July 1954
          (Cheltenham Festival)
f.Eur.p. Niedersachsen Orchestra/Stanley Bate(?) - Hanover, 30 October 1954
f.Lon.p. London Symphony Orchestra/Charles Groves - Royal Festival Hall,
          3 April 1955
f.Austr.p. Sydney Symphony Orchestra/Sir Eugene Goossens - Sydney, 1955
f.Am.p.   Oklahoma City Symphony Orchestra/Guy Fraser Harrison - Oklahoma City,
          1955-56 season
Pub: AMP; Lengnick

Piano Sonatina No. 3 Op.30 (1942)
Dedicated to `Terpander' (MS), to Manuel Jacobs (published score)
Pub: AMP; Schott

Piano Sonatina No. 4 Op.31 (1942)
Dedicated to Vera Brodsky
Pub: AMP; Schott

Piano Sonatina No. 5 Op.32 (1942)
Dedicated to Pamela Boden
Pub: AMP; Schott

Piano Sonatina No. 6 Op.33 (1943)
Dedicated to Ray Lev
Pub: AMP; Schott

Piano Sonatina No. 7 Op.34 (c.1943)
f.p.   probably Stanley Bate during a concert tour of Brazil in 1945
Pub: AMP; Schott

Piano Sonatina No. 8 Op.35 (c.1943)
Pub: AMP; Schott

Piano Sonatina No. 9 Op.36 (1943)
Dedicated to Tapia Caballero - the score is dated 22 February 1943
Pub: AMP; Schott

Overture to a Russian War Relief Concert*, for two pianos Op.37 (c.1943)
Dur: 6′
(* also known as `Overture on Russian Red Army Songs')

Three Pieces for two pianos Op.38 (1943)
[1. Prelude 2. Pastorale 3. Rondo]
Written for Ethel Bartlett and Rae Robertson
Dur: 14′

f.broad.p.   Mary and Geraldine Peppin - Third Programme, 24 July 1958
Pub: AMP; Schott

Three Mazurkas for piano Op.38a (1944)

Sinfonietta No. 2 Op.39 (1944)
Dur: 15′
Instr: 3/2/2/2 - 4/3/3/1 - perc. pno. str.
f.p.   National Orchestra Association/Leon Barzin - Carnegie Hall, New York, 1946
f.Brit.p.   Royal Philharmonic Orchestra/John Pritchard - BBC, 13 May 1952 (LCMC
             Concert)
Pub: AMP

Op.40 (not used)

String Quartet No. 2 Op.41 (1942)
Dedicated to Helen Wilson
Dur: 13′30″
f.p.   Lener Quartet - Town Hall, New York, 1943
f.Brit.p.   Hurwitz String Quartet - BBC, 5 June 1950
f.Brit.conc.p. Wang Quartet - Wigmore Hall, London, 14 November 1955
             (SPNM Concert)
f.S.Am.p.   Quarteto de Cordas Municipal -Sao Paulo, Brazil, 31 July 1956
Pub: Lengnick

Violin Concerto No. 2 Op.42 (1943)
Score dated 6 June, 1943
Dur: 30′
f.p.   Nap de Klijn (Vn.) - Hilversum Radio, February 1951
Pub: AMP

Concerto for two pianos and orchestra Op.43 (1943)
Dur: 15'

Suite No. 1 for piano Op.44 (1943)
[1. Praeludium 2. Hymn 3. Rustico 4. Serenade 5. Burlando 6. Promenade
7. Interludium]
Dedicated to Mac Harshbenger
Dur: 23'
f.p.   probably Stanley Bate during a tour of Brazil in 1945

Piano Sonata No. 1 Op.45 (1943)
Dur: 25'

Viola Concerto Op.46 (1944-46)
Dedicated to Ralph Vaughan Williams - `for William Primrose' on short score
Dur: 36'30″
Instr: 2/2/2/2 - 4/3/3/1 - timp. str.
f.p.   Emmanuel Vardi/NBC Symphony Orchestra/Stanley Bate(?) - New York,

15 June 1947 (NBC Coast to Coast broadcast)
Pub: Schott, 1951

Violin Sonata No. 1 in A minor Op.47 (1945)
Dedicated to the composer's second wife, Margarida Guedes Noguiera
Dur: 13'30″
f.p.   Anselmo Zlatopolsky (Vn.)/Stanley Bate (Pno.) - during a concert tour of
        Brazil in 1945
f.Brit.p.   Maria Lidka (Vn.)/Margaret Kitchin (Pno.) - Guildford, May 1950
        (Guildford Festival)
f.Lon.p.   Amsterdam Duo - Nap de Klijn (Vn.), Alice Heksch (Pno.) - RBA Galleries,
        21 November 1950
f.broad.p.   Amsterdam Duo - Third Programme, 1 December 1956
Pub: Lengnick, 1951

Incantations for high voice and orchestra (or piano) Op.48 (c.1947)
[Words: Eugene Jolas 1. Choral 2. Psalm 3. Mater Dolorosa
4. Vinyard (sic.) in the Sun]
Dur: 15'
Instr: 3/2/2/2 - 4/3/3/1 - perc. hp. pno. str.
f.p.   Vienna, late November 1957
Pub: AMP

Pastorale (English Tune) for military band Op.48a (c.1947-48)
Dur: 7'

Dance Variations - ballet Op.49 (1944-46)
Instr: 2/2/2/2 - 4/2/2/0 - timp. perc. pno. str.
Suite from the above:
Dur: 28'
Instr: 2/2/2/2 - 4/3/3/1 - perc. pno. str.
f.p.   BBC Scottish Orchestra/Alexander Gibson - 8 April 1953
Pub: AMP

Haneen* for flute, gong and string orchestra Op.50 (1944)
Commissioned by Gary Owen for the Arabian American Oil Company
Dur: 8'
f.p.   San Francisco Symphony Orchestra/Efrem Kurtz - 7 January 1945
(* Fantasy on an Arabian Theme)

Sonata for oboe and piano Op.52 (1946)
Score dated 29 June 1946
Dur: 8'
f.p.   James MacGillivray (Ob.)/Jaap Spigt (Pno.) - RBA Galleries, London,
        10 April 1951

Recitative for cello and piano Op.52a (1945)
Dur: 4′
f.p.   Mario Camerini (Vc.)/Stanley Bate (Pno.) - during a concert tour of

Brazil in 1945

Nod - song for voice and piano (1946)
[Words: Walter de la Mare]
Score dated 15 December 1946

We'll go no more a-roving - song for voice and piano (1946)
[Words: W. E. Henley]
Score dated December 1946

Highland Fling - ballet Op. 51 (1946)
Commissioned by Georges Balanchine and Lincoln Kirstein
f.p.   New York Ballet Society - Central High School of Needle Trades, New York,
             26 March 1947
Instr: 2/2/2/2 - 4/2/2/0 - timp. perc. pno. str.
Choreography: William Dollar
Scenery and costumes: David Ffolkes
Suite from the above:
Dur: 32′30″
Instr: 2/2/2/2 - 4/3/3/1 - perc. pno. str.
f.Brit.p.   Scottish National Orchestra/Walter Susskind - St. Andrew's Hall,
             Edinburgh, 1951.

Pomes Penyeach: Thirteen Songs to poems of James Joyce for voice and piano
Op.53 (1946)
[1. Tilly 2. On the beach at Fontana 3. A flower given to my daughter
 4. Watching the needleboats at San Sabba 5. Alone 6. Nightpiece
 7. She weeps over Rahoon 8. Tutto è Sciolto 9. In memory of the players at
 midnight 10. Simples 11. Bahnhofstrasse 12. Flood 13. A Prayer]
Dedicated to Joseph Condon Riley
Dur: 26'
Five songs (Nos. 1, 4, 8, 10 and 11) were later published (1951)
Dur: 7'45"
f.broad.p. John Cameron (Bar.)/Frederick Stone (Pno.) - 20 October 1952
Pub: Ricordi, 1951
also arr. for voice and orchestra (1952)

Ballet - unnamed (1946)
Score dated 19 May 1946

Children's Pieces for piano Op.54 (c.1946-47)

Three Songs for voice and piano Op.55 (1946)
[1. Rest from loving and be living (C. Day-Lewis)
 2. Spinning Song (Edith Sitwell) 3. Ecce Puer (James Joyce)]
Score dated November 1946

Fantasy for cello and piano Op.56 (1946-47)
Dur: 6'

Pastorale for viola and piano Op.57 (c.1947)

His Alms - song for voice and piano (1947)
[Words: Robert Herrick]
Score dated September 1947

Violin Concerto No. 3 Op.58 (1947-48 orch.1950)
Dedicated to Yehudi Menuhin
Dur: 31′30″
Instr: 2/2/2/2 - 4/3/3/1 - timp. str.
f.p.   Antonio Brosa/London Symphony Orchestra/Richard Austin - Royal Festival
          Hall, London, 11 June 1953
f.broad.p. Antonio Brosa/BBC Scottish Orchestra/Ian Whyte - 30 September 1953

Piano Sonata No. 2 Op.59 (1947)
Dur: 15′
f.Brit.p.   John Kersey - St. Martin-in-the-Fields, London, 14 August 1998

Troilus and Cressida - ballet Op.60 (1947)
Instr: Fl. Va. Pno. (or Fl. Vn. Vn. Va. Vc. Pno)
f.p.   New York Ballet Society
Producer: Emy St. Just

Three Songs to words by Hilaire Belloc for voice and piano Op.61 (1947-48)
[1. The Birds 2. The Yellow Mustard 3. The Moon's Funeral]
Dedicated to Margot Rebeil - the score is dated 3 January 1948

Two Songs to poems by e. e. cummings for voice and piano (c.1947)
[1. Sonnet 2. Song]

Piano Sonata No. 3 Op.62 (1949)
Dur: 20′
f.p.   New York/Amsterdam - 1949
f.Brit.p.   Mary Guidon - Wigmore Hall, London, 16 December, 1950

Op.63 (not used)

Seventeen Preludes for piano Op.64 (1949)

Violin Sonata No. 2 (1950)
Dur: 14′
f.p.   Emmanuel Vardi (Vn.)/Stanley Bate (Pno.) - Wigmore Hall, London,
          24 November 1950

Op.65 (not used)

Piano Concerto No. 3 Op.66 (1951-52)
Dur: 31′
Instr: 2+picc./2/2/2 - 2/2/2/0 - timp. perc. str.

f.p.   Stanley Bate/BBC Symphony Orchestra/John Hollingsworth - Royal Albert
            Hall, London, 30 August 1957 (Promenade Concert)
f.Am.p.   Stanley Bate/Oklahoma City Symphony Orchestra/Guy Fraser Harrison -
            Oklahoma City, 4 February 1958

Concerto grosso for piano and string orchestra (1952)
Commissioned by Club d'Essai Radiofusion, Paris - the short score is dated 1 April 1952
Dur: 22'
f.p.   Stanley Bate/Paris Radio Orchestra - Paris, June 1952 (Concert held under the
            auspices of UNESCO and Radio Paris)
f.broad.p. Eric Hope - Hilversum Radio, 3 January 1953
f.Brit.p.   Eric Hope/BBC Scottish Orchestra/Ian Whyte - BBC, 13 October 1954
f.Am.p.   Stanley Bate - Carnegie Hall, New York, Autumn 1954
Pub: Lengnick

Concerto for harpsichord and chamber orchestra (1952 orch. 1955)
Dedicated to Yolanda Penteado Matarazzo - the short score is dated 4 October 1952
Dur: 22'
Instr: 1/1/1/1 - 0/0/0/0 - str.
f.p.   Yolanda Penteado Matarazzo
Pub: Lengnick

Six Songs of Stevie Smith for voice and piano (1952)
[1. O happy dogs of England 2. Duty was his lodestar 3. To a dead vole
4. Arabella 5. Parrot 6. The Boat]
Score dated 22 July - 22 October 1952

Suite No. 2 for piano (1952-54)
Dur: 15'

Suite for violin and orchestra (c.1953)

Concerto for cello and orchestra (1953)
Dur: 25'
f.p.   Eastman Rochester Orchestra - Eastman School of Music, New York,
            late 1954

Prelude, Rondo and Toccata for piano (1953)

Opera - unnamed (1954)
Score dated 17 May 1954

Symphony No. 4 (1954-55)
Commissioned by the London Philharmonic Orchestra and dedicated to Reginald
Goodall. The symphony was later re-dedicated to the composer's second wife, Margarida
Guedes Noguiera - the score is dated 7 October 1955.
Dur: 34'
instr: 2/2/2/2 - 4/3/3/1 - perc. hp. str.

f.p.   London Philharmonic Orchestra/Sir Adrian Boult - Royal Festival Hall,
            London, 20 November 1955
f.Can.p.   cond. Sir Ernest MacMillan - Montreal, January 1956
f.Eur.p.   Niedersachsen Orchestra/Stanley Bate(?) - Hanover, 27 November 1957
f.broad.p. BBC Northern Orchestra/Lawrence Leonard - Third Programme,
            2 January 1958
Pub: Lengnick

Piano Concerto No. 4 (c.1957)
Commissioned by Jean Norris and dedicated to Harriet Cohen

Piano Concerto No. 5 (1958)
Score dated 27 October 1958
Instr: 1/1/1/1 - 2/1/0/0 - str.

Ballad of a King's Progress for voice and piano (1958)
[Words: Dorothy Quick]
Dedicated to Margot Rebeil - the score is dated November 1958

UNDATED WORKS

Four Diversions for piano
Written for Jean Norris

Pastorale for piano

March for piano

When I am old and grey and full of tears - song
[Words: W. B. Yeats]
Dedicated to Aileen Mills

DOCUMENTARY FILM MUSIC

The Fifth Year (1944)
Commissioned by the British Library of Information, New York - the short score is dated
10-14 September 1944
Suite from the above:
Dur: 15'
Instr: 1/1/2/1 - 2/3/2/0 - timp. perc. pno. str.

Careers in Oil (c.1944)
(Based on the music **Haneen Op.50** q.v.)

Jean Helion (1946)
Produced by The Museum of Modern Art (New York and the Sorbonne)
Dur: 6'

The Pleasure Garden (1952-53)
Sponsored by the British Film Institute - the score is dated 1 January 1953
Instr: Voice + Fl. Cl. Bsn. Vc. Hpschd.
Producer: James Broughton

Light through the Ages (1953)
Score dated 19 November 1953
Dur: 9'
Instr: 2+picc./2/2/2 - 4/3/3/1 - timp. perc. pno. str.

INCIDENTAL MUSIC

(a)   Television

Children's Television Show No. 1 for reciter and piano (ND)
[1. The Nightingales (arr. Ruby Mercer) 2. The Ugly Duckling]

Television March No. 1 for orchestra (1956)
Short score dated 12 August 1956

Television March No. 2 for orchestra (ND)

(b)   Stage

The White Guard (c.1938)
f.p.   Phoenix Theatre, London

Twelfth Night (c.1938)
[Shakespeare]
f.p.   Phoenix Theatre, London

Bodas de Sangre (c.1938)
[Lorca]
f.p.   Savoy Theatre, London
Suite from the above:
Instr: 2 Tpt. Fl. Pno.

Electra (1938)
[Sophocles]
f.p.   London Theatre Studio
Exc. Prelude for Piano

Juanita - music for Surica Maejito's ballet-mime (1938)
f.p.   London Theatre Studio

The Cherry Orchard (c.1938)
[Chekhov]
f.p.   Phoenix Theatre, London

The Patriots (1944)
[Sidney Kingsley]
Commissioned by the Playwrights' Society
Instr: Fl. Vn. Va. Vc. Perc. Pno.
f.p. National Theatre, New York, 29 January 1944

MS LOCATION

Majority of MS are held in the library of the Royal College of Music, London **(RCM)**

(N.B. The Royal College of Music also hold a number of sketches of incomplete works, including a Symphonia Concertante, a Cello Concerto and three Musical Plays.)

BL   Seven Pieces for Piano (1938), Piano Sonata No. 3 (1942), Twelve Preludes
            for Piano (1949), Four Songs of A. E. Housman (1938).

RP   Sinfonietta No. 1 (1938), Piano Concertino (1937), Piano Concerto No. 3
            (1951-52)

BIBLIOGRAPHY

Barlow, Michael and Robert Barnett.
            Stanley Bate - Forgotten International Composer. Journal of
                the British Music Society. Vol. 13, 1991.

Hodges, Anthony.
            Stanley Bate 1913-1959 . British Music Society Newsletter No. 47,
                September 1990.

8

Arthur Benjamin (1893–1960)

Four pieces for piano solo (1910)

Clarinet Quintet in C minor (1913)

Three Dance-Scherzi for orchestra (c.1915-16)
f.p. (No. 2 only) Bournemouth Muncipal Orchestra/Sir Dan Godfrey - Winter Gardens, Bournemouth, January 1917

Elegiac Rhapsody for orchestra (c.1916)

Sonata in E minor for violin and piano (1918)
Written in Cologne and partly in Karlsruhe while Benjamin was a prisoner of war.
f.p. Royal College of Music, London, 20 March 1919

Rhapsody on Negro Folk Tunes for orchestra (1919)

Three Pieces for violin and piano (1919)
[1. Arabesque 2. Humoresque 3. Carnavalesque]

Three Impressions for mezzo-soprano and string quartet (or piano) (1920)
[Words: William Sharp 1. Hedgerow 2. Calm sea and mist 3. The Wasp]
Pub: Curwen, 1925

String Quartet No. 1 (1921)
A W.W. Cobbett prize winning work

Eight Songs for voice and piano (1922)
[1. Before Dawn (Walter de la Mare) 2. Diaphena (Henry Constable)
 3. Hey Nonny No! (Anon 16th c.) 4. Man and Woman (Peter Antony Motteux)
 5. The Moon (Hugh McCrae) 6. The Mouse (Hugh McCrae)
 7. The Piper (Seumas O'Sullivan)
 8. To Phyllis, milking the flock (William Drummond)]
Pub: Curwen, 1924 (arr. of No. 1 by Gerard Williams for string orchestra)

No. 7 also arr. for voice, flute and piano

The Passer By, for violin, chorus and orchestra (pre 1924)

Five Pieces for cello (pre 1924)

Two Songs for baritone and orchestra (pre 1924)
[Words: John Masefield]

Rhapsody in D for violin, cello and piano (pre 1924)

Scherzo in B minor for clarinet and piano (pre 1924)

Suite of songs for baritone and piano (pre 1924)
[Words: 18th century poems]

Pastoral Fantasy for string quartet (1924)
Dur: 14'30"
Pub: Stainer & Bell, 1924 (Carnegie award winning work - among the other
          compositions which the Carnegie United Kingdom Trust recommended for
          publication were Walton's **Piano Quartet** and Finzi's **Severn Rhapsody** q.v.)

Odds and Ends for piano (1924)

Sonatina in B minor for violin and piano (1924-25)
Dedicated to Millicent Silver
f.rec.   Frederick Grinke (Vn.)/Arthur Benjamin (Pno.) - *Decca LXT 5143(m)*
Pub: OUP, 1924; Boosey & Hawkes

The Gospel Train for accompanied unison chorus (c.1925)
Pub: Curwen, 1925

Three Mystical Songs for unaccompanied chorus (1925)
[1. I see His Blood upon the Rose (Joseph Mary Plunkett)
 2. The Mystery (Ralph Hodgson)
 3. He is the Lonely Greatness (Madeleine Caron Rock)]
Dedicated to Herbert Howells
Dur: 5' 30"
f.recs.   (No. 3) Adelaide Singers/Patrick Thomas - *Australian Broadcasting
          Commission RRCS 1470*
          (complete) City Chamber Choir of London/Stephen Jones - *British Music
          Society BMS 417(CD)*
Pub: OUP, 1926; Boosey & Hawkes, 1956; Banks Music, 1993

Concertino for piano and orchestra (1927)
Commissioned by Schott
Dur: 12'
Instr: 2/2/3/2 - 2/2/0/0 - timp. perc. str.
f.p.   Arthur Benjamin - Dusseldorf, early 1928

f.Brit.p.   Arthur Benjamin/Queen's Hall Orchestra/Sir Henry Wood - Queen's Hall,
             London, 1 September 1928 (Promenade Concert)
f.rec.   Lamar Crowson/London Symphony Orchestra/Arthur Benjamin - *Everest
             LPBR(m) SDBR 3020, EVC 9029(CD); World Record Club (Austr.) SPE 754*
Pub: Schott

Suite for piano (1927)
[1. Prelude 2. Air 3. Tambourin 4. Toccata 5. Epilogue in canon]
Dur: 14'30"
Pub: OUP, 1927; Boosey & Hawkes, 1927 (No.3 only)
f.p.   (as the ballet `Le Cricket'* using movements 1, 4 and 5)
Commissioned by the Ballet Rambert
f.p.   Ballet Rambert - Lyric Theatre, Hammersmith, 20 December 1930
Choreography and Decor: Susan Salaman
Principals: William Chappell, Walter Gore and Anthony Tudor
(* the other composers who contributed `sporting sketches' of `Le Boxing' and `Le Rugby'
were Lord Berners and Francis Poulenc)

Three Little Pieces for piano (1928)
Pub: Boosey & Hawkes, 1929

Light Music - Suite for orchestra (1928, 1933)
[1. March 2. Pastorale 3. Viennese Waltz 4. Introduction and Final Dance]
Dur: 13' 30"
Instr: 2/1/1/1 - 2/2/1/0 - timp. perc. cel. pno. str.
Pub: Boosey & Hawkes, 1934

The Devil Take Her - comic opera in one Act with a Prologue (1931)
[Libretto: Alan Collard, John B. Gordon]
Dur: 50'
Instr: 2/2/2/2 - 4/2/3/1 - timp. perc. str.
f.p.   Royal College of Music Student Orchestra/Sir Thomas Beecham - Royal
             College of Music, London, 1 December 1931
f.pub.p.   cond. Sir Thomas Beecham - Old Vic Theatre, London, 30 November 1932
f.Am.p.   Brander Matthews Hall, Columbia University, New York, 13 February 1941
f.broad.p.   BBC Northern Symphony Orchestra/Bryden Thomson - Third Programme,
             18 June 1967
Producers: Vivian A. Daniels and David Ellis
Pub: Boosey & Hawkes, 1932 (Vocal score)

Violin Concerto (1932)
Dedicated to "William Walton with great admiration"
Dur: 26'
Instr: 2/2/2/2 - 4/2/3/1 - timp. perc. pno. str.
f.p.   Antonio Brosa/BBC Symphony Orchestra/Arthur Benjamin - BBC Studio,
             29 January 1933
f.conc.p.   above artists - Queen's Hall, London, 5 January 1934
Pub: OUP, 1932; Boosey & Hawkes (arr. violin and piano)

Fantasies - Six Educational Pieces for piano (1933)
[1. A Cloudlet - like a silver Swan it sailed 2. A song with a sad Ending
3. Soldiers in the Distance 4. Waltz
5. Silent and soft and slow descends the snow 6. A Gay Study]
f.rec.   L. Demant - *Columbia (Austr.) DO 3271(78)*
Pub: Boosey & Hawkes, 1933, 1935 (Winthrop and Rogers Ed. in two Books)

Prima Donna - comic opera in one Act (1933)
[Libretto: Cedric Cliffe*]
Dur: 65'
Instr: 2/2/2/2 - 4/2/3/1 - timp. perc. cel. pno. str.
f.p.   London Opera Club - Fortune Theatre, London, 23 February 1949
Principals: Douglas Craig, George James, Marion Perilli, Patricia Hughes,
Bruna Maclean, Max Worthley
f.Am.p.   Philadelphia Co-opera, 26 April 1955
f.broad.p. cond. Stanford Robinson - 19 September 1965
Pub: Boosey & Hawkes, 1935 (Vocal score)
(* Son of Frederick Cliffe who was Benjamin's piano teacher at the Royal College of
Music)

Dancing Schoole - Five Pieces for bamboo pipes* (1934)
[1. Sir Foplin's Airs 2. The Charmer 3. Poor Robin's Maggot 4. Nymph Divine
5. The Tattler]
Pub: Lyre-Bird Press, 1934
(* From 'The Dancing Master' - Nos. 2,4 and 5 were later incorporated in the
Cotillon Suite of 1938 q.v.)

Two Trios for pipes (1934)
[1. A Marching Song 2. Paysage Triste]
Pub: Lyre-Bird Press, 1934

Three Greek Poems for TTBB men's chorus (1934)
[Words: trans. R.H. Benson 1. The Flower Girl (Dionysius)
2. On Deck (Theognis) 3. To A Wine Jug (Anon)]
Pub: (No. 3 only) W.H. Rogers, 1957

Heritage - accompanied unison song (1935)
[Words: Arthur Lewis]
Pub: Boosey & Hawkes, 1952

Heritage - Ceremonial March for orchestra (1935)
Dur: 5'
Instr: 2+picc./2/2/2 - 4/3/3/1 - timp. perc. hp. str. (+ optional solo voice and chorus)
f.rec.   New Concert Orchestra/Frederic Curzon - *Boosey & Hawkes 02213(78)*
Pub: Boosey & Hawkes (also arr. military band)

Romantic Fantasy for violin, viola and orchestra (1935)
Dedicated to Arnold Bax*
Dur: 23'

Instr: 2/2/2/2 - 4/2/0/0 - timp. perc.(2) pno. str.
f.p.   Eda Kersey (Vn.)/Bernard Shore (Va.)/Royal Philharmonic Orchestra/Arthur
          Benjamin - Queens Hall, London, 24 March 1938
f.Am.p.   Isidore Cohen (Vn.)/Abraham Skernick (Va.), cond. Thor Johnson - Ephraim,
          Wisconsin, 19 August 1954 (Peninsula Festival)
f.rec.   Jascha Heifetz (Vn.)/William Primrose (Va.)/RCA Orchestra/Izler Solomon
          (rec. 1 October 1956) - *RCA (USA) LSC 2767, RCA RB(m)/SB 6605, RCA(set)
          09026 61778-2 (CD)*
Pub: Boosey & Hawkes, 1956 (arr. violin, viola and piano)
(* Eda Kersey was to later give the first performance of Bax's **Violin Concerto** in 1943)

The Dreaming of the Day - song for voice, oboe and string quartet (1936)

Shepherd's Holiday - song for voice and piano (1936)
[Words: Elinor Wylie]
f.Brit.p. Eleanor Houston (Sop.)/John Wills (Pno.) - Australia House, London,
           29 January 1953 (Australian Music Association Concert)

Let's Go Hiking - Five Pieces for piano (1936)
Pub: Boosey & Hawkes, 1936 (Winthrop Rogers Ed.)

Chinoiserie for piano (1936)
[1. Gavotte 2. Musette]
Pub: Boosey & Hawkes, 1936 (Winthrop Rogers Ed.)

Wind's Work - song for high voice and piano (1936)
[Words: T.Sturge Moore]
Pub: Boosey & Hawkes (Winthrop Rogers Ed.); Thames, 1993

Scherzino for piano (1936)
Dur: 2'30"
f.recs.   Ronald Smith - *Decca F 10101(78)*
          Lamar Crowson - *Lyrita RCS 20(m); Musical Heritage Society (USA)
          MHS 7003*
Pub: Boosey & Hawkes (Winthrop Rogers Ed.)

Pastorale, Arioso and Finale for piano (1936)
Written in Vancouver, Canada - Dedication "a 21st birthday gift for Jack Henderson"
Dur: 14'
f.rec.   Lamar Crowson - *Lyrita RCS 20(m); Musical Heritage Society (USA)
          MHS 7003*
Pub: Boosey & Hawkes, 1943, 1948

Siciliana for piano (1936)
Dedicated to Lance Dossor
Dur: 3'30"
f.p.   Lance Dossor - Aeolian Hall, London, 1937
f.rec.   Lamar Crowson - *Lyrita RCS 20(m); Musical Heritage Society (USA)
          MHS 7003*

Pub: Boosey & Hawkes (Winthrop Rogers Ed.)

Three Partsongs for two voices and piano (1937)
[Words: Kate Greenaway 1. Bell Song 2. Margery Brown 3. Prince Finnikin]
Pub: Boosey & Hawkes (Winthrop Rogers Ed.)

Three New Fantasies for piano (1937)
[1. Dance at Dawn 2. March 3. Drifting]
Pub: Boosey & Hawkes,1938 (Winthrop Rogers Ed.)

Four Pieces for piano (1937)
[1. Forest Peace 2. Haunted House 3. Rainy Day 4. Squirrel's Parade]
Pub: Boosey & Hawkes (Winthrop Rogers Ed.)

Nightingale Lane for three voices (SSA) and piano (1937)
[Words: William Sharp]
Dur: 2'45"
Pub: W.H. Rogers, 1939

Overture to an Italian comedy* for orchestra (1937)
Dedicated to Muir Mathieson
Dur: 6'
Instr: 2/2/2/2 - 4/2/3/0 - timp. perc. hp. pno. str.
Alt.Instr: 2/2/2/2 - 2/2/0/0 - timp. perc. hp. pno. str.
f.p.   Queen's Hall Orchestra/Sir Henry Wood - Queen's Hall, London,
           2 March 1937
f.recs.   Chicago Symphony Orchestra/Frederick Stock - *Victor (USA) 11-8157(78),*
           Camden CAL 162(m); Biddulph WHL 016(CD)
           Royal Philharmonic Orchestra/Myer Fredman - *Lyrita SRCS 47, Musical*
           Heritage Society (USA) MHS 1750
Pub: Boosey & Hawkes, 1938
(* Used as the overture to `Prima Donna')

Tune and Variations for Little People for violin and piano (1937)

Two Jamaican Pieces for orchestra (1938)
[1. Jamaican Song - Dur: 2'30" 2. Jamaican Rumba - Dur: 2']
Instr: 1/1/1/1 - 2/1/0/0 - str.
Alt.Instr: 1/1/2/1 - 2/1/0/0 - timp. perc. glock. xyl. pno. str. (1/1/1/1)
f.p.   BBC Symphony Orchestra/Joseph Lewis - studio performance,
           31 October 1938
f.Am.p.   (No. 2) WOR Radio Orchestra/Alfred Wallenstein - New York,
           21 January 1942
f.recs.   (No. 2) Los Angeles Symphony Orchestra/Alfred Wallenstein - *Victor (USA)*
           23480(78)
           London Symphony Orchestra/Muir Mathieson - *Decca K 1571(78); London*
           (USA) T 5053(78)
           RTE Concert Orchestra/Ernest Tomlinson - *Marco Polo 8.22352-2(CD); (No.*
           2) 8.55315-2(CD) (and MC)

Pub: Boosey & Hawkes, 1942 (No. 2 also published in an arrangement by the
            composer for string orchestra, 1945)
No. 2 Jamaican Rumba also arr. for two pianos
Written for Joan and Valerie Trimble
Dur: 2'
f.p.   Joan and Valerie Trimble
f.recs.   Rawicz and Landauer - *Columbia DB 2361(78)*
            Cyril Smith and Phyllis Sellick - *Columbia DX 1555(78)*
            Richard McMahon and Martin Jones - *Pianissimo PP 11192(CD)*
Pub: Boosey & Hawkes
also arr. piano duet by Joan Trimble
Pub: Boosey & Hawkes
also arr. piano solo by the composer
Pub: Boosey & Hawkes, 1945
also arr. two pianos (3 hands) by White
f.rec.   Cyril Smith and Phyllis Sellick - *EMI MOM 130(MC)*
Jamaican Rumba (other arrs.)
(i)   Voice and rhythm band
            Instr: 1/0/2 a.sax+2 ten.sax/0 - 0/3/2/0 - dm. gtr. vn. db.
            Pub: Boosey & Hawkes
(ii)   Solo viola (or violin) and orchestra
            (arr. by William Primrose, orch. by H. Carr)
            Instr: 1/1/2/1 - 2/1/0/0 - timp. perc. pno. str.
            f.p. Jascha Heifetz/CBS Orchestra/Donald Voorhees - 29 January 1945
            f.rec. Isaac Stern/Columbia Symphony Orchestra/Milton Katims - *Sony
                    45816 (CD) (and MC)*
            Pub: Boosey & Hawkes, 1944
(iii)   Harmonica and orchestra
            f.rec. Larry Adler/Pro Arte Orchestra/Eric Robinson - *EMI 7 64134-2 (CD)
                    (and MC)*
(iv)   Orchestra (arr. Neil Richardson)
            Instr: 1/1/2+4 sax/1 - 2/3/3/0 - timp. perc. str.
            Pub: Boosey & Hawkes
(v)   Violin (or viola) and piano (arr. by William Primrose)
            f.p.   William Primrose (Va.)/Vladimir Sokoloff (Pno.)
            f.rec. above artists - *Victor (USA) 11-8947(78)*
                    Jascha Heifetz (Vn.)/M. Kaye (Pno.) - *Brunswick (USA) DL 9760(78),
                    LAT 8066(m), AXL 2017(m); RCA (set) 09026 61778-2(CD)*
            Pub: Boosey & Hawkes
(vi)   Clarinet and piano (arr. Reginald Kell)
            f.rec. Emma Johnson (Cl.)/Julius Drake (Pno.) - *ASVCD DCA 8000 (CD)
                    (and MC)*
(vii)   Wind band (arr. Philip J. Lang)
            Pub: Boosey & Hawkes
(viii)   Piano Trio
            f.rec. Compinsky Trio - *Alco (set) (USA) A1(78)*
(ix)   Flute and orchestra
            f.rec. James Galway/Sydney Symphony Orchestra/David Measham - *RCA
                    09026 60917-2 (CD) (and MC)*

(x)   Cello band
           f.rec.   Cologne Philharmonic Cellos - *Schwann 311522(CD)*

Sonatina for cello and piano (1938)
[[1. Preamble 2. Minuet 3. March]
Dur: 11'30"
Pub: Boosey & Hawkes, 1939

Fanfare for a Festive Occasion (1938)*
Instr: 0/0/0/0 - 0/5/3/0
f.recs.   Trumpeters of the Royal Military School of Music, Kneller Hall/ George
           Roberts - *HMV B 9616(78)*
           Locke Brass Consort/James Stobart - *RCA RL 25081; Chandos CHAN
           6573(CD)*
(*Played at the wedding of Princess Elizabeth in November 1947)

Cotillon Suite of English Dance Tunes* for orchestra (1938)
[1. Lord Hereford's Delight 2. Daphne's Delight 3. Marlborough's Victory
4. Love's Triumph 5. Jigg it e foot 6. The Charmer 7. Nymph Divine
8. The Tatler 9. Argyle]
Dur: 11'
Instr: 3/2/2/2 - 4/2/3/1 - timp. perc.(2) hp. str. (2/2/2/2)
f.p.   BBC Symphony Orchestra/Clarence Raybould - studio performance,
           3 February 1939
f.recs.   London Symphony Orchestra/Nicholas Braithwaite - *Lyrita SRCS 115*
           Sydney Symphony Orchestra/John Hopkins - *Australian Broadcasting
           Commission AC 1001*
           London `Pops' Orchestra/Frederick Fennell - *Mercury SR 90440, 434
           356-2MM (CD)*
Pub: Boosey & Hawkes
(* Based on original melodies in `The Dancing Master' pub. London, 1719)

Sonatina for chamber orchestra (1940)
Dur: 11'
Instr: 1+picc./1/1/0 - 0/0/0/0 - perc. hp. (or pno.) str.
Pub: Boosey & Hawkes

Prelude to Holiday: Rondo for orchestra (1940)
Written at the request of Fabien Sebitzky
Dur: 11'
Instr: 2+picc./2/2/2 - 4/2/3/1 - timp. perc.(3) hp. cel. str.
f.p.   Indianapolis Symphony Orchestra/Fabien Sebitzky - Indianapolis,
           17 January 1941
f.Brit.p. BBC Symphony Orchestra/Sir Henry Wood - Royal Albert Hall, London,
           6 August 1942 (Promenade Concert)
Pub: Boosey & Hawkes

Sir Christemas for baritone and SATB chorus (1941)
[Words: Trad.]

Dur: 3'
f.Brit.p. Choir/Ernest Read - Royal Albert Hall, London, 16 December 1954
Pub: W.H. Rogers, 1943

Two Partsongs for SATB chorus (1942)
[Words: David MacGaughie 1. Dirge 2. Spring]
Pub: Boosey & Hawkes, 1942

Symphony No. 1 (1944-45)
Dedicated to Ralph Vaughan Williams
Dur: 41'
Instr: 3/2+ca./2/2+cbsn. - 4/3/3/1 - timp. perc. hp. cel. pno. str.
f.p.   Hallé Orchestra/Sir John Barbirolli - Cheltenham Town Hall, 30 June 1948
           (Cheltenham Festival)
f.Lon.p.   BBC Symphony Orchestra/Arthur Benjamin - Royal Albert Hall,
           6 August 1954 (Promenade Concert)
f.recs.   Queensland Symphony Orchestra/Christopher Lyndon-Gee - *Marco Polo
           8.223764(CD)*
           London Philharmonic Orchestra/Barry Wordsworth - *Lyrita (announced)*
Pub: Boosey & Hawkes, 1945

From San Domingo for orchestra (1945)
Dur: 3′
Instr: 1/1/2+ten.sax./1 - 2/1/0/0 - timp. perc. pno. str.
f.recs.   New Concert Orchestra/Frederic Curzon - *Boosey & Hawkes 02093(78)*
           Cleveland `Pops' Orchestra/Louis Lane - *Columbia 33CX 1702(m), SAX 3545*
Pub: Boosey & Hawkes, 1945
also arr. for violin (or viola) and piano
f.rec.   William Primrose (Va.)/Vladimir Sokoloff (Pno.) - *Victor (USA) 11-8947(78)*
also arr. for two pianos
f.recs.   A. Young/M. Macleod - *T A 11103(78)*
           Richard McMahon/Martin Jones - *Oriana ONA 0003; Pianissimo PP
           11192(CD)*

Red River Jig for orchestra (1945)
Dur: 2'30"
Instr: 2+picc./2/2/2 - 4/3/3/1 - timp. perc. pno. str.
Alt.Instr: 1+picc./2/2/2 - 2/2/1/0 - timp. perc. pno. str.
f.p. cond. Michael Piastro - New York, 1946
f.SA.p.   S.A.B.C. Symphony Orchestra/Averil Coleridge-Taylor - Cape Town,
           June 1952
f.rec.   New Concert Orchestra/Stanford Robinson - *Boosey & Hawkes 02147 (78)*
Pub: Boosey & Hawkes, 1947

Sonata in E minor for viola and piano (1945)
[1. Elegy 2. Waltz 3. Toccata]
Written for William Primrose
Dur: 17'
f.p.   William Primrose - Vancouver, Canada, 1945

f.Brit.p.   Frederick Riddle (Va.)/Arthur Benjamin (Pno,) - Wigmore Hall, London,
             9 October 1946 (Boosey & Hawkes Concert)
f.rec.   William Primrose (Va.)/Vladimir Sokoloff (Pno.) - *Victor (USA)*
             11-9210/1(78); Pearl GEMMCD 9253 (CD)
Pub: Boosey & Hawkes, 1947
also arr. for viola and orchestra as `Elegy, Waltz and Toccata' (1945)
Instr: 2/2/2/2 -4/2/3/1 - timp. perc.(3) hp. pno. str.
f.p.   Frederick Riddle/Hallé Orchestra/Sir John Barbirolli - Cheltenham Town Hall,
             28 June 1949 (Cheltenham Festival)
Pub: Boosey & Hawkes, 1947

Caribbean Dance `A New Jamaican Rumba' for orchestra (1946)
Dur: 2'30"
Instr: 2/1/2/1 - 2/2/1/0 - timp. perc.(2/3) cel. pno. str.
f.rec.   New Concert Orchestra/Frederick Curzon - *Boosey & Hawkes 02093(78)*
Pub: Boosey & Hawkes, 1949
Later arr. for two pianos at the request of Joan and Valerie Trimble
f.p.   Joan and Valerie Trimble - London, November 1947
f.recs.   Phyllis Sellick and Cyril Smith - *Columbia DB 2558(78)*
             Richard McMahon and Martin Jones - *Pianissimo PP 11192(CD)*

Ballade for string orchestra (1947)
Written for the Boyd Neel String Orchestra
Dur: 12'
f.p.   Boyd Neel String Orchestra/Boyd Neel - BBC Third Programme,
             6 February 1948
f.conc.p.   above artists - Wigmore Hall, London, 23 June 1951 (Festival of Britain
             Concert)
f.rec.   Queensland Symphony Orchestra/Christopher Lyndon-Gee - *Marco Polo
             8.223764(CD)*
Pub: Boosey & Hawkes, 1951

Waltz and Hyde Park Galop - from the film `An Ideal Husband' (1947)
Dur: 8'
Instr: 2/2/2/2 - 4/3/3/1 - timp. perc. hp. str.
f.rec.   National Philharmonic Orchestra/Bernard Herrmann - *Decca Phase Four PFS
             4363 (and MC))*
Pub: Boosey & Hawkes

The Fire of Your Love - song from the film `The Master of Bankdam' (1947)
[Words: F. Eyton]
f.rec.   John Cameron - *HMV (Austr.) PA 7687(78)*
Pub: Boosey & Hawkes
Also arr. G. Stacey for small orchestra
Instr: 1/0/1/0 - 0/0/0/0 - pno. str.

Jan - Creole melody for high voice and small orchestra (or piano) (1947)
[Words: Trad. noted down by the composer from Rudolf Camacho]
f.p.   Jennie Tourel (Sop.)/BBC Theatre Orchestra/Walter Goehr - London, 1947

Pub: Boosey & Hawkes, 1947

Linstead Market - song for high voice and small orchestra (or piano) (1947)
[Words: Trad.]
Instr: 1/1/2/1 - 2/2/1/0 - timp. perc. cel. pno. str.
f.p.   Jennie Tourel (Sop.)/BBC Theatre Orchestra/Walter Goehr - London, 1947
f.Brit.p.   (voice and piano) Eleanor Houston (Sop.)/John Wills (Pno.) - Australia
             House, London, 29 January 1953 (Australian Music Association Concert)
Pub: Boosey & Hawkes, 1956

Divertissement for orchestra - from the film `The Steps of the Ballet' q.v. (1948)

Concerto quasi una fantasia for piano and orchestra (1949)
Written to celebrate the fiftieth year of Benjamin's appearance as a pianist since his debut
as a child in Brisbane. The work was played eight times in two weeks in Sydney and
Melbourne and, in the words of the composer, marked his `swansong as a pianist'.
Dur: 25'
Instr: 2/2/2/2 - 4/2/3/1 - timp. perc. str.
f.p.   Arthur Benjamin/Sydney Symphony Orchestra/Sir Eugene Goossens - Sydney,
             5 September 1950
f.Brit.p.   Jacques Abram/City of Birmingham Symphony Orchestra/Rudolf Schwarz -
             Cheltenham Town Hall, 13 July 1952 (Cheltenham Festival)
f.Am.p.   Jacques Abram - San Antonio, 1953
f.Lon.p.   Lamar Crowson/London Symphony Orchestra/Basil Cameron - Royal Albert
             Hall, 20 August 1956 (Promenade Concert)
f.rec.   Lamar Crowson/London Symphony Orchestra/Arthur Benjamin - *Everest
             LPBR(m)/SDBR 3020, EVC 9029; World Record Club (Austr.) SPE 754*
Pub: Boosey & Hawkes (also arr. two pianos)

A Tall Story - song for two-part accompanied chorus (1949)
Pub: W.H. Rogers, 1949

Le Tombeau de Ravel - Valses Caprices for clarinet (or viola) and piano (1949)
Dur: 12'25"
f.Lon.p.   Thea King (Cl.)/Howard Ferguson (Pno.) - Kensington Town Hall, 29 April
             1959 (Redcliffe Festival of British Music)
f.rec.   Gervase de Peyer (Cl.)/Cyril Preedy (Pno.) - *L'Oiseau Lyre SOL 60028*
Pub: Boosey & Hawkes, 1958

Callers - song for unison chorus (1949)
[Words: Caryl Brahms]
Pub: W.H. Rogers, 1949

Two Jamaican Street Songs for two pianos (1949)
[1. Mattie Rag Dur: 1'45" 2. Cookie Dur: 2'35"]
f.p.   Ethel Bartlett and Rae Robertson (for whom it was written)
f.rec.   (No. 1) Cyril Smith and Phyllis Sellick - *Columbia DX 1555(78)*
f.rec.   (complete) Richard McMahon/Martin Jones - *Oriana ONA 0003; Pianissimo
             PP 11192(CD)*

Pub: Boosey & Hawkes
also arr. for orchestra
f.recs.   New Concert Orchestra/Frederic Curzon - *Boosey & Hawkes 02056(78)*
           London Symphony Orchestra/Muir Mathieson - *Decca K 1571(78); London
           (USA) T 5053(78)*
arr. for viola and piano by William Primrose
f.rec.   William Primrose (Va.)/Vladimir Sokoloff (Pno.) - *Victor (USA) 11-8947(78)*

The Tale of Two Cities - opera in 3 Acts (1949-50 rev. 1957)
[Charles Dickens adapted by Cedric Cliffe]
Commissioned for the 1951 Festival of Britain - score completed, London,
17 February 1950
Dur: 130'
Instr: 3/2/2/2 - 4/0/3/1 - timp. perc. hp. cel. pno. str.
f.p.   BBC Chorus/Royal Philharmonic Orchestra/Arthur Benjamin - BBC Third
           Programme, 17 April 1953
Producer: Dennis Arundell
f.p.   (rev. version) New Opera Company/New Opera Chorus/Royal Philharmonic
           Orchestra/Leon Lovett - Sadler's Wells, London, 23 July 1957
Producer: Rudolf Cartier
Decor: Norman James
Choreography: Margaret Dale
Principals: Amy Shuard, Heather Harper, John Cameron, Alexander Young
f.tel.p.   New Opera Company/New Opera Chorus/Royal Philharmonic Orchestra/Leon
           Lovett - BBC Television, 2 October 1958
Pub: Boosey & Hawkes, 1953 (Vocal score)

Brumas Tunes for piano (1950)
Pub: Boosey & Hawkes

Orlando's Silver Wedding - ballet (c.1951)
f.p.   Group Theatre, cond. Joseph Horovitz - Amphitheatre, Festival Pleasure
           Gardens, Battersea, London, May 1951 (Festival of Britain)
Choreography: Andrée Howard
Decor: Kathleen Hale (from her picture books `Orlando, The Marmalade Cat')
Producer: Vera Lindsay
Principals: Sally Gilmour, Harold Turner

North American Square Dance - suite for two pianos and orchestra (1951)
[1. Miller's Reel 2. The Old Plunk 3. The Bundle of Straw
 4. He Piped so Sweet 5. Fill the Bowl 6. Pigeon on the Pier 7. Calder Fair
 8. Salamanca]
Dur: 11'
Instr: 2/2/2/2 - 4/2/3/1 - timp. perc.(2) glock. xyl. hp. pno.(2) str.
f.p.   Vronsky and Babin/Pittsburgh Symphony Orchestra/William Steinberg -
           Pittsburgh, USA, 1 April 1955
f.rec.   Nova Scotia Symphony Orchestra/Georg Tintner - *CBC Records (Can.) SM
           5088 (CD) (and MC)*
Pub: Boosey & Hawkes, 1951

String Quartet No. 2 (1952 rev. 1956)
Dur: 23'
Pub: Boosey & Hawkes, 1959

Harmonica Concerto (1953)
Dedicated to Larry Adler
Dur: 17'30"
Instr: 2/0/2/2 - 2/2/0/0 - xyl. cel. str.
f.p.   Larry Adler/London Symphony Orchestra/ Basil Cameron - Royal Albert Hall,
          London, 15 August 1953 (Promenade Concert)
f.recs.   above artists - *Columbia 33s 1023(m); EMI CDM7 64134-2 (CD) (and MC)*
          Larry Adler/Royal Philharmonic Orchestra/Morton Gould - *RCA SB 6786*, GL
          42747 (and MC)
Pub: Boosey & Hawkes, 1957 (also arr. harmonica and piano)

Fanfare for a State Occasion (1953)
Written for the Coronation of Her Majesty Queen Elizabeth II
Instr: 0/0/0/0 - 0/5/3/0 - timp.
f.p.   State Trumpeters - Westminster Abbey, London, 2 June 1953
f.rec.   Locke Brass Consort/James Stobart - *RCA RL 25081; Chandos CHAN
          6573(CD)*
Pub: Boosey & Hawkes, 1953

Fanfare for a Brilliant Occasion (1953)
Instr: 0/0/0/0 - 0/5/3/0 - timp.
f.rec.   Locke Brass Consort/James Stobart - *RCA RL 25081; Chandos CHAN
          6573(CD)*

Fanfare for a Gala Occasion (1953)
Instr: 0/0/0/0 - 0/5/3/0 - timp.
f.rec.   Locke Brass Consort/James Stobart - *RCA RL 25081; Chandos CHAN
          6573(CD)*

Our Mr. Toad for accompanied unison voices (1954)
Pub: Boosey & Hawkes

Endeavour for two-part accompanied voices (1955)
Pub: Boosey & Hawkes

Mañana - opera for television (1955-56)
[Libretto: Caryl Brahms and George Foa after Brahms: `Under the Juniper Tree']
Dur: 50'
f.p.   Glyndebourne Festival Chorus/Royal Philharmonic Orchestra/Edward Renton
          - BBC Television, 1 February 1956
Designer: Stephen Bundy
Principals: Frederick Sharp, Edith Coates, Heather Harper, Carlos Montes, Ronald Lewis

The Song of the Banana Carriers for voice and piano (1957)
[Words: Trad. - noted down by the composer from Louise Bennett]

Pub: Boosey & Hawkes, 1957

Jamaicalypso for two pianos (1957)
Dur: 2'
f.broad.p. Joan and Valerie Trimble - 6 October 1957
f.rec.   Richard McMahon/Martin Jones - *Oriana OND 0003; Pianissimo PP 11192(CD)*
Pub: Boosey & Hawkes, 1957 (also arr. voice and piano)
also arr. orchestra (1958)
f.p.   BBC Concert Orchestra/Vilem Tausky - Royal Festival Hall, London, 31 May 1958 (BBC Light Music Festival)

Tartuffe - opera (unfinished 1959-60, completed Alan Boustead)
[Libretto: Molière adapted Cedric Cliffe]
f.p.   New Opera Company/Sadler's Wells Orchestra/Alan Boustead - Sadler's Wells, London, 30 November 1964
Producer: Peter Ebert
Principals: Anna Pollack, Jeannette Sinclair, Edward Byles, Eric Garrett
f.broad.p. above performance - 7 December 1964

Divertimento for Wind Quintet (1958-60)
Written for a performance in Dublin in 1958 but the composer withdrew it just before the concert and only a short fragment of the work was played.
Instr: Fl. Ob. Cl. Bsn. Hn.
f.p.   (complete*) Melos Ensemble - Cheltenham Town Hall, 5 July 1960 (Cheltenham Festival)
(*Only four of the six projected movements were completed)

UNDATED WORKS

Etudes Improvisées for piano
Written for Lamar Crowson (a pupil of Benjamin's at the Royal College of Music)
? f.p.   Lamar Crowson
f.rec.   Lamar Crowson - *Lyrita RCS 20(m); Musical Heritage Society (USA) MHS 7003*

Saxophone Blues for piano
Dedicated to Herbert Howells
Pub: Schott, 1929

Elegiac Mazurka for piano
Pub: Boosey & Hawkes, 1942

'Poultry, or Love in E.C.3' - ballet
Instr: piano duet

'Tone Poem' for baritone, piccolo, oboe, violin and bass

A Babe is Born for SATB chorus

FILM MUSIC

(i) Documentary Films

Lobsters - Bury Productions (1936)
Directors: John Mathias/Laszlo Moholy-Nagy
Music conducted by: Muir Mathieson

Toronto Symphony (1945)
A Canadian film documentary featuring works by Tchaikovsky, Kabalevsky and Arthur
Benjamin.

The Cumberland Story - Crown Film Unit (1947)
Director: Humphrey Jennings
Music conducted by: Muir Mathieson

Jamaica Problem - Rank (1947)
[This Modern Age Series No.14]
Music conducted by: Muir Mathieson

The Steps of the Ballet - Crown Film Unit for C.O.I./British Council (1948)
Music played by: Philharmonia Orchestra/Muir Mathieson
Narrator: Robert Helpmann
Choreography: Andrée Howard
Decor and Costumes: Hugh Stevenson
Principals: Gerd Larsen and Alexander Grant
f.rec.   Complete film - *Beulah RT 152(V)*

The Conquest of Everest - Countryman Films with Group 3 (1954)
Awarded `Grand Prix' for Best Film at the Durban Film Festival in 1954
Director: Thomas Stobart
Music conducted by: Muir Mathieson

Under the Caribbean (1954)
Alt. (Swiss) title: Unternehmen Xarifa
Director: Hans Haas

(ii) Feature Films

The Man Who knew Too Much - GFD/Gaumont British (1934)
Director: Alfred Hitchcock
Music conducted by: Louis Levy
f.rec.   complete film (V)
('The Storm Cloud Cantata' - words by D. B. Wyndham-Lewis - was re-used in the 1955
version, re-orchestrated by Bernard Herrmann)

The Clairvoyant - Gaumont British (1935)
US title: The Evil Mind
Director: Maurice Elvey

Music conducted by: Louis Levy
f.rec.   complete film (V)

Turn of the Tide - British National (1935)
Director: Norman Walker
Music conducted by: Arthur Benjamin
f.rec.   complete film (V)

The Scarlet Pimpernel - London Films (1935)
Director: Harold Young
Music conducted by: Muir Mathieson (some of the music was orchestrated by Lionel Salter)
f.rec.   complete film (V)

The Guv'nor - Gaumont British (1935)
US title: Mister Hobo
Director: Milton Rosmer
Music conducted by: Louis Levy

Wharves and Strays - London Films (1935)
Director: Bernard Browne
Music conducted by: Muir Mathieson

Wings of the Morning - New World/Twentieth Century Fox (1936)
Director: Harold Schuster
(The **first** British technicolour feature film)
Music conducted by: Muir Mathieson (music orchestrated by Lionel Salter)

Under the Red Robe - New World/Twentieth Century Fox (1937)
Director: Victor Seastrom
Music conducted by: Muir Mathieson
f.rec.   complete film (V)

The Return of the (Scarlet) Pimpernel - London Films (1937)
Director: Hans Schwartz
Music conducted by: Muir Mathieson

The Master of Bankdam - Holbein Films (1947)
Alt. title: The Crowthers of Bankdam
Director: Walter Forde
Music conducted by: Muir Mathieson

An Ideal Husband - British Lion/London Films (1947)
Director: Alexander Korda
Music conducted by: Hubert Clifford

Melba - Horizon/United Artists (1952)
Co-wrote with Mischa Spoliansky
Director: Lewis Milestone

Music conducted by: Muir Mathieson
f.rec.   complete film

Above us the Waves - Rank/London Independent Producers (1955)
Director: Ralph Thomas
Music conducted by: Muir Mathieson
f.rec.   complete film (V)

The Naked Earth - Foray/Twentieth Century Fox (1957)
Director: Vincent Sherman

Fire down below - Warwick/Columbia (1957)
Co-wrote with Douglas Gamley and Kenneth V. Jones
Director: Robert Parrish
Music conducted by: Muir Mathieson
f.rec.   complete film (V)

ARRANGEMENTS

Five Negro Spirituals arr. for violin (or cello/clarinet) and piano (c.1924)
[1. I'm a-trav'lin' to the grave   2. March on
 3. Gwine to ride up in the chariot 4. I'll hear the trumpet sound
 5. Rise mourners]
Pub: OUP, 1924; Boosey & Hawkes (arr. William Primrose)

Beethoven: Piano Concerto No. 3 in C minor - cadenza for first movement (1941)

Mendelssohn: Praeludium (Prelude in B minor) arr. orchestra (1941)
Dur: 3'30"
Instr: 2/2/2/2 - 4/2/0/0 - timp. perc. str.
Pub: Boosey & Hawkes

Mendelssohn: Prelude and Fugue arr. orchestra (1941)
Dur: 6'30"
Instr: 2/2/2/3 - 4/2/3/1 - timp. perc. str.
Pub: Boosey & Hawkes

Concerto for oboe and string orchestra - adapted from Cimarosa Keyboard Sonatas (1942)
Dur: 10'
f.Brit.p.   Léon Goossens/London Philharmonic Orchestra/Basil Cameron - Royal
             Albert Hall, London, 22 July 1942 (Promenade Concert)
f.p.   (as a ballet 'Primavera') - Juilliard Dance Theatre, New York, 19 April 1955
Choreography: Anna Sokolow
f.rec.   Léon Goossens/Liverpool Philharmonic Orchestra/Sir Malcolm Sargent (rec.
             25 October 1943) - *Columbia DX 1137/8(78); HMV HQM 1087(m)*
Pub: Boosey & Hawkes (also arr. oboe and piano)

Suite for flute and string orchestra - adapted from Scarlatti Keyboard Sonatas (1946)
Dur: 12'
Pub: Boosey & Hawkes (also arr. flute and piano)

Divertimento for oboe and string orchestra on themes from Gluck's Trio Sonatas (1950)
Dur: 14'30"
Pub: Boosey & Hawkes, 1952 (also arr. oboe and piano)

MS LOCATION

There are a number of scores now located at the British Library. **(BL)**

BIBLIOGRAPHY

Anon.   **Arthur Benjamin - list of published works.** London: Boosey
                               & Hawkes, October 1957.

Arundell, Dennis   **Benjamin's Operas.** Tempo No. 15, 1950-51.

Barnett, Robert   **Arthur Benjamin: Australian Symphonist.** The Journal of
                               the British Music Society, Vol. 10, 1988.

Howells, Herbert   **Arthur Benjamin: Obituary.** Tempo No. 55, 1960-61.

Keller, Hans   **Arthur Benjamin and the Problem of Popularity.** Tempo
                               No. 15, 1950-51

Schafer, Murray   **Arthur Benjamin** in his `British Composers in Interview'.
                               London: Faber, 1963.

Seiber, Matyas   **Arthur Benjamin's Symphony.** Tempo No. 32, 1955.

9

Lennox Berkeley
(1903–1989)

Three French Songs for medium voice and piano (c.1924-25)
[1. D'un vanneur de blé aux vents 'The Thresher' (Joachim du Bellay - dedicated
to John Greenidge) 2. Pastourelle (13th cent. Anon.)
3. Rondeau (Charles d'Orléans trans. M. D. Calvocoressi - dedicated to G.M.B.]
Dur: 4'
f.p.   (No. 1) Cecil Day Lewis (Ten.)/Lennox Berkeley (Pno.) - Oxford University
            Musical Club and Union, 12 March 1925
f.Lon.p.   (No. 1) Sophie Wyss (Sop.)/Lennox Berkeley (Pno.) - Fyvie Hall, 20 February
            1945 (International Arts Guild Concert)
f.p.   (No. 2) Oxford University Musical Club and Union, 16 June 1924
f.p.   (complete) Margaret Cable (M/S)/Anthony Legge (Pno.) - BBC Radio 3,
            12 May 1988
f.recs.   (No. 1) Wilfrid Brown (Ten.)/Margaret McNamee (Pno.) - *Jupiter JUR 00A5
            (m) (and MC)*
            Meriel Dickinson (M/S)/Peter Dickinson (Pno.) - *Argo ZRG 788*
Pub: Chester, 1992
No. 1 was revised by the composer in 1925
Dur: 1´30˝
Pub: OUP, 1927; Chester 1992

La Belle Dame sans Merci - song for voice and piano (c.1924)
[Words: John Keats]
f.p.   Oxford University Musical Club and Union, 16 June 1924

Two Ronsard Songs for voice and piano (c.1924)
[1. Sonette de Ronsard 2. Les Dimanches]
f.p.   Oxford University Musical Club and Union, 16 June 1924

March for piano (or harpsichord) (1924)
Dur: 1'45"
f.p.   Anthony Legge - BBC Radio 3, 12 May 1988

Minuet for two recorders (c.1924)

Toccata for piano (1925)
Dedicated to J. F. Waterhouse who later became the music critic of The Birmingham Post.
Dur: 3'
f.p.   Anthony Legge - BBC Radio 3, 12 May 1988
Pub: Chester

Two Dances for piano duet (1925)
f.p.   Oxford University Musical Club and Union, 12 March 1925

Mr. Pilkington's Toye, for piano (or harpsichord) (1925)
Written for Vere Pilkington, a contemporary of Berkeley's at Oxford University, with whom he shared rooms.

Two Auden Songs for voice and piano (c.1926)
[1. Bank Holiday 2. Not traced]
f.p.   Cecil Day Lewis/Lennox Berkeley - Oxford University Musical Club and Union, c.1926

Introduction and Dance for small orchestra (1926)
Written for Anthony Bernard and the London Chamber Orchestra
Instr: 1/1/2/1 - 2/0/0/0 - perc. hp. str.
f.p.   London Chamber Orchestra/Anthony Bernard - New Chenil Galleries, Chelsea, 26 April 1926 (BBC Concert)

Tombeaux - Five Songs for voice and piano (1926)
[Words: Jean Cocteau 1. De Sapho 2. De Socrate 3. D'Un Fleuve (A Rivulet) 4. De Narcisse 5. De Don Juan]
Dur: 7'45"
f.mod.p. Meriel Dickinson (M/S)/Peter Dickinson (Pno.) - British Music Information Centre, London, 4 November 1987
f.broad.p. Margaret Cable (M/S)/Anthony Legge (Pno.) - Radio 3, 12 May 1988
Pub: Chester, 1992
Later arr. for voice and chamber orchestra (c.1929)
Dedicated to Anthony Bernard
f.p.   Sophie Wyss (Sop.)/London Chamber Orchestra/Anthony Bernard - BBC, 11 March 1929
f.conc.p. Jeanne Dusseau (Sop.)/London Chamber Orchestra/Anthony Bernard - Aeolian Hall, London, 10 February 1931

For Vere, for piano (or harpsichord) (1927)
Written for Vere Pilkington
Dur: 0'45"
f.p.   Anthony Legge - BBC Radio 3, 19 May 1988

Petite Suite for oboe and cello (1927)
[1. Prelude 2. Minuet 3. Bourrée 4. Aria 5. Gigue]
Dur: 13'30"
f.p.   London Contemporary Music Centre Concert, 1928

f.mod.p.   Stella Dickinson (Ob.)/Rod McGrath (Vc.) - Purcell Room, London,
           23 June 1981
f.broad.p. Sarah Francis (Ob.)/Rohan de Saram (Vc.) - Radio 3, 12 May 1988

Suite for orchestra (1927)
[1. Sinfonia 2. Bourrée 3. Aria 4. Gigue]
Dur: 18'
Instr: 2/2/2/2 - 4/3/3/1 - timp. perc. hp. str.
f.p.   Straram Orchestra/Walter Straram - Salle Pleyel, Paris, February 1928
f.Brit.p. Henry Wood Symphony Orchestra/Lennox Berkeley - Queen's Hall, London,
           12 September 1929 (Promenade Concert)
Pub: Goodwin & Tabb; Novello

Concertino for chamber orchestra (1927)
Written for Anthony Bernard and the London Chamber Orchestra*
f.p.   London Chamber Orchestra/Anthony Bernard - Court House, Marylebone
           Lane, London, 6 April 1927 (LCMC/BMS Concert)
(* Berkeley conducted the Bournemouth Municipal Orchestra in, probably, the second
performance of this work in November 1928)

Sonatina for solo violin (1927)

Prelude, Intermezzo (Blues) and Finale, for flute, violin, viola and piano (1927)
f.p.   Aeolian Players with Gordon Bryan (Pno.) - London, October 1927

Three Pieces for piano (1927)
f.p.   Jan Smeterlin - London c.1929

Sonatina for clarinet and piano (1928)
f.p.   Frederick Thurston (Cl.)/Harriet Cohen (Pno.) - BBC broadcast, July 1935

Piece for flute, clarinet and bassoon (1929)
Dur: 2'45"
f.broad.p. Richard Adeney (Fl.)/Thea King (Cl.)/William Waterhouse (Bsn.) - Radio 3,
           2 September 1984

Sinfonietta for chamber orchestra (1929)
Written for Anthony Bernard and the London Chamber Orchestra

Piano Sonatina (1929)

Trois Poèmes de Vildrac for medium voice and piano (1929)
[Words: Charles Vildrac 1. Sur quel abre du ciel 2. Ce Caillou Chaud de Soleil 3. Cet
Enfant de Jadis]
Dedicated 'a Mademoiselle Nadia Boulanger en toute admiration et gratitude'
Dur: 3'
f.mod.p.   Sylvia Eaves (Sop.)/Courtney Kenny (Pno.) - Rosslyn Hill Chapel,
           Hampstead, London, 21 May 1983
f.broad.p. Margaret Cable (M/S)/Anthony Legge (Pno.) - Radio 3, 19 May 1988

Pub: Chester, 1992

Serenade for flute, oboe, violin, viola and cello (c.1929)

Suite for flute, oboe, violin, viola and cello (c.1930)

Suite for harpsichord (1930)
Pub: Chester

Symphony for string orchestra (1930-31)
f.p.   London Chamber Orchestra/Anthony Bernard - Queen's Hall, London,
            14 December 1931 (English Music Society Concert)

Sonata No. 1 for violin and piano (1931)
Dedicated to Gladys Bryans

La Poulette Grise for children's voices, two pianos and trumpet (c.1932)
Dur: 3′
f.Brit.p.   L'Ensemble Vocal/Nadia Boulanger - Wigmore Hall, London,
            30 October 1946

Untitled ballet score (1932)
A possible commission from the Ballets Russes de Monte Carlo
Instr: Ob. Cl. Sax. Bsn. Tpt.
Exc. 'Blues' arr. for piano by Peter Dickinson
Dur: 1'45"
f.p.   Anthony Legge - BBC Radio 3, 19 May 1988

Three Pieces for solo clarinet (c.1932)
Dur: 4'45"
f.mod.p.   Thea King - Rosslyn Hill Chapel, Hampstead, London, 21 May 1983
f.broad.p. Colin Parr - Radio 3, 26 May 1988
Pub: Chester (ed. Thea King)

Ode (Partition) for SATB chorus, trumpet and string orchestra (c.1932)

Sonata No. 2 in D for violin and piano Op. 1 (c.1933)
Dur: 20'
f.p.   London Contemporary Music Centre
Pub: Chester, 1934

Trio (Suite) for flute, oboe and piano (1935)
Written for the Sylvan Trio
Dur: 9'45"
f.p.   Sylvan Trio - John Francis (Fl.)/Joy Boughton (Ob.)/Millicent Silver (Pno.) -
            Cowdray Hall, London, November 1935 (LCMC Concert)
f.broad.p. Graham Mayger (Fl.)/Sarah Francis (Ob.)/Gordon Stewart (Pno.) - Radio 3,
            2 June 1988

How love came in - song for medium voice and piano (1935)
[Words: James Herrick]
Dur: 1'30"
f.broad.p. Margaret Cable (M/S), Anthony Legge (Pno.) - Radio 3, 26 May 1988
f.rec.   Peter Pears (Ten.)/Benjamin Britten (Pno.) - *Decca LW5241(m); Eclipse ECS 545(m); London (USA) LLP 1532(m)*
Pub: Boosey & Hawkes, 1936 (in 'A Heritage of Twentieth Century British Song', Vol. 2)

Three Pieces for piano Op. 2 (1935)
[1. Etude 2. Berceuse 3. Capriccio]
The Etude is dedicated to Harriet Cohen, the Berceuse to Alan Searle and the Capriccio to Vere Pilkington
Dur: 8'
f.broad.p. James Walker - Radio 3, 26 May 1988
f.rec.   Christopher Headington - *Kingdom KCLCD 2012(CD) (and MC)*
Pub: Augener, 1937; Galliard, 1973

Jonah - oratorio for three solo voices, chorus and orchestra Op. 3 (1933-35)
[Biblical text adapted by Lennox Berkeley]
Dur: 65'
Instr: 2+picc./2+ca./2+bcl./2+cbsn. - 4/3/3/1 - timp. perc. str.
f.p.   Joan Cross (Sop.)/Jan van der Gucht (Ten.)/William Parsons (Bar.)/ BBC Chorus/BBC Symphony Orchestra/Clarence Raybould - BBC, 19 June 1936 (studio performance)
f.conc.p. Leeds Festival Chorus and Orchestra cond. Lennox Berkeley - Leeds Town Hall, 7 October 1937 (Leeds Triennial Festival)
f.Lon.p. (with organ) Martyn Hill (Ten.)/David Wilson-Johnson (Bar.)/Matthew Morley (Org.) cond. Jonathan Rennert - St. Michael's, Cornhill, 31 March 1990
Pub: Chester

Five Short Pieces for piano Op. 4 (1936)
Dedicated to N. José Raffalli
Dur: 7'
f.broad.p. Anthony Legge - Radio 3, 2 June 1988
f.rec.   Christopher Headington - *Kingdom KCLCD 2012 (CD) (and MC)*
Pub: Chester, 1937

Three Pieces for two pianos Op. 5 (1934-38)
[1. Polka 2. Nocturne 3. Capriccio]
Dedicated to Ethel Bartlett and Rae Robertson
Dur: 7'
f.p.   Ethel Bartlett and Rae Robertson
f.broad.p. Anthony Legge/James Walker - Radio 3, 26 May 1988
f.rec.   (arr. 2 pianos, 3 hands) Cyril Smith and Phyllis Sellick - *HMV CLP 3641(m), CSD 3641*
Pub: Chester, 1934, 1938
Polka arr. for piano solo as Op. 5a (1934)

Dur: 2'
f.rec.   Christopher Headington - *Kingdom KCLCD 2012 (CD) (and MC)*
Pub: Chester, 1934
Polka also arr. for two pianos, trumpet and percussion (1934)
Instr: Cymbal, Tambour de Basque, Triangle

String Quartet No. 1 Op. 6 (1935)
Dedicated to the Pro Arte String Quartet
Dur: 25'
f.p.   Pro Arte String Quartet - Cowdray Hall, London, November 1935
           (LCMC Concert)
f.broad.p. Bochmann String Quartet - 30 November 1983
Pub: Boosey & Hawkes

Three Impromptus for piano Op. 7 (1935)
Dur: 7'
f.broad.p. Anthony Legge - Radio 3, 2 June 1988
f.rec.   (No. 1) Colin Horsley - *Lyrita RCS 9(m)*
Pub: Boosey & Hawkes, Winthrop Rogers Ed., 1937

Overture for orchestra Op. 8 (1934)
Dur: 8'
Instr: 2+picc/2+ca/2/3 - 4/3/3/1 - timp. str.
f.p.   BBC Symphony Orchestra/Lennox Berkeley - Queen's Hall, London,
           1 October 1935 (Promenade Concert)
f.Eur.p.   Barcelona, 23 April 1936 (ISCM Festival)
Pub: Chester

Deux Poemes de Pindar for soloists, SATB chorus and orchestra (c.1936)
[1. Dithyrambe 2. Hymn]
Dedicated to the Princesse de Polignac
Dur: 7′
f.p.   cond. Nadia Boulanger - Queen's Hall, London, 11 November 1936
Pub: Chester

Mont Juic* - suite of Catalan dances for orchestra Op. 9 (1937)
Written in collaboration with Benjamin Britten and dedicated to the memory of Peter
Burra who died in an air accident near Reading in April 1937
Dur: 12'
Instr: 2/2/2+2 sax./2 - 4/2/3/1 - timp. perc.(2) hp. str.
f.p.   BBC Symphony Orchestra/Joseph Lewis - BBC, 8 January 1938 (studio
           performance)
f.conc.p. BBC Symphony Orchestra/Sir Henry Wood - Queen's Hall, London,
           5 September 1939 (Promenade Concert)
f.rec.   London Philharmonic Orchestra/Lennox Berkeley - *Lyrita SRCS 50, SRCD
           226(CD); Musical Heritage Society (USA) MHS 1919*
Pub: Boosey & Hawkes, 1938
(* a district of Barcelona which both composers had visited in company with Peter Burra
during the 1936 ISCM Festival)

Domini est Terra for SATB chorus and orchestra Op. 10 (1937-38)
Dedicated to Nadia Boulanger
Dur: 9'30″
Instr: 2/2/2/2 - 0/3/3/1 - timp. perc. hp. pno. str.
f.p.   London Select Choir/BBC Symphony Orchestra/Arnold Fulton - Queen's Hall,
            London, 17 June 1938 (ISCM Festival)
Pub: Boosey & Hawkes

Seven Songs for medium voice and piano Op. 14 No. 2 (1937-40)
[1. Night covers up the rigid land (W.H. Auden) Dur: 2'40"
 2. Lay your sleeping head, my love (W.H. Auden) Dur: 5'30"
 3. The Beacon Barn (Patrick O'Malley) Dur: 1'25"
 4. Eleven-Fifty (Patrick O'Malley)
 5. The Bells of Cordoba (Federico Garcia Lorca trans. Stanley Richardson)
    Dur: 1'40"
 6. Tant que mes yeux (Louise Labé trans. M.D. Calvocoressi)
 7. Ode du premier jour de Mai (Jean Passerat)]
Nos. 1 and 2 dedicated to Benjamin Britten, No. 6 dedicated to Sophie Wyss
f.p.   (Nos. 1 & 2) (possibly) Sophie Wyss (Sop.)/Lennox Berkeley (Pno.) - Conway
            Hall, London, February 1938 (London Contemporary Music Centre Concert)
f.p.   (Nos. 6 & 7 only) Sophie Wyss (Sop.)/Lennox Berkeley (Pno.) - Fyvie Hall,
            London, 20 February 1945
f.broad.p. (Nos. 1 & 2 only) Margaret Cable (M/S)/Anthony Legge (Pno.) - Radio 3,
            2 June 1988
f.recs.   (Nos. 1 & 2) Philip Langridge (Ten.)/Steuart Bedford (Pno.) - *Collins Classics*
            14902(CD)
            (No. 6) Meriel Dickinson (M/S)/Peter Dickinson (Pno.) - *Argo ZRG 788*
            (No. 7) Wilfrid Brown (Ten.)/Margaret McNamee (Pno.) - *Jupiter JUR*
            0045(m) (and MC)
Pub: (No. 1 only) Boosey & Hawkes, Winthrop Rogers Ed., 1939
            (No. 6 only) OUP, 1941; Chester, 1992
            (No. 7 only) OUP, 1945; Chester, 1992

The Judgement of Paris - ballet Op.10 No.2 (1937-38)
Dur: 15'
Instr: 1/2/2/2 - 4/3/3/0 - timp. hp. str.
f.p.   Vic-Wells Orchestra/Constant Lambert - Sadler's Wells Theatre, London,
            10 May 1938
Choreography: Frederick Ashton
Costumes and decor: William Chappell
Principals: Robert Helpmann, Pearl Argyle, William Chappell
Pub: Boosey & Hawkes

Introduction and Allegro for two pianos and orchestra Op. 11 (1938)
Dedicated to Benjamin Britten
Dur: 14'
Instr: 2/2/2/2 - 4/3/3/1 - timp. perc. hp. str.
f.p.   Lennox Berkeley/William Glock/London Symphony Orchestra/Sir Henry
            Wood - Royal Albert Hall, London, 6 September 1940 (Promenade Concert)

Pub: Chester

Concerto for cello and orchestra (1939)
Written for Maurice Eisenberg who emigrated to America in 1940.
Dur: 20'
Instr: 2/2/2/2 - 4/2/3/1 - timp. perc. str.
f.p.   Moray Welsh/Hallé Orchestra/James Loughran - Cheltenham Town Hall,
            17 July 1983 (Cheltenham Festival)
f.Lon.p.   Moray Welsh/London Symphony Orchestra/Richard Hickox - Royal Festival
            Hall, 23 October 1983 (Great British Music Festival)
Pub: Chester

Serenade for string orchestra Op. 12 (1939)
Dedicated to John and Clement Davenport
Dur: 14'
f.p.   Boyd Neel Orchestra/Boyd Need - Aeolian Hall, London, 30 January 1940
            (LCMC Concert*)
f.p.   (as a ballet entitled 'Common Ground') Royal Ballet - Sadler's Wells Theatre,
            London, 13 April 1984
Choreography: Jennifer (Janet) Jackson
f.recs.   Stuttgart Chamber Orchestra/Karl Munchinger - *Decca LXT 5153(m), Eclipse
            ECS 688; London (USA) LLP 1395(m)*
            London Philharmonic Orchestra/Lennox Berkeley - *Lyrita SRCS 74, SRCD
            226(CD)*
Pub: Chester, 1940
(* Britten's **Les Illuminations** q.v. was also premiered in the same concert)

Mazurka for piano (1939)

Sonatina for treble recorder (or flute) and harpsichord (or piano) Op. 13 (1939)
Commissioned by Carl Dolmetsch and dedicated to Sybil Jackson
Dur: 10'30"
f.p.   Carl Dolmetsch (Rec.)/Joseph Saxby (Pno.) - St. John's Wood, London,
            17 June 1939 (LCMC Concert held at the home of Sir Robert Mayer)
f.pub.p.   Carl Dolmetsch (Rec.)/Christopher Wood (Hpschd.) - Wigmore Hall, London,
            18 November 1939
f.rec.   James Galway (Fl.)/Anthony Goldstone (Pno.) - *RCA LRL1 5127*
Pub: Schott, 1940
later arr. for flute and orchestra by Rodney Newton (1993)
f.p.   Elena Duran/Scottish Ensemble/Jonathan Rees - Pittville Pump Room,
            Cheltenham, 17 July 1990 (Cheltenham Festival)

Four Concert Studies for piano Op. 14 No. 1 (1940)
No. 1 Dedicated to David Ponsonby, No. 2 to Bep Gever, No. 3 to Marc
Chatellier and No. 4 to Claude Berkeley
Dur: 10'
f.p.   (Studies in E minor and B minor) Colin Horsley - BBC, 20 January 1956
f.rec.   (Nos. 2, 3 and 4) Colin Horsley - *Lyrita RCS 9(m)*
Pub: Schott, 1940

Five Housman Songs for high voice and piano Op. 14 No. 3 (1940)
[1. The half moon westers low, my love
 2. The street sounds to the soldiers' tread.   3. He would not stay for me.
 4. Look not in my eyes.   5. Because I liked you better]
Dedicated to Peter Fraser
Dur: c.10′
f.broad.p. Ian Partridge (Ten.)/Jennifer Partridge (Pno.) - Radio 3, 25 September 1978
f.rec.   (Nos. 3 and 5) Anthony Rolfe Johnson (Ten.)/Graham Johnson (Pno.) -
            Hyperion CDA 66471/2(CD)
Pub: Chester, 1983

Impromptu for organ (1941)
Written for Colin Gill `on the occasion of his translation from Holborn to Brighton'
f.p.   Colin Gill, c.October 1941
Pub: Chester

String Quartet No. 2 Op. 15 (1940-41)
Dur: 20'
f.p.   Stratton Quartet - Cambridge Theatre, London, 5 June 1941
Pub: Chester, 1943

Symphony No. 1 in C Op. 16 (1940-41)
Dur: 33'
Instr: 2/2/2/2 - 4/2/3/1 - timp. perc. hp. str.
f.p.   London Philharmonic Orchestra/Lennox Berkeley - Royal Albert Hall,
            London, 8 July 1943 (Promenade Concert)
f.broad.p. BBC Symphony Orchestra/Clarence Raybould - 20 March 1944
f.rec.   London Philharmonic Orchestra/Norman del Mar - *Lyrita SRCS 80; Musical
            Heritage Society (USA) MHS 3696; HNH (USA) 40¹7*
Pub: Chester, 1951

Sonatina for violin and piano Op. 17 (1942)
Dur: 14'
f.p.   Max Rostal (Vn.)/Lennox Berkeley (Pno.) - Hampstead, London,
            25 September 1944 (CPNM Recital)
f.recs.   Frederick Grinke (Vn.)/Lennox Berkeley - *Decca LXT 2978(m); London
            (USA) LLP 1055(m)*
            Michael Davis (Vn.)/Nelson Harper (Pno.) - *Vienna Modern Masters VMM
            2015(CD)*
Pub: Chester, 1945 (ed. Rostal)

The Midnight Murk for unaccompanied SATB chorus (1942)
[Words: Sagittarius]
Dur: 3′
f.p.   BBC Singers(?) - BBC broadcast, 20 June 1942
f.conc.p.   BBC Singers - Cowdray House, London, 11 November 1946 (LCMC Concert)

Divertimento in B flat for orchestra Op. 18 (1942-43)
[1. Prelude 2. Nocturne 3. Scherzo 4. Finale]
Commisioned by the BBC and dedicated to Nadia Boulanger
Dur: 17'30"
Instr: 2/2/2/2 - 2/2/1/0 - timp. str.
f.p.   BBC Symphony Orchestra/Sir Adrian Boult - BBC, 1 October 1943 (studio
            performance from the Corn Exchange, Bedford)
f.Eur.p.   Orchestra Sinfonica Stabile da Camera, Milan/Sir Adrian Boult - Milan, 15
            January 1949
f.recs.   London Chamber Orchestra/Anthony Bernard - *Decca K 1882/3(78)*
            London Philharmonic Orchestra/Lennox Berkeley - *Lyrita SRCS 74, SRCD*
            226(CD)
Pub: Chester, 1946

String Trio Op. 19 (1943)
Dedicated to Frederick Grinke, Watson Forbes and James Phillips
Dur: 16'30"
Instr: Vn. Va. Vc.
f.p.   London String Trio - Frederick Grinke (Vn.), Watson Forbes (Va.), James
            Phillips (Vc.) - Wigmore Hall, London, August 1944
f.broad.p. above artists - 13 July 1947
f.recs.   Troester Trio - *Polydor 68333/4(78)*
            Jean Pougnet (Vn.)/Frederick Riddle (Va.)/Anthony Pini (Vc.) - *Westminster*
            XWN 18515(m); Pye/Nixa WLP 20017(m); Westminster (USA) WL 5316(m)
Pub: Chester, 1944

Two Songs for medium/high voice and piano (1943)
[1. Lullaby (W.B. Yeats) 2. The Ecstatic (C. Day Lewis)]

Legacies for unaccompanied SATB chorus (1943)
[Words: John Donne]

Paysage de France for piano (1944)
Written for an album of ten works "in honour of a redeemed France" and dedicated to
Raymond Mortimer
Dur: 4'
f.p.   Lennox Berkeley - Fyvie Hall, London, 20 February 1945
f.rec.   Christopher Headington - *Kingdom KCLCD 2012(CD) (and MC)*
Pub: Chester

Piano Sonata in A Op. 20 (1943-45 rev.1974)
Dedicated to Clifford Curzon
Dur: 25'
f.p.   Clifford Curzon - London, 28 July 1946
f.broad.p. Clifford Curzon - Third Programme, 16 May 1947
f.rec.   Colin Horsley - *Lyrita RCS 9(m)*
Pub: Chester, 1947

Lord, when the sense of Thy sweet Grace - anthem for SATB chorus and organ Op. 21 No. 1 (1944)
[Words: Richard Crashaw]
f.rec.   Choir of Dean Close School Chapel/Peter Cairns - *Michael Woodward MW 944*
Pub: Chester

There was neither grass nor corn - anthem for SATB chorus (1944)
[Words: Frances Cornford]
Commissioned by the BBC
Dur: 4´
f.p.   BBC Singers/Leslie Woodgate - BBC Home Service, 24 December 1944
           (recorded 5 December 1944 at the Corn Exchange, Bedford)

Festival Anthem for SATB chorus and organ Op. 21 No. 2 (1945)
[1. Sion's Daughters, Sons of Jerusalem (Liturgical text)
 2. O that I once past changing were (George Herbert)
 3. Death and darkness get you packing (Henry Vaughan)]
Commissioned by the Reverend Walter Hussey for St. Matthew's Church, Northampton*
Dur: 15'
f.p.   Choir and organist of St. Matthew's Church, Northampton, c.September 1945
f.rec.   Choir of Clare College, Cambridge/Timothy Brown - *Meridian CDE 84216(CD)*
Pub: Chester

Andantino (No. 2) from above arr. cello and piano as Op. 21 No. 2a (1955)
Dur: 2'30"
Pub: Chester, 1955
Andantino also arr. organ by Jennifer Bate as Op. 21 No. 2b. (1981)
f.p.   Jennifer Bate - Albert Hall, Nottingham, 6 June 1982
f. rec.   Jennifer Bate - *Hyperion A 66061*
Pub: Chester
Andantino also arr. trumpet and piano (1986)
f.p.   Francis Dickinson (Tpt.)/Peter Dickinson (Pno.) - 13 June 1986 (in the
           presence of the composer)
(* two years earlier Britten had contributed his Cantata **Rejoice in the Lamb** for a similar
commission q.v.)

Sonata in D minor for viola and piano Op. 22 (1945)
Dedicated to Watson Forbes
Dur: 20'
f.p.   Watson Forbes (Va.)/Alan Richardson (Pno.) - London Contemporary Music
           Centre, 3 May 1946
f.broad.p. above artists - 13 July 1947
f.rec.   Michael Ponder (Va.)/Raphael Terroni (Pno.) - *Pearl SHE 576*
Pub: Chester, 1949 (ed. Watson Forbes)

Six Preludes for piano Op. 23 (1945)
Commissioned by the BBC to be used as interludes between programmes and dedicated to Val Drewry

Dur: 10'30"
f.p.   Albert Ferber, 13 July 1947 (recorded in the Concert Hall of Broadcasting House on 7 July 1947)
f.rec.   Colin Horsley - *HMV C 3940 (78), HQM 1069(m); Lyrita RCS9(m); Meridian E 77017 (and MC)*
Pub: Chester, 1948

Introduction and Allegro for solo violin Op. 24 (1946)
Dedicated to Ivry Gitlis

Dur: 6'
f.p.   Ivry Gitlis - Wigmore Hall, London, June 1947
f.broad.p.   Ivry Gitlis - 19 September 1947
f.rec.   Michael Davis - *Orion (USA) ORS 78293; Vienna Modern Masters VMM 2015(CD)*
Pub: Chester, 1949 (ed. Ivry Gitlis)

Nocturne for orchestra Op. 25 (1945-46)*
Dur: 10'30"
Instr: 2/2/2/2 - 4/2/3/0 - timp. perc. hp. str.
f.p.   BBC Symphony Orchestra/Sir Adrian Boult - Royal Albert Hall, London, 28 August 1946 (Promenade Concert)
Pub: Chester, 1948
(* Beecham conducted this work in one of his concerts on 17 December 1947)

Five Songs for high voice and piano Op. 26 (1946)
[Words: Walter de la Mare 1. The Horseman 2. Mistletoe 3. Poor Henry
4. The Song of the Soldiers 5. Silver]
Dedicated to Pierre Bernac and Francis Poulenc

f.p.   Pierre Bernac (Ten.)/Francis Poulenc (Pno.) - 1946(47)
f.Lon.p.   Frederick Fuller (Bar.)/Ernest Lush (Pno.) - RBA Galleries, 19 June 1951 (London Contemporary Music Centre Concert)
f.rec.   (No. 3) Simon Woolf (Treb.)/Steuart Bedford (Pno) - *Unicorn RHS 316*
Pub: Chester, 1948

Four Poems of St. Teresa of Avila for contralto and string orchestra
Op. 27 (1947)
[Words: trans. Arthur Symons 1. If Lord, Thy love for me is strong
2. Shepherd, shepherd, hark that calling 3. Let mine eyes see Thee
4. Today, a shepherd and our kin]
Written at the request of Gerald Cooper and dedicated to John Greenidge

Dur: 13'
f.p.   Kathleen Ferrier/Goldsbrough String Orchestra/Arnold Goldsbrough - BBC Third Programme, 4 April 1948
f.conc.p.   Gladys Ripley/Boyd Neel Orchestra/Boyd Neel - Canterbury, 20 July 1951 (Canterbury Festival)

f.Lon.conc.p. Kathleen Ferrier/London Symphony Orchestra/Hugo Rignold -   Royal
Festival Hall, London, 6 April 1952
f.recs.   Pamela Bowden/Collegium Musicum Londinii/John Minchinton - *HMV DLP*
1209(m), HQM 1069(m)
Kathleen Ferrier's radio broadcast was later re-issued by the BBC - *REGL*
368(m), ZCF 368 (MC); Arabesque (USA) 8071
Pub: Chester, 1949 (and piano reduction)

The Lover's Gallery* - ballet (1947)
Choreography: Frank Staff
Designer: George Kirsta
f.p.   Metropolitan Ballet Company, 1947
(* music not traced - it may well have been the **Divertimento Op.18** q.v.)

Stabat Mater for six solo voices (SSATBB) and twelve instruments Op. 28 (1947)
[Latin text attrib. Jacopone da Todi]
Written for the English Opera Group and dedicated to Benjamin Britten. The work was
originally conceived as a concert work for the English Opera Group to take on tour with
two of Britten's chamber operas and therefore accounts for the rather unusual vocal and
instrumental combination.
Dur: 33'
Instr: Fl. Ob. Cl. Bsn. Hn. Hp. Perc. Vn. Vn. Va. Vc. Db.
f.p.   English Opera Group/Benjamin Britten - Zurich, August 1947
f.Brit.p.   above artists - Concert Hall, Broadcasting House, London,
27 September 1947
f.Brit.conc.p. above artists - Aldeburgh, June 1948 (Aldeburgh Festival)
Pub: Chester, 1950
also arr. for full orchestra by Michael Berkeley as Op.28a (1978)
Instr: 1/1/1/2 - 2/0/0/0 - perc. hp. str.
f.p.   Teresa Cahill (Sop.)/Diana Montagu (M/S)/Meriel Dickinson (Con.)/ Brian
Burrows (Ten.)/Richard Jackson (Ten.)/Stephen Varcoe (Bar.)/ Park Lane
Music Group Players/Nicholas Braithwaite - Queen Elizabeth Hall, London,
12 May 1978
Pub: Chester
also arr. for SATB chorus and chamber ensemble by Roy Teed
Instr: perc. str. (+ solo str.qt.)
Pub: Chester

Piano Concerto in B flat Op. 29 (1947-48)
Written for and dedicated to Colin Horsley
Dur: 24'30"
Instr: 2/2/2/2 - 2/2/1/0 - timp. perc. str.
f.p.   Colin Horsley/London Symphony Orchestra/Basil Cameron - Royal Albert
Hall, London, 31 August 1948 (Promenade Concert)
f.Eur.p.   Colin Horsley/Rome Radio Orchestra/Constant Lambert - Theatre Massimo,
Palermo, Sicily, 26 April 1949 (ISCM Festival)
f.rec.   David Wilde/New Philharmonia Orchestra/Nicholas Braithwaite - *Lyrita*
SRCS 94; HNH (USA) 4079
Pub: Chester

Overture for chamber orchestra (1947)
Written for Anthony Bernard and the London Chamber Orchestra.
Dur: 8′
Instr: 2/2/2/2 - 2/0/0/0 - timp. perc. str.
f.p.   London Chamber Orchestra/Anthony Bernard - Canterbury, June 1947
            (Canterbury Festival)
f.broad.p. above artists - 2 November 1947

The Lowlands of Holland - song for high voice and piano (1947)
[Words: Trad.]
Written for Sophie Wyss
Dur: 7′
f.p.   Sophie Wyss (Sop.)/Lennox Berkeley (Pno.) - BBC, 13 July 1947

Concerto for two pianos and orchestra Op. 30 (1948)
Commissioned by the Henry Wood Concert Society and written for Phyllis Sellick and
Cyril Smith
Dur: 30'
Instr: 2+picc./2/2/2 - 4/3/3/0 - timp. perc. hp. str.
f.p.   Phyllis Sellick/Cyril Smith/London Symphony Orchestra/Sir Malcolm Sargent
            - Royal Albert Hall, London, 13 December 1948
f.Eur.p.   Phyllis Sellick/Cyril Smith*/Moscow State Symphony Orchestra/ Clarence
            Raybould - Tchaikovsky Hall, Moscow, 22 April 1956
f.rec.   Garth Beckett/Boyd McDonald/London Philharmonic Orchestra/ Norman del
            Mar - *Lyrita SRCS 80; HNH (USA) 4017; Musical Heritage Society (USA)
            MHS 3696*
Pub: Chester, 1953
(* it was during this tour of Russia that Cyril Smith suffered the stroke which
permanently paralysed one arm)

Colonus' Praise for SATB chorus and orchestra Op. 31 (1949)
[Words: Sophocles trans. W.B. Yeats]
Written in celebration of the twenty-first anniversary of the BBC Choral Society
Dur: 10'
Instr: 2+picc./2/2/2 - 4/2/3/1 - timp. perc. str.
f.p.   BBC Choral Society/BBC Symphony Orchestra/Leslie Woodgate - Royal
            Albert Hall, London, 13 September 1949 (Promenade Concert)

Three Mazurkas "Hommage à Chopin" for piano Op. 32 No. 1 (1949)
Written in response to an invitation from UNESCO to celebrate the centenary of the
death of Chopin - one of Berkeley's favourite composers.
Dur: 7'
f.p.   Colin Horsley - Paris, October 1949
f.Brit.p.   Colin Horsley - BBC, 23 March 1950
f.rec.   Colin Horsley - *Lyrita RCS 9(m)*
Pub: Chester, 1951

Scherzo for piano Op. 32 No. 2 (1949)
Written for and dedicated to Colin Horsley

Dur:	2'
f.p.	Colin Horsley - 1950 (during a tour of Australia and New Zealand)
f.Brit.p.	Colin Horsley - BBC, 23 March 1950
f.rec.	Colin Horsley - *Lyrita RCS 9(m); Meridian E 77017 (and MC)*
Pub:	Chester, 1950

Theme and Variations for solo violin Op. 33 No. 1 (1950)
Written for and dedicated to Frederick Grinke

Dur:	7'30"
f.p.	Frederick Grinke - Zurich, 8 September 1950
f.Brit.p.	Frederick Grinke - BBC, 27 September 1950
f.recs.	Frederick Grinke - *Decca LXT 2978(m); London (USA) LLP 1055(m)*
	Michael Davis (Vn.) - *Vienna Modern Masters VMM 2015(CD)*
Pub:	Chester, 1951

Elegy and Toccata for violin and piano Op. 33 Nos. 2 and 3 (1950)
Written for Frederick Grinke

Dur:	5'
f.p.	Frederick Grinke (Vn.)/Ernest Lush (Pno.) - BBC, 27 September 1950
f.rec.	(Toccata) Michael Davis (Vn.)/Nelson Harper (Pno.) - *Vienna Modern Masters VMM 2015(CD)*
Pub:	Chester, 1951

Elegy also arr. string orchestra as Op. 33 No. 2a (1978)
Written for Essie Craxton's memorial service

Dur:	3'
f.p.	St. John's Smith Square Orchestra/John Lubbock - St. John's Smith Square, London, 26 April 1978
Pub:	Chester

Sinfonietta for chamber orchestra Op. 34 (1950)
Dedicated to Anthony Bernard

Dur:	13'
Instr:	2/2/2/2 - 2/0/0/0 - timp. str.
f.p.	London Chamber Orchestra/Anthony Bernard - Wigmore Hall, London, December 1950
f.broad.p.	above artists - 24 August 1951
f.rec.	English Chamber Orchestra/Norman del Mar - *Lyrita SRCS 111, SRCD 111(CD)*
Pub:	Chester 1951

Variations on a hymn by Orlando Gibbons for tenor, SATB chorus, organ and string orchestra Op. 35 (1951)
[Words: Robert Bridges based on verses by Isaac Watts]
Commissioned by the English Opera Group for the Aldeburgh Festival and dedicated to Dorothy Cranbrook

Dur:	18'
f.p.	Peter Pears/Aldeburgh Festival Choir and Orchestra with Ralph Downes (organ)/Lennox Berkeley - Parish Church, Aldeburgh, 21 June 1952 (Aldeburgh Festival)

Pub: Chester

Concerto for flute and chamber orchestra Op. 36 (1951-52)
Commissioned by and dedicated to John Francis
Dur: 20'30"
Instr: 0/2/0/2 - 2/0/0/0 - timp. str.
f.p.   John Francis/BBC Symphony Orchestra/Sir Malcolm Sargent - Royal Albert
          Hall, London, 29 July 1953 (Promenade Concert)
f.rec.   James Galway/London Philharmonic Orchestra/Lennox Berkeley - *RCA RS
          9011 (and MC), AGLI 5447*
Pub: Chester, 1956 (arr. flute and piano)

Ask me no more - anthem for TTBB chorus Op. 37 No. 1 (1952)
[Words: Thomas Carew]
Pub: Chester

Spring at this Hour - madrigal for SSATBB chorus Op. 37 No. 2 (1953)
[Words: Paul Dehn]
Commissioned by the Arts Council of Great Britain to celebrate the Coronation of Her
Majesty Queen Elizabeth II to whom the work is dedicated. This is the fifth piece from a
collection of ten songs by British composers entitled 'A Garland for the Queen'.
f.p.   Golden Age Singers/Cambridge University Madrigal Society/Boris Ord -
          Royal Festival Hall, London, 1 June 1953 (the eve of Coronation Day)
f.broad.p. above performance - 4 June 1953
f.rec.   Cambridge University Madrigal Society/Boris Ord - *Columbia CX 1063(m)*
Pub: OUP, 1953, Stainer & Bell, 1953

Andante: Movement 3 of 'Variations on Sellinger's Round' - a collaborative work for string orchestra (1953)
Written at the suggestion of Benjamin Britten for performance at the Aldeburgh Festival -
the other composers represented were Arthur Oldham, Humphrey Searle, Michael
Tippett, William Walton and Benjamin Britten.
f.p.   Aldeburgh Festival Orchestra/Benjamin Britten - Aldeburgh Parish Church,
          20 June 1953 (Aldeburgh Festival)
f.Lon.p. Collegium Musicum Londinii/John Minchinton - Wigmore Hall,
          29 May 1957
f.rec.   Aldeburgh Festival Orchestra/Benjamin Britten ('live' recording of the first
          performance) - *Decca LXT 2798(m); London (USA) LLP 808(m)*
Pub: Boosey & Hawkes

Three Greek Songs for medium voice and piano Op. 38 (1951)
[Words trans. F.A. Wright 1. Epitaph of Timas (Sappho)
2. Spring Song (Antipater) 3. To Aster (Plato)]
f.p.   Iris Kells (Sop.)/John Gardner (Pno.) - Morley College, London, 15 March
          1951
f.rec.   Thomas Hemsley (Bar.)/Ernest Lush (Pno.) - *HMV DLP 1209(m), HQM
          1069(m)*
Pub: Chester, 1953

Sonatina for piano duet Op. 39 (c.1953)
Dur: 8'
f.p.   Liza Fuchsova/Paul Hamburger - Wigmore Hall, London, 18 January 1955
f.rec.   Ian Brown/Kathryn Stott - *Hyperion A 66086*
Pub: Chester, 1954

Four Ronsard Sonnets (Set 1) for two tenors and piano Op. 40
(1952 rev. 1977)
[1. Marie levez-vous 2. Comme on void sur la branche 3. Otez votre beauté
 4. Adieu, cruelle, adieu]
Commissioned by Peter Pears to sing with Hugues Cuénod
f.p.   Peter Pears (Ten.)/Hugues Cuénod (Ten.)/George Malcolm (Pno.) - Victoria &
           Albert Museum, London, 8 March 1953
f.p.   (rev. version) Peter Pears (Ten.)/Ian Partridge (Ten.)/Steuart Bedford (Pno.) -
           The Maltings, Snape, 14 June 1978 (Aldeburgh Festival)
Pub: Chester

Nelson - opera in 3 Acts Op. 41 (1949-54)
[Libretto: Alan Pryce-Jones]
Dur: 140'
Instr: 3/2/2/2 - 4/3/3/1 - timp. perc. hp. str.
f.p.   English Opera Group Association with Robert Keys (piano) - Wigmore Hall,
           London, 14 February 1953
Principals: Arda Mandikian, Thomas Hemsley, Peter Pears, Nancy Evans
f.st.p.   Sadler's Wells Opera Chorus and Orchestra cond. Vilem Tausky - Sadler's
           Wells Theatre, London, 22 September 1954
Producer: George Devine
Settings: Felix Kelly
Principals: Victoria Elliott, Arnold Matters, Robert Thomas, Anna Pollack
f.conc.p. Chelsea Opera Group cond. Grant Llewellyn - Queen Elizabeth Hall, London,
           7 April 1988
Pub: Chester

Orchestral suite from the above Op. 41a (1955)
[1. The Sailing of the Victory 2. The Cockpit 3. Portsmouth]
Dur: 15'30"
Instr: 2/2/2/2 - 4/3/3/1 - timp. perc. hp. cel. str.
f.p.   Hallé Orchestra/Sir John Barbirolli - Cheltenham Town Hall, 20 July 1955
           (Cheltenham Festival)
f.Lon.p.   Hallé Orchestra/Basil Cameron - Royal Albert Hall, 30 August 1956
           (Promenade Concert)
Pub: Chester

Interlude from Act III (1955)
Dur: 5'
Instr: 2/2+ca./2/2 - 4/3/3/1 - timp. hp. str.
Pub: Chester

Suite for orchestra Op. 42 (1953)
[1. Intrada 2. Corrente 3. Sarabande 4. Gavotte 5. Aria 6. Hornpipe]
Commissioned by the BBC Third Programme to mark the Coronation
Dur: 21'
Instr: 2+picc./2+ca./2+bcl./2+cbsn. - 4/3/3/1 - timp. perc. hp. str.
f.p.   BBC Symphony Orchestra/Sir Malcolm Sargent - BBC, 6 June 1953   (studio
           performance)
Pub: Goodwin & Tabb

Crux fidelis - hymn for tenor and SATB chorus Op. 43 No. 1 (1955)
Written for Peter Pears and dedicated to Imogen Holst
f.p.   Peter Pears (Ten.)/Purcell Singers/Imogen Holst - Victoria & Albert Museum,
           London, 6 March 1955
f.broad.p. above artists - 23 May 1955
Pub: Chester

Look up sweet Babe - anthem for treble (soprano), SATB chorus and organ
Op. 43 No. 2 (1955)
[Words: Richard Crashaw]
f.rec.   Canterbury Cathedral Choir/Allan Wicks, with Philip Moore (org.) -
           Grosvenor GRS 1030
Pub: Chester, 1955

Sweet was the Song the Virgin Sang - anthem for SATB chorus and organ Op. 43
No. 3 (c.1957)
[Words: William Ballet]
f.rec.   (arr. for TTBB chorus by David Wulstan) The Clerkes of Oxenford/ David
           Wulstan - *Abbey 603*
Pub: Chester

Trio for violin, horn and piano Op. 44 (1953-54)
Commissioned by Colin Horsley and dedicated to Sheila Robertson. The work has the
same scoring as the Brahms Trio Op. 40 and was intended as a companion piece.
Dur: 26'30"
f.p.   Manoug Parikian (Vn.)/Dennis Brain (Hn.)/Colin Horsley (Pno.) - Victoria &
           Albert Museum, London, 28 March 1954
f.rec.   above artists - *HMV CLP 1029 (m), HQM 1057(m), RLS 7701 (and MC);
           Capitol (USA) G 7175(m); Seraphim(USA) M 60073(m)*
Pub: Chester, 1956

A Dinner Engagement - opera in one Act and two Scenes Op. 45 (1954)
[Libretto: Paul Dehn]
Dur: 60'
Instr: 1/1/1+bcl./1 - 1/0/0/0 - perc. hp. pno. str. (1/1/1/1)
f.p.   English Opera Group Chamber Orchestra cond. Vilem Tausky - Jubilee Hall,
           Aldeburgh, 17 June 1954 (Aldeburgh Festival)
Producer: William Chappell
Settings: Peter Snow
Principals: Frederick Sharp, Emelie Hooke, April Cantelo, Alexander Young,

Flora Nielsen, John Ford and Catherine Lawson.

f.broad.p.	above artists - Third Programme, 1 July 1954 (from the York Festival)
f.Lon.p.	above artists - Sadler's Wells Theatre, 7 October 1954
f.Eur.p.	Royal Opera House, Stockholm, 1958-59 season
Pub:	Chester, 1955 (vocal score)

Concerto for piano and double string orchestra Op. 46 (1958)

Commissioned by and dedicated to Colin Horsley

Dur:	25'
f.p.	Colin Horsley/BBC Symphony Orchestra/Lennox Berkeley - Royal Festival Hall, London, 11 February 1959
f.broad.p.	above artists - 14 February 1959
Pub:	Chester

Sextet for clarinet, horn and string quartet Op. 47 (1955)

Commissioned by the BBC for the opening concert of the 1955 Cheltenham Festival

Dur:	15'
f.p.	Members of the Melos Ensemble - Gervase de Peyer (Cl.), Neil Sanders (Hn.), Eli Goren (Vn.), Ivor MacMahon (Vn.), Patrick Ireland (Va.), Bernard Richards (Vc.) - Cheltenham Town Hall, 11 July 1955 (Cheltenham Festival)
f.Lon.p.	above artists - Victoria & Albert Museum, 11 December 1955
f.rec.	Jack Brymer (Cl.)/Alan Civil (Hn.)/Hugh Bean (Vn.)/Frances Routh (Vn.)/Christopher Wellington (Va.)/Eileen Croxford (Vc.) - *Argo ZRG 749*
Pub:	Chester, 1957

Salve Regina - anthem for unison voices and organ Op. 48 No. 1 (1955)

Dur:	3´
f.rec.	London Oratory Junior Choir/John Hoban, with Patrick Russill (org.) - *Abbey MVP 782*
Pub:	Chester

Concert Study in E flat for piano Op. 48 No. 2 (1955)

Dedicated to Colin Horsley

Dur:	3'
f.p.	Colin Horsley - BBC, 20 January 1956
f.rec.	Colin Horsley - *Lyrita RCS 9(m)*
Pub:	Chester, 1956

Concertino for treble recorder, violin, cello and harpsichord Op. 49 (1955)

Dedicated to Carl Dolmetsch who also suggested the particular instrumentation

Dur:	12'
Alt.Instr:	Fl. Vn. Vc. Pno.
f.p.	Carl Dolmetsch (Rec.)/Jean Pougnet (Vn.)/Arnold Ashby (Vc.)/ Joseph Saxby (Hpschd.) - BBC, 24 January 1956
f.rec.	Carl Dolmetsch (Rec.)/Alice Schoenfeld (Vn.)/Eleonore Schoenfeld (Vc.)/Joseph Saxby (Hpschd.) - *Orion (USA) ORS 73104*
Pub:	Chester, 1961

Allegro for two treble recorders (c. 1955)
Pub: Boosey & Hawkes

Ruth - opera in one Act and three Scenes Op. 50 (1955-56)
[Libretto: Eric Crozier]
Dedicated 'To Freda' (the composer's wife)
Dur: 80'
Instr: 2/0/0/0 - 1/0/0/0 - perc. pno. str.
f.p.   English Opera Group cond. Charles MacKerras - Scala Theatre, London,
          2 October 1956
Producer: Peter Potter
Scenery and costumes: Ceri Richards
Principals: April Cantelo, Anna Pollack, Peter Pears, Thomas Hemsley
Pub: Chester

Symphony No. 2 Op. 51 (1956-58 rev. 1972 and 1976)
Commissioned by the Feeney Trust for the City of Birmingham Symphony
Orchestra
Dur: 29'
Instr: 2/2/2/2 - 4/3/3/1 - timp. perc. hp. cel. str.
Instr: (rev.) 2+picc./2+ca./2+bcl./2+cbsn. - 4/2/1/1 - timp. perc.(2) hp. str.
f.p.   City of Birmingham Symphony Orchestra/Andrzej Panufnik - Birmingham
          Town Hall, 24 February 1959
f.Lon.p. BBC Symphony Orchestra/Lennox Berkeley - Royal Albert Hall,
          9 September 1959 (Promenade Concert)
f.rec.   (rev.) London Philharmonic Orchestra/Nicholas Braithwaite - *Lyrita SRCS 94;*
          HNH (USA) 4079
Pub: Chester

Sonatina for guitar Op. 52 No. 1 (1957)
Commissioned by and dedicated to Julian Bream
Dur: 11'
f.p.   Julian Bream - Morley College, London, 9 March 1958
f.rec.   Julian Bream - *RCA (USA)LM 2448(m), LSC 2448; RCA RB 16239(m), SB*
          6891, AGLI 3964, RK 11735 (MC); RCA Gold Seal (set) 09026
          61583-2(CD),09026 61595-2(CD)
Pub: Chester, 1958 (ed. Julian Bream)

Sonatina for two pianos Op. 52 No. 2 (1959)
Commissioned by Sir Ashley Clark, British Ambassador in Rome during the 1950s and a
keen amateur musician
Dur: 12'
f.p.   Rome, 1959 (at a concert organised by Sir Ashley Clark)
f.Brit.p. Joan and Valerie Trimble - BBC, 12 May 1963
Pub: Chester, 1959

Five Poems of W.H. Auden - song cycle for medium voice and piano Op. 53 (1958)
[1. Lauds: Among the leaves the small birds sing
 2. O lurcher-loving collier, black as night

3. What's in your mind, my dove, my coney? 4. Eyes look into the well
5. Carry her over the water
(All from the collected works "Songs and other Musical Pieces")]
Commissioned by and dedicated to the American singer Mrs Alice Esty
Dur: 10'
f.p.   Alice Esty - New York, March 1959
f.Brit.p.   Nancy Evans (Con.)/Norman Franklin (Pno.) - RBA Galleries, London,
              23 October 1959 (Macnaghten Concert)
f.broad.p.   Nancy Evans (Con.)/Ernest Lush (Pno.) - 21 January 1960
f.recs.   Thomas Hemsley (Bar.)/Ernest Lush (Pno.) - *HMV DLP 1209(m), HQM
              1069(m)*
              Philip Langridge (Ten.)/Steuart Bedford (Pno.) - *Collins Classics 14902(CD)*
              (No. 2) Felicity Lott (Sop.)/Graham Johnson (Pno.) - *Chandos ABTD
              1362(MC), CHAN 8722(CD)*
Pub: Chester, 1960

Overture for light orchestra* (1959)
Commissioned by the BBC for the Light Music Festival and dedicated to Vilem and
Peggy Tausky
Dur: 7'
Instr: 2/2/2/2 - 4/2/3/0 - timp. perc. hp. str.
f.p.   BBC Concert Orchestra/Vilem Tausky - Royal Festival Hall, London,   4 July
              1959 (BBC Light Music Festival)
(* originally Op.56)

So sweet love seemed - song for medium voice and piano (c.1959)
[Words: Robert Bridges]
Dur: 1'55"
f.p.   Meriel Dickinson (M/S)/Peter Dickinson (Pno.) - Friend's Meeting House,
              Manchester, 30 October 1975

The Winter's Tale* - Orchestral suite Op. 54 (1960)
[1. Prologue 2. The Banquet 3. Nocturne 4. Mamillius 5. The Storm
 6. Florizel and Perdita 7. Shepherd's Dance 8. The Statue]
Dur: 16'
Instr: 2+picc./2/2/2 - 4/2/3/1 - timp. perc. hp. str.
f.p.   BBC Symphony Orchestra/Lennox Berkeley - St. Andrew's Hall, Norwich, 27
              May 1961 (Norwich Triennial Festival)
Pub: Chester, 1962
(* derived from the incidental music to the play q.v.)

Thou hast made me - anthem for SATB chorus and organ Op. 55 No. 1 (1960)
[Words: John Donne]
Written for the 1960 St. Cecilia's Day Service of the Musician's Benevolent Fund
Dur: 6'
f.p.   Choristers of the Chapel Royal/St. Paul's Cathedral Choir/Westminster Abbey
              Choir/Canterbury Cathedral Choir. cond. John Dykes Bower, with Osborne
              Peasgood (org.) - Church of St. Sepulchre, London, 22 November 1960 (St.
              Cecilia's Day Service)

f.rec.   Canterbury Cathedral Choir/Allan Wicks, with Philip Moore (org.) -
            Grosvenor GRS 1030
Pub: Chester

Improvisations on a theme of Manuel de Falla* for piano Op. 55 No. 2 (1960)

Written for the Centenary Album issued by the House of Chester in 1960 and dedicated to
Douglas Gibson
Dur: 4′
f.rec.   Christopher Headington - *Kingdom KCLCD 2012(CD) (and MC)*
Pub: Chester, 1960 (House of Chester Centenary Album)
(* The theme is taken from the Pantomime movement in 'El amor brujo' - the other
composers who contributed to the album were Goossens (q.v.), Ireland, Malipiero and
Poulenc)

Prelude and Fugue for clavichord Op.55 No.3 (1960)

Dur: 3'30"
f.p.   Michael Thomas (?)
f.rec.   Michael Thomas - *Record Society RSX 16(m)*
Pub: Chester

Five Pieces for violin and orchestra Op. 56 (1961)

Commissioned by and dedicated to Frederick Grinke
Dur: 19'
Instr: 2+picc./2/2/2 - 2/0/0/0 - timp. perc. str.
f.p.   Frederick Grinke/BBC Symphony Orchestra/Lennox Berkeley - Royal Albert
            Hall, London, 31 July 1962 (Promenade Concert)
Pub: Chester

Missa Brevis* for SATB chorus and organ Op. 57 (1960)

Dedicated to Michael and Julian Berkeley and the boys of Westminster Cathedral Choir
Dur: 11′
f.p.   Choir of Westminster Cathedral/Francis Cameron - Westminster Cathedral,
            12 March 1960
f.conc.p.   Elizabethan Singers/Louis Halsey with Alan Harverson (organ) - St. James's,
            Piccadilly, London, 16 November 1960
f.rec.   (excs.) St. Chad's Metropolitan Cathedral Choir/John Harper, with John
            Harper (org.) - *Abbey LPB 768*
Pub: Chester, 1960
(* there is also a version for the Anglican Service dated c.1961)

Melfort (Hail Gladdening Light) - hymn tune (c.1960s)

Autumn's Legacy - song cycle for high voice and piano Op. 58 (1962)

[1. The mighty thoughts of an old world (Thomas Lovell Beddoes)
 2. All night a wind of music (Thomas Lovell Beddoes)
 3. Lesbos (Lawrence Durrell)
 4. Tonight the winds begin to rise (Tennyson)
 5. Hurrahing in Harvest (Gerard Manley Hopkins)
 6. Rich Days (W.H. Davies)

7. When we were idlers with the loitering rills (Hartley Coleridge)]
Commissioned by the Cheltenham Festival and dedicated to Lord Edward Sackville who helped with the choice of poems.

f.p.	Richard Lewis (Ten.)/Geoffrey Parsons (Pno.) - Cheltenham Town Hall, 6 July 1962 (Cheltenham Festival)
f.rec.	(No.3) Maureen Morelle (Sop.)/Diana Wright (Pno.) - *Jupiter jepoc 36(m)*
Pub:	Chester, 1963

Concerto for violin and chamber orchestra Op. 59 (1961)

Commissioned by the Bath Festival Society and dedicated to Yehudi Menuhin

Dur:	22'
Instr:	0/2/0/0/ - 2/0/0/0 - str.
f.p.	Yehudi Menuhin/Bath Festival Chamber Orchestra/Lennox Berkeley - The Abbey, Bath, 1 June 1961 (Bath Festival)
f.Lon.p.	Yehudi Menuhin/London Philharmonic Orchestra/Lennox Berkeley - Royal Festival Hall, 18 (June) 1961
f.rec.	Yehudi Menuhin/Menuhin Festival Orchestra/Sir Adrian Boult - *HMV ASD 2759; EMI CDM5 66121-2 CD)*
Pub:	Chester, 1962

Batter my heart three person'd God - cantata for soprano, SATB chorus, organ and chamber orchestra Op. 60 No. 1 (1962)

[Words: John Donne 'Holy Sonnets']
Commissioned by the Riverside Church Choir, New York

Dur:	13'
Instr:	0/1/0/0 - 1/0/0/0 - str. (Vc. Db. only)
f.p.	Riverside Church Choir/Richard Weagley - New York
f.Brit.p.	BBC Northern Singers/BBC Northern Orchestra/Lennox Berkeley - Leeds University, 19 October 1963
Pub:	Chester, 1962

Justorum Animae - motet for SATB chorus Op. 60 No. 2 (1963)

[Words from 'The Book of Wisdom']

Dur:	5'
f.rec.	Canterbury Cathedral Choir/Allan Wicks - *Grosvenor GRS 1030*
Pub:	Chester

Automne - song for medium voice and piano Op. 60 No. 3 (1963)

[Words: Guillaume Apollinaire]
Written in memory of Francis Poulenc

Dur:	2'30"
f.p.	Nigel Wickens (Bar.)/Peter Croser (Pno.) - Cheltenham Town Hall, 10 July 1968 (Cheltenham Festival)
f.rec.	Meriel Dickinson (M/S)/Peter Dickinson (Pno.) - *Argo ZRG 788*
Pub:	Chester

Counting the Beats - song for high voice and piano Op. 60 No. 4 (1963 rev. 1971)

[Words: Robert Graves]

Commissioned by Patric Dickinson for the 1963 Festival of Poetry - Richard Arnell (q.v.), Nicholas Maw and Humphrey Searle (q.v.) were also asked to contribute their own setting of the poem.

f.p.   Gerald English (Ten.)/John Constable (Pno.) - Royal Court Theatre, London, 16 July 1963

Pub: Thames

Sonatina for oboe and piano Op. 61 (1962)

Dedicated to Janet and John Craxton

Dur: 12'

f.p.   Janet Craxton (Ob.)/John Craxton (Pno.)

f.rec.   Catherine Plugyers (Ob.)/ Matthew Stanley (Pno.) - *Redbridge RBR 1002*

Pub: Chester, 1964

Gartan (Christ is the World's Redeemer) - hymn tune (1963)

[Words attrib. St. Columba trans. Rev. Duncan MacGregor]

Written to celebrate the fourteenth centenary of the death of St. Columba (Britten contributed his **Hymn to St. Columbus** for the same event q.v.)

f.p.   local choirs/Lennox Berkeley - Gartan, Co. Donegal, Eire, 2 June 1963

Pub: Musical Times (Novello), July 1963

Four Ronsard Sonnets (Set 2) for tenor and orchestra* Op. 62 (1963)

[1. Ce premier jour de mai 2. Je sens une douceur
 3. Ma fiévre croist toujours 4. Yeux, qui versez en l'ame]

Commissioned by the BBC and dedicated "in affectionate memory of Francis Poulenc"

Dur: 17'30"

Instr: 2+picc./2/2/2 - 4/2/3/1 - timp. perc.(2) hp. str.

f.p.   Peter Pears/BBC Symphony Orchestra/Lennox Berkeley - Royal Albert Hall, London, 9 August 1963 (Promenade Concert)

f.rec.   William Whitesides (Ten.)/Louisville Orchestra/Robert Whitney - *Louisville (USA) LOU 662(m); LOU S 662*

Pub: Chester, 1964

* Also arr. for tenor and chamber orchestra as Op. 62a (1963)

Instr: 1/1/1/1 - 2/0/0/0 - timp. hp. str.

f.rec.   Peter Pears (Ten.)/London Sinfonietta/Lennox Berkeley - *Decca HEAD 3; London (USA) HEAD 3*

Pub: Chester, 1964

Diversions for eight instruments Op. 63 (1964)

Commissioned by the Delphos Ensemble for the 1964 Cheltenham Festival

Dur: 18'

Instr: Ob. Cl. Bsn. Hn. Vn. Va. Vc. Pno.

f.p.   Delphos Ensemble - David Cowsill (Ob.), Michael Saxton (Cl.), Michael Whewell (Bsn.), Frank Downes (Hn.), Meyer Stolow (Vn.), Kenneth Page (Va.), Oliver Brookes (Vc.), James Walker (Pno.) - Cheltenham, 13 July 1964 (Cheltenham Festival)

f.rec.   Nash Ensemble - *Hyperion A 66086*

Pub: Chester

Mass for five (SSATB) voices Op. 64 (1964)
Commissioned by His Eminence Cardinal Heenan, Archbishop of Westminster, and
dedicated to Colin Mawby and the Choir of Westminster Cathedral.
Dur: 12'
f.p.   Choir of Westminster Cathedral/Colin Mawby, c.1964
f.rec.   Norwich Cathedral Choir/Michael Nicholas - *Vista VPS 1096*
Pub: Chester

Songs of the Half-Light for high voice and guitar Op. 65 (1963-64)
[Words: Walter de la Mare 1. Rachel 2. Full Moon 3. All that's past
 4. The Moth 5. The Fleeting]
Commissioned by and dedicated to Peter Pears
Dur: 13'
f.p.   Peter Pears (Ten.)/Julian Bream (Gtr.) - Jubilee Hall, Aldeburgh, 22 June 1965
            (Aldeburgh Festival)
f.broad.p. above performance - 24 August 1966
f.recs.   (Nos. 2 and 5) Neil Mackie (Ten.)/B. Jeffrey (Gtr.) - *Beltona MBE 111(m),*
            SBE 111
            (complete) Ian Partridge (Ten.)/Jukka Savijoki (Gtr.) - *Ondine ODE*
            779-2(CD)
Pub: Chester, 1966 (ed. Julian Bream)

Partita for chamber orchestra Op. 66 (1964-65)
[1. Prelude 2. Aria I 3. Aria II 4. Rondo]
Commissioned by Crosby & Co. Ltd for the 1965 Farnham Festival
Dur: 12'30"
Instr: 1/1/2/1 - 2/1/1/0 - timp. perc. str.
f.p.   Frensham Heights School Orchestra/Edward Rice - Farnham Parish Church,
            Surrey, 17 May 1965 (Farnham Festival)
f.recs.   (Nos. 2, 3 and 4) above artists (recorded at the first performance) - Waverley
            LLP 1039(m)
            (complete) London Philharmonic Orchestra/Lennox Berkeley - *Lyrita SRCS*
            74, SRCD 226(CD)
Pub: Chester, 1966

Three Songs for four (TTBB) male voices - Op. 67 No. 1 (1965)
[1. Fair Daffodils (Robert Herrick) 2. Spring goeth all in White (Robert Bridges)
 3. Kissing Usurie (Robert Herrick)]
Commissioned by the Men's Chorus of the University of California.
f.p.   The Schubertians/Carl Zytowski - University of California, Santa Barbara, 15
            March 1966
f.Brit.p.   above artists - Pittville Pump Room, Cheltenham, 13 July 1986 (Cheltenham
            Festival)
f.rec.   The Schubertians/Carl Zytowski (private recording) -*Custom Fidelity (USA no*
            number)
Pub: Chester

Nocturne for harp Op. 67 No. 2 (1967)
Written for and dedicated to Hannah Francis

Dur: 3'
f.p.   Hannah Francis c.1967
f.rec.   David Watkins - *RCA LRL 1 5087*
Pub: Stainer & Bell, 1972 (ed. David Watkins)

Castaway* - opera in one Act and four Scenes Op. 68 (1965-67)

[Libretto: Paul Dehn]
Dur: 60'
Instr: 1/1/2/1 - 2/1/1/0 - timp. perc.(2) pno. hp. str.
f.p.   English Opera Group Chorus and Orchestra cond. Meredith Davies - Jubilee
            Hall, Aldeburgh, 3 June 1967 (Aldeburgh Festival)
Producer: Anthony Besch
Settings: Peter Rice
Principals: Geoffrey Chard, Patricia Clark, Kenneth Macdonald, Jean Allister,
            Malcolm Rivers and James Athius
f.Lon.p.   Sadler's Wells Theatre, 12 July 1967
Pub: Chester, 1970 (vocal score)
(* This work was designed as a companion piece to the earlier one Act opera **A Dinner
Engagement**. Peter Dickinson points out that it was not until 1983 that they appeared as
"a double-bill" - with **Castaway** as the first half - in a Trinity College of Music Opera
Group production at the Bloomsbury Theatre, London on 16 June 1983 conducted by
Meredith Davies.)

Three Hymn Tunes (1967)

[1. Boar's Hill (Hearest Thou, my Soul) Words: Richard Crashaw
 2. Wiveton (Lord, by whose Breath) Words: Andrew Young
 3. (I sing of a Maiden) Words: Anon. 15th cent.]
f.rec.   (No. 3) King's College Choir/David Willcocks - *HMV ALP 2290(m)*, *ASD
            2290*
Pub: Cambridge Hymnal, 1967

Signs in the Dark* for SATB chorus and string orchestra Op. 69 (1967)

[Words: Laurie Lee 1. Day of these days 2. Twelfth Night 3. The Three Winds
 4. Poem for Easter]
Commissioned by the Stroud Festival Society (Berkeley's choice of poet was most
appropriate as Laurie Lee was born in Stroud)
Dur: 21'
f.p.   Stroud Festival Choir/Hirsch Chamber Players/Leonard Hirsch - St. Lawrence
            Parish Church, Stroud, Gloucestershire, 22 October 1967 (Stroud Festival)
f.Lon.p.   BBC Chorus/BBC Northern Singers/BBC Northern Symphony
            Orchestra/Lennox Berkeley - Royal Albert Hall, 27 August 1968
            (Promenade Concert)
Pub: Chester
(* The title is a line from the second poem, 'Twelfth Night')

Quartet for oboe and string trio Op. 70 (1967)

Dedicated to Lady Norton who commissioned the work on behalf of the ICA with the aid
of a grant from the Norton Foundation. It was written for the debut of the London Oboe
Quartet.

Dur: 15'
Instr: Ob. Vn. Va. Vc.
f.p.   London Oboe Quartet - Janet Craxton (Ob.), Perry Hart (Vn.), Brian Hawkins
           (Va.), Kenneth Heath (Vc.) - Wigmore Hall, London, 22 May 1968
f.broad.p. above performance - 7 January 1969
f.rec.   Nash Ensemble - *Hyperion A 66086*
Pub: Chester

Magnificat for SATB chorus, organ and orchestra Op. 71 (1967-68)

Commissioned by the City Arts Trust for the opening concert of the 1968 Festival of the
City of London.
Dur: 22'
Instr: 2+picc./2+ca./2+bcl./2+cbsn. - 4/3/3/1 - timp. perc. hp. str.
f.p.   Westminster Abbey Choir/Westminster Cathedral Choir/St. Paul's Cathedral
           Choir/Wandsworth School Boys Choir/London Symphony Chorus and
           Orchestra/Lennox Berkeley - St. Paul's Cathedral, London, (8) 9 July 1968
           (City of London Festival)
f.rec.   BBC Chorus/BBC Choral Society/London Philharmonic Orchestra/Sir Adrian
           Boult - *Intaglio INCD 7451(CD)* (a 'live' performance recorded in the Royal
           Albert Hall, London, at a Promenade Concert on 4 August 1969)
Pub: Chester

Three Pieces for organ Op. 72 No. 1 (1966-68)

[1. Aubade 2. Aria 3. Toccata]
Commissioned by the Cheltenham Festival and dedicated "to Julian" (Julian Berkeley)
Dur: 12'
f.p.   (Aubade only) Simon Preston - Aldeburgh, 17 June 1966 (at an Aldeburgh
           Festival Memorial Concert in tribute to Edith Sitwell)
f.p.   (complete) Simon Preston - Cheltenham College Chapel, 5 July 1969
           (Cheltenham Festival)
f.rec.   S. Hollas (on the organ of Cheltenham College Chapel) - *Wealden WS 149*
Pub: Chester, 1971

The Windhover for SATB chorus Op. 72 No. 2 (1968)

[Words: Gerard Manley Hopkins]
Pub: Novello

Theme and Variations for piano duet Op. 73 (1968)

Dedicated to Annie Alt and Gerald Stofsky
Dur: 8'
f.p.   Annie Alt/Gerald Stofsky - St. Lawrence Parish Church, Stroud,
           Gloucestershire, 20 October 1971 (Stroud Festival)
f.rec.   Raphael Terroni/Norman Beedie - *British Music Society BMS 416(CD)*
Pub: Chester

Symphony No. 3 Op. 74 (1968-69)

Commissioned by the Cheltenham Festival and dedicated to Anthony and Lilli Hornby
Dur: 15'
Instr: 3/2+ca./2/2 +cbsn - 4/3/3/1 - timp. perc.(2) hp. str.

f.p.   L'Orchestre National de l'O.R.T.F./Jean Martinon - Cheltenham Town Hall,
             9 July 1969 (Cheltenham Festival)
f.Lon.p.   BBC Northern Symphony Orchestra/Raymond Leppard - Royal Albert Hall,
             3 August 1973 (Promenade Concert)
f.rec.   London Philharmonic Orchestra/Lennox Berkeley - *Lyrita SRCS 57, SRCD
             226(CD); Musical Heritage Society (USA) MHS 1672*
Pub: Chester, 1971

Windsor Variations for chamber orchestra Op. 75 (1969)

Commissioned by the Windsor Festival with funds provided by the Arts Council of Great
Britain.
Dur: 13'
Instr: 1/2/0/2 - 2/0/0/0 - str.
f.p.   Menuhin Festival Orchestra/Yehudi Menuhin - Windsor, 1969
            (Windsor Festival)
f.Lon.p.   above artists - Southwark Cathedral, 14 July 1970
f.broad.p. BBC Scottish Symphony Orchestra/Meredith Davies - 4 August 1973
Pub: Chester, 1972

Hail Holy Queen* - hymn for unison voice(s) and organ (or piano) (1970)

(* The melodic line of this hymn formed the basis of the slow movement of the String
Quartet No. 3 q.v.)

Andantino for cello and piano (c.1970)

Written for the Annual Lunch of the Performing Right Society on 1 July 1970. Among
the other composers who contributed pieces for an album of music presented to Prince
Charles (who played the cello) were Sir Arthur Bliss - who was then President of the PRS
- John Gardner, Grace Williams and Sir William Walton (q.v.).

String Quartet No. 3 Op. 76 (1970)

Commissioned by Lord Chaplin for the Dartington String Quartet and dedicated to
Anthony Chaplin
Dur: 20'
f.p.   Dartington String Quartet - Dartington, South Devon, November 1970
f.Lon.p.   Alberni Quartet - Purcell Room, 23 March 1971
f.broad.p. Alberni Quartet - August 1971
Pub: Chester

Theme and Variations for guitar Op. 77 (1970)

Written at the request of the Italian guitarist Angelo Gilardino and dedicated to Julian
Bream
Dur: 7'
f.p.   Julian Bream - Salone della Regola, Tronzano-Vercelli, Italy,
            19 December 1971
f.rec.   Julian Bream - *RCA SB 6876,ARD 1 0049; RCA Gold Seal (set) 09026
            61583-2(CD), 09026 61595-2(CD)*
Pub: Berben (Milan); Chester, 1973

Five* Chinese Songs for medium voice and piano Op. 78 (1970-71)
[1. People hide their love (Wu-Ti trans. Arthur Waley)
 2. The Autumn Wind (Wu-Ti trans. Arthur Waley)
 3. Dreaming of a dead lady (Shen-Yo trans. Arthur Waley)
 4. Late Spring (Yang Kuang trans. R. Kotewall and N. D. Smith)
 5. The Riverside Village (Ssu-K'ang Schu trans. R. Kotewall and N. D. Smith)]
Commissioned by the Park Lane Group
Dur: 8'
f.p.   Meriel Dickinson (M/S)/Peter Dickinson (Pno.) - Purcell Room, London,
            22 March 1971 (Park Lane Concert)
f.broad.p. above artists - 29 March 1972
f.rec.   Meriel Dickinson (M/S)/Peter Dickinson (Pno.) - *Argo ZRG 788*
Pub: Chester, 1975
(* there is a draft MS of an additional song `Releasing a Migrant Yen')

Dialogue for cello and chamber orchestra Op. 79 (1970-71 rev.1981)
Commissioned by the King's Lynn Festival
Dur: 17'
Instr: 1/2/0/2 - 2/0/0/0 - str.
f.p.   Maurice Gendron/English Chamber Orchestra/Raymond Leppard - St.
            Nicholas Chapel, King's Lynn, 30 July 1971 (Kings Lynn Festival)
f.Lon.p.   Thomas Igloi/English Chamber Orchestra/Raymond Leppard - Queen
            Elizabeth Hall, 11 February 1972
Pub: Chester

Introduction and Allegro for double bass and piano Op. 80 (1971)
Commissioned with the aid of a grant from the Arts Council of Great Britain and
dedicated to Rodney Slatford
Dur: 7'
f.p.   Rodney Slatford (Db.)/Clifford Lee (Pno.) - London, 1971
Pub: Yorke Ed., 1972, 1984

Duo for oboe and cello (1971)
Dur: 10'
Pub: Chester

Duo for cello and piano Op. 81 No. 1 (1971)
Commissioned by the Park Lane Group
Dur: 9'
f.p.   Elizabeth Wilson (Vc.)/Kathrine Sturrock (Pno.) - Purcell Room, London,
            10 January 1972 (Park Lane Concert Series)
f.rec.   Julian Lloyd Webber (Vc.)/John McCabe (Pno.) - *Oiseau Lyre DSLO 18*
Pub: Chester

Canon: In Memoriam 'Igor Stravinsky' for string quartet (1971)
Dur: 2´
f.p.   John Tunnell (Vn.)/Peter Carter (Vn.)/Brian Hawkins (Va.)/ Charles Tunnell
            (Vc.) - BBC Broadcasting House, London, 8 April 1972

Pub: Boosey & Hawkes, 1971 (in a special Stravinsky issue of 'Tempo' magazine
            No. 97)

Palm Court Waltz for orchestra Op. 81 No. 2 (1971)
Commissioned by and dedicated 'to Burnet with love and gratitude'
(Burnet Pavitt)
Dur: 7'
Instr: 2/2/2/2 - 4/2/3/1 - timp. perc. hp. str.
f.doc.p.   English Sinfonietta/Norman del Mar - Queen Elizabeth Hall, London,
            14 May 1983 (80th Birthday Concert)
Pub: Chester
also arr. for piano duet as Op. 81 No. 2a (1971)
Dur: 4'
f.rec.   Ian Brown/Kathryn Stott - *Hyperion A 66086*
Pub: Chester, 1976

Four Concert Studies for piano Op. 82 (1972)
Commissioned by and dedicated to Lord Chaplin
Dur: 8'30"
f.p.   Margaret Bruce - Purcell Room, London, 9 December 1975
Pub: Chester, 1976

Three Latin Motets for SSATB chorus Op. 83 No. 1 (1972)
[1. Eripe me Domine 2. Veni sponsa Christi 3. Regina coeli]
Commissioned by the North Wales Music Festival and written for the choir of St. John's
College, Cambridge
Dur: 9'
f.p.   Choir of St. John's College, Cambridge/George Guest - St. Asaph Cathedral,
            28 September 1972 (North Wales Music Festival)
f.rec.   Choir of Clare College, Cambridge/Timothy Brown - *Meridian CDE
            84216(CD)*
Pub: Chester

Hymn for Shakespeare's Birthday for SATB chorus and organ Op. 83 No. 2 (1972)
[Words: C. Day Lewis]
Pub: Chester

Fanfare for the Royal Academy of Music Banquet (1972)
Dur: 1'
Instr: 8 Tpt.
Pub: Chester

Sinfonia concertante for oboe and orchestra Op. 84 (1972-73)
Commissioned by the BBC for Berkeley's seventieth birthday and dedicated to Janet
Craxton
Dur: 24'
Instr: 2/0/2/2 - 2/2/0/0 - timp. hp. pno. str.
f.p.   Janet Craxton/BBC Northern Symphony Orchestra/Raymond Leppard - Royal
            Albert Hall, London, 3 August 1973 (Promenade Concert)

f.rec.   (Canzonetta only) Roger Winfield (Ob.)/London Philharmonic
         Orchestra/Lennox Berkeley - *Lyrita SRCS 74, SRCD 226(CD)*
Pub: Chester, 1976
Exc.   Canzonetta arr. for oboe and piano
Pub: Chester

Antiphon* for string orchestra Op. 85 (1973)
Commissioned by the Cheltenham Festival with funds provided by the Arts Council of
Great Britain and dedicated to the Festival's Director, John Manduell
Dur: 13'
f.p.   Academy of St. Martin-in-the-Fields/Neville Marriner - Cheltenham Town
         Hall, 7 July 1973 (Cheltenham Festival)
f.Lon.p. Fine Arts Orchestra/Lennox Berkeley - Queen Elizabeth Hall,
         22 October 1973
f.rec.   Westminster Cathedral String Orchestra/Colin Mawby - *Unicorn UNS 260*
Pub: Chester, 1973
(* The title refers to the plainsong melody from the Antiphonale Romanum on which the
second movement of the work is based)

Voices of the Night for orchestra Op. 86 (1973)
Commissioned by the Three Choirs Festival
Dur: 10'
Instr: 2/2/2/2+cbsn. - 4/3/3/1 - timp. perc. hp. str.
f.p.   City of Birmingham Symphony Orchestra/Lennox Berkeley - Hereford
         Cathedral, 22 August 1973 (Three Choirs Festival)
f.Lon.p. BBC Symphony Orchestra/Sir Adrian Boult - Royal Albert Hall, 4 September
         1975 (Promenade Concert)
Pub: Chester, 1973

Suite for string orchestra Op. 87 (1973-74)
Dur: 11'
f.p.   Westminster Cathedral String Orchestra/Colin Mawby - St. John's Smith
         Square, London, 1 June 1974
Pub: Chester

Guitar Concerto Op. 88 (1974)
Commissioned by the 1974 City of London Festival and dedicated to Julian Bream
Dur: 21'30"
Instr: 1/1/1/1 - 2/0/0/0 - str.
f.p.   Julian Bream/English Chamber Orchestra/Andrew Davis - St. Bartholomew
         The Great, London, 4 July 1974 (City of London Festival)
f.broad.p. above performance - 14 September 1975
f.rec.   Julian Bream/Monteverdi Orchestra/John Eliot Gardiner - *RCA ARL 11181,*
         RK 11734 (MC), GK 81181(MC); RCA Red Seal (set) 09026 61583-2(CD),
         09026 61605-2(CD)
Pub: Chester, 1977 (ed. Julian Bream)

Five Herrick Poems for high voice and harp Op. 89 (1973-74 rev. 1976)
[1. Now is your turne, my dearest 2. Dearest of Thousands

3. These springs were maidens once that lov'd
4. My God! Look on me with eyes of pitie
5. If nine times you your bridegroom kisse]
f.p.   Peter Pears (Ten.)/Osian Ellis (Hp.) - The Maltings, Snape, 19 June 1974
             (Aldeburgh Festival)
Pub: Chester

Quintet for wind and piano Op. 90 (1974-75)
Commissioned by the Chamber Music Society of Lincoln Center, New York
Dur: 26'
Instr: Ob. Cl. Bsn. Hn. Pno.
f.p.   Lincoln Centre Chamber Players - Alice Tully Hall, Lincoln Center, New
             York, 30 January 1976
f.Brit.p.   Melos Ensemble - Peter Graeme (Ob.), Thea King (Cl.), William Waterhouse
             (Bsn.), Timothy Brown (Hn.), Howard Shelley (Pno.) - Wigmore Hall,
             London, 4 December 1976
f.broad.p.   Melos Ensemble - 23 May 1978
f.rec.   Roger Lord (Ob.)/Sidney Fell (Cl.)/Julius Baker (Hn.)/Kerry Camden
             (Bsn.)/Colin Horsley (Pno.) - *Meridian E 77017*
Pub: Chester

Grace for SATB chorus (c.1975)
Written for the Merchant Taylors' Company

The Lord is my Shepherd - anthem for treble,SATB chorus and organ Op. 91 No. 1 (1975)
[Words: Psalm 23]
Commissioned by Chichester Cathedral in celebration of their 900th Anniversary.
Dur: 5′
f.p.   Choir of Chichester Cathedral/John Birch, with Ian Fox (org.) - Chichester
             Cathedral, 14 June 1975
f.rec.   above artists - *Abbey LPB 770*
Pub: Chester

The Hill of the Graces for SATB double chorus Op. 91 No. 2 (1975)
[Words: Edmund Spenser 'The Faerie Queen' Book VI Canto X]
Commissioned by the BBC in celebration of the fiftieth anniversary of the BBC Singer's
first unaccompanied recital and dedicated 'to Nicholas'
Dur: 13'45"
f.p.   BBC Singers/John Poole - St. John's Smith Square, London,
             20 October 1975
f.broad.p.   above artists, 2 November 1975
f.rec.   BBC Northern Singers/Stephen Wilkinson - *Abbey LPB 798*
Pub: Chester, 1977

Fantasia for organ Op. 92 (1976)
Commissioned by the Organ Club in celebration of its Golden Jubilee with funds
provided by the Arts Council of Great Britain and dedicated 'to Julian'
Dur: 10'

f.p.   Nicholas Kynaston - Royal Festival Hall, London, 1 December 1976 (Organ
            Club Golden Jubilee Recital)
f.broad.p. above performance - 14 May 1977
f.rec.   above first performance - *Organ Club JPS G62*
Pub: Berben (Milan); Chester, 1977

Another Spring - song cycle for medium voice and piano Op. 93 No. 1 (1977)
[Words: Walter de la Mare 1. Poetry 2. Another Spring 3. Afraid]
Commissioned by the Chichester Festival for a concert in honour of Dean Walter
Hussey's retirement and dedicated to Dame Janet Baker
Dur: 6'30"
f.p.   Janet Baker (Con.)/Geoffrey Pratley (Pno.) - Chichester Cathedral,   20 July
            1977 (Chichester Festival)
f.rec.   Francis Loring (Bar.)/Colin Horsley (Pno.) - *Meridian E 77017 (and MC)*
Pub: Chester, 1978

Poulenc: Flute Sonata arr. flute and orchestra Op. 93 No. 2 (1977)
Commissioned by James Galway
Dur: 14'
Instr: 1/2/2/2 - 2/0/0/0 - timp. str.
f.rec.   James Galway/Royal Philharmonic Orchestra/Charles Dutoit - *RCA RL 25109
            (and MC), GK 85448(MC)*
Pub: Chester

Four Score Years and Ten - song for voice and piano (1977)
[Words: Vivian Ellis]
f.p.   26 July 1977

Symphony No. 4 Op. 94 (1976-78)
Commissioned by the Royal Philharmonic Orchestra for the composer's 75th birthday
with funds provided by the Arts Council of Great Britain and dedicated to Burnet Pavitt
Dur: 30'
Instr: 2+picc./2+ca./2+bcl./2+cbsn. - 4/3/3/1 - timp. perc.(2) hp. str.
f.p.   Royal Philharmonic Orchestra/Sir Charles Groves - Royal Festival Hall,
            London, 30 May 1978
Pub: Chester

Prelude and Capriccio for piano Op. 95 (1978)
f.p.   Martin Jones - Cardiff, 24 February 1978 (Cardiff Festival)
f.rec.   Raphael Terroni - *Pearl SHE 576*
Pub: Chester

Judica me - anthem for SSATBB chorus Op. 96 No. 1 (1978)
Commissioned by the Three Choirs Festival
Dur: 7'
f.p.   Choir of Worcester Cathedral/Donald Hunt - Worcester Cathedral,
            22 September 1978 (Three Choirs Festival)
f.rec.   above artists - *Alpha ACA 533*
Pub: Chester

Ubi Caritas et Amor - anthem for SSATB chorus Op. 96 No. 2 (1980)
Commissioned in celebration of the 500th Anniversary of the birth of St. Benedict.
f.p.   Westminster Cathedral Choir/Stephen Cleobury - Westminster Cathedral, London, 11 July 1980
Pub: Chester

Sonata for flute and piano Op. 97 (1978 rev. 1983)
Commissioned by the Edinburgh International Festival for James Galway
Dur: 12'
f.p.   James Galway (Fl.)/Philip Moll (Pno.) - Leith Theatre, Edinburgh, 30 August 1978 (Edinburgh International Festival)
f.broad.p. above first performance - 3 June 1979
f.rec.   above artists - *RCA RS 9011 (and MC), ARLI 5447*
Pub: Chester

Una and the Lion - cantata concertante for soprano, recorder, viola da gamba and harpsichord Op. 98 (1978-79)
[Words: Edmund Spenser - 'The Faerie Queen' Canto III]
Commissioned by Carl Dolmetsch with funds provided by the Arts Council of Great Britain
f.p.   Elizabeth Harwood (Sop.)/Jeanne Dolmetsch (Rec.)/Marguerite Dolmetsch (Va.)/ Joseph Saxby (Hpschd.) - Wigmore Hall, London, 22 March 1979
f.broad.p. above artists - 8 August 1979 (recorded 23 March 1979)
Pub: Chester

Magnificat and Nunc Dimittis for SATB chorus and organ Op. 99 (1980)
Commissioned by the Southern Cathedrals' Festival.
Dur: 9'
f.p.   Southern Cathedrals' Choirs/John Birch - Chichester Cathedral, 26 July 1980 (Southern Cathedrals' Festival)
f.rec.   Michael Brewer Singers/Michael Brewer - *Priory PRCD 292(CD)*
Pub: Chester

Faldon Park - opera in two acts Op. 100 (1980, unfinished*)
[Libretto: Winton Dean]
(* an annotated vocal score of Act I has been prepared by Susan Bradshaw)

Bagatelle for two pianos Op. 101 No. 1 (1981)
Dedicated to Lady Helen Dashwood
f.p.   Margaret Bruce/Jennifer Bowring - Purcell Room, London, 1 May 1983
Pub: Chester

Mazurka for piano Op. 101 No. 2 (1982)
Commissioned by the BBC as one of a group of works marking the 250th anniversary of the birth of Haydn.
Dur: 2'

f.p.   John McCabe - BBC Broadcasting House, London, 18 March 1982
f.conc.p.   John McCabe - London, 31 March 1982
f.rec.   Christopher Headington - *Kingdom KCLCD 2012(CD) (and MC)*
Pub: Chester

Sonnet for high voice and piano Op. 102 (1982)
[Words: Louise Labé]
Written 'for Hugues Cuenod with love and admiration'
Dur: 2'30"
Pub: Chester, 1992

In Wintertime - carol for unaccompanied SATB chorus Op. 103 (1983)
[Words: Betty Askwith]
Commissioned by Stephen Cleobury and the Choir of King's College, Cambridge.
Dur: 2'45"
f.p.   King's College Choir/Stephen Cleobury - King's College Chapel, Cambridge,
            24 December 1983 (Festival of Nine Lessons and Carols)
f.rec.   Elysian Singers/Matthew Greenall - *Continuum CCD 1043(CD)*
Pub: Chester

UNDATED WORKS

Andante con moto - movement for piano

A Short Piece for junior wind band
Pub: Chester

Adeste Fidelis - carol for treble and SATB chorus

`i carry your heart' - song
[e. e. cummings]
Draft MS and sketch only

FILM MUSIC

The Voice of the People (1939)

The Sword of the Spirit (1942)
Written for the Catholic Film Society

Out of Chaos - Two Cities (1944)

Hotel Reserve - RKO Radio-British (1944)
Directors: Victor Hanbury, Lance Comfort and Max Greene
Music played by: BBC Northern Orchestra/Muir Mathieson (rec. 28 October 1944)

The First Gentleman - Columbia (1948)
US title: Affairs of a Rogue
Director: Albert Cavalcanti

Music played by: London Symphony Orchestra/Sir Thomas Beecham

Youth in Britain - Basic Films for C.O.L/Colonial Office (1957)

INCIDENTAL MUSIC

(a)   **Radio (all BBC)**

Westminster Abbey - feature (1941)
Instr: 0/0/sax./0 - 2/2/0/0 - timp. perc. str.

Yesterday and Today - documentary (1943)
Music recorded 15 April 1943

A Glutton for life - play (1946)
Instr: 1/1/1/1 - 1/1/1/0 - timp. perc. hp. str.

The Wall of Troy - play (1946)
[Patric Dickinson]
Instr: 1/1/1/1 - 1/0/0/0 - perc. hp. str.
Music played by BBC Midland Light Orchestra/Gilbert Vinter - (rec. 21 November 1946)

Iphigenia in Tauris - play (1954)

Seraphina - play (1956)
Instr: 0/0/sax./0 - 0/0/3/0 - perc. acc. hp. str.

Look back to Lyttletoun - play (1957)
Instr: 1/1/1/1 - 1/0/0/0 - timp. perc. hp. str.

Maupassant (ND)

Sarawack National Anthem (ND)

(b)   **Stage**

Music for a puppet show (1938)
[Montagu Slater - 1.The Seven Ages of Man 2. The Station Master]
f.p.   Helen and Margaret Binyon (puppeteers) - Mercury Theatre, London, 22 June 1938
Music conducted by: Frank Kennard
Designer: Helen Binyon
(* Britten q.v. provided the music for the other play in this trilogy)

The Tempest (1946)
[Shakespeare]
f.p.   Shakespeare Memorial Theatre, Stratford-upon-Avon, 20 April 1946

Pre-recorded music played by: National Symphony Chamber Orchestra/
BBC Singers (recorded by Decca)
Producer: Eric Crozier
Principals: Robert Harris, Joy Parker, Julian Somers
Exc. 'Where the Bee Sucks' - song for voice and orchestra
Instr: 2/2/2/2 - 2/1/3/0 - timp. str.

Oranges and Lemons - review (1946)
[1. Jigsaw 2. Venus Anadyomene]

The Winter's Tale (1960)
[Shakespeare]
f.p. Shakespeare Memorial Theatre, Stratford-upon-Avon, 30 August 1960
Music played by: Wind Band/Brian Priestman
Producer: Peter Wood
Principals: Eric Porter, Elizabeth Sellars, Patrick Allen
Exc. 'Daffodils' - song for high voice and ensemble
f.rec.   Jamie MacDougall (Ten.)/English Serenata - *Meridian CDE
84301(CD)*

MS LOCATION

Majority of MS are held (on loan deposit) at the British Library **(BL)**

Other locations include:

BPL Five Housman Songs (1940), Two Songs (1943)

BIBLIOGRAPHY

Berkeley, Lennox   **Benjamin Britten: a Commentary on his works from a group of
                       specialists** (ed. Donald Mitchell and Hans Keller).
                       London: Rockliff, 1952

Berkeley, Lennox   **Alan Rawsthorne.** Composer No. 42, Winter 1971/72

Berkeley, Lennox   **A Composer Speaks.** Composer No. 43, Spring 1972

Berkeley, Lennox and
Patric Dickinson   **Counting the Beats.** Composer No. 12, Autumn 1963

Brook, Donald   **Lennox Berkeley** in his 'Composers' Gallery'. London:
                       Rockliff,1940

Bryan, Gordon   **The Younger English Composers - V, Lennox Berkeley.**
                       Monthly Musical Record, June 1929

Craggs, Stewart   **A Berkeley Source Book.** Aldershot: Ashgate, 2000

Dickinson, Peter   **The Music of Lennox Berkeley.** Musical Times, May 1963

Dickinson, Peter   **Berkeley's Music Today.** Musical Times, November 1968

Dickinson, Peter   **Senior British Composers 2 - Lennox Berkeley.** Composer No. 36, Summer 1970

Dickinson, Peter(ed.)   **Interview with Sir Lennox Berkeley** in his 'Twenty British Composers'. London: Chester Music, 1975

Dickinson, Peter   **Sir Lennox Berkeley. The Repertoire Guide.** Classical Music, March 1991

Dickinson, Peter   **The Music of Lennox Berkeley.** London: Thames Publishing, 1989 [B]

Flothius, Marius   **Lennox Berkeley** in his 'Modern British Composers'. Stockholm; Continental Book Co./London; Sidgwick & Jackson, 1949

Frank, Alan   **Lennox Berkeley** in his 'Modern British Composers'. London: Dobson, 1953

Hughes, Eric, and
Timothy Day   **Discographies of British Composers - 1 Sir Lennox Berkeley.** Recorded Sound, No. 77, 1979 [D]

Redlich, H. F.   **Lennox Berkeley.** Music Survey, June 1951

Routh, Francis   **Lennox Berkeley** in his 'Contemporary British Composers'. London: Macdonald, 1972

Rushton, James   **Lennox Berkeley at 80: Some reflections on his Church music.** The World of Church Music, 1983

Schafer, Murray   **Lennox Berkeley** in his 'British Composers in Interview'. London: Faber & Faber, 1963

Steptoe, Roger   **Contemporary Composer Series - Sir Lennox Berkeley.** Music Teacher, July 1986

Steptoe, Roger   **Lennox Berkeley: A Tribute.** Composer, No. 90, Spring 1987

Williamson, Malcolm   **Sir Lennox Berkeley (1903-1989).** Musical Times, April 1990

Wordsworth, David   **Sir Lennox Berkeley - a tribute.** Journal of the British Music Society, Vol. 12, 1990

10

Arthur Bliss
(1891–1975)

Quartet (Variations) in C minor (c.1905)
Composed while Bliss was a pupil at Rugby School
Instr: Pno. Cl. Vc. Timp.
f.p.   Arthur Bliss (Pno.), Kennard Bliss (Cl.) and two friends from the Rugby
            School Orchestra - at the house of Basil Johnson, the school organist and
            music master, Rugby c.1905

Trio for piano, clarinet and cello (c.1907)
f.p.   Arthur Bliss (Pno.)/Kennard Bliss (Cl.)/Howard Bliss (Vc.) - at the London
            home of the composer in Bayswater, 19 January 1908

Valse melancolique for piano (c.1910)
f.p.   Arthur Bliss - Bayswater, London, 13 January 1911

May-zeeh - Valse for piano (1910)
`Composée et Dediée à son amie M.W.'
Dur: 2'30"
Pub: Gould, 1910

Suite for piano (c.1910-12)
[1. Prelude 2. Ballade 3. Scherzo]
Dedicated `to my father' - the score is dated 13 May 1912
Dur: 11'30"
Pub: Joseph Williams, 1912

Intermezzo for piano (c.1912)
Dur: 4'
Pub: Stainer & Bell, 1912

The Dark-eyed Gentleman - song for voice and piano (c.1912)
[Words: Thomas Hardy]

Valses Fantastiques for piano (1913)

Dedicated `To A.R.R.' No. 2 `To C.R.' No. 3 `To G.R.'
Dur: 8'45"
Pub: Stainer & Bell, 1913
(Two of the waltzes were later incorporated in the 1974 **Wedding Suite** for piano)

String Quartet in A major `Op.4' (c.1914)

Dedicated to Edward J. Dent
Dur: 28'
f.priv.p.   T. H. Marshall (Vn.)/S. W. Terrell (Vn.)/H. Gardner (Va.)/Howard Bliss (Vc.)
            - Club Room of the Cambridge University Musical Club, 30 May 1914
f.pub.p.   above artists - Hall of Gonville and Caius College, Cambridge, 9 June 1914
f.Lon.p.   Nettie Carpenter (Vn.)/Eugene Goossens (Vn.)/Ernest Yonge (Vn.)/ Howard
            Bliss (Vc.) - at the home of the composer, Bayswater, West London, 7 July
            1914 (Bliss was absent on active service in France)
f.Lon.pub.p. Philharmonic String Quartet - Arthur Beckwith (Vn.), Eugene
            Goossens (Vn.), Raymond Jeremy (Va.), Cedric Sharpe (Vc.) - Aeolian Hall,
            25 June 1915
f.mod.p.   Greenhouse Ensemble - British Music Information Centre, Stratford Place,
            London, 21 June 1993
Pub: Stainer & Bell, 1915

Tis time I think by Wenlock Town - song for voice and piano (c.1914)

[Words: A. E. Housman]
Dur: 2'

Violin Sonata - unfinished (c.1914)

The Hammers - song for voice and piano (c.1915)

[Words: Ralph Hodgson]
Dur: 2'

Piano Quartet in A minor `Op.5' (1915)

`Dedicated to my friend Madame Lily Henkel and to her Quartet' - this piece won the War
Emergency Entertainment Prize (Madame Henkel was the founder of The Guild of
Singers and Players)
Dur: 18'30"
Instr: Pno. Vn. Va. Vc.
f.p.   Mrs. Herbert Withers (Pno.)/Arthur Beckwith (Vn.)/Lionel Tertis (Va)/Herbert
            Withers (Vc.) - Steinway Hall, London, 22 April 1915 (War Emergency
            Concert Series and repeated on 10 June 1915 with Lily Henkel's Quartet)
f.mod.p.   Raphael Terroni (Pno.)/Greenhouse Ensemble - British Music Information
            Centre, Stratford Place, London, 21 June 1993
Pub: Novello, 1915
2nd movement `Intermezzo' later arranged for viola and piano by Watson Forbes (c.1950)
Dur: 2'
Pub: OUP, 1950

Fugue, from Phantasy for String Quartet (1916)

Written for the Elgar Fugue Competition sponsored by 'The Music Student'

The Tramps - song for voice and piano (1916)
[Words: Robert Service]
Dedicated 'to all Hoboes'
Dur: 1'30"
Pub: Boosey & Hawkes, 1918

Album Leaf for Madame Alvar (c.1916-17)
Probably contemporary with that of the **Three Songs Op. 19** by Eugene Goossens, the
third of which was dedicated to, and first performed by, Madam Alvar q.v.

Two Pieces for clarinet and piano (1913-14 and 1916)
[1. Rhapsody (1913-14) 2. Pastoral (1916)]
Dur: 7'45"
f.p.   (No. 1) Kennard Bliss (Cl.)/M. O.Marshall (Pno.) - Cambridge University
            Musical Club, 7 February 1914
f.p.   (complete) Charles Draper (Cl.)/Lily Henkel (Pno.) - Aeolian Hall, London,
            15 February 1917 (Society of Women Musicians' Concert)
f.mod.p.   (No. 2) Geraldine Allen (Cl.)/John Blood (Pno.) - Goldsmith's College,
            London, 2 February 1981
f.broad.p. (No. 2) Geraldine Allen (Cl.)/Roger Vignoles (Pno.) - 20 July 1981
f.rec.   (No. 1) Thea King (Cl.)/Clifford Benson (Pno.) - *Hyperion A 66044 (and
            MC/CD)*
f.rec.   (No. 2) Linda Merrick (Cl.)/Benjamin Frith (Pno.) - *Serendipity SERCD
            4000(CD)*
Pub: Novello, 1980 (No. 2 only)

Madame Noy - A Witchery Song for soprano and instrumental ensemble (1918)
[Words: E. H. W. Meyerstein]
Dedicated to Anne Thursfield
Dur: 3'30"
Instr: Fl. Cl. Bsn. Hp. Va. Db.
f.p.   Anne Thursfield (Sop.)/Ensemble/Arthur Bliss - Wigmore Hall, London,
            23 June 1920
f.recs.   above artists - *Columbia 1476(78)*
            Elizabeth Gale/Nash Ensemble/Lionel Friend - *A 66137 (and MC/CD)*
Pub: Chester, 1921 (also arr. for voice and piano)

Piano Quintet (1919)
Dedicated 'to the City of Bath and three friends met therein: Sir Hugh Miller, Lady Stuart
of Wortley and Leo F. Schuster'
Instr: Pno. Vn. Vn. Va. Vc.
f.p.   Arthur Bliss (Pno.)/Philharmonic Quartet - La Salle Gaveau, Paris,
            26 November 1919
f.Brit.p.   above artists - Aeolian Hall, London, 27 April 1920*
(* at this same concert, Biss conducted the first British performance of Stravinsky's
Ragtime)

Rhapsody - Vocalise for soprano, tenor and chamber orchestra (or piano) (1919)
Dedicated to Gerald Cooper
Dur: 7'
Instr: Fl. Cl. Vn. Vn. Va. Vc. Db.
f.p.   Dorothy Helmrich (Sop.)/Gerald Cooper (Ten.)/Albert Fransella (Fl.)/ Walter
           Hinchliff (Cl.)/Wadsworth String Quartet with Db. - Mortimer Hall, London,
           6 October 1920 (Gerald Cooper Concert)
f.Eur.p.   members of the Vienna Symphony Orchestra/Arthur Bliss - Vienna, 6 April
           1922 (the Rhapsody was also performed at the ISCM Festival in Salzburg the
           following year on 5th August 1923)
f.p.   (as the ballet 'Narcissus and Echo') Theatre Ensemble/Constant Lambert -
           Sadler's Wells Theatre, London, 30 January 1932
Choreography: Ninette de Valois
Scenery and costumes: William Chappell
f.broad.p. Vesuvius Ensemble/Arthur Bliss - 25 April 1975
f.rec.   Elizabeth Gale (Sop.)/Anthony Rolfe Johnson/Nash Ensemble/Lionel Friend -
           Hyperion A 66137(and MC/CD)
Pub: Stainer & Bell, 1921; Novello

Concerto for piano, tenor, xylophone and string orchestra (1920 rev. 1923)
[Words: Arthur Bliss]
Dur: 12'
Written for Myra Hess and Steuart Wilson
f.p.   Myra Hess (Pno.)/Steuart Wilson (Ten.)/Orchestra/Arthur Bliss - Wigmore
           Hall, London, 11 June 1921
f.p.   (rev. version) Gordon Bryan (Pno.)/Archibald Winter (Ten.)/W.W.Bennett
           (Xyl.)/ Bournemouth Municipal Orchestra/Arthur Bliss - Bournemouth,
           29 March 1923 (Bournemouth Festival)
Pub: Goodwin & Tabb
re-written as:
Concerto for two pianos and orchestra (1923)
Written for the American duo-pianists Maier and Pattison
Instr: believed to be brass, woodwind and percussion (no strings)
f.p.   Guy Maier and Lee Pattison/Boston Symphony Orchestra/ Serge Koussevitzky
           - Symphony Hall, Boston, Massachussetts, 19 December 1924
revised version (1925-29)
Instr: 3/2/2/2 - 4/3/3/1 - timp.(2) perc.(3) str.
f.p.   Ethel Bartlett and Rae Robertson/Henry Wood Symphony Orchestra/Sir Henry
           Wood - Queen's Hall, London, 5 September 1929 (Promenade Concert)
f.Am.p.   Ethel Bartlett and Rae Robertson/New York Philharmonic Symphony
           Orchestra/Sir John Barbirolli - Carnegie Hall, New York, 1939-40 season
Pub: OUP, 1933 (arr. 2 pianos with piano reduction)
final version (1950)
Instr: 2/2/2/2 - 4/3/3/0 - timp. perc.(2) str.
f.p.   Ethel Bartlett and Rae Robertson/BBC Northern Orchestra/John Hopkins -
           Manchester, 17 September 1952 (however there is evidence of an earlier BBC
           broadcast on 18 July 1950)
Pub: OUP, 1950

arr. as Concerto for two pianos (three hands) and orchestra by Clifford Phillips (1968)
Specially arranged for Phyllis Sellick and Cyril Smith
Instr: 2/2/2/2 - 4/3/3/0 - timp. perc.(2) str.
f.p.   Phyllis Sellick and Cyril Smith/Tunbridge Wells Orchestra/John Lanchberry -
            Tunbridge Wells, Kent, 8 October 1968
f.Lon.p.   Phyllis Sellick and Cyril Smith/BBC Symphony Orchestra/Sir Arthur Bliss -
            Royal Albert Hall, 16 August 1969 (Promenade Concert)
f.rec.   Phyllis Sellick and Cyril Smith/City of Birmingham Symphony
            Orchestra/Malcolm Arnold - *HMV ASD 2612, ESD 7065 (and MC)*
Pub: OUP, 1968

Conversations for instrumental ensemble (1920)
[1. The Committee Meeting 2. In the Wood 3. In the Ball Room 4. Soliloquy
5. In the Tube at Oxford Circus]
Dedicated to the New Instrumental Quintet
Dur: 14'
Instr: Fl. A.Fl. Ob. Ca. Vn. Va. Vc.
f.priv.p.   New Instrumental Quintet - at the home of Mrs. Lee-Matthews, London,
            19 January 1921
f.pub.p.   Gordon Walker (Fl.)/Charles Souper (A.Fl.)/Léon Goossens (Ob.)/
            J. McDonagh (Ca.)/F. E. Woodhouse (Vn.)/Raymond Jeremy (Va.)/ Cedric
            Sharpe (Vc.) - Aeolian Hall, London, 20 April 1921 (Edward Clark Concert)
f.broad.p. members of the BBC Wireless Orchestra/L.Stanton Jeffries - 31 March 1924
f.recs.   Instrumental Ensemble/Arthur Bliss - *Columbia L 1475/6(78)*
            Nash Ensemble/Lionel Friend - *Hyperion A 66137(and MC/CD)*
Pub: Goodwin & Tabb, 1922; Curwen/Faber

Rout, for soprano and chamber ensemble (1920)
[Words: Arthur Bliss - `a medley of made-up words']
Dedicated to Grace Crawford (the wife of Claude Lovat Fraser to whom the **Mêlée
Fantastique** is dedicated q.v.)
Dur: 7'
Instr: Fl. Cl. Perc. Hp. Vn. Vn. Va. Vc. Db.
f.priv.p.   Grace Crawford (Sop.)/Albert Fransella (Fl.)/Charles Draper (Cl.)/J. H.
            Plowman (Perc.)/Gwendolen Mason (Hp.)/Philharmonic Quartet with Claude
            Hobday (Db.), cond. Arthur Bliss - 139 Piccadilly, the London home of
            Baroness d'Erlanger, 15 December 1920 (this work was 'encored' twice!)
f.pub.p.   Grace Crawford/Chamber Ensemble/Arthur Bliss - Steinway Hall, London,
            4 May 1921 (Guild of Singers and Players Concert)
f.Eur.p.   Dorothy Moulton/Chamber Ensemble/Arthur Bliss - Salzburg, Austria,
            7 August 1922 (ISCM Festival - among the performers was Hindemith, who
            played viola)
f.SA.p.   Cape Town Orchestra/Leslie Heward - Cape Town, c.1924
f.broad.p. (regional) Nell Davis/Orchestra/Sir Dan Godfrey - 27 March 1924
            (from BBC Manchester)
f.broad.p. (national) Odette de Foras/BBC Chamber Orchestra/Constant Lambert -
            18 December 1931 (BBC Contemporary Music Concert)
f.recs.   Stella Power/British Symphony Orchestra/Sir Adrian Boult - *HMV D 574(78)*

Rae Woodland/London Symphony Orchestra/Arthur Bliss - *Lyrita SRCS 55, SRCD 225(CD); Musical Heritage Society (USA) MHS 3096*

Pub: Goodwin & Tabb, 1920; Curwen

also arr. for soprano and orchestra (at the request of Diaghilev)

Instr: 2/1/2/2 - 4/2/0/0 - timp. perc. hp. str.

f.p.   Grace Crawford/Orchestra/Edward Clark - Aeolian Hall, London,
            6 May 1921 (Edward Clark Concert)

f.p.   (as a ballet) Theatre Orchestra/Ernest Ansermet - Princes Theatre, London,
            26 May 1921 (as interval music during the Diaghilev Ballet season)

Pub: Goodwin & Tabb, 1921; Curwen/Faber

also arr. as a concert piece for two pianos (or piano duet)

f.priv.p.   (as a ballet) Arthur Bliss and Malcolm Sargent (piano duet) - de Valois
            Studios, London, 1927

Choreography: Ninette de Valois (after a poem by Ernst Toller)

Principal: Alicia Markova

f.pub.p.   (as a ballet) Walter Leigh and C. J. Leighton (piano duet) - Festival Theatre,
            Cambridge, 31 January 1927

f.Lon.p.   (as a ballet) Vic-Wells Ballet cond. Constant Lambert - Old Vic
            Theatre, 1932

Pub: Goodwin & Tabb, 1921; Curwen/Faber

Two Nursery Rhymes for soprano, clarinet (or viola) and piano (1920)

[Words: Frances Cornford 1. The Ragwort (The Thistle) 2. The Dandelion]

Dedicated to Leslie Howard (No. 1) and Charles Draper (No. 2)

Dur: 3'15"

f.p.   (No. 1 only) Gladys Moger (Sop.)/Frederick Thurston (Cl.)/Arthur Bliss (Pno.)
            - London, 18 January 1921 (Music Society Concert)

f.pub.p.   (No. 1 only) above artists, Aeolian Hall, London, 26 January 1921

f.p.   (complete) Grace Crawford (Sop.)/Charles Draper (Cl.)/Arthur Bliss (Pno.) -
            Steinway Hall, London, 4 May 1921 (Guild of Singers and Players Concert)

f.rec.   Sylvia Eaves(Sop.)/Thea King(Cl.)/Courtney Kenney(Pno.)- Cameo Classics
            GOCLP 9020

Pub: Chester, 1921

later arr. for soprano and viola (or clarinet) by Lionel Tertis (1923)

f.broad.p. Nora Delmarr (Sop.)/S. C. Cotterill (Cl.) - 4 March 1925 (from BBC
            Birmingham)

f.rec.   Judith Howarth (Sop.)/Emma Johnson (Cl.) - *ASV CDDCA 891(CD) (and MC)*

Pub: Chester, 1923

Two Studies for orchestra (1920)

[1. Grave 2. Gay]

Dur: 11'30"

Instr: 1+picc./1+ca./2+bcl./2+cbsn. - 4/2/3/1 - timp. perc.(2) hp. pno. cel. str.

f.p.   New Queen's Hall Orchestra/Arthur Bliss - Royal College of Music, London,
            17 February 1921 (Patron's Fund Concert)

f.pub.p.   City of Birmingham Orchestra/Arthur Bliss - Town Hall, Birmingham,
            c.September 1921

f.rec.   English Northern Philharmonia/David Lloyd-Jones - *Naxos 8.553383(CD)*

Pub: Goodwin & Tabb; Novello

Fanfare for a Political Address (1921)
Written for the musical journal 'Fanfare'
Dur: 0'15"
Instr: Tpt. 2 Cl.(and speaker)
Pub: Goodwin & Tabb, in 'Fanfare', 1921 (ed. Leigh Henry)

Mêlée Fantasque for orchestra (1921, rev. 1937 and 1965)
Written for performance at the 1921 Henry Wood Promenade Concert season and
dedicated 'to the memory of Claude Lovat Fraser, a great and lovable artist' (with whom
Bliss had collaborated in the 1919 production of 'As You Like It' q.v.)
Dur: 11'30"
Instr: 2+picc./2+ca./2+bcl./2+cbsn. - 4/3/3/1 - timp. perc.(3) str.
f.p.   New Queen's Hall Orchestra/Arthur Bliss - Queen's Hall, London,
            13 October 1921 (Promenade Concert)
f.Eur.p.   Czech Philharmonic Orchestra/Sir Adrian Boult - Prague, 5 January 1922
f.Am.p.   Philadelphia Orchestra/Leopold Stokowski - Academy of Music, Philadelphia,
            27 February 1925
f.broad.p. BBC Symphony Orchestra/Arthur Bliss - 18 January 1935 (BBC Con-
            temporary Music Concert)
f.rec.   (rev. version) London Symphony Orchestra/Arthur Bliss - *Lyrita SRCS 50,
            SRCD 225; Musical Heritage Society (USA) MHS 1919*
Pub: Curwen, 1924; Faber

Three Romantic Songs for high voice and piano (1921)
[Words: Walter de la Mare 1. The Hare 2. Lovelocks 3. The Buckle]
Written for Anne Thursfield and dedicated to the three children in the Bliss household -
Patrick Mahony (No. 1), Cynthia Mahony (No. 2) and Enid Bliss (No. 3). (In 1918 Bliss's
father had remarried to a widow with two children of her own, Patrick and Cynthia.)
Dur: 4'30"
f.p.   Anne Thursfield (Sop.)/Arthur Bliss (Pno.) - Wigmore Hall, London,
            18 January 1922 (Classical Concert Society recital)
f.rec.   (No. 3) Lucine Amara (Sop.)/David Benedict (Pno.) - *Cambridge 704(m),
            CRS 1704*
Pub: Goodwin & Tabb, 1922; Novello (as Nos. 1-3 of Nine Songs for voice and
            piano)

A Colour Symphony (1921-22, rev. 1932)
[1. Purple - the colour of Amethysts, Pageantry, Royalty and Death
 2. Red - the colour of Rubies, Wine, Revelry, Furnaces, Courage and Magic
 3. Blue - the colour of Sapphires, Deep Water, Skies, Loyalty and Melancholy
 4. Green - the colour of Emeralds, Hope, Youth, Joy, Spring and Victory]
Commissioned by Edward Elgar for the Three Choirs Festival and dedicated 'to Dr.
Adrian Boult' - the title was suggested by the musicologist Percy Scholes.
Dur: 31'
Instr: 3/2+ca./2+bcl./2+cbsn. - 4/3/3/1 - timp.(6) perc. hp.(2) str.
f.p.   London Symphony Orchestra/Arthur Bliss - Gloucester Cathedral,
            7 September 1922 (Three Choirs Festival)
f.Lon.p.   Royal College of Music Orchestra/Sir Adrian Boult - Royal College of Music,
            December 1922

f.Lon.pub.p. New Queen's Hall Orchestra/Arthur Bliss - Queen's Hall, 10 March
            1923
f.Am.p.   Boston Symphony Orchestra/Pierre Monteux - Symphony Hall, Boston,
            28 December 1923 (and in Carnegie Hall, New York, 5 January 1924)
f.p.   (rev. version) BBC Symphony Orchestra/Sir Adrian Boult - Queen's Hall,
            London, 27 April 1932
f.Eur.p.   (rev. version) Orchestra of Radio Hilversum/Sir Adrian Boult - April 1956
f.Austr.p. Queensland Symphony Orchestra/Arthur Bliss - City Hall, Brisbane,
            2 October 1964
f.Jap.p.   London Symphony Orchestra/Arthur Bliss - Tokyo, October 1964
f.p.   (as the ballet `A Royal Offering') Northern Ballet Theatre - Royal Northern
            College of Music, Manchester, 19 May 1977
Choreography: Robert de Warren
Scenery and Costumes: Michael Holt
f.rec.   (rev. version) London Symphony Orchestra/Arthur Bliss - *Decca LXT*
            5170(m); Ace of Clubs ACL 239(m); Eclipse ECS 625 (es); London (USA) LL
            1402(m); Dutton Laboratories CDLXT 2501(CD)
Pub: Curwen, 1924 (Movement 4, `Pyanepsion',published separately); Boosey &
            Hawkes (rev. version), 1939, 1955, 1988 (Study score)

Three Songs for high voice and piano (1923 rev. 1972*)
[Words: W. H. Davies 1. Thunderstorms 2. This Night 3. Leisure]
Dedicated (in revision) to Elizabeth Poston*
Dur: 6'45"
f.p.   (No. 2 only) Olga Haley (Sop.)/Arthur Bliss (Pno.) - Aeolian Hall, London,
            8 March 1923
f.p.   (rev. version) Janet Price (Sop.)/Antony Saunders (Pno.) - Brecon Music Club,
            21 November 1972
Pub: Composers' Music Corp., 1923; Novello, 1972 (* as Nos. 4-6 of Nine Songs
            for voice and piano)

The Ballads of the Four Seasons - Four Songs for high voice and piano (1923)
[Words: Li-Po, trans. Shigeyoshi Obata 1. Spring 2. Summer 3. Autumn
 4. Winter]
Dedicated to Minnie Untermyer
Dur: 7'30"
f.pub.p.   (Nos. 1 and 4) Elizabeth Simon (Sop.)/Gerald Moore (Pno.) - Cheltenham
            Town Hall, 12 July 1960 (Cheltenham Festival)
f.rec.   (No. 2) Dorothy Dorow (Sop.)/Susan Bradshaw (Pno.) - *Jupiter jepoc 33*
            (45m)
Pub: Composers' Music Corp., 1924; Novello, 1958

Bliss - A One-Step for piano (1923)
Dedicated to Corelli Windeatt and his orchestra
Dur: 2'15"
f.rec.   Richard Rodney Bennett - *Polydor 2383 391; EMI ESD 7164 (and MC),*
            CDM5 65596-2(CD)
Pub: Goodwin, 1923; Novello
later orchestrated by Leighton Lucas (c.1936)

f.p.   probably as a musical interlude between ballets given by the Markova/ Dolin
            Ballet Company on tour in 1936
later re-orchestrated by Victor Fleming (c.1940)
Dur: 3'
Instr: 2+picc./1/2/2 - 2/2/0/0 - perc.(2) hp. str.
f.p.   Victor Fleming Orchestra/Victor Fleming - BBC Midlands, 19 March 1940

Elizabethan Suite for string orchestra (1923)

Three Jolly Gentlemen - song for voice and piano (1923)
[Words: Walter de la Mare]
Dur: 1'
Pub: Composers' Music Corp., 1923

Captions: Five Glimpses of an Anonymous Theme for small orchestra - composite work* (1923)
Bliss's contribution was 'Twone, the House of Felicity' - the other composers were
Herbert Bedford, Felix White, Gerrard Williams and Eugene Goossens (q.v.)
f.p.   Goossens Chamber Orchestra/Eugene Goossens - Aeolian Hall, London,
            15 March 1923
(* this unusual work received a further/final!? performance at the 1925 Bournemouth
Festival, Sir Dan Godfrey conducting the Municipal Orchestra)

The Women of Yueh - song cycle for high voice and piano (1923)
[Words: Li-Po, trans. Shigeyoshi Obata
 1. She is a Southern Girl of Chang-Kan Town 2. Many a Girl of the South
 3. She is gathering Lotus Buds 4. She, a Tungyang Girl
 5. The Water of the Mirror Lake]
Written for the New York Composers' League and dedicated to Ernest Ansermet
Dur: 7'30"
f.p.   Eva Gauthier (Sop.)/Arthur Bliss (Pno.) - Aeolian Hall, New York,
            1 November 1923
f.Brit.p.   Mary Lohden (Sop.)/Manlio di Veroli (Pno.) - Grosvenor House, London,
            6 May 1925
f.Brit.broad.p. Emelie Hooke (Sop.)/Nikita Magaloff (Pno.) - 20 November
            1946
Pub: Chester, 1924
also arr. for high voice and chamber ensemble
Instr: Fl. Ob. Cl. Bsn. Vn. Vn. Va. Vc. Db. Perc.
f.p.   Lilian Gustafson (Sop.)/Chamber Ensemble/Arthur Bliss - Klaw Theatre, New
            York, 11 November 1923 (League of Composers Concert)
f.broad.p. Janet Price (Sop.)/Vesuvius Ensemble/Arthur Bliss - 25 April 1975
f.rec.   Elizabeth Gale (Sop.)/Nash Ensemble/Lionel Friend - *Hyperion A 66137 (and
            MC/CD)*
Pub: Chester

Allegro for string quartet (1923-24)

When I was One and Twenty - song for high/low voice and piano (1924)
[Words: A. E. Housman]
Dur: 3'
Pub: Ricordi (New York), 1924

The Fallow Deer at the Lonely House - song for high voice and piano (1924)
[Words: Thomas Hardy]
Dur: 2'30"
Dedicated to Ursula Grenville
f.p.   Elizabeth Nicol (Sop.)/S.Liddle (Pno.) - Wigmore Hall, London,
           5 October 1925
Pub: Curwen, 1925; Novello (as No. 7 of Nine Songs for voice and piano)

String Quartet (c.1923-24)
Dur: 16'
(Chronologically this is the <u>second</u> string quartet. It was written in America and
submitted for a prize competition, presumed lost, but has since come to light. The first
performance was scheduled for 9 April 1924, to be given by the Philharmonic Quartet at
the Aeolian Hall, London, but cancelled.)

Masks - Four Pieces for piano (1924)
[1. A Comedy Mask 2. A Romantic Mask 3. A Sinister Mask 4.A Military Mask]
Dedicated to Felix Goodwin
Dur: 10'
f.p.   Arthur Benjamin - Faculty of Arts Gallery, Golden Square, London,
           2 February 1926 (Concert Spirituel)
f.rec.   Kathron Sturrock - *Chandos ABTD 1408(MC), CHAN 8870(CD)*
Pub: Curwen, 1925; Curwen/Faber

At the Window - song for voice and piano (c.1925)
[Words: Alfred Lord Tennyson]
Dur: 0'45"

Suite for piano (1925)
[1. Overture 2. Polonaise 3. Elegy* 4. Finale]
Dur: 17'
f.p.   Kathleen Long - Faculty of Arts Gallery, Golden Square, London,
           15 March 1926 (Concert Spirituel)
f.rec.   (No. 2) Cyril Smith - *Decca K 780(78)*
f.rec.   (complete) Philip Fowke - *ABTD 1567(MC),Chandos CHAN 8979(CD)*
Pub: Curwen, 1926; Curwen/Faber
(* subtitled: FKB Thiepval, 1916 - a threnody in memory of his brother, Kennard, who
was killed during the `Battle of the Somme')
No. 2 also arr. for orchestra
Written for and dedicated to Eugene Goossens
Dur: 4'
Instr: 2/2/2/2 - 4/2/3/1 - timp. perc. pno. str.
f.p.   Theatre Orchestra/Eugene Goossens - Her Majesty's Theatre, London,
           14 June 1926 (as interval music during the ballet season)

f.Am.p.   Los Angeles Philharmonic Orchestra/Eugene Goossens - Hollywood Bowl,
             Los Angeles, California, c.1926-27.

Toccata for piano (c.1925)
Dedicated `to my wife'
Dur: 4'30"
f.rec.   Kathron Sturrock - *Chandos ABTD 1408(MC), CHAN 8770(CD)*
Pub: Curwen, 1926; Curwen/Faber

Two Interludes for piano (1925)
Dedicated `To Elizabeth Sprague Coolidge' (No. 1) and `To Ethel Roe Eichheim' (No. 2)
Dur: 8'30"
f.rec.   Kathron Sturrock - *Chandos ABTD 1408(MC), CHAN 8770(CD)*
Pub: Chester, 1925; Novello, 1979

Rich or Poor - song for voice and piano (1925-26)
[Words: W. H. Davies]
Dedicated to Lawrence Strauss
Dur: 2'30"
f.rec.   Frederick Harvey (Bar.)/Gerald Moore (Pno.) - *HMV CLP(m)/CSD 3587*
Pub: Curwen, 1927; Novello (as No. 8 of Nine Songs for voice and piano)

A Child's Prayer - song for voice and piano (1926)
[Words: Siegfried Sassoon]
Dedicated `to Barbara' (the composer's elder daughter)
Dur: 1'
Pub: Curwen, 1927; Novello (as No. 9 of Nine Songs for voice and piano)

Piece for solo clarinet (1926)
f.p.   Frederick Thurston - The Courthouse, Marylebone Lane, London,
             19 January 1927 (London Contemporary Music Centre Concert)

Hymn to Apollo for orchestra (1926 rev. 1965)
Dedicated to Fritz Reiner and the Cincinatti Symphony Orchestra and written as a
`thank-you' to Pierre Monteux who had conducted the first American performance of the
Colour Symphony in Boston. Bliss travelled with Monteux to Amsterdam to hear the
premiere.
Dur: 13'30"
Instr: 3/1+ca./2/2 - 4/3/3/1 - timp.(6) perc.(2) cel. hp. str.
f.p.   Concertgebouw Orchestra/Pierre Monteux - Concertgebouw,
             Amsterdam, 28 November 1926
f.Brit.p.   Queen's Hall Orchestra/Pierre Monteux - Queen's Hall, London,
             27 January 1927 (Royal Philharmonic Society Concert)
f.Am.p.   Cincinnati Symphony Orchestra/Fritz Reiner (1926-27 season)
Pub: Universal, 1928
the work was later revised in 1965
Dur: 10'
Instr: 2/2/2/2 - 4/2/3/0 - timp. perc.(2) cel. hp. str.

f.p.   BBC Northern Symphony Orchestra/Arthur Bliss - Cheltenham Town Hall,
            5 July 1965 (Cheltenham Festival)
f.rec.   London Symphony Orchestra/Arthur Bliss - *Lyrita SRCS 55, SRCD 225(CD);*
            Musical Heritage Society (USA) MHS 3096
Pub: Universal, 1967

Introduction and Allegro for orchestra (1926 rev. 1937)
Dedicated to Leopold Stokowski and the Philadelphia Orchestra
Dur: 12'
Instr: 2+picc./2+ca./2+bcl./2+cbsn. - 4/3/3/1 - timp. perc.(5) hp. str.
f.p.   New Queen's Hall Orchestra/Arthur Bliss - Queen's Hall, London,
            8 September 1926 (Promenade Concert)
f.Am.p.   Philadelphia Orchestra/Leopold Stokowski - Academy of Music, Philadelphia,
            19 October 1928
f.p.   (rev. version) City of Birmingham Orchestra/Arthur Bliss - Birmingham Town
            Hall, 6 October 1938
f.Am.p.   (rev. version) Chicago Symphony Orchestra/Sir Adrian Boult - Ravinia Park,
            Chicago, 7 July 1939
f.recs.   London Symphony Orchestra/Arthur Bliss - *Decca LXT 5170(m); Ace of Clubs*
            ACL 239(m); Eclipse ECS 649 and 783 (es); London (USA) LL 1402(m);
            Dutton Laboratories CDLXT 2501(CD); Belart 461 353-2 (CD)
            Leicestershire Schools Symphony Orchestra/Arthur Bliss - *Argo ZRG 685*
Pub: Universal/Curwen, 1927; Universal, 1937 (rev. version); Boosey & Hawkes,
            1951, 1965

Four Songs for high voice, violin and piano (c.1927)
[1. A Christmas Carol (Arthur S. Cripps) 2. Sea Love (Charlotte Mew)
 3. Vocalise 4. The Mad Woman of Punnet's Town (L. A. G. Strong)]
Dur: 5'30"
f.p.   Sybil Scanes (Sop.)/Paul Belinfonte (Vn.)/George Reeves (Pno.) - Grotrian
            Hall, London, 6 April 1927
Pub: Novello, 1966
No. 2 also published separately
Dur: 1´30˝
Pub: Novello

Oboe Quintet (1927)
Dedicated to Mrs. Elizabeth Sprague Coolidge for performance at the Venice Music
Festival. In the Finale the composer makes use of the old Irish fiddle tune `Connolly's
Jig'.
Dur: 20'30"
Instr: Ob. Vn. Vn. Va. Vc.
f.p.*   Léon Goossens (Ob.)/Venetian Quartet - Conservatorio Benedetto Marcello,
            Venice, 11 September 1927 (Coolidge Invitation Concert)
f.Am.p.   Léon Goossens (Ob.)/Marianne Kneisel Quartet - Guild Theatre, New York,
            22 January 1928
f.Brit.p.   Léon Goossens (Ob.)/Vienna Quartet - Arts Theatre Club, London,
            15 October 1928 (BBC Concert)

f.p.   (as the ballet 'Frontier')Scottish Theatre Ballet - Perth Theatre, Australia, 30
              October 1969
Choreography and designs: John Neumeier
f.Brit.p.   Scottish Theatre Ballet - Sadler's Wells Theatre, London, 26 November 1969
f.rec.   Peter Graeme (Ob.)/Melos Ensemble - *World Record Club CM(m)SCM 42;*
              HMV HQS 1299; Everest SDBR 3153
Pub: OUP, 1928
(* also performed at the ISCM Festival in Vienna on 21 June 1932)

The Rout Trot* - for piano (1927)
Dur: 1'45"
f.rec.   Richard Rodney Bennett - *Polydor 2383 391; EMI ESD 7164 (and MC),*
              CDM5 65596-2(CD)
Pub: Curwen, 1927; Novello
(* see also incidental music to **The White Birds**)

Study for piano (1927)
Dedicated to Edwin Evans
Dur: 1'45"
f.rec.   Philip Fowke - *Chandos ABTD 1567(MC), CHAN 8979(CD)*
Pub: Curwen, 1927; Curwen/Faber

Pastoral: Lie Strewn the White Flocks, for mezzo-soprano, SATB chorus and orchestra (1928)
[1. The Shepherd's Holyday (Ben Jonson) 2. A Hymn to Pan (John Fletcher)
 3. Pan's Saraband (John Fletcher)
 4. Pan and Echo (Poliziano trans. E. Geoffrey Dunlop)
 5. The Naiads' Music (Robert Nichols) 6. The Pigeon Song (Robert Nichols)
 7. Song of the Reapers (Theocritus trans. Andrew Lang)
 8. Finale: The Shepherd's Night Song (Robert Nichols) - Shepherds all, and
    Maiden's Fair (John Fletcher)]
Commissioned by the Harold Brooke Choir and dedicated to Edward Elgar
Dur: 33'
Instr: 1/0/0/0 - 0/0/0/0 - timp. str.
f.p.   Odette de Foras (M/S)/Gilbert Barton (Fl.)/Harold Brooke Choir and
              Orchestra/Harold Brooke - Bishopsgate Institute, London, 8 May 1929
f.recs.   Nancy Evans (Con.)/Gareth Morris (Fl.)/BBC Chorus/BBC Symphony
              Orchestra/Reginald Jacques - *Decca AX 565/8(78)*
              Sybil Michelow (Con.)/Norman Knight (Fl.)/Bruckner-Mahler Choir of
              London/London Chamber Orchestra/Wyn Morris - *Pye Golden Guinea GSGC*
              2042 (and MC) , TPLS 13036, ZCPC 507(MC)
Pub: Novello, 1949, 1953
Exc. No. 5 arr. SATB chorus and piano
Dur: 4´
Pub: Novello, 1949

Serenade for baritone and orchestra (1929)
[1. Overture: The Serenader (orch. only) 2. Fair is my Love (Edmund Spenser)
 3. Idyll: And thus our Delightful Hours, full of Waking Dreams shall Pass

(orch. only) 4. Tune on my Pipe the Praises of my Love (Sir John Wootton)]
Dedicated `to my wife'

Dur:	24'30"
Instr:	2/1/2/2 - 2/2/1/0 - timp. perc. hp. str.
f.p.	Roy Henderson (Bar.)/London Symphony Orchestra/Malcolm Sargent - Queen's Hall, London, 18 March 1930 (Courtauld-Sargent Concert)
f.rec.	John Shirley-Quirk (Bar.)/London Symphony Orchestra/Brian Prestman - *Lyrita SRCS 55, SRCD 225(CD); Musical Heritage Society (USA) MHS 3096*
Pub:	OUP, 1930, 1971 (Nos. 2 and 4 published as Two Love Songs for baritone and piano)

Fanfare for Heroes (1929)

Written in aid of the Musicians' Benevolent Fund. It was also used in the Soviet Newsreel Production `Defeat of the Germans near Moscow' directed by Varlomo and Kopalin

Dur:	1'45"
Instr:	3 Tpt. 3 Tbn. Tba.Timp. Cym.
f.p.	Trumpeters of the Royal Military School of Music, Kneller Hall - Savoy Hotel, London, 8 May 1930 (Annual Dinner of the Musicians' Benevolent Fund)
f.pub.p.	Trumpeters of the Royal Military School of Music, Kneller Hall/members of the BBC Symphony and Royal Philharmonic Orchestras/Capt.H.E.Adkins - Royal Albert Hall, London, 26 May 1932 (in the presence of King George V and Queen Mary)
f.rec.	Trumpeters of the Royal Military School of Music, Kneller Hall/Capt. H. E. Adkins - *HMV C 2445(78)*
Pub:	Novello, 1970

Morning Heroes - Symphony for orator, SATB chorus and orchestra (1930)

[1. Hector's Farewell to Andromache (Homer, `The Iliad', trans. W. Leaf)
 2. The City Arming (Walt Whitman)
 3.* Vigil (Li-Tai-Po) - The Bivouac's Flame (Walt Whitman)
 4. Achilles goes forth to Battle - The Heroes (Homer, `The Iliad', trans. George Chapman)
 5. Spring Offensive (Wilfred Owen) - Dawn on the Somme (Robert Nichols)]
Written for the Norfolk and Norwich Triennial Music Festival and dedicated `to the memory of my brother, Francis Kennard Bliss and all other comrades killed in battle'

Dur:	58'30"
Instr:	2+picc./2+ca./2+bcl./2+cbsn. - 4/3/3/1 - timp.(2) perc.(2) hp. str.
f.p.	Basil Maine (Orator)/Norfolk and Norwich Festival Chorus/New Queen's Hall Orchestra/Arthur Bliss - St. Andrew's Hall, Norwich, 22 October 1930 (Norfolk and Norwich Triennial Music Festival)
f.Lon.p.	Basil Maine/National Chorus/BBC Symphony Orchestra/Arthur Bliss - Queen's Hall, 25 March 1931
f.Am.p.	October 1931 (Worcester Music Festival)
f.recs.	(No. 5) Basil Maine (Orator) with drums - *Decca F 5219(78)* (complete) John Westbrook (Orator)/Royal Liverpool Philharmonic Chorus and Orchestra/Sir Charles Groves - *HMV Angel SAN 365, HMV ESD 7133 (and MC); EMI CDM7 63906-2(CD)*

Pub: Novello, 1930
(* the composer has authorised the separate performance of this movement)

Clarinet Quintet (1932)
Written for Frederick Thurston and dedicated to Bernard van Dieren
Dur: 27'
Instr: Cl. Vn. Vn. Va. Vc.
f.priv.p.   Frederick Thurston (Cl.)/Kutcher Quartet - at the composer's home,
            19 December 1932
f.pub.p.   above artists - Wigmore Hall, London, 17 February 1933
f.broad.p. above artists - 25 April 1933
f.recs.   Frederick Thurston (Cl.)/Griller Quartet - *Decca K 780/3(78)*
            Gervase de Peyer (Cl.)/Melos Ensemble - *World Record Club CM(m) SCM
            42; HMV HQS 1299; Everest SDBR 3153*
Pub: Novello, 1933, 1950

Simples - song for high voice and piano (1932)
[Words: James Joyce from `Pomes Penyeach']
Dur: 2'45"
f.p.   Dorothy Moulton (Sop.)/William Busch (Pno.) - Royal College of Nursing,
            London, 16 March 1932 (LCMC Concert)
f.broad.p. John Armstrong (Ten.)/Hubert Foss (Pno.) - 28 May 1932
Pub: OUP, 1933 (in `The Joyce Book' ed. Herbert Hughes - among the other
            contributors were E. J. Moeran, Bax and Howells q.v.); OUP, 1971 (limited
            edition)

Sonata in D minor for viola and piano (1933)
Dedicated `In admiration - to Lionel Tertis'
Dur: 27'
f.priv.p.   Lionel Tertis (Va.)/Solomon (Pno.) - East Heath Lodge, (the home of the
            composer) Hampstead Heath, London , 9 May 1933*
f.broad.p. above artists - BBC Broadcasting House, London, 3 November 1933 (BBC
            Chamber Concert)
f.conc.p.   Lionel Tertis (Va.)/Artur Rubinstein (Pno.) c.1934
f.recs.   Watson Forbes (Va.)/Myers Foggin (Pno.) - *Decca X 233/5(78)*
            Herbert Downes (Va.)/Leonard Cassini (Pno.) - *Delta DEL 12028(m); Summit
            LSU 3073(m); Revolution RCB 1*
Pub: OUP, 1934
(* In his autobiography **My Viola and I**, p.74, Elek Books, London, 1974, Tertis recalls
that at this first performance the pages were turned by William Walton)

Three Jubilant and Three Solemn Fanfares (1935)
Dur: 6'15"
Instr: 3 Tpt. 3 Tbn. Tba.
f.recs.   Trumpeters of the Royal Military School of Music, Kneller Hall/Roberts -
            HMV B 9616(78)
            above band/Sharpe - *Guild GRSP 7010 (7101)*
Pub: Novello, 1944
later arr. for wind, brass and percussion by Frank Collinson as `Victory Fanfares' (1945)

f.p.   See Music for Radio
also arr. for military band (c.1942)
f.p.   cond. Arthur Bliss - Scotland, July 1942
f.rec.   Royal Artillery Band/Lt. Col. Sidney Hays - *Vanguard VRS 9038; Top Rank
            RRX 7000(m)*
Pub: Novello

Music for Strings (1935)
Dedicated to Rachel and Ernest Makower
Dur: 24'30"
f.p.   Vienna Philharmonic Orchestra/Sir Adrian Boult* - Grossen Saal des
            Mozarteums, Salzburg, 11 August 1935 (Salzburg Summer Festival)
f.Brit.p.   London Philharmonic Orchestra/Sir Malcolm Sargent - London,
            5 November 1935 (London Museum Concerts)
f.broad.p. BBC Symphony Orchestra/Sir Adrian Boult - 27 November 1935
f.Austr.p. Boyd Neel Orchestra/Boyd Neel - Sydney Conservatorium of Music,
            April/May 1947 (during a tour of Australia sponsored by the British Council)
f.p.   (as the ballet `Diversions') Royal Ballet Company/Royal Opera House
            Orchestra/John Lanchberry - Royal Opera House, Covent Garden, London,
            15 September 1961
Choreography: Kenneth MacMillan
Scenery and Costumes: Philip Prowse
f.recs.   BBC Symphony Orchestra/Sir Adrian Boult - *HMV DB 3257/9(78); BBC
            Artium BBC 4001(m)(and MC); RCA Victor (USA) M 464(78)*
            Philharmonia Orchestra/Arthur Bliss - *Columbia 33CX 1205(m); HMV
            1009(m); Angel (USA) 35136(m)*
Pub: Novello, 1936, 1948
(* Bliss first conducted this piece with the City of Birmingham Orchestra during their
1935-36 season)

Things to Come - derived works from the film (1934-35)
(i) Concert Suite arr. by the composer
[1. Ballet for children 2. Attack 3. Pestilence 4. Epilogue 5. Machines
 6. March]
Dedicated to H. G. Wells
Dur: 17'
Instr: 2/2/2/2 - 4/3/3/1 - timp. perc.(2) hp. str.
f.p.   BBC Symphony Orchestra/Arthur Bliss - Queen's Hall, London,
            12 September 1935 (Promenade Concert)
f.Eur.p.   cond. Sir Adrian Boult - Oslo, 12 January 1939
f.Am.p.   Chicago Symphony Orchestra/Sir Adrian Boult - Ravinia Park, Chicago,
            6 July 1939
f.recs.   (Nos. 1, 2,3 and `The World in Ruins') London Symphony Orchestra/ Arthur
            Bliss (rec. 3 March 1935) - *Decca K 810/1(78); Decca (USA) 25606/7(78);
            Dutton Laboratories CDLXT 2501(CD); Symposium 1203(CD)*
            (Nos. 4 and 6) London Symphony Orchestra and Chorus/Muir Mathieson -
            *Decca K 817(78); Decca (USA) 25608(78); Dutton Laboratories CDLXT
            2501(CD); Symposium 1203 (CD)*

(Concert Suite) London Symphony Orchestra/Arthur Bliss - *RCA SB 2026, SDD 255; RCA (USA) LM(m)/LSC 2257; London (USA) STS 15112; Belart 450 143-2(CD) (and MC)*

('March') New Philharmonia Orchestra/Arthur Bliss - *Readers Digest RDM(m)/RDS 2322*

Pub: Chappell, 1936, 1940; Novello, 1946, 1960 (the 'March' was published separately by Novello, 1939)

(ii) also arr. for small orchestra by Denis Wright

[1. Ballet for children 2. March 3. Epilogue]

Dur: 11'

Instr: 2/1/2/1 - 2/2/3/0 - timp. perc. hp. str.

Pub: Chappell

(iii) Concert Suite arr. for brass band by Gary Beresford

[1. Ballet for children 2. Epilogue 3. March]

Dur: 11'

f.rec.   Fodens Motor Works Band/James Scott - *Decca SB 330*

(iv) Concert Suite arr. for military band by Dan Godfrey (c.1942)

f.p.   cond. Arthur Bliss - Scotland, July 1942

f.rec.   Scots Guards Band/Howe - *Philips 6348 145, 6436 021*

Pub: Chappell

(v) Suite for piano

[1. Prologue 2. Ballet for children 3. March 4. Epilogue]

Pub: Chappell, 1936

(vi) Concert Suite reconstructed by Christopher Palmer for the Decca recording (1975)

[1. Prologue 2. Ballet for children 3. Attack 4. March 5. The World in Ruins
6. The Building of the New World 7. Attack on the Moon Gun 8. Epilogue]

Dur: 21'

Instr: 3/3/3/3 - 4/4/4/1 - timp. perc.(3) pno. hp.(2) org. str.

f.recs.   National Philharmonic Orchestra/Bernard Herrmann - *Decca Phase Four PFS 4363 (and MC), Decca 411 837-1(and MC); London 448 954-2LPF(CD)*
          Pub: Novello

(vi) Exc. 'Reconstruction' arr. for piano solo by Stephen Duro

Pub: Chester, 1997 (in 'Contemporary Classics No. 1')

(viii) Exc. 'March' arr. for piano solo by Stephen Duro

Pub: Chester, 1997 (in 'Contemporary Classics No. 2')

Kenilworth - Suite for brass band (1936)

[1. At the Castle gates 2. Serenade on the Lake
3. March: Kenilworth (Homage to Queen Elizabeth)]

Written as a test piece for the 1936 National Brass Band Championships and dedicated to Kenneth A. Wright .This suite was the last work to be played at the Crystal Palace before the disastrous fire of 30 November 1936.

Dur: 8'30"

f.p.   Foden's Motor Works Band/Harry Mortimer - Crystal Palace, London, 26 September 1936 (National Brass Band Championship Concert)

f.recs.   above artists - *Regal-Zonophone MR 2244(78); Beulah IPD 2(CD); Choice CD2 BM2(CD)*

          Harry Mortimer and his All Star Brass - *Columbia 33SX 1530(m), SCX 3484*

Pub: R. A. Smith, 1936

also arr. for military band
f.p.   cond. Joap Stolp - Arnhem, 12 March 1966
Pub: Molenaar NV (Holland)

Checkmate - ballet in one scene with a prologue (1937)
[Scenario: Arthur Bliss]
[1. Prologue: The Players 2. Dance of the Red Pawns
 3. Dance of the Four Knights 4. Entry of the Black Queen
 5. The Red Knight's Mazurka 6. Ceremony of the Bishops
 7. Entry of the Red Castles 8. Entry of the Red King and Queen
 9.The Attack 10. The Duel 11. The Black Queen Dances
 12. Finale: Checkmate]
Written for the British Music Week at the 1937 Paris International Exposition. The work
is dedicated to R. O. Morris
Dur: 47'
Instr: 2/2+ca./2/2 - 4/2/3/0 - timp. perc.(2) hp. str.
f.p.   Vic-Wells Ballet/L'Orchestre des Concerts Lamoureux/Constant Lambert -
            Thêatre des Champs-Elysées, Paris, 15 June 1937
Choreography: Ninette de Valois
Scenery and Costumes: E. McKnight Kauffer
Principals: Frederick Ashton, Harold Turner, Robert Helpmann, Pamela May, Margot
Fonteyn.
f.Brit.p.   Vic-Wells Ballet cond. Constant Lambert - Sadler's Wells Theatre, London,
            5 October 1937
f.broad.p. BBC Symphony Orchestra/Arthur Bliss - 15 October 1937
f.Am.p.   Sadler's Wells Ballet - 2 November 1949 (during their tour of the USA)
f.rec.   Hamburg Philharmonic Orchestra/Horst Werner (pseudonym for BBC
            Symphony Orchestra/Norman del Mar) - *Aries (USA) LP 1602(m)*
Pub: Novello, 1937 (also arr. piano solo)
Concert suite from the above
[1. Prologue: The Players 2. Dance of the Four Knights*
 3. Entry of the Black Queen* 4. The Red Knight's Mazurka*
 5. Ceremony of the Red Bishop* 6. The Attack (last section)
 7. The Duel 8. Finale: Checkmate*]
Dur: 35' (Suite), 25´ (Prologue and Five Dances*)
Instr: 2/2/2/2 - 4/2/3/0 - timp. perc.(2) hp. str.
f.p.   (Prologue and Five Dances) Royal Philharmonic Orchestra/Arthur Bliss -
            Queen's Hall, London, 7 April 1938 (Royal Philharmonic Society Concert)
f.Am.p.   New York Philharmonic Orchestra/Arthur Bliss - Carnegie Hall, New York,
            16 November 1939
f.Eur.p.   Concertgebouw Orchestra/Sir Adrian Boult - Concertgebouw, Amsterdam,
            4 November 1945
f.Russ.p.   Moscow State Symphony Orchestra/Arthur Bliss - Tchaikovsky Hall,
            Moscow, 22 April 1956 (during a British Council sponsored tour of the Soviet
            Union)
f.Jap.p.   London Symphony Orchestra/Arthur Bliss - Tokyo, October 1964
f.recs.   (Excs.) Orchestra of the Royal Opera House, Covent Garden/Robert Irving -
            Columbia DX 1718/20(78); Columbia (USA) ML 4363(m)

(Excs.) Sinfonia of London/Arthur Bliss - *World Record Club T(m)/ST 52;*
HMV SXLP 30153; EMI CDM7 64718-2(CD)
(Excs.) USSR State Symphony Orchestra/Arthur Bliss - *Melodiya (USSR) -*
MK 126720 1(78) and 26726/7(78), D3152(m)

Pub: Novello, 1938 (Suite), 1948 (Five Dances), 1955 (Prologue and Five Dances)
(i)   Two Dances arr. small orchestra by James O. Turner
       [1. Dance of the Red Pawns 2. The Black Queen Dances]
       Dur: 4'
       Instr: 1/2/0/0 - 0/2/1/0 - perc. str.
       Pub: Novello, 1938
(ii)   Four Dances arr. for brass band by Eric Ball
       [1. Dance of the Four Knights 2. The Red Knight's Mazurka
       3. Ceremony of the Red Bishops 4.Finale: Checkmate]
       Arranged and published for the 1978 National Brass Band Championships
       Dur: 15'30"
       f.p. Royal Albert Hall, London, October 1978 (National Brass Band
           Championship Finals)
       f.rec. (Nos. 1, 3 and 4) Yorkshire Imperial Metals Band/Denis Carr -
           Two-ten Records TT 003
       Pub: Novello, 1978
(iii)   Three Dances arr. for military band by Gerrard Williams (c.1942)
       [1. The Red Knight's Mazurka 2. Funeral Procession of the Red Knight
       3. Dance of the Four Knights]
       Dur: 8'
       f.p. cond. Arthur Bliss - Scotland, July 1942
       Pub: Novello

Suite from the film 'Conquest of the Air' (1937)

[1. Prelude: The Wind 2. The Vision of Leonardo da Vinci 3. Stunting
4. Over the Arctic 5. Gliding 6. March: Conquest of the Air]
Dedicated to Muir Mathieson (the fifth movement is dedicated to Mathieson's daughter
Muirné)
Dur: 12'
Instr: 2+picc./2/2/2 - 4/2/3/1 - timp. perc.(3) cel. hp. str.
f.p.   London Film Symphony Orchestra/Muir Mathieson - BBC, 11 February 1938
f.conc.p. BBC Symphony Orchestra/Henry Wood - Queen's Hall, London,
          3 September 1938 (Promenade Concert)
f.rec.   Philharmonia Orchestra/Kenneth Alwyn - *Silva Screen FILMCD 713(CD);*
          (exc.) Silva 3002 (CD and MC)
          (Nos. 1-5 arr. band) RAF Central Band/Barrie Hingley - *Classics for Pleasure*
          CFP 4666 (CD and MC)
Pub: Boosey & Hawkes, 1971

Fanfare for a Dignified Occasion (1938)

Commissioned by Boosey & Hawkes
Dur: 20"
Instr: 4 Tpt. 3 Tbn.
f.rec.   Trumpeters of the Royal Military School of Music, Kneller Hall/Roberts -
          HMV B 9616(78)

Pub: Boosey & Hawkes, 1938

Concerto for piano and orchestra in B flat (1938-39)
Commissioned by the British Council for the British Week at the New York World's Fair in 1939 and dedicated 'to the people of the United States of America'
Dur: 36'
Instr: 2+picc./2/2/2 - 4/2/3/0 - timp. str.
f.p.   Solomon/New York Philharmonic Symphony Orchestra/Sir Adrian Boult - Carnegie Hall, New York, 10 June 1939
f.Brit.p.   Solomon/BBC Symphony Orchestra/Sir Adrian Boult - Queen's Hall, London, 17 August 1939 (Promenade Concert)
f.Eur.p.   Shulamith Shafir/Vienna Philharmonic Orchestra/Arthur Bliss - Vienna, May 1946
f.rec.   Solomon/Royal Liverpool Philharmonic Orchestra/Sir Adrian Boult - *HMV C 3348/52(78); World Record Club H 125(m); HMV set RLS 701(m); EMI CDH 763 821-2(CD)*
Pub: Novello, 1940 (arr. for 2 pianos), 1945, 1947

Karen's Piece, for violin and piano (1939-40)
Written for the composer's younger daughter, Karen
Dur: 1'30"

Christ is Alive! Let Christians Sing, for unison voices and organ (or piano) - hymn tune, 'Mortlake' (1940 rev. 1970)
[Words: Brian Wren]
Written for the Joint Commission on Church Music at the request of Lee H. Bristol Jr.
Dur: 2'
f.Brit.p.   Choir of the Royal College of Music, London/John Wilson - Westminster Abbey, London, 15 May 1974
Pub: American Episcopal Hymnal, 1940; Walton Music Corp. (New York), 1974

Seven American Poems for medium voice and piano (1940)
[Words: Edna St. Vincent Millay (Nos. 1, 2, 3, 5 and 7) and Elinor Wylie (Nos. 4 and 6)
1. Gone, gone again is Summer 2. Siege 3. Feast 4. Little Elegy
5. Rain comes down 6. Fair Annet's song 7. Being Young and Green]
Dedicated 'to Bernhard and Irene Hoffmann in whose house in Santa Barbara these songs were written in August 1940'
Dur: 9'30"
f.p.   (5 songs only) Nicholas Goldschmidt (Bar.)/Arthur Bliss? (Pno.) - San Francisco Museum of Art, California, 6 February 1941 (Third Session of the Composers' Forum)
f.p.   (complete) William Parsons (Bar.)/Arthur Bliss (Pno) - Wigmore Hall, London, 8 November 1941
?f.broad.p. (female voice) Astra Desmond (M/S) - 4 February 1947
f.conc.p.   (female voice) Valerie Heath Davis (M/S)/Una Bradbury (Pno.) - Recital Room, Royal Festival Hall, London, 16 February 1960 (ISM Concert for Young Artists)
f.recs.   Janet Fraser (Sop.)/Gerald Moore (Pno.) - *HMV JH 69/70(78)**

(*a private recording for the British Council)

(No. 4 only) Maureen Lehane (M/S)/Alexander Kelly (Pno.) - *Ensemble ENS 137(MC)*

Pub: Boosey & Hawkes, 1942

Nos. 1, 4 and 7 also arr. for high voice and piano

Pub: Boosey & Hawkes

Two American Poems for medium voice and piano (1940)

[Words: Edna St. Vincent Millay 1. Humoresque 2. The Return from Town]

Dur: 3'

Pub: Boosey & Hawkes, 1980

String Quartet No. 1* in B flat (1941)

Dedicated to Mrs. Elizabeth Sprague Coolidge

Dur: 31'

f.p.   (Movts. 1-3) Coolidge Quartet - New York Public Library, 13 January 1941

f.p.   (complete) Pro Arte Quartet - Antonio Brosa (Vn.), Laurent Halleux (Vn.), Germain Prévost (Va.), Warwick Evans (Vc.) - University of California, Berkeley, USA, 9 April 1941

f.Brit.p.   Griller Quartet - National Gallery, London, 27 March 1942

f.recs.   Griller Quartet - *Decca K 1091/4(78)*

          Delmé Quartet - *Hyperion A 66178 (and CD)*

Pub: Novello, 1942 (* chronologically this is the third string quartet)

When wilt thou save the people - for SATB chorus and band (1941)

[Words: J.Booth, from a Corn Law rhyme]

Commissioned by Miss Lloyd George

Auvergnat - song for medium voice and piano (1943)

[Words: Hilaire Belloc]

Dur: 1'

Pub: Novello, 1944

Birthday Fanfare for Sir Henry Wood (1944)

Commissioned by the Musicians' Benevolent Fund

Dur: 1'15"

Instr: 3 Tpt. 4 Tbn. Timp.

f.p.   Kneller Hall Trumpeters/Lt. Col.M. Roberts - Savoy Hotel, London, 24 March 1944 (at a 75th Birthday Luncheon given by the Musicians' Benevolent Fund)

Pub: Novello

later arr. for orchestra

Dur: 2'

Instr: 2/2/2/2 - 4/3/3/0 - timp. cym.

f.p.   London Philharmonic Orchestra/Basil Cameron - Royal Albert Hall, London, 10 June 1944

f.broad.p.   BBC Symphony Orchestra/Sir Adrian Boult - BBC broadcast (from Bedford), 10 August 1944 (Jubilee Concert in celebration of the fiftieth anniversary of Henry Wood's Promenade Concerts)

Pub: Novello

March: The Phoenix 'Homage to France, August 1944' (1945)
`Written in honour of the France arisen from the defeat of 1940 to the liberation of 1944'
Dur: 6'
Instr: 2+picc./2+ca./2+bcl./2+cbsn. - 4/3/3/1 - timp. perc.(3) str.
f.p.   Paris Conservatoire Orchestra/Charles Munch - Paris 1945
f.Brit.p.   London Philharmonic Orchestra/Charles Munch - Royal Albert Hall, London,
            23 May 1945
f.broad.p. Paris Conservatoire Orchestra/Charles Munch - 5 November 1945
f.rec.   Philharmonia Orchestra/Constant Lambert - *HMV C 3518(78); EMI EH*
            291343-1 (and MC), EMI (set) CZS5 69743-2(CD)
Pub: Novello, 1948
also arr. for military band by Denis Wright (1981)
f.p.   Lewisham Concert Band/Joseph Proctor - Lewisham Concert Hall,
            8 March 1981
Pub: Novello

Miracle in the Gorbals - ballet in one scene (1944)
[Scenario: Michael Benthall 1. Overture 2. The Street 3. The Girl Suicide
 4. The Young Lovers 5. The Prostitute and the Boy 6. The Official
 7. The Discovery of the Suicide's Body 8. The Suicide's Body is Brought in
 9. The Stranger 10. Dance of Deliverance 11. The Official and the Prostitute
12. Intermezzo 13. The Slander Campaign 14. The Conversion of the Prostitute
15. The Killing of the Stranger]
Dedicated `to Trudy, Barbara and Karen - thanksgiving for November 5, 1943' (the date
of the Bliss family reunion in London)
Dur: 35'
Instr: 2+picc./2+ca./2+bcl./2 - 4/2/3/0 - timp. perc.(2) hp. str.
f.p.   Sadler's Wells Ballet cond. Constant Lambert - Prince's Theatre,
            London, 26 October 1944
Choreography: Robert Helpmann
Scenery: Edward Burra
Costumes: Grace Kelly
Principals: Robert Helpmann, Moira Shearer, Pauline Clayden, Alexis Rassine
f.recs.   (Nos. 2, 3, 4, 7, 10, 15) Orchestra of the Royal Opera House, Covent
            Garden/Constant Lambert - *Columbia DX 1260/1(78); Columbia (USA) ML*
            2117(m)
            (Nos. 1, 2, 3, 7, 8, 9, 10, 12, 15) Philharmonia Orchestra/Arthur Bliss -
            Columbia 33CX 1205(m); HMV HQM 1009(m); Angel (USA) 35136(m)
            (complete) Queensland Symphony Orchestra/Christopher Lyndon-Gee -
            Naxos 8.553698(CD)
Pub: Novello (also arr. piano solo, 1945)
Concert Suite from above:
[1. The Street 2. The Girl Suicide 3. The Young Lovers 4. The Stranger
 5. Dance of Deliverance 6. Intermezzo 7. Finale: The Killing of the Stranger]
Dur: 18'30"
f.p.   French National Radio Orchestra/Sir Adrian Boult - Paris, 1 March 1945
f.Brit.p.   (Movements 2, 4, 5, 6 and 7) London Philharmonic Orchestra/Arthur Bliss -
            Cheltenham Town Hall, 15 June 1945 (Cheltenham Festival)
Pub: Novello, 1948, 1959

Theme and Cadenza from the radio play 'Memorial Concert'* - Concert Piece for violin and orchestra (1945)
Dur: 6'30"
Instr: 1/1/2/2 - 2/1/3/0 - timp. hp. str.
f.conc.p.   Alfredo Campoli (Vn.)/London Light Orchestra/Michael Krein - BBC,
            31 March 1949 (BBC Light Music Festival)
f.rec.   Alfredo Campoli/London Philharmonic Orchestra/Arthur Bliss - *Decca LXT
            5166(m); Ace of Clubs ACL 317(m); Eclipse ECS 783(es); London (USA) LL
            1398(m); Beulah 3PD10(CD); Belart 461 353-2 (CD)*
Pub: Keith Prowse, 1946, 1947 (arr. for violin and piano); EMI Music; Novello
(* written by Lady Bliss - see Music for Radio)

Baraza* from the film 'Men of Two Worlds' - Concert Piece for piano, men's chorus and orchestra (1946)
Dur: 8'
Instr: 1+picc./1/2/2 - 2/2/3/0 - timp. perc. str.
f.rec.   Eileen Joyce/National Symphony Orchestra and Chorus/Muir Mathieson -
            Decca K 1174(78); Dutton Laboratories CDLXT 2501(CD)
Pub: Novello, 1946 (arr. for two pianos)
Baraza and Four Excerpts from the film `Men of Two Worlds' arr. Adriano
[* 1. Return to Tanganyika 2. The Challenge 3. Kisenga's Family
4. Village Fire and Finale]
f.rec.   Silvia Capova (Pno.)/Czech-Slovak Radio Symphony Orchestra/ Adriano -
            Marco Polo 8.223 315(CD)
also arr. for piano and brass band by Denis Wright
Pub: Novello
(* `a Swahili word meaning `a discussion in council between an African chief and his head man')

Adam Zero - ballet in one scene (1946)
[Scenario: Michael Benthall 1. Fanfare Overture 2. The Stage
3. The Birth of Adam 4. Adam's Fates 5. Dance of Spring
6. Love Dance (Awakening of Love) 7. Bridal Ceremony
8. Adam Achieves Power 9. Re-entry of Adam's Fates 10. Dance of Summer
11. Approach of Autumn 12. Night Club Scene (Dance of the Son and Daughter)
13. Destruction of Adam's World 14. Approach of Winter 15. Dance with Death
16. Finale: The Stage is set again - Fanfare Coda]
Dedicated to Constant Lambert
Dur: 46'
Instr: 2+2picc./2+ca./2+ten.sax./2 - 4/2/3/1 - timp. perc.(4) cel. gtr. pno. hp. str.
f.p.   Sadler's Wells Ballet and Royal Opera House Orchestra cond.
            Constant Lambert - Royal Opera House, Covent Garden, London, 8 April 1946
Choreography: Robert Helpmann
Scenery and Costumes: Roger Furse
Principals: Robert Helpmann, David Paltenghi, June Brae
f.rec.   (complete) English Northern Philharmonia/David Lloyd-Jones - *Naxos 8.553
            460(CD)*
Pub: Novello, 1948 (also arr. piano solo, 1948)
Concert Suite from the above

[Movts. 1, 5, 6, 7, 10, 11 and 15]
Dur: 18'
f.p.   City of Birmingham Symphony Orchestra/Arthur Bliss - Birmingham Town
            Hall, 28 October 1948
Pub: Novello
Suite from the above
[Movts. 1, 4, 5, 6, 7, 10, 11, 12, 13, 15 and 16]
Dur: 27'
f.p.   BBC Symphony Orchestra/Constant Lambert - Royal Albert Hall, London,
            16 September 1946 (Promenade Concert)
f.recs.   (No. 10) Orchestra of the Royal Opera House, Covent Garden/Robert Irving -
            HMV CLP 1070(m), 7ep 7076 (45m), sdt 1756(t), HQM 1078(m); Angel (USA)
            35521(m)
            (Nos. 5, 7, 10) London Symphony Orchestra/Arthur Bliss - *Lyrita SRCS 47,*
            SRCD 225(CD); Musical Heritage Society (USA) MHS 1750
            (complete) Royal Liverpool Philharmonic Orchestra/Vernon Handley - *HMV*
            ASD 3687(and MC)
Pub: Novello
Exc. `Fun and Games' arr. from movt. 12 for two pianos/three hands (1970)
Dedicated to Cyril and Phyllis
Dur: 5'
f.p.   Cyril Smith and Phyllis Sellick - Morley College, London,
            9 December 1970
Pub: Novello

The Olympians - opera in three Acts (1948-49)
[Libretto: J. B. Priestley]
Dedicated `to my friend and colleague of many years, Harold Brooke' (of Novello &
Company)
Dur: 150' (concert version - 120')
Instr: 2+picc./2/2/2+cbsn. - 4/2/3/1 - timp. perc.(3) cel. hp.(2) str. (+ 6 off-stage
            Tpts.)
f.p.   Sadler's Wells Ballet School and Royal Opera House Chorus and Orchestra
            cond. Karl Rankl - Royal Opera House, Covent Garden, London, 29
            September 1949
Producer: Peter Brook
Choreography: Pauline Grant
Scenery and Costumes: John Bryan
Principals: Murray Dickie, Edith Coates, James Johnson, Shirley Russell, Glynne
            Howell and Ronald Lewis
f.conc.p. (Act II Excs.) Royal Choral Society/London Symphony Orchestra/Sir
            Malcolm Sargent - Royal Albert Hall, London, 28 November 1957
Principals: Amy Shuard, Jacqueline Delman, Edgar Evans, David Galliver and
            Jess Walters
f.conc.p.   (complete) Ambrosian Singers/Polyphonia Orchestra/Bryan Fairfax - Royal
            Festival Hall, London, 21 February 1972 (in the presence of Her Majesty
            Queen Elizabeth, the Queen Mother)
Producer: Anne Anderson

Principals: Shirley Minty, Forbes Robinson, Anne Pashley, Thomas Hemsley, William
            McAlpine, Rae Woodland and Raimund Herincx
f.conc.p.   (full-length opera) Kensington Symphony Orchestra and Chorus/Leslie Head -
            St. John's, Smith Square, London, 2 March 1979
f.recs.   (excs.) first performance - *BBC Discs X 13995/7(m)*
            (complete) Soloists/Ambrosian Singers/Polyphonia Orchestra/Bryan Fairfax -
            Intaglio INCD 7552(CD)
Pub: Novello, 1950 (vocal score)

Two Extracts from the film 'Christopher Columbus' (1949)
[1. The Voyage Begins 2. Return to Spain]
Dur: 4'15"
Instr: 2/2/2/2+cbsn. - 4/3/3/0 - timp. perc.(2) hp. str.
f.p.   cond. Muir Mathieson - BBC, July 1949

Suite from the film 'Christopher Columbus' arr. Marcus Dods (1949 arr. 1979)
Dur: 9'
Instr: 2/2/2/2+cbsn. - 4/3/3/0 - timp. perc.(2) hp. str.
f.p.   BBC Radio Bristol Festival Orchestra/Alistair Jones - Colston Hall, Bristol,
            20 August 1980 (10th anniversary concert of BBC Radio Bristol)
f.recs.   City of Birmingham Symphony Orchestra/Marcus Dods - *HMV ASD 3797, ED
            290109-1*(and MC)
            (arr. Adriano)Czech-Slovak Radio Symphony Orchestra/Adriano - *Marco
            Polo 8.223 315(CD)*
Pub: Novello

String Quartet No. 2 in F minor (1950)
Written for and dedicated to the Griller Quartet on their twentieth anniversary
Dur: 30'
f.p.   Griller Quartet - Edinburgh, 1 September 1950 (Edinburgh Festival)
f.broad.p. above performance - 2 September 1950
f.rec.   above artists - *Decca LX 3038; London (USA) LL 1550(m)*
Pub: Novello, 1951
Movts. 2 and 3 later arr. as `Two Contrasts for string orchestra' (1972)
Dur: 10'30"
f.p.   Academy of St. Martin in the Fields/Neville Marriner - Cheltenham Town
            Hall, 16 July 1972 (Cheltenham Festival)
Pub: Novello

The Enchantress - scena for contralto and orchestra (1951)
[Words: from the `Second Idyll' of Theocritus adapted by Henry Reed]
Dedicated to Kathleen Ferrier
Dur: 16'30"
Instr: 2+picc./1+ca./0/0 - 4/2/3/0 - timp. perc. hp. str.
f.p.*   Kathleen Ferrier/BBC Northern Orchestra/Charles Groves - BBC Manchester,
            2 October 1951
f.conc.p.   Kathleen Ferrier/London Symphony Orchestra/Hugo Rignold - Royal Festival
            Hall, London, 6 April 1952

f.rec.   Linda Finnie/Ulster Orchestra/Vernon Handley - *Chandos ABTD 1443(MC), CHAN 8818(CD)*
Pub: Novello, 1952
(* originally scheduled for the Wigmore Hall on 11 June 1951 but postponed due to illness)

Sonata for piano (1952)
Written for and dedicated to Noel Mewton-Wood
Dur: 22'
f.p.   Noel Mewton-Wood - BBC, 24 April 1953
f.conc.p.   above artist - The Guildhall, St. Ives, Cornwall, June 1953 (St. Ives Music Festival)
f.recs.   Clive Lythgoe - *Concert Artist LPA 1075(m)*
    I. Aptekarev - *Melodiya (USSR) D 3126/7(m)*
Pub: Novello, 1953

Aubade for Coronation Morning, for unaccompanied SATB chorus (1953)
[Words: Henry Reed]
Commissioned by the Arts Council of Great Britain to mark the occasion of the Coronation of Her Majesty Queen Elizabeth II, and written as part of `A Garland for the Queen'*
Dur: 6'15"
f.p.   Cambridge University Musical Society/Boris Ord - Royal Festival Hall, London, 1 June 1953
f.rec.   above artists - *Columbia 33CX 1063(m)*
Pub: Stainer & Bell, 1953 (collection); Novello, 1953 (separately)
(* the other composers were Bax, Tippett, Vaughan Williams, Berkeley, Ireland, Howells, Finzi, Rawsthorne and Rubbra)

Processional for organ and orchestra (1953)
Written to accompany the procession of the Queen Mother from the West Door of Westminster Abbey during the Coronation of Her Majesty Queen Elizabeth II
Dur: 8'
Instr: 3/2/2/2+cbsn. - 4/3/3/1 - timp. perc.(3) str.
f.p.   Coronation Orchestra/Sir Adrian Boult with Osborne Peasgood (organ) - Westminster Abbey, London, 2 June 1953
f.rec.   Royal Liverpool Philharmonic Orchestra/Sir Charles Groves - *HMV ASD 3341 (and MC); Classics for Pleasure CFP 4567(CD and MC)*
Pub: Novello, 1954
also arr. for organ duet by Garrett O'Brien
f.p.   Timothy Farrell/Christopher Herrick - Westminster Abbey, London
f.rec.   above artists, *Vista VPS 1055*

A Salute to Painting - fanfare for brass and timpani (1954)
Dedicated to `Sir Gerald Kelly on the occasion of the Royal Academy Dinner, 28 April 1954'
Dur: 1'10"
Instr: 4 Tpt. 3 Tbn. Timp.

f.p.   Trumpeters of the Royal Artillery Regiment - Royal Academy of Arts,
            Burlington House, London, 28 April 1954
Pub: Novello, 1979

Elegiac Sonnet for high voice and chamber ensemble (1954)
[Words: Cecil Day Lewis]
Dedicated `in memoriam Noel Mewton-Wood'
Dur: 8'
Instr: Vn. Vn. Va. Vc. Pno.
f.p.   Peter Pears (Ten.)/Zorian String Quartet/Benjamin Britten (Pno.) - Wigmore
            Hall, London, 28 January 1955* (Noel Mewton-Wood Memorial Concert)
Pub: Novello, 1955
(* postponed from the original date of 4 December 1954 due to the illness of Peter Pears)

A Song of Welcome for soprano, baritone, SATB chorus and orchestra (1954)
[Words: Cecil Day Lewis]
Written to celebrate the return of the Queen and Prince Philip from their Royal Tour of
the Commonwealth
Dur: 16'
Instr: 2+2picc./2/2/2 - 4/2/3/0 - timp. perc.(2) hp. str.
f.p.   Joan Sutherland/Ian Wallace/BBC Chorus/BBC Concert Orchestra/Sir
            Malcolm Sargent - BBC Camden Studios, 15 May 1954
f.conc.p.   Elsie Morison/Ian Wallace/BBC Choral Society/BBC Symphony Orchestra/Sir
            Malcolm Sargent - Royal Albert Hall, London, 29 July 1954 (Promenade
            Concert)
Pub: Novello, 1954

Welcome the Queen - March (from the film) for orchestra (1954)
Dur: 5'
Instr: 2+picc./1/2/1 - 2/2/3/0 - timp. perc. str.
f.p.   BBC Concert Orchestra/London Light Concert Orchestra/Muir Mathieson -
            Royal Festival Hall, London, 19 June 1954
f.recs.   Philharmonia Orchestra/Arthur Bliss - *Columbia DX 1912(78); HMV HLM
            7093(m)*
            London Symphony Orchestra/Arthur Bliss - *RCA SB 2026 ; Argo SPA 500,
            KCSP 500 (MC); London (USA) STS 15112; RCA (USA) LM(m)/LSC 2257;
            Decca London 425662-2 (CD) (and MC); Decca 436403-2DWO(CD); Belart
            450 143-2 (CD)*
Pub: Chappell, 1954
also arr. for military band by W. J. Duthoit
Dur: 4'30"
f.rec.   Royal Marines Band/Sir Vivian Dunn - *HMV ges 5880(45), 7eg 8866(45m)*
Pub: Army Journal; Chappell, 1954
also arr. for piano
Dur: 4'45"
Pub: Chappell, 1954

A Birthday Greeting* to Her Majesty for orchestra (1955)
Dur: 1'40"

Instr: 2/2/2/2 - 4/3/3/1 - timp. perc. hp. org. str.
f.p.   National Youth Orchestra of Great Britain/Sir Malcolm Sargent - Royal
            Festival Hall, London, 21 April 1955
f.Eur.p.   above artists - Palais des Beux-Arts, Brussels, April 1955 (during the
            orchestra's European tour)
(* on the refrain `Happy Birthday to You, Our Queen Elizabeth')

Concerto for violin and orchestra (1955)
Commissioned by the BBC and dedicated to Alfredo Campoli
Dur: 38'30"
Instr: 2+picc./1/2/2 - 3/2/3/0 - timp. perc. hp. str.
f.p.   Alfredo Campoli/BBC Symphony Orchestra/Sir Malcolm Sargent - Royal
            Festival Hall, London, 11 May 1955
f.Eur.p.   Alfredo Campoli/Moscow Philharmonic Orchestra/Arthur Bliss - Moscow,
            April 1956 (during a tour of the Soviet Union)
f.rec.   (i)   Alfredo Campoli/London Philharmonic Orchestra/Arthur Bliss - *Decca*
                    LXT 5166(m); Ace of Clubs ACL 317(m); Eclipse ECS 783(es);
                    London (USA) LL 1398(m); Beulah 3PD10(CD)
            (ii)   (1968 rec.) Alfredo Campoli/BBC Symphony Orchestra/Arthur Bliss -
                    BBC Radio Classics 15656 91842(CD)
Pub: Novello, 1956 (also arr. for violin and piano, 1957)

Meditations on a theme by John Blow* for orchestra (1955)
[Introduction: The Lord is my Shepherd, I will Fear no Evil
 1. He leadeth me beside the still waters
 2. Thy Rod and Staff they comfort me 3. Lambs 4. He Restoreth my Soul
 5. In Green Pastures
 Interlude: Through the Valley of the Shadow of Death
 Finale: In the House of the Lord]
Commissioned by the City of Birmingham Symphony Orchestra with funds provided by
the John Feeney Charitable Trust and dedicated to the orchestra and its conductor, Rudolf
Schwarz
Dur: 30'
Instr: 3/2+ca./2+bcl./2+cbsn. - 4/3/3/1 - timp. perc.(4) cel. hp. str.
f.p.   City of Birmingham Symphony Orchestra/Rudolf Schwarz - Birmingham
            Town Hall, 13 December 1955
f.Lon.p.   above artists - Royal Festival Hall, 13 February 1956
f.Eur.p.   Moscow Philharmonic Orchestra/Sir Adrian Boult - Moscow, 27 September
            1956
f.recs.   City of Birmingham Symphony Orchestra/Hugo Rignold - *Lyrita RCS 33(m),*
            SRCS 33; Musical Heritage Society (USA) MHS 1251
            Royal Liverpool Philharmonic Orchestra/Sir Charles Groves - *BBC Radio*
            Classics 15656 91682(CD)
Pub: Novello, 1958
(* John Blow was Composer in Ordinary to James II - the theme is taken from his setting
of Psalm xxiii published in Musica Britannica ed. H. Watkins Shaw and Anthony Lewis)

Seek the Lord - anthem for SATB chorus and organ (1955-56)
[Biblical Text; Amos 5]

Written for the centenary service of `The Mission to Seamen'
Dur: 3'30"
f.p.   Choir of Westminster Abbey/William McKie, with Osborne Peasgood (org.) -
           Westminster Abbey, London, 20 February 1956
Pub: Novello, 1956

Edinburgh - overture for full orchestra (1956)
Written to mark the tenth anniversary of the founding of the Edinburgh International
Festival - the opening theme is based on the rhythm of the word `Edinburgh'
Dur: 10'
Instr: 2+picc./2/2/2 - 4/2/3/0 - timp. perc.(3) hp. str.
f.p.   Royal Philharmonic Orchestra/Arthur Bliss - Usher Hall, Edinburgh,
           20 August 1956 (Edinburgh Festival)
f.Eng.p.   Hallé Orchestra/Arthur Bliss - Free Trade Hall, Manchester,
           16 December 1956
f.rec.   City of Birmingham Symphony Orchestra/Vernon Handley - *HMV ASD 3878;*
           EMI CDM 7 69388-2 (CD)
Pub: Novello, 1962

The First Guards - March for military band arr. by W. J. Duthoit (1956)
Written in honour of the tercentenary of the Grenadier Guards
Dur: 6'
f.conc.p. Band of the Grenadier Guards/Arthur Bliss - Royal Festival Hall, London,
           2 June 1956
f.rec.   Band of the Grenadier Guards/Harris - *Decca DFE 6499(45m)*
Pub: Army Journal, 1956; Chappell

Salute to the RAF - fanfare for orchestra (1956)
Written for the first Royal Air Force Anniversary Concert
Dur: 0'40"
Instr: 2/2/2/2 - 4/2/3/1 - timp. perc.(2) str.
f.p.   Central Band of the RAF/Hallé Orchestra/Arthur Bliss - Royal Albert Hall,
           London, 7 April 1956

Three Fanfares for the Service of the Order of the Bath (1956)
Dur: 1'30"
Instr: 3Tpt.2Tbn.Tba.
f.p.   Trumpeters of the Royal Horse Guards/Major J.E.Thirkle - Westminster
           Abbey, London, 15 November 1956
Pub: Novello, 1979

Three orchestral pieces from the film 'Seven Waves Away' (1956)
f.rec.   Czech-Slovak Radio Symphony Orchestra/Adriano - *Marco Polo 8.223*
           315(CD)

Discourse for orchestra (1957)
Commissioned by and dedicated to the Louisville Orchestra
Dur: 21'
Instr: 2+picc./2/2/2 - 2/2/3/0 - timp. perc. str.

f.p.   Louisville Orchestra/Robert Whitney - Columbia Auditorium, Louisville,
            Kentucky, USA, 23 October 1957
f.rec.   above artists - *Louisville LOU 592(m)*
Pub: Novello
The work was extensively revised in 1965
Dur: 20'
Instr   3/3/2/3 - 4/3/3/0 - timp. perc.(2) hp. str.
f.p.   London Symphony Orchestra/Arthur Bliss - Royal Festival Hall, London,
            28 September 1965 (Commonwealth Arts Festival)
f.rec.   City of Birmingham Symphony Orchestra/Vernon Handley - *HMV ASD 3878*
Pub: Novello, 1966

The Lady of Shalott - ballet in one act (1958)
[Scenario: Arthur Bliss and Christopher Hassall after the poem by Tennyson
 1. Prelude 2. The Lady at her Tapestry-frame 3. The Reapers
 4. The Dance of the Villagers 4a. Dance of the Village Belle
 5. The Entry of the Page 6. The Page and the Lady 7. The Entry of the Knight
 8. The Tumblers 9. Re-entry of the Page 10. The Abbot 11. The Young Lovers
 12. The Funeral Cortège 13. Entry of Lancelot 14. The Lady Dances in Delight
 15. The Lady in Love with Lancelot 16. Epilogue]
Commissioned by the University of California for the May T. Morrison Music Festival
Dur: 37'30"
Instr: 2+picc./2/2/2 - 2/2/1/0 - timp. perc. hp. cel. pno. str.
f.p.   San Francisco Ballet and University of California Symphony Orchestra cond.
            Earl Murray - Alfred Hertz Memorial Hall, Berkeley Campus, University of
            California, USA, 2 May 1958
Choreography: Lew Christensen
Scenery and Costumes: Tony Duquette
Principals: Jocelyn Vollmar, Richard Carter, Kent Stowell
f.Brit.p.   BBC Symphony Orchestra/Arthur Bliss - BBC broadcast, 30 December 1968
f.Brit.conc.p.Ballet Group of New Park Girls' School/Leicestershire Schools Symphony
            Orchestra/Eric Pinkett - Haymarket Theatre, Leicester,
            13 May 1975 (for the television programme `Girl in a Broken Mirror')
Choreography: Mary Hockney
f.rec.   BBC Symphony Orchestra/Arthur Bliss - *BBC Radio Classics 15656
            91842(CD)*
Pub: Novello (also arr. piano solo)

Birthday Song for a Royal Child, for unaccompanied SATB chorus (1959)
[Words: Cecil Day Lewis]
Written on the occasion of the birth of H.R.H. Prince Andrew on 19 February 1960
Dur: 3'
f.p.   BBC Chorus/Leslie Woodgate - BBC Light Programme, 20 February 1960
            (pre-recorded 31 December 1959)
f.conc.p.   Purcell Singers/Louis Halsey - Arts Council Drawing Room, London, 18
            March 1960 (Macnaghten Concert)
f.rec.   Glasgow Phoenix Choir/Mooney - *Waverley ZLP(m)/SZLP 2073*
Pub: Novello, 1960

Two Songs for soprano, bass and piano - unfinished (1960s)
[1. Pack Clouds Away (Thomas Heywood)
2. Song of a Man who has come through (D. H. Lawrence)]

Let the People Sing: Two Fanfares (1960)
Dur: 0'25"
Instr: 3 Tpt. 3 Tbn. Timp. Cym.
f.p.   members of the BBC Concert Orchestra/Arthur Bliss - Kingsway Hall,
          London, 28 June 1960 (at the Annual Festival of Choirs `Let the People Sing')
Pub: Novello, 1979

Royal Fanfares and Interlude for the Wedding of H.R.H.Princess Margaret (1960 rev. 1965)
[1. The Sovereign's Fanfare 2. Fanfare for the Bride 3. Interlude
4. Royal Fanfare No. 1 5. A Wedding Fanfare 6. Royal Fanfare No 2]
Dur: 3'(original version) 4'45" (rev. version)
Instr: 3 Tpt. 3 Tbn. Tba. (+ perc. in rev. version)
f.p.   Trumpeters of the Royal Military School of Music, Kneller Hall, and State
          Trumpeters of the Household Cavalry cond. Lt. Col. David McBain -
          Westminster Abbey, London, 6 May 1960
f.conc.p. (No. 4 or 6) New Philharmonia Orchestra/Rudolf Schwarz - Royal Albert Hall,
          London, 21 July 1969 (Promenade Concert celebrating the 150th anniversary
          of the birth of Prince Albert)
f.recs.   (No. 1) Trumpeters of the Royal Air Force Central Band/Wing Commander J.
          L. Wallace - *HMV CLP 1892(m), CSD 1615; Capitol (USA) SP 8685*
          (complete) Locke Brass Consort/James Stobart - *RCA RL 25081; Chandos
          CHAN 6573(CD)*
Pub: Novello 1960, 1965 (rev. version)
original version arr. for organ solo by Basil Ramsey (1964)
f.rec.   (Nos. 1, 2, 5) Christopher Dearnley - *HMV CSD 3677, HQS 1376*
Pub: Novello, 1964

Salute to The Royal Society - fanfare for organ, brass and percussion (1960)
Written to celebrate the tercentenary of The Royal Society, Spring 1960
Dur: 5'45"
Instr: 3 Tpt. 3 Tbn. Timp. Cym.
f.p.   George Thalben-Ball/Kneller Hall Trumpeters/Arthur Bliss - Royal Albert
          Hall, London, 19 July 1960 (Promenade Concert)
f.rec.   William Lloyd Webber/Trumpeters of the Royal Military School of Music,
          Kneller Hall/Sharpe - *Sound News SM 122*
Pub: World Library Publications, 1973; Novello

Stand Up and Bless the Lord your God - anthem for SATB chorus and organ (1960)
[Biblical text from Nehemiah, Isaiah and Kings]
Written for the Llandaff Cathedral Choir on the completion of the restoration of the
Cathedral after War damage
Dur: 8'
f.p.   Llandaff Cathedral Choir/Robert Joyce with V.Anthony Lewis (org.) -
          Llandaff Cathedral, 6 August 1960

Pub: Novello, 1960

Tobias and the Angel - opera in two Acts for Television (1960)

[Libretto: Christopher Hassall from the Apocryphal Book of Tobit]
Commissioned by BBC Television and `Dedicated to Trudy Bliss by the Composer and
the Author'. The opera was to later win an award at a Film(?) Festival in Salzburg.

Dur: 85'
Instr: 2/2/2/2 - 4/2/3/1 - timp. perc.(2) hp. str.
f.p.   London Symphony Chorus and Orchestra/Norman del Mar - BBC Television,
            19 May 1960
Director: Rudolf Cartier
Designer: Clifford Hatts
Choreography: Margaret Dale
Principals: John Ford, Ronald Lewis, Jess Walters, Janet Howe, Trevor Anthony and
            Elaine Malbin
Pub: Novello, 1961 (vocal score of stage version)

The Beatitudes - cantata for soprano, tenor, SATB chorus, organ and orchestra (1961)

[Words arr. by Arthur Bliss and Christopher Hassall
 Orchestral Prelude: A Troubled World
 1. The Mount of Olives (Henry Vaughan) 2. First and Second Beatitudes
 3. Easter: Rise heart, thy Lord is risen (George Herbert)
 4. I got me Flowers to Strew thy Way (George Herbert) 5. Third Beatitude
 6. The Lofty Looks of Man shall be Humbled (Isaiah II) 7. Fourth Beatitude
 8. The Call: Come, my Way, my Truth, my Life (George Herbert) - Orchestral
    Interlude 9. Fifth, Sixth, Seventh and Eighth Beatitudes
 10. And Death shall have no Dominion (Dylan Thomas)
 11. Ninth Beatitude and Voices of the Mob
 12. Epilogue: O Blessed Jesu (Jeremy Taylor)]
Commissioned by the Coventry Cathedral Festival and dedicated `to my grand-daughter,
Susan, born May 10th 1955'

Dur: 50'
Instr: 2/2+ picc./2/2 - 4/2/3/1 - timp.perc.(2) hp.(2) org.str.
f.p.   Jennifer Vyvyan (Sop.)/Richard Lewis (Ten.)/Coventry Cathedral Festival
            Choir/BBC Symphony Orchestra/Arthur Bliss - Belgrade Theatre, Coventry,
            25 May 1962 (Coventry Cathedral Festival)
f.Lon.p.   Jennifer Vyvyan (Sop.)/Gerald English (Ten.)/Rainham Co-operative Ladies'
            Choir/Highgate Choral Society/ Kensington Symphony Chorus and
            Orchestra/Leslie Head - Central Hall, Westminster, 16 February 1963
f.Austr.p. Pearl Berridge (Sop.)/Ronald Dowd (Ten.)/Queensland State and Municipal
            Choir/Queensland Symphony Orchestra/Arthur Bliss - City Hall, Brisbane, 10
            October 1964
f.Am.p.   Choir and Orchestra of Westminster College (Princeton)/Arthur Bliss - New
            York, September 1968
Pub: Novello, 1962

Greetings to a City - flourish for two brass orchestras and percussion (1961)

Commissioned by and dedicated to the American Wind Symphony Orchestra of

Pennsylvania who specialised in giving concerts on rivers

Dur: 6'30"

Instr: 4 Tpt. 4 Flghn. 6 Tbn. Tba. Timp. Cym. BD.

f.p. American Wind Symphony Orchestra/Robert Boudreau - London, 4 July 1961 (on a special 120 foot barge moored on the River Thames at Battersea during the orchestra's first tour of Great Britain)

f.rec. Philip Jones Brass Ensemble - *Decca SDD 274; London 430 369-2LM(CD)*

Pub: Robert King, 1969

Toast to the Royal Household for piano trio (1961)

Composed for the occasions when the Royal Household is toasted by the Royal Company of Archers

Dur: 0'25"

Instr: Vn. Vc. Pno.

f.p. Holyrood House, Edinburgh, July 1962

Call to Adventure, arr. for military band by W. J. Duthoit (1962)

Dedicated to the Air Training Corps on the occasion of their 21st Anniversary Celebration

Dur: 3'15"

f.p. RAF Central Band/Wing Commander J. L. Wallace - Church of St. Clement Danes, London, 4 February 1962

f.rec. Band of the Royal Marines School of Music/Sir Vivian Dunn - *HMV 7eg 8866(45m), ges 5880(45)*

Pub: Army Journal, 1962; Chappell

also arr. for brass band

Pub: Brass and Reed Journal, 1962; Chappell

Gala Fanfare, arr. for military band by W. J. Duthoit (1962)

Commissioned by Professor Frank Callaway for the opening of the 1962 British Empire and Commonwealth Games in Perth, Western Australia

Dur: 1'

f.p. Royal Australian Air Force Band/Squadron Leader L. H. Hicks - Games Stadium, Perth, Western Australia, 22 November 1962

f.rec. Military Band - *Chappell C 868(m)*

Pub: Chappell, 1962

March of Homage in Honour of a Great Man, for orchestra (1961-62)

Written in tribute to Winston Churchill

Dur: 4'15"

Instr: 2/2/2/2 - 4/2/3/1 - timp. perc.(4) str.

f.p. BBC Symphony Orchestra/Arthur Bliss - BBC Maida Vale Studios, London, 30 March 1962 (this performance was subsequently broadcast by the BBC Third Programme on 30 January 1965 immediately before the State Funeral of Sir Winston Churchill)

f.rec. Royal Liverpool Philharmonic Orchestra/David Atherton - *Unicorn DKP 9006; UKCD 2029(CD) (and MC)*

also arr. for military band by W.J.Duthoit

f.rec.   Central Band of the Royal Air Force/Wing Commander J.L.Wallace - HMV
              7EG 8899(45m)
Pub: Chappell
also arr. for organ/piano solo by Felton Rapley
Pub: Chappell

Mary of Magdala - cantata for contralto, baritone, chorus and orchestra (1962)
[Words: Christopher Hassall from Edward Sherburne and `The Gardener' by Roland
Watkins]
Commissioned by the City of Birmingham Symphony Orchestra with funds provided by
the John Feeney Trust and dedicated `to the memory of Christopher Hassall, died 25
April 1963'
Dur: 27'
Instr: 2/2/1/1 - 2/2/0/0 - timp. perc.(2) hp. str.
f.p.   Norma Proctor (Con.)/John Carol Case (Bar.)/Worcester Cathedral Boys'
             Choir/City of Birmingham Choir/City of Birmingham Symphony
             Orchestra/Arthur Bliss - Worcester Cathedral, 2 September 1963 (Three
             Choirs Festival)
f.broad.p.   above artists - 31 October 1963
f.Lon.p.   Meriel Dickinson (Con.)/Neil Howlett (Bar.)/London Orpheus Choir and
             Orchestra/James Gaddarn - Queen Elizabeth Hall, 14 June 1969
Pub: Novello, 1963 (vocal score), 1969

**The Belmont* Variations (Theme, Six Variations and Finale) for brass band arr. by
Frank Wright (1962)**
Commissioned as a test piece for the 1963 National Brass Band Championships
Dur: 11'
f.p.   CWS (Manchester) Brass Band/Alex Mortimer - Royal Albert Hall, London,
             19 October 1963 (National Brass Band Championship of Great Britain
             Festival Concert)
f.rec.   Brighouse & Rastrick Band/Walter Hargreaves - *Pye GGL 0407((m), GSGL
             10407*
Pub: Paxton/Novello, 1963
(* named after the town in Massachusetts where the composer's wife was born)

Cradle Song for a Newborn Child, for SATB chorus and harp (or piano) (1963)
[Words: Eric Crozier]
Written for the birth of H.R.H. Prince Edward on 10 March 1964
Dur: 3'30"
f.p.   BBC Chorus/Peter Gellhorn with Renata Feheffel-Stein (Hp.) - BBC Home
             Service, 11 March 1964 (pre-recorded 5 March 1964)
f.rec.   Bristol Bach Choir/Glyn Jenkins with Valerie Shelton (Pno.) - *Priory PRCD
             352(CD)*
Pub: Novello, 1964

Fanfare: Salute to Shakespeare (1964 rev. 1972)
Written for the Argo recording 'A Homage to Shakespeare' issued in 1964 to celebrate
the quatercentenary of Shakespeare's birth and based on a phrase by the Elizabethan
composer, John Wilbye

Dur: 1'
Instr: 5 Tpt. 3 Tbn. Tba. Perc.
f.p.   (rev.version) Kneller Hall Trumpeters/Lt.Col.Rodney Bashford - Royal Opera
            House, Covent Garden, London, 3 January 1973
f.rec.   Kneller Hall Trumpeters/Lt.Col.Basil H.Brown - *Argo NF(m)/ZNF 4* (recorded
            at the Decca Studios, London, 7 February 1964)
Pub: Robert King Music, 1973 (rev. version)

The Golden Cantata: Music is the Golden Form - cantata for tenor, SATB chorus and orchestra (1963)
[Words: Kathleen Raine]
Written at the invitation of ProfessorThurston Dart for the Quincentenary Celebrations of
the first degree in music given by Cambridge University in 1464 and dedicated to the
Cambridge University Musical Society
Dur: 28'
Instr: 2+picc./2/2/2 - 4/3/3/1 - timp. perc.(3) cel. hp. org. str.
f.p.   Wilfred Brown (Ten.)/Cambridge University Musical Society Choir and
            Orchestra/Arthur Bliss - Cambridge Guildhall, 18 February 1964
f.broad.p. Gerald English (Ten.)/Huddersfield Choral Society/BBC Northern Symphony
            Orchestra/Arthur Bliss - Third Programme, 3 October 1966
Pub: Novello, 1963

The High Sheriff's Fanfare (1963)
Written for and dedicated to Colonel R. J. Longfield when he was High Sheriff of Dorset
Dur: 0'30"
Instr: 2 Tpt.
f.p.   Shaftesbury Silver Band - Garden Party at Lower Silton, Dorset,
            24 August 1963
Pub: Novello, 1979

Music for the Wedding of H.R.H. Princess Alexandra, for brass ensemble (1963)
Dur: 4'
f.p.   Kneller Hall Trumpeters/Lt.Col.Basil H. Brown - Westminster Abbey,
            London, 24 April 1963
Pub: Novello

A Knot of Riddles - song cycle for baritone and ten instruments (1963)
[Words from the Old English of `The Exeter Book' trans. Kevin Crossley-Holland
 1. Fish in River 2. Swallows 3. An Oyster 4. A Weather Cock
 5. A Bookworm (Hommage modeste à Maurice Ravel) 6. A Cross of Wood
 7. Sun and Moon]
Commissioned by the BBC for the Cheltenham Festival and dedicated to William Glock
Dur: 17'
Instr: Fl./Picc. Ob. Cl. Bsn. Hp. Vn. Vn. Va. Vc. Db.
f.p.   John Shirley-Quirk (Bar.)/Melos Ensemble/Arthur Bliss - Cheltenham Town
            Hall, 11 July 1963 (Cheltenham Festival)
f.Lon.p.   John Shirley-Quirk (Bar.)/members of the Bath Festival Orchestra/Arthur Bliss
            - Victoria & Albert Museum, 17 June 1964

f.rec.   John Shirley-Quirk/London Chamber Orchestra/Wyn Morris - *Pye Golden Guinea GSGC 2042 (and MC),TPLS 13036, ZCPC 507(MC)*
Pub: Novello, 1964 (vocal score)

The Linburn Air - March arr. for military band by Leslie Statham (1964)
Dedicated to the Scottish National Institution for the War Blinded
Dur: 4'10"
f.p.   Band of the Gordon Highlanders/Colin Harper - Linburn, 14 November 1965
f.rec.   Royal Highland Fusiliers Band - *Decca SKL 4828; Beltona SBE 161*
Pub: Chappell
also arr. for military band by Colin Harper (1968)

Ceremonial Prelude for organ,brass and percussion (1965)
Commissioned by the Dean of Westminster as processional music for Her Majesty the Queen during the service to commemorate the 900th anniversary of Westminster Abbey
Dur: 5'30"
Instr: 4 Hn. 3 Tpt. 3 Tbn. Perc. Timp.
f.p.   Simon Preston (Org.)/members of the New Philharmonia Orchestra/Arthur Bliss - Westminster Abbey, London, 28 December 1965
f.rec.   above performance - *HMV ALP(m)/ASD 2264*
Pub: World Library Publications, 1972; Novello

Fanfare for the Commonwealth Arts Festival (1965)
Written for the opening of the 1965 Commonwealth Arts Festival
Dur: 1'20"
Instr: 4 Tpt. 4 Tbn. Timp. Cym.
f.p.   Band of the Royal Military School of Music, Kneller Hall/Lt.Col.Basil H. Brown - Banqueting House, Whitehall, London, 16 September 1965
Pub: Novello, 1979

O Give Thanks unto the Lord - anthem for SATB chorus and organ (1965)
[Biblical text: Psalm 106]
Written to commemorate the 400th anniversary of the granting of the Royal Charter to the island of Sark in 1565
Dur   5'15"
f.p.   Westminster Singers/Bernard Wiltshire - St.Peter's Parish Church, Sark, Channel Islands, 8 August 1965 (Thanksgiving Service)
Pub: Novello, 1965 (Musical Times)

The Right of the Line - Fanfare (1965)
Written for the 250th anniversary of the foundation of the Royal Artillery Regiment
Dur: 1'45"
Instr: 4 Tpt. 3 Tbn. Timp. Perc.(2)
f.p.   Band of the Royal Regiment of Artillery/Lt. Col. Sidney Hays - Civic Hall, Hong Kong, 29 January 1966
f.Brit.p.   Band of the Royal Regiment of Artillery/Cpt.R. Quinn - St.Paul's Cathedral, London, 8 July 1966
f.rec.   Band of the Royal Regiment of Artillery/Cpt. R.Quinn - *Gold Star 15-49*
Pub: Novello, 1979

Macclesfield: Fanfare Prelude* for orchestra (1966)
Written for the opening concert of the Macclesfield Arts Festival
Dur: 2'
Instr: 2/2/2/2 - 4/2/3/0 - timp. perc. str.
f.p.   BBC Northern Orchestra/Arthur Bliss - King's School Assembly Hall,
          Macclesfield, Cheshire, 13 May 1966 (Macclesfield Arts Festival)
Pub: Novello
(* based on the Fanfare Overture from **Adam Zero** q.v.)

Fanfare for the Lord Mayor of London (1967)
Dedicated `to Sir Gilbert and Lady Inglefield with every good wish from Arthur Bliss' -
Sir Gilbert Inglefield was the then Lord Mayor of London
Dur: 1'30"
Instr: 4 Hn. 3 Tpt. 3 Tbn. Tba. Timp. Cym.
f.p.   members of the London Symphony Orchestra/Arthur Bliss - on the steps of the
          Royal Exchange, City of London, 21 May 1967
f.conc.p. members of the London Symphony Orchestra/Arthur Bliss - Royal Festival
          Hall, London, 19 November 1967
f.rec.   Locke Brass Consort/James Stobart - *RCA RL 25081; Chandos CHAN
          6573(CD)*
Pub: Robert King Music, 1971

**He is the Way, for unison voices and organ (or piano) - hymn tune, `Santa Barbara'
(1967)**
[Words: W. H. Auden]
Commissioned by Elizabeth Poston for the Cambridge Hymnal
Dur: 2'30"
Pub: CUP, 1967; Novello, 1967

River Music, for unaccompanied SATB chorus (1967)
[Words: Cecil Day Lewis]
Commissioned by the Greater London Council for the opening of the Queen Elizabeth
Hall on London's South Bank
Dur: 7'
f.p.   Ambrosian Singers/Arthur Bliss - Queen Elizabeth Hall, London,
          1 March 1967
f.rec.   Finzi Singers/Paul Spicer - *Chandos ABTD 1568(MC), CHAN 8980(CD)*
Pub: Novello, 1967

**Sweet Day, so Cool, for unaccompanied SATB chorus - hymn tune, `Pen Selwood'
(1967)**
[Words: George Herbert]
Commissioned by Elizabeth Poston for the Cambridge Hymnal
Dur: 2'15"
f.rec.   Benenden School Choir/Hooper - *HMV CLP(m)/CSD 3598*
Pub: CUP, 1967; Novello, 1967

Three Songs for SSAA children's chorus and piano*(1967)
[1. Little Bingo (Nursery Rhyme) 2. A Widow Bird Sate Mourning* (Shelley)

3. A New Year Carol (Anon.)]
Dedicated to Sheila Mossman and the Orpington Junior Singers
Dur: 7'
f.p.   (No.3 only) Orpington Junior Singers/Sheila Mossman, with Iris Claydon
            (Pno.) - Queen Elizabeth Hall, London, 2 January 1969
f.p.   (Nos. 1 and 2) above artists - Orpington, Kent, 29 March 1969
f.p.   (complete) above artists, 13 December 1969
f.rec.   (No. 3) above artists - *BBC RESR 22M(m)*
Pub: Novello, 1968

**Lord, Who shall Abide in Thy Tabernacle? - anthem for SATB chorus and organ
(1968)**
[Biblical Text: Psalms 15 and 22]
Commissioned by Dr.Neville Wallbank and Sir John Russell (Honorary Registrar of the
Imperial Society of Knight's Bachelor) for the Dedication of the Knight's Bachelor
Shrine at the church of St. Bartholomew-the-Great, Smithfield, London
Dur: 4'45"
f.p.   Choir of St. Bartholomew-the-Great/Brian Brockless - St.
            Bartholomew-the-Great, Smithfield, London, 10 July 1968
Pub: Novello, 1968

**One, Two, Buckle my Shoe - Nursery Rhyme for SS children's chorus and piano
(1968)**
Dedicated to `the very young in the Orpington Junior Singers'
Dur: 1'05"
f.p.   Orpington Junior Singers/Sheila Mossman with Iris Claydon (Pno.) -
            Orpington, Kent, 30 March 1968
Pub: Novello, 1968

Enid's Blast, for solo trumpet, or trumpet and piano (1968)
Written for Enid, Bliss's half-sister - the tune was later included in **A Wedding Suite** on
the occasion of her marriage in 1974 q.v.
Dur: 30"
f.p.   Bruce Hudson (Tpt.)/Roger Clarke (Pno.) - Twin Pines Ranch, Carpinteria,
            California, USA, 12 February 1969 (Carpinteria Arts Festival)

A Prayer to the Infant Jesus, for unaccompanied SSAA children's chorus (1968)
[Czech prayer trans.*]
Dedicated to Sheila Mossman and the Orpington Junior Singers
Dur: 5'30"
f.p.   Orpington Junior Singers/Sheila Mossman - All Saints Parish Church,
            Orpington, Kent, 24 May 1968 (during Christian Aid Week)
f.Lon.p.   above artists - Westminster Theatre Arts Centre, 1 December 1968
f.rec.   above artists - *Pilgrim KLPS 42*
Pub: Novello, 1968
(* the words were copied down by the composer when visiting the Church of Our Lady of
Vilbory in Prague in 1966)

Salute to Lehigh University arr. for military band by Jonathan Elkus (1968)

Commissioned by and dedicated to the Marching Band of Lehigh University whose professor was Jonathan Elkus

Dur: 2'
f.p.   Lehigh University Concert Band/Jonathan Elkus - Taylor Stadium, Bethlehem,
            Pennsylvania, USA, 14 September 1968
f.Brit.p.   Marlboro' Brassers/Robert Peel - Embankment Gardens, London,
            11 June 1978
f.rec.   Lehigh University Concert Band/Brown - *Lehigh (USA) STLP 0097*

Angels of the Mind - song cycle for soprano and piano (1968)

[Words: Kathleen Raine   1. Worry about Money 2. Lenten Flowers 3. Harvest
 4. Seed 5. In the Beck 6. Storm 7. Nocturne]
Commissioned by the BBC and dedicated to Kathleen Raine, the poet with whom Bliss collaborated earlier in **The Golden Cantata** q.v.

Dur: 17'
f.p.   Rae Woodland (Sop.)/Lamar Crowson (Pno.) - Lancaster University,
            2 December 1969 (BBC Invitation Concert)
f.Lon.p.   above artists - Queen Elizabeth Hall, 30 June 1971
Pub: Novello, 1969

Miniature Scherzo for piano (1969)

Written for the 125th anniversary of The Musical Times (1969) and based on a phrase from Mendelssohn's Violin Concerto of 1844 - the work is dedicated to Marguerite Wolff

Dur: 1'
f.p.   Marguerite Wolff - BBC, 1 June 1969 (`Music Magazine' series)
f.rec.   Philip Fowke - *Chandos ABTD 1567(MC); CHAN 8979(CD)*
Pub: Novello, 1969

Prince of Wales Investiture Music for brass and military band (1969)

Commissioned by the Duke of Norfolk for the Investiture Ceremony

Dur: 8'15"
Instr: 3 choirs of 3 Tpt. 3 Tbn. each
f.p.   Trumpeters of the Royal Military School of Music directed by Lt. Col. C. H.
            Jaeger and the Band of the Royal Welsh Fusiliers directed by Major H. C. R.
            Bentley - Caernarvon Castle, North Wales, 1 July 1969 (at the Investiture of
            H.R.H. Prince Charles as Prince of Wales)
f.conc.p.   above artists - Royal Festival Hall, London, 22 May 1970
f.rec.   above performance - *Delyse SROY 1*
(i)   Excs. - Antiphonal Fanfares arr. for brass band by Roy Newsome (1974)
            Dur: 1'45"
            f.rec.   Black Dyke Mills Band/Roy Newsome - *Decca SB 308*
            Pub: Paxton/Novello, 1974
(ii)   Exc. - Interlude arr. for military band by Norman Richardson
            f.rec.   Band of the Welsh Guards/Taylor - *AJP 1004 (Music from 25 years of
                    Royal Occasions)*
(iii)   Processional Interlude arr. as Music for a Prince (1970) - composite work.
            Written for the annual luncheon of the Performing Right Society (of which
            Bliss was President) on 1 July 1970 - among the other composers who
            contributed pieces for an album of music, presented to the Prince of Wales on

that occasion, were Lennox Berkeley, John Gardner and Grace Williams q.v.
Instr: Vc. Tpt. Pno.
f.p.   Antonio Lysy (Vc.)/David Short (Tpt.)/Charles Ashworthy (Pno.) -
          Villa Wolkonsky, Rome, 29 April 1985

The World is Charged with the Grandeur of God - cantata for SATB chorus and instrumental ensemble (1969)
[Words: Gerard Manley Hopkins
1. The World is Charged with the Grandeur of God 2. I have Desired to Go
3. Look at the Stars]
Commissioned by the Aldeburgh Festival and dedicated 'to Peter Pears, who selected these poems for me'
Dur: 13'30"
Instr: 2 Fl. 3 Tpt. 4 Tbn.
f.p.   Aldeburgh Festival Instrumental and Choral Ensembles/Philip Ledger -
          Blythburgh Parish Church, 27 June 1969 (Aldeburgh Festival - at a concert
          entitled 'Musica Senectutis: The Over-Seventies')
f.Lon.p. Bach Choir/Instrumental Ensemble/Sir David Willcocks - Wormwood Scrubs,
          14 January 1973
f.Lon.pub!p. BBC Singers/Philip Jones Brass Ensemble/John Poole - Holy Trinity
          Church, Brompton, 2 August 1982 (Promenade Concert)
f.rec.   Ambrosian Singers/London Symphony Orchestra/Philip Ledger - *Lyrita SRCS
          55, SRCD 225(CD); Musical Heritage Society (USA) MHS 3096*
Pub: Novello, 1970
also arr. for SATB chorus and organ by Arthur Wills
Pub: Novello, 1970

Concerto (Concertino*) for cello and orchestra (1970)
Written for and dedicated 'to Mstislav Rostropovitch with admiration and gratitude'
Dur: 26'
Instr: 2+picc./1/2/2 - 2/2/0/0 - timp. cel. hp. str.
f.p.   Mstislav Rostropovitch/English Chamber Orchestra/Benjamin Britten - The
          Maltings, Snape, 24 June 1970 (Aldeburgh Festival)
f.Lon.p. Julian Lloyd Webber/Chanticleer Orchestra/Ruth Gipps - Queen Elizabeth
          Hall, 29 September 1972
f.Am.p.   Ofra Harnoy/Santa Barbara Symphony Orchestra/Frank Collura - Santa
          Barbara, California, 11 March 1984
f.recs.   Arto Noras/Bournemouth Symphony Orchestra/Paavo Burglund - *HMV ASD
          3342 (and MC)*
          Mstislav Rostropovitch/English Chamber Orchestra/Benjamin Britten -
          Intaglio INCD 7151(CD)
Pub: Novello, 1971 (also arr. cello and piano)
(* the work's original title - Bliss was persuaded by Britten to drop the diminutive)

Sailing or Flying? - song for voice and piano (1970)
[Words: Winifred Williams]
Written for the City of Westminster Society for Mentally Handicapped Children
Dur: 1'30"

Tulips - song for voice and piano or guitar (1970)
[Words: Winifred Williams]
Written for the City of Westminster Society for Mentally Handicapped Children
Dur: 1'05"
f.rec.   Barry Alexander (voice and guitar) - *Poplets CP 2600(45)*

Two Ballads for SA chorus and orchestra (1970)
[1. The Mountain Plover: Ushagreaisht (A. W. Moore)
 2. Flowers in the Valley (ed. Edith Sitwell)]
Commissioned by the Isle of Man Arts Council for the schoolchildren of the Isle of Man
Dur: 12'30"
Instr: 2+picc./2/2/2 - 2/2/0/0 - timp. perc.(2) hp. str.
f.p.   Isle of Man Chorus/Leicestershire Schools Symphony Orchestra/Eric Pinkett -
            Villa Marina, Douglas, Isle of Man, 16 April 1971 (April Arts Festival)
Pub: Novello, 1971 (also arr. SA chorus and piano)

Triptych for piano (1970)
[1. Meditation (Romance) 2. Dramatic Recitative 3. Capriccio]
Dedicated `in gratitude and admiration to Louis Kentner'
Dur: 14'
f.p.   Louis Kentner - Queen Elizabeth Hall, London, 21 March 1971
f.rec.   Kathron Sturrock - *Chandos ABTD 1408(MC), CHAN 8870(CD)*
Pub: Novello, 1972

**Birthday Greetings to the Croydon Symphony Orchestra - fanfare for brass
ensemble and percussion (1971)**
Dedicated to the Croydon Symphony Orchestra and their conductor, Arthur Davison, on
the occasion of their fiftieth anniversary
Dur: 1'20"
Instr: 0/0/0/0 - 4/3/3/1 - timp. perc.
f.p.   Croydon Symphony Orchestra/Arthur Davison - Fairfield Halls, Croydon,
            Surrey, 15 May 1971
later revised and published as 'Fanfare for a Coming of Age'(1973)
Written for the Santa Barbara Symphony Orchestra
Dur: 1'35"
f.p.   Santa Barbara Symphony Orchestra/Ronald Oudrejka- Granada Theatre, Santa
            Barbara, California, USA, 24 January 1974
f.rec.   Locke Brass Consort/James Stobart - *RCA RL 25081; Chandos CHAN
            6573(CD)*
Pub: Robert King Music, 1974

Play a Penta for chamber ensemble (1971)
Written for and dedicated to Mary Priestley and her children to be used in music therapy
Dur: 1'10"
Instr: Vn. Chime bars. Pno.
f.p.   Mary Priestley (Vn.) and Marjorie Wardle (Pno.) with chime bars played by
            patients of St.Bernard's Psychiatric Hospital, London

Praeludium for organ and percussion (1971)
Dedicated `to Fred Tulan, friend and artist'
Dur: 8'30"
f.p.   Fred Tulan - Harvard University, Cambridge, Massachusetts, USA,
           24 November 1971
f.Brit.p. Inez (Juez) Pope with James Blades, Heather Corbett and Thomas Corkhill
           (Perc.) cond. Douglas Guest - Westminster Abbey, London, 27 July 1972
f.rec.   Christopher Rathbone - *Wealden WS 106*
Pub: World Library Publications, 1974; Novello

Prayer of St. Francis of Assissi, for unaccompanied SSAA children's chorus (1971)
Written for the Orpington Junior Singers and dedicated `In Memoriam Sheila Mossman'
Dur: 4'30"
f.p.   Orpington Junior Singers/Jane Attfield - Bromley Parish Church, Kent,
           11 June 1972 (Bromley Arts Festival at Sheila Mossman's Memorial Concert)
f.Lon.p.   above artists - St. John's, Smith Square, 11 September 1972
f.rec.   East London Chorus/Harlow Chorus/East Herts Chorus/Michael Kibblewhite -
           Cala CAMC 1010(MC), CACD 1010(CD)
Pub: Novello, 1973 (Musical Times supplement)

Metamorphic Variations for orchestra (1972)
[1. Elements 2. Ballet 3. Assertion 4. Contracts 5. Children's March
 6. Speculation 7. Interjections 8. Scherzo I 9. Contemplation
10. Polonaise 11. Funeral Procession 12. Cool Interlude 13. Scherzo II
14. Duet 15. Dedication to G.D. and A.D. 16. Affirmation]
Commissioned by the Croydon Arts Festival and dedicated `to George and Ann Dannatt
in token of a long and cherished friendship' - the composer makes use of their initials in
Variation 15.
Dur: 37'30"
Instr: 3/3/3/3 - 4/3/3/1 - timp. perc.(4) cel. hp. str.
f.p.   London Symphony Orchestra/Vernon Handley - Fairfield Halls, Croydon, 21
           April 1973
f.broad.p. BBC Symphony Orchestra/Vernon Handley - Radio 3, 22 April 1975
           (rec. Maida Vale Studios, 7 January 1975)
f.recs.   BBC Welsh Symphony Orchestra/Barry Wordsworth - *Nimbus NI 5294(CD),
           NC 5294(MC)*
           BBC Symphony Orchestra/Vernon Handley - *BBC Radio Classics 15656
           91682(CD)*
Pub: Novello, 1976

Ode for Sir William Walton, for speaker and SATB chorus (1972)
[Words: Paul Dehn]
Commissioned by the then Prime Minister, Edward Heath, for the seventieth birthday of
Sir William Walton
Dur: 5'30"
f.p.   St. Margaret's Singers/Martin Neary - 10 Downing Street, London, 29 March
           1972

Put Thou Thy Trust in the Lord - Introit for unaccompanied SATB double chorus (1972)
[Biblical text: Psalm 37]
Commissioned for the Silver Wedding Service of Her Majesty the Queen and His Royal Highness, the Duke of Edinburgh
Dur: 2'45"
f.p.   Westminster Abbey Choir/Douglas Guest - Westminster Abbey,
            London, 20 November 1972
Pub: Novello, 1972

Fanfare for the National Fund for Research into Crippling Diseases (1973)
Commissioned by The National Fund for Research into Crippling Diseases
Dur: 1'15"
Instr: 4 Tpt. 4 Tbn.
f.p.   Trumpeters of the Royal Military School of Music/Bandmaster
            D. H. Mackay - St. Paul's Cathedral, London, 18 October 1973
Pub: Novello, 1979

Mar Portuguese for unaccompanied SATB chorus (1973)
[Words: Fernando Pessoa trans. Alan Goodison]
Commissioned by the then Prime Minister, Edward Heath, and dedicated in commemoration of the 600th anniversary of the Anglo-Portuguese Alliance
Dur: 3'
f.p.   St. Margaret's Singers/Martin Neary - Royal Naval College, Greenwich,
            16 July 1973
f.rec.   Finzi Singers/Paul Spicer - *Chandos ABTD 1568(MC), CHAN 8980(CD)*
Pub: Novello, 1974 (Musical Times Supplement)

Music (Fanfares and Interludes*) for the Wedding of Princess Anne (1973)
Dur: 3'45"
Instr: 3 Tpt. Perc.
f.p.   Regimental Trumpeters of the First Battalion, The Queen's Dragoon Guards/
            J.G. McColl and the Kneller Hall Trumpeters/Lt.Col. Rodney Bashford -
            Westminster Abbey, London, 14 November 1973
f.rec.   above performance - *BBC REW 163*
Pub: Novello, 1979
(*for the hymn 'Glorious Things of Thee are Spoken')

A Wedding Suite for piano* (1973)
A present for Enid Bliss-Morris and Thomas Frame-Thomson on the occasion of their marriage
Dur: 10'
f.p.   Marguerite Wolff - St. John's Wood, London, 18 January 1974
            (pre-recorded tape played at the wedding reception - the recording was made
            at the Decca Studios in London on 11 January 1974)
(* using material from **Valses Fantastiques** and **Enid's Blast** q.v.)

Lancaster - Prelude for orchestra (1974)
Commissioned by Denis McCaldin, Professor of Music at Lancaster University, for the
tenth anniversary of the Lancaster University Concerts
Dur: 4'30"
Instr: picc./0/0/cbsn. - 4/2/3/0 - timp. perc.(2)
f.p.   Lancaster Rehearsal Orchestra/Denis McCaldin - University Concert Hall,
              Lancaster, 24 November 1974
Pub: Novello

Shield of Faith* - cantata for soprano, baritone, SATB chorus and organ (1974)
[Words selected by Canon Stephen Verney from:
1. The Lord is Risen (William Dunbar) Interlude: Gloria in Excelsis Deo
2. Love (George Herbert) 3. An Essay on Man (Alexander Pope)
4. In Memoriam: O Yet We Trust (Tennyson) 5. Little Gidding (T. S. Eliot)]
Commissioned by the Dean of Windsor for the quincentenary of St. George's Chapel,
Windsor and dedicated, by gracious permission, to Her Majesty the Queen
Dur: 35'
f.p.   Jennifer Smith (Sop.)/John Carol Case (Bar.)/Richard Popplewell (Org.)/Bach
              Choir/David Willcocks - St. George's Chapel, Windsor, 26 April 1975
f.Lon.p.   Julie Kennard (Sop.)/Jonathan Roberts (Bar.)/Timothy Farrell (Org.)/ BBC
              Singers/John Poole - St. Augustine's Church, Kilburn, 30 July 1976
f.broad.p.   above (London) performance - Radio 3, 7 October 1976
f.rec.   Finzi Singers/Paul Spicer - *Chandos ABTD 1568(MC), CHAN 8980(CD)*
Pub: Novello, 1975
(* the title is taken from the sixth chapter of St. Paul's Epistle to the Ephesians)

**Sing, Mortals! - a sonnet for the Festival of St. Cecilia, for SATB chorus and organ
(1974)**
[Words: Richard Tydeman]
Commissioned by the St.Cecilia Festival Church Service Committee for the 1974 Festival
Service held in the Church of the Holy Sepulchre, Holborn, London
Dur: 5'30"
f.p.   Choirs of St. Paul's Cathedral, Westminster Abbey and The Chapel Royal with
              Richard Popplewell (Org.) cond. Christopher Dearnley - Church of the Holy
              Sepulchre, Holborn, London, 26 November 1974 (St. Cecilia Festival)
Pub: Novello, 1974

FILM MUSIC

Things to Come - London (1934-35)
Director: Alexander Korda
Music played by: London Film Symphony Orchestra/Muir Mathieson
f.p.   Odeon Cinema, Leicester Square, London, 21 February 1936
f.rec.   complete film (V)

Conquest of the Air - London (1937)
Director: Alexander Korda
Music played by: London Film Symphony Orchestra/Muir Mathieson
f.p.   Phoenix Theatre, London, 20 May 1940

Caesar and Cleopatra - Independent* (1944)

Director: Gabriel Pascal
(* Bliss withdrew from the project before completion and Georges Auric provided the music when the film was released)

Men of Two Worlds - GFD/Two Cities (1945)

US title: Kisenga, Man of Africa (or Witch Doctor)
Director: Thorold Dickinson
Music played by: Eileen Joyce (Pno.)/National Symphony Orchestra/Muir Mathieson
f.p.   Avalon Cinema, Dar es Salaam (Tanganyika), 16 July 1946
f.Brit.p.   Gaumont Cinema, Haymarket, London, 22 July 1946
f.rec.   complete film (V)

Présence au Combat - Ministry of Information (1945-46)*

Director: Marcell Cravenne
Music played by: National Symphony Orchestra/Muir Mathieson
f.p.   Paris, 11 December 1945
(* some of the music was used in a Government film of 1949 - **Faster Than Sound**)

Christopher Columbus - Rank/Gainsborough (1949)

Director: David MacDonald
Music played by: Royal Philharmonic Orchestra/Muir Mathieson
f.p.   Odeon Cinema, Leicester Square, London, 16 June 1949
f.recs.   soundtrack - *Rank F.M. 67-68(78); Citadel (USA) OF-1(m)*
            complete film (V)

The Beggar's Opera - British Lion/Imperado (1952-53)

Director: Peter Brook
Music played by: London Symphony Orchestra/Muir Mathieson
f.p.   Rialto Theatre, Coventry Street, London, 31 May 1953

Welcome the Queen - Associated British Pictures (1954)

Co-wrote with Malcolm Arnold q.v.
Director: Howard Thomas
Music played by: London Symphony Orchestra/Muir Mathieson
f.p.   National Film Theatre, London, 20 May 1954

Seven Waves Away - Columbia/Copa (1956)

US title: Abandon Ship
Director: Richard Sale
Music played by: Sinfonia of London/Muir Mathieson
f.p.   Odeon Cinema, Leicester Square, London, 8 March 1957

INCIDENTAL MUSIC

(a)   **Radio (BBC commissions)**

           In Dominion: Dominion Greetings Fanfare (1935)
           Dur: 0'35"

Instr: brass and percussion
Music played by: BBC Wireless Military Band/B. Walton O'Donnell
(broadcast 6 May 1935 in a programme celebrating the Silver Jubilee of His
Majesty King George V)

Twenty Five Years: The Empire's Tribute (1935)
Dur: 2'40"
Instr: 3 Tpt. 3 Tbn. Tba.
Music played by: BBC Wireless Military Band/B. Walton O'Donnell (broad-
cast 6 May 1935 on the occasion of King George V's Silver Jubilee)

Children's Hour - Peace Fanfare (1944)
Dur: 0'40"
Instr: 3 Tpt. 3 Tbn. Timp. Bells
Music played by: members of the BBC Symphony Orchestra/Clarence
Raybould - broadcast 12 September 1944
Pub: Novello, 1979

Your Questions Answered - title music (1944)
Dur: 0'45"
Instr: 0/2/2/2 - 4/2/3/0 - timp. sd. str.
Music played by: BBC Symphony Orchestra/Clarence Raybould- broadcast 2
March 1944 (rec. 25 February 1944)

Memorial Concert - play (1945)
[Trudy Bliss]
Dur: 14'45"
Instr: 1/1/2/2 - 2/1/3/0 - timp. hp. str.
Music played by: Henry Holst (Vn.)/BBC Symphony Orchestra/ Clarence
Raybould - broadcast 8 November 1945
Producer: Felix Felton

Tribute to the King: Victory Fanfares (1945)
Instr: (max.) 2/2/2/2 - 4/3/3/1 - timp. perc. str.
Music played by: trumpeters of the Royal Military School of Music/ London
Symphony Orchestra/Muir Mathieson - broadcast 8 May 1945
Producers: Cecil MacGivern and Laurence Gilliam

Heritage of Britain - feature signature tune* (1950)
Dur: 1'15"
Instr: 2/2/2/2 - 4/3/3/0 - timp. perc. str.
Music played by: BBC Scottish Orchestra/Ian Whyte - broadcast
1 December 1950
(* Derived from the film score to **Christopher Columbus** q.v.)

(b)   **Television**

War in the Air - opening/closing music* for BBC series (1954)
Commissioned by BBC Television

Dur: 1'30"
Instr: 2/2/2/2 - 4/2/3/0 - timp.(4) perc.(2) str
Music played by: London Symphony Orchestra/Muir Mathieson
f.trans. 8 November 1954
(* an extended version of **Salute to the RAF** q.v.)

ABC Television - title and interlude music (1956)
Commissioned by ABC Television
Dur: 2'
Instr: 2/2/2/2 - 4/2/3/0 - timp. perc.str.

An Age of Kings - title/end music for BBC series (1960)
[Shakespeare]
Commissioned by the BBC
Instr: 2+ picc./2/2/2 - 4/3/3/0 - timp. perc.(2) pno. str.
Music played by: Royal Philharmonic Orchestra/Lionel Salter (pre-recorded at
Maida Vale Studios 29 March 1960)
f.trans. 28 April 1960 et seq.
Producer: Peter Dews
Director: Michael Hoyes
Designer: Stanley Morris
later arr. for concert band by Frank Erikson
[1. Prelude 2. Chorale 3. Postlude]
Dur: 4'30"
f.p.   Lehigh University Band/Jonathan Elkus- Lehigh University , USA,
           1 October 1966
f.rec.   Band of the Coldstream Guards/Sharpe - *Pye GSGL 10443*
Pub: Chappell (New York), 1966

The Royal Palaces of Great Britain - joint BBC/ITV feature (1966)
Commissioned jointly by BBC/ITV
     Instr: 2+picc./1/2/1 - 2/2/3/0 - timp. perc.(2) hp.str
Music played by: Sinfonia of London/Muir Mathieson
f.trans. 25 December 1966 (and on NBC-TV, 29 January 1967)
Director: Anthony de Lotbiniere
Narrator: Kenneth Clark
Suite arr. for concert band by Frank Erikson
[1. Queen Victoria's call to the throne 2. The Ballroom in Buckingham Palace
 3. Joust of the Knights in Armour 4. Melodrama: `The Murder of Rizzio in
Holyrood House' 5. Finale - `Royal Palaces' theme]
Dur: 15'
f.rec.   Band of the Royal Marines, Portsmouth/Lambert - *Philips 6308
           048*
Pub: Chappell, 1969
Suite also arr. for piano
Pub: Chappell

Spirit of the Age - title music for BBC series (1975)
Commissioned by the BBC

Dur: 1'40"
Music played by members of the London Symphony Orchestra/Arthur Bliss
(rec. BBC Television Studios, 11 January 1975)
f.trans. 31 October 1975 et seq.
Producer: John Drummond
arr. for brass ensemble by Robert King
Dur: 1'45"
Instr: 3 Tpt. 3 Tbn. Tba. Pno. Timp. Perc.
Pub: Robert King, 1978

(c)   Stage

As You Like It (1919)
[Shakespeare]
Arrangements and settings from Elizabethan sources
Instr: 2Vn. Va. Vc. (+ solo voices/chorus)
f.p.   Stratford Memorial Theatre, Stratford-upon-Avon, 22 April 1919
Music played by: Theatre String Quartet/Arthur Bliss
Producer: Nigel Playfair
Scenery and costumes: Claude Lovat Fraser
Principals: Athene Seyler, Geoffrey Kerr, Nigel Playfair and Herbert Marshall
f.Lon.p.   Lyric Theatre, Hammersmith, 21 April 1920

The Tempest (1920-21)
[Shakespeare]
Dur: 5'30"
Instr: Tpt. Tbn. Pno. Timp.(4) Perc.(4)
f.p.   Aldwych Theatre, London, 1 February 1921
Music played by: Ensemble with Steuart Wilson (Ten.) and Ivan Firth (Bs.)
Producers: Louis Calvert and Viola Tree
Principals: Henry Ainsley, Louis Calvert, Joyce Carey and Winifred Barnes
f.conc.p.   (Overture) above artists and Ensemble with Harriet Cohen (Pno.)
            cond. Edward Clark - Queen's Hall, London, 8 April 1921 (Edward
            Clark Concert)
f.Eur.p.   members of the Vienna Symphony Orchestra/Arthur Bliss -
            Vienna, 6 April 1922
f.mod.p.   members of the Kensington Symphony Orchestra/Leslie Head - St.
            John's, Smith Square, London, 2 March 1979
Pub: Goodwin & Tabb; Novello

King Solomon (1924)
[Ira Remsen]
f.p.   Community Arts Players - Potter Theatre, Santa Barbara, California,
        21 March 1924
Music conducted by: Arthur Bliss

The White Birds - revue (1927)
[George W. Meyer]
Bliss' contribution was **The Rout Trot** for piano, q.v.

f.p.   His Majesty's Theatre, London, 31 May 1927
Producer: Lew Leslie

Summer Day's Dream (1949)
[J. B. Priestley]
Dur: 1'20"
Instr: Ob. Vn. (`Christopher's Theme')
f.p.   Prince's Theatre, Bradford, Yorkshire, 8 August 1949
f.Lon.p.   St. Martin's Theatre, 8 September 1949
Director: Michael MacOwen

ARRANGEMENTS

Tchaikovsky: 'Nutcracker' ballet excs. arr. for clarinet and cello (c.1907)
[1.Marche 2. Valse des fleurs]
f.p.   Kennard Bliss (Cl.)/Howard Bliss (Vc.) - at the home of the composer,
        Bayswater, West London, 17 January 1908

Pergolesi: La Serva Padrona arr. (1918-19)
[Libretto: Pergolesi trans. Grace Lovat Fraser]
f.p.   Albert Fox's Sextet/Nellie Chaplin (Hpschd.) cond. Arthur Bliss - Lyric
        Theatre, Hammersmith, 29 January 1919
Producer: Nigel Playfair
Scenery: Claude Lovat Fraser
Principals: John Barclay, Tom Reynolds, Grace Crawford

Purcell - Set of Act Tunes and Dances arr. for string orchestra (1919)
[1. Overture 2. Air 3. Saraband 4. Minuet 5. Hornpipe]
Dur: 8'
f.p.   Hammersmith Musical Society Orchestra/Arthur Bliss - Lyric Theatre,
             Hammersmith, 5 October 1919
f.conc.p.   cond. Arthur Bliss - Wigmore Hall, London, 11 June 1921
f.broad.p. BBC Wireless Orchestra/Ernest Ansermet - 9 December 1927
f.rec.   Sinfonia of London/Arthur Bliss - *World Record Club T(m)/ST 52*
Pub: F & B Goodwin, 1923; Curwen, 1966; Curwen/Faber

Christian Sinding: Fire Dance arr. for orchestra (1921)
Dedicated to Tamara Karsavina, a founding member of Diagilev's ballet company and
inspiration for **Checkmate** q.v.
f.p.   London Coliseum, 4 July 1921

Bach: Das Alte Jahr Vergangen Ist - chorale transcribed for piano (1932)
Dedicated to Harriet Cohen
Dur: 1'30"
f.p.   Harriet Cohen - Queen's Hall, London, 17 October 1932
f.rec.   Philip Fowke - *Chandos ABTD 1567(MC), CHAN 8979(CD)*
Pub: OUP, 1932 (`A Bach Book for Harriet Cohen')

The Festival of Flora - masque ballet arr. from the music of Purcell by Arthur Bliss and Cyril Rootham (1927)
[Scenario: Hortensie Mancini]
f.p.   Teatro della Piccole Maschere cond. Leigh Henry - New Scala Theatre,
            London, 31 May 1927

John Gay: The Beggar's Opera arr. (1952-53)
Dur: 60'
Instr: 2/2/2/2 - 2/2/3/1 - timp. perc.(2) hp. cel. str.
f.conc.p.   Marion Studholme (Sop.)/Joyce Gartside (M/S)/Gwent Lewis (Ten.)/ John
            Cameron (Bar.)/Leicestershire School Choirs/BBC Concert Orchestra/Vilem
            Tausky - de Montfort Hall, Leicester, 11 October 1958
Pub: Novello (theatre/concert score)
Exc. Two Songs for men's TTB chorus and piano (or orchestra)
[1. Let us take the road (Christopher Fry) 2. Fill every glass]
Dur: 2'30"
Pub: Novello, 1968
Exc. Two Songs for women's chorus and piano (or orchestra)
[1. Youth's the season made for joys
 2. The modes of the court so common are grown (Lilliburlero)]
Dur: 2'30"
Pub: Novello, 1968
Exc. Two Songs for baritone and orchestra
[1. If the Heart of a Man 2. My Heart was so free]
Dur: 5'
Pub: Novello

Bach: Three Chorales from St. John Passion arr. for brass ensemble (1960)
[1. See Him now, the Righteous one   2. Ah Lord when my last end is come
 3. Peter in forgetfulness twice denies his master]
Dur: 2'30"
Instr: 3 Tpt. 3 Tbn. Tba.
f.p.   members of the City of Birmingham Symphony Orchestra/Melville Cook -
            Worcester Cathedral, 6 September 1960 (Three Choirs Festival)
Pub: Novello, 1979

The National Anthem: God Save the Queen arr. SATB chorus and orchestra (1969)
Written for the Royal Choral Society's American Tour in 1969
Dur: 3'30"
Instr: 2+picc./2+ca./2+bcl./2+cbsn. - 4/3/3/1 - timp. perc.(2) str.
Alt.Instr: 2/2/2/2 - 2/2/0/0 - timp. perc. str.
f.p.   Royal Choral Society/Royal Choral Society Players/Wyn Morris - Memorial
            Auditorium, Burlington, Vermont, USA, 21 October 1969
f.rec.   Royal Choral Society/London Philharmonic Orchestra/Arthur Bliss - *Classics
            for Pleasure CFP 198 (and MC)*
Pub: Novello, 1969

MS LOCATION

The majority of the manuscripts are located in the Bliss Archive at the Cambridge University Library **(CUL)** - see also Craggs, **Arthur Bliss: A Bio-Bibliography,**1988

Other locations include:

BL	Rout (1920), Checkmate (1937)
BML	String Quartet No.2 (1950)
BUL	Meditations (1955) Mary of Magdala (1962)
FMC	Madame Noy (1918) Hymn to Apollo (1926) Introduction & Allegro(1926)
GD	Metamorphic Variations(1972)
JUL	Bach: Chorale arr. (1932)
LHU	Salute to Lehigh (1968)
LOC	Colour Symphony (1921-22) Two Interludes(1925) String Quartet No.1 (1940-41) Greetings to a City (1961)
MBF	Fanfare for Heroes (1930)
NOV	Birthday Fanfare (1944)
NYPL	Three Romantic Songs - No.3 (1921) Ballads of the Four Seasons (1923)
PML	Wedding Music (1960)
RAA	Salute to Painting (1954)
RABL	Right of the Line (1965)
RL	Birthday Song (1959)
RCM	Golden Cantata (1963) Piano Concerto(1938-39)
RMSM	Investiture Music (1969) Wedding Music (1960,1971) Fanfare (1973)
SW	Ode for Sir William Walton (1972)

BIBLIOGRAPHY

Bliss, Arthur	**As I Remember.** London, Faber, 1970; rev. ed. Thames Publishing, 1991.
Bliss, Arthur	**Benjamin Britten's Sixtieth Birthday.** Tempo, September 1973.
Boult, Sir Adrian	**Sir Arthur Bliss.** Royal College of Music Magazine, 1971.
Britten, Benjamin	**Sir Arthur Bliss at 75.** Performing Right, October 1966.
Burn, Andrew	**Arthur Bliss - a survey of his works.** London: Novello, 1995
Craggs, Stewart R.	**Arthur Bliss: A Bio-Bibliography.** Connecticut: Greenwood Press, 1988 [B] [D]
Craggs, Stewart R.	**Arthur Bliss - A Source Book.** Aldershot: Ashgate,1996
Crisp, Clement	**The Ballets of Arthur Bliss.** Musical Times, August 1966.

Evans, Edwin	**Arthur Bliss.** Musical Times, January 1923.
Foreman, Lewis	**Arthur Bliss - catalogue of the complete works.** Sevenoaks: Novello, 1980, supplement 1982. [B] [D]
Frank, Alan	**Arthur Bliss,** in his `Modern British Composers', Dobson, 1953.
Goossens, Eugene	**Arthur Bliss.** Chesterian, June 1921.
Guyatt, Andrew	**Sir Arthur Bliss (1891-1975), Master of the Queen's Music.** Le Grand Baton, March 1977. [D]
Guyatt, Andrew	**Sir Arthur Bliss.** The Journal of the British Music Society, Vol. 1, March 1977.
Guyatt, Andrew	**A Bliss Discography.** The Journal of the British Music Society, Vol. 2, 1980.
Holbrooke, Joseph	**Arthur Bliss,** in his `Contemporary British Composers', Cecil Palmer, 1925
Howells, Herbert	**Master of the Queen's Music.** Royal College of Music Magazine, January 1954.
Howes, Frank	**The Creative Personality of Sir Arthur Bliss.** The Times, 19 July 1966.
Hull, Robert H.	**The Music of Arthur Bliss.** Chesterian, July-August 1935.
Hughes, Patrick	**Arthur Bliss.** Monthly Musical Record, May 1929
Jefferson, Alan	**Bliss: Composer Royal.** Music and Musicians, October 1965.
Keller, Hans	**Four Aspects of Music.** Composer, Winter 1966-67.
Mahoney, Patrick	**Sir Arthur Bliss.** Composer, Summer 1971.
Palmer, Christopher	**Arthur Bliss.** Sevenoaks: Novello, 1976.
Palmer, Christopher	**Aspects of Bliss.** Musical Times, August 1971.
Richards, Denby	**Bliss.** Music and Musicians, September 1971.
Roscow, Dr. Gregory ed.	**Bliss on Music.** (selected writings by Arthur Bliss from 1920-1975), OUP 1991.
Thompson, Kenneth L.	**The Works of Arthur Bliss.** Musical Times, August 1966, rev. August 1971.

11

Benjamin Britten (1913–1976)

(N.B. - This catalogue includes only an abbreviated list of the completed works up to 1930 - for a full account of Britten's compositional output between 1919 and 1929 please refer to 'A Britten Source Book', compiled by John Evans, Philip Reed and Paul Wilson, published by The Britten Estate for The Britten-Pears Library, 1987. Information about the published works is largely drawn from 'Benjamin Britten: A Catalogue of the Published Works', compiled by Paul Banks and others, published by The Britten-Pears Library for The Britten Estate, 1999. For further details about the published works, please refer to that catalogue.)

Symphony in F major/minor (1921-22)
Instr: Vn. Vc. Pno.

The Road Song of the Bandar-Log ('Here we go in a flung festoon'):* song for voice and piano (1923)
[Words: Rudyard Kipling]
(*later used in the Playful Pizzicato movement of the **Simple Symphony** q.v.)

A Country Dance ('Now the King is home again'):* song for voice and piano (1923)
[Words: Tennyson 'The Foresters']
(*later used in the Boisterous Bourrée movement of the **Simple Symphony** q.v.)

Three Early Songs* for medium voice and piano (1922-26, rev.1967-68)
[1. Beware! (Henry Longfellow from 'Des Knaben Wunderhorn') 2. O that I had ne'er been married (Robert Burns#) 3. Epitaph: The Clerk (Herbert Asquith)]
Dur: 3'30"
f.p.   (No.2) Peter Pears (Ten.)/Roger Vignoles (Pno.) - Thames Television, 29 November 1976 (pre-recorded at The Britten-Pears Library, 20 May 1976)
f.p.   (No.1) Peter Pears (Ten./Pno.) - University of East Anglia, Norwich, 4 March 1980 (Arthur Batchelor Lecture)
f.p.   (No.3) Neil Mackie (Ten.)/John Blakely (Pno.) - BBC broadcast, Radio 3, 4 December 1986 (pre-recorded, 18 November 1986)
f.broad.p. (No.1) Peter Pears (Ten.)/Graham Johnson (Pno.) - Radio 3, 4 April 1980 (pre-recorded, 24 August 1979)

f.broad.p. (No.2) Neil Mackie (Ten.)/John Blakely (Pno.) - Radio 3, 23 April 1985
f.rec.   Benjamin Luxon (Bar.)/David Willison (Pno.) - *Chandos ABRD 1224 (and MC), CHAN 8514 (CD)*
Pub: Faber, 1985 (as 'Beware!: three early songs for medium voice and piano')
(*These songs were not composed as a group but were collected together later. #There is also another Burns setting from this period entitled 'Wandering Willie')

Five Walztes (Waltzes) for piano (1923-25, rev.1969)
'Composed by Edward Benjamin Britten Opus 3, 1925, and dedicated to My Father: R. V. Britten Esq.'
Dur: 10'30"
f.p.   (rev. version) Antony Peebles - BBC Radio 3, 10 February 1971
f.rec.   Stephen Hough - *Virgin VC7 91203-2 (CD) (and MC), VC7 59027-2 (CD)*
Pub: Faber, 1970

Quartet in A for two violins, cello and double bass (1923)

Piece in D flat for piano (1923)

Introduction for string orchestra (1924)

Presto con molto fuoco,* for orchestra (1925)
(*there are two further, though incomplete, orchestral movements from this period)

Octet in D for strings (1925)
Instr: 2 Vn. 2 Va. 2 Vc. 2 Db.

6 Variations on 'How bright these glorious spirits shine':* for chorus, string quintet, organ and piano (1925)
Score dated 8-14 November 1925
(*hymn by J.B. Dykes)

Suite No.5* in E for piano (1926)
Score dated 4 January 1926
(*there are also four earlier **Suites** for piano, as well as five other **Waltzes**, six **Scherzos**, seven **Fantasias**, seven **Piano Sonatas**, four **Bourrées**, three **Toccatas**, four **Etudes Symphoniques**, three **Rondos** and several other piano miniatures written between 1923 and 1926!)

Piano Sonata (Grand) No.8 (1926)
Composed between 25 January and 18 March 1926

Sonata in F# minor for violin and viola (1926)
Score dated 13 February 1926
Instr: Vn. Va. Vc. (ad lib.)

Sonata in C minor for viola and piano (1926)
Score dated 14 March 1926

Sonata (No.9) in C# minor for piano (1926)
Score dated 18 March 1926

Sonata in G minor for violin and piano (1926)
Score dated 6 April 1926

First Loss: for viola and piano (1926)
Score dated 6 April 1926
f.p.   Philip Dukes (Va.)/Sophia Rahman (Pno.) - BBC Radio 3, 21 November 1995

(2) Trios in fantastic form (1926)
Score dated 6, 7 April 1926
Instr: Vn. Va. Pno.

Sonate pour orgue ou pedale-pianoforte (1926)
Score dated 16 April 1926

Sonata in A for cello and piano (1926)
Score dated 17 April 1926

Three Canons for two violas and piano (1926)
Score dated 19 April 1926

Overture No. 1 in C for orchestra (1926)
Composed between 23 and 29 April 1926

Ouverture for orchestra* (1926)
Score dated 1-29 June 1926
(*Britten used the pseudonym 'Never Unprepared' when he entered this piece in the
BBC's 1926 Autumn Musical Festival Prize Competition)

Mass in E minor for soloists, chorus and orchestra (1925-26)

Suite fantastique in A minor for piano and orchestra (1926)
Score dated 21 April-5 September 1926

Poème No.1 in D for orchestra (1926)
Score dated 26 September 1926

The Brook: song for voice and violin (1926)

Six Songs* for voice and piano (1926)
Score dated 12 November-5 December 1926
(*one of these was a setting of Robert Burns's 'Of a' the airts' which the composer
revised on 25 August 1928)

String Quartet in G minor (1926)
Score dated 21 November 1926

Poème No.2 in B minor for small orchestra (1926)
Score dated 24 December 1926

Poème No.3 in E for small orchestra (1926-27)
Score dated 29 December 1926-3 January 1927

Symphony in D minor for orchestra (1927)
Score dated 17 January-28 February 1927

Kyrie eleison in B flat minor for chorus and orchestra (1927)

Poème No.4 in B flat for small orchestra (1927)
Score dated 12-14 February 1927
f.p.   Northern Sinfonia/Martyn Brabbins - BBC Radio 3, 21 November 1995

Poème No.5 in F# minor for small orchestra (1927)
Score dated 14-19 February 1927

If I'd as much money as I could spend: song for voice and piano (1927)
[Mother Goose]

String Quartet in G (1927)

String Quartet in A minor (1927)

Cavatina in A for string quartet (1927)
Score dated 15-17 July 1927

The pale stars are gone: for chorus, strings and piano (1927)
[Words: Shelley, from 'Prometheus Unbound']
Composed between 29 July and 2 August 1927

Chaos and Cosmos: Symphonic Poem in E for orchestra (1927)
Composed between 22 August and 5 September 1927

Sonata No.10 in B flat for piano (1927)
Score dated 27 September 1927

Rhapsodie for piano (1927)
Score dated 29 September 1927

Three Poems* for string quartet (1927)
Score dated 23 December 1927
f.p.   (No.2) Sorrel Quartet - BBC Radio 3, 21 November 1995
(*material from the second Poem was used in the **String Quartet in F** of 1928 q.v.)

Sonatina for viola and piano (1927)
Score dated 29 December 1927
f.p.   Philip Dukes (Va.)/Sophia Rahman (Pno.) - BBC Radio 3, 21 November 1995

Tit for Tat: five settings from boyhood of poems by Walter de la Mare for voice and piano (1928-31, rev.1968)
[1. A Song of Enchantment (7 February 1929) 2. Autumn (28 January 1931)* 3. Silver (13 June 1928) 4. Vigil (23 December 1930, rev.17 January 1931, originally dedicated 'For Mr. L. C. Voke') 5. Tit for Tat (13 January 1929 and 25 February 1930)]
Dedicated 'For Dick de la Mare June 4th 1969' (the poet's son on his seventieth birthday)
Dur: 9'
f.priv.p.   (No.4 only) Leonard Voke (Bar.)/Benjamin Britten (Pno.) - 28 December 1930
f.p.   (rev. version) John Shirley-Quirk (Bar.)/Benjamin Britten (Pno.) - Jubilee
            Hall, Aldeburgh, 23 June 1969 (Aldeburgh Festival)
f.broad.p. (No.5 only) Owen Brannigan (Bs.)/Keith Swallow (Pno.) - Radio 3, 16 April
            1970 (pre-recorded, 4 November 1969)
f.broad.p. (complete) Bryan Drake (Bar.)/Paul Hamburger (Pno.) - Radio 3, 23 June
            1971 (pre-recorded, 3 February 1971)
f.recs.   John Shirley-Quirk (Bar.)/Benjamin Britten (Pno.) - *London (USA) OS 26357;*
            Decca SXL 6608
            Benjamin Luxon (Bar.)/David Willison (Pno.) - *Chandos ABRD 1224 (and*
            MC), CHAN 8514 (CD)
Pub: Faber, 1969
(*there is another setting of this poem for voice and string quartet dated 1931 and a
discarded, incomplete, setting for voice and strings of the poem 'Nod' from c.1929)

Dans les Bois:* for orchestra (1928)
Score dated 25 January 1928
(*after the poem by Gérard de Nerval - see the later song setting of June 1928)

Sonata No.11 in B for piano (1927-28)

Humoreske in C for orchestra (1928)
Score dated 6 March 1928
f.p.   City of Birmingham Symphony Orchestra/Simon Rattle - 'Young Apollo',
            BBC Television, 2 October 1985 (recorded 11 December 1984 at the
            University of Warwick, Coventry)

Trio in G minor (1928)
Score dated 28 March 1928
Instr: Vn. Va. Pno.

String Quartet in F (1928)
Score dated 2-11 April 1928
Dur: 20'
f.p.   Sorrel Quartet - BBC Radio 3, 21 November 1995
f.rec.   above artists - *Chandos CHAN 9664 (CD)*
Pub: Faber, 1999

Menuetto for piano (1928)
Score dated 16 April 1928

Elegy for string orchestra (1928)
Score dated 16-23 April 1928

The Waning Moon: song for voice and piano (1928)
[Words: Shelley]
Score dated 3 June 1928

Dans les bois: song for voice and piano (1928)
[Words: Gérard de Nerval]
Scores dated 15, 18 June 1928

Quatre* chansons françaises for high voice and orchestra (1928)
[1. Nuits de juin (Victor Hugo) (17 June 1928)
 2. Sagesse (Paul Verlaine) (4 August 1928)
 3. L'enfance (Victor Hugo) (26 August 1928)
 4. Chanson d'automne (Paul Verlaine) (31 August 1928)]
'To Mr. and Mrs. R. V. Britten on the twenty-seventh aniversary [sic] of their wedding, September 5th 1928'
Dur: 13'
Instr: 2/1/3/2 - 4/0/0/0 - perc. hp. pno. str.
f.p.   Heather Harper (Sop.)/English Chamber Orchestra/Steuart Bedford - BBC
            Radio 3, 30 March 1980 (pre-recorded, 4 June 1979)
f.conc.p.   above artists - The Maltings, Snape, 10 June 1980 (Aldeburgh Festival)
f.Lon.p.   Jill Gomez (Sop.)/London Sinfonietta/Simon Rattle - Queen Elizabeth Hall,
            29 October 1986
f.recs.   above (first) performance - *Carlton Classics 15656 9158-2 (CD)*
            Jill Gomez (Sop.)/City of Birmingham Symphony Orchestra/Simon Rattle -
            EMI ASD 4177 (and MC), CDS7 54270-2 (CD)
Pub: Faber, 1982 (vocal score), 1983 (full score)
(*there is also an incomplete discarded song 'Mon rêve familier' with words by Paul Verlaine)

Novelette for string quartet (1928)
Score dated 28 September 1928

Piano Sonatina (1928)
Score dated 9-13 October 1928
f.p.   Anthony Goldstone - BBC Radio 3, 21 November 1995

Oh, why did e'er my thoughts aspire?: song for voice and piano (1929)
[Words: Charles Sackville]
Score dated 4 January 1929

The Quartette: for unaccompanied SATB quartet (1929)
[Words: Walter de la Mare]
Composed between 7 January and 24 April 1929

Elizabeth Variations: for piano (1929)
Score dated 13 January-25 October 1929

Miniature Suite for string quartet (1929)
Score dated 26 January-8 March 1929
f.p.   (Exc. - Romance) Sorrel Quartet - BBC Radio 3, 29 November 1995

Rhapsody for string quartet (1929)
Score dated 28 January-21 March 1929
Dur: 7'
f.p.   Alexandra Quartet - Royal Northern College of Music, Manchester,
              6 November 1985
f.broad.p. Endellion String Quartet - Radio 3, 28 November 1985
f.rec.   Endellion String Quartet - *EMI EX 270502-3 (and MC), CDC7 47694-2 (CD),*
              CMS5 65115-2 (CD)
Pub: Faber, 1989

Evening Hymn: for unaccompanied SATB chorus (1929)*
Score dated 16 February 1929
(*a revision of an earlier setting in 1923)

Etude for viola (1929)
Score dated 18 February-22 March 1929

Lilian: song for voice and piano (1929)
[Words: Tennyson]
Score dated 15-19 February 1929

Witches' Song: song for voice and piano (1929)
[Words: Ben Jonson]
Score dated 21 February 1929

Two Songs for unaccompanied SATB chorus (1929)
[Words: John Fletcher]
Score dated 22-25 March 1929

Rhapsody for violin, viola and piano (1929)
Score dated 30 March-22 April 1929

The Owl - song for voice and piano (1929)
[Words: Tennyson]
Score dated 6 May-16 June 1929

Children of Love: for SSA solo voices (1929)
[Words: H.H. Munro]
Score dated 18 May 1929

Diaphenia: for tenor and piano (1929)
[Words: Henry Constable]
Score dated 4-8 September 1929

Introduction and Allegro for viola and string orchestra (1929)
Score dated 21-31 October 1929
Dur: 11'
f.p.   Roger Chase (Va.)/Britten-Pears Orchestra/Andrew Schulman -
           The Maltings, Snape, 24 October 1997 (Aldeburgh Festival)

Wild Time: for soprano and strings (1929)
[Words: Walter de la Mare]
Score dated 27-28 October 1929

Two Pieces for violin, viola and piano (1929)
Score dated 17 November-24 December 1929

Quartettino for string quartet (1930)
Score dated 3 January-17 April 1930
Dur: 15'
f.p.   Arditti Quartet - London Weekend Television, 15 May 1983
f.conc.p.   Arditti Quartet - Barbican Hall, London, 23 May 1983 (SPNM 40th
            Anniversary Concert)
f.broad.p. above (concert) performance - Radio 3, 29 September 1983
f.rec.   Endellion String Quartet - *EMI EX 270502-3 (and MC), CDC7 47694-2 (CD),*
            CMS5 65115-2 (CD)
Pub: Faber, 1984

Bagatelle for violin, viola and piano (1929-30)
Score dated 30 March 1929-15 January 1930
f.p.   Miss Chapman (Vn.)/Benjamin Britten (Va.)/Walter Greatorex (Pno.) -
            Gresham's School, Holt, Norfolk, 1 March 1930
f.broad.p. Benedict Holland (Vn.)/Vicki Wardman (Va.)/Anthony Goldstone (Pno.) -
            Radio 3, 29 November 1995

A Poem of Hate: for piano (1930)
Score dated 16 February 1930
f.p.   Anthony Goldstone - BBC Radio 3, 29 November 1995

A Little Idyll: for piano (1930)
Score dated 20 February-8 March 1930
f.p.   Anthony Goldstone - BBC Radio 3, 29 November 1995

Everyone Sang: for tenor and small orchestra (1930)
[Words: Siegfried Sassoon]
Score dated 24 February 1930
f.p.   Michael Bennett (Ten.)/Northern Sinfonia /Martyn Brabbins - BBC Radio 3,
            29 November 1995

Rondo Concertante for piano and strings (incomplete) (1930)
f.p.   Martin Roscoe/Northern Sinfonia/Martyn Brabbins - BBC Radio 3,
            5 December 1995

Reflection: for viola and piano (1930)
Score dated 11 April 1930, rev.1 June 1930 (originally entitled 'Piece')
Dur: 3'
f.p.   Philip Dukes (Va.)/Sophia Rahman (Pno.) - BBC Radio 3, 28 November 1995
f.conc.p   Nobuko Imai (Va.)/Ellen Corver (Pno.) - Kleine Zaal, Concertgebouw,
          Amsterdam, 24 October 1996
f.rec.   Nobuko Imai (Va.)/Roland Pöntinen (Pno.) - *BIS CD-829 (CD)*
Pub: Faber, 1997

A Wealden Trio: The Song of the Women: carol for women's voices (SSA)
unaccompanied (1929-30, rev.1967)
[Words: Ford Madox Ford]
Dedicated (in revision) 'For Rosamund' (Rosamund Strode, Britten's musical assistant) -
the original version of the score is dated 30 May 1930
Dur: 3'
f.p.   (rev. version) Ambrosian Singers/Philip Ledger - Aldeburgh Parish Church,
          19 June 1968 (Aldeburgh Festival)
f.rec.   Wilbye Consort/Peter Pears - *London (USA) OS 26527; Decca SXL 6847 (and*
          MC)
Pub: Faber, 1968, 1998 (in 'Three Carols for Upper Voices')

The Birds: song for medium voice and piano* (1929-30, rev.1934)
[Words: Hilaire Belloc]
Dedicated 'For my Mother' (a version for organ was played at Mrs Britten's funeral in
February 1937) - the score is dated 21 June 1934
Dur: 2'
f.p.   Sophie Wyss (Sop.)/Benjamin Britten (Pno.) - BBC broadcast, 13 March 1936
f.recs.   Billy Neeley (Treb.)/Gerald Moore (Pno.) - *HMV B 10041 (78)*
          John Hahessy (Alto.)/Benjamin Britten (Pno.) - *Argo ZFA 18 (45)*
          Maureen Lehane (Con.)/Alexander Kelly (Pno.) - *Ensemble ENS 137 (MC)*
          (choral version) Lichfield Cathedral Choir - *Abbey XMS 698*
Pub: Boosey & Hawkes, 1935, 1982 (in 'Christmas Song Album', Vol.1),
          1989 (US edition arr. for unison chorus and piano)
(*an earlier version for soprano and string orchestra in 1929 was revised in May 1930 as
part of the composer's submission for a potential scholarship entry into the Royal College
of Music in London)

May in the green wood: for two voices and piano (1930)
[Words: Anon.]
Score dated 8 July 1930

A Hymn to the Virgin: anthem for mixed voices (SATB double chorus),
unaccompanied* (1930, rev. 1934)
[Words: Anon. 13th century]
Composed between 9 July and 3 September 1930, revision dated 29 April 1934
Dur: 3'30"
f.p.   Lowestoft Musical Society/C.J.R. Coleman - St John's Church, Lowestoft,
          5 January 1931
f.broad.p. (rev. version) BBC Singers/Leslie Woodgate - 14 October 1935

f.Lon.conc.p.   Dorian Singers/Mátyás Seiber - Park Lane House, 26 April 1959
f.recs.   Choir of St. John's Church, Upper Norwood - *Croydon Celebrity Recording*
             Society CCI (78 - private issue)
             London Symphony Orchestra Chorus/George Malcolm - *L'oiseau-lyre SOL*
             60037; London 425 153-4 (MC), 436 396-2 (CD)
             Choir of St. John's College, Cambridge/George Guest - *Argo ZK 19;*
             Decca 430 097-2 (CD)
Pub: Boosey & Hawkes, 1935
(*Chorus II may be sung by a semi-chorus or solo quartet)

Passacaglia for organ (1930)
Score dated 10 July 1930

O fly not pleasure: for two women's voices and piano (1930)
[Words: Wilfred S. Blunt]
Score dated 11 July 1930

The Nurse's Song: for soprano, contralto and piano (1930)
[Words: William Blake]
Score dated 25 July 1930

Chamber Music (V): song for soprano (or tenor) and piano (1930)
[Words: James Joyce]
Score dated 28 July-3 August 1930

To Electra: for voice and piano (1930)
[Words: Robert Herrick]
Score dated 29 July 1930

Elegy for solo viola (1930)
Score dated 1 August 1930
Dur: 6'
f.p.   Nobuko Imai - The Maltings, Snape, 22 June 1984 (Aldeburgh Festival)
f.broad.p. Nobuko Imai - Radio 3, 11 December 1986
f.rec.   Garfield Jackson - *EMI EX 270502-3 (and MC), CDC7 47694-2 (CD), CMS5*
             65115-2(CD)
Pub: Faber, 1985

Movement* for Wind Sextet (1930)
Score dated 5 May-June 1930
Dur: 8'
Instr: Fl. Ob. Cl. BsCl. Bsn. Hn.
f.p.   Haffner Wind Ensemble - Aldeburgh Parish Church, 11 June 1993
             (Aldeburgh Festival)
f.broad.p. Haffner Wind Ensemble - Radio 3, 2 December 1996
f.rec.   Nash Ensemble/Lionel Friend - *Hyperion CDA 66845 (CD)*
Pub: Faber
(*A second movement marked 'poco lento' was also played at the Aldeburgh concert -
it is dated 7 August 1930)

Two Portraits* for string orchestra (1930)
[1. D. (David) Layton 2. E.B.B. (featuring Britten's own instrument, the viola)]
Score dated 27 August 1930 (No.1), 10 September 1930 (No.2)
Dur: 15'
f.p.   Michael Gerrard (Va.)/Northern Sinfonia/Martyn Brabbins - BBC Radio 3,
              5 December 1995
f.conc.p.   (No.1) Britten Chamber Orchestra/Andreas Mitisek - Schubert-Saal, Vienna,
              10 February 1996
f.Brit.conc.p.(No.2) Martin Altrim (Va.)/Sinfonia 21/Martyn Brabbins - St. John's, Smith
              Square, London, 8 February 1996
f.Brit.conc.p.(complete) Stephen Tees (Va.)/City of London Sinfonia/Steuart
              Bedford - The Maltings, Snape, 22 June 1996 (Aldeburgh Festival)
Pub: OUP, 1997 (No.2 also arr. for viola and piano by Susan Bradshaw)
(*Britten described the pieces as 'Sketch No.1' and 'Sketch No.2'. There is a third,
unfinished, portrait entitled 'Peter Floud', a fellow pupil at Gresham's School, Holt.)

I saw three ships: for mixed voices (1930, rev.1934)
[Words: Trad.]
Score dated 12 September 1930, revision dated 2 May 1934
Dur: 3'
f.p.   Lowestoft Musical Society/C.J.R. Coleman - St John's Church, Lowestoft,
              5 January 1931

Later revised in November 1967 and published as:-
The Sycamore Tree: carol for SATB unaccompanied
Dedicated (in revision) 'For Imo' (Imogen Holst)
Dur: 3'
f.p.   Ambrosian Singers/Philip Ledger - Aldeburgh Parish Church, 19 June 1968
              (Aldeburgh Festival)
f.broad.p.   BBC Northern Singers/Stephen Wilkinson - Radio 3, 24 December 1974
f.rec.   Wilbye Consort/Peter Pears - *London (USA) OS 26527; Decca SXL 6847 (and
              MC)*
Pub: Faber, 1968

A widow bird sate mourning for her love: for voice and piano (1930)
[Words: Shelley]
Score dated 18 September 1930

Three Character Pieces for piano (1930)
[1. John (Boyd) 2. Daphne (Black) 3.* Michael (Tyler)]
The movements are portraits of three Lowestoft friends. The score is dated 16 September-
27 December 1930.
Dur: 7'
f.p.   Sarah Briggs - St Mary's Centre, Chester, 28 July 1989 (Summer Music
              Festival)
f.rec.   Stephen Hough - *Virgin VC7 91203-2 (CD) (and MC), VC7 59027-2 (CD)*
Pub: Faber, 1989
(*Britten quotes 'Ragamuffin' by John Ireland in this movement)

I saw three witches: for soprano, contralto and piano (1930)
[Words: Walter de la Mare]
Score dated 5 November 1930

Sweet was the song:* carol for women's voices (SSAA) unaccompanied (1931, rev.1966)
[Words: William Ballet's 'Lute Book']
Score dated 13 January 1931, revised April 1966
Dur: 3'30"
f.p.   Purcell Singers/Imogen Holst - Aldeburgh Parish Church, 15 June 1966 (Aldeburgh Festival)
f.rec.   Wilbye Consort/Peter Pears - *London (USA) OS 26527; Decca SXL 6847 (and MC)*
Pub: Faber, 1966, 1998 (in 'Three Carols for Upper Voices')
(*see also **Thy King's Birthday/Christ's Nativity**)

Mass for four voices (1930-31)
Score dated 16 January 1931

Vigil: song for bass and piano (1931)
[Words: Walter de la Mare]
Score dated 17 January 1931

The Moth: song for bass and piano (1931)
[Words: Walter de la Mare]
Score dated 19 January 1931

Sport: song for bass and piano (1931)
[Words: W.H. Davies]
Score dated 21 January 1931

Love me not for comely grace: a madrigal for SSAT (1931)
[Words: Anon.]
Score dated 22-27 January 1931

To the willow-tree: a madrigal for SATB (1931)
Score dated 23-28 January 1931

O Lord, forsake me not: motet for double SATB chorus (1931)
Score dated 31 January-10 February 1931

Thy King's Birthday*: Christmas Suite for soprano, contralto and chorus unaccompanied (1931)
[1. Christ's Nativity (Henry Vaughan) 2. Sweet was the song (William Ballet's 'Lute Book') 3. Preparations (Christ Church MS) 4. New Prince, New Pomp (Scriptures and Robert Southwell) 5. Carol of King Cnut (C.W. Stubbs)]
Score (original version) dated 26 March 1931
Dur: 16'

f.p.   (No.4) Rosamund Strode (Sop.)/Purcell Singers/Imogen Holst - Aldeburgh
            Parish Church, 24 June 1955 (Aldeburgh Festival)
f.p.   (complete) Alison Barlow (Sop.)/Adrienne Murray (M/S)/Britten
            Singers/Stephen Wilkinson - St Edmund's Church, Southwold, 14 June 1991
            (Aldeburgh Festival)
f.broad.p. above (complete) performance - Radio 3, 23 June 1991
f.rec.   Susan Gritton (Sop.)/Catherine Wyn-Rogers (Con.)/Choristers of St Paul's
            Cathedral/Holst Singers/Stephen Layton - *Hyperion CDA 66825(CD)*
Pub: Faber, 1994 (*as 'Christ's Nativity')
No.2 later rev. for women's chorus (SSAA) unaccompanied (1966)

Twelve Variations for solo piano (1931)
Composed between 27 March and 5 May 1931
Dur: 8'
f.p.   Murray Perahia - The Maltings, Snape, 22 June 1986 (Aldeburgh Festival)
f.rec.   Stephen Hough - *Virgin VC7 91203-2 (CD) (and MC), VC7 59027-2 (CD)*
Pub: Faber, 1986

Three Fugues for piano (1931)
Written as student exercises while studying with John Ireland at the Royal College of
Music. The score is dated 14-24 April 1931.
Dur: c.9'
Pub: (No.3 in A only) Associated Board (Grade 7), 1992

String Quartet in D major (1931, rev.1974)
Score dated 8 May-2 June 1931
Dur: 19'
f.priv.p.   Stratton Quartet, 16 March 1932 (a play-through arranged by Evlyn
            Howard-Jones, a friend of Delius)
f.priv.p.   (rev. version) Gabrieli String Quartet - The Red House, Aldeburgh,
            20 March 1974 (in the presence of the composer)
f.pub.p.   (rev. version) Gabrieli String Quartet - The Maltings, Snape, 7 June 1975
            (Aldeburgh Festival)
f.recs.   (original version) Galimir String Quartet - *Counterpoint (USA) CP-504*
            (rev. version) Gabrieli String Quartet - *Decca SDD 497*
Pub: Faber, 1975

Three Small Songs for soprano and small orchestra (1931)
[Words: Samuel Daniel and John Fletcher]
Submitted in May 1932 for the Mendelssohn Scholarship at the Royal College of Music -
among the adjudicators was Malcolm Sargent: the winner was Ivor Walsworth.The work
was composed between 8 and 24 June 1931.
f.p.   Clare Weston (Sop.)/Northern Sinfonia/Martyn Brabbins - BBC Radio 3,
            5 December 1995

Two Pieces for violin and piano (1931)
[1. The Moon (after Shelley)
2. Going down hill on a bicycle (after Henry Charles Beeching)]
Composed between 29 and 30 June 1931

Plymouth Town: ballet for small orchestra (1931)
[Scenario: Violet Alford]
Composed between 12 August and 23 November 1931

Variations on a French Carol (Carol of the Deanery of Saint-Ménéhould): for soprano, contralto, violin, viola and piano (1931)
Score dated 1 December 1931
f.p.   at a 'Musical Evening' at Britten's home in Lowestoft on 9 January 1932

Two Psalms for chorus and orchestra (1931-32)
[1. Psalm 150: Praise Ye the Lord 2. Psalm 130: Out of the Deep]
Submitted in May 1932 for the Mendelssohn Scholarship at the Royal College of Music - the score is dated 26 December 1931 (Psalm 150) and 19 January 1932 (Psalm 130)

Basque Village Ballet (1932)
[Scenario: Violet Alford]
Incomplete: two scenes were drafted on 15-16 June 1932

Phantasy in F minor for string quintet (1932)
Winner of the Cobbett Chamber Music Prize in May 1932, the work was later submitted to the ISCM for performance at the 1933 Festival in Amsterdam but was rejected. The score is dated 25 January-11 February 1932, and was revised 29 August-14 September 1932.
Dur: 11'
Instr: Vn. Vn. Va. Va. Vc.
f.p.   Student Quintet - Royal College of Music, London, 22 July 1932 (Cobbett Prize Concert)
f.pub.p.   (rev. version) Macnaghten Quartet with Nora Wilson (Va.) - Ballet Club (Mercury Theatre), London, 12 December 1932 (Macnaghten-Lemare Concert)
f.broad.p. Mangeot Ensemble with Anthony Collins (Va.) - 17 February 1933 (the first Britten work to be broadcast)
f.rec.   Gabrieli String Quartet with Kenneth Essex (Va.) - *Unicorn DKP 9020, UKCD 2060 (CD)*
Pub: Faber, 1983

Three Two-Part Songs* for boys' (or women's) voices and piano (1932)
[Words: Walter de la Mare 1. The Ride-by-Nights 2. The Rainbow
 3. The Ship of Rio]
Composed between 15 and 29 February 1932 and revised between 25 and 27 May 1932
Dur: 5'30"
f.p.   Carlyle Singers/Iris Lemare with Benjamin Britten (Pno.) - Ballet Club (Mercury Theatre), London, 12 December 1932 (Macnaghten-Lemare Concert)
f.broad.p. (No.1) Kirby Secondary Grammar School Choir/Gertrude Quinn with Gladys Willis (Pno.) - Home Service, 8 April 1954 (from Middlesbrough Town Hall)
f.broad.p. (No.2) London Co-operative Central Junior Choir/Graham Treacher - Home Service, 12 March 1960 (pre-recorded, 4 March 1960)
f.rec.   Toronto Children's Choir/Jean Ashworth Bartle - *Carlton Classics*

PCD 1088 (CD)
Pub: OUP, 1932 (separate publications), 1970 (single volume)
(*Britten's first published work, they were originally entitled 'Three Studies in Canon')
No.3 arr. for medium voice and piano between 16 August and 18 September 1963
Dur: 1'30"
Pub: OUP, 1964

Double Concerto for violin, viola and orchestra (1932)
Score dated 9 March-1 July 1932
Dur: 25'
Instr: 2/2/2/2 - 2/2/0/0 - timp. perc. str.
f.p.   Katherine Hunka (Vn.)/Philip Dukes (Va.)/Britten-Pears Orchestra/Kent
            Nagano - The Maltings, Snape, 15 June 1997 (Aldeburgh Festival)
f.Lon.p.   Tasmin Little (Vn.)/Lars Anders Tomter (Va.)/Royal Philharmonic
            Orchestra/Daniele Gatti - Royal Albert Hall, 31 July 1998 (Promenade
            Concert)
f.rec.   Gidon Kremer (Vn.)/Yuri Bashmet (Va.)/Hallé Orchestra/Kent Nagano -
            Erato 3984-25502-2 (CD)
Pub: OUP, 1999 (ed. by Colin Matthews; also arr. for violin, viola and piano by
            Susan Bradshaw)

Introduction and Allegro for piano trio (1932)
Composed 'For Remo Lauricella & Bernard Richards', members of a student trio which
Britten had formed at the Royal College of Music - the score is dated 20 May 1932
Instr: Vn. Vc. Pno.
f.p.   Marcia Crayford (Vn.)/Christopher van Kampen (Vc.)/Ian Brown (Pno.) -
            Wigmore Hall, London, 22 November 1986

Variations on a theme of Frank Bridge: for piano (1932)
f.p.   Anthony Goldstone - BBC Radio 3, 12 December 1995
f.conc.p.   Roger Vignoles - The Maltings, Snape, 26 October 1997
            (Aldeburgh October Festival)

Sinfonietta for chamber orchestra Op.1 (1932)
Dedicated 'To Frank Bridge'. The score is dated 20 June-9 July 1932. The **Sinfonietta**
was a Sullivan prize-winning work in 1932 and, like the **Phantasy Quintet**, was
submitted for performance at the ISCM Festival in Amsterdam: it was, however, rejected
by the Committee.
Dur: 15'
Instr: Fl. Ob. Cl. Bsn. Hn. Vn. Vn. Va. Vc. Db.
f.p.   Student Chamber Orchestra/Benjamin Britten - Royal College of Music,
            London, Autumn term 1932 (rehearsals only - the work was not given a
            College concert performance until 16 March 1933 under the auspices of the
            Patrons' Fund Scheme)
f.pub.p.   English Wind Players/Macnaghten String Quartet with Adolf Lotter (Db.)/Iris
            Lemare - Ballet Club (Mercury Theatre), London, 31 January 1933
            (Macnaghten-Lemare Concert)
f.broad.p. Strasbourg Municipal Orchestra/Hermann Scherchen - Radio Strasbourg,
            7 August 1933

f.Brit.broad.p. BBC Chamber Orchestra/Edward Clark - Maida Vale Studios, London,
        15 September 1933
f.p.   (as the ballet 'Die Versunkene Stadt') - Stadttheater, St Gallen, Switzerland,
        1950
Choreography: Mara Jovanovits
f.recs.   MGM Chamber Ensemble/Izler Solomon - *MGM E-290 (m)*
        Vienna Octet - *Decca SDD 531; London 425 715-2 (CD)*
Pub: Boosey & Hawkes, 1935
also arr. for small orchestra by the composer (1936)
Instr: 1/1/1/1 - 2/0/0/0 - str.
f.p.   Edric Cundell Chamber Orchestra/Edric Cundell - Aeolian Hall, London,
        10 March 1936
f.rec.   Hallé Orchestra/Kent Nagano - *Erato 3984-25502-2 (CD)*
Pub: Boosey & Hawkes

Phantasy: quartet in one movement for oboe, violin, viola and violoncello Op.2 (1932)

Dedicated 'To Leon Goossens' - the score is dated 25 October 1932
Dur: 14'30"
Instr: Ob. Vn. Va. Vc.
fp.   Leon Goossens (Ob.)/André Mangeot (Vn.)/Eric Bray (Va.)/Jack Shinebourne
        (Vc.) - BBC broadcast, 6 August 1933
f.conc.p.   above artists - St. John's Institute, London, 21 November 1933 (Music Society
        Concert)
f.Eur.p.   Leon Goossens (Ob.)/Sidney Griller (Vn.)/Philip Burton (Va.)/Colin Hampton
        (Vc.) - Florence, 5 April 1934 (ISCM Festival)
f.recs.   Harold Gomberg (Ob.)/Galimir Trio - *Esoteric (USA) ES 504 (m)*
        Vitézslav Hanus (Ob.)/Janáček Quartet - *Supraphon SUAST 50960*
        Derek Wickens (Ob.)/Gabrieli String Quartet - *Unicorn DKP 9020, UKCD
        2060 (CD)*
Pub: Boosey & Hawkes, 1935

Alla Quartetto Serioso 'Go play, boy, play'# - Suite for string quartet (1933)

[1. Alla marcia 2. Alla valse (At the party) 3. Alla romanza 4. Theme and Two
Variations (incomplete) 5. Alla burlesca (Ragging)]
Movement No.1 is dedicated to David Layton and the score is dated 13-14 February 1933.
Further revisions were made between 27 September and 11 October 1933 and re-titled
'All'introduzione' (Physical Training). Movement No.2 is dedicated 'to Stephen' and
No.5 to Francis Barton - these two movements are dated 28 February-20 September 1933.
All three of these movements were extensively revised over the next three years (see
below.*)
Dur: (No.1) 3'
f.priv.p.   (No.1, original version) Antonio Brosa (Vn.)/Ethel Bridge (Vn.)/Frank Bridge
        (Va.)/Bernard Richards (Vc.) - 4 Bedford Gardens, Kensington, West London,
        26 February 1933 (at the London home of Frank Bridge)
f.priv.p.   (No.1, rev.version, and Nos.2 and 5) Student Quartet - Royal College of
        Music, London, 3 November 1933 (as part of Britten's Mendelssohn
        Scholarship submission)

f.pub.p.   (above three movements) Macnaghten Quartet - All Hallows', Barking, Essex, 4 December 1933

f.Lon.pub.p.(above three movements) Macnaghten Quartet - Ballet Club (Mercury Theatre), London, 11 December 1933 (Macnaghten-Lemare Concert)

f.broad.p. (No.1, original version) Gabrieli String Quartet - Radio 3, 31 March 1980 (pre-recorded, 25 September 1979)

f.rec.   (No.1, original version) Gabrieli String Quartet - *Unicorn DKP 9020, UKCD 2060 (CD)*

Pub: Faber, 1983 (No.1, original version)

Nos.2 and 3 also arr. for flute, oboe and piano (1933)

Score dated 4 April 1933

No.2 also arr. for piano solo (1934)

Score dated 2 February 1934

*Nos.1, 2 and 5 were later revised as:

Three Divertimenti for string quartet (1933-36)

[1. March 2. Waltz 3. Burlesque]

Score dated 28 February 1933-15 February 1936

Dur: 12'

f.p.   Stratton Quartet - Wigmore Hall, London, 25 February 1936

f.broad.p. Gabrieli String Quartet - Radio 3, 6 May 1982 (pre-recorded, 15 June 1981)

f.rec.   Gabrieli String Quartet - *Unicorn DKP 9020, UKCD 2060 (CD)*

Pub: Faber, 1983

(#The first movement was also intended as the opening of a suite to be based on the novel 'Emil and the Detectives' by Erich Kästner and was subtitled 'Emil to be' - the sub-title 'Go play, boy, play' is taken from Shakespeare's 'The Winter's Tale')

Two Part-Songs for SATB chorus and piano (1932-33)

[1. I lov'd a lass, a fair one (George Wither) 2. Lift Boy (Robert Graves)]

Score dated 18 July 1932, revised 5-28 June 1933

Dur: 5'

f.p.   Carlyle Singers/Iris Lemare with Benjamin Britten (Pno.) - Ballet Club (Mercury Theatre), London, 11 December 1933 (Macnaghten-Lemare Concert)

f.broad.p. Wireless Singers/Leslie Woodgate - 27 March 1935

f.rec.   Elizabethan Singers/Louis Halsey, with Wilfrid Parry (Pno.) - *Argo ZRG 5424*

Pub: Boosey & Hawkes, 1934

A Boy was Born: choral variations for men's, women's and boys' voices, unaccompanied Op.3 (1932-33, rev.1955 and 1958)

[Theme: A Boy was Born (Anon. 16th century)

 Variation 1: Lullay, Jesu (Anon. before 1536)

 Variation 2: Herod (Anon. 15th century)

 Variation 3: Jesu, as Thou art our Saviour (Anon. 15th century)

 Variation 4: The Three Kings (Anon. 15th century)

 Variation 5: In the bleak mid-winter (Christina Rossetti - Anon. 15th century)

 Variation 6: (Finale): Noel! (Anon. 15th century, Thomas Tusser, Francis Quarles)]

Dedicated 'To my Father' - the score is dated 11 May 1933

Dur: 30'
f.priv.p.   BBC Wireless Singers/Leslie Woodgate - BBC Studios, 10 July 1933
f.broad.p. BBC Wireless Singers/Choirboys of St Mark's, North Audley Street,
            London/Leslie Woodgate - 23 February 1934
f.conc.p.   Carlyle Singers/Choirboys of St Alban the Martyr, Holborn/Iris Lemare -
            Ballet Club (Mercury Theatre), London, 17 December 1934
            (Macnaghten-Lemare Concert)
f.p.   (rev.version) Purcell Singers/Imogen Holst - Grosvenor Chapel, South Audley
            Street, London, 22 November 1955
f.rec.   Purcell Singers/Benjamin Britten - *London (USA) 5398 (m); Decca LXT 5416
            (m), ECS 628 (es), 430 367-2 (CD); London 436 394-2 (CD)*
Pub: OUP, 1934; 1935 (Theme, and Variations 3, 4 and 5 published separately);
            1958 (rev. version); 1961 (Theme, in 'Carols for Choirs' Vol.1); 1962
            (Theme, as part of the series 'Oxford Choral Songs'); 1965 (Variation 3, in
            'Carols of Today')

Corpus Christi Carol (from Variation 5) for voice (or unison voices) and piano or
organ (1961)
Dedicated 'For John Hahessy' - the score is dated 19 January 1961 (there is also a much
earlier version for soprano and piano dated 9 August 1933)
Dur: 2'45"
f.recs.   John Hahessy (Alto.)/Benjamin Britten (Pno.) - *Argo ZFA 18 (45)*
            Janet Baker (M/S)/Gerald Moore (Pno.) - *HMV(set) SLS 5275(and MC), ESD
            100642-1*
Pub: OUP, 1961 (high or low voice with piano), 1962 (high voice with organ);
            1985 (low voice, ed. by John Carol Case in 'Sing Solo Baritone')

Simple Symphony: for string orchestra (or string quartet) Op.4 (1933-34)
[1. Boisterous Bourrée 2. Playful Pizzicato 3. Sentimental Saraband
4. Frolicsome Finale]
'Dedicated to Audrey Alston (Mrs. Lincolne Sutton)', Britten's viola teacher in the
twenties and close friend of Mr. & Mrs. Frank Bridge. Each movement is based on piano
pieces and songs composed between 1923 and 1926 - the score is dated 10 February 1934
Dur: 18'
f.p.   Norwich String Orchestra/Benjamin Britten - Stuart Hall, Norwich,
            6 March 1934
f.broad.p. Boyd Neel Orchestra/Boyd Neel - BBC Regional, 25 May 1935
f.Eur.p.   Boyd Neel Orchestra/Boyd Neel - Lisbon, 1939
f.p.   (as the ballet 'Simple Symphony') Ballet Rambert - Theatre Royal, Bristol,
            19 November 1944
Choreography: Walter Gore
Scenery: Ronald Wilson
Principals: Sally Gilmour, Walter Gore
f.Austr.p. Boyd Neel Orchestra/Boyd Neel - Sydney Conservatorium, April/May 1947
            (during their tour of Australia)
f.recs.   Boyd Neel Orchestra/Boyd Neel - *Decca (AX) K 245-7 (78); Dutton
            Laboratories CDAX 8007 (CD)*

English Chamber Orchestra/Benjamin Britten - *London (USA) CS 6618;*
Decca SXL 6405 (and MC), 410 171-1 (and MC), 417 312-1 (and MC), 417
509-1 (and MC/CD), 425 160-2 (CD), 436 990-2 (CD) (and MC),
448 569-2 (CD)

Pub: OUP, 1935
Nos.2 and 3 also arr. for piano duet by Howard Ferguson
Pub: OUP, 1972
also arr. for brass ensemble by Colin Matthews and Simon Wright
f.rec.   Wallace Collection/Simon Wright - *Collins 1115-2 (CD) (and MC)*

Te Deum in C major for treble solo, choir (SATB) and organ (1934)

'Written for Maurice Vinden and the Choir of St Mark's, N. Audley St,
London' - the score is dated 17 September 1934
Dur: 8'30"
f.p.   May Bartlett (Sop.)/St Michael's Singers/Harold Darke, with George
            Thalben-Ball (organ) - St Michael's, Cornhill, London, 13 November 1935
f.recs.   Washington Cathedral Choir/Paul Calloway - *WCFM (USA) LP-11(m)*
            Choir of King's College, Cambridge/Philip Ledger - *HMV ASD 3035; EMI*
            CDM7 64653-2 (CD)
Pub: OUP, 1935 (vocal score) (new edition forthcoming)

later arr. for harp and string orchestra (1936)
Commissioned by the BBC - the score is dated 20 January 1936
f.p.   Choir of St Alban's, Holborn/Lemare Orchestra/Reginald Goodall - Ballet
            Club (Mercury Theatre), London, 27 January 1936 (Lemare Concert)
f.broad p. May Bartlett (Sop.)/St Michael's Singers/BBC Orchestra/Harold Darke -
            28 February 1936
Pub: OUP, 1998 (full score) (study score forthcoming)

Jubilate Deo in E flat for chorus (SATB) and organ (1934)

'Written for Maurice Vinden & the Choir of St. Mark's, North Audley Street, London'
The score is dated 8-10 August 1934
Dur: 3'
f.p.   Winchester Cathedral Choir/Martin Neary, with James Lancelot (organ) -
            Winchester Cathedral, 4 March 1984
f.rec.   Choir of Westminster Cathedral/David Hill, with James O'Donnell (organ) -
            Hyperion CDA 66220 (CD)
Pub: Faber, 1984

May - unison song with piano (1934)

[Words: Anon]
Score dated 28 September 1934
Dur: 1'
f.p.   Meriel St. Clair (Sop.)/Millicent Silver (Pno.) - BBC Home Service,
            24 June 1942
f.rec.   Aldeburgh Festival Singers/Peter Aston, with Graham Barber (Pno.) -
            University of East Anglia UEA 82015
Pub: The Year Book Press, Ascherberg, Hopwood & Crew (originally A. & C.
            Black), 1935; now distributed by IMP

Holiday Diary - Suite for piano Op.5 (1934)
[1. Early Morning Bathe 2. Sailing 3. Funfair 4. Night]
Dedicated 'To Arthur Benjamin', Britten's piano teacher - the work was completed on 14 October 1934. It was first published as 'Holiday Tales'.

Dur:	16'
f.p.	Betty Humby - Wigmore Hall, London, 30 November 1934
f.broad.p.	Millicent Silver - 4 June 1936
f.recs.	Sandra Bianca - *MGM E-3366 (m)*
	Eric Parkin - *Chandos(set) DBRD 2006 (and MC)*
	Christopher Headington - *Kingdom KCLCD 2017 (CD) (and MC)*
Pub:	Boosey & Hawkes, 1935

A Poison Tree:* song for medium voice and piano (1935)
[Words: William Blake]
Score dated 2 March 1935

Dur:	3'
f.p.	Henry Herford (Bar.)/Ian Brown (Pno.) - Wigmore Hall, London, 22 November 1986
f.rec.	Ian Bostridge (Ten.)/Graham Johnson (Pno.) - *Hyperion CDA 66823 (CD)*
Pub:	Faber, 1994 (in 'The Red Cockatoo & Other Songs')

(*a later setting was used in the **Songs and Proverbs of William Blake** q.v.)

Two Insect Pieces: for oboe and piano (1935)
[1. The Grasshopper 2. The Wasp]
Dedicated 'For Sylvia Spencer' - the score is dated 21 April 1935

Dur:	5'
f.priv.p.	Sylvia Spencer (Ob.)/Benjamin Britten (Pno.) - 26 April 1935
f.pub.p.	Janet Craxton (Ob.)/Margot Wright (Pno.) - Royal Northern College of Music, Manchester, 7 March 1979 (at a Memorial Concert for Sylvia Spencer)
f.broad.p.	Janet Craxton (Ob.)/Ian Brown (Pno.) - Radio 3, 3 April 1980 (pre-recorded, 28 March 1979)
f.recs.	Robin Canter (Ob.)/Linn Hendry (Pno.) - *Phoenix DGS 1022*
	Derek Wickens (Ob.)/John Constable (Pno.) - *Unicorn DKP 9020, UKCD 2060 (CD)*
Pub:	Faber, 1980

Friday Afternoons: Twelve* Children's Songs with piano Op.7 (1933-35)
[1. Begone, dull care (Anon.) 2. A Tragic Story (William Thackeray) 3. Cuckoo! (Jane Taylor) 4. Ee-Oh! (Anon.) 5. A New Year Carol (Anon.) 6. I mun be married on Sunday (Nicholas Udall) 7. There was a man of Newington (Anon.) 8. Fishing Song (Izaak Walton) 9. The Useful Plough (Anon.) 10. Jazz-Man (Eleanor Farjeon) 11. There was a Monkey (Anon.) 12. Old Abram Brown (Anon.)]
Dedicated 'To R. H. M. Britten and the boys of Clive House, Prestatyn, 1934'
(Robert Britten was the headmaster of Clive House School) - the score is dated 2 August 1935

Dur:	22'
f.broad.p.	(Nos.10 & 11) Sophie Wyss (Sop.)/Adolph Hallis (Pno.) - 26 October 1937
f.broad.p.	(complete) St Felix School Choir, Southwold/Ruth Railton - Home Service, 18 May 1949

f.recs.   (Nos.3, 5, 6, 8, 11) John Hahessy (Alto.)/Benjamin Britten (Pno.) -
          Argo ZFA 18 (45)
          (omitting No.4) Downside School Choir/Viola Tunnard (Pno.) cond.
          Benjamin Britten - *London (USA) OS 25993, STS 15173; Decca SXL 6264;*
          London 436 394-2 (CD)
          (complete) Australian Boys' Choir - *Classics for Pleasure CFP 178*
Pub: Boosey & Hawkes, 1936 (in 2 volumes) (Nos.2, 3, 10 and 12 also published
          separately); 1951, 1965, 1966 (vocal score), 1994 (new edition)

Nos.1, 2, 3, 4, 5, 7, 10, 11 and 12 arr. for SSA chorus and orchestra by Heuwell Tircuit
Dur: 16'
Instr: 3/2+ca./2+bcl./2+cbsn. - 4/2/3/1- timp.perc.(3) hp.str.
No.5 arr. for SSA chorus and piano (1971)
Dur: 2'30"
f.rec.   Bristol Cathedral Choir - *Abbey ACA 552*
Pub: Boosey & Hawkes, 1971
No.12 arr. for SATB chorus and piano
Dur: 5'30"
Pub: Boosey & Hawkes, 1947(?)
(*There is another song 'Lone Dog' [Words: Irene McLeod], dated 10 November 1933,
originally omitted due to copyright difficulties but published as an Appendix in the 1994
edition)

Suite for violin and piano Op.6 (1934-35)
[Introduction - 1. March 2. Moto perpetuo 3. Lullaby 4. Waltz]
Score dated 27 June 1935
Dur: 18'
f.p.   (Nos.1, 3 and 4) Henri Temianka (Vn.)/Betty Humby (Pno.) - Wigmore Hall,
          London, 17 December 1934
f.p.   (complete) Antonio Brosa (Vn.)/Benjamin Britten (Pno.) - BBC broadcast,
          13 March 1936
f.Eur.p. above artists - Casal del Metge, Barcelona, 21 April 1936 (ISCM Festival)
f.Brit.conc.p. Frederick Grinke (Vn.)/Benjamin Britten (Pno.) - London, 20 June 1938
          (ISCM Festival)
f.rec.   Ladislav Jasek (Vn.)/Josef Hala (Pno.) - *Supraphon SUAST 50707*
Pub: Boosey & Hawkes, 1935

later revised and republished as
Three Pieces for violin and piano (1976)
[1. March 2. Lullaby 3. Waltz]
Dur: 12'
Pub: Boosey & Hawkes, 1977

Rossini Suite: for boys' voices and chamber ensemble (1935)
Score dated 18 July 1935
Dur: 12'
Instr: 1/1/1/0 - 0/0/0/0 - perc.(2) pno. (+wordless boys' voices)
f.p.   Finchley Children's Music Group/London Sinfonietta/Lukas Foss -
          The Maltings, Snape, 18 June 1987 (Aldeburgh Festival)

f.rec.   Paisley Abbey Choir/Scottish Chamber Orchestra/Steuart Bedford - *EMI*
            CDC7 49480-2 (CD)
Pub: Boosey & Hawkes
(Movements 1, 2 and 5 were used in the film, **The Tocher** q.v. Four movements were
later rescored to form part of **Soirées musicales** and **Matinées musicales** q.v.)

Russian Funeral:* for brass and percussion ensemble (1936)
Score dated 2 March 1936
Dur: 6'
Instr: 4 Hn. 3 Tpt. 3 Tbn. Tba. Perc.
f.p.   South London Brass Orchestra/Alan Bush - Westminster Theatre, London,
            8 March 1936 (London Labour Choral Union Concert)
f.broad.p. Philip Jones Brass Ensemble - Radio 3, 11 April 1980
f.rec.   Philip Jones Brass Ensemble - *London 430 369-2 (CD)*
Pub: Faber, 1981
also arr. for brass band and percussion by Ray Farr
f.p.   Grimethorpe Colliery Band/Ray Farr - Framlingham Castle, 15 June 1984
            (Aldeburgh Festival)
Pub: Studio Music, 1987
(*the work includes a Russian revolutionary song used by Shostakovich in his **Symphony
No.11** and was originally entitled 'War and Death, an impression for brass orchestra')

**When you're feeling like expressing your affection: song for high voice and piano
(c.1935-36)**
[Words: W.H. Auden?]
Possibly the song Hedli Anderson remembered singing in connection with a GPO film
during Auden's time at the Film Unit
Dur: 0'45"
f.p.   Lucy Shelton (Sop.)/Ian Brown (Pno.) - Holy Trinity Church, Blythburgh,
            15 June 1992 (Aldeburgh Festival)
f.broad p. above first performance - Radio 3, 8 July 1992
f.rec.   Jill Gomez (Sop.)/Martin Jones (Pno.) - *Unicorn DKPCD 9138 (CD)*
Pub: Faber, 1994 (in 'The Red Cockatoo & Other Songs')

Two Lullabies for two pianos (1936)
[1. Lullaby 2. Lullaby for a Retired Colonel]
Written for a BBC audition with Adolph Hallis - the score is dated 16 March 1936
Dur: 6'
f.p.   (No.2) Benjamin Britten/Adolph Hallis - Concert Hall, Broadcasting House,
            London, 19 March 1936
f.conc.p.   (complete) Peter Frankl/Tamás Vásáry - The Maltings, Snape, 22 June 1988
            (Aldeburgh Festival)
f.rec.   Stephen Hough/Ronan O'Hora - *Virgin VC7 91203-2 (CD) (and MC)*,
            VC7 59027-2 (CD)
Pub: Faber, 1990

**Our Hunting Fathers: symphonic cycle for high voice and orchestra Op.8 (1936,
rev.1961)**
[Text devised by W.H. Auden - Prologue (W.H. Auden) - 1. Rats Away! (Anon.)

2. Messalina (Anon.) 3. Dance of Death (Thomas Ravenscroft) - Epilogue and Funeral March (W.H. Auden)]
'Dedicated to Ralph Hawkes, Esq.' Written to be performed by Sophie Wyss at the Norwich Festival, the work was composed between 13 May and 23 July 1936.

Dur:	27'
Instr:	2/2/1+E flat cl.+a.sax./2 - 4/2/3/1 - timp. perc.(2) hp. str.
f.p.	Sophie Wyss (Sop.)/London Philharmonic Orchestra/Benjamin Britten - St Andrew's Hall, Norwich, 25 September 1936 (Norfolk and Norwich Triennial Music Festival)
f.broad.p.	Sophie Wyss (Sop.)/BBC Orchestra/Sir Adrian Boult - BBC, 30 April 1937 (BBC Contemporary Music Concert)
f.Lon.p.	Peter Pears (Ten.)/Chelsea Symphony Orchestra/Norman del Mar - Chelsea Town Hall, 6 June 1950
f.Am.p.	Heather Harper (Sop.)/BBC Symphony Orchestra/Antal Dorati - Boston, 25 April 1965
f.recs.	Peter Pears (Ten.)/London Symphony Orchestra/Benjamin Britten (BBC Third Programme broadcast 11 June 1961) - *BBC REGL 417, BBCB 8014-2 (CD)* Elizabeth Söderström (Sop.)/Welsh National Opera Orchestra/Richard Armstrong - *HMV ASD 4397 (and MC); EMI CDM7 69522-2 (CD)*
Pub:	Boosey & Hawkes, 1936 (vocal score), 1964 (full score)

Soirées musicales: Suite of five movements from Rossini for orchestra Op.9 (1935-36)
[1. March 2. Canzonetta 3. Tirolese 4. Bolero 5. Tarantella]
Dedicated 'To M. Alberto Cavalcanti' (Producer of the GPO film **The Tocher** in which Britten had first used these orchestral arrangements of Rossini's music - see also **Rossini Suite**) - the work was composed between 4 December 1935 and 24 August 1936

Dur:	11'
Instr:	2/2/2/2 - 4/2/3/0 - timp. perc.(2) hp. str.
Alt.Instr:	1/1/1/0 - 0/1/1/0 - perc. hp.(pno.) str.
f.p.	BBC Symphony Orchestra/Joseph Lewis - BBC, 16 January 1937 (studio performance)
f.conc.p.	BBC Orchestra/Sir Henry Wood - Queen's Hall, London, 10 August 1937 (Promenade Concert)
f.priv.p.	(as the ballet 'Soirée musicale') London Ballet Company - Scala Theatre, London, 26 November 1938 (Cecchetti Society Matinée)
Choreography:	Anthony Tudor
Decor:	Hugh Stevenson
Principals:	Gerd Larsen, Hugh Laing, Maude Lloyd, Anthony Tudor
f.pub.p.	(as the ballet 'Soirée musicale') above artists - Toynbee Hall Theatre, London, 12 December 1938
f.p.	(with **Matinées musicales** as the ballet 'Divertimento') American Ballet Company cond. Emanuel Balaban - Teatro Municipal, Rio de Janeiro, 27 June 1941 (on their South American tour)
Choreography:	Georges Balanchine
f.Eur.p.	(with **Matinées musicales** as the ballet 'Fantaisie Italienne') Théâtre de la Monnaie, Brussels, 1948
f.Am.p.	(as the ballet 'Soirée') Metropolitan Opera, New York, 1955
Choreography:	Zachary Solov
Decor and costumes:	Cecil Beaton

f.recs.   Charles Brill Orchestra/Charles Brill - *Decca AK 873-4 (78)*
           New Symphony Orchestra/Edgar Cree - *Decca ECS 712 (es)*
           Philharmonia Orchestra/Robert Irving - *HMV CLP 1172 (m); Bluebird (USA)*
           LBC 1078 (m); Capitol (USA) G 7105 (m)
           National Philharmonic Orchestra/Richard Bonynge - *Decca SXDL 7539*
           (and MC), 410 139-2 (CD)
Pub: Boosey & Hawkes, 1938, 1965, 1997 (Orchestral Anthology, Vol.1)
also arr. for military band by T. Conway Brown
Pub: Boosey & Hawkes, 1946
also arr. for two pianos by Brian Easdale
f.broad.p. (No.3) Joan and Valerie Trimble - 15 June 1940
Pub: Boosey & Hawkes, 1938

Two Ballads for two voices and piano (1936-37)
[1. Mother Comfort (Montagu Slater) 2. Underneath the Abject Willow (W.H. Auden)*]
Written for Sophie and Colette Wyss. The Auden poem from his collection 'Look
Stranger' is dedicated to Benjamin Britten and the score is dated 25 November 1936
Dur: 6'
f.p.   Sophie Wyss (Sop.)/Betty Bannerman (Sop.)/Benjamin Britten (Pno.) -
           Wigmore Hall, London, 15 December 1936 (Adolph Hallis Concert)
f.broad.p. (No.1) Mary MacDougall (Sop.)/Anne Wood (Con.) - Home Service,
           7 March 1941
f.rec.   Kathleen Livingstone (Sop.)/Neil Mackie (Ten.)/John Blakely (Pno.) -
           Unicorn DKPC 9072 (MC), UKCD 2009 (CD)
Pub: Boosey & Hawkes, 1937
(*there is also a version of this song for voice and piano dating from c.1941 q.v.)

Theme for improvisation* (1936)
f.p.   André Marchal - St John's, Red Lion Square, London, 12 November 1936
           (Organ Music Society Concert)
Pub: (themes) Organ Music Society, 1936
(*For a four-movement symphony for organ. Britten's theme was used for the Scherzo
movement, placed second: the other three movements were based on themes provided by
Alan Bush [Movt.I - Fugue], William Walton [Movt.III - Adagio] and Constant Lambert
[Movt.IV - Toccata])

Temporal Variations: for oboe and piano (1936)
[Theme - 1. Oration 2. March 3. Exercises 4. Commination 5. Chorale 6. Waltz
7. Polka 8. Resolution]
Dedicated 'To Montagu Slater' - the score is dated 12 December 1936
Dur: 14'30"
f.p.   Natalie Caine (Ob.)/Adolph Hallis (Pno.) - Wigmore Hall, London,
           15 December 1936 (Adolph Hallis Concert)
f.broad.p. Janet Craxton (Ob.)/Ian Brown (Pno.) - Radio 3, 3 April 1980 (pre-recorded,
           28 March 1979)
f.rec.   Janet Craxton (Ob.)/Ian Brown (Pno.) - *BBC REM 635 (and MC/CD)*
Pub: Faber, 1980
later arr. for oboe and string orchestra by Colin Matthews

f.p.   Nicholas Daniel/English Chamber Orchestra/Steuart Bedford - The Maltings,
            Snape, 12 June 1994 (Aldeburgh Festival)
f.rec.   Nicholas Daniel/Northern Sinfonia/Steuart Bedford - *Collins 5 023391*
            152627 (CD)
Pub: Faber, 1995

Philip's Breeches for SATB chorus (1936)
[Words: Charles and Mary Lamb]
Score dated 31 December 1936

Pacifist March - unison song with orchestra (1936-37)
[Words: Ronald Duncan]
Written for The Peace Pledge Union founded by Rev. Canon Dick Sheppard, the vicar of
St Martin-in-the-Fields, London - the work was composed between 30 November 1936
and 27 January 1937.
Dur: 4'
f.p.   untraced - the March was later rejected by the PPU membership and was not
            performed by them*
Pub: Peace Pledge Union, London, 1937 (chorus parts only)
(*Ronald Duncan in his memoir **Working with Britten**, The Rebel Press, 1981, tells us
that the **Pacifist March** was originally conceived as a cantata for large choir and
orchestra of Berlioz dimensions. Britten completed the orchestration in a month.)

Reveille:* Concert Study for violin with piano accompaniment (1937)
Dedicated 'For Toni Brosa' - the draft score is dated 15 March 1937
Dur: 5'
f.p.   Antonio Brosa (Vn.)/Franz Reizenstein (Pno.) - Wigmore Hall, London,
            12 April 1937
f.broad.p. Antonio Brosa (Vn.)/unnamed pianist - 15 August 1937
f.rec.   Lorraine McAslan (Vn.)/John Blakely (Pno.) - *Continuum CCD 1022 (CD)*
Pub: Faber, 1983 (ed. Hugh Maguire)
(*Michael Kennedy points out that the title 'was an in-joke, Brosa being noted as a late
riser'.)

Johnny: cabaret song for voice and piano* (1937)
[Words: W.H. Auden]
Composed 5 May 1937
Dur: 4'30"
[f.p.]   Hedli Anderson (Sop.)/Benjamin Britten (Pno.) - Hammersmith, West
            London, 18 January 1938 (at a 'farewell' party for Auden and Isherwood held
            at the home of the artist, Julian Trevelyan)
f.broad.p. Hedli Anderson (Sop.)/Norman Franklin (Pno.) - Third Programme,
            29 June 1949
f.recs.   Hedli Anderson (Sop.)/Benjamin Britten (Pno.) - *Columbia (rec. 1938-39 but*
            not issued)
            Sarah Walker (Sop.)/Roger Vignoles (Pno.) - *Meridian E 77056,*
            CDE 84167 (CD)
Pub: Faber, 1980 ('Cabaret Songs')
also arr. for female voice and chamber ensemble by Daryl Runswick (1990)

Instr: Al.Sax. Tpt. Vn. Db. Pno. Drum kit
f.p.   Mary King (M/S)/Daryl Runswick All-Stars - Jubilee Hall, Aldeburgh,
          8 June 1990 (Aldeburgh Festival)
f.broad.p. above performance - Radio 3, 8 July 1990
Pub: Faber
(*two further Auden settings from this period, 'Give up love' and 'I'm a jam tart' were
also recorded by Hedli Anderson and Britten for Columbia, but these are now lost)

Variations on a Theme of Frank Bridge:* for string orchestra Op.10 (1937)
[Introduction and Theme - Var. 1. Adagio 2. March 3. Romance
4. Aria Italiana 5. Bourrée classique 6. Wiener Walzer 7. Moto perpetuo
8. Funeral March 9. Chant 10. Fugue and Finale]
Written at Boyd Neel's suggestion for his orchestra to play at the 1937 Salzburg Festival
and dedicated 'To F.B. A tribute with affection and admiration' - the score is dated
12 July 1937
Dur: 25'
f.p.   Boyd Neel Orchestra/Boyd Neel - Hilversum Radio broadcast, Holland,
          25 August 1937 (both Bridge and Britten attended the last rehearsals on 23
          August in the Kensington Studios before the journey to Holland)
f.conc.p. above artists - Mozarteum Grossersaal, Salzburg, 27 August 1937
          (Salzburg Festival)
f.Brit.p. above artists - Wigmore Hall, London, 5 October 1937 (the work was also
          performed at the ISCM Festival in London the following year, on 20 June
          1938)
f.Brit.broad.p. above artists - 31 October 1937
f.Am.p.   Cincinnati Symphony Orchestra/Eugene Goossens - Cincinnati, 4 March 1939
          (the New York première took place at Carnegie Hall on 21 August 1939,
          Sir John Barbirolli conducting the New York Philharmonic Orchestra)
f.Can.p. CBC Symphony Orchestra/Alexander Chuhaldin - Toronto, June 1939
f.p.   (as the ballet 'Jinx') Dance Players - National Theatre, New York,
          24 April 1942 (later to London's Covent Garden in July 1950)
Instr: a two-piano transcription by Colin McPhee (see f.recs.)
Choreography: Lew Christensen
Scenery: James Morcom
Costumes: Felipe Fiocca
Principals: Janet Reed, Conrad Linden, Lew Christensen
f.Austr.p. Boyd Neel Orchestra/Boyd Neel - Sydney Town Hall, 16 April 1947
          (and broadcast by ABC)
f.NZ.p.   Boyd Neel Orchestra/Boyd Neel - Auckland Town Hall, August 1947
f.p.   (as the ballet 'La Rêve de Leonore' arr. for full orchestra by Arthur Oldham)
          Ballets de Paris de Roland Petit - Princes Theatre, London, 26 April 1949
Choreography: Frederick Ashton
f.p.   (as the ballet 'Variations on a theme' arr. for small orchestra by James
          Bernard) Ballet Rambert, 21 June 1954
Choreography: John Cranko
f.Eur.p. (as the ballet 'House of Shadows') Bavarian State Opera and Ballet
          Company, Munich - February 1955
Choreography: Alan Carter
f.p.   (as the ballet 'Winter's Eve') American Ballet Theatre - New York, 1957

Choreography: Kenneth MacMillan
Decor: Nicholas Georgiadis
f.p.   (as the ballet 'Eaters of Darkness') Frankfurt State Opera Ballet - Frankfurt,
              29 January 1958
Choreography: Walter Gore
f.recs.   Boyd Neel Orchestra/Boyd Neel (rec. 1938) - *Decca (X) K 226-8 (78); Dutton
              Laboratories CDAX 8007 (CD)*
              Boyd Neel Orchestra/Boyd Neel (rec. 1952) - *London set (USA) LA 100 (78);
              Decca AK 2307-9 (78)*
              English Chamber Orchestra/Benjamin Britten - *London (USA) OS 26032, CS
              6671; Decca SXL 6316, SXL 6450 (and MC), 417 509-1 (and MC/CD)*
              (two-piano arrangement by Colin McPhee) Anthony Goldstone/Caroline
              Clemmow - *Olympia OCD 648 (CD)*
Pub: Boosey & Hawkes, 1938 (full score), 1951 (miniature score), 1998 (Orchestral
              Anthology, Vol.2)
also arr. for small orchestra by James Bernard (c.1954)
Instr: 1/1/1/1 - 1/1/0/0 - timp. perc. str.
Pub: Boosey & Hawkes
(*the theme is taken from the second of **Three Idylls** for string quartet of 1906. Britten
had also used the theme for an incomplete set of piano variations in 1932 q.v.)

Not even summer yet: song for high voice and piano (1937)
[Words: Peter Burra]
Written for Nell Moody (Nella Burra) to sing at her brother's memorial service - the
score is dated 9 October 1937
Dur: 2'
f.p.   Nella Burra (Sop.)/Gordon Thorne (Pno.) - Downe House, Berkshire,
              3 December 1937
f.Lon.p.   (possibly) Sophie Wyss (Sop.)/Benjamin Britten (Pno.) - Cowdray Hall,
              London, February 1938 (London Contemporary Music Centre Concert)
f.broad.p. Neil Mackie (Ten.)/John Blakely (Pno.) - Radio 3, 23 April 1985
f.mod.p.   Neil Mackie (Ten.)/Iain Burnside (Pno.) - Wigmore Hall, London,
              22 November 1983
f.rec.   Ian Bostridge (Ten.)/Graham Johnson (Pno.) - *Hyperion CDA 66823 (CD)*
Pub: Faber, 1994 (in 'The Red Cockatoo & Other Songs')

On This Island: five songs for high voice and piano Op.11 (1937)
[Words: W.H. Auden, from 'Look Stranger'
1. Let the florid music praise! (12 October 1937) 2. Now the leaves are falling fast
(27 May 1937) 3. Seascape (12 October 1937) 4. Nocturne: Now through night's
caressing grip (5 May 1937) 5. As it is, plenty (9 October 1937)]
Dedicated: 'To Christopher Isherwood' (No.3 is also inscribed 'For Kit Welford')
Dur: 12'30"
f.p.*   Sophie Wyss (Sop.)/Benjamin Britten (Pno.) - Concert Hall, Broadcasting
              House, London, 19 November 1937 (BBC Contemporary Music Recital)
f.recs.   (No.1) Peter Pears (Ten.)/Benjamin Britten (Pno.) - *London (USA) LL 1532
              (m), 5324 (m); Decca LW 5241 (m), ECS 545 (es)*
              (complete) Peter Pears (Ten.)/Benjamin Britten (Pno.) (broadcast from the
              Aldeburgh Festival, 18 June 1969) - *BBC REGL 417, BBCB 8015-2 (CD)*

Pub: Boosey & Hawkes, 1938, 1949 (No.4 only), 1977 (No.4 only, in 'A Heritage
            of 20th Century British Song', Vol.4)
(*Donald Mitchell points out in his book **Britten and Auden in the Thirties**, Pub. Faber
and Faber, that Peter Pears and Britten had given an earlier - private - performance of the
work on 15 October 1937 in the presence of Lennox Berkeley and Christopher
Isherwood. Other Auden settings from this period were probably included in a broadcast
recital of Britten songs given in Toronto for CBC in June 1939 - the following three songs
were probably intended to form part of a projected second Auden song cycle.)

To lie flat on the back: for high voice and piano (1937)
[Words: W.H. Auden]
Completed on 26 October 1937
f.p.   Neil Mackie (Ten.)/John Blakely (Pno.) - BBC Radio 3, 23 April 1985
f.conc.p.   above artists - Blythburgh Church, 27 October 1989
f.rec.   Ian Bostridge (Ten.)/Graham Johnson (Pno.) - *Hyperion CDA 66823 (CD)*
Pub: Faber, 1997 (in 'Fish in the Unruffled Lakes: Six Auden Settings')

Night covers up the rigid land: for high voice and piano (1937)
[Words: W.H. Auden (this text is dedicated to Britten)]
Score dated 27 October 1937
Dur: 2'30"
f.p.   Patricia Rozario (Sop.)/Graham Johnson (Pno.) - Wigmore Hall, London,
            22 November 1985
f.broad.p. Neil Mackie (Ten.)/John Blakely (Pno.) - Radio 3, 4 December 1986
            (pre-recorded, 18 November 1986)
f.rec.   Ian Bostridge (Ten.)/Graham Johnson (Pno.) - *Hyperion CDA 66823 (CD)*
Pub: Faber, 1997 (in 'Fish in the Unruffled Lakes: Six Auden Settings')

The sun shines down: for high voice and piano (1937)
[Words: W.H. Auden]
Dur: 2'
f.rec.   Philip Langridge (Ten.)/Steuart Bedford (Pno.) - *Collins Classics 14902 (CD)*
Pub: Faber, 1997 (in 'Fish in the Unruffled Lakes: Six Auden Settings')

Mont Juic: Suite of Catalan Dances for orchestra Op.12 (1937)
Written jointly with Lennox Berkeley* with whom Britten had visited the Mont Juic Park
in Barcelona during the 1936 ISCM Festival in company with Peter Burra. The work is
dedicated 'In memory of Peter Burra' who had died in an aeroplane crash near Reading
on 27 April 1937 - the score is dated 12 December 1937.
Dur: 12'
Instr: 2/2/2 + ten.sax/a.sax. (ad.lib)/2 - 4/2/3/1 - timp. perc.(2) hp. str.
f.p.   BBC Orchestra/Joseph Lewis - BBC, 8 January 1938 (studio performance)
f.conc.p.   BBC Symphony Orchestra/Sir Henry Wood - Queen's Hall, London,
            5 September 1939 (Promenade Concert)
f.rec.   London Philharmonic Orchestra/Sir Lennox Berkeley - *Musical Heritage
            Society (USA) MHS 1919; Lyrita SRCS 50, SRCD 226 (CD)*
Pub: Boosey & Hawkes, 1938 (full score), 1980 (study score)
(*There are four movements in the Suite - the first two are by Berkeley, the remaining
two by Britten - the third movement, a Lament, is subtitled 'Barcelona, July 1936')

Fish in the unruffled lakes: song for high voice and piano (1938, rev.1942-43)
[Words: W.H. Auden]
Composed between 15 and 16 January 1938
Dur: 3'
f.p.   Peter Pears (Ten.)/Benjamin Britten (Pno.) - Friends House, Euston Road,
              London, 28 February 1943
f.broad.p.   above artists - BBC Third Programme, 26 November 1947
f.recs.   Sylvia Eaves (Sop.)/Courtney Kenney (Pno.) - *Cameo Classics GOCLP 9020*
              Felicity Lott (Sop.)/Graham Johnson (Pno.) - *Chandos ABTD 1362 (MC),*
              CHAN 8722 (CD)
Pub: Boosey & Hawkes, 1947, 1972 and 1973, 1977 (version II, in 'A Heritage of
              20th Century British Song', Vol.3), 1997 (original version ed. Colin Matthews
              in 'Fish in the Unruffled Lakes: Six Auden Settings')

The Red Cockatoo: song for high voice and piano (1938)
[Words: Po Chü-i, trans. Arthur Waley*]
Score dated Peasenhall, Suffolk, 24 January 1938
Dur: 0'45"
f.p.   Lucy Shelton (Sop.)/Ian Brown (Pno.) - The Maltings, Snape, 17 June 1991
              (Aldeburgh Festival)
f.broad.p.   above first performance - Radio 3, 24 June 1991
f.rec.   Ian Bostridge (Ten.)/Graham Johnson (Pno.) - *Hyperion CDA 66823(CD)*
Pub: Faber, 1994 (in 'The Red Cockatoo & Other Songs')
(*Britten returned to translations by Waley in his **Songs from the Chinese** q.v.)

Tell me the Truth about Love: cabaret song for voice and piano (1938)
[Words: W.H. Auden]
Composed January 1938
Dur: 5'
[f.p.]   Hedli Anderson (Sop.)/Benjamin Britten (Pno.) - Hammersmith, West
              London, 18 January 1938 (at a 'farewell' party for Auden and Isherwood
              held at the home of the artist, Julian Trevelyan)
f.broad.p.   Hedli Anderson (Sop.)/Daphne Ibbott (Pno.) - Third Programme, 14 June 1949
f.rec.   Sarah Walker (Sop.)/Roger Vignoles (Pno.) - *Meridian E 77056,*
              CDE 84167 (CD)
Pub: Faber, 1980 ('Cabaret Songs')
also arr. for female voice and chamber ensemble by Daryl Runswick (1990)
Instr: Al.Sax. Tpt. Vn. Db. Pno. Drum kit
f.p.   Mary King (M/S)/Daryl Runswick All-Stars - Jubilee Hall, Aldeburgh,
              8 June 1990 (Aldeburgh Festival)
f.broad.p.   above performance - Radio 3, 8 July 1990
Pub: Faber

A Cradle Song* ('Sleep, beauty bright'): for soprano, contralto and piano (1938)
[Words: William Blake]
Written for Mary MacDougall and Anne Wood - the score is dated 8 March 1938
Dur: 3'
f.p.   Victoria Bell (Sop.)/Kathleen Roland (M/S)/Julian West (Pno.) -
              Britten-Pears School, Snape, 23 July 1994

Pub: Faber, 1994
(*a later setting appeared in **A Charm of Lullabies** q.v.)

Piano Concerto Op.13 (1938, rev.1945)
[1. Toccata 2. Waltz 3. Recitative and Aria 4. March]
Dedicated 'To Lennox Berkeley' - the score is dated 26 July 1938
Dur: 35'30"
Instr: 2/2/2/2 - 4/2/3/1 - timp. perc.(2) hp. str.
f.p.   Benjamin Britten/BBC Symphony Orchestra/Sir Henry Wood - Queen's Hall,
           London, 18 August 1938 (Promenade Concert)
f.Am.p.   Benjamin Britten/Illinois Symphony Orchestra/Albert Goldberg - Blackstone
           Theatre, Chicago, Illinois, 15 January 1940
f.mod.p.   Peter Donohoe/English Chamber Orchestra/Steuart Bedford - The Maltings,
           Snape, 13 June 1989 (Aldeburgh Festival)
f.rec.   Joanna MacGregor/English Chamber Orchestra/Steuart Bedford - *Collins
           1102-2 (CD) (and MC)*

The Concerto was revised in 1945, the original third movement (Recitative and Aria)
being replaced by an Impromptu - much of the material used was contemporary, with the
rest of the work being derived from the incidental music to **King Arthur**. (Walton later
used the theme from the Impromptu for his 1970 orchestral **Improvisations on an
Impromptu of Benjamin Britten** q.v.)

Dur: 33'
f.p.   Noel Mewton-Wood*/London Philharmonic Orchestra/Benjamin Britten -
           Cheltenham Town Hall, 2 July 1946 (Cheltenham Festival)
f.Lon.p.   Noel Mewton-Wood/London Symphony Orchestra/Basil Cameron - Royal
           Albert Hall, 2 August 1946 (Promenade Concert)
f.Am.p.   Jacques Abram/New York Philharmonic Orchestra/Leopold Stokowski -
           Carnegie Hall, New York, 24 November 1949
f.Russ. p. Sviatoslav Richter/London Symphony Orchestra/Benjamin Britten -
           Moscow/Leningrad, April 1971
f.Jap.p.   Michael Roll/BBC Symphony Orchestra/Sir Charles Groves - May 1975
           (during a British Council tour of Japan)
f.p.   (as a ballet) English National Ballet - Royal Festival Hall, London,
           17 June 1996
Choreography: Matthew Hart
f.recs.   Jacques Abram/Philharmonia Orchestra/Herbert Menges -
           HMV CLP 1118 (m)
           Sviatoslav Richter/English Chamber Orchestra/Benjamin Britten - *London
           (USA) CS 6723; Decca SXL 6512 (and MC), 417 308-1 (and MC/CD)*
Pub: Boosey & Hawkes, 1939 (arr. for two pianos by Brian Easdale), 1946 (rev.
           version), 1967 (full score)
(*the intended soloist was to have been Clifford Curzon)

Advance Democracy: for chorus (SSAATTBB) unaccompanied (1938)
[Words: Randall Swingler]
Commissioned by the London Co-operative Society - the score is dated
29 November 1938
Dur: 3'

f.p.   (probably) Workers' Music Association Choir/Alan Bush
f.broad.p.   BBC Chorus/Myer Fredman - BBC Music Programme, 30 December 1964
f.rec.   The Sixteen/Harry Christophers - *Collins 1343-2 (CD)*
Pub: Boosey & Hawkes, 1939

(Song Setting of a love poem by Stephen Spender) (c.1938-39)
f.p.   Peter Pears (Ten.) - at his London flat, January 1939.
(see Mitchell and Reed, **Letters from a Life**, pp.608-9)

Ballad of Heroes: for tenor (or soprano) solo, chorus and orchestra Op.14 (1939)
[Words: Randall Swingler and W.H. Auden 1. Funeral March 2. Scherzo (Dance of Death) 3. Recitative and Choral - Epilogue (Funeral March)]
Written specially for the Festival of 'Music for the People' in honour of those men of the British Battalion of the International Brigade who fell in the Spanish Civil War and dedicated 'To Montagu and Enid Slater' - the score is dated 29 March 1939
Dur: 15'
Instr: 3/2+ca./2+E flat cl./2+cbsn.- 4/2/3/1 - timp. perc.(2) hp. str. (+optional off-stage tpts. SD)
f.p.   Walter Widdop (Ten.)/Twelve Co-operative and Labour Choirs/London Symphony Orchestra/Constant Lambert - Queen's Hall, London, 5 April 1939 (Festival of 'Music for the People')
f.Eur.p.   Collegium Musicum Londonii/John Minchinton - Abbaye St Michel-de-Cuxa, July 1959 (Prades Festival)
f.mod.p.   Nigel Douglas (Ten.)/Festival Singers/Tavenham Hall School Choir/City of Birmingham Symphony Orchestra/Philip Ledger - The Maltings, Snape, 1 July 1973 (Aldeburgh Festival)
f.recs.   Robert Tear (Ten.)/City of Birmingham Symphony Chorus and Orchestra/Simon Rattle - *EMI CDS7 54270-2 (CD)*
             Martyn Hill (Ten.)/London Symphony Chorus and Orchestra/Richard Hickox - *Chandos DBTD 2032 (MC), CHAN 8983/4 (CD)*
Pub: Boosey & Hawkes, 1939 (vocal score), 1992 (study score)

Young Apollo:* for piano, string quartet and string orchestra Op.16 (1939)
[Chant - Fanfare - Chorale - Coda (these titles were later deleted by the composer)]
Commissioned by the Canadian Broadcasting Corporation, Toronto. 'Dedicated to Alexander Chuhaldin' - the score is dated 2 August 1939
Dur: 9'
f.p.   Benjamin Britten/CBC String Orchestra/Alexander Chuhaldin - CBC broadcast, Toronto, 27 August 1939
f.Am.p.   Benjamin Britten/CBS Orchestra/Bernard Herrmann - CBS broadcast, New York, 20 December 1939
f.Brit.p.   Michael Roll/English Chamber Orchestra/Steuart Bedford - The Maltings, Snape, 20 June 1979 (Aldeburgh Festival)
f.broad.p.   above Aldeburgh performance - 11 October 1979
f.p.   (as a ballet) Royal Ballet Company - Royal Opera House, Covent Garden, London, 17 November 1984
Choreography: David Bintley
f.rec.   Peter Donohoe/City of Birmingham Symphony Orchestra/Simon Rattle - *HMV ASD 4177 (and MC); EMI CDS7 54270-2 (CD)*

Pub: Faber, 1982
(*the title is derived from the last words of Keats's unfinished poem 'Hyperion')

A.M.D.G. (Ad majorem Dei gloriam):* seven settings of Gerard Manley Hopkins for SATB unaccompanied (1939)

[1. Prayer I 2. Rosa Mystica 3. God's Grandeur 4. Prayer II 5. O Deus, ego amo te
6. The Soldier 7. Heaven-Haven]
Written for the Round Table Singers - the work was composed between 5 and
30 August 1939

Dur: 17'
f.p.   (Excs.) Round Table Singers - possibly at Riverhead, New York,
            19 November 1939 (the intended première at the Aeolian Hall, London on 24
            November 1939 had been abandoned with the outbreak of war in Europe)
f.Brit.p.   (Nos.1, 2, 5 and 7) BBC Northern Singers/Stephen Wilkinson - Beccles
            Church, 18 June 1984 (Aldeburgh Festival)
f.p.   (complete) London Sinfonietta Voices/Terry Edwards - Purcell Room,
            London, 21 August 1984
f.broad.p. BBC Northern Singers/Stephen Wilkinson - Radio 3, 20 May 1985
            (pre-recorded, 7 October 1984)
f.rec.   London Sinfonietta Voices/Terry Edwards - *Virgin VC7 90728-1 (and MC)*
Pub: Faber, 1989
(*the opus number originally given to **A.M.D.G.**, Op.17, was later allocated to **Paul Bunyan** in the 1974 revision q.v.)

Calypso: cabaret song for voice and piano (1939)

[Words: W.H. Auden]
Dur: 2'
f.p.   Peter Pears (Ten.)/Benjamin Britten (Pno.) - Southold High School
            Auditorium, Long Island, New York, 14 December 1941
f.broad.p. Hedli Anderson (Sop.)/Daphne Ibbott (Pno.) - Third Programme, 14 June 1949
f.rec.   Sarah Walker (Sop.)/Roger Vignoles (Pno.) - *Meridian E 77056,*
            CDE 84167 (CD)
Pub: Faber, 1980 ('Cabaret Songs')
also arr. for female voice and chamber ensemble by Daryl Runswick (1990)
Instr: Al.Sax. Tpt. Vn. Db. Pno. Drum kit
f.p.   Mary King (M/S)/Daryl Runswick All-Stars - Jubilee Hall, Aldeburgh,
            8 June 1990 (Aldeburgh Festival)
f.broad.p. above performance - Radio 3, 8 July 1990
Pub: Faber

Violin Concerto Op.15 (1938-39, rev.1950, 1954 and 1965)

Dedicated 'To Henry Boys' - the score is dated Amityville, New York,
20 September 1939
Dur: 31'
Instr: 3/2/2/2 - 4/3/3/1 - timp. perc.(2) hp. str.
f.p.   Antonio Brosa/New York Philharmonic Orchestra/Sir John Barbirolli -
            Carnegie Hall, New York, 28 March 1940
f.Brit.p.   Thomas Matthews/London Philharmonic Orchestra/Basil Cameron -
            Queen's Hall, London, 6 April 1941

f.broad.p.   Thomas Matthews/BBC Orchestra/Clarence Raybould -
             Home Service, 28 April 1941
f.Eur.p.   Theo Olof/BBC Symphony Orchestra/Sir Adrian Boult - Kurhaus,
             Scheveningen, 26 June 1947
f.p.   (rev. version) Bronislav Gimpel/Royal Philharmonic Orchestra/Sir Thomas
             Beecham* - Royal Festival Hall, London, 12 December 1951
f.p.   (as a ballet) Royal Ballet Company - Royal Opera House, Covent Garden,
             London, 7 February 1996
Choreography: Matthew Hart
f.recs.   Nora Grumlikova/Prague Symphony Orchestra/Peter Maag -
             Supraphon SUA 50959
             Mark Lubotsky/English Chamber Orchestra/Benjamin Britten - *London (USA)*
             CS 6723; Decca SXL 6512 (and MC), 417 308-1 (and MC/CD)
Pub: Boosey & Hawkes, 1940 (arr. for violin and piano by the composer),
             1958 (rev. version, piano reduction), 1965 (full score)
(*Beecham had programmed the **Violin Concerto** and the **Four Sea Interludes** in a
concert as early as October 1945)

Les Illuminations: for high voice and string orchestra Op.18 (1939)
[Words: Arthur Rimbaud 1. Fanfare 2. Villes 3a. Phrase 3b. Antique
4. Royauté 5. Marine 6. Interlude 7. Being Beauteous 8. Parade   9. Départ]*
Dedicated 'For Sophie Wyss'. The work was composed between March and 25 October
1939. No.3b is dedicated to Wulff Scherchen ('K.H.W.S.') No.6 to Elizabeth Mayer
('E.M.') and No.7 to Peter Pears ('P.N.L.P.')
Dur: 21'
f.p.   (No.7 only) Sophie Wyss (Sop.)/Birmingham Philharmonic String
             Orchestra/Johan C. Hock - Queen's College Chambers Lecture Hall,
             Birmingham, 21 April 1939
f.p.   (No.5 only) Sophie Wyss (Sop.)/BBC Symphony Orchestra/Sir Henry Wood -
             Queen's Hall, London, 17 August 1939 (Promenade Concert)
f.p.   (complete) Sophie Wyss (Sop.)/Boyd Neel Orchestra/Boyd Neel - Aeolian
             Hall, London, 30 January 1940
f.broad.p.   (complete) Sophie Wyss (Sop.)/BBC Symphony Orchestra/Sir Adrian Boult -
             Home Service, 12 April 1940
f.Am.p.   Peter Pears (Ten.)/CBS Orchestra/Benjamin Britten - CBS Studios, New York,
             18 May 1941 (ISCM Festival and broadcast on the CBS network. The
             performance was recorded by Guild Recordings of New York - see f.recs.)
f.Brit.p.   Peter Pears (Ten.)/Walter Goehr Orchestra/Walter Goehr - Wigmore Hall,
             London, 30 January 1943
f.Austr.p.   Peggy Knibb (Sop.)/Boyd Neel Orchestra/Boyd Neel - Sydney
             Conservatorium, April/May 1947
f.p.   (as the ballet 'Les Illuminations') New York City Ballet - New York City
             Centre, 2 March 1950
Choreography: Frederick Ashton
Decor: Cecil Beaton
Principals: Nicholas Magallanes, Tanaquil LeClerq, Melissa Hayden,
             Robert Barnett (with Angelene Collins as the soprano soloist)
f.Lon.p.   (as the ballet) New York City Ballet - Royal Opera House, Covent Garden,
             London, 22 July 1950 (with Peter Pears as the tenor soloist)

f.Jap.p.   Peter Pears (Ten.)/Japanese Radio Symphony Orchestra/Benjamin Britten - Tokyo, 8 February 1956 (during their tour of the Far East)

f.recs.   Peter Pears (Ten.)/CBS Orchestra/Benjamin Britten - *NMC D030 (CD)* (CBS broadcast, 18 May 1941)

Maggie Teyte (Sop.)/John Ranck (Pno.) - *GHP 4003 (m)* (rec. 'live' in 1948)

Alice Mock (Sop.)/La Jolla Orchestra, California/Nicolai Sokoloff - *Alco (USA) Y-1211(m)*

Peter Pears (Ten.)/New Symphony Orchestra/Eugene Goossens (rec. 25 January 1954) - *Decca LXT 2941(m), ECM 507(m), ECS 507(es)*

Peter Pears/English Chamber Orchestra/Benjamin Britten - *London (USA) OS 26032, OS 26161; Decca SXL 6316, SXL 6449, 417 311-1 (and MC), 417 153-2 (CD), London 436 395-2 (CD)*

Jill Gomez (Sop.)/Endymion Ensemble/John Whitfield - *EMI CDC7 42952-2 (CD)*

Pub: Boosey & Hawkes, 1940 (full score), 1944 (vocal score by the composer), 1999 (Masterworks Library)

(*there are three discarded songs 'Aube', dated 5 July 1939, 'A une raison' and 'La cascade sonne' and an incomplete sketch entitled 'Un prince était vexé')

Canadian Carnival* (Kermesse Canadienne) Op.19 (1939)

Written at the initial request of Sir Robert Mayer - the score is dated 10 December 1939

Dur: 14'

Instr: 2/2/2/2 - 4/3(2)/3/1 - timp. perc.(2) hp. str.

f.p.   BBC Orchestra/Clarence Raybould - BBC Home Service, Bristol, 6 June 1940

f.conc.p. London Philharmonic Orchestra/Benjamin Britten - Cheltenham Town Hall, 13 June 1945 (Cheltenham Festival)

f.Lon.p. City of Birmingham Symphony Orchestra/Simon Rattle - Royal Festival Hall, 22 October 1982

f.rec.   City of Birmingham Symphony Orchestra/Simon Rattle - *HMV ASD 4177 (and MC); EMI CDS7 54270-2 (CD), CDM7 64440-2 (CD), HMV5 68334-2 (CD)*

Pub: Boosey & Hawkes, 1948 (full score), 1979 (study score)

(*Four French-Canadian folk songs 'Là-bas sur les montagnes!', 'Jardin d'amour', 'La perdriole' and 'Alouette' are quoted in the work)

Sinfonia da Requiem Op.20 (1939-40, rev.1941)*

[1. Lacrymosa 2. Dies irae 3. Requiem aeternam]

Commissioned from Japan through the British Council for a symphony to celebrate the 2,600th anniversary of the foundation of the Mikado Dynasty - the authorities rejected the work for its underlying Christian dogma but further discussion was halted by Japan's involvement in the Second World War - the Sinfonia da Requiem is dedicated 'In memory of my parents'.

Dur: 20'

Instr: 3+afl./2+ca./2+bcl.+a.sax./2+cbsn. - 6(4)/3/3/1 - timp. perc.(4) hp.(2) pno. str.

f.p.   New York Philharmonic Orchestra/Sir John Barbirolli - Carnegie Hall, New York, 29 March 1941 (An earlier première was scheduled for 27 May 1940 in Chicago with Albert Goldberg conducting. However the concert was cancelled for financial reasons, eventually taking place on 24 November 1941. The work was also performed in America by the Boston Symphony Orchestra

conducted by Serge Koussevitzky in Boston on 2 January 1942 and later that
year at the ISCM Festival held in Berkeley, California on 8 August 1942)

f.broad.p.   above artists - CBS, 30 March 1941 (the second performance - see f.recs.)

f.Brit.p.   London Philharmonic Orchestra/Basil Cameron - Royal Albert Hall, London,
             22 July 1942 (Promenade Concert)

f.Eur.p.   Vienna Philharmonic Orchestra/Sir Adrian Boult - Vienna, 23 June 1948

f.Russ.p.   Moscow/Leningrad - March 1963 (Festival of British Music)

f.p.   (as the ballet 'Dances of Albion' with **Serenade**) Royal Ballet Company, 1980
Choreography: Glen Tetley

f.recs.   New York Philharmonic Orchestra/Sir John Barbirolli - *NMC D030 (CD)*
             (recorded 30 March 1941 at the second performance)

             Danish State Radio Symphony Orchestra/Benjamin Britten - *London (USA) LL
             1123 (m); Decca LXT 2981 (m), ACL 314 (m), ECS 799 (es)*

             New Philharmonia Orchestra/Benjamin Britten - *London (USA) OS 25937, CS
             6852; Decca SXL 6175, SXL 6641, 417 312-1 (and MC); London 425 100-2
             (CD)*

             German South-West Radio Symphony Orchestra/Benjamin Britten - *Polydor
             0629 029 (CD)*

Pub: Boosey & Hawkes, 1942 (full score, US), 1944 (miniature score, UK),
             1998 (Orchestral Anthology, Vol.2)

(*discovery of the autograph score in Tokyo in 1987 made possible the first performance
of the original 1940 version given by Simon Rattle and the City of Birmingham
Symphony Orchestra in Symphony Hall, Birmingham on 2 February 1989 - this one
performance was given by permission of the Britten Estate)

Sonatina Romantica for piano (1940)
[1. Moderato 2. Nocturne 3. Burlesque 4. Toccata]
Dedicated 'For Dr. William B. Titley to play'. Dr Titley was an enthusiastic amateur
pianist and Director of the Long Island Home in Amityville, Long Island, USA.

Dur: 13'

f.p.   George Benjamin - Jubilee Hall, Aldeburgh, 16 June 1983 (Aldeburgh
            Festival)

f.broad.p. Anthony Goldstone - Radio 3, 19 June 1984 (pre-recorded 1 December 1983)

f.rec.   Stephen Hough - *Virgin VC7 91203-2 (CD) (and MC), VC7 59027-2 (CD)*

Pub: Faber, 1986 (Nos.1 and 2 only)

Diversions for piano (left hand) and orchestra Op.21 (1940, rev.1950 and 1953-54)
[Theme - Var. 1. Recitative 2. Romance 3. March 4. Arabesque 5. Chant
6. Nocturne 7. Badinerie 8. Burlesque 9a. Toccata I 9b. Toccata II
10. Adagio - Finale: Tarantella]
Written 'For Paul Wittgenstein' (who demanded exclusive performing rights for 15 years)
- the score is dated 24 August 1940

Dur: 30'

Instr: 2/2/2+a.sax./2+cbsn. - 4/2/3/1 - timp. perc.(3) hp. str.

f.priv.p.   Benjamin Britten - Bideford Pool, Maine, USA, 21 September 1940 (at a
            dinner party held at the house of the composer John Hausserman)

f.p.   Paul Wittgenstein/Philadelphia Orchestra/Eugène Ormandy - Academy of
            Music, Philadelphia, 16 January 1942

f.Brit.p.   Paul Wittgenstein/Bournemouth Municipal Orchestra/Trevor Harvey -
Bournemouth, 14 October 1950
f.Lon.p.   Paul Wittgenstein/London Symphony Orchestra/Sir Malcolm Sargent -
Royal Albert Hall, 29 October 1950
f.broad.p.   Ross Pratt/BBC Scottish Orchestra/Ian Whyte - Third Programme,
16 September 1955
f.recs.   (original version) Siegfried Rapp/Radio Symphony Orchestra of Berlin/Arthur
Rother - *Urania URLP 7101 (m)*
(rev. version) Julius Katchen/London Symphony Orchestra/Benjamin Britten -
*London (USA) LL 1123 (m); Decca LXT 2981 (m), ACL 314 (m), ECS 799
(es), 421 855-2 (CD)*
Pub: Boosey & Hawkes, 1941 (full score), 1955 (rev. version arr. for two pianos by
the composer), 1988 (miniature score)

Seven Sonnets of Michelangelo: for tenor and piano Op.22 (1940)
[Sonnet Nos. are: XVI, XXXI, XXX, LV, XXXVII, XXXII and XXIV, trans. Peter Pears
and Elizabeth Mayer]
Dedicated 'To Peter' (Pears), the work was composed between March and 30 October
1940
Dur: 15'30"
f.priv.p.   Peter Pears (Ten.)/Benjamin Britten (Pno.) - USA, October 1940 or 1941
f.pub.p.   above artists - Wigmore Hall, London, 23 September 1942 (Boosey & Hawkes
Concert)
f.broad.p.   above artists - Home Service, 20 July 1943 (and on the newly-launched Third
Programme, 18 November 1946)
f.Russ.p.   Peter Pears (Ten.)/Benjamin Britten (Pno.) - Moscow Conservatoire,
25 December 1966 (and repeated a few days later in Leningrad)
f.recs.   above artists (1941) - *NMC D030 (CD)* (a private recording made in New
York in early 1941 and preserved in the Britten archives)
above artists (rec. 20 November 1942) - *HMV B 9302 (78) and C 3312 (78),
RLS 748 (m); EMI CDC7 54605-2 (CD); Pearl GEMMCD 9177 (CD)*
above artists (1954) - *London (USA) LL 1204 (m), 5154 (m); Decca LXT 5095
(m), ECS 629 (es), 417 183-1 (and MC), 425 996-2 (CD)*
above artists (1966) - *Melodiya M10 46091 009* (a 'live' recording of the
Moscow concert)
Pub: Boosey & Hawkes, 1943

Introduction and Rondo alla Burlesca for two pianos Op.23 No.1 (1940)
Written in California for the British piano duo Bartlett and Robertson at whose home they
were staying*
Dur: 9'
f.p.   Ethel Bartlett/Rae Robertson - Town Hall, New York, 5 January 1941
f.Brit.p.   Clifford Curzon/Benjamin Britten - Arts Theatre, Cambridge, 25 April 1943
f.broad.p.   Clifford Curzon/Benjamin Britten - Home Service, 9 November 1943
f.Lon.p.   Clifford Curzon/Benjamin Britten - Wigmore Hall, 29 March 1944
f.recs.   Clifford Curzon/Benjamin Britten (rec. January 1944) - *London (USA) EDA
17 (78), T 5269 (78); Decca K 1117 (78); Pearl GEMMCD 9177 (CD)*
Sviatoslav Richter/Vassilli Lobanov - *Philips 420 157-2 (CD)*
Pub: Boosey & Hawkes, 1944

(*Michael Kennedy points out that Bartlett and Robertson 'had drawn Britten's music to the attention of their old friend Barbirolli - Ethel Bartlett had begun her career as Barbirolli's partner in cello recitals - and this had led to the first performance (both) of the **Violin Concerto** and **Sinfonia da Requiem** ... Barbirolli in later years was hurt that the composer had never acknowledged the help he had been given at this point of his career' - **Britten**, Michael Kennedy, J.M. Dent, rev. ed. 1993)

Paul Bunyan: operetta in two acts and a prologue Op.17* (1939-41, rev.1974-75)
[Libretto: W.H. Auden]
Dur: 114'
Instr: 2/1/2+bcl.+a.sax./1 - 2/2/2/1 - timp. perc.(2) hp. pno. gtr. str.
Alt.Instr: Two pianos and percussion (arr. by David Matthews)
f.p.   New York Schola Cantorum Chorus/Columbia Theatre Associates/Columbia
              University Department of Music/Hugh Ross - Brander Matthews Hall,
              Columbia University, New York, 5 May 1941 (there had been a preview for
              the League of Composers on 4 May 1941)
Producer: Milton Smith
Designer: John W. Love
Principals: Milton Warchoff, Bliss Woodward, Helen Marshall, William Hess,
              Mordecai Bauman
f.Brit.conc.p. (rev. version - extracts only) Heather Harper (Sop.)/Janet Baker (M/S)/Peter
              Pears (Ten.)/John Shirley-Quirk (Bar.) cond. Steuart Bedford - The Maltings,
              Snape, 23 June 1974 (Aldeburgh Festival - there had also been a preview of
              some of the extracts given by Peter Pears at the Royal Society of Arts,
              London, on 2 May 1974)
f.Brit.broad.p. (rev. version - extracts) above Aldeburgh performance - Radio 3,
              24 December 1974
f.Brit.p.   (rev. version - complete) BBC Northern Singers/BBC Northern Symphony
              Orchestra/Steuart Bedford - BBC Radio 3, 1 February 1976 (recorded
              April 1975)
Producers: Ernest Warburton and Charles Lefeaux
Principals: Russell Smythe, Neil Jenkins, Iris Saunders, Philip Doghan, Peter
              Pears, Norma Burrowes, George Hamilton IV
f.Brit.stage p. (rev. version) English Music Theatre Orchestra/Steuart Bedford -
              The Maltings, Snape, 4 June 1976 (Aldeburgh Festival)
Producer: Colin Graham
Principals: Russell Smythe, Paul Maxwell,Neil Jenkins, Iris Saunders, Donald
              Stephenson, Michael Bulman
Designer: Margaret Harris
f.Lon.p.   above artists - 1 September 1976
f.Eur.p.   above artists - Florence, Italy, May 1976 (Florence Festival)
f.rec.   soloists/Plymouth Music Series Choir and Orchestra/Philip Brunelle -
              Virgin VC7 90710-1 (and MC/CD), VCD7 59249-2 (and MC)
Pub: Faber, 1978 (vocal score by David Matthews), 1993 (full score)
(*the original opus number for the choral work **A.M.D.G.** q.v.)

Excs. Five Choruses for chorus and piano
[1. Prologue I (Since the birth of the earth) 2. Prologue II (Once in a while) 3. Blues
 4. Hymn 5. Litany]

Dur: 25'
Pub: Schirmer, 1978
Excs. Ballads for voice and piano or guitar
[1. The cold wind blew 2. The spring came and the summer and fall
3. So Helson smiled and Bunyan smiled]
Dur: 10'
f.p.   Wandsworth School Choir/Russell Burgess - The Maltings, Snape,
            10 June 1974 (Aldeburgh Festival)
Pub: Faber, 1978
Exc. 'Carry her over the water': partsong for unaccompanied chorus (SSATTBB), arr. by
Colin Matthews
Dur: 1'
f.rec.   Trinity College Choir, Cambridge/Richard Marlow - *Pearl SHE 593*
Pub: Faber, 1980
Excs. omitted from the 1974-75 revised score ed. Colin Matthews
[Lullaby of Dream Shadows. Inkslinger's Love Song]
Dur: 11'
f.rec.   soloists/London Philharmonic Choir/English Chamber Orchestra/
            Philip Brunelle - *Virgin VC5 45093-2(CD)*
Pub: Faber

Exc. 'Paul Bunyan' Overture for piano duet
Dur: 5'
f.rec.   Anthony Goldstone/Caroline Clemmow - *Olympia OCD 648 (CD)*
Exc. 'Paul Bunyan' Overture orch. Colin Matthews (1977)
Instr: 2/1/2+bcl./1 - 2/2/2/1 - timp. perc.(3) hp. (pno.) str.
f.p.   European Community Youth Orchestra/James Judd - Royal Albert Hall,
            London, 6 August 1978 (Promenade Concert)
f.broad.p. above artists - Radio 3, 5 December 1979
f.recs.   English Chamber Orchestra/Philip Brunelle - *Virgin VC5 45093-2 (CD)*
            London Symphony Orchestra/Steuart Bedford - *Collins 1102-2 (CD) (and MC)*
Pub: Faber, 1980 (full score)
Also transcribed for concert band by Charles Fussell
Pub: Studio Music, 1985; Hal Leonard (USA)

Exc.   'Blues' arr. for six-piece cabaret ensemble by Daryl Runswick (1990)
Dur: 4'45"
Instr: Cl./Sax. Tpt. Vn. Db. Pno.Drum kit
f.p.   Daryl Runswick All-Stars - Jubilee Hall, Aldeburgh, 8 June 1990
            (Aldeburgh Festival)
f.broad.p. above first performance - Radio 3, 8 July 1990
f.Lon.p.   Nash Ensemble - Barbican Hall, March 1993 (Britten-Rostropovich Festival,
            Foyer Concert)
f.rec.   Instrumental Ensemble - *Unicorn DKP 9138 (CD)*

Matinées musicales: second suite of five movements from Rossini Op.24 (1941)
[1. March 2. Nocturne 3. Waltz 4. Pantomime 5. Moto perpetuo]
Dedicated 'To Lincoln Kirstein' at whose request the suite was written.
Dur: 13'

Instr: 2/2/2/2 - 4(2)/2/3/1(0) - timp. perc.(2) hp. cel. (pno.) str.
f.p.   (with **Soirées musicales** as the ballet 'Divertimento') American Ballet
             Company cond. Emanuel Balaban - Teatro Municipal, Rio de Janeiro,
             27 June 1941 (on their South American tour)
Choreography: Georges Balanchine
f.Brit.p.   BBC Midland Light Orchestra/Rae Jenkins - BBC Midland broadcast,
             23 December 1942
f.Eur.p.   (with **Soirées musicales** as the ballet 'Fantaisie Italienne') Thèâtre de la
             Monnaie, Brussels, 1948
f.recs.   Boston Pops Orchestra/Arthur Fiedler - *Victor (USA) LM 1093(m)*
             Philharmonia Orchestra/Robert Irving - *HMV CLP 1172 (m); Bluebird (USA)*
             LBC 1078 (m); Capitol G 7105 (m)
             National Philharmonic Orchestra/Richard Bonynge - *Decca SXDL 7539 (and*
             MC); 410 139-2 (CD)
Pub: Boosey & Hawkes, 1943 (full score), 1965 (miniature score), 1997 (Orchestral
             Anthology, Vol.1)

String Quartet No.1 in D Op.25 (1941)

Commissioned by and dedicated to 'Mrs Elizabeth Sprague Coolidge' - with this work
Britten won the 1941 Elizabeth Sprague Coolidge Medal of the Library of Congress for
services to chamber music. The composition draft is dated 28 July 1941.
Dur: 26'
f.p.   Coolidge String Quartet - Belle Wilber Thorne Hall, Occidental College, Los
             Angeles, 21 September 1941 (there was a second performance in the Library
             of Congress, Washington D.C. given on 30 October 1941 - the quartet was
             first played in New York on 17 January 1944 in a programme which included
             the **String Quartet No.2** by Eugene Goossens q.v.)
f.Brit.p.   Griller Quartet - Wigmore Hall, London, 28 April 1943
f.broad.p.   Griller Quartet - Home Service, 30 May 1943
f.p.   (with **String Quartet No.2** as the ballet 'Ruins and Visions') - Jose Limon
             Ballet Company - New London, Connecticut, USA, 20 August 1953
Choreography: Jose Limon
f.Lon.p.   (as the ballet) above performers - Sadler's Wells Theatre, 1957
f.recs.   Galimir Quartet - *Esoteric (USA) ES 504 (m)*
             Allegri Quartet - *Decca SXL 6564*
             Alberni Quartet - *CRDC 4051 (MC), CRD 1051 (CD), CRD 3351 (CD)*
Pub: Boosey & Hawkes, 1942 (miniature score), 1945 (parts)

Mazurka Elegiaca:* for two pianos Op.23 No.2 (1941)

Written for the British piano duo Bartlett and Robertson and dedicated 'In memoriam I. J.
Paderewski' who had died on 29 June 1941.
Dur: 6'30"
f.p.   Ethel Bartlett/Rae Robertson - Town Hall, New York, 9 December 1941
f.Brit.p.   Clifford Curzon/Benjamin Britten - Arts Theatre, Cambridge, 25 April 1943
f.broad.p.   Clifford Curzon/Benjamin Britten - Home Service, 9 November 1943
f.Lon.p.   Clifford Curzon/Benjamin Britten - Wigmore Hall, 29 March 1944
f.recs.   Clifford Curzon/Benjamin Britten - *London (USA) EDA 17 (78); Decca*
             K1118 (78), 5BB 119-20 (es); Pearl GEMMCD 9177 (CD);
             Beulah IPD 14 (CD)

Sviatoslav Richter/Vassalli Lobanov - *Philips 420 157-2 (CD)*
Pub: Boosey & Hawkes, 1942 (US ed.), 1945 (UK ed.)
(*originally intended for publication in a memorial volume to Paderewski -
Britten's **Mazurka** was not included, however, as it was mistakenly written for
two rather than one piano)

An American Overture* (1941)
Composed for Artur Rodzinski, it was originally entitled 'Occasional Overture' - the
work was composed between 7 and 16 October 1941.
Dur: 10'
Instr: 3/3/3/3 - 4/3/3/1 - timp. perc.(2) hp.(2) cel.(pno.) str.
f.p.   City of Birmingham Symphony Orchestra/Simon Rattle - Birmingham Town
          Hall, 8 November 1983
f.Lon.p. above artists - Royal Festival Hall, 22 February 1984 (Royal Philharmonic
          Society Concert)
f.Eur.p. above artists - Berlin, 24 September 1984 (Berlin Festival)
f.rec.   City of Birmingham Symphony Orchestra/Simon Rattle - *EMI 270263-1 (and
          MC), CDC7 47343-2 (CD), CDS7 54270-2 (CD)*
Pub: Faber, 1985
(*the work was withdrawn and its opus number (27) allocated to **Hymn to St Cecilia** q.v.
- the manuscript had been housed at the New York Public Library and news of its
existence was communicated to the composer in 1972!)

Scottish Ballad* for two pianos and orchestra Op.26 (1941)
Written for Ethel Bartlett and Rae Robertson - the score is dated 27 October 1941
Dur: 13'
Instr: 2/2/2/2 + cbsn. - 4/2/3/1 - timp. perc.(2) hp. str.
f.p.   Ethel Bartlett/Rae Robertson/Cincinnati Symphony Orchestra/Eugene
          Goossens - Music Hall, Cincinnati, USA, 28 November 1941
f.broad.p. Clifford Curzon/Benjamin Britten/BBC Symphony Orchestra/Clarence
          Raybould - BBC European Service, 16 February 1943
f.Brit.p. Clifford Curzon/Benjamin Britten/London Philharmonic Orchestra/Basil
          Cameron - Royal Albert Hall, London, 10 July 1943 (Promenade Concert)
f.Eur.p. unnamed soloists/Netherlands Radio Orchestra/Sir Adrian Boult - Brussels,
          7 November 1945
f.p.   (with Arnold's **Scottish Dances** as the ballet 'Flowers of the Forest')
          Sadler's Wells Royal Ballet - Covent Garden, London, 1986 (and later on tour
          in the United States)
Choreography: David Bintley
f.rec.   Peter Donohoe/Philip Fowke/City of Birmingham Symphony Orchestra/Simon
          Rattle - *HMV ASD 4177 (and MC); EMI CDS7 54270-2 (CD)*
Pub: Boosey & Hawkes, 1946 (arr. for two pianos); 1969 (full score)
(*The work includes the Scottish psalm tune 'Dundee' and the folksongs 'Turn ye to me'
and 'Flowers of the forest')

What's in your mind?: for high voice and piano (1941)
[Words: W.H. Auden]
Dur: 2'
f.rec.   Philip Langridge (Ten.)/Steuart Bedford (Pno.) - *Collins Classics 14902 (CD)*

Pub: Boosey & Hawkes, 1997 (in 'Fish in the Unruffled Lakes: Six Auden Settings')

Underneath the abject willow:* for high voice and piano (1941)
[Words: W.H. Auden (text dedicated to Britten)]
Dur: 1'30"
f.rec.   Philip Langridge (Ten.)/Steuart Bedford (Pno.) - *Collins Classics 14902 (CD)*
Pub: Boosey & Hawkes, 1997 (in 'Fish in the Unruffled Lakes: Six Auden Settings')
(*there is another, incomplete, Auden setting from this period entitled 'O, what is the sound that so thrills the ear?')

Hymn to St Cecilia: for 5-part chorus (SSATB) with solos, unaccompanied Op.27 (1941-42, rev.1966)
[Words: W.H. Auden (which are dedicated to Britten)]
Dedicated 'To Elizabeth Mayer' - the work was completed on 2 April 1942
Dur: 12'
f.p.   BBC Singers/Leslie Woodgate - BBC, 22 November 1942 (St Cecilia's Day and the composer's birthday)
f.conc.p. above artists - Wigmore Hall, London, 28 November 1942
f.Eur.p. BBC Choral Society/Leslie Woodgate - Aachen, 15 July 1958
f.recs.   Fleet Street Choir/T.B. Lawrence - *Decca AK 1088-9 (78)*
           Chamber Chorus of Washington/Paul Calloway - *WCFM (USA) LP-11 (m)*
           London Symphony Chorus/George Malcolm - *Oiseau Lyre SOL 60037; London 425 153-4 (MC), 436 396-2 (CD)*
Pub: Boosey & Hawkes, 1942, 1967 (new ed.)

Clarinet Concerto (unfinished) (1941-42)
Commissioned by Benny Goodman, the concerto was originally designated as Op.28 (later allocated to **A Ceremony of Carols** q.v.) - the first, and only completed, movement was orchestrated by Colin Matthews in 1989.
Dur: 6'
Instr: 2/2/0+bcl./2 - 4/2/3/0 - timp. perc. hp. str.
f.p.   Michael Collins/Britten-Pears Orchestra/Tamás Vásáry - Barbican Hall, London, 7 March 1990
f.rec.   Thea King/English Chamber Orchestra/Barry Wordsworth - *Hyperion CDA 66634 (CD)*
Pub: Faber (as 'Movement for Clarinet and Orchestra')

Chorale Prelude in D - voluntary for organ (c.1942)

God, who created me - school anthem for mixed chorus and organ (c.1942)
[Words: Henry Charles Beeching]

Who is this in garments gory? - hymn tune (c.1942)

Wild with Passion: song for high voice and piano (1942)
[Words: Thomas Lovell Beddoes]

Both this, and the following Beddoes setting, were written on board the M.S. Axel
Johnson on Britten's return to England with Peter Pears in April 1942
Dur   2'30"
f.p.   Lucy Shelton (Sop.)/Ian Brown (Pno.) - Holy Trinity Church, Blythburgh,
           15 June 1992 (Aldeburgh Festival)
f.broad.p. above first performance - Radio 3, 8 July 1992
f.rec.   Ian Bostridge (Ten.)/Graham Johnson (Pno.) - *Hyperion CDA 66823 (CD)*
Pub: Faber, 1994 (in 'The Red Cockatoo & Other Songs')

If thou wilt ease my heart: song for high voice and piano (1942)
[Words: Thomas Lovell Beddoes]
Score dated 4 April 1942
Dur: 2'
f.p.   Lucy Shelton (Sop.)/Ian Brown (Pno.) - Holy Trinity Church, Blythburgh,
           15 June 1992 (Aldeburgh Festival)
f.broad.p. above first performance - Radio 3, 8 July 1992
f.rec.   Ian Bostridge (Ten.)/Graham Johnson (Pno.) - *Hyperion CDA 66823 (CD)*
Pub: Faber, 1994 (in 'The Red Cockatoo & Other Songs')

Cradle Song* ('Sleep, my darling, sleep'): song for high voice and piano (1942)
[Words: Louis MacNeice]
Possibly written for Hedli Anderson whom MacNeice had married in 1942
Dur: 3'
f.p.   Lucy Shelton (Sop.)/Ian Brown (Pno.) - Holy Trinity Church, Blythburgh,
           15 June 1992 (Aldeburgh Festival)
f.broad.p. above first performance - Radio 3, 8 July 1992
f.rec.   Ian Bostridge (Ten.)/Graham Johnson (Pno.) - *Hyperion CDA 66823 (CD)*
Pub: Faber, 1994 (in 'The Red Cockatoo & Other Songs')
(*there is also an unfinished setting of Louis MacNeice's 'Cradle Song for Eleanor' from
the same year)

A Ceremony of Carols: for treble voices and harp Op.28 (1942, rev. 1943)
[1. Procession 2. Wolcum Yole! (Anon.) 3. There is no rose (Anon.)
 4. (a) That yongë child (Anon.) (b) Balulalow (James, John and Robert Wedderburn)
 5. As Dew in Aprille (Anon.) 6. This little Babe (Robert Southwell)
 7. Interlude (for harp) 8. In Freezing Winter night (Robert Southwell)
 9. Spring Carol (William Cornish) 10. Deo gracias (Anon.) 11. Recession]
Written 'For Ursula Nettleship' (Pears and Britten shared her house in Cheyne Walk on
their return from America)
Dur: 23'
f.p.   Women's voices of the Fleet Street Choir/Gwendolen Mason (Hp.)/
           T.B. Lawrence - Norwich Castle, 5 December 1942
f.Lon.p.   above artists - National Gallery, 21 December 1942
f.broad.p. above artists - Home Service, 25 January 1943
f.p.   (rev. version) Morriston Boys' Choir/Maria Korchinska (Hp.)/Benjamin
           Britten - Wigmore Hall, London, 4 December 1943
f.broad.p. (rev. version) BBC Chorus/Sidonie Goossens (Hp.)/Leslie Woodgate -
           Home Service, 24 December 1943

f.Eur.p.   Copenhagen Boys' Choir*/Enid Simon (Hp.)/Benjamin Britten - Copenhagen, Denmark, September 1953
f.recs.   Morrison Boys' Choir/Maria Korchinska (Hp.)/Ivor Sims - *Decca set (USA) EDA 86; Decca AK 1155-7 (78); London (USA) LPS 57 (m); Pearl GEM 0002 (CD); Beulah IPD 14 (CD)*
            Boys of Washington Cathedral Choir/Paul Calloway - *WCFM (USA) LP-11(m)*
            above (Copenhagen) performers - *London (USA) LD 9102 (m), LL 1336 (m), CM 9146 (m); Decca LW 5070 (m), ECS 507 (es), London 436 394-2 (CD)*
Pub: Boosey & Hawkes, 1943 (score), 1946 (Nos.2, 3, 4b, 5, 6 and 9), 1949 (No.8), 1954 (No.10), 1970 (rev. ed.), 1994 (new ed.)
(*Britten had conducted this choir in the **Ceremony of Carols** at the 1952 Aldeburgh Festival)

arr. for SATB chorus and harp (or piano) by Julius Harrison (1948)
Pub: Boosey & Hawkes, 1948 (Nos.2, 3, 4b, 6, 8 and 10), 1955 (complete), 1994 (new edition)
f.doc.p.   Hampstead Parish Church Choir/Martindale Sidwell with Gwendolen Mason (Hp.) - Royal Festival Hall, London, 19 December 1956
No.6 also arr. for piano solo by Christopher Norton
Pub: Boosey & Hawkes, 1998 (in 'Twentieth Century Classics', Vol.2)

Prelude and Fugue for 18-part string orchestra Op.29 (1943)
Commissioned by and dedicated 'To Boyd Neel and his orchestra, on the occasion of their 10th birthday, 23 June 1943'
Dur: 8'30"
Instr: 10 Vn. 3 Va. 3 Vc. 2 Db.
f.p.   Boyd Neel Orchestra/Boyd Neel - Wigmore Hall, London, 23 June 1943
f.broad.p. Boyd Neel Orchestra/Benjamin Britten - Third Programme, 21 April 1948
f.recs.   New Symphony Orchestra/Eugene Goossens (rec. 27 January 1954) - *Decca (not issued)*
            Royal Philharmonic Orchestra/Norman del Mar - *Argo ZRG 754*
            English Chamber Orchestra/Benjamin Britten - *Decca SXL 6847 (and MC), 425 160-2 (CD), 448 569-2 (CD)*
Pub: Boosey & Hawkes, 1951 (full score), 1981 (study score)

Rejoice in the Lamb: festival cantata for chorus (SATB) with treble, alto, tenor and bass solos, and organ Op.30 (1943)
[Words: Christopher Smart]
Written 'For the Rev.Walter Hussey and the choir of St Matthew's Church, Northampton, on the occasion of the 50th anniversary of the consecration of their church, 21 September 1943' - the score is dated 17 July 1943. (Tippett's **Fanfare No.1** for brass immediately preceded the cantata's first performance q.v.)
Dur: 16'
f.p.   Choir of St Matthew's Church/Benjamin Britten with Charles Barker (org.) - St Matthew's Church, Northampton, 21 September 1943
f.broad.p. above artists - Home Service, 31 October 1943
f.recs.   Washington Presbyterian Church Choir/Theodore Schaefer - *WCFM (USA) LP-4 (m)*
            Purcell Singers/Benjamin Britten - *London (USA) 5398 (m);*

Decca LXT 5416 (m), ECS 628 (es), 425 714-2 (CD)
Pub: Boosey & Hawkes, 1943 (vocal score), 1964 (new ed.)
arr. for chorus and orchestra by Imogen Holst (1952)
Instr: 1/1/1/1 - 1/0/0/0 - timp. perc. org. str.
f.p.   Aldeburgh Festival Choir & Orchestra/Imogen Holst with Ralph Downes
              (org.) - Aldeburgh Parish Church, 20 June 1952 (Aldeburgh Festival)
f.Lon.p.   London Bach Society/Riddick Orchestra/Paul Steinitz -
              Church of St Bartholomew the Great, Smithfield, 17 June 1953
Pub: Boosey & Hawkes
arr. for SSAA chorus and organ by Edmund Walters
f.p.   I.M. Marsh College Choir/Edmund Walters with Brian Hodge (org.) -
              Mossley Hill Church, Liverpool, 3 July 1966
f.broad.p.   above first performance - Third Programme, 19 December 1966
Pub: Boosey & Hawkes, 1973

Serenade for tenor, horn and strings Op.31 (1943)

[Prologue (Horn solo) 1. Pastoral (Charles Cotton) 2. Nocturne (Alfred, Lord
Tennyson) 3. Elegy (William Blake) 4. Dirge (Anon.) 5. Hymn (Ben Jonson)
6. Sonnet (John Keats)   Epilogue (Horn solo)]
Dedicated 'To E.S.-W.', Edward Sackville-West, with whom Britten had recently
collaborated on the radio play 'The Rescue' q.v.
Dur: 24'
f.p.   Peter Pears (Ten.)/Dennis Brain (Hn.)/String Orchestra/Walter Goehr -
              Wigmore Hall, London, 15 October 1943
f.broad.p.   Peter Pears (Ten.)/Dennis Brain (Hn.)/Boyd Neel Orchestra/Boyd Neel -
              Home Service, 20 April 1944
f.Eur.p.   Peter Pears (Ten.)/Collegium Musicum, Zurich/Benjamin Britten - Zurich,
              Switzerland, January 1947
f.Russ.p.   Moscow/Leningrad, March 1963 (Festival of British Music)
f.p.   (with **Sinfonia da Requiem** as the ballet 'Dances of Albion') - Royal Ballet
              Company, 1980
Choreography:Glen Tetley
f.recs.   Peter Pears/Dennis Brain/Boyd Neel Orchestra/Benjamin Britten (rec. 1944)
              *London (USA) EDA 7 (78); Decca AK 1151-53 (78), ECM 814 (m), 417 183
              (and MC), 425 996-2 (CD)*
              Peter Pears/Dennis Brain/New Symphony Orchestra/Eugene Goossens -
              (rec. November 1953) - *Decca LXT 2941 (m), ECM 507 (m), ECS 507 (es)*
              Peter Pears/Barry Tuckwell/London Symphony Orchestra/Benjamin Britten
              *London (USA) CS 6398, OS 26161; Decca SXL 6110, SXL 6449, 417 311-1
              (and MC), 417 153-2 (CD), London 436 395-2 (CD)*
Pub: Boosey & Hawkes, 1944 (also arr. for tenor, horn and piano), 1999
              (Masterworks Library)

There is a discarded song 'Now sleeps the crimson petal'(another Tennyson setting)
which has now been performed and published (ed. Colin Matthews) - the score was
completed on 22 March 1943
Dur: 3'

f.p.   Neil Mackie (Ten.)/Alan Civil (Hn.)/English Chamber Orchestra/Steuart
            Bedford - Friends House, London, 3 April 1987 (Peter Pears Memorial
            Concert)
f.tel.p.   Neil Mackie (Ten.)/Michael Thompson (Hn.)/Scottish Chamber
            Orchestra/Steuart Bedford - BBC2 Television, 28 February 1988
f.rec.   Neil Mackie (Ten.)/Barry Tuckwell (Hn.)/Scottish Chamber Orchestra/Steuart
            Bedford - *EMI HMV5 68334-2 (CD), CDC7 49480-2(CD)*
Pub: Boosey & Hawkes, 1989 (also arr. for tenor, horn and piano), 1999
            (Masterworks Library)

The Ballad of Little Musgrave and Lady Barnard: for male voices and piano (1943)

[Words: Anon.]
Written 'For Richard Wood* and the musicians of Oflag VIIb - Germany - 1943' - the
score is dated 13 December 1943
Dur: 9'
f.p.   Chorus of Prisoners of War/Richard Wood with Barrie Grayson and Fred
            Henson (pianos) - Eichstätt P.O.W. Camp, Germany, 20 February 1944
f.Brit.p.   Singers in Consort/Richard Wood - Wigmore Hall, London, 7 March 1951
f.broad.p. above artists - Third Programme, 19 June 1958
f.rec.   Elizabethan Singers/Louis Halsey, with Wilfrid Parry (Pno.) - *Argo ZRG 5424*
Pub: Boosey & Hawkes, 1952
(*Lieutenant Richard Wood - later director of the Singers in Consort - was a
prisoner-of-war during the winter of 1942-43 in Camp Oflag VIIb. As a direct result of
hearing a recording of the **Michelangelo Sonnets** the Ballad was 'commissioned'.
Despite initial problems with censorship and fears that the music itself may have been a
coded message, the manuscript was allowed through thanks to the efforts of the British
Red Cross.)

Cadenzas to Haydn's Harpsichord Concerto in D, Hoboken XVIII/11 (1943-44?)

Written for Lucille Wallace (wife of the pianist, Clifford Curzon) to play at a Henry
Wood Promenade Concert

Festival Te Deum for treble solo, chorus (SATB) and organ Op.32 (1944)

'Written for the Centenary Festival of St Mark's, Swindon' - the score is dated 8-9
November 1944
Dur: 5'
f.p.   Choir of St Mark's Church, Swindon/ J.J. Gale with G.W. Curnow (org.) -
            St Mark's Church, Swindon, 24 April 1945
f.broad.p. Elizabethan Singers/Louis Halsey - Third Programme, 29 July 1961
            (pre-recorded, 4 July 1961 at Holy Trinity Church, Dockhead)
f.rec.   Choir of St John's College, Cambridge/George Guest - *Argo RG 340 (m), ZRG
            5340, ZK 19, 430 097-2 (CD)*
Pub: Boosey & Hawkes, 1945

A Shepherd's Carol:* for chorus (SATB) unaccompanied (1944)

[Words: W.H. Auden]
Composed between 8 and 11 November 1944
Dur: 3'
f.p.   BBC Singers/Leslie Woodgate - BBC Home Service, 24 December 1944

f.conc.p.   Purcell Singers/Imogen Holst - Grosvenor Chapel, South Audley Street,
             London, 14 December 1961
f.recs.   Wilbye Consort/Peter Pears - *Decca SXL 6847*
             Elizabethan Singers/Louis Halsey - *Argo ZRG 5424*
             Westminster Abbey Choir - *DGG 410 590-1 (and MC/CD)*
Pub: Novello, 1962 (and in 'The Musical Times'), 1963 (in 'Sing Nowell')
(*see also Music for Radio)

Chorale after an Old French Carol:* for unaccompanied chorus (SSAATTBB) (1944)

[Words: W.H. Auden]
Score dated 15 November 1944
Dur: 4'
f.p.   BBC Singers/Leslie Woodgate - BBC Home Service, 24 December 1944
f.conc.p. Purcell Singers/Imogen Holst - Grosvenor Chapel, South Audley Street,
           London, 14 December 1961
f.rec.   Elizabethan Singers/Louis Halsey - *Argo ZRG 5424*
Pub: Faber, 1992
(*see also Music for Radio)

Peter Grimes: opera in three acts and a prologue Op.33 (1944-45)

[Libretto: Montagu Slater from a poem by George Crabbe]
Written at the request of Serge Koussevitzky and the Koussevitzky Music Foundation for
performance at the Berkshire Festival, Massachusetts - the score is dated 10 February
1945 and inscribed 'For the Koussevitzky Music Foundation, dedicated to the memory of
Natalie Koussevitzky'
Dur: 147'
Instr: 2/2/2/2+cbsn. - 4/3/3/1 - timp. perc.(2) cel. hp. str. (+ off stage organ, bells,
           tuba and stage band: 2 Cl. Perc. Vn. Db. Pno.)
f.p.   Sadler's Wells Opera Company cond. Reginald Goodall - Sadler's Wells
           Theatre*, London, 7 June 1945 (a concert introduction with Eric Crozier
           narrating the story accompanied by Britten was given at the Wigmore Hall
           on 31 May 1945)
Producer: Eric Crozier
Scenery and costumes: Kenneth Green
Principals: Peter Pears, Joan Cross, Owen Brannigan, Edith Coates, Roderick Jones
f.broad.p. above first performance - Home Service, 17 July 1945 (some extracts had
           been broadcast earlier on 15 July 1945 with Peter Pears and Joan Cross
           accompanied by the composer)
f.recs.   (excs.) Soloists/Royal Opera House Chorus and Orchestra/Reginald Goodall
           (rec. 1948) - *EMI CMS7 64727-2 (CD)*
           Soloists/Royal Opera House Chorus & Orchestra/Benjamin Britten - *London
           (USA) 1305; Decca SXL 2150-2 (Excs.) SXL 2189, K71K33 (MC), 414 577-2
           (CD)*
           Royal Opera House Production cond. Colin Davis - *Castle Vision CVI 2015(V)*
Pub: Boosey & Hawkes, 1945 (vocal score by Erwin Stein), 1963 (study score),
           1967 (vocal score 2nd ed.)
(*the opera was first produced at the Royal Opera House, Covent Garden on 6 November
1947 conducted by Karl Rankl and produced by Tyrone Guthrie)

Other performances:
f.Eur.p.   cond. Herbert Sandberg - Kungliga Teatern, Stockholm, 21 March 1946
Principals: Elisabeth(?) Sundström, Set Svanholm, Sigurd Björling
f.Am.p.   cond. Leonard Bernstein - Berkshire Music Centre, Tanglewood, Lenox,
            Massachusetts - 6 August 1946 (Tanglewood Festival* - the New York
            première took place at the Metropolitan Opera House in March 1948 with
            Emil Cooper conducting)
Producer: Eric Crozier
Principals: Richard Manning, James Pease, William Horne
f.Austr.p. Sydney Conservatorium - 8 March 1947 (concert performance broadcast)
f.Can.p.   Toronto - CBC Broadcast, 27 February 1952 (rec. October/November 1949)
f.Russ.conc.p. Leningrad Radio Chorus/Leningrad Philharmonic Orchestra/Dzhemal
            Dalgat - Leningrad Conservatorium, March 1964
f.Russ.st.p.Kirov Theatre, Leningrad, 20 March 1964
f.S.Am.p.   Rio de Janeiro, October 1967
f.tel.p.   cond. Benjamin Britten - BBC TV, 2 November 1969 (rec. February 1969)
Producer: John Culshaw
Principals: Peter Pears, Heather Harper
(*the fiftieth anniversary of the American premiere was celebrated with three
performances conducted by Seiji Ozawa at the Tanglewood Festival between 18 and 30
July 1997 - the producer was David Kneuss)

Excs. from the above
(i)   Four Sea Interludes Op.33a
           [1. Dawn 2. Sunday Morning 3. Moonlight 4. Storm]
           Dur: 16'
           Instr: 2/2/2/2+cbsn. - 4/3/3/1 - timp. perc.(2) hp. str.
           f.conc.p.* London Philharmonic Orchestra/Benjamin Britten -
                      Cheltenham Town'Hall, 13 June 1945 (Cheltenham Festival)
           f.Lon.conc.p. (with Passacaglia Op.33b) BBC Symphony Orchestra/Sir
                      Adrian Boult - Royal Albert Hall, London, 29 August 1945
                      (Promenade Concert)
           f.broad.p. BBC Symphony Orchestra/Sir Adrian Boult - Home Service,
                      30 September 1945
           f.Eur.p.   Czech Philharmonic Orchestra/Sir Adrian Boult - Prague, 23 May
                      1946 (Prague Festival)
           f.Am.p.   Cincinnati Symphony Orchestra/Eugene Goossens - 1946-47
           f.Russ.p. Moscow/Leningrad, March 1963 (Festival of British Music)
           f.recs.   (with Passacaglia) Concertgebouw Orchestra/Eduard van Beinum -
                      London set (USA) LA 201 (78); Decca AK 1702-4 (78);
                      440 063-2DM (CD)
                      (with Passacaglia) Orchestra of the Royal Opera House, Covent
                      Garden/Benjamin Britten - *London (USA) CS 6179; Decca SXL
                      2189, London 425 659-2 (CD) (and MC), 436 990-2(CD) (No.2)*
           Pub: Boosey & Hawkes, 1945, 1998 (Orchestral Anthology, Vol.2)
           (*Britten had hoped to have had these Interludes ready for the 1944
           Promenade Concerts - Arthur Jacobs: **Henry J. Wood, Maker of the Proms**)
(ii)   Passacaglia Op.33b (edited for concert performance)
           Dur: 7'

	Instr:	2/2/2/2+cbsn. - 4/3/3/1 - timp. perc.(2) hp. cel. str.
	f.p.	see above London performance (due to lack of rehearsal time the Passacaglia was not included in the Cheltenham Festival performance)
	f.recs.	see (i)
Pub:		Boosey & Hawkes, 1945, 1998 (Orchestral Anthology, Vol.2)
(iii)		Church Scene (Ellen's Aria): for soprano and piano (or orchestra)
	Dur:	3'30"
	Instr:	2/2/2/2 - 2/2/0/0 - timp. perc. hp. org. str.
	Pub:	Boosey & Hawkes, 1945
(iv)		Embroidery Aria: for soprano and piano (or orchestra)
	Dur:	4'
	Instr:	2/1+ca./0/2+cbsn. - 4/3/3/1 - timp. perc. hp. str.
(v)		Peter's Dreams: for tenor and piano (or orchestra)
	Dur:	3'
	Instr:	2/2/2/0 - 2/2/1/0 - hp. str.
(iv)		Old Joe has gone fishing: round for chorus (SATB) and piano
	Dur:	2'
	Pub:	Boosey & Hawkes, 1947 (US), 1948 (UK)
(v)		Song of the Fishermen: Working chorus for chorus (SATB) and piano
	Dur:	3'30"
	Pub:	Boosey & Hawkes, 1947 (US), 1948 (UK)

The Young Person's Guide to the Orchestra: variations and fugue on a theme of Henry Purcell, for speaker and orchestra, or orchestra alone Op.34* (1945)
[Words: Eric Crozier]
'This work is affectionately dedicated to the children of John and Jean Maud: Humphrey, Pamela, Caroline and Virginia, for their edification and entertainment.'
The score is dated 31 December 1945.

Dur:	17' (19' with narration)
Instr:	2+picc./2/2/2 - 4/2/3/1 - timp. perc.(3) hp. str.
f.p.	Liverpool Philharmonic Orchestra/Sir Malcolm Sargent - Philharmonic Hall, Liverpool, 15 October 1946
f.Lon.p.	London Symphony Orchestra/Sir Malcolm Sargent - Empire Theatre, Leicester Square, 29 November 1946 (on the soundtrack of the film 'The Instruments of the Orchestra' q.v.)
f.Lon.conc.p.	Orchestra/Sir Malcolm Sargent - Royal Albert Hall, 6 January 1947 (Promenade Concert - winter series)
f.Am.p.	Philadelphia Orchestra/Eugene Ormandy - Philadelphia, 13 December 1947
f.Eur.p.	Collegium Musicum, Zurich/Benjamin Britten - Kleiner Tonhallesaal, Zurich, Switzerland, 30 January 1948
f.SA.p.	Johannesburg City Orchestra/Sir Malcolm Sargent - City Hall, Johannesburg, 1948
f.p.	(as the ballet 'Oui ou Non?') Association des Amis de la Danse - Théâtre National Populaire du Palais de Chaillot, Paris, June 1949
f.S.Am.p.	Colón Orchestra/Sir Malcolm Sargent - Teatro Colón, Buenos Aires, May 1950

f.Russ.p.   Royal Philharmonic Orchestra/Sir Malcolm Sargent - Great Hall of the
Moscow Conservatoire, February 1963 (on a tour taking in Leningrad, Kiev
and Moscow)

f.Am.p.   (as the ballet 'Fanfare') New York City Ballet - New York, 2 June 1953
(the Coronation Day of Queen Elizabeth for whom this ballet performance
was an American tribute)

Choreography: Jerome Robbins

Scenery and costumes: Irene Sharaff

Principals: Yvonne Mounsey, Todd Bolender

f.Brit.p.   (as the ballet 'Variations on a theme of Purcell') Sadler's Wells Ballet - Royal
Opera House, Covent Garden, London, 6 January 1955

Choreography: Frederick Ashton

Scenery and costumes: Peter Snow

Principals: Elaine Fifield, Nadia Nerina, Jennifer Jackson, Alexander Grant

f.recs.   London Symphony Orchestra/Sir Malcolm Sargent - *Beulah 1PD 13 (CD)*
Liverpool Philharmonic Orchestra/Sir Malcolm Sargent - *Columbia (USA)
72228-30 (78), ML 4197 (m); Columbia DX 1307-9 (78)*
London Symphony Orchestra/Benjamin Britten - *London (USA) CS 6398, CS
6671; Decca SXL 6110, SXL 6450 (and MC), 417 509-1 (and MC/CD),
London 425 659-2 (CD) (and MC), 436 928-2(CD) (and MC), 436 990-2 (CD)
(and MC)*

Pub: Boosey & Hawkes, 1947, 1997 (Orchestral Anthology, Vol.1)

Theme arr. for piano solo by Christopher Norton

Pub: Boosey & Hawkes, 1989 (in 'Twentieth Century Classics', Vol.1)

Theme arr. for piano duet by Roger Brison

Pub: Boosey & Hawkes, 1990 (in 'Twentieth Century Classics for Piano Duet',
Vol.1)

(*the theme is taken from Purcell's incidental music to the play 'Abdelazar' or 'The
Moor's Revenge')

Birthday Song for Erwin: song for high voice and piano (1945)

[Words: Ronald Duncan]

Dur: 1'30"

f.priv.p.   Peter Pears (Ten.)/Benjamin Britten (Pno.) - at Erwin Stein's sixtieth birthday
party, 7 November 1945

f.pub.p.   Christopher Hobkirk (Ten.)/Rosalind Jones (Pno.) - Royal College of Music,
London, 22 November 1988

Pub: Faber, 1994 (in 'The Red Cockatoo & Other Songs')

Themes (for a Prelude and Fugue) for organ improvisation (1945)

Written at the request of John Lowe (of the BBC) for a broadcast by Marcel Dupré.
Britten had fulfilled a similar request for the blind French organist André Marchal in
1936 q.v.

f.p.   Marcel Dupré - BBC Home Service, 24 July 1945 (from St Mark's, North
Audley Street, London)

Pub: Boosey & Hawkes, 1945 (in *Tempo*, 15)

The Holy Sonnets of John Donne:* for high voice and piano Op.35 (1945)

[1. Oh my blacke Soule! (2 August 1945) 2. Batter my heart (6 August 1945)

3. Oh might those sighes and teares (3 August 1945)
4. Oh, to vex me (7 August 1945) 5. What if this present (14 August 1945)
6. Since she whom I loved (8 August 1945)
7. At the round Earth's imagined corners (8 August 1945)
8. Thou has made me (9 August 1945) 9. Death, be not proud (19 August 1945)]
Written 'For Peter' (Pears), shortly after Britten had returned from a concert tour with
Yehudi Menuhin during which they had played to survivors of the Nazi concentration
camps.

Dur:	26'
f.p.	Peter Pears (Ten.)/Benjamin Britten (Pno.) - Wigmore Hall, London, 22 November 1945 (at a concert commemorating the 250th anniversary of Purcell's death)
f.broad.p.	above artists - Home Service, 1 September 1946
f.recs.	above artists (1947) - *HMV DB 6689-91 (78), RLS 748 (m), EMI CDC7 54605-2 (CD)*
	above artists (1967) - *London (USA) OS 26099; Decca SXL 6391, 417 310-1 (and MC), London 417 428-2 (CD)*
Pub:	Boosey & Hawkes, 1947 (No.6 also published separately in 'A Heritage of 20th Century British Song', Vol.4, 1977)

(*there is also an Epilogue, 'Perchance he for whom the bell tolls be so ill', dated 15
August 1945, which was later discarded)

String Quartet No.2 in C Op.36 (1945)
Written to commemorate the 250th anniversary of Purcell's death with the dedication
'For Mrs J.L. Behrend' - the score is dated 14 October 1945. The work was first
performed on the exact anniversary of Purcell's death.

Dur:	31'
f.p.	Zorian String Quartet - Wigmore Hall, London, 21 November 1945
f.broad.p.	Zorian String Quartet - Home Service, 11 March 1946
f.p.	(with **String Quartet No.1** as the ballet 'Ruins and Visions') Jose Limon Ballet Company - New London, Connecticut, USA, 20 August 1953
Choreography:	Jose Limon
f.Lon.p.	(as the ballet) above performers - Sadler's Wells, 1957
f.recs.	Zorian String Quartet - *HMV C 3536-9 (78)*
	Amadeus Quartet - *London (USA) CS 7116; Decca SXL 6893, 425 715-2 (CD)*
Pub:	Boosey & Hawkes, 1946

The Rape of Lucretia: opera in two acts Op.37 (1946, rev.1947)
[Libretto: Ronald Duncan after André Obey]
'Dedicated to Erwin Stein' - the work was completed on 3 May 1946

Dur:	107'
Instr:	Fl. Ob. Cl. Bsn. Hn. Perc. Hp. Pno. Vn. Vn. Va. Vc. Db.
f.p.	Glyndebourne Festival Opera cond. Ernest Ansermet - Glyndebourne Opera House, Sussex, 12 July 1946 (and by the second cast on 16 July 1946 conducted by Reginald Goodall)
Producer:	Eric Crozier
Designer:	John Piper
Principals:	Peter Pears, Joan Cross, Owen Brannigan, Kathleen Ferrier, Anna

Pollak (and a second cast including Aksel Schiøtz, Flora Nielsen, Norman Walker, Nancy Evans and Catherine Lawson)

f.recs.   (excs.) Soloists/English Opera Group Orchestra/Hans Oppenheim - *Educ. Media (USA) IGI 369* ('live' Holland Festival broadcast on Dutch Radio, 4 October 1946)

(excs.) Soloists/English Opera Group Orchestra/Reginald Goodall - *Victor set (USA) M 1288 (78); HMV C 3699-3706 (78), RLS 290023 (and MC); EMI CMS7 64727-2 (CD)*

(complete) Soloists/English Chamber Orchestra/Benjamin Britten - *London (USA) OSA 1288; Decca SET 492-3, 425 666-2 (CD)*

English National Opera Production cond. Lionel Friend - *Virgin & Vision VVD 617 (V)*

Pub: Boosey & Hawkes, 1946 (vocal score by Henry Boys), 1947 (rev. version vocal score), 1949 (full score), 1958 (full score 2nd ed.)

Other performances:

f.Lon.p.   Glyndebourne Productions cond. Reginald Goodall - Sadler's Wells Theatre, 26 August 1946

f.Eur.p.   Glyndebourne Productions (on tour) cond. Benjamin Britten and Hans Oppenheim - Municipal Theatre, Amsterdam, 2 October 1946 (Holland Festival)

f.broad.p.   Glyndebourne Productions cond. Reginald Goodall - Third Programme, 11 October 1946 (from the Camden Hippodrome)

Principals: Kathleen Ferrier, Joan Cross, Peter Pears, Owen Brannigan

f.Am.p.   (rev. version) Chicago Opera cond. Paul Briesach - Shubert Theatre, Chicago, 1 June 1947 (the first New York performance was staged on Broadway on 29 December 1948 and by New York Opera conducted by Paul Breisach early the following year)

f.p.   (rev. version) Glyndebourne Productions cond. Reginald Goodall - Glyndebourne, 7 July 1947

Principals: Nancy Evans, Joan Cross, Peter Pears, Norman Lumsden

f.Eur.p.   (rev. version) English Opera Group (on tour) cond. Reginald Goodall - Holland, 24 July 1947 (Scheveningen Festival)

f.Austr.p.   Sydney - 25 October 1947 (concert performance)

f.Can.p.   Stratford, Ontario, August 1956 (Stratford Festival)

f.Austr.st.p. cond. Donald Peart - Sydney University, 1957

f.Russ.p.   English Opera Group (on tour) - Riga/Leningrad/Moscow, October 1964

Principals: Sylvia Fisher, Janet Baker, Peter Pears

Flower Song: for contralto and piano (or orchestra)

Dur: 2'30"
Instr: Ob. Bsn. Hp. Vn. Vn. Va. Vc. Db.
Pub: Boosey & Hawkes, 1947

The Ride: for tenor and piano (or orchestra)

Dur: 3'
Instr: Picc. Ob. Cl. Bsn. Hn. Perc. Hp. Vn. Vn. Va. Vc. Db.
Pub: Boosey & Hawkes, 1947

Slumber Song: for soprano and piano (or orchestra)
Dur: 3'
Instr: A.Fl. B.Cl. Hn. Hp.
Pub: Boosey & Hawkes, 1947

Occasional Overture Op.38* (1946)
Commissioned by Victor Hely Hutchinson for the opening concert of the BBC Third
Programme - the score is dated 14 September 1946
Dur: 8'
Instr: 3+picc./2+ca./2+Eflat cl./2+cbsn. - 4/3/3/1 - timp. perc.(3) cel. hp. str.
f.p.   BBC Symphony Orchestra/Sir Adrian Boult - BBC Third Programme,
          29 September 1946 (the *Radio Times* gave the work's title as 'Festival
          Overture')
f.conc.p. Chicago Symphony Orchestra/Raymond Leppard - Orchestra Hall, Chicago,
          28 April 1983
f.Brit.conc.p.City of Birmingham Symphony Orchestra/John Carewe - Birmingham
          Town Hall, 6 October 1983
f.rec.   City of Birmingham Symphony Orchestra/Simon Rattle - *EMI EL 270263-1
          (and MC), CDC7 47343-2 (CD), CDS7 54270-2 (CD)*
Pub: Faber, 1984
(*after the first performance Britten, who was dissatisfied with the overture, gave the
manuscript to Hans Keller saying it was not to be performed)

Prelude and Fugue on a Theme of Vittoria:* for organ (1946)
Written 'For St Matthew's Church, Northampton, St Matthew's Day, 1946' - the score is
dated 18 September 1946
Dur: 5'30"
f.p.   Alec Wyton - St Matthew's Church, Northampton, 21 September 1946
f.broad.p. Geraint Jones - BBC European Service, 7 January 1947
          (pre-recorded, 22 November 1946)
f.Brit.broad.p. above European broadcast - Third Programme, 27 January 1947
f.Lon.p. Alan Harverson (?) - St James's Church, Piccadilly, 18 November 1959
f.recs.   Richard Ellsasser - *MGM E-3064 (m)*
          David Lumsden - *Saga 5274 (m)*
          Herrick Bunney - *HMV HQS 1376*
Pub: · Boosey & Hawkes, 1952
(*from the motet 'Ecce sacerdos magnus' Pub. 1585, the Prelude and Fugue was played
at Britten's funeral service on 7 December 1976)

Albert Herring: comic opera in three acts Op.39 (1947)
[Libretto: Eric Crozier after Guy de Maupassant]
Written for the English Opera Group's first season and 'Dedicated to E.M. Forster, in
admiration'
Dur: 137'
Instr: Fl. Ob. Cl. Bsn. Hn. Perc. Hp. Pno. Vn. Vn. Va. Vc. Db.
f.p.   English Opera Group cond. Benjamin Britten - Glyndebourne Opera House,
          Sussex, 20 June 1947
Producer: Frederick Ashton*
Scenery and costumes: John Piper

Principals: Peter Pears, Joan Cross, Frederick Sharp, William Parsons, Nancy Evans,
        Margaret Ritchie, Gladys Parr, Norman Lumsden
f.recs.   Soloists/English Chamber Orchestra/Benjamin Britten - *London (USA) OSA
        1378; Decca SET 274-6, 421 849-2 (CD)*
        Glyndebourne Festival Production (1985) cond. Bernard Haitink - *Castle
        Vision CVI 2051(V)*
Pub: Boosey & Hawkes, 1948 (vocal score by Henry Boys); 1970 (study score)
(*Carl Ebert had been the original choice but declined after listening to a play-through)

Other performances:
f.Eur.p.   English Opera Group (on tour) - Holland, 22 July 1947 (Scheveningen
        Festival)
f.Lon.p.   English Opera Group - Covent Garden, 8 October 1947 (and first performed at
        the Aldeburgh Festival on 7 June 1948)
f.Am.p.   Berkshire Music Centre, Tanglewood, Lenox, Massachusetts - 8 August 1949
        (Tanglewood Festival - and later in New York, June 1952)
f.Can.p.   CBC broadcast, Toronto - 10 January 1951
f.Russ.p. English Opera Group - Riga/Leningrad/Moscow, October 1964

Canticle I 'My Beloved is Mine': for high voice and piano Op.40 (1947)
[Words: Francis Quarles]
'This Canticle was written for the Dick Sheppard Memorial Concert on 1 November
1947, when it was performed by Peter Pears and the composer' - the score is dated 12
September 1947
Dur: 7'
f.p.   Peter Pears (Ten.)/Benjamin Britten (Pno.) - Central Hall, Westminster,
        London, 1 November 1947 (Dick Sheppard Memorial Concert)
f.broad.p. above artists - Third Programme, 26 November 1947
f.recs.   above artists - *Argo ZRG 5277, ZRG 946; London 425 716-2 (CD)*
Pub: Boosey & Hawkes, 1950

A Charm of Lullabies:* for mezzo-soprano and piano Op.41 (1947)
[1. A Cradle Song (William Blake) 2. The Highland Balou (Robert Burns)
 3. Sephestia's Lullaby (Robert Greene) 4. A Charm (Thomas Randolph)
 5. The Nurse's Song (John Philip)]
Dedicated 'For Nancy Evans'
Dur: 11'30"
f.p.   Nancy Evans (M/S)/Felix de Nobel (Pno.) - The Hague, 3 January 1948
f.Brit.p   Nancy Evans (M/S)/Ernest Lush (Pno.) - BBC Third Programme,
        18 October 1948
f.Brit.conc.p. Nancy Evans (M/S)/Ernest Lush(?) (Pno.) - RBA Galleries,
        London, 8 February 1949 (LCMC Concert)
f.rec.   Helen Watts (Con.)/Benjamin Britten (Pno.) - *BBC REGL 417* (BBC Third
        Programme, broadcast 31 March 1962)
Pub: Boosey & Hawkes, 1949 (Nos.3 and 4 also published separately in 'A
        Heritage of 20th Century British Song', Vols. 3 and 4, 1977)
(*there are 2 discarded songs: 'Somnus the humble god' [Sir John Denham] and 'Come,
Little Babe' [Nicholas Breton])

also arr. for mezzo-soprano and orchestra by Colin Matthews (1990)

Instr: 2/2/2+b.cl./2 - 2/0/0/0 - hp. str.

f.p.   Maureen Forrester (Con.)/Indianapolis Symphony Orchestra/Raymond
            Leppard - Circle Theatre, Indianapolis, 17 January 1991

f.Brit.p.   Barbara Rearick (M/S)/City of Birmingham Symphony Orchestra/Steuart
            Bedford -The Maltings, Snape, 25 June 1992 (Aldeburgh Festival)

f.rec.   Catherine Wyn-Rogers (M/S)/Northern Sinfonia/Steuart Bedford - *Collins 5
            023391 152627 (CD)*

Pub: Boosey & Hawkes (vocal score)

**The Beggar's Opera: a ballad-opera by John Gay (1728) realized from the original
airs Op.43 (1947-48)**

[Libretto: John Gay and Tyrone Guthrie]

'Dedicated to James Lawrie'

Dur: 105'

Instr: Fl. Ob. Cl. Bsn. Hn. Perc. Hp. Vn. Vn. Va. Vc. Db.

f.p.   English Opera Group cond. Benjamin Britten - Arts Theatre, Cambridge, 24
            May 1948

Producer: Tyrone Guthrie assisted by Basil Coleman

Scenery and costumes: Tanya Moiseiwitsch

Principals: Peter Pears, Nancy Evans, Flora Nielsen, George James

f.broad.p. above artists - Third Programme, 21 September 1948 (from Camden Theatre,
            London)

Producer: Tyrone Guthrie

f.rec.   Soloists/Orchestra/Steuart Bedford - *Argo 436 850-2 (CD)*

Pub: Boosey & Hawkes, 1949 (vocal score by Arthur Oldham); 1997 (study score)

Other performances:

f.Eur.p.   English Opera Group (on tour) - Municipal Theatre, Amsterdam,
            25 June 1948 (Amsterdam Festival)

f.Lon.p.   English Opera Group - Sadler's Wells Theatre, 6 September 1948

f.Am.p.   Julliard School of Music, New York, 24 March 1949

later rescored for a baritone Macheath by Julius Harrison

f.p.   English Opera Group cond. Norman del Mar - Jubilee Hall, Aldeburgh,
            19 June 1950 (Aldeburgh Festival)

Producer: Basil Coleman

Principals: David Franklin, Esther Salaman, Nancy Evans, Bruce Boyce

f.broad.p. above artists - Third Programme, 31 July 1950 (from the Lyric Theatre,
            Hammersmith)

Pub: Boosey & Hawkes

**Saint Nicolas: cantata for tenor solo, chorus (SATB), semi-chorus (SA), four boy
singers and string orchestra, piano duet, percussion and organ Op. 42 (1948)**

[Words: Eric Crozier 1. Introduction 2. The Birth of Nicolas 3. Nicolas devotes himself
to God 4. He journeys to Palestine 5. He comes to Myra and is chosen Bishop
6. Nicolas from prison 7. Nicolas and the pickled boys 8. His piety and marvellous
works 9. The Death of Nicolas]

Written at the suggestion of Esther Neville-Smith for performance at the centenary
celebration of Lancing College, Sussex (where Pears had been a pupil and whose patron
saint was Saint Nicolas) on 24 July 1948 (courtesy of Lancing College the first
performance was given at the first Aldeburgh Festival) - the score is dated 31 May 1948

Dur: 50'
Instr: Pno.duet, perc. org. str.
f.p.   (Aldeburgh) Peter Pears (Ten.)/Aldeburgh Festival Chorus and
               Orchestra/Leslie Woodgate - Aldeburgh Parish Church, 5 June 1948
               (Aldeburgh Festival)
f.p.   (Lancing) Peter Pears (Ten.)/Woodard Schools Choirs/Southern Philharmonic
               Orchestra/Benjamin Britten - Lancing College, Sussex, 24 July 1948
f.Eur.p.   Peter Pears (Ten.)/Chorus and Orchestra of Volksuniversiteit,
               Rotterdam/Benjamin Britten - Radio Hilversum broadcast (from Lutherse
               Kerk, Amsterdam), 9 December 1948
f.Brit.broad.p. Peter Pears (Ten.)/BBC Chorus/BBC Choral Society/Jacques String
               Orchestra/Leslie Woodgate - Third Programme, 6 January 1949
f.Lon.p.   Peter Pears (Ten.)/Mixed Choirs/Southwark Cathedral Choristers/
               Aldeburgh Festival Chorus/Jacques Orchestra/Benjamin Britten - Southwark
               Cathedral, 23 June 1949 (in the presence of Queen Mary)
f.Am.p.   School of Sacred Music, Union Theological Seminary, New York,
               c.January 1951
f.rec.   Soloists/Aldeburgh Festival Chorus and Orchestra/Benjamin Britten - *London
               (USA) LL 1254 (m), 5173 (m); Decca LXT 5060 (m), ECM 765 (m),
               425 714-2 (CD)*
Pub: Boosey & Hawkes, 1948, 1949 (vocal score by Arthur Oldham)

**The Little Sweep: the opera from 'Let's make an Opera', an entertainment for
young people Op.45 (1949)**
[Libretto: Eric Crozier]
'Affectionately dedicated to the real Gay, Juliet, Sophie, Tina, Hughie, Jonny and Sammy
- the Gathorne-Hardys of Great Glemham, Suffolk'

Dur: 45' (opera only), 130' (complete entertainment)
Instr: Str.Qt. Pno.(4 hands) Perc.
f.p.   English Opera Group cond. Norman del Mar - Jubilee Hall, Aldeburgh,
               14 June 1949 (Aldeburgh Festival)
Producers: Basil Coleman and Stuart Burge
Scenery and costumes: John Lewis
Principals: Norman Lumsden, Max Worthley, John Moules, Gladys Parr, Anne Sharp
f.broad.p.   above artists - Third Programme, 7 October 1949
Producers: Eric Crozier and Basil Coleman
f.tel.p.   English Opera Group cond. Norman del Mar - BBC Television,
               5 February 1950 (from the Theatre Royal, Stratford)
Director: Michael Henderson
f.rec.   Soloists/Alleyn's School Choir/English Opera Group Orchestra/ Benjamin
               Britten - *London (USA) LL 1439 (m), 5296 (m); Decca LXT 5163 (m), ECM
               2166 (m), 430 367-2 (CD), London 436 393-2 (CD)*
Pub: Boosey & Hawkes,1950 (vocal score for piano duet by Arthur Oldham), 1965
               (full score),1968 (vocal score for solo piano and percussion by Martin Penny)

Other performances:
f.Lon.p.   English Opera Group - Lyric Theatre, Hammersmith, 15 November 1949
f.Am.p.   Kiel Auditorium, Saint Louis, Missouri - 22 March 1950 (Music Educators'
           National Conference)
f.Eur.p.   Städtische Bühnen, Nurnberg-Furth, West Germany - September 1950
f.Austr.p. Palace Theatre, Sydney, New South Wales - 7 September 1951

Excs. arr. for mixed voices and piano
[1. Sweep's Song 2. Sammy's Bath 3. Night Song 4. Coaching Song]
Dur: 11'30"
Pub: Boosey & Hawkes, 1950 (separately)

Spring Symphony: for soprano, contralto and tenor solos, chorus, boys' choir and orchestra Op.44 (1949)

[Pt.1   Introduction (Anon. 16th cent.) The Merry Cuckoo (Edmund Spenser)
            Spring (Thomas Nashe) The Driving Boy (George Peele - John Clare)
            The Morning Star (John Milton)
Pt.2   Welcome, Maids of Honour (Robert Herrick)
            Waters above (Henry Vaughan) Out on the Lawn (W.H. Auden)
Pt.3   When will my May come? (Richard Barnefield)
            Fair and Fair (George Peele) Sound the flute (William Blake)
Pt.4   Finale: London, to thee I do present (Francis Beaumont and
            John Fletcher)]
'For Serge Koussevitzky and the Boston Symphony Orchestra' - the draft score is dated
15 March 1949
Dur: 45'
Instr: 3/2+ca./2+bcl./2+cbsn. - 4/3/3/1+cow horn - timp. perc.(4) hp.(2) str.
f.p.   Jo Vincent (Sop.)/Kathleen Ferrier (Con.)/Peter Pears (Ten.)/Dutch Radio
            Chorus/Boys' Choir of St Willibrorduskerk, Rotterdam/Concertgebouw
            Orchestra/Eduard van Beinum - Concertgebouw, Amsterdam, 14 July 1949
            (Holland Festival)
f.broad.p. above first performance - Third Programme, 14 July 1949
f.Am.p.   Boston Symphony Chorus and Orchestra/Serge Koussevitzky - Tanglewood,
            Massachusetts, 13 August 1949 (Berkshire Festival)
f.Brit.conc.p.   Joan Cross (Sop.)/Anne Wood (Con.)/Peter Pears (Ten.)/London Schools'
            Music Association Choir/London Philharmonic Choir and Orchestra/Eduard
            van Beinum - Royal Albert Hall, London, 9 March 1950
f.recs.   above (first) performance - *Decca 440 063-2 (CD), (Exc.) 436 990-2 (CD)
            (and MC)*
            Jennifer Vyvyan (Sop.)/Norma Proctor (Con.)/Peter Pears (Ten.)/Royal Opera
            House Chorus and Orchestra/Benjamin Britten - *London (USA) OS 25242;
            Decca SXL 2264, 410 171-1 (and MC); London 425 153-4 (MC),
            436 396-2 (CD)*
Pub: Boosey & Hawkes, 1949 (vocal score by Arthur Oldham), 1951 (min. score)

A Wedding Anthem* (Amo Ergo Sum): for soprano and tenor solos, choir (SATB) and organ Op.46 (1949)

[Words: Ronald Duncan]

Written 'For Marion and George, 29 September 1949', the Earl and Countess of
Harewood, on the occasion of their wedding
Dur: 9'30"
f.p.   Joan Cross (Sop.)/Peter Pears (Ten.)/Choir of St Mark's Church/Benjamin
            Britten - St Mark's Church, North Audley Street, London, 29 September 1949
            (at the wedding of the Earl and Countess of Harewood and in the presence of
            King George VI and Queen Elizabeth)
f.conc.p.   above artists - Parish Church, Aldeburgh, 24 June 1950 (Aldeburgh Festival)
f.broad.p. April Cantelo (Sop.)/Ian Partridge (Ten.)/Thames Chamber Choir/Louis
            Halsey - Third Programme, 9 March 1967 (pre-recorded 23 February 1966)
f.rec.   Mary Seers (Sop.)/Philip Salmon (Ten.)/Westminster Cathedral Choir/
            Corydon Singers cond. Matthew Best - *Hyperion CDA 66126 (CD)*
Pub: Boosey & Hawkes, 1950 (vocal score)
(*a manuscript of this anthem was buried, among other artefacts, in the foundations of
the Royal Festival Hall in London on 13 October 1949)

Five Flower Songs: for chorus (SATB) unaccompanied Op.47 (1950)
[1. To Daffodils (Robert Herrick) 2. The Succession of the Four Sweet Months
(Robert Herrick) 3. Marsh Flowers (George Crabbe) 4. The Evening Primrose
(John Clare) 5. The Ballad of Green Broom (Anon.)]
Dedicated 'To Leonard and Dorothy Elmhirst on the occasion of their twenty-fifth
wedding anniversary - 3rd April 1950'. (A few years earlier the Elmhirsts had made a
generous donation towards the English Opera Group - the Elmhirsts were both amateur
botanists - hence the choice of subject)
Dur: 10'30"
f.priv.p.   (excs.) Choir - Dartington Hall, Totnes, South Devon, 3 April 1950 (sung to
            the dedicatees on the exact anniversary date)
f.p.   Student Choir/Imogen Holst - Dartington Hall, Totnes, South Devon,
            23 July 1950
f.broad.p. BBC Midlands Chorus/John Lowe - Home Service, 24 May 1951
f.Lon.p.   Elizabethan Singers/Louis Halsey - June 1951
f.Eur.p.   King's College Choir, Cambridge/Boris Ord - Bern, Switzerland, March 1955
f.recs.   Elizabethan Singers/Louis Halsey - *Argo ZRG 5424*
            Cambridge Singers/John Rutter - *Collegium COLCD 104 (CD)*
Pub: Boosey & Hawkes, 1951

Lachrymae: Reflections on a song of John Dowland,* for viola and piano Op.48
(1950, rev.1970)
Written 'For William Primrose' - the score is dated 16 May 1950
Dur: 14'30"
f.p.   William Primrose (Va.)/Benjamin Britten (Pno.) - Aldeburgh Parish Church,
            20 June 1950 (Aldeburgh Festival)
f.p.   (rev.version) Cecil Aronowitz (Va.)/Benjamin Britten (Pno.) - The Maltings,
            Snape, June 1970 (Aldeburgh Festival)
f.recs.   Milton Thomas (Va.)/George Akst (Pno.) - *Esoteric (USA) CPT 605 (m)*
            Josef Kadousek (Va.)/Kveta Novotna (Pno.) - *Supraphon 1111 2694*
            Yuri Bashmet (Va.)/Sviatoslav Richter (Pno.) - *MK (Russia) MK 418015 (CD)*
            Margaret Major (Va.)/Benjamin Britten (Pno.) - *BBCB 8014-2 (CD)*
Pub: Boosey & Hawkes, 1951 (ed. William Primrose), 1974 (rev. version)

(* 'If my complaints could passions move' - the work also includes a quotation from Dowland's 'Flow my tears')

later arr. for viola and string orchestra Op.48a (1976)
Arranged at the request of Cecil Aronowitz
f.p.   Rainer Moog (Va.)/Westphalian Symphony Orchestra/Karl Anton
             Rickenbacker - Recklinghausen, West Germany, 3 May 1977
f.Brit.p.   Cecil Aronowitz/Northern Sinfonia/Steuart Bedford - The Maltings, Snape,
             21 June 1977 (Aldeburgh Festival)
f.Lon.p.   Keith Crellin/Australian Sinfonia/Geoffrey Simon - Queen Elizabeth Hall,
             London, 12 October 1977
f.broad.p.   Duff Burns/BBC Scottish Symphony Orchestra/Karl Anton Rickenbacker -
             18 November 1977
f.rec.   Roger Best/English String Orchestra/William Boughton - *Nimbus NI 5025*
             (CD) (and MC)
Pub: Boosey & Hawkes, 1977
also arr. for viola and harp
f.rec.   Nobuko Imai (Va.)/Naoko Yoshino (Hp.) - *Philips 442 012-2 (CD)*

Six Metamorphoses after Ovid: for oboe solo Op.49 (1951)
[1. Pan 2. Phaeton 3. Niobe 4. Bacchus 5. Narcissus 6. Arethusa]
Written 'For Joy Boughton'
Dur: 12'30"
f.p.   Joy Boughton - on The Meare at Thorpeness, 14 June 1951 (Aldeburgh
             Festival - both performer and audience sat in punts)
f.broad.p.   Joy Boughton - Third Programme, 3 October 1952 (pre-recorded,
             29 September 1952)
f.Lon.p.   Koen van Slogteren - Wigmore Hall, 9 October 1958
f.p.   (as a ballet) Kirov Ballet - Philharmonic Hall, Leningrad, December 1966
f.recs.   James Lyon - *Concert Hall Society H-4 (m)*
             Vitezlav Hanus - *Supraphon SUAST 50694*
             Sarah Francis - *Argo ZRG 842*
Pub: Boosey & Hawkes, 1952 (No.1 also published separately in 'Contemporary
             Music for Oboe', 1981)

Billy Budd: opera in two acts Op.50 (1951, rev.1960)
[Libretto: E.M. Forster and Eric Crozier from the story by Herman Melville]
Commissioned by the Arts Council of Great Britain for the Festival of Britain and
dedicated 'To George and Marion, December 1951' - the work was completed on
2 November 1951
Dur: 158' (rev. version in 2 Acts) or 152' (original version in 4 Acts)
Instr: 4/2+ca./2+bcl.+a.sax./2+cbsn. - 4/4/3/1 - timp. perc.(6) hp. str.
             (+ drums on stage)
f.p.   Chorus and Orchestra of the Royal Opera House cond. Benjamin Britten -
             Royal Opera House, Covent Garden, London, 1 December 1951 (Britten
             conducted in place of Josef Krips who was indisposed)
Producer: Basil Coleman
Designer: John Piper
Principals: Theodor Uppmann, Peter Pears, Frederick Dalberg, Geraint Evans

f.recs.   original version première cond. Benjamin Britten - *VAI 1034-3 (CD)*
          Soloists/Ambrosian Opera Chorus/London Symphony Orchestra/Benjamin
          Britten - *London (USA) OSA 1390; Decca SET 379-81, 417 428-2 (CD),*
          (excs.) 436 990-2(CD) (and MC)
          English National Opera Production cond. David Atherton - *Virgin Vision VVD*
          545(V)
Pub: Boosey & Hawkes, 1952 (vocal score by Erwin Stein), 1961 (vocal score, rev.
          version), 1985 (study score, rev. version)

Other performances:
f.Eur.p.   Covent Garden Opera Company (on tour) - Théâtre des Champs-Elysées,
            Paris, 26 May 1952 (Festival of Twentieth Century Art)
f.Am.p.   (abridged version) cond. Peter Herman Adler - NBC Television,
            18 October 1952 (TV Opera Workshop)
Producer: Samuel Chotzinoff
Director: Kirk Browning
Designer: William Molyneux
Principals: Theodor Uppmann, Andrew McKinley, Leon Lishner, Warren Galjour
f.Am.st.p. Indiana University Opera Theatre Company - Bloomington, Indiana,
            7 December 1952
f.p.   (rev. version) cond. Benjamin Britten - BBC Third Programme, 13 November
            1960 (pre-recorded, Camden Theatre, London, 8 November 1960)
Principals: Joseph Ward, Peter Pears, Michael Langdon, John Noble
f.st.p.   (rev. version) cond. Sir Georg Solti - Royal Opera House, Covent Garden,
            London, 9 January 1964
Producer: Basil Coleman
Designer: John Piper
Principals: Richard Lewis, Forbes Robinson, Robert Kerns, John Shaw
f.Eur.p.   (rev. version) Florence, Italy, May 1965 (Florence Festival)
f.Am.p.   (rev. version) American Opera Society, cond. Sir Georg Solti - Carnegie Hall,
            New York, 4 January 1966 (concert performance)
f.Am.st.p. (rev. version) cond. Sir Georg Solti - Civic Opera House, Chicago,
            6 November 1970
f.conc.p.   (original version) Hallé Orchestra cond. Kent Nagano - Bridgewater Hall,
            Manchester, 27 May 1997

Canticle II 'Abraham and Isaac': for alto and tenor voices and piano Op.51 (1952)
[Words from the Chester Miracle Play]
Written 'For Kathleen Ferrier and Peter Pears'
Dur: 17'
f.p.   Kathleen Ferrier* (Con.)/Peter Pears (Ten.)/Benjamin Britten (Pno.) -
          Albert Hall, Nottingham, 21 January 1952 (as part of a fund-raising tour for
          the English Opera Group)
f.Lon.p. above artists - Victoria and Albert Museum, 3 February 1952
f.broad.p. above artists - Home Service, 18 February 1952 (pre-recorded at Birmingham
          Town Hall, 22 January 1952)
f.recs.   John Hahessy (Alto.)/Peter Pears (Ten.)/Benjamin Britten (Pno.) - *Argo ZRG*
          5277, ZRG 946; London 425 716-2 (CD)
          Janet Baker (Con.)/Peter Pears (Ten.)/Graham Johnson (Pno.) - *CBS 79316*

Pub: Boosey & Hawkes, 1953
(*Kathleen Ferrier's only Aldeburgh Festival appearance was to sing **Canticle II** with
Pears and Britten in June 1952)

Variation 4 of Variations on an Elizabethan theme 'Sellinger's Round' for string orchestra (1953)

Written at the suggestion of Benjamin Britten for performance at the 1953 Aldeburgh
Festival. The identities of the six composers - Oldham, Tippett, Walton, Searle,*
Berkeley and Britten were not revealed until after the performance - Britten's variation
includes a quotation from **Gloriana**.The theme, scored by Imogen Holst, uses William
Byrd's harmonisation from his own set of variations.

Dur: 2' (Var.4), 16' (complete work)
f.p.   Aldeburgh Festival Orchestra/Benjamin Britten - BBC Third Programme,
            16 June 1953
f.conc.p.   above artists - Aldeburgh Parish Church, 20 June 1953 (Aldeburgh Festival
            Coronation Choral Concert)
f.Lon.p.   Collegium Musicum Londinii/John Minchinton - Wigmore Hall, 29 May 1957
f.recs.   above first concert performance - *London (USA) LL 809 (m)*;
            Decca LXT 2798 (m)
            Toulouse National Chamber Orchestra/B. Bratoev - *Auvidis A 6124 (CD)*
Pub: Boosey & Hawkes
(*both Alan Rawsthorne and Edmund Rubbra had been approached before Humphrey
Searle was invited to contribute his variation movement)

Gloriana: opera in three acts Op.53 (1953, rev.1966)

[Libretto: William Plomer after Lytton Strachey's 'Elizabeth and Essex']
Commissioned for the Coronation, 'This work is dedicated by gracious permission to Her
Majesty Queen Elizabeth II, in honour of whose Coronation it was composed' - the score
is dated 13 March 1953

Dur: 148'
Instr: 3/2+ca./2+bcl./2+cbsn. - 4/3/3/1 - timp. perc.(4) hp. str. (+ on-stage band)
f.priv.p.   (excs.) Peter Pears (Ten.)/Joan Cross (Sop.)/Benjamin Britten (Pno.) - 18 May
            1953 (at the London home of the Harewoods in Orme Square, Bayswater)
f.p.   Chorus and Orchestra of the Royal Opera House cond. John Pritchard -
            Royal Opera House, Covent Garden, London, 8 June 1953 (in the presence of
            Her Majesty the Queen and the Royal family)
Producer: Basil Coleman
Designer: John Piper
Choreography: John Cranko
Principals: Joan Cross, Peter Pears, Geraint Evans, Monica Sinclair, Jennifer
            Vyvyan, Michael Langdon, Adèle Leigh, Arnold Matters
f.recs.   English National Opera cond. Mark Elder - *Virgin VVD 344 (V)*
            Welsh National Opera cond. Charles Mackerras - *Argo 440 213-2 (CD)*
Pub: Boosey & Hawkes, 1953 (vocal score by Imogen Holst), 1968 (rev. version,
            vocal score), 1981 (rev. version, vocal score, 2nd ed.),
            1990 (rev. version, study score)

Other performances:
f.Afr.p.   Covent Garden Opera Company (on tour), Bulawayo, Southern

Rhodesia - 8 August 1953 (Rhodes Centennial Exhibition)
f.Am.conc.p. cond. Josef Krips - Music Hall, Cincinnati, 8 May 1956 (May
       Festival concert)
Principals: Inge Borkh, Eugene Conley
f.conc.p.   Polyphonia Chorus and Orchestra/Bryan Fairfax - Royal Festival Hall,
       London, 22 November 1963 (50th birthday concert)
Principals: Sylvia Fisher, Peter Pears, Thomas Hemsley, Forbes Robinson
f.p.   (rev. version) Sadler's Wells Opera cond. Mario Bernardi - Sadler's Wells,
       London, 21 October 1966 (and repeated at the 1968 Aldeburgh Festival)
Producer: Colin Graham
Designers: Alix Stone and Colin Graham
Principals: Sylvia Fisher, John Wakefield, Jennifer Vyvyan, Donald McIntyre
Choreography: Peter Darrell
f.Eur.p.   (rev. version) English National Opera - Munich, October 1972 (as part of the
       Olympic Games celebrations)
f.Am.st.p. English National Opera cond. Mark Elder - Lila Cockrell Theatre, San
       Antonio, Texas, 6 June 1984 (and later at the Metropolitan, New York)
Principals: Sarah Walker, Arthur Davies

Symphonic Suite 'Gloriana': for orchestra and tenor solo (ad lib.) Op.53a (1953)
[1. The Tournament 2. The Lute Song* (Words: Robert Devereux, Earl of Essex)
3. The Courtly Dances 4. Gloriana moritura]
Score dated 14 December 1953
Dur: 26'
Instr: 2+picc./2+ca./2+bcl./2+cbsn. - 4/3/3/1 - timp. perc.(4) hp. str.
f.p.   Peter Pears (Ten.)/City of Birmingham Symphony Orchestra/Rudolf Schwarz
       - Birmingham Town Hall, 23 September 1954
f.Lon.p. above artists - Royal Festival Hall, 16 May 1955
f.broad.p. Richard Lewis (Ten.)/City of Birmingham Symphony Orchestra/Rudolf
       Schwarz - Home Service, 5 June 1955
f.recs.   London Symphony Orchestra/Steuart Bedford - *Collins 1019-2 (CD) (and MC)*
       BBC Northern Symphony Orchestra/Norman del Mar - *BBC RD 9129 (CD)*
Pub: Boosey & Hawkes (Movement 3 in 'Orchestral Anthology', Vol.1, 1997)
(*the tenor voice may be replaced by an oboe)

Other excs. from above:
(i)   Courtly Dances - suite arr. for orchestra by the composer (1957)
       [1. March 2. Coranto 3. Pavane 4. Morris Dance 5. Galliard
       6. Lavolta 7. (Reprise of the March)]
       Dur: 10'
       f.p.   members of the Aldeburgh Festival Orchestra/Charles Mackerras -
              Jubilee Hall, Aldeburgh, 23 June 1957 (Aldeburgh Festival)
       f.Lon.p. English Chamber Orchestra/Imogen Holst - Royal Festival Hall,
              10 January 1968
(ii)   Courtly Dances arr. for symphonic band by Jan Bach
       f.p.   Northern Illinois University Wind Ensemble/Stephen Squires -
              Jacobs High School, Algonquin, Illinois, USA, 5 October 1989
       Pub: Boosey & Hawkes, 1995
(iii)   Courtly Dances arr. for lute consort by Julian Bream (1959)

Dur: 10'

f.rec. Bream Consort - *RCA VL 89030 (and MC), ARL3 0997, 09026 61583-2 (CD set), 09026 61589-2 (CD)*

(iv) Five* Courtly Dances arr. for school orchestra by David Stone

Dur: 9'30"

Instr: 1/1/2/1 - 2/2/1/0 - timp. perc. pno. str.

Pub: Boosey & Hawkes, 1965 (*omitting the Galliard)

(v) Choral Dances for unaccompanied SATB chorus

[1. Time 2. Concord 3. Time and Concord 4. Country Girls 5. Rustics and Fishermen 6. Final Dance of Homage]

Dur: 8'

f.p. BBC Midland Chorus/John Lowe - BBC Home Service, 7 March 1954

f.conc.p. Elizabethan Singers/Louis Halsey - ICA, London, 14 December 1954

f.rec. London Symphony Chorus/George Malcolm - *Oiseau Lyre SOL 60037; Argo ZRG 947*

Pub: Boosey & Hawkes, 1954

also arr. for tenor, chorus and harp (1967)

Written for the opening of the Queen Elizabeth Hall in London

Dur: 10'

f.p. Peter Pears (Ten.)/Osian Ellis (Hp.)/Ambrosian Singers/Benjamin Britten - Queen Elizabeth Hall, London, 1 March 1967

f.broad.p. above first performance - Home Service, 2 March 1967

f.recs. above first performance - *BBCB 8009-2 (CD)*

Martyn Hill (Ten.)/T. Owen (Hp.)/Holst Singers cond. Hilary Davan Wetton - *Hyperion CDA 66175 (CD)*

Pub: Boosey & Hawkes, 1982

(vi) The Second Lute Song of the Earl of Essex arr. for voice and piano by Imogen Holst (1953)

[Words: Robert Devereux]

'For Peter Pears'

Dur: 4'

f.p. Peter Pears (Ten.)/Benjamin Britten (Pno.) - Jubilee Hall, 28 June 1953 (Aldeburgh Festival)

Pub: Boosey & Hawkes, 1954

also arr. for tenor and lute

f.rec. Peter Pears (Ten.)/Julian Bream (Lute) - *London (USA) LSC 2718, AGLI 1281; RCA SB 6621, GL 42752 (and MC), 09026 61583-2 (CD set), 09026 61601-2(CD)*

also arr. for tenor and harp

f.rec. Peter Pears (Ten.)/Osian Ellis (Hp.) - *London (USA) OS 26477; Decca SXL 6788*

(vii) Morris Dance arr. for two descant recorders by Imogen Holst

Dur: 1'

Pub: Boosey & Hawkes, 1957

(viii) March arr. for descant recorder by Imogen Holst

Dur: 1'

Pub: Boosey & Hawkes, 1959 (in 'The Book of the Dolmetsch

Recorder')
(ix)   Fanfare, for trumpets (1967)
            Arranged for the opening of The Maltings Concert Hall at Snape
            Dur: 30"
            f.conc.p.   Herald Trumpeters of the Royal Artillery Band, Woolwich -
                        The Maltings, Snape, 2 June 1967 (Aldeburgh Festival)
            f.rec.   above performance - *Decca 5BB 119-20*
(x)   Concord arr. for piano solo by Christopher Norton
            Dur: 2'
            Pub: Boosey & Hawkes, 1989 (in 'Twentieth Century Classics',Vol.1)

Winter Words: lyrics and ballads of Thomas Hardy for high voice and piano Op.52 (1953)

[1. At Day-close in November 2. Midnight on the Great Western 3. Wagtail and Baby
(28 March 1953) 4. The Little Old Table (13 September 1953) 5. The Choirmaster's
Burial 6. Proud Songsters (15 September 1953) 7. At the Railway Station, Upway
(7 September 1953) 8. Before Life and After]
Dedicated 'To John and Myfanwy Piper'
Dur: 19'30"
f.p.   Peter Pears (Ten.)/Benjamin Britten (Pno.) - Harewood House, Yorkshire,
            8 October 1953 (Leeds Festival)
f.broad.p. above artists - Third Programme, 28 November 1953
            (pre-recorded, 22 October 1953)
f.Lon.p.   above artists - Victoria & Albert Museum, 24 January 1954
f.Ind.p.   above artists - Bombay, 15 December 1955 (during a world tour)
f.Russ.p.   above artists - Great Hall, Moscow Conservatory, 8 March 1963
            (during a Festival of British Music)
f.NZ.p.   above artists - Auckland Town Hall, North Island, 7 April 1970
f.recs.   above artists - *London (USA) LL 1204 (m), 5154 (m); Decca LXT 5095 (m),*
            ECS 629 (es), 417 183-1 (and MC), 425 996-2 (CD)
            (above f.Russ.p.) - *Melodiya M10 46091009*
            above artists - *Aldeburgh Festival AF 001* (live 1972 recording)
Pub: Boosey & Hawkes, 1954, 1994 (new ed.) (Nos.3 and 5 also published
            separately in 'A Heritage of 20th Century British Song', Vols.3 and 4)

2 songs were discarded from the original song-cycle but later published and performed:-
[1. The Children and Sir Nameless 2. If it's ever spring again]
f.p.   Neil Mackie (Ten.)/Iain Burnside (Pno.) - Wigmore Hall, London,
            22 November 1983
f.broad.p. Neil Mackie (Ten.)/John Blakely (Pno.) - Radio 3, 23 April 1985
f.recs.   Neil Mackie (Ten.)/Roger Vignoles (Pno.) - *HMV EL 270653-1;*
            EMI CDC7 49257-2 (CD)
            Philip Langridge (Ten.)/Steuart Bedford (Pno.) - *Collins 1468-2 (CD)*
Pub: Boosey & Hawkes, 1994 (as an Appendix to the complete cycle)

The Turn of the Screw: opera in a prologue and two acts Op.54 (1954)

[Libretto: Myfanwy Piper after Henry James]
'This opera was written for and is affectionately dedicated to those members of the
English Opera Group who took part in the first performance' - the opera was

commissioned by the Fenice Theatre in Venice and was completed by August/September 1954.

Dur: 105'
Instr: Fl. Ob. Cl. Bsn. Hn. Perc. Hp. Pno. Vn. Vn. Va. Vc. Db.
f.p.   English Opera Group cond. Benjamin Britten - Teatro La Fenice, Venice, 14 September 1954 (Festival of Contemporary Music)
Producer: Basil Coleman
Designer: John Piper
Principals: Jennifer Vyvyan, Joan Cross, Peter Pears, David Hemmings
f.Brit.p.   above artists - Sadler's Wells Theatre, London, 6 October 1954
f.recs.   Soloists/English Opera Group Orchestra/Benjamin Britten - *London (USA) LL 1207-8 (m), A 4219 (m), RS 62021 (m); Decca LXT 5038-9 (m), GOM 560-1 (m), 425 672-2 (CD)*
            Royal Opera House Production cond. Colin Davis - *Philips 410 426-1 (and MC), 070 400-3(V) (and L)*
Pub: Boosey & Hawkes, 1955 (vocal score by Imogen Holst), 1958 (full score), 1966 (study score)

Other performances:
f.Can.p.   English Opera Group (on tour) - Stratford, Ontario, 20 August 1957 (Stratford Shakespeare Festival)
f.Am.p.   New York College of Music, 19 March 1958 (amateur production)
f.tel.p.   cond. Charles Mackerras - Television House, 25 and 28 December 1959 (Associated Rediffusion Production)
f.Russ.p.   English Opera Group (on tour) - Riga/Leningrad/Moscow, October 1964
f.prof.Am.p. cond. Julius Rudd - Boston, August/September 1961 (and in April 1962 by New York City Opera)
Principals: Patricia Neway, Naomi Farr, Ruth Kobart, Richard Cassilly

Scherzo for recorder quartet (1954)
Dedicated 'To the Aldeburgh Music Club'
Dur: 2'30"
Instr: Desc. Treb. Ten. Bs.(or Ten.)
f.p.   Aldeburgh Music Club - The Meare, Thorpeness, 26 June 1955 (Aldeburgh Festival)
f.rec.   Munrow Recorder Consort - *HMV (set) SLS 5022*
Pub: Boosey & Hawkes, 1955

Canticle III 'Still falls the Rain - The raids, 1940, Night and Dawn': for tenor voice, horn and piano Op.55 (1954)
[Words: Edith Sitwell 'The Canticle of the Rose']
Dedicated 'To the memory of Noel Mewton-Wood' - the score is dated 27 November 1954
Dur: 11'30"
f.p.   Peter Pears (Ten.)/Dennis Brain (Hn.)/Benjamin Britten (Pno.) - Wigmore Hall, London, 28 January 1955* (Noel Mewton-Wood Memorial Concert)
f.broad.p. above artists - Third Programme, 22 June 1955 (from the Aldeburgh Festival)
f.recs.   above artists (recorded at the 1956 Aldeburgh Festival) - *BBCB 8014-2 (CD)*

Peter Pears (Ten.)/Barry Tuckwell (Hn.)/Benjamin Britten (Pno.) - *Argo ZRG 5277, ZRG 946; London 425 716-2 (CD)*

Peter Pears (Ten.)/Alan Civil (Hn.)/Graham Johnson (Pno.) - *CBS 79316*

Pub: Boosey & Hawkes, 1956

(*postponed from the original date of 4 December 1954 due to the illness of Peter Pears who had sung in the première of Walton's **Troilus and Cressida** the night before q.v.)

Alpine Suite: for recorder trio (1955)

[1. Arrival at Zermatt 2. Swiss (Romance) 3. Nursery Slopes 4. Alpine Scene
5. Moto perpetuo: Down the Piste 6. Farewell to Zermatt]

'For Mary Potter'* and written for her to play (with Pears and Britten) while recovering from a ski-ing accident in Zermatt

Dur: 7'30"
Instr: 2 Desc. Treb.
f.priv.p. Mary Potter, Peter Pears and Benjamin Britten (Recs.) - The Red House,
           Aldeburgh, c.February/March 1955
f.pub.p.   Aldeburgh Music Club - The Meare, Thorpeness, 26 June 1955
           (Aldeburgh Festival)
f.broad.p. Stanley Taylor Recorder Consort - Home Service, 8 December 1956
Pub: Boosey & Hawkes, 1956

(*The painter Mary Potter, wife of the author of 'Gamesmanship', Stephen Potter, was the then owner of The Red House in Aldeburgh to which Pears and Britten moved in November 1957 in an ingenious house-swap)

Farfield* (1928-30): for voice and piano (1955)

[Words: John Lydgate (The Monk of Bury)]

Written in celebration of the 400th anniversary of the foundation of Gresham's School

Dur: 1'
Pub: 'Grasshopper' (the school magazine), 1955

(*Farfield was Britten's House at Gresham's School)

Hymn to St Peter: for choir (SATB) with treble solo (or semi-chorus) and organ Op.56a (1955)

[Words from the Gradual of the Feast of St Peter and St Paul]

'Written for the Quincentenary of St Peter Mancroft, Norwich, 1955'

Dur: 5'30"
f.p.   Choir of St Peter Mancroft, with C.J.R. Coleman* (org.) - Norwich,
           20 November 1955
f.broad.p. Choir of Exeter Cathedral, with Reginald Moore (org.) - Home Service,
           22 January 1957
f.rec.   Choir of St John's College, Cambridge/George Guest - *Argo ZK 19*;
           Decca 430 097-2 (CD)
Pub: Boosey & Hawkes, 1955

(*the former organist of St John's Church in Lowestoft who had taken part in several first performances of early Britten works q.v.)

Timpani Piece for Jimmy - for timpani and piano (1955)

Written for James Blades

f.rec.   James Blades (Perc.)/Joan Goossens (Pno.) - *Discourses ABK 13*

Antiphon for choir (SATB with optional solos) and organ Op.56b (1956)

[Words: George Herbert]
Written 'For the centenary of St Michael's College, Tenbury Wells' - the score is dated
30 March 1956

Dur: 6'
f.p.   Choir of St Michael's College with Kenneth Beard (org.) - Tenbury Wells,
            Worcs., 29 September 1956 (during Evensong)
f.broad.p. BBC West of England Singers/Reginald Redman - Home Service,
            25 June 1958 (pre-recorded at St Mary Redcliffe, Bristol, 24 March 1958)
?f.Lon.conc.p. Winchester Cathedral Choir/Martin Neary - Royal Albert Hall,
            10 September 1979 (Promenade Concert)
f.rec.   Choir of St Michael's College, Tenbury Wells - *Alpha APR 303*;
            Argo ZRG 5423
Pub: Boosey & Hawkes, 1956

Three Songs from 'The Heart of the Matter': for tenor, horn and piano (1956)

[Words: Edith Sitwell 1. Prologue: Where are the Seeds of the Universal Fire?
2. Song: We are the darkness in the heat of the day 3. Epilogue: So, out of the dark]
Written for a special Aldeburgh Festival concert entitled 'The Heart of the Matter' during
which Edith Sitwell read a sequence of her poetry interspersed with Britten's settings of
these three poems, a linking Fanfare and the complete **Canticle III Op. 55** (q.v.). - the
score of No.2 is dated 17 May 1956.

Dur: 8' (songs only)
f.p.   Edith Sitwell (Narr.)/Peter Pears (Ten.)/Dennis Brain (Hn.)/Benjamin Britten
            (Pno.) - Aldeburgh Parish Church, 21 June 1956 (Aldeburgh Festival)
Pub: Boosey & Hawkes, 1994

A shortened version of 'The Heart of the Matter' was prepared for performance by Sir
Peter Pears in 1983.

Dur: 28' (including texts)
f.p.   Peter Pears (Narr.)/Neil Mackie (Ten.)/Richard Watkins (Hn.)/Iain Burnside
            (Pno.) - Wigmore Hall, London, 22 November 1983
f.rec.   Peter Pears (Narr.)/Neil Mackie (Ten.)/Barry Tuckwell (Hn.)/Roger Vignoles
            (Pno.) - *EMI EL 270 653-1; CDC7 49257-2 (CD)*

No.2 also arr. for unaccompanied five-part mixed choir (1956?)
Arranged for Imogen Holst and the Purcell Singers

Dur: 1'30"
Pub: Boosey & Hawkes, 1997

The Prince of the Pagodas: ballet in three acts Op.57 (1956)

Dedicated 'To Imogen Holst and Ninette de Valois'

Dur: 115'
Instr: 3/3/2+E flat cl.+a.sax./3 - 4/3/3/1 - timp. perc.(7) hp. cel. pno.(4 hands) str.
            (+ 2 or more on stage tpts.)
f.p.   Sadler's Wells Ballet/Orchestra of the Royal Opera House/Benjamin Britten -
            Royal Opera House, Covent Garden, London, 1 January 1957 (the original
            planned date was 19 September 1956)

Choreography: John Cranko
Decor: John Piper
Costumes: Desmond Heeley

Principals: Svetlana Beriosova, David Blair, Julia Farron, Leslie Edwards
f.Eur.p.   La Scala, Milan, April/May 1957
f.Am.p.   Royal Ballet Company - Metropolitan Opera House, New York,
            18 September 1957
f.recs.   (cut version) above artists - *London (USA) LL 1690-1 (m), CM 9198-9 (m),*
            STS 15081-2; Decca LXT 5336-7 (m), GOS 558-9, 421 855-2 (CD)
            (complete) London Sinfonietta/Oliver Knussen - *Virgin VCD7 91103-2 (CD)*
            (and MC), VCD7 59578-2 (CD) (and MC)
            Royal Ballet Production (1990) cond. Ashley Lawrence - *Teldec 9031-73826*
            (V) (and L)
Pub: Boosey & Hawkes, 1989 (study score)

Exc. Pas de six: for orchestra Op.57a
[1. Entrée 2. Variation I - Pas de deux 3. Variation II - Girl's solo
4. Variation III - Boy's solo 5. Pas de trois 6. Coda]
Dur: 12'
Instr: 2+picc./2+ca./2+E flat cl./2+cbsn. - 4/3/3/1 - timp. perc.(2) hp. pno. str.
f.p.   City of Birmingham Symphony Orchestra/Rudolf Schwarz - Birmingham
            Town Hall, 26 September 1957
f.broad.p. City of Birmingham Symphony Orchestra/Andrzej Panufnik - Home Service,
            1 November 1957 (pre-recorded, 26 October 1957)
f.Lon.p.   London Symphony Orchestra/Basil Cameron - Royal Albert Hall,
            2 August 1958 (Promenade Concert)
f.rec.   Royal Liverpool Philharmonic Orchestra/Takuo Yuasa - *Eminence*
            EMX 2231 (CD)
Pub: Boosey & Hawkes

Exc. Prelude and Dances arr. by Norman Del Mar Op.57b (1963)
[1. Prelude 2. March and Gavotte 3. The Four Kings 4. Belle Epine and Belle Rose
5. Variations of the Prince and Belle Rose 6. Finale]
Dur: 33'
Instr: 3/2+ca./2+E flat cl.+a.sax./2+cbsn. - 4/3/3/1 - timp. perc.(3) hp. pno. str.
f.p.   BBC Scottish Orchestra/Norman Del Mar - BBC Home Service,
            26 December 1963 (pre-recorded, 7 December 1963)
f.conc.p.   above artists - Usher Hall, Edinburgh, 29 August 1964 (Edinburgh Festival)
f.recs.   Adelaide Symphony Orchestra/David Measham - *Unicorn Kanchana KP 8007*
            Bournemouth Symphony Orchestra/Uri Segal - *EMI CDM7 69422-2 (CD)*
Pub: Boosey & Hawkes, 1980

Symphonic Suite arr. by Michael Lankester (1976)
Dur: 55'
f.p.   BBC Symphony Orchestra/Michael Lankester - Royal Albert Hall, London,
            21 July 1979 (Promenade Concert)

Suite from the Ballet arr. by Mervyn Cooke and Donald Mitchell
[Part I - Prelude Part II - The Four Kings Part III - The Strange Journey of Belle Rose to
the Pagoda Land - Pas de deux - Coda Part IV - The Arrival and Adventures of Belle
Rose in the Kingdom of the Pagodas - Pas de deux Part V - The Pagoda Palace:
Darkness to Light - Pas de six - Pas de trois Part VI - Finale - Apotheosis]

Dur: 47'
Instr: 3/2+ca./2+E flat cl.+a.sax./3 - 4/3/3/1 - timp. perc.(3) hp. pno.(4 hands) str.
f.p.   (omitting Part III) Deutsches Symphonie-Orchester, Berlin/Vladimir
          Ashkenazy - Concertgebouw, Amsterdam, 4 June 1997 (and broadcast by
          Netherlands Radio)
f.Brit.p. (including Part III) Royal Scottish National Orchestra/Steuart Bedford -
          Royal Concert Hall, Glasgow, 25 February 1999
Pub: Boosey & Hawkes

Malayan National Anthem, for military band (1957)
Commissioned by the Malaysian Chief Minister - it was not used.

Songs from the Chinese: for high voice and guitar Op.58 (1957)
[Words: trans. Arthur Waley 1. The Big Chariot (from 'The Book of Songs')
 2. The Old Lute (Po Chü-i) 3. The Autumn Wind (Wu-ti) 4. The Herd-Boy (Lu Yu)
 5. Depression (Po Chü-i) 6. Dance Song (from 'The Book of Songs')]
Dedicated 'To Peg and Lu,* from Ben, Peter and Julian'
Dur: 10'
f.p.   Peter Pears (Ten.)/Julian Bream (Gtr.) - Great Glemham House, 17 June 1958
          (Aldeburgh Festival)
f.broad.p. above first performance - Home Service, 15 July 1958
f.rec.   above artists - *RCA (USA) LSC 2718, AGLI 1281; RCA SB 6621, GL 42752
          (and MC), 09026 61583-2 (CD set), 09026 61601-2 (CD)*
Pub: Boosey & Hawkes, 1959 (ed. Julian Bream)
(*The Princess and Prince of Hesse and the Rhine, with whom Pears and Britten had
spent several holidays)

Noye's Fludde: the Chester Miracle Play, set for adults' and children's voices, children's chorus, chamber ensemble and children's orchestra Op.59 (1957-58)
[Words from the Chester Miracle Play, additional words by Bishop Synesius, William
Whiting and Joseph Addison]
Dedicated 'To my nephew and nieces, Sebastian, Sally and Roguey Welford, and my
young friend Roger Duncan' - the draft score was completed on 18 December 1957
Dur: 50'
Instr: (Professional ensemble) Treb.Rec. Pno.(4 hands) Org. Timp. Vn. Vn. Va. Vc.
          Db.
          (Amateur/children's orchestra) Recs., Bugles, Handbells, Perc., Str.
f.p.   English Opera Group cond. Charles Mackerras - Orford Church, 18 June 1958
          (Aldeburgh Festival)
Producer: Colin Graham
Costumes: Ceri Richards
Principals: Owen Brannigan, Gladys Parr, Trevor Anthony, Michael Crawford
f.tel.p. above artists - Associated Television, 22 June 1958
Director: Quentin Lawrence
f.Lon.p. above artists cond. Benjamin Britten - Southwark Cathedral,
          14 November 1958
f.rec.   Soloists/English Chamber Orchestra/Norman Del Mar - *Argo ZNF1(m), ZK1;
          London 436 397-2 (CD), (excs.) 436 990-2 (CD) (and MC)*

Pub: Boosey & Hawkes, 1958 (vocal score by Imogen Holst), 1959 (full score),
            1965 (miniature score)

Other performances:
f.Am.p.   New York, 31 July 1958 (radio broadcast)
f.Am.st.p. School of Sacred Music, Union Theological Seminary, New York,
            16 March 1959
f.Can.p.   Vancouver, October 1960

Excs. arr. for accompanied chorus
[1.Tallis's Canon 2. Eternal Father]
Dur: 8'30"
Pub: CUP, 1967 (Nos.34 and 26 in 'The Cambridge Hymnal')

Einladung zur Martinsgans - eight part canon for voices and piano (1958)
Written for the 60th birthday of Martin Hürlimann

Nocturne for tenor voice, seven obligato instruments and string orchestra Op.60 (1958)
[1. Shelley: 'Prometheus Unbound' (strings only);
 2. Alfred Lord Tennyson: 'The Kraken' (bassoon obligato);
 3. Samuel Taylor Coleridge: 'The Wanderings of Cain' (harp obligato);
 4. Thomas Middleton: 'Blurt, Master Constable' (horn obligato);
 5. William Wordsworth: 'The Prelude' (timpani obligato)
 6. Wilfred Owen: 'The Kind Ghosts' (cor anglais obligato);
 7. John Keats: 'Sleep and Poetry' (flute and clarinet duet);
 8. William Shakespeare: Sonnet 43 (full ensemble)]
Dedicated 'To Alma Mahler' whom Britten had first met in New York in the early 1940s
Dur: 25'
Instr: Fl. Ca. Cl. Bsn. Hn. Timp. Hp. Str.
f.p.   Peter Pears (Ten.)/BBC Symphony Orchestra/Rudolf Schwarz - Leeds Town
            Hall, 16 October 1958 (Leeds Centenary Festival)
f.Lon.p.   Peter Pears (Ten.)/Aldeburgh Festival Orchestra/Benjamin Britten - Friends
            House, 30 January 1959 (Erwin Stein commemorative concert)
f.rec.   Peter Pears/London Symphony Orchestra/Benjamin Britten - *London (USA)*
            CS 6179; Decca SXL 2189, SWL 8025, 417 310-1 (and MC), 417 153-2 (CD);
            London 436 395-2 (CD)
Pub: Boosey & Hawkes, 1959 (full score), 1960 (vocal score by Imogen Holst),
            1999 (Masterworks Library)

Sechs Hölderlin-Fragmente: for voice and piano Op.61 (1958)
[Words: Friedrich Hölderlin trans. Elizabeth Mayer and Peter Pears
 1. Menschenbeifall (The Applause of Men) 2. Die Heimat (Home) 3. Sokrates und
Alcibiades (Socrates and Alcibiades) 4. Die Jugend (Youth)
 5. Hälfte des Lebens (The Middle of Life) 6. Die Linien des Lebens (Lines of Life)]
'Meinem Freund, dem Prinzen Ludwig von Hessen und bei Rhein, zum fünfzigsten
Geburtstag' (Written for the 50th birthday of Prince Ludwig of Hesse and the Rhine)
Dur: 12'
f.p.   Peter Pears (Ten.)/Benjamin Britten (Pno.) - BBC Third Programme,

14 November 1958 (pre-recorded, 20 October 1958)

f.conc.p.   above artists - Schloss Wolfsgarten, Darmstadt, 20 November 1958
             (Prince Ludwig's birthday)

f.Brit.conc.p. above artists - Wigmore Hall, London, 1 February 1960
             (ICA Concert)

f.Russ.p.   above artists - The Great Hall of Moscow Conservatory, 10 March 1963
             (during a Festival of British Music)

f.rec.   above artists - *London (USA) OS 25321; Decca SWL 8507, SDD 197, 417*
             313-1 (and MC); London 433 200-2 (CD)

Pub: Boosey & Hawkes, 1963

**Cantata academica, 'carmen basiliense': for soprano, alto, tenor and bass solos,
chorus and orchestra Op.62 (1959)**
[Latin text compiled by Bernhard Wyss
Pars I - 1. Corale 2. Alla rovesco 3. Recitativo 4. Arioso 5. Duettino 6. Recitativo
7. Scherzo. Pars II - 8. Tema seriale con fuga 9. Soli e duetto 10. Arioso con canto
popolare 11. Recitativo 12. Canone ed ostinato 13. Corale con canto]
'Composuit Universitati Basiliensi, sollemnia saecularia quinta celebranti, dedicavit
Benjamin Britten MCMLX' (Commissioned to celebrate the 50th anniversary of the
foundation of the University of Basle, Switzerland)

Dur: 22'

Instr: 2/2/2/2 - 4/2/3/1 - timp. perc.(4) hp.(2) pno.(cel.) str.

f.p.   Agnes Giebel (Sop.)/Elsa Cavelti (Con.)/Peter Pears (Ten.)/Heinz Rehfuss
             (Bs.)/Basle Chamber Choir and Orchestra/Paul Sacher - Basler Kongresshalle,
             Basle, Switzerland, 1 July 1960

f.Brit.p.   Jennifer Vyvyan (Sop.)/Helen Watts (Con.)/Peter Pears (Ten.)/Owen
             Brannigan (Bs.)/Cambridge University Musical Society Choir and Orchestra -
             Guildhall, Cambridge, 29 November 1960

f.Lon.p.   Jennifer Vyvyan (Sop.)/Helen Watts (Con.)/Peter Pears (Ten.)/Owen
             Brannigan (Bs.)/London Symphony Choir and Orchestra/George Malcolm -
             Royal Festival Hall, 10 March 1961

f.recs.   above first performance - *Ars Musici (Freiburg) AM 1155-2 (CD)*
             above (Lon.) artists - *L'oiseau- lyre SOL 60037; Decca SXL 6640; London*
             425 153-4 (MC), 436 396-2 (CD)

Pub: Boosey & Hawkes, 1959 (vocal score by Imogen Holst), 1960 (full score)

Fanfare for St Edmundsbury: for three trumpets (1959)

Dur: 3'30"

f.p.   Cathedral of Bury St Edmunds - 10 June 1959 (on the occasion of the Pageant
             of Magna Carta and performed in the precincts of the Cathedral with a
             recorded performance of trumpeters from the Suffolk Regiment)

f.conc.p.   Philip Jones Brass Ensemble - Royal Albert Hall, London, 9 August 1976
             (Promenade Concert)

f.broad.p.   Philip Jones Brass Ensemble - Radio 3, 20 October 1979

f.rec.   Philip Jones Brass Ensemble - *Decca SDD 274, SPA 419, KCSP 419 (MC);*
             London 430 369-2 (CD)

Pub: Boosey & Hawkes, 1969 (also in 'Contemporary Music for Trumpet', 1968)

Missa Brevis in D for boys' voices and organ Op.63 (1959)
[1. Kyrie 2. Gloria 3. Sanctus-Benedictus 4. Agnus Dei]
Written 'For George Malcolm and the boys of Westminster Cathedral Choir' on the
occasion of his retirement - the work was completed on 24 May 1959
Dur: 11'
f.p.   Westminster Cathedral Choristers/George Malcolm - Westminster Cathedral,
              London, 22 July 1959
f.broad.p.   above first performance - Home Service, 7 December 1959
f.recs.   above artists - *Decca CEP 654 (45), ECM (m)/ECS 507 (es)*
              New College Choir, Oxford/Edward Higginbottom - *Proud Sound PROUCD*
              1140-2 (CD)
Pub: Boosey & Hawkes, 1959 (choral score), 1960 (organ/vocal score)

Um Mitternacht: song for high voice and piano (1960?)
[Words: Goethe* trans. Andrew Porter]
Dur: 3'30"
f.p.   Lucy Shelton (Sop.)/Ian Brown (Pno.) - Holy Trinity Church, Blythburgh,
              15 June 1992 (Aldeburgh Festival)
f.broad.p.   above first performance - Radio 3, 8 July 1992
f.rec.   Ian Bostridge (Ten.)/Graham Johnson (Pno.) - *Hyperion CDA 66823 (CD)*
Pub: Faber, 1994 (in 'The Red Cockatoo & Other Songs')
(*Britten was considering a Goethe cycle but this is the only known setting. He had
received a 1959 edition of Goethe's complete poetry as a gift from Prince Ludwig of
Hesse, the dedicatee of the **Sechs Hölderlin-Fragmente** q.v.)

A Midsummer Night's Dream: opera in three acts Op.64 (1959-60)
[Libretto: Shakespeare adapted by Benjamin Britten and Peter Pears]
'Dedicated to Stephen Reiss' who was then managing both the Aldeburgh Festival and
the English Opera Group - the draft score is dated 15 April 1960
Dur: 144'
Instr: 2/1/2/1 - 2/1/1/0 - perc.(2) hp.(2) hpschd. str. (+stage band)
f.p.   English Opera Group cond. Benjamin Britten - Jubilee Hall, Aldeburgh,
              11 June 1960 (Aldeburgh Festival)
Producer: John Cranko
Scenery and costumes: John Piper assisted by Carl Toms
Principals: Alfred Deller, Jennifer Vyvyan, April Cantelo, Peter Pears, Owen
              Brannigan, Forbes Robinson, Thomas Hemsley, Marjorie Thomas
f.broad.p.   above artists - Home Service, 24 June 1960 (pre-recorded at the dress
              rehearsal, 10 June 1960)
f.recs.   Soloists/London Symphony Orchestra/Benjamin Britten - *London (USA) OSA*
              1385; Decca SET 338-40; London 425 663-2 (CD)
              Glyndebourne Festival Production (1981) cond. Bernard Haitink - *Castle*
              Vision CVI 2008(V)
Pub: Boosey & Hawkes, 1960 (vocal score by Imogen Holst and Martin Penny);
              1962 (study score)

Other performances:
f.Eur.p.   English Opera Group cond. George Malcolm - Amsterdam, June 1960
              (Holland Festival)

f.Lon.p.   cond. Sir George Solti - Royal Opera House, Covent Garden,
            2 February 1961
Producer: Sir John Gielgud
Principals: Juan Carlyle, Irene Salemka, Russell Oberlin, Geraint Evans, John
            Lanigan, Marjorie Thomas
f.Am.p.   War Memorial Opera House, San Francisco, 10 October 1961 (and later in
            New York by the City Opera Company on 25 April 1963)
f.Can.p.   Vancouver, October 1961
f.S.Am.p. Buenos Aires, Argentina, October/November 1962
f.Russ.p. Bolshoi Theatre Company cond. Gennadi Rozhdestvensky - Moscow,
            28 October 1965
Producer: Boris Bokrovsky
Designer: Nicolai Benois

Exc. Bottom's Dream: song for bass-baritone and orchestra, or piano Op.64a
Dur: 3'30"
Instr: 2/ca./2/1 - 2/1/0/0 - perc.(2) hp.(2) hpschd. str.
f.rec.   as above but also in *Decca (compilation) SPA 321*
Pub: Boosey & Hawkes, 1965

Fanfare for Oriana (1960)
Score dated 4 October 1960
Instr: 3Tpt.
f.p.   at the launching of the vessel by Princess Alexandra - Vickers Shipyard,
           Barrow-in-Furness, Cumbria, 3 November 1960

Sonata in C for cello and piano Op.65 (1960-61)
[1. Dialogo 2. Scherzo-pizzicato 3. Elegia 4. Marcia 5. Moto perpetuo]
Written 'For Mstislav Rostropovich'
Dur: 18'
f.p.   Mstislav Rostropovich (Vc.)/Benjamin Britten (Pno.) - Jubilee Hall,
           Aldeburgh, 7 July 1961 (Aldeburgh Festival - the last two movements were
           repeated as an encore)
f.broad.p. above first performance - Third Programme, 26 November 1961
f.Russ.p. above artists - Moscow, March 1963 (as part of a Festival of British Music)
f.rec.   above artists - *London (USA) CS 6237; Decca SXL 2298, SWL 8503,
           410 168-1 (and MC); London 421 859-2 (CD)*
Pub: Boosey & Hawkes, 1961 (ed. Mstislav Rostropovich)

Te Deum, for choir and organ - incomplete (1961)

Venite exultemus Domino:* for choir (SATB) and organ (1961)
[Psalm 95]
Dur: 3'
f.p.   Choir of Westminster Abbey/Simon Preston with Geoffrey Morgan (org.) -
           Westminster Abbey, London, 2 October 1983
f.rec.   Trinity College Choir, Cambridge/Richard Marlow - *Pearl SHE 593*
Pub: OUP, 1983
(*intended as one of the companion pieces to the **Te Deum in C** of 1934 q.v.)

Jubilate Deo in C:* for choir (SATB) and organ (1961)
[Psalm 100]
'Written for St George's Chapel,Windsor, at the request of H.R.H. The Duke of
Edinburgh'
Dur: 2'30"
f.p.   Choir of St George's Chapel, with William Harris (org.) - Windsor Castle,
            16 July 1961
f.broad.p. Choir of St Matthew's Church, Northampton with John Bertalot (org.) -
            Home Service, 21 January 1962
f.rec.   Choir of St John's College, Cambridge/George Guest - *Argo ZRG 5340,*
            ZK 19
Pub: OUP, 1961
(*intended as one of the companion pieces to the **Te Deum in C** of 1934 q.v.)

Fancie: for unison voices and piano (1961, rev.1965)
[Words: William Shakespeare]
Written 'For M.H.' (Marion Harewood) - the score is dated 9 May 1961
Dur: 1'
f.recs.   Aldeburgh Festival Singers - *University of East Anglia UEA 82015*
            New London Children's Choir/Ronald Corp - *Naxos 8.553183 (CD)*
Pub: Boosey & Hawkes, 1965 (rev. version)
also for voice and piano
f.broad.p. Rupert Oliver Forbes (Bar.)/Julian Dawson (Pno.) - Scottish Home Service,
            2 March 1969 (pre-recorded, 8 January 1969)
f.rec.   Sarah Walker (M/S)/Graham Johnson (Pno.) - *Hyperion CDA 66136 (CD)*
Pub: Anthony Blond, 1964 (original version in 'Classical Songs for Children')

**War Requiem: for soprano, tenor and baritone solos, chorus, orchestra, chamber
orchestra, boys' choir and organ Op.66 (1961)**
[Words: The Missa pro Defunctis and extracts from poems by Wilfred Owen]
Dedicated 'In loving memory of Roger Burney, Sub-Lieutenant R.N.V.R.,
Piers Dunkerley, Captain Royal Marines, David Gill, Ordinary Seaman, Royal Navy,
Michael Halliday, Lieutenant R.N.Z.N.V.R.' (Four of Britten's friends, three of whom
had been killed during the Second World War. One, Piers Dunkerley, had committed
suicide in 1959.) The draft score is dated 20 December 1961.
Dur: 85'
Instr: 3/2+ca./3/2+cbsn. - 6/4/3/1 - timp. perc.(4) pno. org. str.
            (+chamber orchestra - Fl. Ob. Cl. Bsn. Hn. Timp. Perc. Hp. Harm.[Ch.Org.]
            Vn. Vn. Va. Vc. Db.)
f.p.   Heather Harper* (Sop.)/Peter Pears (Ten.)/Dietrich Fischer-Dieskau
            (Bar.)/Coventry Festival Chorus/boys of Holy Trinity, Leamington,, and Holy
            Trinity, Stratford/City of Birmingham Symphony Orchestra cond. Meredith
            Davies and the Melos Ensemble cond. Benjamin Britten - St Michael's
            Cathedral, Coventry, 30 May 1962 (at the Festival to celebrate the
            consecration of the Cathedral)
f.Eur.p.   above artists cond. Colin Davis - Berlin, 11 November 1962
            (on the anniversary of the Armistice)

f.Lon.p.   Heather Harper (Sop.)/Peter Pears (Ten.)/Vladimir Ruzdjak (Bs.)/BBC
Chorus/BBC Symphony Orchestra cond. Meredith Davies and the Melos
Ensemble cond. Benjamin Britten - Westminster Abbey, 6 December 1962

f.Am.p.   cond. Erich Leinsdorf - Tanglewood, Lenox, Massachusetts, 27 July 1963
(Berkshire Music Festival - and later in New York, November 1963)

f.Russ.p.   (complete) Moscow, c.September 1966 (there had been an earlier, though
incomplete, performance given in March 1964 by the students of Leningrad
University in the presence of the composer)

f.rec.   Soloists/Choirs/London Symphony Orchestra/Melos Ensemble cond.
Benjamin Britten - *London (USA) OSA 1255 (set); Decca SET 252-3, K27K22
(MC), 414 383-2 (CD), (excs.) 436 990-2 (CD)*

Pub: Boosey & Hawkes, 1962 (study score, vocal score by Imogen Holst), 1963
(chorus score, boys' chorus score), 1997 (full score)

Exc. 'Agnus Dei' arr. for tenor solo, SATB and organ by Philip Brunelle

Dur: 3'30"

Pub: Boosey & Hawkes, 1989

(*the original soprano soloist was to have been Galina Vishnevskaya, the wife of
Rostropovich. However the Soviet authorities had forbidden her appearance in a
'political work'. It was not until the performance at the Royal Albert Hall on 9 January
1963 that Vishnevskaya sang the part which had been written expressly for her.)

Psalm 150 for two-part children's voices and instruments Op.67 (1962)

'Written for the centenary celebrations of Old Buckenham Hall School - formerly South
Lodge School, Lowestoft* - July 1962' - the score is dated 1 May 1962

Dur: 5'

Instr: Treble and bass instruments, percussion and keyboard (+optional 2Cl. Tpt.
Hn. Tbn. Va.)

f.p.   Choir of Old Buckenham Hall School, Lowestoft/instrumental ensemble/Kay
Foster - St Mary's Church, Thorpe Morieux, 29 July 1962

f.pub.p.   Northgate School Choir and Orchestra/Benjamin Britten - Jubilee Hall,
Aldeburgh, 24 June 1963 (Aldeburgh Festival)

f.rec.   Boys of Downside School/Benjamin Britten - *London (USA) OS 25993, STS
15173; Decca SXL 6264; London 436 394-2 (CD)*

Pub: Boosey & Hawkes, 1963

(*Britten's preparatory school)

A Hymn of St Columba - Regis regum rectissimi: for chorus (SATB) and organ (1962)

[Words attrib. St Columba trans. John Andrewes]

'For Derek Hill' (the artist) to mark the fourteenth centenary of St Columba's missionary
journey from Ireland to Iona, the birthplace of St Columba - the score is dated 29
December 1962

Dur: 2'30"

f.p.   Ulster Singers/Havelock Nelson with R.A. McGraw (org.) - Churchill,
Co. Donegal, Southern Ireland, 2 June 1963 (a pre-recorded tape was played
over loudspeakers - however a gusting wind rendered the performance
virtually inaudible!)

f.broad.p.   above artists - Northern Ireland Home Service, 20 June 1963 (pre-recorded at
Gartan, Co. Donegal, 28 May 1963)

f.rec.   Choir of St John's College, Cambridge/George Guest - *Argo ZRG 621, ZK 19;*
            Decca 430 097-2 (CD)
Pub: Boosey & Hawkes, 1963, 1975 (Latin and English)

Symphony for Cello and Orchestra Op.68 (1963, rev.1964)
Written for Mstislav Rostropovich - the score is dated 3 May 1963
Dur: 34'
Instr: 2/2/2/1+cbsn. - 2/2/1/1 - timp. perc.(2) str.
f.p.   Mstislav Rostropovich/Moscow Philharmonic Orchestra/Benjamin Britten -
            Great Hall of Moscow Conservatory, 12 March 1964
f.Brit.p.   Mstislav Rostropovich/English Chamber Orchestra/Benjamin Britten -
            Blythburgh Church, Aldeburgh, 18 June 1964 (Aldeburgh Festival*)
f.Lon.p.   above artists - Guildhall, 15 July 1964
f.Am.p.   Mstislav Rostropovich/London Symphony Orchestra/Gennadi Rozhdestvensky
            - New York, May 1967
f.recs.   above artists (f.p.) - Russian Disc *RDCD 11108 (CD)*
            above artists - *London (USA) CS 6419, CS 6852; Decca SXL 6138, SXL 6641,*
            417 312-1 (and MC); London 425 100-2 (CD)
            above (f.Am.p.) artists - *Intaglio INCD-7151(CD)*
Pub: Boosey & Hawkes, 1964 (ed. Mstislav Rostropovich), 1965 (arr. for cello and
            piano by Imogen Holst)
(*the first performance was planned for the 1963 Festival but had to be postponed owing
to the illness of Rostropovich)

Night Piece (Notturno) for piano solo (1963)
Commissioned by Marion Thorpe (Harewood) for the first Leeds International Pianoforte
Competition - it was used again for the competition in 1978 in memory of Britten
Dur: 5'
f.p.   Michael Roll (the winner) - Great Hall of Leeds University, between 13-18
            September 1963 (first Leeds International Pianoforte Competition)
f.broad.p. Michael Roll - Home Service, 13 November 1963
f.conc.p.   John McCabe - Royal Manchester College of Music, 13 July 1964
f.recs.   John McCabe - *Pye Golden Guinea GSGC 2069 (and MC)*
            Stephen Hough - *Virgin VC7 91203-2 (CD) (and MC), VC7 59027-2 (CD)*
Pub: Boosey & Hawkes, 1963

Cantata Misericordium: for tenor and baritone solos, small chorus and string quartet, string orchestra, piano, harp and timpani Op.69 (1963)
[Latin text: Patrick Wilkinson]
'In honorem Societatis Crucis Rubrae kalendis septembribus A.S. MCMLXIII sollemnia
saecularia Genavae celebrantis hoc opus compositum illo primum die auditum est'
Written for the celebration of the centenary of the International Red Cross Society in
Geneva and dedicated 'To Fidelity Cranbrook', the Chairman of the Aldeburgh Festival
Council - the draft score is dated 25 May 1963
Dur: 19'30"
f.p.   Peter Pears (Ten.)/Dietrich Fischer-Dieskau (Bar.)/Le Motet de
            Genève/L'Orchestre de la Suisse Romande/Ernest Ansermet - Grand Théâtre,
            Geneva, 1 September 1963

f.Brit.p.   Peter Pears (Ten.)/Thomas Hemsley (Bar.)/BBC Chorus/London Symphony
            Orchestra/Benjamin Britten - Royal Albert Hall, London, 12 September 1963
            (Promenade Concert)
f.Am.p.   Philadelphia Chorus and Orchestra/Eugene Ormandy - Philadelphia,
            26 February 1965
f.rec.   Peter Pears (Ten.)/Dietrich Fischer-Dieskau (Bar.)/London Symphony Chorus
            and Orchestra/Benjamin Britten - *London (USA) OS 25937, OS 26389; Decca
            SXL 6175, SXL 6640; Argo ZRG 947; London 425 100-2 (CD)*
Pub: Boosey & Hawkes, 1963 (chorus score), 1964 (full score, miniature score,
            vocal score by Imogen Holst)

Nocturnal after John Dowland: reflections on 'Come, heavy sleep' for guitar Op.70 (1963)

[1. Musingly 2. Very agitated 3. Restless 4. Uneasy 5. March-like
6. Dreaming 7. Gently rocking 8. Passacagalia]
'For Julian Bream' - the work is based on Dowland's song, 'Come, heavy Sleep, the
image of true Death'. The score is dated 11 November 1963.
Dur: 18'
f.p.   Julian Bream - Jubilee Hall, Aldeburgh, 12 June 1964 (Aldeburgh Festival)
f.broad.p. above artist - Home Service, 20 August 1964 (from Leith Town Hall,
            Edinburgh)
f.Lon.p.   above artist - 19 November 1965
f.recs.   above artist - *RCA (USA) LSC 2964, VCS 7057; RCA SB 6723, DPS 2003,
            SER 5638-42, 09026 61583-2 (CD set), 09026 61601-2 (CD)*
            above artist (rec. 1992) - *EMI CDC7 54901-2 (CD)*
Pub: Faber, 1965 (ed. Julian Bream)

Curlew River:* a parable for church performance Op.71 (1964)

[Libretto: William Plomer after the medieval Japanese Nō play 'Sumidagawa'
('The Sumida River') by Jūrō Motomasa]
Dedicated 'To Michael Tippett, in friendship and admiration' - the work was completed
on 26 March 1964
Dur: 71'
Instr: Fl. Hn. Va. Db. Hp. Perc. Ch.Organ
f.p.   English Opera Group (no conductor) - Orford Church, Suffolk, 12 June 1964
            (Aldeburgh Festival)
Producer: Colin Graham
Costumes: Annena Stubbs
Principals: Peter Pears, John Shirley-Quirk, Don Garrard, Bryan Drake
f.broad.p. above first performance - Third Programme, 21 June 1964
f.rec.   above artists - *London (USA) OSA 1156; Decca SET 301, IBB 101-3, 421
            858-2 (CD)*
Pub: Faber, 1964, 1965 (rehearsal score by Imogen Holst), 1983 (full score), 1997
            (rehearsal score 2nd ed.)

Other performances:
f.Eur.p.   English Opera Group - Municipal Theatre, Amsterdam, June 1964 (Holland
            Festival)

f.Lon.p.   English Opera Group - Southwark Cathedral, 13 July 1964 (City of London
            Festival)
f.Am.p.   Spanish Courtyard, Katonah, New York, 26 June 1966 (Caramoor Festival)
f.Can.p.   English Opera Group (on tour) - Montreal, 1967 (Expo '67)
f.Austr.p. English Opera Group (on tour) - Adelaide, March 1970 (Adelaide Festival)
(*the film of 'Curlew River' made at Louvain in 1965 by Belgian Television was
awarded first prize in the Monte Carlo 'Unda' Festival)

Cadenzas to Haydn's Cello Concerto in C (Hoboken VIIb/1) (1964)
Dur: 3'
f.p.   Mstislav Rostropovich/English Chamber Orchestra/Benjamin Britten -
            Blythburgh Church, 18 June 1964 (Aldeburgh Festival)
f.rec.   above artists - *Decca 430 633-2 (CD)*
Pub: Boosey & Hawkes, 1966 (cadenzas to movements I and III ed. Rostropovich)

First Suite for Cello Op.72 (1964)
[Canto primo - Fuga - Lamento - Canto secondo - Serenata - Marcia - Canto terzo -
Bordone - Moto perpetuo e Canto quarto]
Written 'For Slava' (Mstislav Rostropovich)
Dur: 21'
f.p.   Mstislav Rostropovich - Aldeburgh Parish Church, 27 June 1965
            (Aldeburgh Festival)
f.broad.p. above first performance - Third Programme, 28 December 1965
f.Russ.p.   above artist - Philharmonic Concert Hall, Yerevan, Armenia, 28 August 1965
            (Britten Festival)
f.Lon.p.   above artist - 30 June 1966
f.rec.   above artist - *London (USA) CS 6617; Decca SXL 6393, 417 309-1 (and MC);
            London 421 859-2 (CD)*
Pub: Faber, 1966 (ed. Mstislav Rostropovich), 1986 (in 'Three Suites for Cello')

Gemini Variations: Twelve Variations and Fugue on an Epigram of Kodály* - quartet for two (or four) players Op.73 (1965)
Written 'For Zoltán and Gábor Jeney', two gifted children the composer had met in
Budapest during the spring of 1964 - the score is dated 5 March 1965
Dur: 15'
Instr: Fl. Vn. Pno.(4 hands)
f.p.   Zoltán Jeney (Pno./Fl.) and Gabriel Jeney (Pno./Vn.) - Aldeburgh Parish
            Church, 19 June 1965 (Aldeburgh Festival)
f.broad.p. above first performance - Third Programme, 14 June 1966
f.rec.   above artists - *London (USA) OS 25993, STS 15183; Decca SXL 6264, 436
            393-2 (CD)*
Pub: Faber, 1966
(*from the fourth of Kodály's 'Epigrams' for piano of 1954)

Songs and Proverbs of William Blake: for baritone and piano Op.74 (1965)
[Proverb I - London Proverb II - The Chimney-Sweeper Proverb III - A Poison Tree
 Proverb IV - The Tyger Proverb V - The Fly Proverb VI - Ah, Sun-flower!
 Proverb VII - Every Night and Every Morn]
Written 'For Dieter: the past and the future' - the score is dated 6 April 1965

Dur: 22'
f.p.   Dietrich Fischer-Dieskau (Bar.)/Benjamin Britten (Pno.) - Aldeburgh Parish
           Church, 24 June 1965 (Aldeburgh Festival)
f.broad.p. above first performance - Third Programme, 2 August 1965
f.Lon.p.   Benjamin Luxon (Bar.)/Sheila Amit (Pno.) - Conway Hall, 18 November 1969
           (Music In Our Time Festival)
f.rec.   Dietrich Fischer-Dieskau/Benjamin Britten - *London (USA) OS 26099; Decca
           SXL 6391, 417 313-1 (and MC); London 417 428-2 (CD)*
Pub: Faber, 1965

Voices for Today: anthem for chorus (men, women and children) with ad libitum accompaniment for organ Op.75 (1965)

[Words from Virgil's 'Eclogue IV' and others]
Commissioned by Secretary General U Thant for the twentieth anniversary of the
founding of the United Nations
Dur: 10'
f.p.   (simultaneous triple première/broadcast) 24 October 1965
           (i)   Schola Cantorum/Farmingdale Boys' Choir/Richard Foster (organ) cond.
                 Hugh Ross and Arpad Darazs - General Assembly Hall of the United
                 Nations Building, New York
           (ii) O.R.T.F. Chorus and Boys' Choir cond. Jacques Jouineau and Jean-Paul
                 Kreder - O.R.T.F. Studios, Paris
           (iii) LSO Chorus/Choristers of Westminster Abbey/Ralph Downes (organ)
                 cond. István Kertész and Douglas Guest - Royal Festival Hall, London
f.rec.   King's College & Cambridge University Musical Society Choirs/David
           Willcocks and Benjamin Britten - *Argo ZRG 947; Decca 5BB 119-20*
Pub: Faber, 1965, 1995 (new edition)

The Poet's Echo: for high voice and piano Op.76 (1965)

[Words: Alexander Pushkin trans. Peter Pears   1. Echo 2. My Heart ... 3. Angel
4. The Nightingale and the Rose 5. Epigram 6. Lines written during a sleepless night]
Written 'For Galya and Slava' - the score is dated 23 August 1965
Dur: 12'
f.p.   (Nos.2 and 5 only) Galina Vishnevskaya (Sop.)/Mstislav Rostropovich (Pno.) -
           Philharmonic Concert Hall, Yerevan, Armenia, 29 August 1965 (Britten
           Festival)
f.p.   (complete) above artists - Small Hall of the Conservatoire of Music, Moscow,
           2 December 1965
f.Am.p.   above artists - New York, 19 December 1965
f.Brit.p. above artists - Royal Festival Hall, London, 2 July 1966
f.broad.p. above first (British) performance - Third Programme, 2 February 1967
f.rec.   above artists - *London (USA) OS 26141; Decca SXL 6428, 417 313-1 (and
           MC); London 433 200-2 (CD)*
Pub: Faber, 1967

The Burning Fiery Furnace: second parable for church performance Op.77 (1965-66)

[Libretto: William Plomer from the Book of Daniel]
Dedicated 'To Donald and Kathleen Mitchell' - the score is dated 5 April 1966

Dur: 64'
Instr: Fl. Hn. Al.Tbn. Va. Db. Hp. Perc. Ch.Organ
f.p.   English Opera Group (no conductor) - Orford Church, Suffolk, 9 June 1966
            (Aldeburgh Festival)
Producer: Colin Graham
Costumes: Annena Stubbs
Principals: Bryan Drake, Peter Pears, John Shirley-Quirk, Robert Tear
f.broad.p. Bryan Drake, Kenneth Macdonald, John Shirley-Quirk, Robert Tear/English
            Opera Group instrumentalists - Third Programme, 20 June 1966
f.rec.   above (f.p.) artists - *London (USA) OSA 1163; Decca SET 356, IBB 101-3,*
            414 663-2 (CD)
Pub: Faber, 1966, 1968 (rehearsal score by Martin Penny and David Matthews),
            1983 (full score)

Other performances:
f.Eur.p.   English Opera Group (on tour) - Municipal Theatre, Amsterdam, June 1966
            (Holland Festival) (also recorded for Belgian Television at Louvain in 1966)
f.Am.p.   Spanish Courtyard, Katonah, New York, 25 June 1967 (Caramoor Festival)
f.Lon.p.   English Opera Group - Southwark Cathedral, 24 July 1967
            (City of London Festival)
f.Can.p.   English Opera Group (on tour) - Montreal, 1967 (Expo '67)
f.Austr.p. English Opera Group (on tour) - Adelaide, March 1970 (Adelaide Festival)
f.Brit.tel.p. cond. Benjamin Britten - BBC Television, 18 April 1971

Cadenzas to Mozart's Piano Concerto in E flat major, K482 (1966)
Written 'For Slava Richter'
f.p.   Sviatoslav Richter - Tours, France, July 1966
f.Brit.p.   Sviatoslav Richter/English Chamber Orchestra/Benjamin Britten -
            The Maltings, Snape, 13 June 1967 (Aldeburgh Festival)
f.broad.p. above first (British) performance - Third Programme, 1 February 1968
f.rec.   above first (British) performance - *Nuovo Era 013 6339*
Pub: Faber, 1967 (cadenzas to movements I and III)

The Golden Vanity: a vaudeville for boys and piano after the old English ballad Op.78 (1966)
[Libretto: Colin Graham]
Written at the request of the Vienna Boys' Choir to perform on tour - the score, dedicated
'Für die Wiener Sängerknaben', is dated 26 August 1966
Dur: 17'
f.p.   Vienna Boys' Choir/Anton Neyder (Pno.) - The Maltings, Snape, 3 June 1967
            (Aldeburgh Festival)
f.broad.p. above first performance - Third Programme, 19 October 1967
f.Lon.p.   above artists - Royal Festival Hall, 24 November 1967
f.tel.p.   above artists - London Weekend Television, October 1968
f.rec.   Wandsworth School Boys' Choir/Benjamin Britten (Pno.) cond. Russell
            Burgess - *London (USA) OS 26156; Decca SET 445; London 436 397-2 (CD)*
Pub: Faber, 1967

Hankin Booby: Folk Dance for wind and drums (1966)
Commissioned by the Greater London Council for the opening of the Queen Elizabeth
Hall on London's South Bank - the score is dated 11 December 1966
Dur: 2'
Instr: 2/2/2/2 - 0/2/0/0 - tamburo
f.p.   English Chamber Orchestra/Benjamin Britten - Queen Elizabeth Hall, London,
            1 March 1967 (at the inaugural concert given in the presence of Her Majesty
            Queen Elizabeth II)
f.broad.p. above artists - Home Service, 2 March 1967
f.rec.   as part of **Suite on English Folk Tunes Op.90** q.v.
Pub: Faber, 1976 (as No.3 of **Suite on English Folk Tunes Op.90** q.v.)

The Building of the House: overture with or without chorus Op.79 (1967)
[Words: Psalm 127, adapted by Imogen Holst]
Written for the opening of the original Maltings Concert Hall, Snape, by Her Majesty the
Queen - the score is dated 16 March 1967
Dur: 5'15"
Instr: 2/2/2/2 - 2/2/0/1 - timp. perc. org.(ad lib.) str.
f.p.   East Anglian Choirs/English Chamber Orchestra/Benjamin Britten - The
            Maltings, Snape, 2 June 1967 (Aldeburgh Festival)
f.broad.p. above first performance - Third Programme, 4 June 1967
f.Lon.p.   New Philharmonia Orchestra/Carlo Maria Giulini - Royal Festival Hall,
            16 January 1968
f.recs.   above first performance - *BBCB 8007-2 (CD)*
            City of Birmingham Symphony Chorus and Orchestra/Simon Rattle - *EMI
            CDS7 54270-2 (CD)*
Pub: Faber, 1968
also transcribed for concert band by Thad Marciniak
Pub: Faber/Studio Music, 1977; Hal Leonard (USA)

The Oxen: Carol for women's voices (two parts) and piano (1967)
[Words: Thomas Hardy]
Written 'For Cecily Smithwick* and the East Coker W. I.' - the score is dated
19 April 1967
Dur: 3'
f.p.   East Coker Women's Institute Choir - 25 January 1968
f.rec.   New London Children's Choir/Ronald Corp - *Naxos 8.553183 (CD)*
Pub: Faber, 1968
(*Peter Pears's sister)

Second Suite for Cello Op.80 (1967)
[1. Declamato 2. Fuga 3. Scherzo 4. Andante lento 5. Ciaccona]
Written 'For Slava' - the score is dated 17 August 1967
Dur: 22'
f.p.   Mstislav Rostropovich - The Maltings, Snape, 17 June 1968
            (Aldeburgh Festival)
f.Lon.p.   above artist - Queen Elizabeth Hall, 12 September 1968
f.rec.   above artist - *London (USA) CS 6617; Decca SXL 6293, 417 309-1 (and MC);
            London 421 859-2 (CD)*

Pub: Faber, 1969 (ed. Mstislav Rostropovich), 1986 (in 'Three Suites for Cello')

The Prodigal Son:* third parable for church performance Op.81 (1968)
[Libretto: William Plomer after Luke]
Dedicated 'To Dmitri Shostakovich' - the draft score is dated 22 April 1968
Dur: 72'
Instr: Al.Fl. Tpt. Hn. Va. Db. Hp. Perc. Ch.Org.(+on-stage perc.)
f.p.   English Opera Group (no conductor) - Orford Church, Suffolk, 10 June 1968
           (Aldeburgh Festival)
Producer: Colin Graham
Costumes: Annena Stubbs
Principals: Peter Pears, John Shirley-Quirk, Bryan Drake, Robert Tear
f.broad.p. above artists - Third Programme, 28 June 1968
f.rec.   above artists - *London (USA) OSA 1164; Decca SET 438, IBB 101-3, 425
           713-2 (CD)*
Pub: Faber, 1968, 1971 (rehearsal score by David Matthews), 1986 (full score)

Other performances:
f.Lon.p.   English Opera Group - Southwark Cathedral, 13 July 1968 (City of London
           Festival)
f.Am.p.   Spanish Courtyard, Katonah, New York, 29 June 1969 (Caramoor Festival)
f.Austr.p. English Opera Group (on tour) - Adelaide, March 1970 (Adelaide Festival)

(*all three church parables were given, for the first time in one evening, by the City of
Birmingham Touring Opera conducted by Simon Halsey in Symphony Hall, Birmingham
on 2 March 1977)

Children's Crusade: a ballad for children's voices and orchestra Op.82 (1968)
[Words: Bertolt Brecht trans. Hans Keller]
'Written for the members of Wandsworth School Choir (director Russell Burgess) to
perform on the 50th anniversary of The Save The Children Fund at St Paul's Cathedral,
May 19th 1969' and dedicated 'To Hans Werner Henze' - the score is dated 10 November
1968
Dur: 19'
Instr: 6 solo perc. tutti perc. 2 pnos. chamber/elec. organ
f.p.   Wandsworth School Boys' Choir and Orchestra/Russell Burgess - St Paul's
           Cathedral, London, 19 May 1969
f.conc.p. above artists - Royal Albert Hall, London, 31 August 1969 (Promenade
           Concert)
f.rec.   above artists - *London (USA) OS 26156; Decca SET 445; London 436 393-2
           (CD)*
Pub: Faber, 1970, 1972 (full score), 1973 (limited edition)

Suite for harp Op.83 (1969)
[1. Overture 2. Toccata 3. Nocturne 4. Fugue 5. Hymn (St Denio)]
'For Osian Ellis' - the score is dated 18 March 1969
Dur: 14'
f.p.   (Nos.2, 3 and 4) Osian Ellis - BBC2 Television, 1 June 1969
           (pre-recorded, 20 May 1969)

f.conc.p.   (complete) Osian Ellis - Jubilee Hall, Aldeburgh, 24 June 1969
            (Aldeburgh Festival)
f.Lon.p.   above artist - Queen Elizabeth Hall, 28 September 1969
f.broad.p. above (Aldeburgh) performance - Home Service, 6 October 1969
f.rec.   above artist - *London (USA) OS 26477; Decca SXL 6788; Meridian KE 77119
            (MC), CDE 84119 (CD)*
Pub: Faber, 1970 (ed. Osian Ellis)

Who are these Children?: lyrics, rhymes and riddles by William Soutar for tenor and piano Op.84 (1969)
[1. A Riddle (The Earth) 2. A Laddie's Sang 3. Nightmare   4. Black Day 5. Bed-time
6. Slaughter 7. A Riddle (The Child You Were) 8. The Larky Lad   9. Who are these
Children? 10. Supper 11. The Children 12. The Auld Aik]
Dedicated 'To Tertia Liebenthal' for whose 700th National Gallery of Scotland Concert it
was written
Dur: 19'
f.p.   (Nos.1, 2, 3, 4, 7, 9 and 12) Peter Pears (Ten.)/Benjamin Britten (Pno.) -
            New Hall, Department of Music, University College, Cardiff, 7 March 1971
            (Cardiff Festival)
f.p.   (omitting No.5) above artists - National Gallery of Scotland, Edinburgh,
            4 May 1971
f.p.   (complete) above artists - The Maltings, Snape, 26 September 1971
f.Lon.p.   above artists - St James's Palace, 27 September 1971
f.broad.p. above (Snape) performance - Radio 3, 21 May 1972
f.rec.   above (Snape) performance - *BBCB 8014-2 (CD)*
            above artists - *London (USA) OS 26357; Decca SXL 6608*
Pub: Faber, 1972, 1997 (rev. ed.)

3 songs were discarded from the original cycle but later published:
[(i) Dawtie's Devotion (ii) Tradition (iii) The Gully]
f.p.   Neil Mackie (Ten.)/Iain Burnside - Wigmore Hall, London, 22 November 1983
f.broad.p. Neil Mackie (Ten.)/John Blakely (Pno.) - Radio 3, 23 April 1985
Pub: Faber, 1997 (as an Appendix to the revised edition)

A Fanfare for D.W. (David Webster*) for brass ensemble (1970)
f.p.   members of the Royal Opera House Orchestra/Sir Georg Solti - Royal Opera
            House, Covent Garden, London, 30 June 1970 (at a Farewell Gala marking Sir
            David Webster's retirement)
(*The General Administrator of the Royal Opera House from 1945 to 1970. Britten's
Fanfare is based on a series of rising fifths, a musical cryptogram of the names 'Covent
Garden' [C......E......G] and 'David Webster' [DA......EB......E])

Owen Wingrave: opera in two acts Op.85 (1969-70)
[Libretto: Myfanwy Piper after Henry James]
Commissioned by BBC Television and dedicated to Joan and Isador Caplan
Dur: 106'
Instr: 2/2/2/2 - 2/2/2/1 - timp.(4) perc.(3) hp. pno. str. (+off-stage perc.)

f.p.   English Opera Group and English Chamber Orchestra cond. Benjamin Britten
              - BBC2 Television and PBS-TV in New York, 16 May 1971 (pre-recorded,
              23-30 November 1970)
Directors: Brian Large and Colin Graham
Designer: David Myerscough-Jones
Costumes: Charles Knode
Principals: Benjamin Luxon, John Shirley-Quirk, Nigel Douglas, Janet Baker,
              Peter Pears, Jennifer Vyvyan, Heather Harper, Sylvia Fisher
f.st.p.   English Opera Group/English Chamber Orchestra cond. Steuart Bedford -
              Royal Opera House, Covent Garden, London, 10 May 1973
Producer: Colin Graham
Designer: John Piper
Costumes: Charles Knode
f.rec.   Soloists/Wandsworth School Boys' Choir/English Chamber
              Orchestra/Benjamin Britten - *London (USA) OSA 1291; Decca SET 501-2;*
              London 433 200-2 (CD)
Pub: Faber, 1973 (vocal score by David Matthews), 1995 (full score)

Other performances:
f.Am.p.   Santa Fe Opera - New Mexico, 9 August 1973
f.Eur.p.   Hanover Opera - Lower Saxony, Germany, September 1973

Canticle IV 'Journey of the Magi': for counter-tenor, tenor, baritone and piano Op.86 (1971)
[Words: T.S. Eliot]
Dedicated 'To James, Peter and John' - the work was composed between 12 and
22 January 1971
Dur: 11'
f.p.   James Bowman (C/Ten.)/Peter Pears (Ten.)/John Shirley-Quirk (Bar.)/
              Benjamin Britten (Pno.) - The Maltings, Snape, 26 June 1971
              (Aldeburgh Festival)
f.tel.p.   above artists - BBC2, 12 December 1971 (rec.13-14 November 1971 in
              Blythburgh Church)
f.broad.p. above artists - Radio 3, 30 January 1972
f.Lon.p.   above artists - National Gallery, 28 May 1972
f.rec.   above artists - *London (USA) OS 26357; Decca SXL 6608; Argo ZRG 946;*
              London 425 716-2 (CD)
Pub: Faber, 1972

Third Suite for cello Op.87 (1971, rev.1974)
[1. Introduzione 2. Marcia 3. Canto 4. Barcarola 5. Dialogo 6. Fuga
 7. Recitativo 8. Moto perpetuo 9. Passacaglia]
Written 'For Slava' - the score is dated 3 March 1971
Dur: 22'
f.p.   Mstislav Rostropovich - The Maltings, Snape, 21 December 1974
f.Lon.p.   Julian Lloyd Webber - Bishopsgate Institute, 11 October 1977
f.broad.p. Rohan de Saram - Radio 3, 22 November 1979
f.recs.   Julian Lloyd Webber - *Alpha ACA 1001 (and MC)*
              Alexander Baillie - *Etcetera KTC 1166 (CD), KTC 2006 (CD)*

Pub: Faber, 1976 (ed. Mstislav Rostropovich), 1986 (in 'Three Suites for Cello')

Alleluia! for Alec's 80th Birthday: a canon (on a well-known tune) (1971)
Written at the request of Donald Beswick as part of a symposium published to celebrate the 80th birthday of Alec Robertson. The three-part canon is based on the Alleluia from the Procession and Recession in **A Ceremony of Carols.**
Dur: 30"
Pub: Stanbrook Abbey Press, 1972 (limited ed.)

Death in Venice: opera in two acts Op.88 (1971-73, rev.1973-74)
[Libretto: Myfanwy Piper after Thomas Mann]
Dedicated 'To Peter' (Pears) - the draft score is dated 17 (24) December 1972
Dur: 145'
Instr: 2/2/2/2 - 2/2/2/1 - timp. perc.(5) hp. pno. str.
f.p.   English Opera Group/Royal Ballet Company and children of the Royal Ballet School/English Chamber Orchestra/Steuart Bedford - The Maltings, Snape, 16 June 1973 (Aldeburgh Festival)
Producer: Colin Graham
Choreography: Frederick Ashton
Designer: John Piper
Costumes: Charles Knode
Principals: Peter Pears, John Shirley-Quirk, Robert Huguenin, James Bowman
f.broad.p. above artists - Radio 3, 22 June 1973
f.Lon.p.   above artists - Royal Opera House, Covent Garden, 18 October 1973
f.recs.   Soloists/English Chamber Orchestra/Steuart Bedford - *London (USA) OSA 13109; Decca SET 581-3, 425 669-2 (CD)*
            Glyndebourne Festival Production (1990) cond. Graeme Jenkins - *Virgin VVD 545(V)*
Pub: Faber, 1975 (vocal score by David Matthews), 1979 (full score)

Other performances:
f.Eur.p.   Teatro La Fenice, Venice, September 1973
f.Am.p.   cond. Steuart Bedford - Metropolitan Opera, New York, 18 October 1974
f.Austr.p. Adelaide, 1980 (Adelaide Festival)
f.Can.p.   Canadian Opera cond. Steuart Bedford, January 1990
f.SA.p.   Performing Arts Council of Transvaal, Pretoria, 14 April 1992

Suite from 'Death in Venice' Op.88a, compiled by Steuart Bedford (1984)
[Summons to Venice - Overture to Venice - First Beach Scene - Tadzio -
I love you - Pursuit]
Dur: 26'
Instr: 2/2/2/2 - 2/2/2/1 - timp. perc.(4) hp. pno. str.
f.p.   English Chamber Orchestra/Steuart Bedford - The Maltings, Snape, 13 June 1984 (Aldeburgh Festival)
f.rec.   above artists - *Chandos ABRD 1126 (and MC), CHAN 8363 (CD)*
Pub: Faber, 1993

Canticle V 'The Death of Saint Narcissus': for tenor and harp Op.89 (1974)
[Words: T.S. Eliot]

Dedicated 'In loving memory of William Plomer' (who had died in September 1973)
Dur: 7'
f.p.   Peter Pears (Ten.)/Osian Ellis (Hp.) - Schloss Elmau, Upper Bavaria,
            15 January 1975
f.Brit.p.   above artists - Fairfield Halls, Croydon, Surrey, 23 January 1975
f.broad.p. above artists - Radio 3, 4 February 1975
f.Lon.p.   above artists - Queen Elizabeth Hall, 14 January 1976
f.rec.   above artists - *London (USA) OS 26477; Decca SXL 6788; Argo ZRG 946;*
            London 425 716-2 (CD)
Pub: Faber, 1976

Suite on English Folk Tunes 'A time there was ...'* Op.90 (1967, 1974)
[1. Cakes and Ale 2. The Bitter Withy 3. Hankin Booby (1967) 4. Hunt the Squirrel
 5. Lord Melbourne]
'Lovingly and reverently dedicated to the memory of Percy Grainger' - the score is dated
16 November 1974
Dur: 14'
Instr: 2/2/2/2 - 2/2/0/0 - timp. perc.(2) hp. str.
f.p.   English Chamber Orchestra/Steuart Bedford - The Maltings, Snape,
            13 June 1975 (Aldeburgh Festival - and in the presence of the Festival's
            patron, Her Majesty, Queen Elizabeth the Queen Mother)
f.Lon.p.   above artists - Royal Albert Hall, 17 September 1975 (Promenade Concert)
f.Am.p.   New York Philharmonic Orchestra/Leonard Bernstein - New York, 1976
f.recs.   New York Philharmonic Orchestra/Leonard Bernstein - *CBS 76640 (and MC);*
            Sony SMK 47541 (CD)
            City of Birmingham Symphony Orchestra/Simon Rattle - *EMI EL 270263-1*
            (and MC), CDC7 47343-2 (CD), CDS7 54270-2 (CD)
Pub: Faber, 1976 (full score prepared by Rosamund Strode)
(*a quotation from Thomas Hardy's poem 'Before Life and After' which Britten had also
set as the last of **Winter Words** q.v.)

**Sacred and Profane: eight medieval lyrics for unaccompanied voices (SSATB) Op.91
(1974-75)**
[1. St Godric's Hymn 2. I Mon Waxe Wod 3. Lenten is come
 4. The Long Night 5. Yif Ic of Luve Can 6. Carol 7. Ye that pasen by 8. A Death]
'Written for P.P. and the Wilbye Consort'
Dur: 15'
f.p.   Wilbye Consort/Peter Pears - The Maltings, Snape, 14 September 1975
f.broad.p   above first performance - Radio 3, 30 May 1976
f.Lon.p.   Hilliard Ensemble - Fenton House, Hampstead, 24 June 1977
f.rec.   Wilbye Consort/Peter Pears - *London (USA) OS 26527; Decca SXL 6847 (and*
            MC)
Pub: Faber, 1977

A Birthday Hansel: for high voice and harp Op.92 (1975)
[Words: Robert Burns 1. Birthday Song 2. My Early Walk
 3. Wee Willie Gray 4. My Hoggie 5. Afton Water 6. The Winter 7. Leezie Lindsay]
'These songs were written at the special wish of Her Majesty The Queen for her mother's
seventy-fifth birthday, August 4th 1975' - the score is dated 21 March 1975

Dur: 16'30"
f.p.   Peter Pears (Ten.)/Osian Ellis (Hp.) - Schloss Elmau, Upper Bavaria,
         11 January 1976
f.Brit.priv.p. above artists - Uphall, near Sandringham, 16 January 1976 (at the home of
         Ruth, Lady Fermoy, and in the presence of Her Majesty the Queen, Her
         Majesty, Queen Elizabeth the Queen Mother, and Princess Margaret)
f.Brit.pub.p. above artists - New Hall, Department of Music, University College,
         Cardiff, 19 March 1976 (Cardiff Festival)
f.Lon.p.   above artists - Wigmore Hall, 1 June 1977
f.rec.   above artists - *London (USA) OS 26477; Decca SXL 6788, 417 310-1 (and*
         MC); London 425 716-2 (CD)
Pub: Faber, 1978 (ed. Osian Ellis)
Nos.3, 4, 5 and 6 arr. for high voice and piano by Colin Matthews (1975)
Dur: 12'
f.p.   Julian Pike (Ten.)/Graham Johnson (Pno.) - Wigmore Hall, London,
         4 April 1979
f.rec.   Yvonne Kenny (Sop.)/Tan Crone (Pno.) - *Etcetera KTC 1046 (CD) (and MC)*
Pub: Faber, 1978 (as 'Four Burns Songs')

Phaedra: dramatic cantata for mezzo-soprano and small orchestra Op.93 (1975)

[Words: Robert Lowell, after Racine's Phèdre]
Written 'For Janet Baker' - the score is dated 12 August 1975
Dur: 15'30"
Instr: timp. perc.(2) hpschd. str.
f.p.   Janet Baker (M/S)/English Chamber Orchestra/Steuart Bedford - The
         Maltings, Snape, 16 June 1976 (Aldeburgh Festival)
f.Lon.p.   Janet Baker (M/S)/Academy of St. Martin-in-the-Fields/Neville Marriner -
         Royal Festival Hall, 7 August 1977
f.rec.   above artists - *London (USA) OS 26527; Decca SXL 6847 (and MC), 417*
         313-1 (and MC), 425 666-2 (CD)
Pub: Faber, 1977 (vocal score by David Matthews), 1992 (full score)

String Quartet No. 3 Op.94 (1975)

[1. Duets 2. Ostinato 3. Solo 4. Burlesque
 5. Recitative and Passacaglia (La Serenissima)]
Written for the Amadeus Quartet and dedicated 'To Hans Keller' - the draft score was
completed by 20 November 1975
Dur: 28'
f.p.   Amadeus Quartet - The Maltings, Snape, 19 December 1976 (they had
         rehearsed the work with Britten on 28 and 29 September, only a few weeks
         before his death on 4 December 1976)
f.broad.p. above artists - Radio 3, 29 September 1977
f.Lon.p.   above artists - National Gallery, 1 February 1978
f.rec.   above artists - *London (USA) CS 7116; Decca SXL 6893;*
         London 425 715-2 (CD)
Pub: Faber, 1977

Tema 'Sacher': for solo cello* (1976)
Written at the invitation of Mstislav Rostropovich in celebration of Paul Sacher's
seventieth birthday - the score is dated 5 January 1976 and uses the musical letters of the
recipient's name as the basis for the theme.
Dur: 1'
f.p.   Mstislav Rostropovich - Tonhalle, Zurich, 2 May 1976
f.Brit.p.   Rohan de Saram - The Maltings, Snape, 16 June 1985 (Aldeburgh Festival)
f.broad.p.   above first (British) performance - Radio 3, 30 December 1985
f.rec.   Julian Lloyd Webber - *ASV CDDCA 592 (CD) (and MC)*
Pub: Faber, 1990 (ed. Mstislav Rostropovich)
(*among the eleven other composers who contributed 'variations' were Witold
Lutoslawski, Hans Werner Henze, Pierre Boulez and Luciano Berio)

Welcome Ode: for young people's chorus and orchestra Op.95 (1976)
[1. March (Thomas Dekker and John Ford) 2. Jig (orchestra) 3. Roundel (Anon.)
 4. Modulation (orchestra) 5. Canon (Henry Fielding)]
Written for Suffolk schoolchildren to perform during Silver Jubilee year - the draft score
is dated 19 August 1976 (the orchestration was later undertaken by Colin Matthews)
Dur: 8'
Instr: 2/2/2/2 - 4/2/3/1 - timp. perc.(3) pno. str.
Alt.Instr: 2/1/2/1 - 2/2/2/0 - timp. perc.(2) str.
f.p.   Suffolk Schools' Choir and Orchestra/Keith Shaw - Corn Exchange, Ipswich,
             11 July 1977 (in the presence of Her Majesty the Queen on the occasion of
             her Silver Jubilee visit to Suffolk)
f.broad.p.   above performance - Radio 3, 27 October 1977
f.Lon.p.   Choir and Orchestra of Pimlico School/Roderick Spencer - Queen Elizabeth
             Hall, 31 October 1977
f.rec.   City of London Schools' Choir/London Symphony Orchestra/Richard Hickox -
             Chandos ABTD 1472 (MC), CHAN 8855 (CD)
Pub: Faber, 1977 (vocal score by Colin Matthews), 1992 (full score)
Excs. from the above arr. for string orchestra by Tony Osborne
[1. Jig 2. Roundel 3. Canon]
Dur: 6'
Pub: Faber, 1994 (as 'Welcome Suite')

Praise We Great Men: for soloists, chorus and orchestra* (1976)
[Words: Edith Sitwell - the poem is dedicated to Britten]
Written for performance by Rostropovich as conductor of the National Symphony
Orchestra of Washington
Dur: 7'
Instr: 3/2/2/2 - 4/2/2(1)/0 - timp. perc.(2) hp. pno. str.
f.p.   Marie McLaughlin (Sop.)/Heather Harper (Sop.)/Philip Langridge
             (Ten.)/Richard Jackson (Bs.)/Philharmonia Chorus and Orchestra/Mstislav
             Rostropovich - The Maltings, Snape, 11 August 1985
f.rec.   Alison Hargan (Sop.)/Mary King (M/S)/Robert Tear (Ten.)/Willard White
             (Bs.)/City of Birmingham Symphony Chorus and Orchestra/Simon Rattle -
             EMI CDS7 54270-2 (CD)
Pub: Faber
(*edited and orchestrated for performance by Colin Matthews in 1977)

FILM MUSIC

(N.B. More detailed information, including instrumentation, on all of Britten's film music may be found in 'A Britten Source Book')

The King's Stamp - GPO Film Unit (1935)
Director: William Coldstream
Coal Face* - GPO Film Unit (1935)
Producer: John Grierson
Director: Alberto Cavalcanti
(*including a setting of Auden's poem 'O lurcher loving collier' for female chorus)

The Tocher - GPO Film Unit (1935)
Producer: Alberto Cavalcanti
Animator: Lotte Reiniger

C.T.O. - The Story of the Central Telegraph Office - GPO Film Unit (1935)
Producer: Stuart Legg

God's Chillun - GPO Film Unit (1935)
Editors: Max Anderson, Gordon Hales and Rona Morrison

Men Behind the Meters - British Commercial Gas Association (1935)
Director: Arthur Elton

Dinner Hour - British Commercial Gas Association* (1935)
Producer: Arthur Elton
Director: Edgar Anstey
(*there are two manuscripts not matched to films for the British Commercial Gas Association - 'Gas Abstract' and 'Title Music III')

How the Dial Works - GPO Film Unit (1935)
Producers: Ralph Elton and Rona Morrison

Conquering Space: The Story of Modern Communications - GPO Film Unit (1935)
Producer: Stuart Legg

Sorting Office - GPO Film Unit (1935)
Director: Harry Watt

The Savings Bank - GPO Film Unit (1935)
Producer: Stuart Legg

The New Operator - Empire Marketing Board Film Unit/GPO Film Unit (1935)
Producer: John Grierson
Director: Stuart Legg

Night Mail* - GPO Film Unit (1935-36)
Composed between 22 November 1935 and 13 January 1936
Producer: John Grierson

Directors: Harry Watt and Basil Wright
Music played by: Chamber Ensemble/Benjamin Britten (recorded 15 January 1936)
f.tel.p.   BBC Television, 16 October 1949 (broadcast of the original film)
f.conc.p.   Cicely Herbert (Narr.)/Gerard Benson (Narr.)/Apollo Chamber
            Orchestra/David Chernaik - Conway Hall, London, 7 November 1997
f.rec.   (End sequence) Nigel Hawthorne (Narr.)/Nash Ensemble/Lionel Friend -
            Hyperion CDA 66845 (CD)
Excs. from the film
[1. Title Music 2. Percussion Interlude 3. End sequence]
Dur: 5'
Pub: Chester (study score)
(*including a setting of Auden's verse 'This is the night mail crossing the border')

Calendar of the Year - GPO Film Unit (1936)
Producer: Alberto Cavalcanti
Director: Evelyn Spice

Peace of Britain - Strand Films (1936)
Producer: Paul Rotha

Around the Village Green - Travel and Industrial Development Association (1936)
Alt. title: Village Harvest
Producer: Marion Grierson
Director: Evelyn Spice
Music played by: Orchestra/Benjamin Britten (recorded 21 October 1936)
Exc. 'Irish Reel'
Score dated 2 April 1936, rev.1937
Dur: 2'40"
Instr: (original version) 2/1/1/0 - 0/1/1/0 - timp. hp. str.
Instr: (rev. version) 1/1/1/1 - 1/0/0/0 - timp. hp. str.
f.broad.p. BBC Concert Orchestra/Carl Davis - BBC Radio 3, 21 March 1995*
            ('Fairest Isle' series)
f.conc.p. City of London Sinfonia/Richard Hickox - The Maltings, Snape, 17 June 1995
            (Aldeburgh Festival)
f.tel.p.   BBC Symphony Orchestra/Andrew Davis - Royal Albert Hall, London,
            13 September 1997 (Promenade Concert)
f.rec.   Charles Brill Orchestra/Charles Brill (rec. 9 November 1937) - *Decca K 874
            (78)*
Pub: Faber, 1996 (rev. version)
(*however, the Decca gramophone recording was broadcast on 21 April 1938)

Men of the Alps* - GPO Film Unit/Pro Telephon, Zurich (1936)
Co-written with Walter Leigh q.v.
Producer: Harry Watt
Director: Alberto Cavalcanti
(*including more Rossini arrangements)

Line to the Tschierva Hut - GPO Film Unit/Pro Telephon, Zurich (1936)
Producer: John Grierson

Director: Alberto Cavalcanti

Message from Geneva - GPO Film Unit/Pro Telephon, Zurich (1936)
Director: Alberto Cavalcanti

Four Barriers - GPO Film Unit/Pro Telephon, Zurich (1936)
Co-written with John Foulds
Producer: Harry Watt

The Savings of Bill Blewitt - GPO Film Unit (1936)
Producers: John Grierson and Alberto Cavalcanti
Director: Alberto Cavalcanti

Love from a Stranger - Trafalgar Films* (1936)
Commissioned by Boyd Neel - the score was composed between 18 and 26 November 1936
Producer: Max Schach
Director: Rowland V. Lee
Music conducted by: Boyd Neel (rec. 25 and 27 November 1936)
f.rec.   complete film (V)
Music from the film transcribed by Colin Matthews
[1.Title Music 2. Traffic Music 3. Brighton 4. Love Music 5. Channel Crossing
6. End Titles]
f.p.   BBC Concert Orchestra/Carl Davis - Barbican Hall, London, 20 May 1995
f.broad.p. above first performance - Radio 3, 27 December 1995
Pub: Chester (study score)
(*Britten's only feature film and first shown in London on 7 January 1937)

The Way to the Sea - Strand Films for Southern Railway (1936)
Producer: Paul Rotha
Director: John B. Holmes

Book Bargain - GPO Film Unit (?1937)
Director: Norman McLaren

Mony a Pickle - GPO Film Unit (?1938)
Co-written with John Foulds and Victor Yates
Producer: Richard Massingham
Director: Alberto Cavalcanti

Advance Democracy* - Realistic Film Unit (1938)
Director: Ralph Bond
(*not the same music as the motet q.v.)

The Instruments of the Orchestra* - Crown Film Unit for the Ministry of Education (1945)
Producer: Alexander Shaw
Director: Muir Mathieson

Music played by: London Symphony Orchestra/Sir Malcolm Sargent (with spoken commentary by Montagu Slater)
f.rec.   complete film - *Beulah RT 152(V)*
(* 'The Young Person's Guide to the Orchestra' Op.34 q.v.)

INCIDENTAL MUSIC

(N.B. More detailed information, including instrumentation, on all of Britten's incidental music may be found in 'A Britten Source Book')

a)   **Radio** (all BBC unless stated)

King Arthur (1937)

[D. Geoffrey Bridson]
Producer: Val Gielgud
f.p.   23 April 1937
Music played by: London Symphony Orchestra/Clarence Raybould
later adapted as a symphonic suite by Paul Hindmarsh
[1. Overture (Fanfare, Introduction, The Lady of the Lake, Wedding March)
2. Scherzo (Doom, Wild Dance, Death Music) 3. Variations (Galahad, Graal
Music) 4. Finale (Battle)]
Dur: 24'
Instr: 3/2/2+E flat cl./2 - 4/3/3/1 - timp. perc.(2) hp. str.
f.p.   Royal Academy of Music Orchestra/Lutz Köhler - The Maltings,
            Snape, 21 October 1995
f.broad.p BBC Philharmonic Orchestra/Richard Hickox - Radio 3,
            6 December 1995
f.rec.   BBC Philharmonic Orchestra/Richard Hickox - *Chandos CHAN
            9487 (CD)*
Pub: OUP, 1996

Up the Garden Path (1937)

[Verses chosen by W.H. Auden and the music *chosen* by Britten]
f.p. 13 June 1937
Music played by Henry Bronkhurst and Denis Arundell
Principals: Charlotte Leigh, Felix Aylmer, Denis Arundell
(N.B. This programme did not contain music *composed* by Britten)

The Company of Heaven (1937)

[Compiled by R. Ellis Roberts.
Part I - Before the Creation - 1. Chaos 2. The Morning Stars (St Joseph)
Part II - Angels in Scripture - 3a. Jacob 3b. Elisha 3c. Hail, Mary!
4. Christ, the fair glory (Archbishop Rabanus Maurus trans. Athelstan Riley)
5. War in Heaven.
Part III - Angels in Common Life and at our Death - 6. Heaven is here
7. A thousand, thousand gleaming fires* (Emily Brontë) 8. Funeral March for
a Boy 9. Whoso dwelleth under the defence of the most High (Psalm 91)
10. Lento (John Bunyan) 11. Ye watchers and ye holy ones (Athelstan Riley)]
Producer: Robin Whitworth

f.p.   29 September 1937 (the feast day of St Michael and All Angels)
Music performed by: Sophie Wyss (Sop.)/Peter Pears (Ten.)/BBC Chorus and
                Orchestra/Trevor Harvey
Cast: Felix Aylmer, Leo Genn, Robert Speaight
later arr. for concert performance (1956)
Dur: 20' (45' with narration)
Instr: timp. org. str. (+soprano, tenor, SATB chorus)
f.p.   BBC, 20 May 1956
f.conc.p.   (complete) Sheila Allen (Spkr.)/Peter Barkworth (Spkr.)/Cathryn
                Pope (Sop.)/Dan Dressen (Ten.)/London Philharmonic
                Choir/English Chamber Orchestra/Philip Brunelle - The Maltings,
                Snape, 10 June 1989 (Aldeburgh Festival)
f.Am.p.   cond. Philip Brunelle - Plymouth, Minneapolis, 3 December 1989
                (Plymouth Music Series)
f.rec.   above (Brit.) artists - *Virgin VC7 91107-2 (CD), VC5 45093-2(CD)*
Pub: Faber, 1990, 1992 (revised edition)
Exc. 'Whoso dwelleth under the defence of the most High' - anthem for
unaccompanied chorus (SSAATTBB)
Dur: 4'
Pub: Faber, 1990
(*the first music Britten composed for Peter Pears)

Hadrian's Wall* (1937)

[W.H. Auden]
Producer: John Pudney
f.p.   25 November 1937 from Newcastle-upon-Tyne
Music performed by: Felling Male Voice Choir/Leslie Russell Quartet/
                Benjamin Britten
(*including a setting of Auden's 'Roman Wall Blues')

Lines on the Map - series (1938)

[1. Communication by Land (Stephen Potter)
 2. Communication by Sea (James Miller)
 3. Communication by Wireless (D.F. Aitken and E.J. Alway)
 4. Communication by Air (Stephen Potter)]
Producers: John Pudney and Leslie Stokes
f.p.   (four monthly programmes) 27 January-22 April 1938

The Chartists' March (1938)

[J.H. Miller]
Producer: John Pudney
f.p.   13 May 1938
Music performed by: BBC Men's Chorus/Benjamin Britten

The World of the Spirit (1938)

[Compiled by R. Ellis Roberts
Part I - Prologue
1. Prelude 2. O Thou that movest all (Mary Duclaux) 3. The Sun, the Moon,
the Stars (Alfred, Lord Tennyson) 4a. This is my commandment (St John)

4b. With wide-embracing love (Emily Brontë)
Part II - The Fruits of the Spirit
5. O Life, O Love, now undivided (Mary Duclaux) 6a. A voice within our souls has spoken 6b. The fruit of the spirit is love 6c. The fruit of the spirit is faith 6d. The fruit of the spirit is goodness 6e. The fruit of the spirit is long-suffering 6f. The fruit of the spirit is joy 7. The Spirit of the Lord
Part III - Epilogue 8. O knowing, glorious Spirit! (Henry Vaughan) 9. The world is charged* (Gerard Manley Hopkins) 10. Come, O Creator Spirit, Come (trans. Robert Bridges)]
Producer: Robin Whitworth
f.p.   Sophie Wyss (Sop.)/Anne Wood (Con.)/Emlyn Bebb (Ten.)/Victor Harding (Bs.)/BBC Singers and Orchestra/Trevor Harvey - 5 June 1938 (Whit Sunday)
Cast: Felix Aylmer, Leo Genn, Robert Speaight

later made available for public performance in 1996 with abridged texts by Donald Mitchell
Dur: 36'
Instr: 2/2/2/2 - 4/2/3/1 - timp. perc. hp. org. str.
f.mod.p. BBC Philharmonic Orchestra/Richard Hickox - Radio 3, December 1995
f.conc.p. Daniel Evans (Spkr.)/Janice Watson (Sop.)/Catherine Wyn-Rogers (M/S)/Timothy Robinson (Ten.)/Neal Davies (Bar.)/Joyful Company of Singers/City of London Sinfonia/Steuart Bedford - The Maltings, Snape, 27 June 1998 (Aldeburgh Festival)
f.rec.   BBC Philharmonic Orchestra/Richard Hickox - *Chandos CHAN 9487 (CD)*
Pub: OUP, forthcoming (full score, with vocal score by Olivia Kilmartin)
(*see also **A.M.D.G.** for a further setting)

The Sword in the Stone - series (1939)
(T.H. White adapted by Marianne Helweg]
Producer: John Cheatle
f.p.   (six weekly programmes) 11 June-16 July 1939
Music performed by: BBC Singers/BBC Orchestra/Leslie Woodgate

Concert Suite for chamber ensemble compiled from the above by Oliver Knussen and Colin Matthews:-
[1. Introduction and Boys' Tunes 2. Merlyn's Tune and Tree Music
 3. Merlyn's Spell and Witch Tune 4. Bird Music 5. Lullaby
 6. Water Theme and End Music]
Dur: 10'
Instr: Fl. Cl. Bsn. Tpt. Tbn. Hp. Perc.
f.p.   Aldeburgh Festival Chamber Ensemble/Oliver Knussen - The Maltings, Snape, 14 June 1983 (Aldeburgh Festival)
f.broad.p. above first performance - Radio 3, 22 January 1984
f.rec.   Nash Ensemble/Lionel Friend - *Hyperion CDA 66845(CD)*
Pub: Faber, 1989

Johnson over Jordan* (1939)

[J.B. Priestley]

f.p.   (Act III only) Home Service, 11 August 1940
f.p.   (complete play) 23 July 1951
f.p.   (complete music) Elaine MacKillop (Sop.)/BBC Scottish
            Orchestra/John Carewe - Radio 4, 9 September 1985
            (rec. 2 August 1985)

(*originally music for the stage play q.v.)

The Dark Valley - CBS* (1940)

[W.H. Auden]
A monologue especially written for Dame May Whitty, including two
unaccompanied songs
Producer: Brewster Morgan
f.p.   CBS (Columbia Workshop), New York, 2 June 1940
Music conducted by: Bernard Herrmann
(*the first of a series of scores commissioned by the CBS network in
New York)

The Dynasts - CBS (1940)

[Thomas Hardy]
f.p.   CBS (Columbia Workshop), New York, 24 November 1940
?f.Brit.p. BBC Third Programme, from 3 June 1951 (in six episodes)
Producer: Douglas Cleverdon

The Rocking Horse Winner - CBS (1941)

[W.H. Auden and James Stern]
Producer: Guy della Cioppa
f.p.   CBS (Columbia Workshop), New York, 6 April 1941
Music conducted by: Bernard Herrmann

Appointment (1942)

[Norman Corwin]
Producer: Norman Corwin
f.p.   20 July 1942

An American in England - CBS/BBC drama series (1942)

[Norman Corwin 1. London by Clipper 2. London to Dover
3. Ration Island 4. Women of Britain 5. The Yanks are Here
6. The Anglo-American Angle]
Producer: Edward R. Murrow
f.p.   (six programmes) 27 July-7 September 1942
Music played by: RAF Orchestra/Rudolf P. O'Donnell

The Man Born to be King - series (1942)

[Dorothy L. Sayers - Britten provided music for No.10 'The Princes of
this World' and No.11 'King of Sorrows']
Producer: Val Gielgud
f.p.   23 August and 20 September 1942

Lumberjacks of America (1942)
[Ranald MacDougall]
Producer: Charles A. Schenk Jr.
f.p.   24 August 1942
Music conducted by: Benjamin Britten

Britain to America - BBC series for NBC, New York (1942-43)
[Louis MacNeice - Britten provided music for Series I, No.9, 'Britain
Through American Eyes'; Series II, No.4, 'Where Do I Come In?' and
Series II, No.13, 'Where Do We Go From Here?']
Producer: Lawrence Gilliam
f.p.   20 September, 7 November 1942; 3 January 1943
Music played by: London Symphony Orchestra/Muir Mathieson

The Four Freedoms - series 1943)
[Louis MacNeice - Britten composed music for the first in this series of
six programmes - No.1, 'Pericles']
Producer: Louis MacNeice
f.p.   21 February 1943

The Rescue - epic drama (1943)
[Edward Sackville-West from Homer's Odyssey]
Producer: John Burrell
f.p.   25 and 26 November 1943 (in two episodes)
Music performed by: Hedli Anderson (Sop.)/Veronica Mansfield(M/S)/
            Stephen Manton (Ten.)/Donald Munro (Bs.)/BBC Symphony
            Orchestra/Clarence Raybould

later adapted for concert performance by Chris de Souza in association with
Donald Mitchell and Colin Matthews (1993)
Dur: 45'
Instr: 2/2/2 +a.sax./2 - 4/3/3/1 - timp. perc.(2) pno. hp. str.
f.p.   Janet Suzman (Narr.)/Alison Wells (Sop.)/Sarah Connolly (M/S)/
            Thomas Randle (Ten.)/Christopher Foster (Bar.)/BBC Symphony
            Orchestra/Nicholas Cleobury - The Maltings, Snape, 23 October
            1993
f.broad.p. above first performance - Radio 3, 25 April 1995
f.Am.p.   Sally Ann Howes (Narr.)/Indianapolis Symphony Orchestra/
            Raymond Leppard - Indianapolis, 17 October 1996
f.Eur.p.   Radio Philharmonic Orchestra of Hilversum/Gennadi
            Rozhdestvensky - Concertgebouw, Amsterdam, 16 February 1997
f.rec.   Janet Baker (Narr.)/Hallé Orchestra/Kent Nagano - *Erato 0630
            12713-2 (CD)*
Pub: Faber, 1998 (as 'The Rescue of Penelope'- vocal score by Alan
            Boustead)

A Poet's Christmas* (1944)
Producer: Edward Sackville-West
f.p.   BBC Home Service, 24 December 1944

Music: BBC Singers/Leslie Woodgate
(*Britten's contribution was two choral settings to texts by W.H. Auden -
'A Shepherd's Carol' and 'Chorale' q.v. Among the other composers who
provided new settings were Berkeley and Tippett q.v.)

The Dark Tower (1946)
[Louis MacNeice]
Producer: Louis MacNeice
f.p.   BBC Home Service, 21 January 1946
Music conducted by: Walter Goehr

Men of Goodwill: The Reunion of Christmas (1947)
Producers: Lawrence Gilliam and Leonard Cottrell
f.p.   25 December 1947 (immediately preceding King George VI's
            Christmas Day broadcast to the nation)
Music played by: London Symphony Orchestra/Walter Goehr

later published as:-
Variations on a Christmas Carol 'God Rest Ye Merry Gentlemen' for
orchestra
Dur: 8'
Instr: 2+picc./2/2/2 - 4/2/3/1 - timp. perc.(2) hp. str.
f.conc.p.   London Symphony Orchestra/Neville Marriner - Royal Festival
            Hall, London, 8 February 1982
f.rec.   Minnesota Orchestra/Neville Marriner - *EMI ASD 143628-1 (and
            MC); CDC7 49300-2 (CD)*
Pub: Faber, 1982

b)   **Stage**

Timon of Athens (1935)
[William Shakespeare]
Instr: 2Ob. Perc. Hpschd.
f.p.   Group Theatre Company, Westminster Theatre, London,
            19 November 1935
Music conducted by: Herbert Murrill q.v.
Producer: Nugent Monck
Designer: Robert Medley
Choreography: Rupert Doone

Easter 1916 (1935)
[Montagu Slater]
Instr: Perc. Acc. (+2 voices)
f.p.   Left Theatre Company (in association with A.E.U.) - Islington
            Town Hall, London, 4 December 1935
Music conducted by: Charles Kahn
Producer: André van Gyseghem

Stay Down Miner (1936)
[Montagu Slater]
Instr: Cl. Perc. Vn. Vc. (+Ten./Bar. and TB chorus)
f.p.   Left Theatre Company - Westminster Theatre, London,
            10 May 1936
Music conducted by: Charles Kahn
Producer: Wilfred Walter

The Agamemnon (1936)
[Aeschylus trans. Louis MacNeice]
Instr: 2Fl. Ca. Cl. Perc. (+SATB chorus)
f.p.   Group Theatre Company - Westminster Theatre, London,
            1 November 1936
Music conducted by: Brian Easdale*
Producer and Choreographer: Rupert Doone
Designer: Robert Medley
(*Grace Williams q.v. also assisted Britten in this production)

The Ascent of F6 (1937)
[W.H. Auden and Christopher Isherwood]
Instr: Perc. Uke. 2Pno. (+3 voices and SATB chorus)
f.p.   Group Theatre Company - Mercury Theatre, London,
            26 February 1937
Music conducted by: Brian Easdale
Producer: Rupert Doone
Designer: Robert Medley
f.broad.p. 5 December 1938

Exc. 'Funeral Blues': cabaret song for voice and piano
Arranged 17 June 1937
Dur: 3'
f.pub.p.   Peter Pears (Ten.)/Benjamin Britten (Pno.) - Southold High School,
            Long Island, New York, 14 December 1941
f.recs.   Hedli Anderson (Sop.)/Benjamin Britten (Pno.) - *Columbia
            (recorded 1938-39, not issued)*
            Sarah Walker (Sop.)/Roger Vignoles (Pno.) - *Meridian E 77056,
            CDE 84167 (CD)*
Pub: Faber, 1980 (in 'Cabaret Songs')
Exc. 'Funeral Blues' arr. for female voice and chamber ensemble by Daryl
Runswick (1990)
Instr: Al.Sax. Tpt. Vn. Db. Pdo. Drum kit
f.p.   Mary King (M/S)/Daryl Runswick All-Stars - Jubilee Hall,
            Aldeburgh, 8 June 1990 (Aldeburgh Festival)
f.broad.p. above performance - Radio 3, 8 July 1990
Pub: Faber

Suite from the above arr. by Mervyn Cooke
f.p.   Faye Newton (Sop.)/Philip Weller (Bar./Narr.)/Kieran
            O'Riordan (Perc.)/Martin Leigh (Pno.) - The Maltings, Snape,

14 June 1996 (Aldeburgh Festival)

Pageant of Empire - satirical review (1937)
[Montagu Slater]
Instr: Cl. Sax. Tpt. Perc. Pno. Vn. Vc. Db. (+2 voices and male chorus)
f.p.   Left Theatre Company - Collins's Music Hall, London,
          28 February 1937
Music conducted by: Charles Kahn

Out of the Picture* (1937)
[Louis MacNeice]
Instr: Tpt. Perc. Pno.(2 and 4 hands) (+2 voices and SATB chorus)
f.p.   Group Theatre Company - Westminster Theatre, London,
          5 December 1937
Music conducted by: Brian Easdale
Producer: Rupert Doone
Designers: Robert Medley and Geoffrey W. Monk
(*includes the song 'Sleep and Wake' performed in this production by Sophie Wyss)

Spain - puppet show* (1938)
[Montagu Slater]
Instr: Cl. Vn. Pno. (+2 voices)
f.p.   Helen and Margaret Binyon (puppeteers) - Mercury Theatre,
          London, 22 June 1938
Music conducted by: Frank Kennard
Designer: Helen Binyon
(*Lennox Berkeley q.v. provided the music for the other two plays in this trilogy)

On the Frontier (1938)
[W.H. Auden and Christopher Isherwood]
Instr: 2Tpt. Perc. Acc. Pno.(2 and 4 hands) (+1 voice and mixed chorus)
f.p.   Group Theatre Company - Arts Theatre, Cambridge,
          14 November 1938
f.Lon.p. Globe Theatre, 12 February 1939 (a single performance)
Music conducted by: Brian Easdale (pre-recorded music sung by the
          London Labour Choral Union)
Producer: Rupert Doone
Designer: Robert Medley

Exc. 'The clock on the wall gives an electric tick' (Blues) arr. for six-piece cabaret ensemble by Daryl Runswick
Dur: 4'30"
Instr.   Cl./Sax. Tpt. Vn. Db. Pno. Drum kit
f.p.   Daryl Runswick All-Stars - The Maltings, Snape, 8 June 1990
          (Aldeburgh Festival)
f.broad.p. above first performance - Radio 3, 8 July 1990

f.Lon.p.   Nash Ensemble - Barbican Hall, March 1993 (Britten-Rostropovich
            Festival, Foyer Concert)
f.rec.   Instrumental Ensemble - *Unicorn DKPCD 9138 (CD)*
Pub: Faber (as No.3 of 'Britten's Blues')

They Walk Alone (1938)
[Max Catto]
Instr: organ
f.p.   'Q' Theatre, London, 21 November 1938 (and later to the
            Shaftesbury and Comedy Theatres the following year)
Producer: Bertold Viertel
Designer: Herman Herrey

Johnson over Jordan* (1939)
[J.B. Priestley]
Instr: 1/1/2+bcl./1 - 0/2/1/0 - perc. pno. gtr. str.(+solo soprano)
Instr: (in 'The Spider and the Fly') 2Al.Sax. 2Ten.Sax. 3Tpt. 2Tbn. Perc.
            Pno. Gtr. Vn. Db.
f.p.   New Theatre, London, 22 February 1939
Music conducted by: Ernest Irving (some pre-recorded music was played by
Geraldo's Orchestra whose assistance in the orchestration of 'The Spider and
the Fly' dance was acknowledged in the theatre programme)
Producer: Basil Dean
Designer: Edward Carrick
Costumes: Elizabeth Haffenden
Choreography: Anthony Tudor
Principal: Ralph Richardson (in the title role)

Suite later arr. for concert performance by Paul Hindmarsh (1988)
[1. Overture 2. Incinerator's Ballet 3. The Spider and the Fly   4. End Music]
Dur: 18'
Instr: 1/1/2+a.sax./1 - 0/2/1/0 - perc.(2) pno. str.
f.p.   Northern Sinfonia/Odaline de la Martinez - Radio 3,
            25 February 1990
f.conc.p.   English Chamber Orchestra/Steuart Bedford - The Maltings,
            Snape, 22 June 1990 (Aldeburgh Festival)
f.rec.   English Chamber Orchestra/Steuart Bedford - *Collins 1192-2 (CD)*
Pub: Faber, 1993

Exc.   'The Spider and the Fly' arr. for six-piece cabaret ensemble by
            Daryl Runswick
Dur: 3'45"
Instr: Cl./Sax. Tpt. Vn. Db. Pno. Drum kit
f.p.   Daryl Runswick All-Stars - Jubilee Hall, Aldeburgh, 8 June 1990
            (Aldeburgh Festival)
f.broad.p. above first performance - Radio 3, 8 July 1990
f.Lon.p.   Nash Ensemble - Barbican Hall, March 1993 (Britten-Rostropovich
            Festival, Foyer Concert)
f.rec.   Instrumental Ensemble - *Unicorn DKPCD 9138 (CD)*

Pub: Faber (as No.1 of 'Britten's Blues')
Exc.   'The Spider and the Fly' arr. for brass band by Darrol Barry (1990)
Dur: 4'
f.p.   Besses o'th' Barn Band/Paul Hindmarsh - Spenmoor,
            Co. Durham, 18 November 1990 ('Brass in Concert' series)
f.rec.   above artists - *Polyphonic QPRL 060D(CD)*
Pub: Faber/Studio Music, 1993
(*see also Radio music)

This Way to the Tomb - masque (1945)
[Ronald Duncan]
Instr: Perc. Pno.duet (+4 voices and SATB chorus)
f.p.   Pilgrim Players - Mercury Theatre, London, 11 October 1945 (and
            first broadcast on the Light Programme on 14 November 1945)
Music conducted by: Arthur Oldham
Producer: E. Martin Browne
Principals: Robert Speaight, Eric Shilling

Exc. Three Songs for medium voice and harp (or piano)
[1. Evening 2. Morning 3. Night]
Dur: 4'15"
f.rec.   Ian Bostridge (Ten.)/Graham Johnson (Pno.) - *Hyperion CDA
            66823 (CD)*
Pub: Boosey & Hawkes, 1988
Exc. 'Deus in adjutorium meum': for unaccompanied SATB chorus
Dur: 4'
f.conc.p.   Elizabethan Singers/Louis Halsey - St Clement Danes Church,
            London, 26 October 1962 (Macnaghten Concert)
f.broad.p. Rochester Cathedral Choir/Barry Ferguson - Radio 4, 2 April 1980
f.rec.   Westminster Cathedral Choir/David Hill - *Hyperion A 66220 (and
            MC/CD)*
Pub: Boosey & Hawkes, 1983

Exc. 'Boogie-Woogie' arr. for six-piece cabaret ensemble by Daryl Runswick
Dur: 3'
Instr: Cl./Sax. Tpt. Vn. Db. Pno. Drum kit
f.p.   Daryl Runswick All-Stars - Jubilee Hall, Aldeburgh,
            8 June1990 (Aldeburgh Festival)
f.broad.p. above first performance - Radio 3, 8 July 1990
f.Lon.p.   Nash Ensemble - Barbican Hall, March 1993 (Britten-Rostropovich
            Festival, Foyer Concert)
f.rec.   Instrumental Ensemble - *Unicorn DKPCD 9138 (CD)*
Pub: Faber (as No.4 of 'Britten's Blues')

The Eagle has Two Heads (1946)
[Jean Cocteau trans. Ronald Duncan*]
Instr: 4Cnt. 3Tpt. 3Tbn. Euph. Bs. Perc.
f.p.   Company of Four - Lyric Theatre, Hammersmith,
            4 September 1946

Producer: Murray MacDonald
Exc. 'Fanfare'
f.rec.   Philip Jones Brass Ensemble - *Argo ZRG 912 (and MC);*
London 430 369-2 (CD)

(*in his memoir **Working with Britten**, Duncan mentions that the music included a 'National Anthem' played by the Band of the Royal Household Brigade)

The Duchess of Malfi (1946)
[John Webster adapted by W.H. Auden]
f.p.   Metropolitan Theatre, Providence, Rhode Island, USA
20 September 1946 (and later at the Ethel Barrymore Theatre, New York, on 15 October 1946)
Producer: George Rylands
Scenery: Harry Bennett
Costumes: Miles White

Stratton (1949)
[Ronald Duncan]
f.p.   Theatre Royal, Brighton, 31 October 1949
Music recorded by: English Opera Group Orchestra/Norman Del Mar*
Producer: John Fernald
Designer: Reece Pemberton
(*according to Ronald Duncan, Britten conducted the orchestra - a copy of the recording is in the possession of the Ronald Duncan Literary Foundation)

Am Stram Gram* (1954)
[André Roussin]
Instr: Pno. (+2 voices)
f.p.   Toynbee Hall Theatre, London, 4 March 1954
Producer: Victor Azavia
(*Britten's contribution was a song, set in French, for unison voices and piano dated 31 January 1954 - a facsimile of the MS was published in *Tempo*, December 1973)

The Punch Review* (1955)
[Ronald Duncan]
Compiled at the suggestion of the then editor of *Punch*, Malcolm Muggeridge
Instr: Pno. (+female voice)
f.p.   Duke of York's Theatre, London, 28 September 1955
Producer: Vida Hope
(*Britten's contribution included the songs 'Tell me the truth about love' - a W.H. Auden setting from 1938 q.v. and a specially written song, words by William Plomer, entitled 'Old friends are best'. Ronald Duncan also recalls that both Walton and Tippett had been asked to contribute but 'of the so-called high-brows, only Britten, as usual, turned in a piece on time. It was a waltz. A particularly haunting melody, subtle, elusive and memorable ... (it) was to my mind the only outstanding piece in the evening. The pity is his

score was lost and he had taken no copy.' See **Working with Britten** - The Rebel Press, 1981.)

ARRANGEMENTS

(N.B. More detailed information on all the Purcell realizations, folk songs and other arrangements may be found in **Benjamin Britten: A Catalogue of the Published Works**, compiled and edited by Paul Banks. Pub: The Britten-Pears Library for The Britten Estate, 1999)

(i) Other composers

Bridge: There is a Willow Grows Aslant a Brook arr. for viola and piano (1932)
Composed between 11 and13 December 1932
Dur: 8'
f.p.   Nobuko Imai (Va.)/Roger Vignoles (Pno.) - Erin Arts Centre, Port Erin,
           Isle of Man, 27 August 1988
f.broad.p. above first performance - Radio 3, 12 September 1988
Pub: Thames, 1990
also arr. for reduced orchestra by the composer (c.1948)
f.p.   Festival Orchestra/Benjamin Britten - Jubilee Hall, Aldeburgh, June 1948
           (First Aldeburgh Festival)

Bridge: The Sea (movements 2 and 3) arr. for piano and organ (1934)
f.p.   (movement 3 'Moonlight' only) Benjamin Britten (Pno.)/C.J.R. Coleman
           (organ) - St John's Church, Lowestoft, 9 July 1934

Mozart: Symphony No.39 K543 (finale) arr. for piano and organ (1934)
f.p.   Benjamin Britten (Pno.)/C.J.R. Coleman (organ) - St John's Church,
           Lowestoft, 9 July 1934

Edward Carpenter: England Arise! - revolutionary song arr. SATB chorus and piano (c.1939)
Dur: 4'
f.p.   (probably) Workers' Music Association Chorus/Alan Bush
Pub: Workers' Music Association, 1939 (orchestrated by Will Sahnow)

Schubert: Gretchens Bitte, D564 - song completion for high voice and piano (1938)
[Words: Goethe trans. Andrew Porter]
Commissioned by the BBC for a programme of Schubert songs
Dur: 7'
f.p.   May Blyth (Sop.) - BBC Regional broadcast, 27 December 1938
f.rec.   Marie McLaughlin (Sop.)/Graham Johnson (Pno.) - *Hyperion CDJ
           33013 (CD)*
Pub: Faber, 1998

Chopin: Les Sylphides arr. for small orchestra (1941)
Arranged for Ballet Theatre, New York City for their 1941 season
f.p.   Ballet Theatre Company - Majestic Theatre, New York, 11 February

1941 (and used by them for their Covent Garden performances in London
between 4 July and 31 August 1946)
Choreography:Michael Fokine

Mahler: What the Wild Flowers tell Me: the second movement from Symphony No.3, arr. for reduced orchestra (1941)

Dur:	10'
Instr:	2/2/2/2 - 4/3/1/0 - perc. hp. str.
f.p.	BBC Scottish Orchestra/Guy Warrack - BBC Home Service, 14 November 1942
Pub:	Boosey & Hawkes, 1950

Schubert: The Trout (Die Forelle) arr. for voice and orchestra (1942)
[Words: C.F.D. Schubart]

Dur:	4'
Instr:	0/0/2/0 - 0/0/0/0 - str.(4/3/2/2/2)
Pub:	Boosey & Hawkes

Schumann: Spring Night (Frühlingsnacht) arr. for voice and orchestra (1942)
[Words: Friedrich Eichendorff]

Dur:	1'30"
Instr:	1/1/2/1 - 2/2/1/0 - perc. hp.(or pno.) str.
Pub:	Boosey & Hawkes

Purcell: The Golden Sonata - for two violins, cello and piano (1945)

Dur:	11'
f.p.	members of the Zorian String Quartet/Benjamin Britten (Pno.) - Wigmore Hall, London, 21 November 1945
f.broad.p.	above artists - Third Programme, 10 June 1948
Pub:	Boosey & Hawkes, 1946

The National Anthem arr. chamber orchestra (1946)

Instr:	Fl. Ob. Cl. Bsn. Hn. Perc. Hp. Pno. Vn. Vn. Va. Va. Vc.
f.p.	Glyndebourne Festival Opera Orchestra/Ernest Ansermet - Glyndebourne Opera House, Sussex, 12 July 1946 (at the first night of **The Rape of Lucretia**)

Purcell: Chacony in G minor for string quartet or string orchestra (1947-48, rev.1963)

Dur:	7'
f.p.	Collegium Musicum, Zurich/Benjamin Britten - Kleiner Tonhallesaal, Zurich, 30 January 1948
f.p.	(rev. version) London Symphony Orchestra/Benjamin Britten - Royal Albert Hall, London, 12 September 1963 (Promenade Concert)
f.rec.	English Chamber Orchestra/Benjamin Britten - *Decca SXL 6405, 448 569-2 (CD)*
Pub:	Boosey & Hawkes, 1965

Purcell: Dido and Aeneas - opera in three acts (1950-51, rev.1958-59)
[Libretto: Nahum Tate]
Dur: 50'
f.p.   English Opera Group cond. Benjamin Britten - Lyric Theatre, Hammersmith,
            1 May 1951*
Producer: Joan Cross
Designer: Sophie Fedorovich
Principals: Nancy Evans, Bruce Boyce, Pamela Woolmore
f.broad.p. English Opera Group cond. Benjamin Britten - Third Programme,
            10 July 1951 (from the Cheltenham Festival)
Principals: Joan Cross, Peter Pears, Pamela Woolmore
f.p.   (rev. version) cond. Benjamin Britten - Drottningholmsteater, Stockholm,
            Sweden, 16 May 1962 (Drottningholm Festival)
Producer: Colin Graham
Principals: Janet Baker, John Lawrenson, Jeanette Sinclair
f.recs.   English Opera Group/Benjamin Britten - *BBCB 8003-2 (CD)*
            English Opera Group/Steuart Bedford - *Decca SET 615 (and MC)*
            (excs.) above (Stockholm) performance - *Denon CD 295 (CD)*
Pub: Boosey & Hawkes, 1960 (vocal score by Imogen Holst), 1961 (full score)

Charles Dibdin: Tom Bowling arranged for high voice and piano (1959)
Dur: 4'30"
f.p.   Peter Pears (Ten.)/Benjamin Britten (Pno.) - Jubilee Hall, Aldeburgh,
            22 June 1959 (Aldeburgh Festival)
f.rec.   above artists - *Decca cep 711(45), 430 063-2 (CD)*
f.tel.p.   above artists - BBC2 Television, 21 June 1964
Pub: Boosey & Hawkes, forthcoming (in 'Tom Bowling and Other Song
            Arrangements')

The National Anthem arranged for chorus (double SATB) and orchestra (1961, rev.1967)
Written 'For the Leeds Festival, 1961' - the work was completed by 17 August 1961
Dur: 2'30"
Instr: 2/2/2/2 - 4/2/3/1 - timp. perc.(2) str.
Alt.Instr: 2/2/2/2 - 2/2/0/(0) - timp. perc. str.
f.p.   Leeds Festival Chorus/Royal Liverpool Philharmonic Orchestra/John Pritchard
            - Leeds Town Hall, 7 October 1961 (Leeds Festival)
f.Lon.p.   Philharmonia Chorus and Orchestra/Sir Adrian Boult - Royal Festival Hall,
            22 November 1961 (St. Cecilia Concert)
f.p.   (rev. version) English Chamber Orchestra/Benjamin Britten - Queen Elizabeth
            Hall, London, 1 March 1967 (at the opening of the Queen Elizabeth Hall)
f.broad.p. (rev. version) East Anglian Choirs/English Chamber Orchestra/Benjamin
            Britten - Third Programme, 4 June 1967
f.recs.   London Symphony Chorus and Orchestra/Benjamin Britten - *Decca sec 5119
            (45), SPA 419; London 436 403-2 (CD)*
            (rev. version) East Anglian Choirs/English Chamber Orchestra/Benjamin
            Britten - *Decca 5BB 199-20*
Pub: Boosey & Hawkes, 1961 (vocal score)

Purcell: The Fairy Queen - a masque for soloists, SATB chorus and orchestra (1967)
[1. Oberon's Birthday 2. Night and Silence 3. The Sweet Passion 4. Epithalamium]
Dur: 96'
Instr: 2/2+ca./0/1 - 0/2/0/0 - timp. hpschd. str.
f.p.   English Opera Group/Benjamin Britten - The Maltings, Snape, 25 June 1967
         (Aldeburgh Festival)
Principals: Jennifer Vyvyan, Alfreda Hodgson, James Bowman, Peter Pears,
         Owen Brannigan
f.Lon.p.   cond. Benjamin Britten - Royal Albert Hall, September 1971 (Promenade
         Concert)
f.rec.   Soloists/Ambrosian Opera Chorus/English Chamber Orchestra/Benjamin
         Britten - *Decca SET 499-500, 433 163-2 (CD)*
Pub: Faber, 1970

J.S. Bach: Five Spiritual Songs - Geistliche Lieder for high voice and piano (1969)
[Words trans. Peter Pears 1. Gedenke doch, mein Geist, zurücke 2. Kommt, Seelen,
dieser Tag 3. Liebster Herr Jesu 4. Komm, süsser Tod 5. Bist du bei mir]
Dur: 9'
f.p.   Peter Pears (Ten.)/Benjamin Britten (Pno.) - Blythburgh Church, 18 June 1969
         (Aldeburgh Festival)
Pub: Faber, 1971
Nos.3 and 4 also arr. for SATB chorus
Pub: Faber, 1971 (in 'New Catholic Hymnal')

God Save the Queen - orchestral arrangement of the national anthem (1971)
Completed 9 May 1971
Dur: 1'
Instr: 2+picc./3/3/2+cbsn. - 4/4/3/1 - timp. perc.(3) hp. str.
Alt.Instr. 2/2/2/1+cbsn. - 4/2/3/1 - timp. perc.(2) str.
f.p.   English Chamber Orchestra/Benjamin Britten - The Maltings, Snape,
         13 June 1971 (Aldeburgh Festival in the presence of Her Majesty Queen
         Elizabeth, the Queen Mother)
Pub: Faber

(ii) Folk Song Volumes

Volume 1, British Isles, for high or medium voice and piano (1941-42)
Dur: (complete) 18'
Pub: (complete) Boosey & Hawkes, 1943 (high voice), 1946 (medium voice)
         (orchestral arrangements of Nos.1-4 & 7 in 'Fourteen Folk Songs Arranged for
         Voice and Orchestra', forthcoming)

Individual songs:
1.   **The Salley Gardens** (Ireland)
        [Words: W.B. Yeats]
        Dedicated 'To Clytie Mundy', Pears's singing teacher
        Dur: 3'
        Instr: 0/0/0/1(or solo vc.) - 0/0/0/0 - hp.(pno.) str. (or strings alone)

f.rec.   Peter Pears (Ten.)/Benjamin Britten (Pno.) - *London (USA) LA 30 (78), R 10008 (78), LD 9136 (m); Decca M 555 (78), LW 5122 (m); EMI CMS7 64727-2 (CD)*

also arr. for unison voices and piano
Pub: Boosey & Hawkes, 1955
also arr. for TTBB men's chorus and piano by Edmund Walters
Pub: Boosey & Hawkes, 1986 (as No.2 of 'Three Folk Songs')
also arr. for voice and guitar by Gregg Nestor
Pub: Boosey & Hawkes, 1984 (in 'Twelve Folksong Arrangements')

2.   **Little Sir William** (Somerset)
Dedicated 'To William Mayer'
Dur: 2'30"
Instr: 2/2/2/2 - 2/2/0/0 - timp. str.
f.rec.   Peter Pears (Ten.)/Benjamin Britten (Pno.) - *London (USA) LA 30 (78), R 10008 (78), LD 9136 (m); Decca M 555 (78), LW 5122 (m), EMI CMS7 64727-2 (CD)*

3.   **The Bonny Earl o'Moray** (Scotland)
Dedicated 'To Mildred Titley'
Dur: 2'30"
Instr: 2/2/2/2 - 2/2/0/0 - timp. perc. str.
f.rec.   *London (USA) LA 30 (78), R 10010 (78), LD 9136 (m), OS 25327; Decca M 594 (78), LW 5122 (m), SXL 6007, 430 063-2 (CD) (and MC); EMI CMS7 64727-2 (CD)*

also arr. for TTBB men's chorus and piano by Edmund Walters
Pub: Boosey & Hawkes, 1986 (as No.1 of 'Three Folk Songs')

4.   **O can ye sew cushions?** (Scotland)
Dedicated 'To Meg Mundy', a member of the Elizabethan Singers
Dur: 2'30"
Instr: 2/1+ca./1+bcl./2 - 2/0/0/0 - hp. str.
also arr. for SSA chorus and piano by Imogen Holst
Pub: Boosey & Hawkes, 1955

5.   **The trees they grow so high** (Somerset)
Dedicated 'To Bobby Rothman'
Dur: 3'30"

6.   **The Ash Grove** (Wales)
Dedicated 'To Beata Mayer'
Dur: 3'
f.rec.   Peter Pears (Ten.)/Benjamin Britten (Pno.) - *London (USA) LA 30 (78), R 10009 (78), LD 9136 (m), OS 25327; Decca LW 5122 (m), SXL 6007, 430 063-2 (CD) (and MC); EMI CMS7 64727-2 (CD)*

7.   **Oliver Cromwell** (Suffolk)
Dedicated 'To Christopher Mayer'
Dur: 1'
Instr: 1+picc./2/2/2 - 2/2/0/0 - timp. str.
f.rec.   Peter Pears (Ten.)/Benjamin Britten (Pno.) - *London (USA) LA 30 (78), R 10008 (78), LD 9136 (m); Decca M 555 (78), LW 5122 (m); EMI CMS7 64727-2 (CD)*

also arr. for unison voices and piano
Pub: Boosey & Hawkes, 1959

also arr. for TTBB men's chorus and piano by Edmund Walters
Pub: Boosey & Hawkes, 1986 (as No.3 of 'Three Folk Songs')

Documented performances:
f.p.	(Nos.1, 2, 3 and 7) Peter Pears (Ten.)/Benjamin Britten (Pno.) - Congregational Church, Grand Rapids, Michigan, USA, 26 November 1941
f.p.	(No.6) above artists - Southold High School Auditorium, Long Island, New York, 14 December 1941
f.p.	(No.4) above artists - St Margaret's Church, Lowestoft, 14 October 1943
f.Brit.p.	(Nos.1, 2, 3, 6 and 7) above artists - Hockerill Training College, Bishop's Stortford, 18 November 1942
f.p.	(Nos.1, 2, 3 and 7 - orch. version) Peter Pears (Ten.)/New London Orchestra/Alex Sherman - Odeon Theatre, Southgate, London, 13 December 1942
f.p.	(No.4 - orch. version) Helena Cook (Sop.)/BBC Midland Light Orchestra/Rae Jenkins - BBC broadcast, 6 November 1944
f.p.	(No.5) Anne Marie O'Neil (Sop.)/Andrew Bryson (Pno.) - BBC Scottish Home Service, 8 February 1950
f.p.	(No.1 - TB/chorus version) Chorus and Orchestra of the Schools Music Association/Sir Adrian Boult - Royal Albert Hall, London, 6 May 1956

Volume 2, France, for high or medium voice and piano (1942)
[Words trans. Iris Rogers]
Dedicated 'To my young friends, Arnold and Humphrey Gyde' - the sons of Arnold Gyde and Sophie Wyss for whom they were written. The orchestral arrangements of Nos.3, 4, 5, 7 and 8 were made for the baritone, Martial Singher.
Dur: (complete) 20'
Pub: (complete) Boosey & Hawkes,1946 (high voice), 1947 (medium voice)
              (orchestral arrangements of Nos.1, 3, 4, 5, 7 and 8 in 'Fourteen Folk Songs Arranged for Voice and Orchestra', forthcoming)

Individual songs:
1.   **La Noël passée** (The Orphan and King Henry)
        Dur: 4'
        Instr: string orchestra
2.   **Voici le printemps** (Hear the voice of spring)
        Dur: 1'45"
        f.rec.   Sophie Wyss (Sop.)/Benjamin Britten (Pno.) - *EMI CMS7 64727-2 (CD)*
3.   **Fileuse**
        Dur: 2'
        Instr: 0/1+ca./0/0 - 0/2/0/0 - perc. hp. str. (no vns.)
        f.rec.   Sophie Wyss (Sop.)/Benjamin Britten (Pno.) - *EMI CMS7 64727-2 (CD)*
4.   **Le roi s'en va-t'en chasse** (The King is gone a-hunting)
        Dur: 2'15"

Instr: 0/2/2/2 - 0/2/0/0 - str. (no Db.)

f.recs.   Sophie Wyss (Sop.)/Benjamin Britten (Pno.) - *Decca M 568 (78);*
            EMI CMS7 64727- 2 (CD)

            Peter Pears (Ten.)/Benjamin Britten (Pno.) - *London (USA) OS*
            25327; Decca SXL 6007, 430 063-2 (CD) (and MC); HMV RLS
            748 (m); EMI CHS7 69741-2 (CD), CMS7 64727-2 (CD)

5.   **La belle est au jardin d'amour** (Beauty in love's garden)

Dur: 3'15"

Instr: 2/0/2/1 - 0/0/0/0 - str.

f.recs.   Sophie Wyss (Sop.)/Benjamin Britten (Pno.) - *Decca M 568 (78);*
            EMI CMS 7 64727- 2 (CD)

            Peter Pears (Ten.)/Benjamin Britten (Pno.) - *London (USA) OS*
            25327; Decca SXL 6007, 430 063-2 (CD) (and MC)

6.   **Il est quelqu'un sur terre** (There's someone in my fancy)

Dur: 5'

7.   **Eho! Eho!**

Dur: 2'

Instr: 2/2/0/2 - 2/0/0/0 - str.

8.   **Quand j'étais chez mon père (Heigh ho! heigh hi!)**

Dur: 2'

Instr: 1+picc./2/2/2 - 2/2/0/0 - timp. perc. str.

f.recs.   Sophie Wyss (Sop.)/Benjamin Britten (Pno.) - *EMI CMS7 64727-2*
            (CD)

            Peter Pears (Ten.)/Benjamin Britten (Pno.) - *London (USA) LA 30*
            (78), R 10010 (78); Decca M 594 (78); EMI CMS7 64727-2 (CD)

Documented performances:

f.p.   (Nos.5 and 8) Peter Pears (Ten.)/Benjamin Britten (Pno.) - Friends
            House, London, 28 February 1943

f.p.   (complete) Sophie Wyss (Sop.)/Gerald Moore (Pno.) - National
            Gallery, London, 25 March 1943

f.Eur.p.   (Nos.1 and 4) Peter Pears (Ten.)/Benjamin Britten (Pno.) - Paris,
            March 1945

f.p.   (Nos.3, 4, 5, 7 and 8 - orch. version) Martial Singher (Bar.)/
            Chicago Symphony Orchestra/Fritz Busch - Orchestra Hall,
            Chicago, 23 December 1948

f.Brit.p.   (No.4 - orch. version) Esther Salaman (Sop.)/Montmartre
            Players/Henry Krein - BBC Light Programme, 5 November 1949

f.rec.   (orch. version) Thomas Allen (Bar.)/Northern Sinfonia/Steuart
            Bedford - *Collins 7039-2(CD)*

Volume 3, British Isles, for high or medium voice and piano (1945-46)

Dedicated 'To Joan Cross'

Dur: (complete) 14'45"

Pub: (complete) Boosey & Hawkes, 1948
            (orchestral arrangements of Nos.1, 6 and 7 in 'Fourteen Folk Songs Arranged
            for Voice and Orchestra', forthcoming)

Individual songs:
1.   **The Plough Boy** (tune by William Shield)
        Dur: 2'
        Instr: picc. and string orchestra/quartet (without Db.)
        f.recs.   Peter Pears (Ten.)/Benjamin Britten (Pno.) - *London (USA) OS
                    25327; Decca SXL 6007, 430 063-2 (CD) (and MC); HMV DA
                    1873 (78), 7 ep 7071 (45), RLS 748 (m); EMI CMS7 64727-2 (CD)
                    above artists - Aldeburgh Festival AF 001* ('live' recording)
        Pub: Boosey & Hawkes, 1953 (high voice), 1955 (medium voice)
2.   **There's none to soothe** (Scotland)
        Dur: 1'45"
        f.rec.   Peter Pears (Ten.)/Benjamin Britten (Pno.) - *London (USA) LA 30
                    (78), R 10009 (78), LD 9136 (m); Decca M 678 (78), LW 5122 (m);
                    EMI CMS7 64727-2 (CD)*
3.   **Sweet Polly Oliver** (17th-century tune)
        Dur   2'15"
        f.rec.   Peter Pears (Ten.)/Benjamin Britten (Pno.) - *London (USA) LA 30
                    (78), R 10009 (78), LD 9136 (m), OS 25327; Decca M 678 (78),
                    LW 5122 (m), SXL 6007, 430 063-2 (CD) (and MC); EMI CMS7
                    64727-2 (CD)*
4.   **The Miller of Dee** (England)
        Dur: 2'
        f.recs.   Peter Pears (Ten.)/Benjamin Britten (Pno.) - *London (USA) LD
                    9136 (m), OS 25327; Decca LW 5122 (m), SXL 6007, 430 063-2
                    (CD) (and MC)*
                    above artists - *Aldeburgh Festival AF 001* ('live' recording)
5.   **The Foggy, Foggy Dew** (Suffolk)
        Dur   2'30"
        f.recs.   Peter Pears (Ten.)/Benjamin Britten (Pno.) - *HMV DA 1873 (78),
                    cep 711 (45), 7 ep 7071 (45), RLS 748 (m); EMI CMS 7 64727-2
                    (CD), Decca sec 5102 (45), SDD 197, 430 063-2 (CD) (and MC)*
                    above artists - *Aldeburgh Festival AF 001* ('live' recording)
        also arr. for voice and guitar by Gregg Nestor
        Pub: Boosey & Hawkes, 1984 (in 'Twelve Folksong Arrangements')
6.   **O Waly, Waly** (Somerset)
        Dur: 3'45"
        Instr: string orchestra
        f.rec.   Peter Pears (Ten.)/Benjamin Britten (Pno.) - *HMV DA 2032 (78),
                    7 ep 7071 (45), RLS 748 (m); EMI CMS7 64727-2 (CD); London
                    (USA) OS 25327; Decca SXL 6007, 430 063-2 (CD) (and MC)*
        also arr. for voice and guitar by Gregg Nestor
        Pub: Boosey & Hawkes, 1984 (in 'Twelve Folksong Arrangements')
7.   **Come you not from Newcastle?** (England)
        Dur: 1'15"
        Instr: 2/2/2/2 - 2/0/0/0 - timp. perc. str.(4 Vn. Db.)
        f.rec.   Peter Pears (Ten.)/Benjamin Britten (Pno.) - *HMV DA 1873 (78),
                    7 ep 7071 (45), RLS 748 (m); EMI CMS7 64727-2 (CD); London
                    (USA) OS 25327; Decca SXL 6007, 430 063-2 (CD) (and MC)*

Documented performances:

f.p.   (No.3) Peter Pears (Ten.)/Benjamin Britten (Pno.) -
          Bristol Grammar School, 26 September 1945

f.p.   (Nos.1, 2 and 5) above artists - Melksham, Wiltshire,
          27 September 1945 (Melksham Music Club)

f.p.   (No.7) Joan Cross (Sop.)/Nina Milkina(Pno.) - BBC Light
          Programme, 21 February 1946

f.p.   (No.4) Peter Pears (Ten.)/Benjamin Britten (Pno.) - National
          Gallery, London, 11 March 1946

f.p.   (No.6) above artists - Concertgebouw Recital Hall, Amsterdam,
          31 October 1946

f.p.   (No.1 - fl./str.qt. version) Peter Pears (Ten.)/John Francis (Fl.)/
          Zorian String Quartet - BBC Light Programme, 21 November 1946

f.rec.   (Nos.1, 6 and 7 - orch. version) Philip Langridge (Ten.)/Northern
          Sinfonia/Steuart Bedford - *Collins 7039-2 (CD)*

Volume 4, Moore's Irish Melodies, for high voice and piano (1957)
[1. **Avenging and bright** (Crooghan a venee) Dur: 1'45"
 2. **Sail on, sail on** (The Humming of the Ban) Dur: 2'30"
 3. **How sweet the answer** (The Wren) Dur: 2'
 4. **The minstrel boy** (The Moreen) Dur: 2'30"
 5. **At the mid hour of night** (Molly, my Dear) Dur: 2'45"
 6. **Rich and rare** (The summer is coming) Dur: 3'
 7. **The dear harp of my country** (Kate Tyrrel) Dur: 2'30"
 8. **Oft in the stilly night** Dur: 2'45"
 9. **The Last Rose of Summer** (Groves of Blarney) Dur: 3'45"
 10. **O the sight entrancing** (Planxty Sudley) Dur: 2'15"]
Dedicated to Anthony Gishford
Dur: 24'30" (complete)

f.p.   (Nos.3 and 4) Peter Pears (Ten.)/Benjamin Britten (Pno.) - Mozartsaal,
          Vienna, 23 April 1957

f.p.   (Nos.1, 8 and 9) above artists - Victoria & Albert Museum, London,
          26 January 1958

f.broad.p. (Nos.1, 4 and 9) above artists - BBC Third Programme, 27 March 1958

f.broad.p. (Nos.3 and 8) above artists - BBC Home Service, 1 July 1958 (pre-recorded,
          20 May 1958)

f.broad.p. (complete) Ian Caddy (Bar.)/Jennifer Coultas (Pno.) - Radio 3,
          14 September 1979 (pre-recorded, 20 January 1979)

f.rec.   (Nos.1, 3, 4, 8 and 9) above artists - *London (USA) OS 25327; Decca SXL
          6007, 430 063-2 (CD) (and MC)*

Pub: Boosey & Hawkes, 1960

Volume 5, British Isles, for high voice and piano (1951-59)
[1. **The Brisk Young Widow** (Trad.) Dur: 2'
 2. **Sally in our Alley** (Words and music: Henry Carey) Dur: 4'30"
 3. **The Lincolnshire Poacher** (Trad.) Dur: 2'
 4. **Early one morning** (Trad.) Dur: 3'15"
 5. **Ca' the yowes** (Words: Robert Burns) Dur: 4'30"]
Dur: 15'45"

f.p.	(No.5) Peter Pears (Ten.)/Benjamin Britten (Pno.) - Mozartsaal, Vienna, 9 April 1951
f.p.	(No.1) above artists - Victoria & Albert Museum, London, 24 January 1954
f.p.	(No.4) above artists - Mozartsaal, Vienna, 23 April 1957
f.p.	(Nos.2 and 3) above artists - Jubilee Hall, Aldeburgh, 22 June 1959 (Aldeburgh Festival)
f.recs.	(No.1) Peter Pears (Ten.)/Benjamin Britten (Pno.) - *London (USA) LD 9136 (m), Decca LW 5122 (m)*
	(Nos.2 and 3) Peter Pears (Ten.)/Benjamin Britten (Pno.) - *HMV cep 711 (45); Decca sec 5102 (45), SDD 197, 430 063-2 (CD) (and MC)*
	(Nos.1, 4 and 5) Peter Pears (Ten.)/Benjamin Britten (Pno.) - *London (USA) OS 25327; Decca SXL 6007, 430 063-2 (CD) (and MC)*
Pub:	Boosey & Hawkes, 1961

No.3 also arr. for voice and guitar by Gregg Nestor

Pub:	Boosey & Hawkes, 1984 (in 'Twelve Folksong Arrangements')

Volume 6, England, for high voice and guitar (1956-58?)
[1. **I will give my love an apple** (Dorset) Dur: 1'15"
 2. **Sailor-boy** (Appalachian Mountains) Dur: 2'
 3. **Master Kilby** (Somerset) Dur: 2'
 4. **The Soldier and the Sailor** (Oxfordshire) Dur: 2'30"
 5. **Bonny at Morn** (Northumberland) Dur: 2'30"
 6. **The Shooting of his Dear** (Norfolk) Dur: 2'45"]

Dur:	12'15" (complete)
f.p.	(Nos.1, 4, 6) Peter Pears (Ten.)/Julian Bream (Gtr.) - Wigmore Hall, London, 6 May 1956
f.p.	(Nos.2 and 3) above artists - Great Glemham House, Suffolk, 17 June 1958 (Aldeburgh Festival)
f.rec.	(Nos.1, 2, 3, 4 and 6) above artists - *London (USA) LSC 2718, AGLI 1281; RCA SB 6621, GL 42752, 09026 61583-2 (CD)*
Pub:	Boosey & Hawkes, 1961 (ed. Julian Bream)

Eight Folk Song Arrangements for high voice and harp (1976)
[1. **Lord! I married me a wife** (Southern Appalachians) Dur: 1'15"
 2. **She's like the Swallow** (Newfoundland) Dur: 2'45"
 3. **Lemady** (British Trad.) Dur: 3'15"
 4. **Bonny at Morn** (North Country) Dur: 1'30"
 5. **Bugeilio'r Gwenith Gwyn (I was lonely and forlorn)** (Welsh trans. Osian Ellis) Dur: 2'15"
 6. **David of the White Rock (Dafydd y Garreg Wen)** (Welsh trans. Thomas Oliphant) Dur: 3'
 7. **The False Knight upon the Road** (Southern Appalachians) Dur: 3'30"
 8. **Bird Scarer's Song** (British) Dur: 1']
Written for Peter Pears and Osian Ellis

Dur:	18'45" (complete)
f.p.	(Nos.2 and 8) Peter Pears (Ten.)/Osian Ellis (Hp.) - The Maltings, Snape, 17 June 1976 (Aldeburgh Festival)
f.broad.p.	(Nos.2 and 8) above first performance - Radio 3, 17 January 1978

f.p.   (Nos.3 and 7) above artists - Mandel Hall, University of Chicago,
               10 November 1977
f.recs.   (Nos.1 and 2) above artists - *London (USA) OS 26477; Decca SXL 6788*
               John Shirley Quirk (Bar.)/Osian Ellis (Hp.) - *Meridian KE 77119 (MC), CDE
               84119 (CD)*
Pub: Faber, 1980
also arr. for medium voice and piano by Colin Matthews
Pub: Faber, 1980

(iii) Other folksongs

The Twelve Days of Christmas, for high voice and piano (1941)
f.p.   Peter Pears (Ten.)/Benjamin Britten (Pno.) - Southold High School
               Auditorium, Long Island, New York, 14 December 1941

Greensleeves, for high voice and piano (1941?)
Dur: 2'
f.rec.   Philip Langridge (Ten.)/Graham Johnson (Pno.) - *Collins 7039-2 (CD)*
Pub: Boosey & Hawkes, forthcoming (in 'Tom Bowling and Other Song
               Arrangements')

I wonder as I wander, for high voice and piano (1940-41?)
[Collected and arranged by John Jacob Niles]
Dur: 4'
f.p.   Peter Pears (Ten.)/Benjamin Britten (Pno.) - Haywards Heath, Sussex,
               20 March 1943 (CEMA Concert)
f.Lon.p.   above artists - Central Hall, Westminster, 7 November 1944 (Society of
               Friends Concert)
f.rec.   Philip Langridge (Ten.)/Graham Johnson (Pno.) - *Collins 7039-2 (CD)*
Pub: Boosey & Hawkes, forthcoming (in 'Tom Bowling and Other Song
               Arrangements')

The Crocodile, for high voice and piano (1941)
Dur: 4'45"
f.p.   Peter Pears (Ten.)/Benjamin Britten (Pno.) - Southold High School
               Auditorium, Long Island, New York, 14 December 1941
f.rec.   Philip Langridge (Ten.)/Graham Johnson (Pno.) - *Collins 7039-2 (CD)*
Pub: Boosey & Hawkes, forthcoming (in 'Tom Bowling and Other Song
               Arrangements')

Pray Goody, for high voice and piano (1945-46?)
[Words: Kane O'Hara, from John Hullah's 'The Song Book']
Dur: 2'30"
f.rec.   Philip Langridge (Ten.)/Graham Johnson (Pno.) - *Collins 7039-2 (CD)*
Pub: Boosey & Hawkes, forthcoming (in 'Tom Bowling and Other Song
               Arrangements')

The Stream in the Valley, for tenor, cello and piano (1946)
[German folksong 'Da unten im Tale' trans. Iris Rogers]

Probably written for a joint recital with Maurice Gendron
Dur: 2'30"
f.p.   Peter Pears (Ten.)/Maurice Gendron (Vc.)/Benjamin Britten (Pno.) - BBC
            Light Programme, 21 November 1946
f.rec.   Philip Langridge (Ten.)/Christopher van Kampen (Vc.)/Graham Johnson
            (Pno.) - *Collins 7039-2 (CD)*
Pub: Boosey & Hawkes, forthcoming (in 'Tom Bowling and Other Song
            Arrangements')

The holly and the ivy, for chorus (SATB) unaccompanied (1957)
[Words: Trad.]
Written for June Gordon (Marchioness of Aberdeen and Temair) and the Haddo House
Choral Society
Dur: 3'15"
f.broad.p. Haddo House Choral Society/June Gordon - BBC Scottish Home Service,
            22 December 1957 (pre-recorded at Haddo House, Aberdeen, 14 December
            1957 during their annual Carol Concert)
f.rec.   BBC Singers/Simon Joly - *Collins 7039-2 (CD)*
Pub: Boosey & Hawkes, 1957, 1963 (in 'Sing Nowell: 51 carols new and
            arranged')

Soldier, won't you marry me? for two voices and piano (1958)
[Southern Appalachian words and melody collected by Cecil Sharp]
Written for Peter Pears and Norma Procter for their joint recital tours in the 1950s.
Dur: 1'45"
f.p.   Norma Procter (Con.)/Peter Pears (Ten.)/Benjamin Britten (Pno.) -
            Düsseldorf, 15 March 1958
f.Brit.p.   Kathleen Livingstone (Sop.)/Neil Mackie (Ten.)/John Blakely (Pno.) - BBC
            Radio 3, 4 December 1986 (pre-recorded, 18 November 1986)
f.rec.   Felicity Lott (Sop.)/Philip Langridge (Ten.)/Graham Johnson (Pno.) - *Collins
            7039-2 (CD)*
Pub: Boosey & Hawkes, forthcoming (in 'Tom Bowling and Other Song
            Arrangements')

The Deaf Woman's Courtship, for two voices and piano (c.1950s)
Written for Peter Pears and Norma Procter for their joint recital tours in the 1950s.
Dur: 1'15"
f.rec.   Felicity Lott (Sop.)/Philip Langridge (Ten.)/Graham Johnson (Pno.) - *Collins
            7039-2 (CD)*
Pub: Boosey & Hawkes, forthcoming (in 'Tom Bowling and Other Song
            Arrangements')

The Bitter Withy,* for tenor, boys' chorus and piano (1962)
Written for the London Boy Singers
Dur: 5'15" (unfinished)
f.rec.   Philip Langridge (Ten.)/Wenhaston Boys' Choir/David Owen Norris (Pno.)
            cond. Christopher Barnett - *Collins 7039-2 (CD)*
(*Originally intended to be the fourth Canticle)

King Herod and the Cock, for unison voices and piano (1962, rev.1965)
[Words and melody: Trad. - collected by Cecil Sharp]
Written 'For the London Boy Singers' - the arrangement was completed on 3 May 1962
Dur: 2'
f.p.   London Boy Singers - Aldeburgh Parish Church, 16 June 1962 (Aldeburgh
             Festival)
f.recs.   Aldeburgh Festival Singers - *University of East Anglia UEA 82015*
             Wenhaston Boys' Choir/David Owen Norris (Pno.) cond. Christopher Barnett
             - *Collins 7039-2 (CD)*
Pub: Boosey & Hawkes, 1965

The Twelve Apostles, for tenor, unison chorus and piano (1962)
[Folk Songs from the Southern Appalachians]
Written for the London Boy Singers
Dur: 6'15"
f.p.   Peter Pears (Ten.)/London Boy Singers/Benjamin Britten (Pno.) - Aldeburgh
             Parish Church, 16 June 1962 (Aldeburgh Festival)
f.recs.   David Mattinson (Bar.)/Trinity College Choir, Cambridge/Charles Matthews
             (Pno.) cond. Richard Marlow - *Pearl SHE 593*
             Wenhaston Boys' Choir/David Owen Norris (Pno.) cond. Christopher Barnett
             - *Collins 7039-2 (CD)*
Pub: Faber, 1981

The holly and the ivy, for voice and piano (ND)
Dur: 2'30"
f.rec.   Felicity Lott (Sop.)/Graham Johnson (Pno.) - *Collins 7039-2 (CD)*
Pub: Boosey & Hawkes, forthcoming (in 'Tom Bowling and Other Song
             Arrangements')

Dink's Song, for voice and piano (ND)
[Words: Trad. American]
Dur: 3'30"
f.rec.   (arr. cello and piano) Christopher van Kampen (Vc.)/Graham Johnson (Pno.) -
             Collins 7039-2 (CD)
Pub: Boosey & Hawkes, forthcoming (in 'Tom Bowling and Other Song
             Arrangements')

MS LOCATION

The majority of manuscripts, including those owned by the British Library (but on
permanent loan), are housed in The Britten-Pears Library, Aldeburgh. (**BPL**)

Other locations include:

NYPL An American Overture (1941)
YUL Seven Sonnets of Michelangelo (1940)

BIBLIOGRAPHY

Banks, Paul (ed.)	**Benjamin Britten: A Catalogue of the Published Works**. Aldeburgh: The Britten-Pears Library for the Britten Estate, 1999 [D] [B]
Blyth, Alan (ed.)	**Remembering Britten**. London: Hutchinson, 1981
Blythe, Ronald (ed.)	**Aldeburgh Anthology**. Aldeburgh: Snape Maltings. Foundation/Faber Music, 1972
Britten, Benjamin	**On Receiving the First Aspen Award.** London: Faber and Faber, 1964
Britten, Beth	**My Brother Benjamin**. The Kensal Press, 1987
Carpenter, Humphrey	**Benjamin Britten: A Biography**. London: Faber and Faber, 1992
Duncan, Ronald	**Working with Britten**. Bideford: The Rebel Press, 1981
Evans, John; Philip Reed and Paul Wilson	**A Britten Source Book**. Aldeburgh: The Britten-Pears Library, 1987 [D] [B]
Evans, Peter	**The Music of Benjamin Britten**. London: J.M. Dent USA: University of Minnesota Press, 1979, rev. ed. 1989
Flothuis, Marius	**Benjamin Britten**. In his 'Modern British Composers' Stockholm: Continental Book Co./London: Sidgwick & Jackson, 1949
Foreman, Lewis (ed.)	**From Parry to Britten: British Music in Letters 1900-1945** London: Batsford, 1987
Gishford, Anthony (ed.)	**Tribute to Benjamin Britten on his Fiftieth Birthday**. London: Faber and Faber, 1963
Headington, Christopher	**Britten**. London: Eyre Methuen, 1981
Headington, Christopher	**Peter Pears: A Biography**. London: Faber and Faber, 1992
Herbert, David (ed.)	**The Operas of Benjamin Britten**. London: Hamish Hamilton, 1979
Holst, Imogen	**Britten** (Great Composer Series). London: Faber and Faber, 1966; rev. ed. 1980

Kennedy, Michael   **Britten** (Master Musician Series). London:
                    J.M. Dent, 1981, rev. ed. 1993 [B] [D]

Mark, Christopher   **Early Benjamin Britten, a Study of Stylistic and Technical
                    Evolution**. New York: Garland Publishing Inc., 1995

Mitchell, Donald   **Britten and Auden in the Thirties**. London:
                    Faber and Faber/USA: University of Washington Press,
                    1981

Mitchell, Donald and John Evans
                    Benjamin Britten, 1913-1976: Pictures from a Life.
                    London: Faber and Faber/USA: Scribners, 1978

Mitchell, Donald and Hans Keller (ed.)
                    **Benjamin Britten - A Commentary on his Works
                    from a Group of Specialists**. London: Rockliff,1952
                    Westport, Conn., USA: Greenwood Press, 1972 [B] [D]

Mitchell, Donald and Philip Reed (eds.)
                    Letters from a Life: Vols.1 and 2. London: Faber and
                    Faber, 1991

Palmer, Christopher (ed.) **The Britten Companion**. London: Faber and Faber, 1984

Parsons, Charles H.   **A Benjamin Britten Discography**. Lampeter: Edwin Mellen
                    Press, 1990 [D]

Routh, Francis   **Benjamin Britten** in his 'Contemporary British
                    Music'. London: Macdonald, 1972

Schafer, Murray   **Benjamin Britten** in his 'British Composers in
                    Interview'. London: Faber and Faber, 1963

Thorpe, Marion (ed.)   **Peter Pears: A Tribute on his 75th birthday**.
                    Aldeburgh: The Britten-Pears Library, 1985

White, Eric Walter   **Benjamin Britten: A Sketch of his Life and Works**.
                    London: Boosey & Hawkes, 1948; 2nd ed. 1954

White, Eric Walter   **Benjamin Britten: His Life and Operas**.
                    London: Faber and Faber/USA: California University
                    Press, 1970; rev. ed. 1983 (ed. John Evans)

Whittall, Arnold   **The Music of Britten and Tippett: Studies in Themes
                    and Techniques**. Cambridge/New York: Cambridge University
                    Press, 1982

12

Alan Bush
(1900–1995)

Sonata in G for violin and piano (c.1918)
f.p.   (Andante and Presto only): Gladys Chester (Vn.)/Alan Bush (Pno.) -
      Royal Academy of Music, London, 15 June 1918

Variations on an original theme for piano (c.1919)
f.p.   Warwick Braithwaite - Royal Academy of Music, London, 1 February 1919

Sonata in E for violin and piano (c. 1920)
f.p.   Florence Lockwood (Vn.)/Alan Bush (Pno.) - Royal Academy of Music,
      London, 3 July 1920

Three Pieces for two pianos Op. 1 (1921)
[1. On the Warpath 2. Pastoral Scene 3. * At the Cinema]
A Charles Mortimer prize-winning work
Dur: 11'
f.p.   Alan Bush/Reginald Paul - Royal Academy of Music, London, 2 March 1921
Pub: Chappell, 1921 (* Also published as a piano solo)

Piano Sonata No. 1 in B minor Op. 2 (1921)
A Philip Agnew prize-winning work
Dur: 22'
f.p.   Alan Bush - Royal Academy of Music, London, 6 July 1921
Pub: Chappell, 1922

Louis N. Parker's Masque 'A Wreath of a Hundred Roses' - No. 5 Festive March for organ (1922)
f.p.   Benjamin Dale - Queen's Hall, London, 17 July 1922

Last Days of Pompeii - opera (1923 - unfinished)
[Libretto: Hamilton Brinsley Bush based on the novel by Bulwer Lytton]
Instr: not orchestrated - piano part only

f.priv.p.   Brinsley Bush (Ten.)/May Murphy (Sop.)/Dorothy Giles (M/S.)/Alan Bush
             (Pno.) - Highgate, North London, c.1923

Fantasy for violin and piano Op. 3 (1923)
Commissioned by W.W. Cobbett
Dur: 13'
f.priv.p.   Evelyn Cooke (Vn.)/Alan Bush (Pno.) - Wigmore Studios, London,
             10 May 1924
f.pub.p.   Florence Lockwood (Vn.)/Alan Bush (Pno.) - Hampstead Town Hall, London,
             4 December 1924
f.Eur.p.   Florence Lockwood (Vn.)/Alan Bush (Pno.) - Bechstein Hall, Berlin,
             9 September 1926

String Quartet in A minor Op. 4 (1923)
A Carnegie Award-winning composition
Dur: 20'
f.p.   Spencer Dyke String Quartet - Spencer Dyke (Vn.), Ernest Tomlinson (Vn.),
             Edwin Quaife (Va.), B. Patterson Parker (Vc.) - Hampstead Town Hall,
             London, 4 December 1924
f.broad.p.   Virtuoso Quartet - 11 June 1925
f.Eur.p.   Brosa Quartet - Bechstein Hall, Berlin, 6 November 1928
Pub: Stainer & Bell, 1925

Quartet for piano, violin, viola and cello Op. 5 (1924)
Dur: 29'
f.p.   (2 movts. only): Alan Bush (Pno.) and members of the Spencer Dyke String
             Quartet - Hampstead Town Hall, London, 4 December 1924
f.p.   (complete): Alan Bush (Pno.)/John Pennington (Vn.)/James Lockyer
             (Va.)/Anthony Pini (Vc.) - Faculty of Arts Gallery, London, 24 May 1927
f.Eur.p.   Alan Bush and members of the Brosa Quartet - Bechstein Hall, Berlin,
             6 November 1928

Five Pieces for violin, viola, cello, clarinet and horn Op. 6 (1925)
Dedicated to John Ireland (who, at that time, was his teacher)
Dur: 18'
f.p.   Antonia Brosa (Vn.)/Leonard Rubens (Va.)/Anthony Pini (Vc.)/
             Carl Essberger (Cl.)/ Ernest Friere (Hn.) - Bechstein Hall, Berlin,
             6 November 1928
f.Brit.p.   Antonio Brosa (Vn.)/Leonard Rubens (Va.)/Anthony Pini (Vc.)/ Haydn
             Draper (Cl.)/A.D. Hyde (Hn.) - Cowdray Hall, London,
             29 January 1930
f.broad.p.   Vesuvius Ensemble - Radio 3, 12 October 1977
Also arr. for wind and strings by the composer (1925)

Two Songs for soprano and chamber orchestra Op. 7 (1925)
[Words: 1. The Moth (Walter de la Mare)
 2. Heard on a Saltmarsh (Harold Munro)]
Dur: 8'
Instr: 1/1/1/1 - 2/0/0/0 - hp. str.

Symphonic Impression Op. 8 (1926-27)
Dur: 18'
Instr: 3/3/3/2 - 4/3/3/1 - timp. perc.(2) str.
f.priv.p.   Royal College of Music, London, 19 November 1929
              (Patron's Fund Rehearsal)
f.pub.p.   Queen's Hall Orchestra/Alan Bush - Queen's Hall, London,
              11 September 1930 (Promenade Concert)
Also arr. for piano duet (1927)
f.p.   Alan Bush/William Busch - Faculty of Arts Gallery, London, 21 June 1927

Song to Labour for SATB chorus and piano (1926)
[Words: Charlotte Perkin Gilman]
Pub: W.M.A., c.1926

Prelude and Fugue for piano Op. 9 (1927)
Dedicated `To Edward J. Dent Esq.'
Dur: 11'
f.p.   Alan Bush - Faculty of Arts Gallery, London, 21 June 1927
f.Eur.p.   Alan Bush - Bechstein Hall, Berlin, 6 November 1928
Pub: OUP, 1927

Song to the Men of England for unaccompanied SATB chorus Op. 10 (1928)
[Words: Shelley]
Written for the London Labour Choral Union
Dur: 3'
Pub: Curwen, 1928; Joseph Williams, 1950

Relinquishment for piano Op. 11 (1928)
Dedicated `To C.K.'
Dur: 8'
f.p.   Alan Bush - Bechstein Hall, Berlin, 6 November 1928
f.rec.   Piers Lane - Redcliffe Recordings RR 008(CD)
Pub: OUP, 1929 (originally written as a contribution to a series of contemporary
              compositions edited by John Ireland for OUP. It was at first rejected due to its
              extreme difficulty, but was published separately a few months later).

The Road for unaccompanied SATB chorus Op. 13 No. 1 (1929)
[Words: Violet A. Friedlander]
Dur: 2'30'
Pub: Curwen, 1930

Three Contrapuntal Studies for violin and viola Op. 13 No. 2 (1929)

**Songs of the Doomed - song cycle for tenor and piano with Epilogue for female
chorus and piano Op. 14 (1929)**
[Words: Poems taken from `Out of the Coalfields' by F.C. Boden
 1. Despair is at heart and hatred for ever 2. When daylight's breaking
 3. Here they lie, not nice to see   Epilogue - Hush be still you bitter strings]
Dur: 15'

f.p.   Geoffrey Dunn/London Labour Choral Union/Alan Bush - Morley College,
            London, 7 March 1933

Dialectic for string quartet Op. 15 (1929)
Dur: 14'30'
f.p.   Brosa Quartet - BBC Broadcasting House, London, 29 March 1935
            (BBC Chamber Concert)
f.Eur.p.   New Hungarian Quartet - Sandor Vegh (Vn.), L. Halmos (Vn.),
            D. Koromzay (Va.), V. Palotai (Vc.) - Prague, 2 September 1935
            (ISCM Festival)
f.rec.   Aeolian String Quartet - *Decca K 1852/3 (78), London (USA) LA 50 (78)*
            (recorded under the auspices of the British Council)
Pub: Boosey & Hawkes, 1938
Later arr. string orchestra Op. 15a (1938)
f.p.   London String Orchestra/Alan Bush - Wigmore Hall, London,
            30 January 1939

Dance Overture for military band Op. 12 (1930)
Dedicated to Edward Clark
Dur: 14'
f.broad.p. BBC Wireless Military Band - 25 April 1931
Later arr. for orchestra Op. 12a (1935)
Instr: 3/2/3+sax./2 - 4/3/3/1 - timp. perc. str.
f.p.   BBC Symphony Orchestra/Alan Bush - Queen's Hall, London,
            30 August 1935 (Promenade Concert)

Question and Answer for SATB chorus and piano (1931)
[Words: Roy Atterbury]
Pub: W.M.A., c.1931, reprinted 1970

Hunger Marchers Song for SATB chorus and piano (1934)
[Words: Randall Swingler]
Pub: W.M.A., c. 1934, reprinted 1970

Prologue for a Workers Meeting for brass band* Op. 16 (1935)
Written for the International Music Bureau, Moscow
Dur: 7'
(* later re-cast as **Overture: Resolution Op. 25 q.v.**)

His War or Yours - Ballet (1935)
f.p.   London Workers Ballet/David Ellenberg

Mining - ballet (1935)
f.p.   London Workers Ballet/Alan Bush

Concert Piece for cello and piano Op. 17 (1936)
Dur: 19'
f.p.   Norina Semino (Vc.)/Alan Bush (Pno.) - Mercury Theatre, London,
            January 1937 (Iris Lemare Concert Series)

f.Eur.p.   V. Palotai (Vc.)/Alan Bush (Pno.) - Paris, 21 June 1937 (ISCM Festival)
f.broad.p. Jonathan Williams (Vc.)/Alan Bush (Pno.) - Radio 3, 18 October 1978

Labour's Song of Challenge for SATB chorus and piano (1936)
[Words: Randall Swingler]
Pub: London Labour Choral Union, 1936

Concerto for piano and orchestra Op. 18 (1937)
[Words: Randall Swingler]
Dur: 57'
Instr: 3/3/3/3 - 4/3/3/1 - timp. perc. hp. str. (with baritone solo and male voice
            chorus in last movement)
f.p.   Alan Bush/Dennis Noble/BBC Male Voice Chorus/BBC Symphony
            Orchestra/Sir Adrian Boult - BBC Broadcasting House, London,
            4 March 1938
f.Eur.p.   Alan Bush - Moscow, 20 September 1938
f.conc.p.   (Lento and Finale only): Alan Bush/Dennis Noble/Co-operative and Labour
            Choirs/London Symphony Orchestra/Constant Lambert
            Queen's Hall, London, 5 April 1939 (during Festival of Music)
f.conc.p.   (complete) Margaret Kitchin/John Hargreaves/Modern Symphony
            Orchestra/Arthur Dennington - Northern Polytechnic, Holloway, London,
            15 May 1954
Pub: Joseph Williams, 1938

Pages from 'The Swallow Book' (also known as 'The Prison Cycle') for mezzo-soprano and piano Op. 19 (1939)
[Words: Ernst Toller's Schwalbenbuch:
Introduction - Sechs Schritte her, sechs Schritte hin, ohne Sinn (Alan Bush)
Song - Die Dinge, die erst feindlich zu dir schauen (Alan Bush)
Interlude - Sechs Schritte her, sechs Schritte hin, ohne Sinn (Alan Rawsthorne)
Song - Uber mir aug dem Holzrahmen des halbgeoeffneten Gitterfensters
(Alan Rawsthorne)
Epilogue - Sechs Schritte her, sechs Schritte hin, ohne Sinn (Alan Bush)]
Written in collaboration with Alan Rawsthorne
Dur: 10'
f.p.   Anne Wood (M/S)/Alan Bush (Pno.) - Conway Hall, London,
            15 December 1939
f.broad.p. Graham Titus (Bar.)/Alan Bush (Pno.) - Radio 3, 26 February 1978

Make Your Meaning Clear for SATB chorus and piano (1939)
[Words: Randall Swingler]
f.p.   Combined W.M.A. Choirs/Alan Bush - Conway Hall, London,
            15 December 1939
Pub: W.M.A. 1939, reprinted 1970; Kahn & Averill for the W.M.A. 1989 (in a
            collection of `Peace Songs' ed. John Jordan)

Against the People's Enemies for baritone solo, SATB chorus and piano (1939)
[Words: Randall Swingler]

f.p.   Martin Lawrence/Combined W.M.A. Choirs/Alan Bush - Conway Hall,
            London, 15 December 1939
Pub: W.M.A. 1939

Symphony No. 1 in C Op. 21 (1939-40)
Dur: 32'
Instr: 2/2/3/3 - 4/3cnts./3/1 - timp. perc. hp. pno. str.
f.p.   London Philharmonic Orchestra/Alan Bush - Royal Albert Hall, London,
            24 July 1942 (Promenade Concert)
f.broad.p. Royal Philharmonic Orchestra/Eugene Goossens - 3 January 1955
Pub: Joseph Williams, 1940

March of the Workers for SATB chorus and piano (1940)
[Words: William Morris]
Pub: W.M.A. 1950

The Ice Breaks for SATB chorus and piano (1940)
[Words: Randall Swingler]
Pub: W.M.A. 1940, 1947, and reprinted 1970 (also arr. for SSAA chorus and
            piano); Kahn & Averill for the W.M.A. 1989 (in a collection of `Peace Songs'
            ed. John Jordan)

Russian Glory for military band Op. 20 (March on Soviet Songs) (1941)
Dur: 5'
f.broad.p. BBC Wireless Military Band - 15 March 1943

Unite and be Free for SATB chorus and piano (1941)
[Words: Alan Bush]
Dedicated to `the peoples of India and Britain'
Pub: W.M.A. 1941

Meditation on a German Song* of 1848 for violin and string orchestra
Op. 22 (1941)
Dur: 9'
f.p.   Max Rostal/London String Orchestra/Alan Bush - Aeolian Hall, London,
            6 December 1941
Pub: Joseph Williams, 1948
Also arr. for violin and piano Op. 22a (1941)
f.doc.p.   Max Rostal (Vn.)/Alan Bush (Pno.) - London Contemporary Music Centre,
            15 May 1944
Pub: Joseph Williams, 1948 (ed. Max Rostal)
(* Reiterlied or 'The Trooper's Pledge with words by Georg Herwegh translated by
Nancy Bush - a song of a German conscript in the army of the Holy Roman
Empire.)

Overture: Festal Day* Op. 23 (1942)
Written as a seventieth birthday greeting to Ralph Vaughan Williams
Dur: 5'
Instr: 1/1/2/2 - 2/2/1/0 - perc. pno. str.

f.p.   London Symphony Orchestra/Clarence Raybould - BBC broadcast,
            12 October 1942
f.Russ.p.   USSR State Symphony Orchestra/Alan Bush - Great Hall of the Moscow
            Conservatory, 3 October 1963
f.rec.   above Russian performance - *Melodiya (USSR) D 012687/90(m)*
(* Original title `Birthday Greeting in Honour of Vaughan Williams')

Fantasia on Soviet Themes Op. 24 (1942)

Dur: 11'
Instr: 2/2/2/2 - 4/2/3/1 - timp. perc. glock. str.
f.p.   London Symphony Orchestra/Alan Bush - Royal Albert Hall, London,
            27 July 1945 (Promenade Concert)
Pub: Novello, 1944

The Great Red Army for SATB chorus and piano (1942)

[Words: Randall Swingler]
Pub: W.M.A. c.1942, reprinted 1970 (also arr. 2-part female voice with piano
            accompaniment)

Song of the Commons of England for SATB chorus and piano (1942)

[Words: Miles Carpenter]
f.p.   W.M.A. Singers/Alan Bush - Unity Theatre, London, 2 December 1945
Pub: W.M.A. 1944

Till Right is Done - part song (1940s)

[Words: Will Sahnow]
Dur: 2'
Pub: W.M.A.

Once is Enough for unaccompanied SATB chorus (1940s)

[Words: Miles Tomalin]

Britain's Part for speaker, SATB chorus, piano and percussion (or orchestra) (1942)

[Words: Alan Bush]
Dur: 8'
f.p.   W.M.A. Chorus/Alan Bush - Conway Hall, London, 24 October 1942
Pub: W.M.A. 1942 (chorus parts only)

Toulon for mezzo-soprano with SATB chorus and piano (1942)

[Words: Nancy Bush]
Dur: 4'
f.p.   Birmingham, 26 May 1943 (W.M.A. Concert, Birmingham Anglo-Soviet
            Unity Group)
f.Lon.p.   Jane Charlton (M/S)/W.M.A. Singers/Alan Bush - Unity Theatre,
            2 December 1945

Le Quatorze Juillet - Esquisse for piano Op. 38 (1943)

Written in commemoration of the French resistance movement - the piece makes use of
two of the most famous songs of the Revolution `La Carmagnole' and `Ca ira'

Dur: 3'30'
f.p.   Kyla Greenbaum - Academy Hall, London, 17 February 1948 (Institute of
            Contemporary Arts Concert)
f.broad.p. Margaret Kitchin - 15 June 1953
f.rec.   Eric Parkin - *Chandos DBRD 2006-2 (and MC)*
Pub: Joseph Williams, 1953

Lyric Interlude for violin and piano Op. 26 (1944)
Dedicated to Nancy Bush
Dur: 16'
f.p.   Max Rostal (Vn.)/Alan Bush (Pno.) - Queen Mary Hall, London,
            6 January 1945
f.rec.   Clio Gould (Vn.)/Sophia Rahman (Pno.) - *Redcliffe Recording RR 008(CD)*
Pub: Joseph Williams, 1948 (ed. Max Rostal)

Overture: Resolution Op. 25 (1944)
Dur: 7'
Instr: 2/2/2/2 - 4/2/3/0 - timp. perc. pno. str.
f.p.   BBC Symphony Orchestra/Clarence Raybould - BBC, 1 February 1944
f.Eur.p.   Concertgebouw Orchestra/Alan Bush - Amsterdam, 19 March 1950
Pub: Joseph Williams (also arr. for piano solo)

The Press Gang (or 'The Escap'd Apprentice') - Children's Operetta (1946)
[Libretto: Nancy Bush]
Dur: 60'
f.p.   St. Christopher School, Letchworth, Herts., 7 March 1947
f.Lon.p.   Opera Group of the Workers' Music Association/Geoffrey Corbett - Rudolph
            Steiner Hall, 26 April 1948
f.p.   (as a ballet) Newcastle-upon-Tyne Ballet Club c.1947
Choreography: Lyn Oxenford
Pub: W.M.A. and Mitteldeutscher, 1953

A World for Living for SATB chorus and piano (1946)
[Words: Randall Swingler]
Pub: W.M.A. 1948

'Homage to William Sterndale Bennett'* for string orchestra Op. 27 (1946)
Dur: 9'
f.p.   London String Orchestra/Alan Bush - Wigmore Hall, London,
            9 February 1946
(* Based on the Piano Sonata Op. 46 `The Maid of Orleans')

English Suite for string orchestra Op. 28 (1945-46)
[1. Fantasia 2. Soliloquy on a Sailor's Song 3. Passacaglia on `The Cutty Wren']
Dur: 22'30'
f.p.   London String Orchestra/Alan Bush - Wigmore Hall, London,
            9 February 1946
f.rec.   Northern Chamber Orchestra/Nicholas Ward - *Redcliffe Recordings RR008
            (CD)*

Pub: Joseph Williams, 1951

The Winter Journey - A Christmas Cantata for soprano, baritone, SATB chorus, string quintet and harp Op. 29 (1946)

[Words: Randall Swingler 1. The City 2. The Journey
3. The Sleepers in the City 4. Mary's Song 5. Final Chorale]

Dur: 22'30'

f.p.   Frederick Hudson (Bar.)/Alnwick Choral Society/Maria Korchinska
            (Hp.)/Alan Bush - Alnwick Parish Church, Northumberland, December 1946

f.Lon.p.   Jane Charlton (Sop.)/Robert Rowell (Bar.)/Hurwitz String Quartet and Martin
            Lovett (Vc.)/Maria Korchinska (Hp.)/Radlett and W.M.A. Singers/Alan Bush -
            Conway Hall, 22 March 1948

Pub: Joseph Williams, 1947 (vocal score)

Piers Plowman's Day - Symphonic Suite Op. 30 (1946-47)

Dur: 27'

Instr: 2/2/2/2 - 4/2/3/0 - timp. perc. str.

f.p.   Orchestra/Alan Bush - Prague Radio broadcast, October 1947

f.Brit.p.   BBC Symphony Orchestra/Alan Bush - Royal Albert Hall, London,
            7 September 1951 (Promenade Concert)

Three Concert Studies for piano, violin and cello Op. 31 (1947)

[1. Moto perpetuo 2. Nocturne 3. Alla Bulgara]

Written for the London International Trio

Dur: 18'

f.p.   London International Trio - Tom Bromley (Pno.), Jan Sedivka (Vn.), Sela
            Trau (Vc.) - Conway Hall, London, 13 February 1948

f.rec.   David Parkhouse (Pno.)/Hugh Bean (Vn.)/Eileen Croxford (Vc.) - *Argo ZRG
            749*

Pub: Novello, 1965

Lidice* for unaccompanied SATB chorus (1947)

[Words: Nancy Bush]

Dur: 3'

f.p.   W.M.A. Singers/Alan Bush - Lidice, Prague Radio broadcast, October 1947

Pub: W.M.A. 1947

(* The village in Czechoslovakia razed to the ground by German occupying forces on 10
June 1942)

Concerto for violin and orchestra Op. 32 (1948)

Dedicated `to Max Rostal as a grateful tribute to his artistry as a violinist and
encouragement as a friend'.

Dur: 26'

Instr: 2/2/2/2 - 4/3/3/0 - timp. perc. str.

f.p.   Max Rostal/London Philharmonic Orchestra/Basil Cameron - Royal Albert
            Hall, London, 25 August 1949 (Promenade Concert)

f.broad.p. Max Rostal/BBC Scottish Orchestra/Ian Whyte - 16 July 1952

f.rec.   Manoug Parikian/BBC Symphony Orchestra/Norman del Mar - *Hyperion A
            66138*

Pub: Joseph Williams, 1948 (also arr. violin and piano, ed. Max Rostal, 1951)

Wat Tyler - opera in two Acts with Prologue (1948-50)

[Libretto: Nancy Bush]

Commissioned by the Arts Council of Great Britain in The Festival of Britain Opera
Competition

Dur: 160'

Instr: 3/2/2/3 - 4/3/3/1 - timp. perc.(2) hp. str. (+ 2 stage tpts.)

f.conc.p.   Soloists/W.M.A. Singers/Bernard Stevens with Alan Bush (Pno.) - Conway
            Hall, London, 15 December 1950

f.broad.p. East Berlin Radio Production - 3 April 1952

f.stage.p. Leipzig Opera Chorus/Leipzig Gewandhaus Orchestra/Helmut Seidelmann -
            Stadtisches Theater, Leipzig, 6 September 1953

Producer: Heinrich Voigt

Designer: Max Elten

f.Brit.stage.p. Keynote Opera Society/City Philharmonic Choir/Royal
            Philharmonic Orchestra/Stanford Robinson - Sadler's Wells Theatre, London,
            19 June 1974

Producer: Tom Hawkes

Designer: Alan Barrett

Pub: Henschelverlag, Berlin; Novello, London, 1959

Our Song for SATB chorus and piano (1948)

[Words: Nancy Bush]

Commissioned for the opening of the Nottingham Co-operative Arts Centre Theatre

f.p.   Nottingham Co-operative Arts Centre Choir/David Ellenberg - Arts Centre
            Theatre, Nottingham, 7 November 1948

f.Lon.p.   W.M.A. Singers/Alan Bush - King George's Hall, 16 June 1949

Pub: W.M.A. c.1948, reprinted 1970

Symphony No. 2 'The Nottingham'Op. 33 (1949)

[1. Sherwood Forest 2. Clifton Grove 3. Castle Rock 4. Goose Fair]

Commissioned by the Nottingham Co-operative Society in celebration of the 500th
anniversary of the founding of the City.

Dur: 36'

Instr: 2/2/2/2 - 4/3/3/1 - timp. perc. str.

f.p.   London Philharmonic Orchestra/David Ellenberg - Albert Hall, Nottingham,
            27 June 1949

f.Eur.p.   Orchestra Santa Cecilia/David Ellenberg - Argentina Theatre, Rome,
            14 June 1951

f.Lon.p.   London Philharmonic Orchestra/Clarence Raybould - London Contemporary
            Music Centre, 20 June 1951 (studio performance)

f.Lon.conc.p. London Philharmonic Orchestra/Sir Adrian Boult - Royal Festival
            Hall, 11 December 1952

f.Russ.p.   USSR State Symphony Orchestra/Alan Bush - Great Hall of the Moscow
            Conservatory, 3 October 1963

f.rec.   above Russian performance - *Melodiya (USSR) D 012687/90(m)*

Pub: Joseph Williams, 1949

Song of Friendship - cantata for bass, SATB chorus and orchestra Op. 34 (1949)
[Words: Nancy Bush]
Written for the British Soviet Friendship Society
Dur: 11'
Instr: 2/0/3+2sax./1 - 0/3/4/1 - timp. perc.
f.p.   Soloist/Massed Choirs and Orchestra of the W.M.A./Alan Bush - Empress
            Hall, London, 6 November 1949
Pub: W.M.A. 1949

The Dream of Llewelyn Ap Gruffydd for male voice chorus and piano Op. 35 (1950)
[Words: Randall Swingler]
Dedicated to the Treorchy and District Male Voice Choir
Dur: 8'
f.p.   Treorchy and District Male Voice Choir/John Davies - Treorchy, South
            Wales, 11 April 1952
Pub: Joseph Williams, 1951

Times of Day - Four piano pieces for children (1950)
[1. Wake up! 2. Noon ramble 3. After School 4. Bedtime]
Dur: 8'
Pub: Joseph Williams, 1950

Shining Vision: A Song for Peace - for SATB chorus and piano (1950)
[Words: Montagu Slater]
Pub: W.M.A. 1950; Kahn & Averill for the W.M.A. 1989 (in a collection of `Peace
            Songs' ed. John Jordan)

Trent's Broad Reaches for horn and piano Op. 36 (1951)
Dur: 4'
f.p.   Dennis Brain (Hn.)/Alan Bush (Pno.) - Wigmore Hall, London,
            28 January 1955 (Concert in memory of Noel Mewton-Wood)
f.broad.p. Barry Tuckwell (Hn.)/Ernest Lush (Pno.) - 12 March 1959
Pub: Schott, 1952

Two Easy Pieces for cello and piano (1951)
[1. Song across the Water 2. Fireside Story]
Dur: 3'
Pub: Joseph Williams, 1952 (ed. Herbert Withers)

Concert Suite for cello and orchestra Op. 37 (1952)
[1. Introduction and Divisions on a Ground 2. Ballet 3. Poem 4. Dance]
Dur: 28'
Instr: 2/2/2/2 - 4/2/3/0 - timp. perc. hp. str.
f.p.   Vera Denes/Budapest Philharmonic Orchestra/Alan Bush - Budapest, 1952
f.Brit.p.   Zara Nelsova/BBC Scottish Orchestra/Alan Bush - 14 October 1953
f.Lon.p.   Florence Hooton/BBC Symphony Orchestra/Alan Bush - Royal Albert Hall,
            7 September 1956 (Promenade Concert)
Pub: Joseph Williams, 1957 (also arr. for cello and piano)

Defender of (the) Peace* - Character Portrait for orchestra Op. 39 (1952)

Dur: 6'
Instr: 2/2/2/2 - 4/3/3/1 - timp. perc. pno. str.
f.p.   Orchestra/Alan Bush - Vienna Radio broadcast, 24 May 1952
f.conc.p.   Orchestra/Alan Bush - Moscow Youth Festival, 1957
Pub: Soviet Music Publishers, Moscow, 1966
(* Last movement of Symphony No. 1 re-composed)

Three English Song Preludes for organ Op. 40 (1952)

[1. Worldes blis ne last no throwe - 13th Century Song
 2. Be Merry - 15th Century Carol
 3. Lowlands, my lowlands - 17th Century Shanty]
Dur: 8'
f.p.   Caleb Henry Trevor - St. Mark's Church, North Audley Street, London,
            21 April 1954
Pub: Joseph Williams, 1954

Voices of the Prophets - cantata for tenor and piano Op. 41 (1953)

[1. From the 65th chapter of the book of the Prophet Isaiah `For behold I create new heavens'. 2. From the Oration "Against the Scholastic Philosophy" by John Milton `So at length the spirit of man' 3. From "Selections from Milton" by William Blake `Rouse up, O Young Man' 4. From "My Song for all Men" by Peter Blackman `Over the Years']
Dedicated to Peter Pears and Noel Mewton-Wood
Dur: 18'30'
f.p.   Peter Pears (Ten.)/Noel Mewton-Wood (Pno.) - Recital Room, Royal Festival
            Hall, London, 22 March 1953
f.broad.p. above artists - Third Programme, 9 January 1954
f.rec.   Peter Pears (Ten.)/Alan Bush (Pno.) - *RG 439(m) Argo ZRG 5439, ZK 28*
Pub: Joseph Williams, 1953

The Spell Unbound - operetta for girls in an Elizabethan Setting (1953)

[Libretto: Nancy Bush - the music is based in part on Elizabethan airs by William Byrd, John Bull, John Dowland, Thomas Campion and William Playford with five principal singing parts and simple 2 part chorus with piano solo accompaniment]
Dur: 70'
f.p.   Bournemouth School for Girls, 6 March 1955
Pub: Novello, 1954

Northumbrian Impressions for Northumbrian small pipes Op. 42* (1953)

[1. Prelude 2. Lament 3. Dance]
These pieces were written for the Northumbrian pipe virtuoso Jack Armstrong, who met Alan Bush during the composition of **Men of Blackmoor**.
Dur: 10'
f.p.   Richard Butler (a pupil of Jack Armstrong) - Wigmore Hall, London,
            28 October 1979
f.broad.p. Richard Butler - 13 July 1981
Also arr. oboe and piano Op. 42a (1953)
f.p.   Joy Boughton (Ob.)/Alan Bush (Pno.) - Arts Council Drawing Room, London,
            14 December 1953 (Macnaghten Concert)

f.broad.p. Roger Lord (Ob.)/Josephine Lees (Pno.) - 13 February 1958
Pub: Novello, 1956

Pavane for the Castleton Queen for brass band Op. 43 (1953)
Written for the Castleton Wakes Committee
Dur: 3'30'
f.p.   Castleton Brass Band/Alan Bush - Castleton, Derbyshire, 1953

The Ballad of Freedom's Soldier for tenor, bass-baritone, SATB chorus and orchestra Op. 44 (1953)
[Words: John Manifold]
Written in memory of the British hero of World War II, Major Frank Thompson, who died in action in Bulgaria in 1944. (The work uses the irregular rhythms of Bulgarian folk dances)
Dur: 21'
Instr: 2/2/2/2 - 4/3/3/0 - timp. perc. hp. str.
f.p.   Soloists/Choir/Ilya Temkov - Russe, Bulgaria, April 1962
f.Brit.p.   Robin Legatte (Ten.)/Andrew Golder(Bs./Bar.)/Putney Choral Society and Orchestra/Stephen Rhys - Battersea Town Hall, 6 November 1975

Autumn Poem for horn and piano Op. 45 (1954)
Written as a tribute to Noel Mewton-Wood
Dur: 3'
f.p.   Dennis Brain (Hn.)/Alan Bush (Pno.) - Wigmore Hall, London, 28 January 1955 (Concert in memory of Noel Mewton-Wood)
f.broad.p. Barry Tuckwell (Hn.)/Ernest Lush (Pno.) - 12 March 1959
Pub: Schott, 1955

Men of Blackmoor - opera in two Acts (1954-55)
[Libretto: Nancy Bush]
Dur: 130'
Instr: 3/3/3/3 - 4/3/3/1 - timp. perc.(2) str.
f.p.   German National Opera Chorus and Orchestra/Heinz Finger - Weimar, 18 November 1956
Producer: Alan Bush
Designer: Jochen Schube
f.Brit.p.   Oxford University Opera Club, cond. Jack Westrup - Oxford Town Hall, 30 November 1960
Producer: Eddie Gilbert
Designer: Christopher Denyer
f.Brit.broad.p. BBC Northern Singers/BBC Northern Symphony Orchestra/ Stanford Robinson - 1965*
Producer: Ernest Warburton
Pub: Henschelverlag, Berlin, Joseph Williams, 1959
(* This performance was re-broadcast in December 1995 as a memorial tribute to the composer, who had died on 31 October 1995, two months short of his 95th birthday.)

Allegro Molto - movement No. 2 for variations (1955)
In 1955, at the suggestion of Vaughan Williams, eight British composers contri-buted a
set of variations on a theme attributed to Alfred Scott- Gatty (1847-1918) entitled
'Where's my little basket gone?' The eight composers represented were - Alan Bush,
Howard Ferguson, Gerald Finzi, Gordon Jacob, Elisabeth Lutyens, Elizabeth Maconchy,
Alan Rawsthorne and Grace Williams q.v.

f.p.   Anne Macnaghten/Elizabeth Rajna/Maxwell Ward/Arnold Ashby/ Nigel
            Amherst (strings) and Gordon Heard/James Brown/George Draper/Roger
            Birnstingl/Richard Walton/Robert Young (wind) Ensemble conducted by Iris
            Lemare - Arts Council Drawing Room, London, 16 May 1955 (Macnaghten
            Concert)

Variations, Nocturne and Finale for piano Op. 46 (1956)
Dur: 6' (Nocturne only)
f.p.   Edna Iles - Arts Council Drawing Room, London, 21 March 1958
            (Macnaghten Concert)
f.rec.   (Nocturne) Peter Jacobs - *Altarus AIR-2-9004 (2) (and CD)*
Pub: Novello, 1970 (Nocturne only - the first two movements were withdrawn after
            the first performance and later re-scored as Op. 60 q.v.)

Two Melodies for viola and piano Op. 47 (1957)
[1. Song Melody 2. Dance Melody]
Dedicated 'In admiration and affection to Lionel Tertis'
Dur: 6'
f.broad.p. Bernard Shore (Va.)/Alan Bush (Pno.) - 8 January 1959
Pub: Joseph Williams, 1959

Like Rivers Flowing - part song for SSATB chorus (1957)
[Words: Nancy Bush]
Dur: 2'50'
Pub: Joseph Williams, 1957

Two Songs for mezzo-soprano and piano Op. 48 (see Op. 79)

**Nicht den Tod aus der Ferne for baritone, mixed unison chorus and instrumental
ensemble (1958)**
[Words: Armin Mueller]
Dur: 2'30'
Instr: Cl. Tpt. Perc. Pno.
f.p.   Weimar, 1958

**Ballad of the March to Aldermaston ('Ballade vom Marsch auf Aldermaston') for
speaker, SATB chorus and instrumental ensemble (1958)**
[Words: Armin Mueller. English version text: Nancy Bush]
Dur: 4'
Instr: 2 Hn. 2 Tpt. 2 Gtr. Perc. Db.
f.p.   Weimar, 1958
f.Brit.p.   Glyn Davys (Spkr.)/Combined Glasgow Y.C.L. and London Choirs/ Alan
            Bush - St. Pancras Town Hall, London, 1 April 1961

Mister Playford's Tunes - a Little Suite for piano Op. 49 (1958)
[1. Argeers 2. The Whish and Peppers Black 3. Nonesuch 4. The Beggar Boy
5. The Slip, a Going-out]
Dur: 5'
Pub: Joseph Williams, 1959

Two Ballads of the Sea for piano Op. 50 (1957-58)
[1. The Cruel Sea Captain 2. Reuben Ranzo]
Dedicated 'In friendship and admiration to John Ireland'
Dur: 6'30'
f.p.   Alasdair Graham - Morley College, London, 19 November 1961
f.broad.p. Alan Bush - 7 April 1962
f.rec.   (No. 1) Alan Bush - *Argo ZRG 749*
Pub: Joseph Williams, 1961

**The World is his Song for mezzo-soprano (or baritone), SATB chorus and
instrumental ensemble Op. 51 (1958)**
[Words: Nancy Bush]
Dedicated to Paul Robeson
Dur: 6'
Instr: 2 Hn. 2 Tpt. 3 Tbn. Tba. Gtr. Perc. Pno.
f.p.   Martin Lawrence (Bar.)/W.M.A. Massed Choirs/Ensemble/Alan Bush - Royal
           Albert Hall, London, 15 February 1959 (Daily Worker Birthday Rally)

Dorian Passacaglia and Fugue for orchestra Op. 52 (1959)
Dur: 16'
Instr: 2/1+ca./2/3 - 4/3/3/1 - timp. perc. str.
f.p.   BBC Symphony Orchestra/Rudolf Schwarz - BBC Studios, London,
           11 June 1961
f.conc.p. BBC Symphony Orchestra/Rudolf Schwarz - Cheltenham Town Hall,
           14 July 1961 (Cheltenham Festival)
f.Lon.conc.p. BBC Symphony Orchestra/Alan Bush - Royal Albert Hall,
           27 August 1964 (Promenade Concert)
Pub: Novello, 1962

Symphony No. 3 'The Byron Symphony' Op. 53 (1959-60)
[1. Newstead Abbey 2. Westminster 3. Il Palazzo Savioli 4. Missolonghi*]
A Handel prize-winning work presented by the City Council of Halle in 1962 and
commissioned by G.D.R. Radio (*The text of this movement is taken from "Ode on the
Death of Lord Byron" by Dionysios Solomos.)
Dur: 50'
Instr: 3/3/3/3 - 4/3/3/1 - timp. perc. hp. str. (with baritone solo and mixed chorus in
           last movement)
f.p.   Robert Lauhofer/Leipzig Radio Choir and Symphony Orchestra/ Herbert
           Kegel - Leipzig, 20 March 1962
f.Brit.p. Neil Howlett/Kensington Symphony Orchestra and Chorus/ Leslie Head -
           Friends House, London, 6 June 1962
f.broad.p. Peter Walker/BBC Northern Singers/BBC Northern Symphony
           Orchestra/Bernard Keeffe - 7 December 1971

On Lawn and Green - suite for harpsichord (or piano) Op. 54 (1960)
[1. Pavan 2. Galliard 3. Air 4. Longway Set]
Dedication `A present to my friend and colleague Hans Pischner as a small recompense for his invaluable support and help eight years ago'(a reference to the first performance of **Wat Tyler**)
Dur: 9'
f.p.   Hans Pischner - Berlin, 1960
f.Brit.p.   Millicent Silver, BBC broadcast, 12 October 1961
f.rec.   (Nos. 2 and 3) Alan Bush - *Argo ZRG 749*
Pub: Peters, 1962

Three African Sketches for flute and piano Op. 55 (1960)
[1. Southern Rhodesia 2. Zululand 3. Congo]
Dur: 8'
f.p.   Alexander Murray (Fl.)/Alan Bush (Pno.) - Morley College, London,
            19 November 1961
f.broad.p. Colin Chambers (Fl.)/Daphne Ibbott (Pno.) - 2 April 1964
Pub: Peters Edition, 1962

Two Occasional Pieces for organ Op. 56 (1960)
[1. For a Solemn Occasion 2.* For a Festal Occasion]
Dedicated to `To C.H. Trevor' (professor of organ at the R.A.M.)
Dur: 9'
Pub: Novello, 1962
(* No. 2 also arranged for organ and orchestra, see Op. 58)

Seafarers Songs for baritone and piano Op. 57 (1961)
[Texts from the Penguin Book of English Folksongs 1. The Ship in Distress
2. Ratcliffe Highway 3. The Greenland Whale Fishery 4. Jack the Jolly Tar]
Dur: 11'
f.p.   Philip Lewtas (Bar.)/Alan Bush (Pno.) - Morley College, London,
            19 November 1961
Pub: Joseph Williams (Galliard), 1964

The Tide that will never turn - a Declaration by Hugh McDiarmid for two speakers, bass (or baritone), SATB chorus, piano, percussion and string orchestra (1961)
Dur: 15'
f.p.   Marjorie Mason/Glyn Davys/Martin Lawrence/Glasgow Y.C.L. Choir/
            W.M.A. Massed Choirs/Ensemble/Alan Bush - St. Pancras Town Hall,
            London, 1 April 1961

For a Festal Occasion for organ and orchestra Op. 58 (1961)
Dur: 5'
Instr: 2/2/2/2 - 4/2/3/0 - timp. perc. str. (optional)
f.p.   Peter Hurford/London Symphony Orchestra/Melville Cook - Hereford
            Cathedral, 3 September 1961 (Three Choirs Festival)

The Ferryman's Daughter - an opera of the Thames Waterside for schools (1961)
[Libretto: Nancy Bush - five principal singing parts and SAB chorus in two
 scenes]
Dur: 60'
f.p.   St. Christopher School, Letchworth, Herts., 6 March 1964
Pub: Novello, 1963

Three Raga Melodies for unaccompanied violin Op. 59 (1961)
[1. Himavirdani Raga 2. Nadatha-Rangini Raga 3. Garundavirdani Raga]
These studies were part of the composer's preparation for his opera `The Sugar Reapers'
in which both Indian and African national idioms are used.
Dur: 6'
f.p.   Hazel Smith - South Hill Park Arts Centre, Bracknell, Berkshire,
           25 April 1980
Pub: Galliard, 1965

The Sugar Reapers - opera in two Acts (1961-64)
[Libretto: Nancy Bush]
Dur: 145'
Instr: 3/3/3+sax./3 - 4/3/3/1 - timp. perc. (2) gtr.(2) pno. hp. str.
f.p.   Leipzig Opera Chorus/Leipzig Gewandhaus Orchestra/Rolf Reuter - Leipzig
           Opera House, 11 December 1966
Producer: Fritz Bennewitz
Designer: Bernhard Schroter
Choreographer: Johannes Richter
f.Brit.p. BBC, 24 September 1976 (above performance with added English narration)
Pub: Henschelverlag, Berlin, 1965
Exc.   Three Negro Songs arr. unison chorus and piano by the composer
           [1. Hurry on, my weary soul 2. Many Thousands go
            3. It makes a long time Man feel bad]

**Variations, Nocturne and Finale on an English Sea-Song (`Blow ye winds') for piano
and orchestra Op. 60 (1962)**
Dedicated to Sir Thomas Armstrong
Dur: 21'
Instr: 2/2/2/2 - 4/2/3/1 - timp. perc.(2) str.
f.p.   David Wilde/BBC Northern and Midland Light Orchestras/Meredith Davies -
           Cheltenham Town Hall, 7 July 1965 (Cheltenham Festival)
f.rec.   David Wilde/Royal Philharmonic Orchestra/John Snashall - *Pye Golden
           Guinea GGC 4073(m), GSGC 14073*
Pub: Novello, 1973 (also arr. for 2 pianos/4 hands ed. Lyon)

**Prelude, Air and Dance for solo violin, string quartet and percussion Op. 61
(1963-64)**
Dur: 14'30'
f.p.   Ralph Holmes (Vn.)/Aeolian String Quartet/Eric Allen (Perc.)/Alan Bush -
           BBC Invitation Concert, 28 April 1964
Pub: Novello, 1965 (also arr. for violin and piano)

Song of the Cosmonaut for baritone, SATB chorus and piano (or orchestra) (1963)
[Words: Miles Tomalin]
Dedicated to Major Yuri Gagarin
Dur: 3'
Pub: W.M.A., 1963

During Music - for unaccompanied SATB chorus Op. 62 (1963)
[Words: Dante Gabriel Rossetti]
Dur: 2'30'
f.p.   Inaugural concert of the Borough Arts Council Festival, Wood Green,
            London, 4 April 1964
Pub: Novello, 1964

Partita Concertante for orchestra Op. 63 (1965)
[1. Overture 2. Hornpipe 3. Air 4. Cheviot Reel]
Dur: 12'30'
Instr: 2/1/2/1 - 2/2/1/0 - timp. perc.(2) str.
f.doc.p.   Dartford Symphony Orchestra/Leonard Davis - N.W. Kent College of
            Technology, Dartford, May 1975
Pub: Novello, 1966

Joe Hill: The Man Who Never Died - opera in two Acts (1965-67)
[Libretto: Barrie Stavis]
Commissioned by the Berlin State Opera
Dur: 130'
Instr: 2/3/3+bcl./2 - 4/3/3/1 - timp. perc.(2) acc. pno. hp. str.
f.p.   Berlin Opera Chorus/Berlin State Opera Orchestra/Heinz Fricke - Deutsche
            Staatsoper, Berlin, 29 September 1970
Producer: Erhard Fischer
Designer: Wilfried Werz
f.Brit.p.   BBC Singers/BBC Concert Orchestra/James Judd, BBC, 29 July 1976
Producer: Elaine Padmore

Two Dances for cimbalom ' Ket Tanc Cimbalomara' Op. 64 (1965)
Specially composed for the British Hungarian Friendship Society to celebrate the
twentieth anniversary of the liberation of Hungary and dedicated to John Leech.
Dur: 7'
f.p.   John Leech - Arts Council Drawing Room, London, 10 March 1965
Pub: Editio Musica, Budapest, 1965 (ed. John Leech)

Suite for two pianos Op. 65 (1967)
[1. Prologue 2. Volga Harvest 3. Kinloch Iorram 4. Samarkand Dugokh
5. Pennine Round]
Dur: 19'30'
f.p.   John Ogdon/Brenda Lucas - Queen Elizabeth Hall, London, 23 September
            1967 (at an Anniversary Concert on the occasion of the 50th Birthday of the
            Soviet Union)
f.broad.p. above performance - 4 April 1969

The Alps and Andes of the Living World - cantata for speaker, tenor, SATB chorus and orchestra Op. 66 (1968)
[Words: Hamlet (Shakespeare), Man's Place in Nature (T.H. Huxley),
 April the Twelfth, 1961 (Nancy Bush)]
Dur: 11'
Instr: 0/0/0/0 - 4/3/3/1 - pno. perc. str. (2/1/2/0)
f.p.   John Amis/Joseph Ward/Ensemble including the Devon Brass Consort/Philip
            Simms - Dartington Summer School, 9 August 1968

Time Remembered - a piece for chamber orchestra Op. 67 (1968)
Commissioned by the Cheltenham Festival and dedicated to Nancy Bush
Dur: 11'30'
Instr: 1/1/1/1 - 1/0/0/0 - hp. str. (2/1/1/1)
f.p.   Members of the Melos Ensemble/Alan Bush - Cheltenham Town Hall, 8 July
            1969 (Cheltenham Festival)

Scherzo for wind orchestra with percussion Op. 68 (1969)
Commissioned by the BBC
Dur: 10'
Instr: 4/3/4/3 - 4/4/3/1 - xyl. perc.(2)
f.p.   BBC Symphony Orchestra/Alan Bush - Royal Albert Hall, London,
            29 July 1969 (Promenade Concert)
Pub: Novello, 1969

Songs of Asian Struggle arr. for SATB chorus and piano (1969)
[Words trans. Nancy Bush: 1. `Polishing the Gun' - song of the Malayan partisans 2.
`The Rice Harvest' - song from North Korea
 3. `My Country in Captivity' - song of the Huk partisans of the Phillipine Islands
 4. `The Jacket-Makers' Song' - song from North Vietnam
 5. `Chinese Students' Song' - song against the Japanese invaders of the 1930's]
Dur: 12'
f.p.   The London Co-operative Youth Choir and Alan Bush (Pno.)/Jonathan Cohen
            - Wigmore Hall, London, 17 January 1970

The Freight of Harvest - song cycle for tenor and piano Op. 69 (1969)
[Words: Poems by Sylvia Townsend Warner
 1. Country Thought from a Town 2. The Sailor 3. The Maiden
 4. The Load of Fern]
Commissioned by the Dartington Summer School of Music and dedicated to Joseph
Ward
Dur: 19'
f.p.   Joseph Ward (Ten.)/Alan Bush (Pno.) - Dartington Summer School of Music,
            8 August 1969
f.pub.p.   above artists - Newcastle, 14 October 1969
f.Lon.p.   above artists - Wigmore Hall, London, 19 January 1970
f.broad.p. above artists, 20 August 1970

Serenade for string quartet Op. 70 (1969)
[1. Romance 2. Musette 3. Air and variation 4. March 5. Postlude]
Commissioned by the BBC and dedicated `with admiration and affection to my old friend
Ernst Hermann Meyer'
Dur: 19'
f.p.   Gabrieli String Quartet - Kenneth Sillito (Vn.), Brendan O'Reilly (Vn.),
             Ian Jewel (Va.), Keith Harvey (Vc.) - Wigmore Hall, London,
             17 January 1970
f.broad.p.   above artists - 20 August 1970

Piano Sonata No. 2 in A flat* Op. 71 (1970)
Dedicated `in friendship and high esteem to Ronald Stevenson'
Dur: 20'
f.p.   Ronald Stevenson - Bath, 28 May 1972 (Bath Festival)
f.broad.p.   Ronald Stevenson - above performance, 30 July 1972
f.Lon .p.   Ronald Stevenson - Wigmore Hall, 5 May 1974
f.Eur.p.   Ronald Stevenson - Berlin State Opera House, 12 October 1980
(* the Sonata is sub-titled `He Hedone Ipikureia' or `concerning the rapture of Epicurus')

Men of Felling for male TTBB chorus and piano Op. 72 (1971)
[Words: Nancy Bush]
Dedicated to the Felling Male Voice Choir
Dur: 2'30'
f.p.   The Felling Male Voice Choir and Ken Murray (Pno.)/Norman Williams -
             Newcastle City Hall, 15 October 1971

Concert Overture for an Occasion Op. 74 (1971-72)
Dedicated `to the student orchestral players of the Royal Academy of Music' in
celebration of the 150th anniversary of the Academy's foundation.
Dur: 8'
Instr: 3/3/3/3 - 4/3/3/1 - timp. perc. cel. pno. str.
f.p.   Royal Academy of Music First Orchestra/Maurice Handford - Royal Festival
             Hall, London, 5 July 1972
f.broad.p.   BBC Welsh Symphony Orchestra/Bryden Thomson - 1 October 1981
also arr. for wind band
f.p.   RNCM Wind Orchestra/Northern Wind Ensemble/Clark Rundell - Royal
             Northern College of Music, Manchester, 22 June 1985

Africa - Symphonic movement for piano and orchestra Op. 73 (1972)
Dur: 25'
Instr: 4/4/4/4 - 4/3/3/1 - timp. perc.(2) str.
f.p.   Alan Bush/Halle Philharmonic Orchestra/Olaf Koch - Halle, GDR,
             16 October 1972
f.Brit.p.   Alan Bush/London Senior Orchestra/Terence Lovett - St. John's, Smith
             Square, London, 20 November 1976
f.broad.p.   William Langford/BBC Welsh Symphony Orchestra/Bryden Thomson -
             1 October 1981
Pub: Peters, 1974

Earth has Grain to Grow for SATB chorus (1972)
[Words: C. Day Lewis]
Dur: 2'30'
Pub: Novello, 1972

The Earth Awaking - carol for female SSAA chorus and organ (1972)
[Words: Nancy Bush]
Written for the Perse Girls School, Cambridge
Dur: 2'
f.p.   Choir of Perse Girls School, Cambridge - Great St. Mary's Church,
           Cambridge, 18 December 1972

Song for Angela Davis for unaccompanied SATB chorus Op. 75 (1972)
[Words: Nancy Bush]
Dur: 5'
f.p.   Sheila Searchfield (M/S.)/W.M.A. Summer School Chorus with Brian
           Trueman (Pno.)/Alan Bush - W.M.A. Summer School, Wortley Hall,
           Sheffield, 25 August 1972
Pub: W.M.A. (also arr. chorus and piano)

'Corentyne Kwe-Kwe'* - Toccata for piano Op. 76 (1972)
Dedicated `to those men and women of Guyana who faced a British warship and stood
their ground'
Dur: 4'
f.p.   William Langford - Wigmore Hall, London, 11 January 1976
f.rec.   Alan Bush - *Argo ZRG 749*
(* `Kwe-Kwe' - songs of Guyana sung by a group of villagers around a new bride's house -
the toccata is based on an African song which commemorates
the abolition of slavery in Guyana in 1842)

The Liverpool Overture Op. 77 (1973)
Commissioned by the Liverpool Trades Council for their 125th Anniversary celebrations
Dur: 9'
Instr: 3/3/3/3 - 4/3/3/1 - timp. perc. pno. str.
f.p.   Royal Liverpool Philharmonic Orchestra/Sir Charles Groves -
           Philharmonic Hall, Liverpool, 1 May 1973

Festival March for (of) British Youth Op. 78 (1973)
Dur: 4'
Instr: 3/2/5/2 - 0/3/3/3 - timp. perc. gtr.(2) db.
f.p.   Berlin, August 1973

Song and Dance Duet for clarinet and cello with piano Op.78 Nos. 1 and 2 (1973)*
No. 1 written for the composer's two grandchildren
(* This may be a later work)

Life's Span - song cycle for mezzo-soprano and piano Op. 79 (1958, 1961, 1974)
[Words: 1. A Child Asleep (Nancy Bush - 1958)
 2. Learning to Talk (C. Day Lewis - 1961)

3. The Long Noonday (Nancy Bush - 1974)
4. Beauty's end is in sight (C. Day Lewis - 1974]

Dur:	18'
f.p.	(Nos. 1 and 2 only - originally designated as Op. 48): Anna Pollack (M/S.)/Alan Bush (Pno.) - Morley College, London, 19 November 1961
f.p.	(complete): Katinka Seiner (M/S.)/Alan Bush (Pno.) - Shenstone New College, Bromsgrove, 4 April 1973
f.broad.p.	Laura Sarti (M/S.)/Alan Bush (Pno.) - Radio 3, 21 December 1975
f.Lon.p.	Laura Sarti (M/S.)/Alan Bush (Pno.) - Wigmore Hall, 11 January 1976

Suite in English Style for string orchestra Op.79 No. 2 (1974)
[1. Pavan 2. Cheviot Rant 3. Soliloquy on a Sailor's Song 4. March]

Letter Galliard for piano Op. 80 (1974)
Written as a tribute to Shostakovitch using the letters D.S.C.H. and A.B.S.H.

Dur:	2'30'
f.p.	William Langford - Wigmore Hall, London, 11 January 1976
f.rec.	Peter Jacobs - *Altarus AIR-2-9004 (2) (and CD)*
Pub:	Sovietskya Musika, 1974

Suite for Six for string quartet Op. 81 (1975)
[Introduction - Pavan - Interlude I - Reel - Interlude II - Andamento - Interlude
III - Air - Interlude IV - Moto Perpetuo - Interlude V - Sword Dance - Postlude]
Commissioned by the BBC

Dur:	26'
f.p.	Chilingirian String Quartet - Levon Chilingirian (Vn.), Mark Butler (Vn.), Simon Rowland-Jones (Va.), Philip de Groote (Vc.) - St. John's, Smith Square, London, 15 December 1975 (BBC Lunchtime Concert)

Duo Sonatina for recorders and piano Op. 82 (1975)
Dedicated to Ross Winters

Instr:	Desc. Treb. Ten. (one player)
Dur:	15'
f.p.	Ross Winters (Recs.)/Alan Bush (Pno.) - Wigmore Hall, London, 11 January 1976
Pub:	Nova Music

Compass Points - A suite for pipes Op. 83 (1976)
[1. North, based on `Dance to your Shadow' and `Islay Reaper's Song'
2. West, based on `Watching the wheat' and `Black Sir Harry'
3. East, based on `The Cruel Sea Captain'
4. South, based on `Bedlam City' and `The Scolding Wife']
Commissioned by The Bamboo Pipe Association

Dur:	12'
f.p.	Canterbury, August 1976

Africa is my name for mezzo-soprano, SATB chorus and piano (or orchestra) Op. 85 (1976)
[Words: Nancy Bush and from African Songs]

Dur: 10'
f.p.   Annette Gavin/W.M.A. Summer School Chorus with Alan Bush (Pno.) -
            W.M.A. Summer School, Wortley Hall, Sheffield, 20 August 1976

De Plenos Poderes* - song cycle for baritone and piano Op. 86 (1976-77)
[Spanish text by Pablo Neruda:
 1. El Pueblo (The People)   2. Nada Mas (Nothing More)
 3. El Perezoso (The Lazy Man)]
Dur: 14'
f.p.   (Nos. 2 and 3 only): Graham Titus (Bar.)/Alan Bush (Pno.) - Wigmore Hall,
            London, 11 January 1976
f.p.   (complete): above artists - Wigmore Hall, London, 30 October 1977
f.broad.p. Peter Savidge (Bar.)/Alan Bush (Pno.) - 13 July 1981
(* translated as 'From Fully Empowered')

Twenty Four Preludes for piano Op. 84 (1977)
Dur: 37'
f.p.   Alan Bush - Wigmore Hall, London, 30 October 1977
f.broad.p. Alan Bush - 8 April 1979
f.rec.   Peter Jacobs - *Altarus AIR-2-9004(2) (and CD)*

Woman's Life - song cycle for soprano and piano Op. 87 (1977)
[Words: Poems by Nancy Bush 1. Prologue 2. Weaving Song 3. Factory Day
 4. Epilogue]
Commissioned by Woking Music Club
Dur: 14'
f.p.   Sylvia Eaves (Sop.)/Alan Bush (Pno.) - Woking, Surrey, 12 February 1978
f.Lon.p.   above artists - Wigmore Hall, 28 October 1979
f.rec.   (No.2)Sylvia Eaves (Sop.)/Courtney Kenney (Pno.)- *Cameo Classics
            GOCLP 9020*

Sonatina for viola and piano Op. 88 (1978)
Later dedicated to the memory of Cecil Aronowitz who had given the first performance.
Dur: 17'
f.priv.p.   Cecil Aronowitz (Va.)/Alan Bush (Pno.) - Royal College of Music, London,
            10 June 1978 (during the Sixth International Viola Research Society
            Congress)
f.pub.p.   John White (Va.)/Alan Bush (Pno.) - Wigmore Hall, London,
            28 October 1979
Pub: Schauer, 1978 (ed. John White)

Pro Pace et Felicitate Generis Humani* - rhapsody for cello and piano Op. 89 (1979)
[Based on melodies from U.S.A. (Earl Robinson 'The Ballad of Joe Hill') G.B. (Carl
Dallas 'The Family of Man') and the U.S.S.R. (Borodin 'Prince Igor' and a song by
Dunayevsky]
Dur: 8'
f.p.   Cathy Giles (Vc.)/Alan Bush (Pno.) - Camden Town Hall, London,
            18 May 1979
(* 'For the peace and happiness of mankind')

Souvenir d'une Nuit d'été après Sergei Liapunov for piano* Op. 90 (1979)
Dur: 3'
(* Re-composition of two Liapunov Transcendental Studies - Nuit d'été and Berceuse)

Voices from Four Continents* - trio for clarinet, cello and piano Op. 91 (1980)
[1. Africa: Mozambique - Hymn of the Revolution (Dombo)
2. Asia: Vietnam - Song of Liberation (Van Chung)
3. Americas: Chile -Song (Victor Jara)
4. Europe: USSR - Song of the Plains (Lev Knipper)]
Dur: 6'
f.p.   Rory Allam (Cl.)/Cathy Giles (Vc.)/Alan Bush (Pno.) - Camden Town Hall,
            London, 10 May 1980 (British Soviet Friendship Society, 2nd International
            Festival)

Two Shakespeare Sonnets for baritone and chamber orchestra Op. 92 (1980)
[Introduction - Sonnet No. 18: Shall I compare thee to a Summer's Day? - Idyll -
Sonnet No. 60: Like as the Waves make towards the pebbled shore - Dance]
Dedicated to Nancy Bush
Dur: 15'
Instr: 1/1/1/0 - 2/0/4/0 - timp. perc. pno. str.
f.p.   Graham Titus/BBC Welsh Symphony Orchestra/Bryden Thomson - Royal
            Albert Hall, London, 5 August 1981 (Promenade Concert)

Meditation and Scherzo for double bass and piano Op. 93 (1964, 1980)
Dur: Meditation (5') Scherzo (4')
f.p.   (Meditation only - originally designated as Op. 62) Roger Dean (Db.)/ Alan
            Bush (Pno.) - South Hill Park Arts Centre, Bracknell, Berkshire, 25 April 1980
f.p.   (complete) Roger Dean (Db.)/Alan Bush (Pno.) - British Music Information
            Centre, London, 11 December 1980
Pub: Yorke Edition, 1981

Concertino for two violins and piano Op. 94 (1980-81)
Dedicated to Hazel and Maureen Smith
Dur: 29'
f.p.   Hazel Smith (Vn.)/Maureen Smith (Vn.)/Alan Bush (Pno.) -
            Aldeburgh, 18 June 1981 (Aldeburgh Festival)

Scots Jigganspiel (Scottish Dances*) for piano Op. 95 (1981)
Dedicated 'in warm affection to Ronald Stevenson'
(* Based on 'Sweet Molly', 'Duke of Pert', 'Tullodogrum', 'Strathspern', 'Marquis of
Huntley's Farewell' and 'Stumpie' published in 'The Select Melodies of Scotland',
Edinburgh, 1822)

Song and Dance* for junior string orchestra Op. 96 (1981-82)
(* The Dances are based on the folksongs 'Dance to your Shadow' and 'The Islay
Reaper's Song')

A Song from the North* for piano Op. 97 (1983)
Dedicated to Thomas Pitfield

Pub: Forsyth (Manchester), 1983 (`A Birthday Album for Thomas Pitfield')
(* Based on a calling-on song used by the sword-dancers of Earsdon, Northumberland)

Lascaux* Symphony for orchestra Op. 98 (1982-84)

[1. The Wild 2. The Children 3. Ice Age Remembered 4. Mankind Emergent]
f.broad.p. BBC Philharmonic Orchestra/Edward Downes, 25 March 1986
(* inspired by a visit the composer made to the cave paintings of Lascaux in the
Dordogne during May 1982)

Six Short Pieces for piano Op. 99 (1980)

[1. Invention for two voices 2. Ceremonial 3. Evening Lyric 4. Song
 5. Tyneside Reel 6. Rondino]
f.p.   Alan Bush - Queen Elizabeth Hall, London, 10 January 1986
f.rec.   Alan Bush - *Hyperion A 66138*
Pub: Roberton, 1988

Two Impressions for clarinet and piano Op. 100 (1983)

[1. Summer Fields 2. Hedgerows]
Dedicated to Nancy Bush

Turkish Workers' Marching Song Op. 101 (1983-84)

The Earth in Shadow for SATB chorus and orchestra Op. 102 (1984)

[Words: Nancy Bush]
Dedicated to Nancy Bush

Op. 103 (not used)

Piano Quintet Op. 104 (1984-85)

Instr: Pno. Vn. Vn. Va. Vc.
f.p.   John Bingham/Medici String Quartet - BBC Birmingham, 12 December 1985
f.conc.p.   above artists - Queen Elizabeth Hall, London, 10 January 1986

Octet for flute, clarinet, horn, string quartet and piano Op. 105 (after 1985)

Canzona for flute, clarinet, violin, cello and piano Op. 106 (after 1985)

Dedicated to Nancy Bush

Meditation for orchestra in memory of Anna Ambrose* Op. 107 (after 1985)

Anna Ambrose was the producer of the film on Alan Bush `Pages from a Life' first shown
at the National Film Theatre in 1984

Two Preludes and Fugues for viola and piano Op. 108 (after 1985)

Distant Fields for piano Op. 109 No. 1 (after 1985)

Song Poem and Dance Poem for string orchestra and piano Op. 109 No. 2 (after 1985)

Dedicated to John Amis

Mandela Speaking for baritone, SATB chorus and orchestra Op. 110 (after 1985)
[Words: Nelson Mandela]
f.p.   August 1986

Serenade and Duet for violin and piano Op. 111 (after 1985)
Dedicated to Nancy (Bush) "my life's companion for more than fifty years."
Pub: Stainer & Bell, 1988

Op. 112 (not used)

Piano Sonata No. 3 in G (Mixolydian) Op. 113 (after 1985)
f.p. Leslie Howard - British Music Information Centre, London, 28 October 1986

Three Easy Pieces for Piano Op.114 (after 1985)
Pub: Bardic Edition; Ludwig Music (USA)

Three Pieces `for Nancy' for piano Op. 115 (after 1985)
Dedicated to Nancy Bush

Prelude and Concert Piece for organ Op.116 (after 1985)
Dedicated to Robert Crowley

Song and Dance for violin and piano Op.117 (after 1985)

Two Pieces for piano Op.118 No. 1 (after 1985)
[1. Spring Woodland 2. Summer Garden]

Septet for woodwind and strings Op. 118 No. 2 (after 1985)

Two Etudes for piano Op.118 No. 3 (after 1985)

Op. 119 (not used)
Originally allocated to the **Six Modes for Piano Duet Op.122 q.v.**

Sonata for cello and piano Op.120 (after 1985)

A Heart's Expression, for piano Op. 121 No. 1 (unfinished, after 1985)
Dedicated to Nancy Bush

Two Preludes and Fugues for piano Op. 121 No. 2 (after 1985)
[1. Prelude No. 1 in B flat, Dorian 2. Prelude No. 2 in F sharp, Mixolydian]

The Six Modes for piano duet Op.122 (after 1985)

UNDATED WORKS

It's Up to Us - unison song for chorus and orchestra (or piano)
[Words: Etta Fennell]

Song of Age - for chorus and piano(?)
[Words: Randall Swingler]
Probably dates from c.1939-42

Song of the Engineers - for chorus and piano(?)
[Words: Rhoda Fraser]

Song of the Peace-lovers - for baritone, SATB chorus and piano
[Words: Randall Swingler]
Probably dates from c.1939-42

Two Yeats Songs, for voice and piano
[1. Down by the Sally Gardens 2. The Lake Isle of Innisfree]

Priscilla's Pavan for cello and piano

Summer Valley for cello and piano

FILM MUSIC

Hiroshima (1953-54)
Instr: Fl. Hp.

Fifty Fighting Years (1971)
[Directed by Stanley Forman and Roland Bischoff - story of the `Labour Monthly'
founded by Palme Dutt in 1921, narrated by Robin Page Arnot and Palme Dutt]
Instr: 0/0/1/0 - 0/2/2/0 - pno. perc. str. (and chorus)
First screening: National Film Theatre, Waterloo, 10 June 1973

INCIDENTAL MUSIC

The Pageant of Labour (1934)
[Scenario: Matthew Anderson
 Musical numbers include:
 Episode 1 - Capital Enslaves the Worker
 Episode 2 - The Martyrdom of the Children (1800)
 Episode 3 - Consolations of Philanthropy and Religion (1800-1820)
 Episode 4 - London received the Chartists (1848)
 Episode 5 - The Triumph of the Trade Union
 Episode 6 - the Fletcher Family (1900-1919)]
Instr: 2/1/1/0 - 2/1/2/0 - timp. perc. str. and mixed chorus (and in the Ballet
           scenes: 3 Tpt. 3 Tbn.)
f.p.   Orchestra/Choir conducted by Michael Tippett and Alan Bush - Crystal
           Palace, London, 15 October 1934
Producer: Edward P. Genn
N.B.   The composer has also made a concert version of Episode 2 and the Finale:
Instr: 2/2/2/2 - 4/3/3/1 - timp. perc. str. (and men's chorus)

Towards Tomorrow - A Pageant of Co-operation (1938)
[Scenario by Montagu Slater and André van Gyseghem]
Choreography: Margaret Barr, Katie Eisenstaedt, Teda de Moor
Instr: 2/2/3/1 - 2/3+4cnts./3/2 - timp. perc. str. (db only)
f.p.   Members of the London/South Suburban/Watford Co-operative Societies
          (with speaking parts and ensemble directed by Alan Bush) - Wembley
          Stadium, 2 July 1938

Pageant 'Music for the People'(1939)
[Scenario: Randall Swingler - the pageant was arranged in 10 episodes, Alan Bush
contributing the music to Episode 7 `Prisoners']
Instr: 1/1/4/1 - 4/2/3/3 - timp. perc. org.
f.p.   People's Festival Wind Band/Alan Bush with Arnold Goldsbrough (org.) -
          Royal Albert Hall, London, 1 April 1939

Freedom on the Air (1940)
[Words: Randall Swingler 1. Thrillers 2. Leave your brains in bed 3. And then
4. There's a reason 5. The hope concealed 6. Truth on the March]
f.p.   Unity Theatre Music Hall c. 1940
f.rec.   (No. 6) Topic Singers/Alan Bush - *Topic TRC 10*
Pub: W.M.A. 1940 (No. 6 published separately 1970)

The Star Turns Red (1940)
[Sean O'Casey]
Instr: 3 Tpt. Vn. Pno. Perc.(2)
f.p.   Unity Theatre, 12 March 1940

The Duke in (of) Darkness (1942)
[Patrick Hamilton]
Instr: 1/1/1/1 - 2/2/1/0 - perc. str. (2/1/1/1)
f.p.   St. James's Theatre, London, 8 October 1942

Macbeth (1947)
[Shakespeare]
Instr: picc./0/3/1 - 2/3/3/0 - timp. perc. hp. str. (2/0/3/1)
f.p.   Aldwych Theatre, London, 18 December 1947
Producer: Norris Houghton
Principals: Michael Redgrave, Ena Burrill

Communist Manifesto Centenary Pageant (1948)
[1. The Red Flag (Jim Connell - Tune, Maryland)
 2. The Internationale (Eugene Pottier - Tune by Pierre Degeyter)]
Instr: picc./1/4+2sax./2 - 2/3/3/1 - timp. perc.
f.p.   Royal Albert Hall, London, April 1948
Nos. 1 and 2 also arr. for mixed voice chorus
f.rec.   (No. 2) Topic Singers *Topic TRC 1 (78)*
f.rec.   (complete) Centenary Choir *Topic TRC 23 (78)*
No. 2 also arr. for chorus, two pianos, brass and percussion

ARRANGEMENTS

(i)   **Folk/Traditional Songs**

Comrade dear, come home (1940s)
[Trad: song of the Partisans arr.]
f.p.   W.M.A. Singers/Alan Bush - Fyvie Hall, London, 12 December 1944
          (International Arts Guild Concert)

Twenty English Folk Songs for mixed 2 or 3 part chorus accompanied or unaccompanied (1945)
Pub: Joseph Williams

Ten English Folk Songs for mixed 3 or 4 part chorus accompanied or unaccompanied (1951)
Pub: Joseph Williams, 1953

Folk song arrangements (c.1960s)
[1. Westron Wynd 2. The Peat Bog Soldiers
3. She walked through the Fair 4. The Islay Reaper's Song
5. The Sons of Liberty 6. Time for us to leave her
7. Rise up now ye shepherds]
f.doc.p.(No. 7) Elizabethan Singers/Louis Halsey - BBC (rec. 27/28 March 1963)
Pub: Novello, 1965

(ii)   **Miscellaneous**

(a) Choral - many written/arranged for performance by the choir at the Workers' Music Association.

> Parry: These things shall be arr. SATB
> Purcell: Fairest Isle arr. SAT
> Dunstable: O Rosa Bella arr. T. Bar. B.
> The Agincourt Song: arr. SATB
> Soviet Cradle Song arr. SA
> Easter Bells (Norwegian) arr. SSA or SATB
> Dark is the Night (Greek) arr. SATB
> Chinese Students Song arr. SATB
> Carmagnole (French) arr. SATB
> Lowlands, My Lowlands away arr. SATB

(b) String Orchestra (22 Players) - many written for performance by the London String Orchestra.

> Bach: Ricercar a 6 voci (from the Musical Offering)
> Bach: Chorale Prelude `Gott, heiliger Geist'
> Bach: Fuga super `Jesus Christus unser Heiland'
> Bach: Contrapuncti: I, V, IX, and XI (from the Art of Fugue)

Dowland: 3 Pavans from 'Lacrymae or Seaven Teares'
Gabrieli: Ricercar 8 per sonar
Hasler: Ricercar VII Toni
Krein: Dance
Pachelbel: Chorale Prelude 'Ach Herr, mich Armen Sunder'
Retakin: Romance
Senfl: Carmen in re
Senfl: Lamentatio Carmen
Sterndale-Bennett: Allegro agitato Op. 11 No. 6
Sterndale-Bennett: Nocturne No. 14 in C
Sterndale-Bennett: Rondo from Sonata in C minor Op. 1
Sterndale-Bennett: Serenade from Chamber Trio Op. 26
From Peter Schoffer's Liederbuch (1513):
[1. Mich trubt schwerlich (Anon) 2. Ach Unfall gross (Wolff)]
100 years of the Viennese Waltz (Haydn, Beethoven, Hummel, Ries
and Lanner)

(c) Full Orchestra

Suite from Purcell's 'The Fairy Queen' arr. (1955)
[1. Symphony 2. Rondo 3. Hornpipe
 4. Dance of the Haymakers 5. Monkey's Dance
 6. Dance of the Followers of Night 7. Chaconne]
Instr: 0/2/0/0 - 0/2/0/0 - timp. cemb. str.
f.p.   Rumanian State Philharmonic Orchestra/Alan Bush -
          Bucharest, 2 December 1955

(d) Piano/Chamber

Borodin: Mazurka arranged for piano duet
Dur: 2'
Pub: W.M.A.

Schumann: Carnival arr.
[Preamble - Harlequin, Eusebius, Chopin & Renaissance]

**The People Sing - a collection of revolutionary songs arranged for
two pianos**
f.p.   Mary and Geraldine Peppin (and dedicated to them)
f.rec.   above artists - *Topic TRC 7 (78)*

Two Spanish Songs arranged for cello and piano
f.p.   B. Rickelmann and Alan Bush
f.rec.   above artists - *Topic TRC 11 (78)*

MS LOCATION

Majority of MS are held by The British Library. **(BL)**

Other locations are:

BBC   Russian Glory (1941)

BL   Diabelleries (1955)

BPA   Compass Points (1976)

BPL   Prison Cycle (1939)

NCC   Symphony No. 2 (1949)

RAM   Festive March (1922), Prison Cycle (1939)

BIBLIOGRAPHY

Amis, John   **Songs for the Working Man.** BBC Music Magazine, January 1996

Bush, Alan   **Ronald Stevenson's `Passacaglia'.** Composer, No. 14, 1964.

Bush, Alan   **Franz Reizenstein 1911-1968.** Royal Academy of Music Magazine
                  No. 196, Summer 1969.

Bush, Alan   **In my Seventh Decade.** London: Kahn & Averill, 1970.

Bush, Alan   **In my Eighth Decade and other essays.** London: Kahn & Averill,
                  1980.

Bush, Alan   **The vocal compositions of Michael Head.** (in 'Michael Head, a
                  memoir'). London: Kahn & Averill, 1982.

Conway, Paul   **Alan Bush's Piano Concerto - a suitable case for fair treatment?**
                  British Music Society Newsletter No. 79, September 1998

Gardner, John   **Alan Bush 1900-1995.** British Music Society Newsletter No. 69,
                  March 1996.

Jacobs, Peter   **Recording Alan Bush.** British Music Society Newsletter No. 30,
                  June 1986.

Orga, Ates   **Alan Bush, musician and Marxist.** Music & Musicians, August
                  1969.

Orga, Ates   **Senior British Composers 1 - Alan Bush.** Composer, No. 35, Spring
                    1970

Payne, Anthony   **Alan Bush.** Musical Times, April 1964

Ross, Patience   **Alan Bush.** Monthly Musical Record, October 1929

Schafer, Murray   **Alan Bush,** in his `British Composers in Interview'. London: Faber and
                    Faber, 1963.

Stevenson, Ronald
                    Alan Bush - Committed Composer. Music Review, Vol. 25, 1964

Stevenson, Ronald
(ed.)   **Time Remembered: An 80th birthday symposium.**
                    Kidderminster: Bravura Publications, 1981 [B] [D]

13

Geoffrey Bush
(1920–1998)

Te Deum in C for SATB chorus and organ (1938)
Written in memoriam, E. Lawrence Griffiths
Dur: 6'30"
Pub: Augener, 1961; Stainer & Bell

Natus est Immanuel - A Christmas Piece, for string orchestra*   (1939)
Dedicated to the composer's mother.
Dur: 6'
f.p.   BBC Northern Orchestra/John Hopkins - BBC, 11 March 1952
Pub: Elkin, 1954; Novello
(* a re-scoring of an earlier piano piece written while the composer was still a
 schoolboy at Lancing College)

Rhapsody for clarinet and string orchestra (or string quartet) (1940)
Dedicated to Kenneth Hunt
Dur: 8'30"
f.p.   (qt.) Kenneth Hunt (Cl.)/Student Quartet - Balliol College, Oxford,
            17 November 1940
f.broad.p. (qt.) Philip Cardew (Cl.)/Hirsch String Quartet - 18 December 1943
Pub: Elkin, 1953 (arr. clarinet and piano); Novello

Epigrams: Suite for piano (1941)
[1. Marcia 2. Ostinato 3. Presto 4. Siciliana 5. Rondo 6. Marcia]
Dedicated to Francis Harvey
Dur: 4'
f.broad.p. Geoffrey Bush - Radio 3, 28 April 1971
f.rec.   Eric Parkin - *J. Martin Stafford JMSCD 3 (CD)*
Pub: Augener, 1951; Stainer & Bell

Five Choral Dances for unaccompanied SATB chorus (1941)
[Words: Trad. 1. Comin' through the rye 2. Barbara Allen 3. Bobby Shaftoe
 4. Green Gravel 5. Dame, get up and bake your pies]

Dur: 10'
f.p.   Tudor Singers/Harry Stubbs - Wigmore Hall, London, 16 May 1952
f.broad.p. BBC Singers/Cyril Gell - 8 July 1952
Pub: Augener, 1951; Stainer & Bell

Overture: The Spanish Rivals * (1941 rev.1969)

Dur: 6'
Instr: 2/2/2/2 - 4/2/3/0 - timp. perc. str.
f.p.   BBC Northern Orchestra/Basil Douglas - BBC, 13 September 1944
f.conc.p.   BBC Midland Light Orchestra/Gilbert Vinter - Cheltenham Town Hall,
            20 July 1952 (Cheltenham Festival)
Pub: Novello, 1969
(* orignally the overture to a one act comic opera after Sheridan's `The Duenna',
subsequently withdrawn by the composer. The opera received its first performance at the
Mercury Theatre, London on 19 June 1951, the Intimate Opera Company directed by
Frederick Woodhouse, as part of the Festival of Britain)

Portraits: Five Songs about Musicians, for unaccompanied SATB chorus (1942)
[1. Orpheus (Shakespeare `Henry VIII') 2. Thomas Morley (Michael Drayton)
 3. Henry Lawes (Robert Herrick) 4. Giles Farnaby (John Dowland)
 5. Pan (John Fletcher)]
Dur: 10'
f.p.   BBC Singers/Leslie Woodgate - BBC, 22 September 1944
Pub: Augener, 1961; Stainer & Bell; Thames

Two Choral Songs for unaccompanied SATB chorus (1942)
[1. Christmas Night 2. La Belle Dame sans Merci (John Keats)]
No. 2 dedicated to Bruce Montgomery
Dur: 11'
f.p.   (No. 1) BBC Chorus/Leslie Woodgate - BBC, 23 December 1944
f.p.   (No. 2) William McAlpine (Ten.)/London Bach Society/Paul Steinitz - BBC,
            3 April 1952
Pub: OUP, 1949 (No. 2), 1955 (No.1)

Sinfonietta Concertante for cello and small orchestra (1943)
Dedicated to Francis Harvey
Dur: 18'
Instr: 1/1/2/1 - 2/1/0/0 - timp. str.
f.p.   John Shinebourne/BBC Symphony Orchestra/Clarence Raybould - BBC,
            28 September 1945
Pub: Elkin; Novello

Divertimento for string orchestra (1943)
Dedicated to Basil Douglas
Dur: 22'
f.p.   Riddick String Orchestra/Kathleen Riddick - Wigmore Hall, London,
            6 January 1947
f.broad.p. Harvey Phillips String Orchestra/ Harvey Phillips - 20 March 1955

f.rec.   Touring Chamber Orchestra of the Soviet Union/L. Markes - *Melodiya (USSR)*
            D.015133-4 (recorded at a live concert in the Concert Hall of the Composer's
            Union, Moscow, 2 October 1964)
Pub: Galliard, 1964; Stainer & Bell

In Praise of Salisbury* - Overture for SATB chorus (optional) and orchestra (1944)
Dur: 16'
Instr: 2/2/2/2 - 4/2/3/1 - timp. perc. str.
f.p.   BBC Scottish Orchestra/Ian Whyte - BBC, 4 March 1952
(* Geoffrey Bush had been a chorister at Salisbury Cathedral for five years)

Five Spring Songs for high voice and piano (1944)
[1. Diaphenia (Henry Constable) 2. Lay a garland on my hearse (John Fletcher) 3. What
thing is love? (George Peele) 4. Weep you no more, sad fountains*
(Anon) 5. Now the lusty spring is seen (John Fletcher)]
Dur: 9'
f.p.   Richard Lewis (Ten.)/Frederick Stone (Pno.) - BBC, 2 January 1946
f.conc.p.   David Galliver (Ten.) - Jubilee Hall, Stoke-on-Trent, 3 April 1958
Pub: Novello, 1953
* No. 4 later arr. by the composer for high voice and orchestra q.v.
Pub: Novello (as No. 4 of Five Songs)

Overture: The Rehearsal* (1945)
Dur: 6'
Instr: 2/2/2/2 - 4/2/3/0 - timp. perc. str.
f.p.   BBC Northern Orchestra/Charles Groves - BBC, 14 March 1946
f.conc.p.   City of Birmingham Symphony Orchestra/Rudolf Schwarz - Cheltenham
            Town Hall, 14 June 1953 (Cheltenham Festival)
Pub: Augener, 1961; Stainer & Bell
(* The work originated in a reading of the Duke of Buckingham's Restoration Comedy
`The Rehearsal')

Sonata for violin and piano (1945)
Dedicated to John Ireland
Dur: 18'
f.p.   Peter Gibbs (Vn.)/Geoffrey Bush (Pno.) - Balliol College, Oxford,
            24 February 1946
f.broad.p. Frederick Grinke (Vn.)/Kendall Taylor (Pno.) - 31 October 1949
f. Lon. p. Peter Gibbs (Vn.)/Geoffrey Bush (Pno.) - RBA Galleries, 12 April 1953
Pub: Augener, 1959; Stainer & Bell

Three Elizabethan Songs for high voice and piano (c.1945)
[1. Fire! Fire!* (Thomas Campion) 2. Sweet, stay a while (John Donne)
 3. Sigh no more ladies (Shakespeare: `Much Ado about Nothing')]
No. 1 dedicated to J. and J. H. (Horder)
No. 2 dedicated to H. and M. F. (Furze)
No. 3 dedicated to G. and M. S. (Sedgwick)
Dur: 5'30"
f.p.   Stephen Manton (Ten.)/Margaret Schofield (Pno.) - BBC, 11 July 1952

f.conc.p.   David Galliver (Ten.)/Geoffrey Bush (Pno.) - RBA Galleries, London,
            12 April 1953
f.recs.   (No.3) Anthony Rolfe Johnson (Ten.)/Graham Johnson (Pno.) - *Hyperion*
            CDA 66480(CD)
            Felicity Lott (Sop.)/Graham Johnson (Pno.) - *Chandos CHAN 8722(CD)*
Pub: Novello, 1948
* No. 1 later arr. by the composer for high voice and string orchestra q.v.
Pub: Novello (as No. 1 of Three Songs)

Five Songs for high voice and orchestra (1945, 1950)
[1. There is a garden in her face (Thomas Campion)
 2. Come away, death (Shakespeare 'Twelfth Night')
 3. It was a lover and his lass (Shakespeare 'As You Like It')
 4. Weep you no more, sad fountains (Anon.) from 'Five Spring Songs' q.v.
 5. When daffodils began to peer (Shakespeare 'Winter's Tale')]
Instr: 1/1/2/1 - 2/2/1/0 - timp. str.
f.p.   Helen Wells (Sop.)/Bernard Rose (Ten.)/Orchestra/Christopher
            Longuet-Higgins - Oxford, 11 March 1946
f.broad.p. William Herbert (Ten.)/London Chamber Orchestra/Anthony Bernard -
            21 February 1956
Pub: Novello

Four Pieces for piano - Set 1 (1946)
Dur: 7'
f.p.   Geoffrey Bush - Lady Margaret Hall, Oxford, 27 April 1947
f.rec.   (No. 3, Novelette) Eric Parkin - *J. Martin Stafford JMSCD3 (CD)*
Pub: Augener, 1950; Stainer & Bell; Thames (No. 3)

Nocturne and Toccata for piano (1947)
Dur: 5'
f.p.   Geoffrey Bush - Lady Margaret Hall, Oxford, 27 April 1947
f.rec.   Eric Parkin - *J. Martin Stafford JMSCD3 (CD)*
Pub: Augener,1950; Stainer & Bell; Galaxy, New York (Toccata only)

A Christmas Cantata for soprano, SATB chorus, oboe and string orchestra (1947)
[1. Prelude 2. Theme and Variations: The Seven Joys of Mary (Trad.)
 3. Chorale: The Birds (Hilaire Belloc)
 4. Lullaby: The Rocking Carol (Czech. carol trans. Percy Dearmer)
 5. Scherzo: Make we merry both more and less (c.1500)
 6. Carol: This Endris Night (15th C) 7. I Sing of a Maiden (15th C)
 8. Lament: The Coventry Carol (15th C) 9. Finale: I saw three ships (Trad.) -
Epilogue]
Written for the Musical Society of Balliol College, Oxford and dedicated to A.R.McD.G
(Ronald Gordon) and other Oxford friends.
Dur: 35'
f.p.   Musical Society of Balliol College, cond. Ronald Gordon - Balliol College,
            Oxford, 30 November 1947
f.broad.p. Honor Sheppard (Sop.)/BBC Northern Singers/Alfred Livesley (Ob.)/ BBC
            Northern Orchestra/Gordon Thorne - 24 December 1957

f.rec.   Cardiff Polyphonic Choir and Orchestra/Richard Elfyn Jones - *Saydisc SDL 352 (and MC)*
Pub: Novello, 1948 (vocal score)

Seven Songs for medium voice and piano (1945-1947)

[1. Fain would I change that note** (Anon)
 2. When daffodils begin to peer* (Shakespeare `Winter's Tale)
 3. She hath an eye (Robert Jones)
 4. My true love hath my heart (Sir Philip Sidney)
 5. It was a lover and his lass* (Shakespeare `As You Like It')
 6. There is a garden in her face* (Thomas Campion)
 7. A Song of Praise - Let all the world in every corner sing** (George
    Herbert)]
No. 7 dedicated to P. D. (Powell Davies)
Dur: 13´
f.p.   (No. 5) Maurice Bevan (Bar.)/Geoffrey Bush (Pno.) - RBA Galleries, London,
          12 April 1953
f.rec.   (No.5) Sarah Walker (M/S)/Graham Johnson (Pno.) - *Hyperion A 66136 (and
          CD)*
Pub: Novello (Nos. 1-5); Stainer & Bell (Nos. 6 & 7 in an Album of Eight Songs)
* Nos. 2, 5 and 6 also arr. by the composer for high voice and orchestra q.v.
Pub: Novello (as Nos. 5, 3 and 1 of Five Songs)
** Nos. 1 and 7 later arr. by the composer for high voice and string orchestra q.v.
Pub: Novello (as Nos. 2 and 3 of Three Songs)

Two Miniatures for string orchestra (1948)

[1. Lullaby 2. Promenade]
Dur: 7'
Pub: Novello

Concerto for oboe and string orchestra (1948)

[1. Prelude 2. Siciliana 3. Rondo alla giga]
Commissioned for the Centenary of Lancing College (where the composer had been a
pupil) and dedicated to Tamara Coates
Dur: 16'
f.p.   Tamara Coates/Southern Philharmonic Orchestra/Geoffrey Bush - Lancing
          College, Sussex, 24 July 1948
f.broad.p. Evelyn Rothwell/Boyd Neel String Orchestra/Boyd Neel - 3 June 1952
f.Lon.p. Evelyn Rothwell/Hallé Orchestra/George Weldon - Royal Albert Hall,
          London, 27 August 1956 (Promenade Concert)
Pub: Elkin, 1960; Novello (arr. oboe and piano)

A Summer Serenade for tenor, SATB chorus, timpani, piano and string orchestra (1948)

[1. Worship ye that lovers be this May (King James I of Scotland)
 2. Madrigal: Love is a sickness (Daniel)
 3. Scherzo: Love is a pretty frenzy (Anon.)
 4. Dirge: O Rose, thou art sick! (William Blake)
 5. Aubade: Pack, clouds, away! (John Heywood)

6. Nocturne: Music, when soft voices die (Shelley)

7. Finale: Pleasure it is (Anon.)]

Commissioned by the Eglesfield Musical Society of Queen's College, Oxford and dedicated to Bernard Rose and the Society

Dur: 20'

f.p.   Eglesfield Musical Society/Bernard Rose - Queen's College, Oxford, June 1949

f.Lon.p.   David Galliver (Ten.)/South London Bach Choir/London Classical Orchestra/Trevor Harvey - Wigmore Hall, 26 April 1951

f.broad.p. BBC Northern Singers/BBC Northern Orchestra/John Hopkins - 8 October 1955

f.rec.   Adrian Thompson (Ten)/Westminster Singers/City of London Sinfonia/Richard Hickox - *Chandos ABTD 1479(MC), CHAN 8864(CD)*

Pub: Elkin, 1951; Novello (vocal score)

An Oxford Scherzo for two pianos (1949)

Dedicated to Lina and Margaret Deneke

Dur: 3'30"

f.p.   Bruce Montgomery*/Geoffrey Bush - Lady Margaret Hall, Oxford, 16 October 1949

f.Lon.p.   above artists - Wigmore Hall, London, 1949

f.broad.p. Eileen and Joan Lovell - February 1964

Pub: Augener; Stainer & Bell

(* Bruce Montgomery's pseudonym when writing detective stories was Edmund Crispin - he and Geoffrey Bush once collaborated on a short story entitled `Baker Dies' and published in a collection called `Fen Country')

Overture: Yorick (1949)

Commissioned by the National Association of Boys' Clubs to be played at a concert in memory of Tommy Handley. The overture was awarded a Royal Philharmonic Society Open Prize in the same year and is dedicated to Trevor Harvey.

Dur: 8'30"

Instr: 2/2/2/2 - 4/2/3/0 - timp. perc. str.

f.p.   New Philharmonic Orchestra/John Woolf - Royal Albert Hall, London, 19 March 1949

f.broad.p. BBC Welsh Orchestra/Mansel Thomas - 12 August 1950

f.Austr.p. Sydney Symphony Orchestra/Sir Eugene Goossens - Sydney, 1955

f.rec.   New Philharmonia Orchestra/Vernon Handley - *Lyrita SRCS 95, SRCD 252(CD)*

Pub: Elkin, 1955; Novello

Four Songs from Herrick's Hesperides - song cycle for baritone and piano (1949)

[1. The Impatient Lover 2. Upon the loss of his Mistresses 3. To Electra

4. Upon Julia's clothes]

Dedicated to the composer's fiancée (now his wife)

Dur: 7'30"

f.p.   Donald Munro (Bar.)/Geoffrey Bush (Pno.) - BBC, 28 March 1950

Pub: Elkin, 1951; Novello

Also arr. by the composer for baritone and string orchestra (1950)

f.p.   Maurice Bevan (Bar.)/London Classical Orchestra/Trevor Harvey - Wigmore
            Hall, London, 26 April 1951
f.rec.   Stephen Varcoe (Bs./Bar.)/City of London Sinfonia/Richard Hickox - *Chandos
            ABTD 1479(MC), CHAN 8864(CD)*
Pub: Elkin, 1959; Novello

Farewell, Earth's Bliss, for baritone and string orchestra (or string quartet) (1950)
[1. Sweet day, so cool (George Herbert)
 2. O, the month of May (Thomas Dekker)
 3. Do not fear to put thy feet naked in the river sweet (John Fletcher)
 4. Fear no more the heat o' the sun (Shakespeare `Cymbeline')
 5. When May is in his prime (Richard Edwardes)
 6. Fair pledges of a fruitful tree (Robert Herrick)]
Dur: 18'
f.p.   Denis Dowling/Welbeck String Orchestra/Trevor Harvey - BBC Latin
            American Service broadcast, 9 April 1951
f.conc.p.   Richard Bowen/Capriol Orchestra/Roy Budden - Wigmore Hall,
            London, 14 December 1951
f.Brit.broad.p. (qt. version) Roderick Jones/MacGibbon String Quartet -
            18 November 1953
f.recs.   Stephen Varcoe (Bs./Bar.)/City of London Sinfonia/Richard Hickox - *Chandos
            ABTD 1479(MC), CHAN 8864(CD)*
            Martin Oxenham (Bar.)/Bingham String Quartet - *Meridian DUOCD
            89026(CD) (and MC)*
Pub: Novello
Nos. 2 and 5 also arr. by the composer for baritone and piano
Pub: Novello (in an Album of Eight Songs)

**Twelfth Night - an Entertainment for tenor, SATB chorus and chamber
orchestra (1950)**
[Shakespeare 1. Prelude   2. If music be the food of love
 3. Farewell, dear love 4. O mistress mine 5. Come away death
 6. I am gone, sir 7. When that I was and a little tiny boy]
Commissioned for the Festival of Britain by the London Choral Society
Dur: 22'
Instr: 1/1/1/0 - 1/0/0/0 - timp. str.
f.p.   Stephen Manton (Ten.)/London Choral Society/ Tobin Chamber
            Orchestra/John Tobin - Central Hall, Westminster, London, 1 June 1951
f.broad.p. Wilfred Brown (Ten.)/BBC West of England Singers/BBC West of England
            Light Orchestra/Reginald Redman - 18 May 1952
Pub: Elkin, 1951; Novello (vocal score)
Exc. Come away death, arr. by the composer for high voice and orchestra q.v.
Pub: Novello (as No. 2 of Five Songs)

Three Dance Variations - for harpsichord (or piano) (1951)
[Theme - Siciliana - March - Saraband]
Dur: 6'
f.p.   Ruth Dyson - Wigmore Hall, London, 5 May 1951
Pub: Elkin, 1957; Novello

Three Songs of Ben Jonson for high voice and piano (1952)
[1. Echo's lament for Narcissus 2. The Kiss 3. A Rebuke]
Dur: 6'
f.p.   David Galliver (Ten.)/Geoffrey Bush (Pno.) - RBA Galleries, London,
           12 April 1953
f.broad.p. John Tainsh (Ten.)/Geoffrey Bush (Pno.) - 24 November 1955
f.rec.   (No. 1) Ian Partridge (Ten.)/Jennifer Partridge (Pno.) - *Enigma VAR 1027*
           (complete) Ian Partridge (Ten)/Geoffrey Bush (Pno.) - *Chandos ABRD 1053*
           (and MC), CHAN 8830(CD)
Pub: Elkin, 1959; Novello

The Blind Beggar's Daughter of Bethnal Green - a ballad opera (1952 rev. 1964)
[Libretto Sheila Bathurst and Geoffrey Bush]
Dur: 60'
Instr: 1/1/2/2 - 2/2/0/0 - timp. perc. pno. str. (+ 3 soloists, 4 speaking parts and S. A.
           Bar. chorus)
f.p.   Farnham Operatic Society, cond. Leonard Starling - Farnham, Surrey,
           21 January 1954
Producer: Gladys Starling
f.Lon.p.   South Middlesex Operatic and Dramatic Society, cond. Ronald Bateman -
           Acton Town Hall, 6 May 1955
Producer: Eileen Bateman
Pub: Elkin, 1953; Novello (vocal score)
Excs.   Suite: 'Old London' (on themes from the above) arr. for concert band by
           Robert Leist
Dedicated to Major C. H. Jaeger
Dur: 7'30"
Pub: Galaxy Music, New York, 1967

Trio for oboe, bassoon and piano (1952)
Written for and dedicated to the Camden Trio
Dur: 11'
f.p.   Camden Trio - Evelyn Rothwell (Ob.), Archie Camden (Bsn.), Wilfrid Parry
           (Pno.) - Canterbury, 18 November 1952
f.broad.p. above artists - 15 December 1953
f.rec.   Neil Black (Ob.)/Graham Sheen (Bsn.)/Geoffrey Bush (Pno.) - *Chandos ABRD*
           1196 (and MC), CHAN 8819(CD)
Pub: Novello, 1955

Concertino No. 1 for piano and orchestra (1953 rev. 1961)
Dur: 17'
Instr: 2/1/2/1 - 4(2)/2/3/0 - timp. perc. str.
f.p.   Eric Parkin/Yorkshire Symphony Orchestra/Maurice Miles - Leeds Town Hall,
           24(25) June 1953
f.p.   (rev. version) Eric Parkin/Modern Symphony Orchestra/Arthur Dennington -
           Northern Polytechnic, London, 11 February 1961
f.broad.p. Eric Parkin/BBC Concert Orchestra/Ashley Lawrence - 27 September 1985
Pub: Novello

The End of Love - song cycle for baritone and piano (1954)
[Words: Kathleen Raine 1. Lament 2. Far-darting Apollo 3. The End of Love
4. Introspection]
Dur: 13'
f.p.   Thomas Hemsley (Bar.)/Geoffrey Bush (Pno.) - BBC, 25 June 1956
f.rec.   Benjamin Luxon (Bar.)/Geoffrey Bush (Pno.) - *Chandos ABRD 1053 (and
            MC), CHAN 8830(CD)*
Pub: Stainer & Bell, 1984 (in an Album of Eight Songs)

Symphony No. 1 (1954)
Dedicated to the composer's fellow composer Bruce Montgomery - the second movement
was written in memory of Constant Lambert and contains a brief reference to `The Rio
Grande'
Dur: 26'
Instr: 2/2/2/2 - 4/3/3/1 - timp. perc.(2). str.
f.p.   City of Birmingham Symphony Orchestra/Rudolf Schwarz - Cheltenham
            Town Hall, 8 July 1954 (Cheltenham Festival)
f.broad.p. BBC Scottish Orchestra/Ian Whyte - 7 April 1956
f.Lon.p.   BBC Symphony Orchestra/Maurice Miles - Royal Albert Hall,
            12 September 1958 (Promenade Concert)
f.rec.   London Symphony Orchestra/Nicholas Braithwaite - *Lyrita SRCS 115, SRCD
            252(CD)*
Pub: Elkin, 1962; Novello

Sonata for trumpet and piano (c.1955)
f.broad.p. David Mason (Tpt.)/Joyce Hedges (Pno.) - 16 March 1955

Two Pieces for organ (1955)
[1. Carillon 2. Toccata]
Dedicated to Christopher Dearnley (No.1) and Erik Routley (No.2)
Dur: 5'30"
f.rec.   (No. 1) Christopher Dearnley - *Motette M 10915(MC), CD 10911(CD)*
Pub: No. 1 - OUP (Christmas Album); No. 2 - OUP (Festive Album), 1956

In Praise of Mary, for soprano, SATB chorus and orchestra (1955)
[Words: Medieval English carols - 1. Hail Mary, full of grace
2. There is no rose of such virtue 3. A maid peerless
4. Adam lay y-bounden 5. Lully, lullay 6. Alleluia]
Dedicated to the composer's wife
Dur: 20'
Instr: 2/2/2/2 - 4/2/3/1 - timp. perc. str.
Alt.Instr: organ. timp. str.
f.p.   Isobel Baillie/Festival Chorus/London Symphony Orchestra/Meredith Davies -
            Hereford Cathedral, 7 September 1955 (Three Choirs Festival)
f.Lon.p.   Cynthia Thorn/Arnold Foster Choir/Arnold Foster Orchestra/Arnold Foster -
            Central Hall, Westminster, 1 December 1955
f.rec.   Valery Hill (Sop.)/Royal College of Music Chamber Choir/Royal
            Philharmonic Orchestra/Sir David Willcocks - *Unicorn DKPCD 9057 (CD)*
Pub: Elkin, 1955; Novello (vocal score)

Two Anthems for SATB chorus and organ (1955)
[1. O love, how deep, how broad, how high 2. Praise the Lord, O my soul]
The first anthem is dedicated `In memoriam, Hallam Fordham'
The second anthem was written for the St. Cecilia's Day Festival Service
Dur: 5' each
f.p.   (No.2) St. Sepulchre's, Holborn, London, 21 November 1956
              (St. Cecilia's Day Festival Service)
f.rec.   (No.2) Canterbury Cathedral Choir/Allan Wicks - *Alpha ACA 502*
Pub: Novello, 1956; Laurel Press, Nashville, Tennessee, USA (No. 1 only)

If the Cap Fits - opera in one Act (1956)
[Libretto: Geoffrey Bush after Molière's `Les Precieuses Ridicules']
Dedicated to J. B. R. and A. W. B. W. (Jasper Rooper and Alan Webb)
Dur: 35'
Instr: 1/1/1/1 - 2/1/1/0 - perc. pno. str. (+ Sop. Ten. Bar. soloists)
f.p.   Intimate Opera Company, cond. Anthony Hopkins - Cheltenham Town Hall,
              12 July 1956 (Cheltenham Festival)
Principals: Ann Dowdall, Stephen Manton, Leyland White
Producer: Eric Shilling
Pub: Galliard, 1964; Stainer & Bell (vocal score)

Three Songs for high voice and string orchestra (c.1956)
[1. Fire! Fire! (Thomas Campion) 2. Fain would I change that note (Anon.)
 3. Let all the world in every corner sing (George Herbert)]
Arrangements by the composer of earlier settings for voice and piano q.v.
Dur: 6′
f.p.   Stephen Manton (Ten.)/Welbeck String Orchestra/Boyd Neel - BBC
              broadcast, 24 July 1956
Pub: Novello

Symphony No. 2 'The Guildford' (1957)
Commissioned by Alderman Lawrence Powell for the 700th anniversary of the granting
of the Royal Charter to the City of Guildford and dedicated to Elsie and Lawrence Powell
Dur: 30'
Instr: 2/2/2/2 - 4/3/3/0 - timp. perc. str.
f.p.   Guildford Municipal Orchestra/Geoffrey Bush - Guildford Town Hall, Surrey,
              3 November 1957
f.Lon.p.   Modern Symphony Orchestra/Arthur Dennington - Northern Polytechnic,
              10 December 1966
f.broad.p.   BBC Welsh Symphony Orchestra/Bryden Thomson - 15 June 1987
f.rec.   Royal Philharmonic Orchestra/Barry Wordsworth - *Lyrita SRCD 252(CD)*
Pub: Elkin, 1965; Novello

Concerto for light orchestra (1958)
[1. Introduction and Toccata 2. Siciliana 3. Notturno 4. Hornpipe
 5. Air 6. Finale alla Giga]
Commissioned for the BBC Light Music Festival and dedicated `for Julie', the composer's
wife - the movements of the concerto are based on six songs by Thomas Arne
Dur: 16'

Instr:	2/2/2/2 - 4/2/3/0 - timp. perc. str.
f.p.	BBC Concert Orchestra/Vilem Tausky - Royal Festival Hall, London, 5 July 1958 (BBC Light Music Festival)
Pub:	Elkin, 1958; Novello

Songs of Wonder, for high voice and string orchestra (1959)

[Words: Trad. 1. Prologue: How many miles to Babylon? 2. Here comes a lusty wooer
3. Polly Pillicote 4. The Wonder of Wonders 5. Old Abram Brown 6. The little nut-tree
7. The noble Duke of York 8. Epilogue: How many miles to Babylon?]
Dedicated `to my family'

Dur:	14'
f.p.	Jacqueline Delman (Sop.)/Welbeck String Orchestra/Maurice Miles - BBC, 17 December 1961
Pub:	Elkin, 1962; Novello

N.B. There is a shorter version of this song cycle for high voice and piano, omitting Nos.
1, 7 and 8.

Dur:	9'
f.p.	Thelma Godfrey (Sop.) - Wigmore Hall, London, 27 May 1963
f.broad.p.	Barbara Yates (Sop.)/Viola Tunnard(Pno.) - 16 October 1963
f.recs.	(No.4) Ian Partridge (Ten.)/Jennifer Partridge (Pno.) - *Enigma VAR 1027* (complete)Ian Partridge (Ten)/Geoffrey Bush (Pno.) - *Chandos ABRD 1053 (and MC), CHAN 8830(CD)*

Hornpipe - second movement from the Suite for St. Cecilia's Day (composite work*) (1960)

Dur:	2' (complete suite: 10')
Instr:	2/2/2/2 - 4/2/3/0 - timp. perc. str.
f.p.	City of Birmingham Symphony Orchestra/Hugh Rignold - Royal Festival Hall, London, 22 November 1960 (Royal Concert)
Pub:	Mills Music

(* the other composers were Alun Hoddinott, Thea Musgrave and Iain Hamilton q.v.)

Dialogue for oboe and piano (1960)

[1. Preamble 2. Chorale 3. March]
Commissioned by the Hampton Music Club

Dur:	15'
f.p.	Léon Goossens (Ob.)/Geoffrey Bush (Pno.) - Arts Council Drawing Room, London, 25 March 1960 (Hampton Music Club Concert)
f.broad.p.	Ian Wilson (Ob.)/Geoffrey Bush (Pno.) - 8 September 1962
f.rec.	Neil Black (Ob.)/Geoffrey Bush (Pno.) - *Chandos ABRD 1196 (and MC), CHAN 8819(CD)*
Pub:	Augener, 1962; Thames, 1988

The Sweet Season - Four Simple Songs for unaccompanied SATB chorus (1961)

[1. Spring, the sweet Spring (Thomas Nashe) 2. Chopcherry (George Peele)
 3. How should I your true love know? (Shakespeare `Hamlet')
 4. It was a lover and his lass (Shakespeare `As You Like It')]
Dedicated to Neil Saunders

Dur:	6'

f.broad.p. (complete) BBC Chorus/Peter Gellhorn - 17 February 1965 (No.3 had been
                 broadcast 13 March 1964)
Pub: Stainer & Bell, 1963; Thames
Later arr. for high voice and string quartet (1992)

A Lover's Progress - song cycle for tenor, oboe, clarinet and bassoon (1961)
[Words: Anon. 16th century poems 1. Hope 2. Resolution 3. Doubt 4. Jealousy   5.
Grief 6. Despair]
Dur: 16'
f.p.   David Galliver (Ten.)/Léon Goossens (Ob.)/Thea King (Cl.)/Archie Camden
                 (Bsn.) - London, 26 April 1961
f.broad.p. David Galliver (Ten.)/London Reed Trio - 4 May 1963
Pub: Novello, 1965

Whydah variations on a theme by Balfour Gardiner, for two pianos (1961)
Commissioned by the Redcliffe Festival of British Music and dedicated to the memory of
Balfour Gardiner - the work is based on a theme from Balfour Gardiner's Choral Settings
of John Masefield's `News from Whydah' (Whydah Roads was once a pirate anchorage)
Dur: 11'
f.p.   Ian Lake/Geoffrey Bush - London, 30 October 1964
                 (Music in Our Time Festival)
f.broad.p. above artists - 23 June 1968
f.rec.   Eric Parkin - *J. Martin Stafford JMSCD3 (CD)*
Pub: Novello, 1966

Homage to Matthew Locke for brass sextet (1962)
[1. Trumpet Tune 2. Hornpipe 3. Air 4. Round-O 5. Ground 6. Jig]
Commissioned by the City of Birmingham Symphony Orchestra Brass Ensemble and
dedicated to Francis Harvey
Dur: 14'
Instr: 3 Tpt. 3 Tbn.
f.p.   City of Birmingham Symphony Orchestra Brass Ensemble - Wrekin College,
                 27 October 1962
f.broad.p. above artists - 9 November 1962
Pub: Galliard, 1965; Stainer & Bell
Movements 3 and 4 also arr. for wind quintet
Dedicated to Francis Harvey
Dur: 4'30"
f.rec.   English Chamber Orchestra Wind Ensemble - *Chandos ABRD 1196 (and
                 MC), CHAN 8819(CD)*
Pub: Stainer & Bell

Concerto for trumpet, piano and string orchestra (1962)
[1. Toccata 2. Nocturne 3. Finale]
Dur: 20'
f.p.   David Mason (Tpt.)/Ian Lake (Pno.)/Riddick Orchestra/Geoffrey Bush - Royal
                 Festival Hall, London, 16 December 1963
Pub: Braydeston Press, 1976

Two Latin Hymns for unaccompanied SATB chorus (1963)
[1. O Salutaris Hostia 2. Tantum ergo]
Written for the Choir of All Saints Church, Margaret Street, London
Dur: 4'30"
f.p.   Sine Nomine Singers/Michael Rose - Holy Trinity Church, Brompton Road,
             London, 20 November 1963
f.broad.p. BBC Chorus/Peter Gellhorn - 27 July 1966
f.rec.   Canterbury Cathedral Choir/Allan Wicks - *Alpha ACA 502*
Pub: Novello, 1963

Wind Quintet (1963)
Commissioned by the New London Wind Ensemble and dedicated to the memory of
Prokofiev
Dur: 18'
Instr: Fl. Ob. Cl. Bsn. Hn.
f.p.   New London Wind Ensemble - Victoria and Albert Museum, London,
             5 April 1964
f.broad.p. Nash Ensemble - 23 March 1970
f.rec.   English Chamber Orchestra Wind Ensemble - *Chandos ABRD 1196 (and
             MC), CHAN 8819(CD)*
Pub: Galliard, 1968; Stainer & Bell

Finale for a Concert for orchestra (1964)
Dedicated to Stanford Robinson
Dur: 4'30"
Instr: 2/1/2/1 - 2/2/1/0 - timp. perc.(4). pno. (duet) str.
f.broad.p. BBC Concert Orchestra/Stanford Robinson - December 1967
Pub: Novello, 1965

The Merchant of Venice - incidental music (1964)
[Shakespeare]
Commissioned by the British Council
Director: David William
Two Fragments:
(No. 1)   Tell me where is Fancy bred? for soprano, tenor, SATB chorus and solo cello
           Dedicated to David William
           Dur: 2'
(No. 2)   The Prince of Morocco's Fanfare and March,
           Dedicated to B. W. T. H. (Basil Handford)
           Dur: 2'
           Instr: 2/2/2/1 - 2/2/3/0 - timp. perc.(3)
           Alt.Instr: 3/2/3/2 - 4/2/3/1 + contrabass
f.broad.p. (No. 1) Jonathan Hastings (Treb.)/Ian Partridge (Ten.) Norman Jones (Vc.) -
             6 July 1966
f.p.   (No. 2) Blackburn Sinfonia/Roy Rimmer - Blackburn Cathedral,
             18 December 1965
f.broad.p. (No. 2) Northern Junior Philharmonic Orchestra/Myers Foggin -
             15 January 1970
Pub: Novello, 1964 (No. 1), 1965 (No. 2)

Seven Greek Love Songs - song cycle for baritone and piano (1964)
[Words: Meleager trans. Dudley Fitts - 1. Fanfare 2. Flowers 3. A Curse
4. The Mosquito 5. Night 6. Lullaby 7. The Poet's Epitaph]
Commissioned by the Bridport and West Dorset Music Club
Dur: 12'
f.p.   John Shirley Quirk (Bar.)/Geoffrey Bush (Pno.) - Bridport, Dorset 30
             November 1964 (Bridport and West Dorset Music Club)
f.Lon.p.   Benjamin Luxon (Bar.)/Geoffrey Bush (Pno.) - 27 February 1970
f.rec.   Benjamin Luxon (Bar.)/Geoffrey Bush (Pno.) - *Chandos ABRD 1053 (and*
             MC), CHAN 8830(CD)
Pub: Galliard, 1969; Stainer & Bell

Cantata Piccola for baritone, SATB chorus, two violins, cello and harpsichord (or piano) (1965)
[Words: Shakespeare
1. Take, O, take those lips away, from `Measure for Measure'
2. Did not the heavenly rhetoric of thine eye, from `The Passionate Pilgrim']
Dedicated to Ron and Peggy Mason
Dur: 6'
f.p.   London Recital Group/Richard Sinton - Wigmore Hall, London,
             17 February 1965
f.broad.p.   Michael George/BBC Singers/Hamilton Ensemble/Nicholas Cleobury -
             23 March 1980
Pub: Novello, 1969 (vocal score)

Piano Sonatina No. 1 (1965)
Dedicated to Lyn (Leonard Pearce)
Dur: 9'
f.p.   Geoffrey Bush - BBC Radio 3, 25 October 1967
f.conc.p.   Geoffrey Bush - Leighton House, London, 5 July 1972
f.recs.   Eric Parkin - *Chandos DBRD 2006-2 (and MC)*
             Eric Parkin - *J. Martin Stafford JMSCD3 (CD)*
Pub: Elkin, 1966; Novello

The Equation - opera in one Act (1965-67)
[Libretto by Geoffrey Bush after John Drinkwater's play "X=0"]
Commissioned by the Sacred Music Drama Society and dedicated to Penny and Michael
Self
Dur: 40'
Instr: 1/1/1/1 - 1/2/1/0 - perc. organ. Vc. (+ 2 Sop. 2 Ten. Bar. Bs-Bar. BS soloists
             and offstage female chorus)
f.p.   Sacred Music Drama Society, cond. Geoffrey Bush - All Saints Church,
             Margaret Street, London, 11 January 1968
f.broad.p.   cond. Meredith Davies - Radio 3, 7 February 1976
Producer: Julian Budden
Pub: Elkin, 1967; Novello (vocal score)

Two Shelley Songs for unaccompanied SATB chorus (1967*)
[1. Music when soft voices die 2. Ozymandias]

No. 2 dedicated to John and Elizabeth Elliott
Dur: 5'30"
f.broad.p. BBC West of England Chorus/Philip Moore - September 1968
Pub: Novello, 1956 (No. 1), 1967 (No. 2)
No. 2 also arr. for unaccompanied TTBB men's chorus
Pub: Galaxy Music, New York
(* completion date - the first song originates from c.1945)

Music for Orchestra (1967)

Commissioned by Jones & Crossland Limited on behalf of the County of Shropshire for
the Shropshire Schools Symphony Orchestra and dedicated to the composer's friends
Patricia and Richard Bishop
Dur: 13'30"
Instr: 3/2/2/1 - 4/3/2/1 - timp. perc.(4/6). pno.(1/2). str.
f.p.   Shropshire Schools Symphony Orchestra/Geoffrey Bush - Shrewsbury,
            28 March 1968
f.broad.p. BBC Training Orchestra/Meredith Davies - Radio 3, 25 August 1971
f.rec.   London Philharmonic Orchestra/Vernon Handley - *Lyrita SRCS 57, SRCD 252*
            (CD)

Seven Limericks for two-part choir and school orchestra (1968)

[1. The Man with the Nose like a Trumpet 2. The Suicide
 3. The Girl who played Jigs on her Flute 4. The Girl with the Tyrian Lyre
 5. The Nautical Lady of Portugal 6. The Confusing Curate
 7. The Composer and the Critic]
Written for University College Junior School, Hampstead
Dur: 5'
Instr: (max.) 1/1/1/0 - 0/1/0/0/ - perc(5). glock. xyl. pno. str. (no Vas.or Dbs.) +
            recorders
f.p.   University College Junior School Choir and Orchestra/David Norman -
            Hampstead, London, 1968
Pub: Novello, 1970
Later re-worked for two-part (SA or TB) chorus and piano (1993)
Pub: Novello

Missa Brevis Salisburiensis (Salisbury Mass) for SATB chorus and organ (1968)

Dur: 8'
f.p.   Choir of Salisbury Cathedral - Eucharist, Easter Day, Salisbury Cathedral,
            6 April 1969
f.rec.   Canterbury Cathedral Choir/Allan Wicks - *Alpha ACA 502*
Pub: Novello, 1969

Magnificat and Nunc Dimittis, Collegium Magdalenae Oxoniense for SATB chorus and organ (1968)

Dedicated to Bernard Rose
Dur: 6'
f.p.   Choir of Magdalen College, Oxford/Bernard Rose with Jeremy Suter (organ) -
            Evensong, Magdalen College, Oxford, 4 June 1969
f.rec.   above artists - *Argo ZRG 722*

Pub: Novello, 1969

A Menagerie for unaccompanied SATB chorus (1969)
[1. Tiger (William Blake) 2. Cuckoo (Shakespeare `Love's Labours Lost')
3. Monkey house (Anon.)]
Dedicated to Peter and Elaine (Self)
Dur: 5'
f.broad.p. BBC Chorus/Peter Gellhorn - 14 December 1970
f.rec.   Westminster Singers/Richard Hickox - *Chandos ABTD 1479(MC), CHAN
           8864(CD)*
Pub: Elkin, 1971; Novello

Psalm 24 for SATB chorus and organ* (1969)
Commissioned for the centenary of Croydon Parish Church
Dur: 4'
Instr:*   (optional) 2 Tpt. 2 Tbn. Timp.
f.p.   Croydon Parish Church Choir/Michael Fleming - Croydon, Surrey,
           4 January 1970
f.rec.   Cantebury Cathedral Choir/Allan Wicks - *Alpha ACA 502*
Pub: Novello, 1969 (vocal score)

Piano Sonatina No. 2 (1969)
Dur: 7'30"
f.p.   Geoffrey Bush - Purcell Room, London, 27 February 1970
f.broad.p. Geoffrey Bush - Radio 3, 27 April 1970
f.rec.   Eric Parkin - *J. Martin Stafford JMSCD3 (CD)*
Pub: Braydeston Press, 1974

Two Choruses for unaccompanied SATB chorus (1969)
[1. Fog (Charles Dickens `Bleak House')
2. Drop, drop slow Tears (Phineas Fletcher)]
Dur: 7'
f.broad.p. BBC Singers/Nicholas Cleobury - 23 March 1980
f.rec.   (No.2) Canterbury Cathedral Choir/Allan Wicks - *Alpha ACA 502*
Pub: Basil Ramsey,1976

Five Medieval Lyrics - song cycle for baritone and piano (1970)
[1. Colloquy (Anon.) 2. Confession (Charles of Orleans) 3. Carol (Anon.)
4. The Vanity of Human Wishes (Anon.) 5. Rutterkin (attrib. John Skelton)]
Written for John Barrow and dedicated to Julie, the composer's wife
Dur: 9'
f.p.   John Barrow (Bar.)/Geoffrey Bush (Pno.) - Balliol College, Oxford,
           3 December 1972
f.broad.p. above artists - 31 January 1973
f.Lon.p.   above artists, Purcell Room, 10 April 1974
Pub: Elkin, 1971; Novello

A Nice Derangement of Epitaphs*, for unaccompanied SATB chorus (1971)
[1. Prologue: Death be not proud (John Donne) 2. A Baby (Robert Herrick)

3. A Sailor (Shakespeare and `Greek Anthology', trans. Dudley Fitts)
4. A Bartender (Geoffrey Bush) 5. A Veteran (Shakespeare)
6. A Critic (`Greek Anthology' trans. Dudley Fitts)
7. A Bootlegger (Raymond Chandler and 16th cent. Anon.)
8. A Beast of Burden (Anon.)]
Commissioned by the Collegiate Choir of Illinois Wesleyan University, USA and written in memory of the painter, Maurice de Sausmarez and the English musician, Thurston Dart

Dur:	13'
f.p.	Collegiate Choir of Illinois Wesleyan University/David Nott - Illinois, USA, 14 May 1972
f.Brit.p.	BBC Singers/Kerry Woodward - BBC, 22 September 1975
Pub:	Elkin, 1972; Novello

(* The title is taken from Sheridan's play `The Rivals')

Lord Arthur Savile's Crime - opera in one Act (1972)
[Libretto: Geoffrey Bush after Oscar Wilde]
Commissioned by the Guildhall School of Music and Drama

Dur:	50'
Instr:	2/1/1/2 - 2/2/1/0 - timp. perc. pno. str. (+ 2 Sop. MS. Con. 2 Ten. 3 Bar. 1/2 Bs.Bar. + optional SATB chorus)
f.p.	Guildhall School of Music and Drama, cond. Vilem Tausky, 5 December 1972
Producer:	Dennis Maunder
f.broad.p.	soloists/Musicians of London/Simon Joly - Radio 3, 27 July 1986
Producer:	Chris de Souza
Pub:	Novello

Daffydd in Love - Three Poems for baritone, SATB chorus and piano (1974)
[Words: Daffydd ap Gwilym trans. Joseph Clancy
1. The Seagull 2. In a Tavern 3. The Judgement]
Commissioned by the Redcliffe Festival of British Music

Dur:	12'
f.p.	John Barrow (Bar.)/Vaughan Williams Singers/Geoffrey Bush (Pno.) - Purcell Room, London, 10 April 1974 (Redcliffe Concert)
f.broad.p.	Michael George (Bar.)/BBC Singers/Harold Lester (Pno.) cond. Nicholas Cleobury - 23 March 1980
Pub:	Basil Ramsey

The Cat who went to Heaven - music theatre piece in one Act (1974)
[Libretto: Geoffrey Bush after Elizabeth Coatsworth]
Written for the London University Extra-Mural Summer School and dedicated to Margaret (Cottier) and Joanne (Verden)

Dur:	35'
Instr:	1/1/1/1 - 1/1/1/0 - timp. perc. pno. Vc. (+ Sop. Ten. Bar. Narr. mime group and 3 speaking parts. SAB chorus)
Alt.Instr:	perc.(2). pno.
f.p.	members of the London University Extra-Mural Summer School, cond. Geoffrey Bush - Westonbirt, Gloucestershire, 8 August 1974
Producers:	Margaret Cottier and Joanne Verden

Pub: Basil Ramsey, 1990; Thames (vocal score)

Magnificat and Nunc Dimittis: St. Paul's Service for SATB chorus and organ (1976)
Written for performance in St. Paul's Cathedral and dedicated to Christopher Dearnley
Dur: 5'30"
f.p.   St. James' Church Choir - Evensong, St. James' Church, Sussex Gardens,
            London, 22 October 1978
f.rec.   Canterbury Cathedral Choir/Allan Wicks with David Flood (Organ) - *Alpha
            ACA 502*
Pub: Basil Ramsey, 1978

A Little Love Music - song cycle for soprano, tenor and piano (1976)
[1. Hide Absalom, thy guilty tresses clear (Geoffrey Chaucer)
 2. The bailey beareth the bell away (Anon.)
 3. Merry Margaret, a midsummer flower (John Skelton)
 4. With margerain gentle (John Skelton)
 5. Sweet, let me go (Anon.)
 6. I love and I hate (Caius Valerius Catullus, trans. Geoffrey Bush)
 7. And wilt thou leave me thus? (Thomas Wyatt)
 8. This is the key of the Kingdom (Anon.)]
Dur: 10'
f.p.   Teresa Cahill (Sop.)/Ian Partridge (Ten.)/Geoffrey Bush (Pno.) - BBC Radio 3,
            3 February 1979
f.rec.   above artists - *Chandos ABRD 1053 (and MC), CHAN 8830(CD)*
Pub: Basil Ramsey, 1978

Concertino No. 2 for piano and instrumental ensemble (1976)
Dur: 10'30"
Instr: 1/1/1/1 - 1/2/1/0 - perc. str. (0/0/1/1/1)
f.p.   Hamish Milne/Hamilton Ensemble/Nicholas Cleobury - BBC,
            23 March 1980
Pub: Basil Ramsey

Two Carols for SATB chorus and organ (1977)
[1. 'Twas in the year that King Uzziah died (Advent)
 2. Gabriel of high degree (The Annunciation)]
No. 2 dedicated to John Boulton Smith
Dur: 5'
f.rec.   Canterbury Cathedral Choir/Allan Wicks with David Flood (organ) - *Alpha
            ACA 502*
Pub: Novello, 1963 (No. 1); Basil Ramsey, 1980 (No. 2)

The Holy Innocent's Carol - for unison voices, piano and percussion (1978)
Dedicated to Jane (Fisher)
Dur: 2'30"
Pub: Novello, 1968; Hinshaw Music, North Carolina, USA.

The Bookrest Carol for unison voices, organ (piano duet) and optional percussion (1978)

Dedicated to Julie (Bush)
Dur: 2'
Pub: Basil Ramsey, 1980 (vocal score)

Phantoms for soprano, girls' (boys') chorus and instrumental ensemble* (1978)
[1. The bloody brothers (ballad) 2. Lowlands away (sea shanty)
 3. The unfortunate Miss Bailey (George Colman the Younger)]
Commissioned by the Leeds Girls' choir and dedicated to Bruce Montgomery and his wife
Anne
Dur: 11'30"
Instr: 1/1/1/1 - 1/1/1/0 - timp. pno. str. (0/0/0/1/1)
f.p.   Sarah Leonard (Sop.)/BBC Singers/Hamilton Ensemble/Nicholas Cleobury -
           BBC, 23 March 1980
Pub: Basil Ramsey, 1984 (vocal score)
* also arr. by the composer for brass band accompaniment

A Stevie Smith Cycle for high voice, oboe, cello and piano (1981)
[Words: Stevie Smith 1. Admire Cranmer! 2. The broken heart 3. My cats
 4. Avondale 5. Farewell 6. Is it wise?]
Commissioned by the BBC and dedicated to the composer's sister-in-law,
Jo McKenna, who introduced him to Stevie Smith's poetry
Dur: 14'
f.p.   Ian Partridge (Ten.)/Valerie Darke (Ob.)/Christopher van Kampen
           (Vc.)/Jennifer Partridge (Pno.) - Manchester, 20 November 1981
Pub: Novello
Nos. 3 and 4 also arr. by the composer for high voice and piano
Pub: Novello, 1990

Trumpet March for organ (1981)
Written in memory of my friend David Munir
Dur: 5'
f.p.   Christopher Dearnley - St. Paul's Cathedral, London, 29 July 1981 (at the
           Royal Wedding)
f.rec.   Allan Wicks - *Alpha ACA 502*
Pub: Basil Ramsey, 1982

Daystar in Winter - Carol sequence for SATB chorus and organ (1982)
[Words: Charles Causley]
Commissioned by the Harrow Choral Society
Dur: 13'
f.p.   Harrow Choral Society/Bryan Fairfax - Trinity Church, Harrow,
           20 November 1982
Pub: Basil Ramsey, 1982

Cuisine Provençale - scena for medium voice and piano (1982)
[Words: Virginia Woolf from `To the Lighthouse']
Commissioned by the Songmaker's Almanac and dedicated to M. et Mme. Paul Dunand
Dur: 4'
f.p.   Felicity Palmer (M/S)/Graham Johnson (Pno.) - London, 4 September 1982

Pub: Stainer & Bell, 1984 (in an Album of Eight Songs for medium voice and
            piano)

Two Legends for SATB chorus and piano/organ (1984)
[1. Joseph of Arimathea 2. Clerk Stephen]
Dur: 5'30"
f.p.   Illinois Wesleyan University Collegiate Choir/David Nott - Illinois Wesleyan
            University, Bloomington, USA, 8 December 1991
Pub: Stainer & Bell, 1985

Two Love Lyrics for medium voice and piano (1984)
[1. Love, for such a cherry lip (Thomas Middleton)
 2. Venus and Adonis* (Robert Greene)]
* Commissioned by the English Song Award for the 1985 Brighton Festival and
dedicated to the memory of Frances Poulenc
Dur: 4'
f.p.   (complete) Susannah Self (Con.)/Geoffrey Bush (Pno.) - British Music
            Information Centre, London, 18 March 1985
f.p.   (No. 2 only) the competitors - 13 May 1985 (Brighton Festival)
Pub: Stainer & Bell (No.1), 1984 (in an Album of Eight Songs for medium voice
            and piano); Novello, 1983 (No.2)

Mirabile Misterium (A great and mighty wonder): song cycle for high voice and piano* (1985)
[1. A marvellous thing have I mused in my mind
 2. Tyrly, tyrlow 3. There is a Flower sprung of a tree
 4. Jesu Christ, my leman sweet 5. Blessed Mary, mother virginal
 6. When I see on Rood, Jesu my leman
 7. Out of your sleep arise and wake]
Commissioned by Warren Hoffer of Arizona State University, USA and dedicated to
Warren Hoffer and Mary Pendleton
Dur: 12'
Alt.   Instr: *Vn. Vn. Va. Vc. Hpschd.
f.p.   David Johnston (Ten.)/Virginia Black (Hpschd.)/Britten String Quartet -
            Concert Hall, BBC Broadcasting House, London, 26 October 1988
Pub: Novello, 1988

Love's Labours Lost - symphonic cycle for soprano, baritone and orchestra (1986)
[Words: Shakespeare]
Dur: 18'
Instr: 2/2/2/2 - 2/3/3/0 - timp. perc. str.

Tributes - Five respectful pieces for clarinet and piano (1986)
[1. Artie Shaw 2. Harold Arlen 3. Darius Milhand 4. Erik Satie
 5. Joseph Horovitz]
Dur: 9'
Pub: Thames, 1986

Four Chaucer Settings, for baritone, oboe and piano (1987)
[1. Saint Valentine 2. Hymn to the Virgin 3. Merciless Beauty 4. Envoy]
Dur: 9'
f.p.   John Shirley Quirk (Bar.)/Sara Watkins (Ob.)/Geoffrey Bush (Pno.) - BBC,
            20 February 1990
Pub: Novello
No. 3 also transcribed by the composer for baritone and piano
Pub: Novello, 1990

Consort Music - Six Victorian Sketches for string orchestra (1987)
Dedicated to Roderick Swanston
Dur: 9'
f.p.   BBC Concert Orchestra/Ashley Lawrence - BBC, 15 October 1990
Pub: Thames, 1989

Old Rhymes Re-set for high voice and piano (1987)
[Trad. or Anon. texts 1. The Test 2. Aubade 3. Severn Sand
4. An Encounter 5. Nonsense Song]
Dur: 9'
f.Brit.p.   Ian Partridge (Ten.)/Geoffrey Bush (Pno.) - Lauderdale House, Highgate,
            London, 10 May 1995
Pub: Stainer & Bell, 1990

Love's Labours Lost - opera in 2 Acts (1988)
[Libretto by Geoffrey Bush after Shakespeare]
Dur: 120'
Instr: 2/2/2/2 - 2/3/3/0 - timp. perc. hpschd. str. (+ 3 Sop. 2 M/S. 2 Bs-Bar and SATB
            chorus)

Zodiac Variations - song cycle for high voice and piano (1989)
[Words: David Gascoyne 1. Aries 2. Gemini 3. Taurus 4. Cancer 5. Leo
6. Virgo 7. Libra 8. Scorpio 9. Sagittarius 10. Capricorn 11. Aquarius
12. Pisces]
Dur: 12'
f.p.   The Song Maker's Almanac - Lilian Watson (Sop.), Henry Herford (Bar.),
            Anthony Rolfe Johnson (Ten.), Graham Johnson (Pno.) - Wigmore Hall,
            London, 20 March 1990
Pub: Novello

Yesterday: song cycle for high voice and piano, `Nine Songs for Kay' (1990)
Words: Charles Causley
[1. Daniel Brent 2. Lady Jane Grey 3. Smugglers' Song 4. Mistletoe
5. Sleigh Ride 6. By the Tamar 7. Morwenstow: a dialogue 8. Transience
9. Wishes]
Commissioned by Music at Leasowes Bank Farm and dedicated to Lewis Kay Bush, the
composer's youngest grandson.
Dur: 11′
f.p.   Ian Partridge (Ten.)/Jennifer Partridge (Pno.) - Leasowes Bank Farm,
            31 August 1990 (Leasowes Bank Festival)

f.Am.p.   Maria Jette (Sop.)/Rees Allison (Pno.) - Hamline University, 13 January 1991
Pub: Thames

Suite Champêtre for piano (1990)
[1. Prélude 2. Siciliene 3. Hornpipe à l'Anglaise 4. Marche et Musette
5. Passacaille 6. Final]
Dedicated to Eric Parkin
Dur: 13′
f.p.   Geoffrey Bush - Illinois Wesleyan University, Bloomington, USA,
           3 October 1991
f.rec.   Eric Parkin - *J. Martin Stafford JMSCD3 (CD)*
Pub: Thames

A Little Triptych (for a birthday) for unaccompanied SATB chorus (1991)
[1. Soliloquy (Anon.) 2. The Vigil (Anon.) 3. Hymn to Diana (Ben Jonson)]
Dedicated "for the Carringtons - `rejoice with me for I have found that which was lost'"
Dur: 6′
Pub: Thames

Pavans and Galliards, for wind quintet (1992)
Dur: 13′
f.p.   Syrinx - British Music Information Centre, London, 21 October 1993
Pub: Thames

Four Pieces for piano - Set 2 (1993)
Dur: 9′
f.rec.   Eric Parkin - *J. Martin Stafford JMSCD3 (CD)*
Pub: Thames

Matthew's Tunes for piano, 4 hands (1993)
[1. March 2. Musical Box 3. Barcarolle 4. Hornpipe]
Written for the composer's eldest grandson
Dur: 5'
f.rec.   Eric Parkin - *J. Martin Stafford JMSCD3 (CD)*
Pub: Thames, 1994

archy at the zoo, for high voice and piano (1994)
[Words: don marquis 1. centipede 2. camel and giraffe 3. hippopotamus
4. hen 5. octopus 6. man and monkey 7. penguin 8. ichneuman 9. shark
10. young whale]
Commissioned by maria jette (Sop.) and rees alison (Pno.)
Dur: 8′
Pub: Thames

Rudi's Blues for two guitars (pupil and teacher) (1994)
Written in memory of the conductor, Rudolf Schwarz, who had premiered the composer's
Symphony No. 1 at the 1954 Cheltenham Festival
Dur: 1'30"
Pub: Chanterelle Verlag (Heidelberg, Germany)

Rudi's Blues for piano (1995)
Extended version of the above.
Dur: 2´
f.rec.   Eric Parkin - *J. Martin Stafford JMSCD3 (CD)*
Pub: Thames

Laus Deo - four settings of familiar texts for SATB chorus and organ (1996)
[1. The Lord is my Shepherd (Psalm 23) 2. God be in my Head (Anon.)
 3. Jesu, the very thought is sweet (St. Bernard trans. J. M. Neale)
 4. O praise God in his holiness (Psalm 150)]
Pub: Thames

Cradle Song (Berceuse sur les touches blancs) for soprano, recorder (or flute) and piano (1996)
[Words: Geoffrey Bush - Welsh text by Nerys Jones]
Commissioned by John Turner and dedicated to Ian Parrott on his birthday.
Dur: 2'30"
f.rec.   Alison Wells (Sop.)/John Turner (Rec.)/Keith Swallow (Pno.) - *TAB IPI (CD)*

Albatross - music for the film* (1997)
Instr: Cl. Hn. Vn. Vn. Va. Vc. Db. (and SATB Chorus)
(*An animated film by Paul Bush based on Coleridge's **The Rime of the Ancient Mariner**)

ARRANGEMENTS

(1)   Orchestral

Two Schubert Scherzos (1938-40)
[1. completed from the unfinished Piano Sonata in C, D.840
 2. completed from the unfinished Symphony in B minor, D.759]
Dur: 14'
Instr: 2/2/2/2 -2/2/3/0 - timp. str.
f.p.   BBC Midland Orchestra/Gilbert Vinter - BBC, 14 September 1949
Pub: Elkin, 1957; Novello

Sonata for two pianos in B flat major (after Thomas Arne*) (1939)
Dur: 4'30"
f.broad.p. Robert and John South, 16 June 1958
Later arr. for orchestra and published as `Sinfonietta' (c.1946)
Instr: 1/1/1/1 - 2/1/0/0 - timp. str.
f.broad.p. BBC Scottish Orchestra/Robert Irving - 6 August 1946
Pub: Augener, 1952; Stainer & Bell
(* The Fifth Sonata for harpsichord with an additional second piano part. Bush had heard a performance of a Mozart piano sonata to which a second piano part had been added by Greig)

A Little Concerto on themes by Arne for piano and string orchestra (1939)
Dedicated to Julian Herbage and Anna Instone
Dur: 8'
f.p.   John Wills/BBC Symphony Orchestra/Trevor Harvey - BBC Bristol,
        29 April 1941
Pub: Elkin, 1966; Novello

Martini Fantasia for piano and string orchestra (arr. from John Field c.1949)
Dur: 10'
f.p.   Eric Parkin/Welbeck String Orchestra/Maurice Miles - BBC Latin
        American Service, January 1950
Pub: Novello

Henry Bishop: Overture - The Miller and his Men (Concert ending c.1949)
Dur: 7'
Instr: 1/2/2/2 - 2/2/1/0 - timp. str.
f.p.   Bournemouth Municipal Orchestra/Trevor Harvey - Bournemouth,
        16 January 1949
f.broad.p. BBC Welsh Orchestra/Arwel Hughes - 3 February 1953
Pub: Novello

Matthew Locke: Suite - Psyche arr. for string orchestra (in collaboration with Francis Harvey c. 1957)
Dur: 8'
f.p.   Riddick String Orchestra/Kathleen Riddick - BBC, 1 February 1959
Pub: Novello, 1957

Prelude in the style of Handel arr. from Mozart K.399 for string orchestra (c.1958)
Dedicated to Ruth and Christopher Fisher
Dur: 5'
f.p.   BBC West of England Light Orchestra/Frank Cantell - November 1959
Pub: Augener, 1958; Stainer & Bell

(2)   Keyboard

Sonata for two pianos in C major, after Sterndale Bennett
Based on the one movement concerto for two pianos
Dur: 7'
f.broad.p. Ian Lake/Geoffrey Bush - Radio 3, 20 March 1969

Mozart: Piano Sonata in F (K.497) re-scored for two pianos
Dur: 23'

(3)   **Choral**

Castle Gordon (after Sterndale Bennett) arr. for unaccompanied SATB chorus
[Words: Robert Burns]
Dur: 2'30"
Pub: Novello, 1972

(4)   **Vocal**

Nine Songs from the Ballad Operas arr. for voice (Sop. Ten. Bar.) and piano
[1. By the simplicity of Venus's doves (Bishop: `A Midsummer Night's Dream')
 2. Pleasing tales in dear romances (Arne: `The Guardian Outwitted')
 3. Softly lulling, sweetly thrilling (Hook: `Wilmore Castle')
 4. Though cause for suspicion appears (Linley: `The Duenna')
 5. Ere bright Rosina met my eyes (Shield: `Rosina')
 6. Come, every man now give his toast (Dibdin: `Poor Vulcan')
 7. Should you ever find her complying (Arne: `Achilles in Petticoats')
 8. By the beer as brown as a berry (Lampe: `The Dragon of Wantley')
 9. In the grove, friend to love (Attwood: `The Escape')
Pub: Novello, 1982
Nos. 3, 6 and 8 arr. by the composer for baritone and small orchestra.
Dur: 5'30"
Instr: 2/2/2/2 - 2/2/0/0 - timp. str.
Pub: Novello

(5)   **Arrangements of the music of John Ireland**
All commissioned by the John Ireland Trust

Two Symphonic Studies
[1. Fugue 2. Toccata]
Dedicated to Norah Kirby and the John Ireland Trust
Dur: 10'30"
Instr: 2/2/2/2 - 4/3/3/1 - timp. perc.(2). str.
Pub: Boosey & Hawkes, 1971

Scherzo and Cortège, from Julius Caesar
Dur: 6'
Instr: 2/2/2/2 - 3/3/3/1 - timp. perc.(2). db.(2).
Pub: Boosey & Hawkes, 1971

A Downland Suite - completed transcription for string orchestra
Dur: 16'30"
f.p.   BBC Concert Orchestra/Christopher Adey - BBC broadcast,
        27 July 1981
Pub: R. Smith

Elegiac Meditation - transcription for string orchestra
Dur: 6'30"
Pub: Novello, 1988

Missa Brevis: St. Stephen's Mass for unaccompanied SATB Chorus - completed
Dur: 5'30"
Pub: Braydeston Press

BIBLIOGRAPHY

Anon.   **Geoffrey Bush - catalogue of published works**. Novello.

Bush, Geoffrey   **Musical Form** (in) **Chambers Encyclopaedia.** 1950 rev. 1966.

Bush, Geoffrey   **Musical Creation and the Listener.** London: Frederick Muller, 1954 rev. 1967; USA: Hawthorn Books Inc., 1966.

Bush, Geoffrey   **Prophet in his own country - Sterndale Bennett.** Composer No. 21, Autumn 1966.

Bush, Geoffrey   **Heard near Tiflis.** Composer No. 29, Autumn 1968.

Bush, Geoffrey   **People who live in Glasshouses.** Composer No. 37, Autumn 1970.

Bush, Geoffrey   **Hugh the Drover Rides Again.** Records and Recordings, June 1979.

Bush, Geoffrey   **Song and chamber music** (in) **The Athlone History of Music in Britain, V: The Romantic Age.** ed. Nicholas Temperley. London: The Athlone Press, 1981.

Bush, Geoffrey   **Left, Right and Centre.** London: Thames Publishing, 1983.

Bush, Geoffrey   **An Unsentimental Education and other musical recollections.** London: Thames Publishing, 1990

Bush, Geoffrey   Introduction to **John Ireland: a catalogue, discography and bibliography** by Stewart Craggs. London: OUP, 1993.

Palmer,
Christopher   **Geoffrey Bush and his Music.** Novello

Rooper, Jasper   **Geoffrey Bush.** Musical Times, December 1967.

14

Francis Chagrin
(1905–1972)

Historiette d'amour for piano (1927)
Score dated: Zurich, 13 September 1927
Dur: 2'30"

Movement for string quartet (1927)
Score dated: Zurich, 2 October 1927

Violin Sonata (1927 rev. 1931)
Score dated: (in revision) 14 March 1931
Dur: 10'

Intermezzo for piano (c.1927-28)
Dur: 4'

Fromm - song for voice and piano, with violin or cello obligato (1928 rev. 1971)
[Words: Gustav Falke]
Score dated: Zurich, 22 October 1928
Dur: 2'15"
Pub: Novello, 1971 (as Two German Songs)

Bitte - song for voice and piano (1928 rev. 1971)
[Words: Hermann Hesse]
Dur: 2'
Pub: Novello, 1971 (as Two German Songs)

Piano Quintet (1928)
Score dated: 23 October 1928
Dur: 11'
f.broad.p. Norbert Wethman Quintet - 20 May 1940

Suite in the ancient style for piano (c.1928-30)
Dur: 2'40"

Theme and Variations for piano 'Hommage to Schumann' (1930)
Dur: 9'15"

Rondo for piano (1930)
Score dated: 6 April 1930

Suite Roumaine for piano (1932)
Dur: 5'
f.Brit.p.   Kathleen Cooper - BBC, 27 November 1939
Pub: Augener (Galliard) 1950

Sonatine for piano (1932)
Score dated: 19 September 1932

Two Marches for piano (1933)
Score dated: 19-27 July 1933

Lamento for string quartet (1935)
Dur: 5'10"
Also arr. as wordless SATB part-song
Scored dated: Paris, 13 March 1935
Pub: Chester

Only Tell Her that I Love - song for voice and piano (1936)
[Words: Lord Cutts]
Score dated: 29 June 1936
Dur: 1'15"

Mother, I cannot mind my wheel - song for voice and piano (1936)
[Words: Walter Savage Landor]
Score dated: 23 September 1936
Dur: 1'30"
Pub: Les Editions de Paris, 1939; Ricordi, 1965
Also arr. SATB chorus
Pub: Ricordi, 1970

We'll go no more a-roving - song for voice and piano (1936)
[Words: Lord Byron]
Score dated: 25 September 1936
Dur: 2'
f.Brit.broad.p. Ernest Frank - 29 November 1948
Pub: Les Editions de Paris, 1939; Novello (as No. 1 of Four English Songs)

Absence - song for voice and piano (1936)
[Words: Walter Savage Landor]
Score dated: 28 September 1936
Dur: 1'30"
Pub: in France 1937; Novello (as No. 2 of Four English Songs)

Time of Roses - song for voice and piano (1936)
[Words: Thomas Hood]
Score dated: 2 October 1936
Dur: 1'

It was a Lover and his Lass - song for voice and piano (1936)
[Words: Shakespeare]
Score dated: 7 October 1936
Dur: 1'30"
Pub: privately in France c.1936

Dirge: Come away death - song for voice and piano (1936)
[Words: Shakespeare]
Score dated: 10 October 1936
Dur: 2'
f.Brit.broad.p. Ernest Frank - 29 November 1948
Pub: Les Editions de Paris, 1939; Novello (as No. 3 of Four English Songs)

Blow, blow thou winter wind - song for voice and piano (1936)
[Words: Shakespeare]
Score dated: 12 October 1936
Dur: 2'
Pub: in France, 1936; Novello (as No. 4 of Four English Songs)
Also arr. for voice and chamber ensemble:
Instr: Fl. Cl. (or Ob.d'amore) string quintet (or string orchestra)
f.p.   Sybil Michelow (M/S)/Christopher Hyde-Smith (Fl.)/Jennifer Paul
            (Ob.d'am)/English String Quartet, with Francis Baines (Db.)/Francis Chagrin -
            BBC Radio 3, 19 May 1971

Can't you do the samba? - song for voice and piano (1937)
[Words: Roger Macdougall]
Pub: Latin American, 1937

The Angelus - song for voice and piano (1937)
[Roger Macdougall]
Pub: Sun Music, 1937

Etude for piano (1937)
Score dated: 29 June 1937
Dur: 2'

Fairy Tale - suite for piano (1937)
Dur: 5'

Lento for violin, clarinet and piano (1937)
Score dated: 20 July 1937
Dur: 2'30"

Cradle Song for voice and piano (1937)

[Words: William Blake]
Dur: 2'15"
Pub: Les Editions de Paris 1939; Francis, Day & Hunter 1952
(also pub. as piano solo and SSA Chorus and piano)
(N.B. An orchestral version also exists in MS)

Two Piano Pieces (1937-38)
[1. Moment perdu 2. Sicilienne]
Written for Chagrin's wife, Eileen
Dur: 3'
f.p.   Geoffrey Philippe
Pub: Chappell, 1951 (also arr. for string orchestra/quintet)

Capriccio for string orchestra (1938)
Dur: 4'
Alt.instr: string quartet with db. (ad.lib)

Scherzo for flute and violin (or two violins) (1939)
Dur: 4'15"

Echoes of Hungary for salon orchestra (1939)
Instr: 2Vn. Va. Vc. Db. Gtr. Acc. Pno.
f.broad.p. Michaeloff Orchestra - 6 August 1939

The Three Souls - ballet (1939)
[1. The Soul of Ambition (from `Melody for Life')
 2. The Soul of Faith 3. The Soul of Love - Mazurka]
Instr: 1/1/1/1 - 0/1/1/0 - perc. str. (or quintet)
f.broad.p. Charles Brill Orchestra/Charles Brill - 9 June 1939

Divertimento for flute and violin (1939)
Score dated: 11 November 1939
Dur: 4'15"

Toccata for piano (1939)
Score dated: 18 November 1939
Dur: 5'45"
f.p.   Lance Dossor - BBC, 28 March 1940
f.conc.p.   Hedwig Stein - RBA Galleries, London, 31 October 1950
Pub: Lengnick, 1948

Berceuse tendre for flute, clarinet, violin and piano (1939)
Score dated: 13 December 1939
Dur: 7'30"

String Quartet (1940)
Dur: 22'30"

Scherzo for violin, clarinet and piano (1940)

Score dated: 6 February 1940

Berceuse for light orchestra (1940)
Dur: 3'
Instr: 1/1/1/1 - pno. str.
f.broad.p.   Westminster Players - 28 July 1940
Pub: Clef-Music, 1953

Piano Concerto (1941 rev. 1971)
Score dated: March 1941
Dur: 25'
Instr: 2/2/2/2 - 4/2/3/1 - timp. perc.(3) str.
f.p.   Franz Osborn/London Symphony Orchestra/Francis Chagrin - Royal College
             of Music, London, 4 February 1944 (CPNM Concert)
f.broad.p.   Alice Heksch/Radio Hilversum Orchestra/Paul van Kempen - Hilversum
             Radio, April 1951 (recorded in Paris)
f.Eur.conc.p. Yvonne Loriod/Orchestre Radio Symphonique de Paris/Francis
             Chagrin - Paris
Pub: Lengnick, 1948 (arr. for two pianos by the composer)

Legende Orientale for cello and piano (1941)
Dedicated "to Margaret and Bill with great admiration and friendship"
Dur: 7'
f.p.   William Pleeth (Vc.)/Margaret Good (Pno.)

Down the Road to Nowhere - Gipsy ballad for voice and piano (1941)
[Words: G. Korel and Fred S. Tysh]
Dur: 2'
f.broad.p.   Louis Voss - 2 August 1941
Pub: Schauer & May, 1942

Two Contrasted Moods for chamber orchestra (1940s)
[1. Desolation (after floods) 2. Exuberance]
Dur: 6'
Instr: 1/1/2/1 - 2/2/1/0 - perc. hp. str.
Pub: Charles Brull

Cuban Beguinne and Samba for orchestra (1940s)
Alt. arr. by Phil Cardew
Instr: 2Asax. 2Ten.sax. 3Tpt. 2Tbn. Db. Perc. Pno.

Aubade d'Automne for small orchestra (c.1940s)
Dur: 6'30"
Instr: 2/1/2/1 - 1/1/1/0 - perc. hp. str.

Suite Bretonne for orchestra (c.1940s)
[1. Berceuse Bretonne (Breton Peasant Lullaby)
 2. La Bourée d'Auvergne (French Country Dance)
 3. Quand Biron voulet danser (Rustic Frolic)]

Dur: 6'
Instr: 1/1/2/1 - 2/1/1/0 (or 2/0/0/0) - perc. hp. pno. str.
f.p.   BBC Midland Light Orchestra/Gilbert Vinter - October 1946
Pub: Charles Brull

Capricco for saxophone quartet (1945)
Dedicated to the Michael Krein Saxophone quartet
Dur: 4'
Instr: Sop. Al. Ten. Bar.(Bs.)
f.p.   Michael Krein Saxophone Quartet

Scherzo for wordless SATB chorus (1945)
Score dated: 4 June 1945
f.p.   cond. Francis Chagrin - London, 26 June 1946

Prelude and Fugue for two violins (1945)
Score dated: 20 July 1945
Dur: 7'
f.p.   Max Rostal/Maria Lidka - London, 13 July 1946 (CPNM Recital)
f.broad.p. above artists - BBC European Service, 22 January 1947
f.Brit.broad.p. above artists - Third Programme, 5 June 1950
f.Eur.p. Francine Villers/Nicole Lepinte - Unesco House, Paris, 27 February 1951
          (International Music Council Concert)
Pub: Augener (Galliard), 1950

Symphony No. 1 (1946-59 rev. 1965)
"Dedicated to Jo Jo and Lawrence Leonard with affectionate friendship"
Dur: 28'30"
Instr: 2+picc./2/2/2 - 4/3/3/1 - timp. perc. vib. xyl. hp. str.
f.p.   BBC Northern Orchestra/Stanford Robinson - BBC Home Service, 24
          November 1963
f.p.   (rev. version) Royal Philharmonic Orchestra/Francis Chagrin - Odeon Cinen
          Swiss Cottage, London, 15 March 1966 (St. Pancras Festival)
f.Eur.p. Orchestre Philharmonique/Francis Chagrin - ORTF, Paris, 23 June 1971
Pub: Novello, 1967

Prelude and Fugue for orchestra (1946)
Dur: 11'
Instr: 2/2/2/2 - 4/2/2/0 - timp. perc.(2) str.
f.p.   London Philharmonic Orchestra/Basil Cameron - Royal Albert Hall,
          London, 2 September 1947 (Promenade Concert)
f.Eur.p. French National Orchestra/Roger Desormière - Paris, 8 July 1948
Pub: Mills, 1957

Serenade boiteuse (Farewell Serenade) for orchestra (c.1940s)
Dur: 5'45"
Instr: 2/2/2/2 - 4/2/1/0 - perc. hp. str.

Serenata Sentimentale for wind band (c.1940s)

Dur: 2'45"
Instr: 3/2/2/2 - 4/3/3/1 - perc.(2)

Marcia Eroica for wind band (c.1940s)
Dur: 4'30"
Instr: 3/2/2/2 - 4/3/3/1 - perc.(2)

The Wings of England* for brass band (c.1940s)
Dur: 4'15"
(* Derived from the music to `The Black Cobra' q.v.)

Rêverie for light orchestra (c.1940s)
Dur: 3'
Instr: 1/0/1/0 - 0/0/0/0 - str.
Alt.Instr: (i) Fl. Cl. Hp. Perc. (Cel.) Vn. Va. Vc.
            (ii) Saxophone quartet
Pub: Inter Art

Concert Rumba for two pianos (1948)
Dedicated to "My Eileena", the composer's wife, Eileen
Dur: 8'30"
f.broad.p. Joan and Valerie Trimble - 1948
Pub: Lengnick, 1948
Later in 1948 Chagrin orchestrated the Concert Rumba, at the suggestion of Walter
Goehr:
Dur: 7'30"
Instr: 2+picc./2/2/2 - 4/3/3/1 - timp. perc.(2) hp. pno. str.
Alt.Instr: 2/1/2/1 - 2/2/3/0 - perc. pno. str.
f.p.   BBC Theatre Orchestra/Walter Goehr - 1948
Pub: Lengnick, 1948
In 1951 Roy Douglas made a shortened version of the Concert Rumba with reduced
orchestration:
Dur: 4'
Instr: 1/1/2/0 - 0/2/1/0 - perc. pno. str.
Pub: Lengnick, 1951

Lamento Appassianato for string orchestra (1948)
Written in memory of Chagrin's parents - the score is dated: London,
6 September 1948
Dur: 11'
f.p.   broadcast on BBC's Latin American Service, January 1950
f.Brit.broad.p. London Philharmonic Orchestra/Norman del Mar - Third
            Programme, 9 November 1953
f.conc.p.   Hallé Orchestra/Sir John Barbirolli - Free Trade Hall, Manchester,
            5 May 1954
f.Eur.p.   Orch/Pierre Capdevielle - French Radio
Pub: Augener (Galliard), 1951

Alpine Holiday for orchestra (1949)
Dur: 4'
Instr: 2/1/2+3sax./1 - 2/2/2/0 - timp. perc. acc. hp. str.
Pub: Dix, 1949 (arr. Ronald Hanmer)

Scherzo for saxophone quartet (1949)
f.broad.p. Michael Krein Saxophone Quartet - 10 October 1949

Promenade for orchestra (1949)
Dur: 3'
Instr: 1/1/2/1 - 1/1/1/0 - perc.(2) hp. pno. str.
f.broad.p. BBC Midland Light Orchestra/Gilbert Vinter - Home Service,
            10 November 1949
Pub: Francis, Day and Hunter, 1953

Aquarelles: Portraits of Five Children* for piano solo/duet (1950)
Dur: 5'
f.p.   Wilfrid Parry - BBC, 18 February 1952
Pub: Augener (Galliard), 1951
Also arr. for string orchestra
f.p.   cond. Stanford Robinson
(* The portraits are of friends the composer knew as a child)

Thrills of Spring 'Joyeux Printemps' for light orchestra (1950)
Dur: 3'
Instr: 1/1/2/1 - 2/2/1/0 - perc. glock. hp. str.
f.broad.p. BBC Midland Light Orchestra/Gilbert Vinter - Home Service,
            16 March 1950
Pub: Charles Brull, 1950 (orch. Roy Douglas)

The Counsel - unaccompanied SATB part song (1950)
[Words: Alexander Brome]
Dur: 3'45"
Pub: Augener (Galliard), 1952

Divertimento for wind quintet (1950)
Dur: 9'
Instr: Fl. Ob. Cl. Bsn. Hn.
f.broad.p. Virtuoso Chamber Ensemble - Edward Walker (Fl.), Roger Lord (Ob.), Sidney
            Fell (Cl.), Ronald Waller (Bsn.), John Burden (Hn.) - 9 June 1955
Pub: Augener, 1952
Later arr. for brass quintet (March 1968)
Instr: 2Tpt. Hn. Tbn. Tba
f.broad.p. Northern Brass Ensemble - June 1970
Pub: Galliard, 1969

Elegy for string quartet (or string orchestra) (1950-51)
Score composed between 12 March 1950 and 10 February 1951
Dur: 7'

f.p.   (qt. version) Virtuoso Ensemble
f.p.   (str. orch. version) Harvey Phillips String Orchestra/Harvey Phillips - BBC
            Third Programme, 3 September 1956
Pub: Mills, 1956

Sarabande for string orchestra (1951)
Dur: 6'
f.p.   Guildford Philharmonic Orchestra/Crossley Clitheroe - St. Mary's Church,
            Guildford, 31 May 1951
f.broad.p. BBC Northern Orchestra/John Hopkins - 10 June 1953
Pub: Lengnick, 1951
Also arr. for oboe* and string orchestra (or string quintet)
f.p.   Peter Newbury/London Studio Players
Alt.Instr: *Fl. Cl. Hn. Tpt. Sop.Sax. Ten.Sax. Hn. Vn.
f.p.   Michael Krein (Sax.); Max Jaffa (Vn.); John Burden (Hn.) - all with London
            Studio Players
Pub: Lengnick, 1952 (also arr. with piano acc.)

Noel - song for voice and piano (1951)
[Words: Theophile Gautier]
Dur: 2'
Pub: OUP and 'Time and Tide' 1951 (Children's Christmas number)

London Sketches for light orchestra (1950s)
Dur: 3'
Instr: 2/2/2/1 - 2/2/1/0 - perc. hp. pno. str.

Three Pieces for harp (1950s)
[1. Impromptu   2. Sarabande 3. Toccata]
Dur: 10'15"

Two Soliloquies for solo cello or viola (1950s)
Dur: 7'

Bagatelles for string quartet (1952)
Dur: 8'30"
f.broad.p. Element Quartet
Pub: Augener (Galliard), 1954
Also arr. for string orchestra (1952)
f.p.   Royal Philharmonic Orchestra/John Pritchard - BBC Maida Vale Studios,
            12 May 1953 (ICA/LCMC Concert in association with the BBC)
f.conc.p.   Goldsbrough Orchestra/Harry Samuel - Chelsea Town Hall,
            28 October 1954
f.Am.p.   Albany Symphony Orchestra/Edgar Curtis - New York

Charme d'amour for light orchestra (1952)
Dur: 3'30"
Instr: 1/1/2/1 - 0/0/0/0 - pno. str. (1/1/1/1)
Pub: Southern Music, 1952 (arr. B. Thompson)

Dream of Vienna for orchestra (1952)
Dur: 3'15"
Instr: 2/1/2/1 - 2/2/3/0 - hp. pno. str.
f.broad.p. Northern Ireland Orchestra/David Curry - 9 October 1957
Pub: Metro Music, 1952 (also arr. piano solo)

Improvisation and Toccatina for solo clarinet (1953)
Written for and dedicated to Jack Brymer - the score is dated 25 April 1953
Dur: 9'30"
f.p.   Jack Brymer - BBC Third Programme, 9 April 1954
Pub: Augener (Galliard), 1955

Trois Pièces Tendres for piano (1954)
Dur: 4'40"
Pub: Augener (Galliard), 1955
Also arr. for string orchestra
f.p.   London Studio Strings/Francis Chagrin - BBC, 15 June 1971
Also arr. for oboe d'amore (or clarinet) and string trio (or piano)
Dedicated to Jennifer Paul

Nocturne for chamber orchestra (1956)
Dur: 6'
Instr: 2/1/2/1 - 2/1/1/0 - perc. hp. str.
f.p.   BBC Scottish Orchestra/Colin Davis
Pub: Mills, 1956

Roumanian Fantasy (Rhapsody) for harmonica (or violin) and orchestra (1956)
Commissioned by the BBC and dedicated to Larry Adler - the score is dated London, 8
May 1956
Dur: 16'
Instr: 2/2/2/2 - 4/2/3/0 - timp. perc. vib. xyl. hp. str.
f.p.   Larry Adler/BBC Concert Orchestra/Francis Chagrin - Royal Festival Hall,
           London, 9 June 1956 (Light Programme Music Festival)
f.Am.p.   John Sebastian/Florida Symphony Orchestra
f.rec.   Larry Adler/Pro Arte Orchestra/Francis Chagrin - *EMI EG7 64134-4(MC),
           CDM7 64134-2(CD)*
Pub: Mills, 1956 (also arr. harmonica/violin and piano)
Arr. for light orchestra by Malcolm Binney (1969)
f.p.   Midland Light Orchestra/Francis Chagrin - December 1969

Two Sea Shanties - accompanied part songs for tenor, TTBB chorus and piano (or violin) (1956)
[Trad. 1. A-roving 2. Early in the morning*]
Dur: 4'
Alt.Instr: *(No. 2) Picc. Vn.(s) Perc.(2)
Pub: Novello, 1967

Suite No. 1 for orchestra (1957)
[1. Toccata 2. Fughetta 3. Finale]
Dur: 17'15"
Instr: 2/2/2/2 - 4/2/2/0 - timp. perc. glock. vib. xyl. tam. str.
f.p.   BBC Scottish Orchestra/Norman del Mar - BBC, 30 July 1963
Pub: Mills, 1957

Tango Mirage for orchestra (1957)
Dur: 2'30"
Instr: acc. pno. str.
Pub: Inter Art, 1957 (arr. piano solo)

Dialogue* for piano and orchestra (1957)
Dedicated to Peter Sachs - the score is dated 11 August 1957
Dur: 24'
Instr: 2/1/2/1 - 4/2/2/1 - perc.(2) str.
f.p.   John McCabe/BBC Northern Symphony Orchestra/Francis Chagrin - BBC,
          6 December 1971 (pre-recorded 20 August 1971)
(* Subtitled `Four Arguments on one theme')

Fives and Sevens for orchestra - incomplete (1950s)

Clockwork Revels for light orchestra* (1958)
Dur: 2'
Alt.Instr: *Pno. (Cel.) and Wind Quintet
Pub: Francis, Day & Hunter, 1958

Concerto for conductor and orchestra (1958)
Commissioned by Gerard Hoffnung
f.p.   Joseph Cooper (Pno.)/Hoffnung Symphony Orchestra/Gerard Hoffnung -
          Royal Festival Hall, London, 21 November 1958   (Hoffnung Interplanetary
          Music Festival)
f.rec.   (exc.) above performance - *EMI CMS7 63302-2(CD)*

Cobbler's Polka for light orchestra (1959)
Dur: 2'35"
Pub: Dominant, 1959 (arr. piano solo)

Two Studies for jazz quartet (1959)
Dur: 7'
Instr: Tpt. Ba.Sax. Db. Drums

Tussle for piano (1960)
Dur: 1'10"
Pub: Ricordi, 1963

Six duets for treble and tenor recorders* (1960)
Dur: 9'45"
Alt.Instr: *2 Vn. 2 Fl. 2 Ob. 2 Cl. 2 Sax. 2 Harm.

Pub: Schott, 1963

Album for Nicholas for piano (1960)
Written for the composer's son, Nicholas.
Dur: 6'15"
Pub: Chappell
Also arr. for recorder quartet
Instr: 2 Desc. Treb. Ten.
Pub: Chappell, 1963
arr. string orchestra
Pub: Chappell, 1968

Serenade for piano (1960)
Dur: 1'15"
Pub: Ricordi, 1963

Mazurka for descant and treble recorders with piano (1961)
Dur: 4'
Pub: Schott, 1963

Viennese Waltz for descant and treble recorders with piano (1961)
Dur: 3'
Pub: Schott, 1963 (version for piano solo in MS)

Barcarolle and Berceuse for descant (or tenor) recorder* and piano (1961)
Dur: 2'20"
Alt.Instr: *Fl. Ob. Cl. Vn. Va.
Pub: Schott, 1962

The Ballad of County Down (mostly in D major) (1961)
Dur: 5'
Instr: 2+picc./2/2/2 - 4/2/3/1 - perc. hp. str.
f.p.   Forbes Robinson (Spkr.)/Hoffnung Symphony Orchestra/Francis Chagrin -
              Royal Festival Hall, London, 28 November 1961 (Hoffnung Astronautical
              Musical Festival)
f.recs.   above performance - *EMI CMS7 63302-2(CD)*
              Philharmonia Orchestra/Michael Massey - *Decca (set) 444 921-2DF2 (CD)*

Three French Folk Songs for recorder trio and piano* (1961)
[1. Chantons, je vous en prie 2. Las! En mon doux printemps
 3. Le Chanson du Marie (Chanson bretonne)]
Dur: 4'15"
Instr: Desc. Treb. Ten. (with tamb. ad.lib.)
Pub: Schott, 1962
(* Derived from earlier orchestral material c.1941)

Renaissance Suite for chamber orchestra* (1962)
[1. Intrada marziale 2. Pavana e Gagliarda
 3. Canzona Lamentevole 4. Rondo Gioioso]

Dur: 7'30"
Instr: 1/1/1/1 - 0/0/0/0 - str.
Alt.Instr: *(i.) Fl. Ob. Cl. Bsn.
            (ii.) Fl. Ob. Cl. Bsn. and String Quintet
Pub: Novello, 1969
Also arr. string orchestra
f.broad.p. London Studio Strings/Francis Chagrin - 2 December 1963

Lullaby for chamber orchestra* (1962)
Dur: 3'30"
Instr: 2/0/2/1 - 0/0/0/0 - str.
Alt.Instr: *(i.) 2 Fl. 2 Cl. Bsn. (or Vc.) and Pno. (or String Quintet)
            (ii.) 2 Desc.Rec. 2 Treb.Rec. Vc. (or Bsn.) Pno.
            (iii.) 4 Vns. Bsn. (or Vc.) Pno.
Pub: Novello, 1970

Four Lyric Interludes for solo instrument and strings* (1963)
Dur: 5'15"
Alt.Instr: *solo instrument or piano/string quartet
f.p.   (oboe d'amore and piano version) - Nottingham Festival, July 1970
Pub: Novello, 1969
Also arr. for string orchestra
f.broad.p. London Studio Strings/Francis Chagrin - 15 June 1971

Three Pieces for descant/treble recorders and piano (1960s)
[1. Jota Aragonesa 2. Serenata Napolitana (Annabella) 3. Tarantella]

Marriage Bureau - ballet (1963)
Dur: 15'
Instr: Cl. Tpt. Hn. Db. Perc. Pno.
f.p.   "Collages" Company, Edinburgh Festival
f.Lon.p.   Savoy Theatre
Choreography: Gillian Lynne

Sonatina for solo oboe (or flute) (1964)
Dur: 9'
f.broad.p. Sarah Francis - 27 November 1970
f.Lon.p.   Malcolm Messiter - Purcell Room, 21 May 1972
Pub: Novello, 1969

Symphony No. 2 (1965-70)
Score written between November 1965 and March 1970
Dur: 30'
Instr: 3/2/2/2 - 4/3/3/1 - timp. perc. vib. org. xyl. hp. str.
f.p.   Bournemouth Symphony Orchestra/Francis Chagrin - Winter Gardens,
            Bournemouth, 20 May 1971
Pub: Novello

Serenade 'Jottings for Jeremy' for string orchestra* (1966)
Dur: 9'30"
Alt.Instr: *(i.) String Quartet (ii.) Wind Quartet (2 Fl. 2 Cl.)
           (iii.) Sax. Quartet (iv.) Recorder Quartet
Pub: Novello, 1968
Also arr. Wind Quartet
Instr: Fl. Ob. Cl. Bsn.
f.broad.p. Gerald Jackson (Fl.)/Michael Dobson (Ob.)/Sidney Fell (Cl.)/Anthony Judd
           (Bsn.) - 29 October 1968
Pub: Novello, 1968

Sept Piecès pour 8 instruments (or piano duet) (1966)
[1. Promenade 2. Etude 3. Rêverie 4. En Bateau 5. Nostalgie 6. Petite Valse
7. Parade des soldats de bois]
Dedicated "To Judy"
Dur: 9'45"
Instr: Picc. Fl. Ob. 2 Cl. Hn. 2 Bsn.
Pub: Novello, 1969 (instrumental version)

Concerto for double bass and orchestra (1966)
Sketches only

Six duets for equal (or mixed) instruments (1967)
Dur: 12'55"
Pub: Novello

Two Fanfares for 3 equal instruments and percussion (1967)
Dur: 2'15"
Pub: Novello, 1971

Two Fanfares for 4 equal instruments and percussion (1967)
Dur: 1'50"
Pub: Novello

Two Fanfares for Kneller Hall (1967)
Dur: 40" each
Instr: (No. 1) 4 Tpt. Perc. (No. 2) 3 Tpt. (or Tbn.) Perc.

Two Pieces for solo bassoon (or cello) (1967)
[1. Souvenir lointain 2. Conversation animée]
Dur: 5'45"
Pub: Novello, 1969

Castellana - Spanish Dance for light orchestra (c.1968)
Dur: 2'45"
Instr: 1/1/1/1 - 1/1/1/0 - perc. pno. str.
Pub: Novello, 1968

Lullaby for a China Doll for light orchestra (1968)
Score dated: 29 February 1968
Dur: 3'30"
Instr: 1/1/2/1 - 2/1/0/0 - hp. (pno.) cel. str.
Pub: Dominant

Fanfare for 'Adam' (per ardua ad astra) (1968)
Dedicated to Miron Grindea - the score is dated 10 October 1968
Dur: 2'
Instr: 3 Trb. (or 3 Vc./3 Bsn.)
Pub: Novello, 1969

Jeunesse 'Youth' for piano (early work but rev. 1969/70)
[1. Sad Story 2. Mist]

Preludes for 4 (1970)
Dedicated to the Dolmetsch - Schoenfeld Ensemble
Dur: 12'45"
Instr: Rec. Vn. Vc. Hpschd.
Alt.Instr: Fl. Vn. Vc. Pno.
f.p.   Carl Dolmetsch (Rec.)/Alice Schoenfeld (Vn.)/Eleonore Schoenfeld
            (Vc.)/Joseph Saxby (Hpschd.) - Wigmore Hall, London, 6 February 1970
f.broad.p. above artists - 17 November 1970
Pub: Novello, 1972

Etude for solo violin (1970)
Score dated: 21 April 1970
Dur: 2'30"

Duo Concertante for violin and cello (1971)
Dedicated to Alice and Eleonore (Schoenfeld Duo) - the score is dated
6 November 1971
f.p.   Peter Thomas (Vn.)/Sharon Schoenfeld McKinley (Vc.) - Purcell Room,
            London, 21 April 1972 (SPNM Concert)
f.broad.p. Schoenfeld Duo - Radio Zurich, March 1974

Etudes 'sur blanches et noires' for piano* (1971-72)
[1. Andantino 2. Lento 3. Moderato 4. Lento 5. Vivace]
Score written between January 1971 and July 1972
Dur: 25'15"
(* or harpischord/organ)

Seven Simple Duets for 2 violins (1972)

Nine Miniatures for wind quartet* (1972)
Dur: 18'
Alt.Instr: *(i)String Quartet
            (ii) String Orchestra
            (iii)   Keyboard

CONCERT MUSIC DERIVED FROM THE FILM SCORES

Two Songs from 'Ca Colle' (1934)
[1. Ca Colle (co-wrote with Ouvard - lyrics: F. de Manse)
2. Petite femme (co-wrote with Raymond Wraskoff - lyrics: Charlie Davson)]
Pub: Campbell Connelly, 1934

Five Faces - suite (1937)
Instr: 1/1/1/1 - 0/1/1/0 - perc. pno. str. (2/2/1/1/1)
f.broad.p. Charles Brill Orchestra/Charles Brill - 17 April 1939

Behind the Maginot Line - theme (1938)
f.broad.p. BBC Theatre Orchestra

Animal Legends - suite from the film (1938)
[1. Dragon Legend 2. Barnacle Goose 3. Monsters 4. The Mermaids
5. Roc Legend 6. Unicorn Legend]
Dur: 8'30"
Instr: 1/1/1/1 - 0/1/1/0 - perc. pno. str. (2/2/1/1/1)
Alt.Instr: (i) 1/1/2/1 - 2/1/1/0 - perc. hp. pno. str.
            (ii) Ob. Cl. Bsn. Vn. Vc.
            (iii)   Fl. Ob. Vn. Vc. Hp
f.broad.p. Charles Brill Orchestra/Charles Brill - 19 September 1938

Ripe Earth - suite (1939)
f.broad.p. Charles Brill Orchestra/Charles Brill - 9 June 1939

En Voyage - scherzo and trio from 'Law and Disorder' (1940)
Instr: small orchestra

Folk Song, Pastorale and Scherzo from 'Britain's Youth' (1940)
f.broad.p. Charles Brill Orchestra/Charles Brill - 30 August 1940

Behind the Guns - suite for orchestra (1940)
[1. Steel 2. Guns 3. Shells (Conveyor Belt) 4. Tanks 5. Shipyard Activity 6. Convoy]
Dur: 10'30" (*alt. version 5'15")
Instr: 2/2/2/2 - 4/2/3/1 - perc.(2) pno. str.
Alt.instr: * 2/1/2/1 - 2/2/3/0 - perc. str.
f.p.   * International Radio Orchestra/Louis Voss - recorded 1951 (issued on
            Bosworth's commercial library music label, 3 discs, *BX 517, 518 & 519*)
Pub: Bosworth (movts. 1,3 and 5 only)

Nursery Suite from 'Bringing up Babies' (1941)
[1. Daybreak 2. Mischief 3. Daydreams 4. Playtime]
Dur: 8'
Instr: 1/1/2/1 - 2/1/1/0 - perc. hp. str.
f.p.   Light Concert Orchestra/Michael Krein - BBC Home Service,
            29 November 1949
Pub: Francis, Day & Hunter, 1951

Fughetta* from 'Castings' (1944)
Instr: 1/1/2/1 - 2/1/1/0 - perc. str.
(* Later incorporated in Suite No. 1 for orchestra q.v.)

Yougoslav Sketches* for chamber orchestra from 'The Bridge' (1946)
[1. Village Feast 2. Omladina (Childhood) 3. Dusk 4. The New Bridge]
Dur: 9'50"
Instr: 2/1/2/1 - 2/2/3/0 - perc. hp. str.
f.p.   BBC Midland Light Orchestra/Gilbert Vinter
Pub: Metro Music, 1950

'Il basso ostinato' - Divertimento from 'Easy Money' (1947)
Instr: 2+picc./2/2/2 - 4/3/3/1 - timp. perc. hp. str.

The River and the Jungle - suite from 'Tree of Life'* (1948)
[1. Arrival: The River and the Jungle 2. "Yaligimba"
 3. The Village awakens 4. Ride to the market (Scherzo)
 5. Forest aflame 6. Return: The Mountains and the Sea]
Dur: 15'10"
Instr: 2/1/2/1 - 2/2/2/0 - perc.(2) hp. str.
(* Originally entitled Symphonietta Fouristique)

Beggar Theme* from 'Last Holiday' (1950)
Dur: 3'
Instr: 2/1/2/1 - 2/2/2/0 - timp. perc. hp. str.
f.rec.   *Columbia DB 2702(78)*
Pub: Chappell, 1950 (arr. Cecil Milner)
Also arr. for barrel organ
(* Chagrin composed the theme in two minutes and was played in the film by David McCallum as the blind street fiddler)

Dance Music from 'Last Holiday' (1950)
[1. Samba 2. Quick Step 3. Blues 4. Pack up your troubles]

Helter Skelter* - a comedy overture (1950-51)
Dur: 7'
Instr: 3/2/2/2 - 4/3/3/1 - perc.(3) hp. str.
f.p.   Film Festival Orchestra/Roger Desormière - Biarritz Film Festival, 1950
f.Brit.p.   London Philharmonic Orchestra/Sir Adrian Boult - Royal Festival Hall, London, 16 January 1952
f.rec.   London Philharmonic Orchestra/Sir John Pritchard - Lyrita SRCS 95
Pub: Augener (Galliard), 1951
(* Subtitled 'The Girl with the Hiccups')

Riverside Rondo from 'The Happy Family' (1952)
Dur: 3'
Instr: 1/1/1/1 - 2/2/3/0 - hp. perc. str.
Pub: Dick James, 1952 (arr. Ernest Tomlinson)

Four Orchestral Episodes from 'The Intruder' (1953)
[1. Preamble 2. Conflagration 3. Pursuit at night - Nocturne 4. Vindication]
Dur: 12'30"

Suite from 'The Beachcomber' (1953)
[1. Arrival at the Island 2. Amao (Serenade) 3. Promenade au Marche
4. Dramatic Interlude "Elephant"]

The Eva Smith theme from 'An Inspector Calls' (1954)
Dur: 3'
Instr: 2/1/2/1 - 2/2/2/0 - perc. hp. pno. str.
Pub: Francis, Day and Hunter, 1954 (piano solo)

Theme from 'The Deep Blue Sea' (1955)
[Words: Roy Hamilton]
Dur: 2'
Pub: Robbins Music, 1955

Gone - Foxtrot from 'The Deep Blue Sea' (1955)
[Words: Guy Morgan]
Dur: 2'
Pub: Charles Brull, 1955

Prelude - March from 'The Colditz Story' (1955)
Dur: 3'30"
Instr: 3/2/2/2 - 4/3/3/1 - timp. perc.(3) hp. pno. str.

Don't say Goodbye - Foxtrot from 'The Colditz Story' (1955)

March from 'The Cockleshell Heroes' (1955)
f.broad.p. BBC Concert Orchestra/Francis Chagrin - Light Programme, 6 May 1956
            (Melody Hour)

Theme from 'The Scamp' (1957)
[Words: Tony Rima]
Dur: 2'
f.broad.p. Northern Ireland Orchestra/David Curry - October 1957
Pub: B.F. Wood Music, 1957 (arr. piano solo)

Primavera - theme from 'The Snorkel' (1958)
Dur: 3'
Pub: Mills, 1958 (arr. piano solo)

Marcia Rustica from 'Danger Within' (1958)
Instr: 1/1/1/1 - 1/1/1/0 - perc.(2) hp. pno. str.

FILM MUSIC

(i)   **Documentary Films**

Five Faces - Strand Films for M.O.I. Malaya (1937)
Director: Alex Shaw

Animal Legends - Strand Films for M.O.I. (1938)
Director: Alex Shaw

Derrière la ligne Maginot (Behind the Maginot Line) - March of Time for M.O.I., Paris (1938)

Silent Battle - Pinebrook, Denham (1939)
US Title: Continental Express
Director: Herbert Mason

Britain's Youth - Strand Films for M.O.I. (1939)
Director: Alex Shaw

Ripe Earth - Charter (1939)
Director: Roy Boulting
Music conducted by: Charles Brill

Law and Disorder - British Consolidated (1940)
Director: David MacDonald

Behind the Guns - Merton Park for M.O.I. (1940)
Director: Montgomery Tully

Carnival in the Clothes Cupboard - J. Walker Thompson cartoon for Lux Soapflakes (1941)
Directors: John Halas and Joy Batchelor

Telefootlers - Verity Films for M.O.I. (1941)
Director: John Paddy Carstairs

A-tish-oo - Verity Films for M.O.I. (1941)
Director: Maxwell Munden

Canteen on Wheels - Verity Films for M.O.I. (1941)
Director: Jay Lewis

Fable of the Fabrics - J. Walter Thompson cartoon for Lux Soapflakes (1941)
Directors: John Halas and Joy Batchelor

Shunter Black's Night Off - Verity Films for M.O.I. (1942)
Director: Max Munden

What's Underneath? - Verity Films (1942)
Director: Henry Cass

Bringing up Babies - Strand Films for Odham's (1942)
Director: Alex Shaw

Free House - Verity Films for M.O.I. (1942)
Director: Henry Cass

The Great Harvest - Rotha Films for C.O.I. (1943)
Director: Jack Chambers

Compost Heaps - Halas & Batchelor cartoon for C.O.I. (1943)
Directors: John Halas and Joy Batchelor

Rationing in Britain - World Wide for C.O.I. (1943)
Director: Ralph Bond

Tank Pranks - Sidney Box for Lintas (1943)
Director: Muriel Box

Barbara Takes a Bath - Verity Films for Sunlight Soap (1943)
Director: Muriel Box

Als drie willen Koppen - W. Larkins cartoon for Dutch Govt. (1944)
Director: William Larkins

Rotterdam - W. Larkins cartoon for Dutch Govt. (1944)
Director: William Larkins

Mrs. Sew and Sew - Halas & Batchelor cartoon for M.O.I. (1944)
Directors: John Halas and Joy Batchelor

Post Early - Halas & Batchelor cartoon for M.O.I. (1944)
Directors: John Halas and Joy Batchelor

How the Motor Car Engine Works - Horizon/Verity Films for Ford Motor Co. (1944)
Director: Max Munden

Castings - Merton Park for High Duty Alloys (1944)
Director: James Rogers

Salvage Trailer - Halas & Batchelor cartoon (1944)
Directors: John Halas and Joy Batchelor

Homes for the People - Basic Films for Odham's (1945)
Director: Kay Mander

The Big Four (What to Eat) - W. Larkins cartoon for Ministry of Food (1945)
Director: William Larkins

Near Home - Basic Films for C.O.I./Ministry of Education (1945)
Director: Kay Mander

Picture Paper - Verity Films for British Council/Illustrated (1945)
Director: Eric Cripps

Victory in the Netherlands - Canadian Army Film Unit (1945)

(Seven) National Savings trailers - W. Larkins cartoons for National Savings Committee (1946)
(Subtitled: Frivolous variations on a simple theme)
Director: William Larkins

Train Trouble - J. Walter Thompson cartoon for Kellogg's (1946)
Directors: John Halas and Joy Batchelor

Radio Ructions - J. Walter Thompson cartoon for Kellogg's (1946)
Directors: John Halas and Joy Batchelor

The Bridge - Data Films for C.O.I. (1946)
Director: Jack Chambers

(Two) Army trailers - W. Larkins cartoons for the War Office (1946)
Director: William Larkins

In Grandma's Day - W. Larkins cartoon for Rowntrees (1946)
Director: William Larkins

(Three) T.C.P. trailers - W. Larkins cartoons for T.C.P. (1946)
Director: William Larkins

(Three) Mars trailers - W. Larkins cartoons for Mars (1946)
Director: William Larkins

What's Cooking? - Halas & Batchelor cartoon for Bovril (1946)
Directors: John Halas and Joy Batchelor

University of Flying - Horizon Films for Ministry of Aviation (1947)
Directors: Max Munden and Albert Rayner
Music conducted by : John Hollingsworth

T. for Teacher - W. Larkins cartoon for Tea Bureau (1947)
Director: William Larkins

Naval Demolition - Concord for Department of Naval Training (1947)

Director: William Larkins

Designing Woman - Merlin Films for Council of Industrial Design (1947)
Director: Roger MacDougall

Long, Long Ago - Basic Films cartoon for Coal Board (1947)
Director: R. K. Neilson-Baxter

Halibut Oil - Merton Park (1947)
Director: Eric Cripps

Just Janie - W. Larkins cartoon for Halex (1948)
Director: William Larkins

How, Which and Why? (series) - Basic Films (1948)
Director: Kay Mander

Men of Merit - W. Larkins cartoon for Electricity Board (1948)
Director: William Larkins

Tree of Life - Lintas/Veritas for Unilever (1948)
Director: G. de Boe

A Fly About the House - Halas & Batchelor cartoon for C.O.I./ Ministry of Health (1949)
Directors: John Halas and Joy Batchelor

R.A.F. - The First Line of Defence - Halas & Batchelor cartoon for C.O.I./R.A.F. (1949)
Directors: John Halas and Joy Batchelor

The Best of Two Worlds - Film Producer's Guild for Pilkington Bros. (c. 1949/50)
Director: Cecil Musk

And Now Today (1949)

Once Upon a Time - Film Workshop for C.O.I. (1949)
(The story of British Clock-making from 1713 to the present day.)

Another Case of Poisoning - Massingham for Ministry of Health with Central Council for Health Education (1949)
Director: John Waterhouse

The British Army (at your service) on Guard - Halas & Batchelor cartoon for C.O.I. (1949)
Directors: John Halas and Joy Batchelor

Mining Review - E.C.T. (c. 1949/50)

Enterprise - W. Larkins cartoon for I.C.I. (1949/50 rev. 1952)
Directors: Peter Sachs and Nancy Hanna

Without Fear - W. Larkins cartoon for E.C.A. (1950)
Director: Peter Sachs

A Family Affair - W. Larkins cartoon for C.O.I./Home Office (1950)
Director: Peter Sachs

Congo Harvest (Tree of Life) - Pathe (1950)

Voices Under the Sea - Concord for Cable & Wireless Ltd. (1951)
Director: Maurice Harvey

The Flying Squad (1951)

In on the Beam - Crown Film Unit for C.O.I./Ministry of Civil Aviation (1951)

Aspro - Halas & Batchelor cartoon (1951)
Directors: John Halas and Joy Batchelor

Energy Foods - Crown Film Unit for C.O.I./Ministry of Food (1951)

A Postcard from Paris - International Realist (1951)
Director: Alex Strasser

Britain's Civil Airways - Crown Film Unit (1951)

Minarets of Santa Sophia - W. Larkins cartoon for E.C.A. (c. 1951)
Director: Peter Sachs

East Meets West - W. Larkins cartoon for Anglo-Iranian Oil Co. (c. 1951)
Director: Peter Sachs

Balance - 1950 - W. Larkins cartoon for I.C.I. (1951)
Director: Peter Sachs

Full Circle - W. Larkins cartoon for British Petroleum (1952)
Director: Peter Sachs

Parents Take Hart - W. Larkins cartoon for Lemon Hart Rum (1952)

Happy Families - W. Larkins cartoon for Lemon Hart Rum (c. 1952)

It's Magic - Film Workshop (1953)
Director: Max Munden

Guinness Clock - Green Park for Guinness (1953)

The Last Straw - W. Larkins cartoon (c. 1953)

Kores - W. Larkins cartoon (1953)

Lux - W. Larkins cartoon (c. 1953)

Air in your Hair - W. Larkins cartoon for Silvikrin (1953)

Cool Custom - W. Larkins cartoon for Frigidaire (1956)

All Lit Up - Halas & Batchelor cartoon for the Gas Board (1957)
Directors: John Halas and Joy Batchelor

Mr. Finlay's Feelings - W. Larkins cartoon for Mental Health (USA Insurance Co.) (1958)

(Six) Road Safety Films - Halas & Batchelor cartoons for C.O.I./ Ministry of Transport (1958-59)
[1. Learning to Bike 2. Boot Bumper 3. Crossing with a Pram
4. Muleheaded Motor-Cyclists 5. Rude on the Road
6. Vehicles Parking]
Directors: John Halas and Joy Batchelor

Piping Hot - Halas & Batchelor cartoon for the Gas Board (1959)
Directors: John Halas and Joy Batchelor

Ways to Security - W. Larkins cartoon for German Insurance Company (1963)

Project `Spear' - Wallace Film Productions for United Steel Co. (1964)
Director: Bill Mason

Prototype - Lion Pacesetters Productions for Ford (1970)

Deadlock - John Halas cartoon (1971)
Director: Janusz Wiktorowsky

Formica for Me - cartoon for Guild Television (c. 1960s)

Gentleman Farmer (ND)

Pool Games (ND)

(ii)   **Feature Films**

Ca Colle - Frogerais, Paris (1934)
Director: Christian Jacque

La Lutte pour la Vie - Gold Star, Paris (1935)

La Grande Croisière - Gold Star, Paris (1935)

David et Goliath - Gold Star, Paris (1935)

Le Bouif chez les Pur-Sangs - Romain Piñes, Paris (1936)

Easy Money - Sydney Box for Gainsborough (1947)
Director: Bernard Knowles
Music conducted by: Muir Mathieson

Helter Skelter - Sydney Box for Gainsborough (1949)
Director: Ralph Thomas
Music played by: London Symphony Orchestra/Muir Mathieson

Last Holiday - Watergate/Associated British (1950)
Director: Henry Cass
Music conducted by: Louis Levy
f.rec.   complete film (V)

The Happy Family - London Independent (1952)
U.S. title: Mr. Lord Says No
Director: Muriel Box

Castle in the Air - Hallmark/Associated British (1952)
Director: Henry Cass

The Good Beginning (1953)
(Chagrin's contribution was the Waltz - the main score was composed by
Robert Gill)

The Intruder - British Lion/Ivan Foxwell (1953)
Director: Guy Hamilton
First screening: Empire Theatre, Leicester Square, London, 15 October 1953
Music played by: Royal Philharmonic Orchestra/Muir Mathieson

An Inspector Calls - Watergate/British Lion (1953)
Director: Guy Hamilton

The Beachcomber - GFD/London Independent (1954)
Director: Muriel Box
f.rec.   complete film (V)

The Deep Blue Sea* - London Films 1955)
Director: Anatole Litvak
(* Francis Chagrin's contribution was the theme song - the main score was composed by Malcolm Arnold q.v.)

The Colditz Story - British Lion/Ivan Foxwell (1955)
Director: Guy Hamilton
First screening: Gaumont Theatre, Haymarket, London, 27 January 1955
Music played by: Goldsbrough Orchestra/Francis Chagrin
f.rec.   complete film (V)

The Cockleshell Heroes* - Warwick/Columbia (1955)
Director: José Ferrer
(Francis Chagrin's contribution was the March - the main score was composed by John Addison q.v.)

Simba - GFD/Group Films (1955)
Director: Brian Desmond Hurst
First screening: Leicester Square Theatre, London, 20 January 1955
f.rec.   complete film (V)

Charley Moon - Colin Lesslie Productions (1956)
Director: Guy Hamilton
First screening: 14 May 1956
Music conducted by: Francis Chagrin

No Time for Tears - Associated British (1956)
Director: Cyril Frankel

The Scamp - Minter/Lawrie Productions - Renown (1957)
Director: Wolf Rilla
Music conducted by: Francis Chagrin

The Snorkel - Columbia/Hammer (1958)
Director: Guy Green

Danger Within - Colin Lesslie Productions (1958)
US Title: Breakout
Director: Don Chaffey

(Three) Edgar Wallace Films - Merton Park (1960)
1. Clue of the Twisted Candle   Director: Allan Davis
2. Marriage of Convenience   Director: Clive Donner
3. The Man Who was Nobody   Director: Montgomery Tully
Music conducted by: Francis Chagrin

Greyfriars Bobby - Walt Disney (1961)
Director: Don Chaffey
f.rec.   complete film (V)

The Monster of Highgate Ponds - Halas & Batchelor for Children's Film Foundation (1961)
Director: Alberto Cavalcanti

In the Cool of the Day - MGM (1963)
Director: Robert Stevens

INCIDENTAL MUSIC

(a)   **Radio**

The Marriage of St. Francis (1942)
[Henri Ghéon]
Instr: 2/1/2/1 - 2/1/1/0 - timp. perc. vib. hp. str.
f.broad.p. BBC Home Service - 4 October 1942
Music played by: Orchestra/Francis Chagrin
Producer: John Burrell
Principals: Alan Wheatley, Penelope Dudley-Ward, Belle Chrystall

The Rhine is a River - BBC series 'The Battleground for Peace' (1940s)
Instr: 1/1/1/1 - 2/1/0/0 - perc. hp. str.

Focus: opening and closing theme music - BBC series (1940s)
Instr: 2/0/2/0 - 0/0/0/0 - timp. perc. vib. hp. pno. str.

These Simple Things: 'Clocks' (1946)
Instr: 1/1/4/1 - 1/1/0/0 - perc. hp. pno. str.
f.broad.p. Home Service, 27 September 1946
Music played by: BBC Variety Orchestra/Rae Jenkins
Producer: William Worsley
Narrator: Reginald Arkell

The Bronze Horse (1948)
[James Forsyth]
f.broad.p. BBC Third Programme, 9 January 1948 (recorded in the Aeolian
        Hall, 5 January 1948)
Music conducted by: Francis Chagrin
Producer: Michel St. Denis
Principals: Peggy Ashcroft, Yvonne Mitchell and Paul Scofield
Later arr. for orchestra as Suite Médiévale
[1. Passamezzo 2. Saltarello 3. Pavane 4. Basse danse
 5. Rondo giubilante]
Dur: 9'30"
Instr: 2/1/2/1 - 2/1/1/0 - perc.(2) hp. str.
f.p.   BBC Northern Orchestra/Stanford Robinson
Pub: Charles Brull

Excs. arr. for military band as French Patrol No. 1 (1948)
Dur: 5'30"
Arr. for wind band as French Patrol Nos. 1 and 2 (c.1958)
Dur: 9'30"
Instr: 3Picc. 3Fl. 2Ob. Perc.(3)
f.p.   (exc.) Band of the Royal Military School of Music, Kneller
         Hall/Francis Chagrin - Royal Festival Hall, London, 21 November
         1958 (Hoffnung Interplanetary Music Festival)
f.rec.   above performance - *EMI CMS7 63302-2(CD)*
Other excs. arr. for wind band as Intermezzo Gioviale (1948)
Dur: 3'15"
Instr: 3/2/2/2 - 4/3/3/1 - perc.(2)
Pub: Inter Art, 1968

An Englishman looks at Turkey (1949)
Producer: D. G. Bridson

We speak of France (1950)
[A programme in honour of the visit of President Auriol of France and written
by Christopher Sykes]
f.p.   BBC Home Service, 7 March 1950
Music played by: Goldsbrough Orchestra/Francis Chagrin
Producer: W. Farquaharson-Small
Narrator: Colin Wills

La Surprise de l'Amour (1954)
[Marivaux]
Producer: Weltman
Suite from above (Mouret arr.)
Dur: 6'45"
Instr: 1/2/0/1 - hpschd. str. (2/1/1/1)
f.broad.p. Francis Chagrin Ensemble/Francis Chagrin - Home Service,
         9 January 1957

Danton's Death (1954)
[Georg Buchner]
Instr: 1/0/1/0 - 1/1/0/0 - perc. str. (2/1/1/1)
f.broad.p. 11 and 12 July 1954
Music played by: Orchestra/Francis Chagrin (recorded 5 July 1954)
Producer: R.D. Smith
Suite arr. from above
f.p.   Francis Chagrin Ensemble/Francis Chagrin

(b)   **Television**

(i)   **Series**

Music for BBC TV Newsreel (1957)
Instr: 0/0/1/1 - 2/1/1/0 - perc. pno. str. (1/0/1/0)
Music recorded: 2 May 1957

Uncle Silas (1957)
Music conducted by: Francis Chagrin
First transmission: October 1957

Lullaby for a Baby Planet for solo tuba and orchestra (c.1958-59)
Commissioned by BBC Television for Gerard Hoffnung
Dur: 3'
Instr: 2/2/2/2 - 0/2/3/0 - perc.(2) cel. hp. str.
f.p.   Gerard Hoffnung/Eric Robinson Orchestra/Eric Robinson, BBC
           Television, c.1958-59 ('Music for You' series)

The Four Just Men - ATV (1959)
Producers: Sidney Cole/Jud Kinberg
Directors: Basil Dearden/Don Chaffey/Anthony Bushell/Harry
Watt/William Fairchild/Compton Bennett
First transmission: from 12 September 1959 (39 episodes)

Hotel Imperial - Associated Rediffusion (1960)
Director: Christopher Hodson

Dr. Who (The Dalek Invasion of Earth) - BBC (1964)
[Terry Nation]
Producers: Verity Lambert and Mervyn Pinfield
Director: Richard Martin
Music conducted by: Francis Chagrin
First transmission: BBC 1, from 21 November 1964

Tales from Hoffnung - Halas & Batchelor cartoons for BBC TV Enterprises (1965)
[6 cartoons based on drawings by Gerard Hoffnung
 1. The Symphony Orchestra 2. The Music Academy
 3. The Palm Court Orchestra 4. The Maestro
 5. Professor Ya-Ya's Memoirs 6. The Vacuum Cleaner]
Instr: 2/1/1/1 - 1/1/1/0 - perc. pno. hp. vn. vc. (and solo tuba)
Director: John Halas
Narrator: Peter Sellers

(ii) Commercials (late 1950s)

Cussons Gift Set	Phensic (W. Larkins)
Haliborange	Phoenix
Halibut Oil (Cripps)	Players
Harris Paint Brushes	Shell X100
Horlicks	Silvikrin
Kelloggs	T.C.P.
Milo (Rank Screen Services)	Westclox

(All music conducted by Francis Chagrin)

(c)   Stage

Parade Tricolore de la revue des 'Folies Bergère' (1936)
[Words: Maurice Hermite]
Pub: Enoch, 1936

Haji Baba - an oriental romance in 3 Acts (1937)
[Libretto: Frank Cochrane and Cyril Roberts]
Score dated: 25 November 1937
Instr: piano acc.
Exc. [1. Prelude 2. Street in Teheran]
Dur: 4'30"
Instr: 1/1/1/1 - 0/1/1/0 - perc. pno. str.
f.broad.p. Charles Brill Orchestra/Charles Brill - 11 August 1939

Villa Carlotta - musical play in 3 Acts (c. 1938)
Instr: piano acc. (10 numbers)

The Black Cobra - musical in 2 Acts (1938)
Dur: 36'
Instr: piano acc. (16 numbers)

Topsy Turvy - a musical comedy (1938)
[Libretto: Roger Macdougall and Allan MacKinnon]
Dur: c.40'
Instr: piano acc. (15 numbers)

Melody for Life - play with music (c. 1938-39)
[Words: Lewis Wallace]
See also the ballet 'The Three Souls'

Heartbreak House (1943)
[George Bernard Shaw]
Instr: 2/1/2/1 - 2/1/1/0 - perc. pno. str.
f.p.   Cambridge Theatre, London, 18 March 1943
Music played by: Orchestra/Francis Chagrin
Producer: John Burrell
Principals: Robert Donat, Deborah Kerr

The King Stag (1946)
[Carlo Gozzi]
Instr: Fl. Ob. Hn. Vn. Vc. Hpschd. Pno. Cel.
f.p.   Young Vic Company - Lyric Theatre, Hammersmith,
             26 December 1946
Music conducted by: Francis Chagrin
Producer: George Devine
Principals: Joan Hopkins and John Byron
Later arr. for chamber ensemble as Suite Galante (1952)
[1. Sunset Song "Angela" 2. Deramo 3. Gavotte 4. Rejoicing]
Dur: 9'45"
Instr: Fl. Ob. Hn. Vn. Vc. Hpschd.

Volpone (1952)
[Ben Jonson]
f.p.   Memorial Theatre, Stratford-on-Avon, 15 July 1952
Music played by: Theatre Orchestra/Harold Ingram
Producer: George Devine
Principals: Ralph Richardson, Anthony Quayle and Siobhan
                McKenna

The White Countess (1954)
[J.B. Priestley and Jacquetta Hawkes]
Instr: Vn. Pno.
f.p.   Savile Theatre, London, March 1954
Producer: Hugh Hunt

ARRANGEMENTS

Handel: Water Music arr. orchestra (1940s)
Instr: 2/2/2/2 - 4/2/0/0 - timp. str.

Saint Saens: Dance Macabre arr. orchestra (1940s)

Offenbach: Orpheus in the Underworld (Roi de Beotie arr.) (1940s)

Offenbach: La Belle Helène re-orch. for BBC (1942)
Score dated: 7 January 1942
Instr: 1/1/1/1 - 0/1/1/0 - perc. pno. str.

Tchaikovsky: The Snow Maiden arr.* (1940s)
[* Excerpt - Scene Dansante (Invitation au Trepek)]
Dur: 10'
Instr: 3/3/3/2 - 4/2/3/1 - timp. perc.(2) hp. str.

Purcell: Organ Voluntary in C orch. (c. 1940s)
Dur: 2'30"
Instr: 0/0/0/1 - 2/0/0/0 - str.

Byrd: Earl of Salisbury Pavanne orch. (c. 1940s)
Dur: 1'30"
Instr: 0/0/0/0 - 2/2/0/0 - hp. str. (or str. quintet)

APPENDIX I

SONGS FOR VOICE AND PIANO (1934-36)

L'amour vole (1934)
[Words: Louis Sauvat]
Dur: 1'15"
f.p.   Adrienne Gallon
Pub: Eds. Margueritat c. 1936

Berceuse: Lied (1934)
[Words: Louis Sauvat]
f.p.   Constantin Stroescu - Bucarest, 9 January 1936
f.Brit.broad.p. Mark Raphael - 15 October 1940
Pub: Eds. France Musique, 1934

Ceux du maquis (1934)
[Words: M. van Moppés]
Pub: Salabert, 1934

Le collier rouge: Chanson Dramatique (1934)
[Words: Louis Sauvat]
f.p.   Maud Mary - Bucarest, 9 January 1936
Pub: Eds. France Musique, 1934

Coup de Grisou (1934)
[Words: Louis Potérat]
Dur: 5'
Pub: Eds. France Musique, 1934

Echos d'Andalousie (1934)
[Words: Suzette Desty]
Dur: 2'30"
Pub: Eds. France Mélodie, 1935

Paris, la village et les fauborgs - Waltz (1934)
[Words: M. van Moppés]
Pub: Salabert, 1934

Poème flou (1934)
[Words: Francis Carco]
Score dated: 8 October 1934
Dur: 2'30"
f.p.   Constantin Stroescu - Bucarest, 9 January 1936

f.Brit.broad.p. Mark Raphael - 15 October 1940
Pub: Eds. France Musique, 1934
Also arr. voice and orchestra:
Instr: 2/2/0/2 - 2/0/0/0 - pno. perc. str.

La Rumba du danseur nègre (1934)
[Words: Louis Sauvat]
Pub: Eds. Musicalles Universalles, 1934

Les trois saisons (1934)
[Words: Louis Sauvat]
Written for Adrienne Gallon
Dur: 1'30"
f.p.   Constantin Stroescu - Bucarest, 9 January 1936
Pub: Eds. Margueritat c. 1936

A travers prés, a travers champs (1935)
[Words: Louis Sauvat]
f.p.   Denisys
Pub: Eds. France Mélodie, 1935

Le Bateau Ivre: Chanson Dramatique (1935)
[Words: Louis Sauvat]
f.p.   Marianne Oswald
Pub: Phillipe Parès, 1935

Bella Donna - Tango (1935)
[Words: Charlie Davson]
Pub: Eds. France Mélodie, 1935 ᾽

Complainte (1935)
[Words: Francis Carco]
Dur: 1'50"
f.p.   Constantin Stroescu - Bucarest, 9 January 1936
Pub: Eds. France Mélodie, 1935
Also arr. voice and orchestra:
Instr: 2/2/0/2 - 2/0/0/0 - perc. pno. str.

De toute ma tendresse: Mélodie (1935)
[Words: Charlie Davson]
f.p.   Constantin Stroescu - Bucarest, 9 January 1936
Pub: Eds. H. Benjamin, 1935
Also arr. voice and orchestra:
Instr: 1/1/2/1 - 2/0/0/0 - str.

Les deux amants - Valse Lente (1935)
[Words: Charlie Davson]
f.p.   Constantin Stroescu - Bucarest, 9 January 1936
Pub: Bourcier, 1935

Fii atent la roşu de buze (1935)
f.p.   Viorica Anghel/Tedy Cosma - Sambata, 28 March 1936

La Java Serieuse - Java (1935)
[Words: Louis Sauvat]
f.p.   Hélène Seni - Bucarest, 9 January 1936
Pub: Eds. France Mélodie, 1935

Je n'ai qu'un seul Dieu, c'est l'amour - Blues (1935)
[Words: Jean Bernard-Derosné]
f.p.   Maud Mary - Bucarest, 9 January 1936
Pub: Eds. France Mélodie, 1935

Jet d'eau (1935)
[Words: Suzette Desty]
Dur: 3'

Julot-c'est le plus beau - Java (1935)
[Words: Henri le Pointe]
f.p.   Bordas
Pub: Eds. Musicalles Universalles, 1935

Laisse-moi partir - Tango (1935)
[Words: Charlie Davson]
f.p.   Maud Mary - Bucarest, 9 January 1936
Pub: Eds. Musicalles Universalles, 1935

Loin de Paris (1935)
[Words: Henri le Marchand]
Pub: Lionel Caseaux, 1935

Madrigal (1935)
[Words: Francis Carco]
Dur: 1'
f.p.   Constantin Stroescu - Bucarest, 9 January 1936
Pub: Lionel Cazaux, 1935
Also arr. SATB chorus (1963)

Manola - English Waltz (1935)
[Words: Suzette Desty/Max-Blot]
Pub: Max-Blot, 1935

Un mot sur le sable - Valse Anglaise (1935)
[Words: Charlie Davson]
Pub: Eds. Musique Bourcier, 1935

Un mot tout petit - Slow Foxtrot (1935)
[Words: Louis Sauvat]
f.p.   Hélène Seni - Bucarest, 9 January 1936

Pub: Eds. Musicalles Universalles, 1935

Les Naufragés: Chanson Dramatique (1935)
[Words: Charlie Davson]
f.p.   Damia
Pub: Eds. France Mélodie, 1935

Perle de Cacao - Rumba (1935)
[Words: Louis Potérat]
f.p.   Hélène Seni - Bucarest, 9 January 1936
Pub: Eds. Musicalles Universalles, 1935

Si vous avez souffert: Chanson Dramatique (1935)
[Words: Suzette Desty]
f.p.   Maud Mary - Bucarest, 9 January 1936
Pub: Les Editions de Paris, c. 1935

Le Tango de l'hacienda (1935)
[Words: Louis Potérat]
Pub: Lionel Cazaux, 1935

Ti-ta-ti-del-dou - Slow Foxtrot (1935)
[Words: Charlie Davson]
Pub: Eds. France Mélodie, 1935

Tournez, dansez - Valse Viennoise (1935)
[Words: Louis Potérat]
f.p.   Hélène Seni - Bucarest, 9 January 1936
Pub: Lionel Cazaux, 1935

10 heurs ... Père Lachaise: Chanson Dramatique (1935)
[Words: Suzette Desty/Max-Blot]
f.p.   Maud Mary - Bucarest, 9 January 1936

Haut et court - Marche (1936)
[Words: Louis Sauvat]
f.p.   Bordas
Pub: Coda, 1936

Je cherche partout - Rumba Russe (1936)
[Words: Louis Potérat - English lyrics `If you see my love' by Gene Martin]
f.p.   Charlotte Dauvia
Pub: Francis, Day & Hunter

Madina - tempo di blues (1936)
[Words: Louis Potérat]
Pub: Ray Ventura, 1936

Prenez garde à la peinture (1936)

[Words: Charlie Davson]
Pub: Eds. France Mélodie, 1936

APPENDIX II

SALON MUSIC (1937-40) DERIVED FROM SONG MATERIAL (q.v.)
[Arr. alphabetically]
(* Piano solo versions first performed by Francis Chagrin and Theodor Zweibel
- Bucarest, 9 January 1936)

Bella Donna - Tango
Instr: (i) Vn. Vn. Va. Vc. Vc. Pno.
            (ii) Vn. Vn. Vc. Db. Acc. Sax. Tpt.
f.p.   Mario Melfi and his orchestra
f.broad.p. Cedric Sharpe Sextet - 15 December 1938

Can't you do the Samba?
Pub: Latin American Music, 1949

Ceux du maquis

Cradle Song
Instr: Vn. Vn. Va. Vc. Db. Pno. Fl. Cl.
f.broad.p. Frank Walker Octet - 29 September 1938

De toute ma tendresse - Mélodie
f.broad.p. Frank Walker Octet - 29 September 1938

Les deux amants - Valse Lente
Instr: Vn. Vn. Va. Vc. Db. Pno. Acc. Gtr.
f.broad.p. Eugene Pini Octet - 19 September 1938

Echos d'Andalousie
Instr: (i) 2 Tpt. 2 Tbn. Pno.
            (ii) 2 Cl. 2 Tpt. 2 Vn. Va. Vc. Db.
            (iii) Cl. Acc. Vn. Vc. Perc.
            (iv) string quartet
            (v) string quintet, Pno.
            (vi) Vn. Vn. Va. Vc. Db. Pno. Acc. Gtr.
            (vii) 2/2/0/2 - 2/0/0/0 - perc. pno. str.
f.broad.p. (vi) Eugene Pini Octet - 23 October 1938

Jet d'eau
Instr: 2/2/0/2 - 2/0/0/0 - perc. pno. str.

Je cherche partout - Rumba Russe*
f.broad.p. Eugene Pini Octet - 25 September 1938

Laisse-moi partir - Tango
f.broad.p.   Eugene Pini Octet - 25 September 1938

Loin de Paris
Instr: Vn. Vn. Vc. Db. Pno. Acc. Gtr. (and vocals)
f.broad.p.   Falkman Septet - 20 September 1938

(3) Love Lyrics
[1. Only tell her that I love 2. Time of Roses 3. It was a lover and his lass]
Instr: string orchestra
f.broad.p.   (No. 1 only) The Alphas/Frank Stewart - 9 July 1939

Madina*
Instr: Vn. Vn. Vn. Va. Vc. Db. Gtr. Pno. Acc.
f.broad.p.   Julius Kantrovitch Ensemble - 15 June 1939

Madrigal
Instr: (i) harp quintet (arr. for Leslie Bridgewater)
             (ii) octet
             (iii) Vn. Va. Va. Vc.
f.broad.p.   (ii) Frank Walker Octet - 29 September 1938

Manola - English Waltz

Un mot sur le sable - Valse Anglaise*

Un mot tout petit - Slow Foxtrot

Les Naufragés: Chanson Dramatique

Parade Tricolore ('Folies Bergere')
Instr: (i) organ (arr. for Sandy MacPherson)
             (ii) septet
             (iii) 2 Vn. Vc. Db. Acc. Gtr.
f.broad.p.   (ii) Falkman Septet - 20 September 1938

Paris, la ville et les Fauborgs - Waltz
Instr: string sextet, Acc. Hp. Perc.
f.broad.p.   20 January 1943

Perle de Cacao - Rumba
Instr: octet
f.broad.p.   Walford Hyden - 23 July 1938

Pour valser avec vous*
Instr: (i) trio (ii) octet
f.broad.p.   (ii) Eugene Pini Octet - 25 September 1938

Prenez garde à la peinture

520   Francis Chagrin

Instr: 3 Sax. 2 Tpt. Trb. Gtr. Db. (arr. R. Monta)

Rumba du danseur nègre

Si vos yeux étaient moins bleu*
Pub: Chappell

Soul of love
f.broad.p. Bernard Crooke Piano Quintet - 11 November 1938

Ti-ta-ti-del-dou* - Slow Foxtrot
Instr: 0/0/2/0 - 0/2/1/0 - perc. pno. acc. str. (6/1/1/1)
f.broad.p. Arthur Dulay Orchestra - 24 July 1939

Tango de l'Hacienda
Instr: (i) string quintet, Gtr. Acc. Pno.
           (ii) Vn. Vc. Gtr. Acc. Pno. Drums
f.broad.p. Eugene Pini Octet - 5 September 1938

Tournez, dansez - Valse Viennoise

MS LOCATION

Majority of MS are held by the British Library **(BL)** and by Nicholas Chagrin **(NC)**

Other locations are:

BPL   Fromm (1928 rev. 1971)

BIBLIOGRAPHY

Chagrin, Francis   **A Quartercentury of new music.** Composer, No. 26. Winter
                         1967/68

Frankel, Benjamin   **Francis Chagrin.** SPNM 30th anniversary concert programme, 5
                         February 1973

Tichler, Jonathan   **Francis Chagrin - Music and Tape Catalogue.** April 1976

15

Arnold Cooke
(1906–)

Piano Sonata (1921)

Piano Trio (1923-25)

Air in F minor for piano (c.1924)
f.p. Arnold Cooke - Repton School, 28 June 1924

Violin Sonata (1926-27)

Horn Concerto (1928-29)

String Trio (1929)

Passacaglia, Scherzo and Finale - Octet (1931)
Dur: 15'
Instr: Fl. Ob. Cl. Bsn. Vn. Vn. Va. Vc.
also arr. for string orchestra (1937)
Pub: OUP

Suite for brass sextet (1931)
Dur: 12'
Instr: 2Tpt. 2Hn. 2Tbn.

Harp Quintet (1932)
Dur: 18'
Instr: Hp. Fl. Cl. Vn. Vc.
f.p. Maria Korchinska (Hp.), John Francis (Fl.), Alan Frank (Cl.) Anne
    Macnaghten (Vn.), Olive Richards (Vc.) - Ballet Club Theatre, London,
    17 December 1934 (Macnaghten - Lemare Concert)

String Quartet No. 1 (1933)
Dedicated to the Griller Quartet
Dur: 25'

f.p.   Griller Quartet - Manchester, March 1935
f.broad.p. Griller Quartet - 1936
Pub: OUP

Holderneth: Cantata for baritone solo, chorus and orchestra (1933-34)
[Words: Edward B. Sweeney]
Dur: 30'
Instr: 2/2+ca./2/2 - 4/2/3/1 - timp. str.

Concert Overture No. 1 for orchestra* (1934)
Dur: 8'
Instr: 2/2/2/2 - 4/2/2/1 - timp. perc. str.
f.p.   Hallé Orchestra/R. J. Forbes - Royal Manchester College of Music,
            17 May 1934 (Patron's Fund Concert)
f.Lon.p.   BBC Symphony Orchestra / Sir Henry Wood - Queen's Hall, 30 August 1934
            (Promenade Concert)
(* Third prize in the Daily Telegraph overture competition - the winner was Cyril Scott.)

Three Pieces for piano (1934)
[1. Ostinato 2. Intermezzo 3. Capriccio]
Dur: 7'
f.broad.p. John Wills - 19 April 1936

Duo for violin and viola (1935)
Dur: 15'
Pub: A-AMP

Flute Quartet (1935-36)
Dur: 15'
Instr: Fl. Vn. Va. Vc.
f.p.   Brunner (Fl.)/Student Quartet - Manchester College of Music, 1936
Pub: A-AMP

Viola Sonata (1936-37)
Dur: 20'
f.p.   Keith Cummings (Va.) / Lucy Pierce (Pno.) - Wigmore Hall, London,
            October 1937
Pub: OUP, 1940; (ed. Keith Cummings) A-AMP

Sonata for 2 pianos (1936-37)
Written for the Adolph Hallis concert series and dedicated to Adolph Hallis and Franz
Reizenstein.
Dur: 18'
f.p.   Adolph Hallis/Franz Reizenstein - Wigmore Hall, London, March 1937
f.broad.p. Joan and Valerie Trimble - 14 August 1953
Pub: OUP, A-AMP

Piano Sonata No. 1 (1938)
Dur: 16'

f.p.   Lucy Pierce - Royal Manchester College of Music, c. 1939
f.broad.p. Lamar Crowson - 8 September 1958
f.Lon.p.   Lamar Crowson - Arts Council Drawing Room, London, 1959?
            (Macnaghten Concert)

Violin Sonata No. 1 in G (1939)
Dedicated to Thomas Matthews and Dora Gilson
Dur: 15'
f.p.   Thomas Matthews (Vn.)/Dora Gilson (Pno.)
f.Lon.p.   Maria Lidka (Vn.)/Frank Reizenstein (Pno.) - Cowdray Hall, 21 January 1946
Pub: OUP, 1940

Bedtime Songs - 12 children's songs (1939)
[Words: Arthur Rathkey]
Dur: 8'
Pub: Augener

Labrador - song for voice and piano (1939)
[Words: Hart Crane]

Piano Concerto (1940)
Written at the suggestion of Adolph Hallis who had hoped to premiere the work.
However, he was prevented from doing so as he returned to his native South Africa at the
outbreak of the Second World War.
Dur: 34'
Instr: 2+picc/2/2/2 - 4/3/3/1 - timp. perc. str.
Alt.instr: 1/2/2/2 - 2/2/0/0 - timp. str.
f.p.   Louis Kentner/BBC Symphony Orchestra/Clarence Raybould - 11 November
            1943 (studio performance)

Cello Sonata in B flat (1941)
Dur: 26'
f.p.   William Pleeth (Vc.)/Margaret Good (Pno.) - Wigmore Hall, London, April
            1948
f.broad.p. Amaryllis Fleming (Vc.)/Lamar Crowson (Pno.) - 21 January 1950
f.Eur. p.   Amaryllis Fleming (Vc.)/Lamar Crowson (Pno.) - Paris, 1 February 1950
Pub: Novello, 1960 A-AMP

Four Shakespeare Sonnets for soprano and string orchestra (1941)
[1. Shall I compare thee to a summer's day?
 2. That time of year thou may'st in me behold
 3. How like a winter hath my absence been
 4. From you I have been absent in the spring]
Written at the suggestion of Sophie Wyss and dedicated to her.
Dur: 11'
f.p.   Sophie Wyss (Sop.)/Kathleen Merritt String Orchestra/Kathleen Merritt -
            Wigmore Hall, London, 28 January 1947 (Gerald Cooper Concert Series)
f.broad.p. Max Worthley (Ten.)/London Classical Orchestra/Trevor Harvey -
            13 August 1951

Piano Trio in C (1941-44)

Partly written while his ship was anchored off the Normandy coast during the Allied invasion.

Dur: 23'
Instr: Vn. Vc. Pno.
f.broad.p. Kantrovitch Trio - Hilda Bor (Vn.), Vera Kantrovitch (Vc.), Lilly Phillips (Pno.)

Suite in C for piano (1943)

[1. Capriccio 2. Sarabande 3. Finale - orginally in five movements]

Dur: 7'30" (original version 15')
f.p.   (orginal version) Malcolm Troup - Park Lane House, London, 9 March 1958
f.broad.p. (rev. version) Jean Mackie - BBC, 9 February 1963
f.rec.   Colin Horsley - *Meridian E 77064*
Pub: OUP, 1943 A-AMP (rev. version) 1962
Sarabande - arranged by the composer for organ
Pub: OUP

Variations on an original theme for string quartet (1945)

Dur: 10'

Song for tenor and small orchestra (1945)

[Words: Hoelderlin trans. Frederick Prokosch - Da ich ein Knabe war (Once when I was a boy)]

Dur: 6'
Instr: 2/2/2/2 - 2/0/0/0 - hp. str.

Concert Overture No. 2 'Processional'* for orchestra (1945)

Dur: 8'
Instr: 2/2/2/2 - 4/3/3/1 - timp. perc. str.
f.p.   BBC Symphony Orchestra/Sir Adrian Boult - Cambridge, 26 February 1948 (Cambridge Festival)
f.Lon.p.   London Symphony Orchestra/Basil Cameron - Royal Albert Hall, 20 August 1948 (Promenade Concert)

(* The title was suggested to the composer by the various processions and celebrations which marked the end of the War)

Alla Marcia for clarinet and piano (1946)

Dur: 4'30"
f.p.   Hovingham Hall, 29 July 1951 (Hovingham Festival)
Pub: OUP, 1947; Emerson, 1989

Four Songs for high voice and piano (1946-47)

[1. Soldier from the Wars Returning (A.E. Housman)
2. The Song of Soldiers (Walter de la Mare) 3. Spring (Thomas Nash)
4. Song on May Morning (John Milton)]

Dur: 7'30"
f.p.   Sophie Wyss (Sop.) - Wigmore Hall, London

Two Songs for baritone and piano (1946-47)
[1. O What is that sound that so thrills the ear? (W.H. Auden)
 2. Reconciliation (Walt Whitman)]
Dur: 5'

Symphony No. 1 in B flat (1946-47)
Dur: 35'
Instr: 2/2/2/2 - 4/3/3/1 - timp. perc. str.
f.p.   BBC Symphony Orchestra/Sir Adrian Boult - BBC, 26 February 1949
f.conc.p.   Yorkshire Symphony Orchestra/Maurice Miles c.1950-51
Pub: Goodwin & Tabb/Novello; A-AMP

String Quartet No. 2 in F (1947)
Dur: 29'
f.p.   Kathleen Sturdy String Quartet - Wigmore Hall, London, 6 October 1948
f.broad.p. MacGibbon String Quartet - 9 June 1959

Concerto in D for string orchestra (1947-48)
Commissioned by the South American division of the BBC Overseas Service.
Dur: 13'30"
f.p.   BBC Overseas Service (?) 1948
f.conc.p.   London Philharmonic Orchestra/Sir Adrian Boult - Winter Gardens, Malvern,
            Worcs. 5 June 1951 (Malvern Festival)

Oboe Quartet (1948)
Written for Léon Goossens and the Carter String Trio and dedicated to them.
Dur: 17'
Instr: Ob. Vn. Va. Vc.
f.p.   Léon Goossen (Ob.)/Carter String Trio - Mary Carter (Vn.), Anatole Mines
            (Va.), Antonia Butler (Vc) - Cambridge, 1 December 1950 (Thursday
            Concerts series)
f.Lon.p.   above artists - RBA Galleries, London, 12 December 1950 (LCMC Concert)
f.rec.   Roger Lord (Ob.)/Roger Garland (Vn.)/Andrew McGee (Va.)/Roger Smith
            (Vc.) - *Meridian E 77064*
Pub: Novello, 1956

Piano Quartet in A (1948-49)
Commissioned by Patrick Hadley for the Cambridge Summer Festival
Dur: 27'
Instr: Pno. Vn. Va. Vc.
f.p.   Alan Richardson (Pno.)/Aeolian String Quartet - St. John's College,
            Cambridge, 11 August 1949 (Cambridge Summer Festival)

Rain - song for voice and piano(1949)
[Words: W.R. Morrison]
Dur: 2'

Mary Barton - opera in a Prologue and 3 Acts (1949-54)
[Libretto: Arthur Rathkey - based on the novel by Mrs. Gaskell.]

Entered for the Arts Council sponsored opera competition. The scene is set in Manchester in 1840 at the time of the Chartist movement.

Dur: 180′
Instr: 2/2/2/2 - 4/3/3/1 - timp. perc. str.
Prelude and Interlude from above:
Dur: 7′
Instr: 2/2/2/2 - 4/3/3/1 - timp. perc. str.

String Trio in B flat (1950)
Written for the Carter String Trio and dedicated to them.
Dur: 16′30″
Instr: Vn. Va. Vc.
f.p.   Carter String Trio - Cambridge, January 1952
f.broad.p   above artists - 2 July 1952
Pub: Novello, 1951

Rondo in B flat for horn and piano (1950)
Written at the request of Schott, the publishers.
Dur: 3′30″
f.recs.   Ifor James (Hn.)/John McCabe (Pno.) - *Phoenix DGS 1020*
            Frank Lloyd (Hn.)/Roger Vignoles (Pno.) - *Merlin MRFD 92092(CD)*
Pub: Schott, 1952

Violin Sonata No. 2 in A (1951)
Commissioned by Gerard Heller for Rosemary Rapaport and Else Cross
Dur: 21′30″
f.p.   Rosemary Rapaport (Vn.)/Else Cross (Pno.) - Wigmore Hall, London,
            17 May 1951
f.broad.p. Yfrah Neaman (Vn.)/Howard Ferguson (Pno.) - 31 July 1953
Pub: Novello, 1961

Lord, Thou hast been our refuge - motet for unaccompanied chorus (1952)
[From Psalms 90 and 81]
Dur: 10′
f.p.   Leeds Philharmonic Society Choir/Allan Wicks - Hovingham Hall,
            25/27 July 1952 (Hovingham Festival)
f.broad.p. BBC Midland Chorus - 15 June 1953
Pub: OUP, 1953   A-AMP

Concerto for oboe and string orchestra (1953-54)
Written for Léon Goossens
Dur: 21′
f.p.   Léon Goossens/Jacques String Orchestra/Reginald Jacques - Cambridge,
            6 August 1954 (Cambridge Festival)
f.Lon.p.   Léon Goossens/Royal Philharmonic Orchestra/Basil Cameron - Royal Albert
            Hall, 5 August 1955 (Promenade Concert)
f.Eur.p.   Léon Goossens/Moscow State Symphony Orchestra/Clarence Raybould -
            Tchaikovsky Hall, Moscow, 19 April 1956
Pub: Novello, 1956

Sinfonietta for chamber orchestra (1954)
Written for the Macnaghten Concerts
Dur: 25'
Instr: 1/1/1/1 - 1/1/0/0 - str. (2/1/1/1)
f.p.   Lemare Chamber Orchestra/Iris Lemare - Arts Council Drawing Room,
            London, 16 May 1955 (Macnaghten Concert)
Pub: Belwyn-Mills, 1961

This Worlde's Joie - song for solo tenor (1954)
Written for Peter Pears for a competition initiated by him.
Dur: 3'30"
f.priv.p.   Peter Pears - Morley College, London, 22 December 1954
f.pub.p.   Peter Pears - Parish Church, Aldeburgh, 24 June 1955 (Aldeburgh Festival)

Arioso and Scherzo - Horn Quintet (1955)
Written for Dennis Brain and the Carter String Trio at the suggestion of
Mrs. Hackforth, the wife of a Cambridge don and organiser of the Thursday Concerts
Society
Dur: 9'
Instr: Hn. Vn. Va. Va. Vc. (the same scoring as Mozart's Horn Quintet K.407)
f.p.   Dennis Brain (Hn.)/Carter String Trio and Marjorie Lempfert (Va.)
            Cambridge 1955 (Thursday Concert Series).
f.Lon.p.   above artists - Wigmore Hall, 26 May 1956
f.broad.p. above artists - 3 November 1956
Alternative version arranged at the suggestion of Dennis Brain
Instr: Hn. Vn. Pno.

Concerto for clarinet and string orchestra (1955-56)
Dedicated to William Morrison
Dur: 25'
f.p.   Gervase de Peyer/Goldsborough Orchestra/Charles Mackerras - Cheltenham,
            11 July 1957 (Cheltenham Festival)
Pub: Novello, 1964 (also arr. clarinet and piano)

Nocturnes: Five Songs for soprano, horn and piano (1956)
[1. The Moon (Shelley) 2. Returning, we hear the larks (Isaac Rosenberg)
 3. River Roses (D.H. Lawrence) 4. The Owl (Tennyson)
 5. Boat Song (John Davidson)]
Written at the request of Sophie Wyss
Dur: 12'
f.p.   Sophie Wyss (Sop.)/John Burden (Hn.)/Ruth Dyson (Pno.) - Arts Council
            Drawing Room, London, 19 March 1956 (Macnaghten Concert)
f.broad.p. Sophie Wyss (Sop.)/John Burden (Hn.)/Clifton Helliwell (Pno) -
            22 May 1957
f.rec.   Jean Danton (Sop.) - *Albany TROY 264(CD)*
Pub: OUP, 1963

Flute Sonatina (1956 rev. 1961)
Dur: 10'

f.p.   Mary Benchley (Fl.)/Mary Hicks (Pno.) - July 1964 (Ashwell Festival)
f.broad.p. Harold Clarke (Fl.)/Hubert Dawkes (Pno.) - Third Programme,
            24 November 1964
Pub: OUP, 1964

Concerto for treble recorder (or flute) and string orchestra (1956-57)
Written for Philip Rodgers
Dur: 15'
f.p.   Philip Rodgers/Radio Hilversum, 1 October 1957
f.Brit.broad.p. Philip Rodgers/BBC Midland Orchestra/Leo Wurmser -
            16 March 1959
Pub: Schott, 1957 (arr. treble recorder and piano)

Three Songs of Innocence for soprano, clarinet and piano (1957)
[Words: William Blake 1. Piping down the Valleys Wild 2. The Shepherd
3. The Echoing Green]
Written for the Clarion Trio
Dur: 6'30"
f.p.   Clarion Trio - Jean Broadley (Sop.)/Pamela Weston (Cl.)/Eileen Nugent
            (Pno.) - 26 November 1957
f.broad.p. Clarion Trio - 27 March 1959
f.recs.   Sylvie Eaves (Sop.)/Thea King (Cl.)/Courtney Kenney (Pno.)- *Cameo Class
            GOCLP 9020*
            Jean Danton (Sop.) - *Albany TROY 264(CD)*
Pub: OUP, 1960

Oboe Sonata (1957)
Written for Léon Goossens
Dur: 20'
f.p.   Léon Goossens (Ob.) - Cambridge, 1958 (Cambridge Festival)
f.broad.p. Léon Goossens (Ob.)/Clifton Helliwell (Pno.) - 19 February 1959
Pub: Novello, 1963

Little Suite for flute and viola (1957)
Dur: 9'30"
Pub: Schott; A-AMP

Scherzo for piano (1957)
Dur: 3'30"
Pub: Novello, 1960

Two Pieces for piano (1957)
[1. Dance of the Puppets 2. Pastorale]
Dur: 4'
Pub: Ricordi, 1959 (`Modern Festival Pieces')

Suite for three clarinets (1958)
Dur: 9'
f.p.   Stephen Waters/Archibald Jacobi/Basil Tchaikov - 17 October 1959

f.rec.   Daphne Down/Thea King/Georgina Dobree - *Chantry CHT 004*
Pub: OUP, 1959; Emerson, 1989

Violin Concerto (1958)
Dedicated to Yfrah Neaman
Dur: 27'
Instr: 2/2/2/2 - 4/3/3/0(1) - timp. perc. hp. cel. str.
f.p.   Yfrah Neaman/Hallé Orchestra/Sir John Barbirolli - Cheltenham Town Hall,
            7 July 1959 (Cheltenham Festival)
f.broad.p. above artists - BBC Overseas Service, 25 October 1959
f.Brit.broad.p. above artists - Home Service, 22 January 1960
Pub: Novello

Clarinet Sonata in B flat (1959)
Commissioned by the Hampton Music Club for Thea King
Dur: 20'
f.p.   Thea King (Cl.)/James Gibb (Pno.) - Arts Council Drawing Room, London,
            13 March 1959
f.broad.p. above artists - 17 March 1960
f.rec.   Thea King (Cl.)/Clifford Benson (Pno.) - *Hyperion CDA 66044(CD)*
Pub: Novello, 1962

Three Elizabethan Love Songs for tenor and guitar (1959)
[1. Lullaby of a lover (George Gascoigne) 2. Love is a sickness (Samuel Daniel)
 3. A song of comparisons (Anon)]
Written for Wilfred Brown and John Williams
Dur: 10'
f.p.   Wilfred Brown (Ten.)/John Williams (Gtr.) - Wigmore Hall, London, 1960
f.broad.p. above artists - 12 April 1962

Five part-songs for SATB unaccompanied chorus (1959)
[1. Dawn (John Ford) 2. Hey Nonny No! (Anon)
 3. Hymn in praise of Neptune (Thomas Campion)
 4. Fall leaves, Fall (Emily Bronte) 5. God Lyaeus (John Fletcher)]
Written at the request of Novello, the publishers
Dur: 10'
Pub: Novello, 1959, 1960, 1961

Divertimento for treble recorder and string quartet (1959)
Written for Carl Dolmetsch
Dur: 10'30"
Instr: Tr.rec. Vn. Vn. Va. Vc.
f.p.   Carl Dolmetsch (Tr.rec.)/Aeolian String Quartet - Wigmore Hall, London,
            8 February 1960
f.broad.p. above artists - 19 September 1960
Pub: A-AMP

Jabez and the Devil - ballet (1959)
[Based on a story by Stephen Vincent Benet `The Devil and Daniel Webster']

Commissioned by the Royal Ballet at the suggestion of Denis ApIvor.

Dur: c.45'
Instr: 2/2/2/2 - 4/3/3/1 - timp. perc. bells hp. xyl. str.
f.p.   Royal Ballet cond. John Lanchberry - Royal Opera House, Covent Garden,
          15 September 1961
Choreography: Alfred Rodrigues
Scenery/Costumes: Isabel Lambert
Principals: Donald Macleary, Antoinette Sibley, Alexander Grant
Ballet Suite from the above (1961):
[1. Introduction - The Devil's Dance and Fiddle Polka 2. Waltz
3. Dance of the Devils 4. Slow Dance and Percussion Dance
5. Finale: Square Dance]
Dur: 17'
f.p.   London Philharmonic Orchestra/Basil Cameron - Royal Albert Hall, London,
          5 September 1962 (Promenade Concert)
f.rec.   London Philharmonic Orchestra/Nicholas Braithwaite - *Lyrita SRCS 78*
Pub: OUP, 1962

Concerto for small orchestra (1960)
Commissioned by the Bath Festival
Dur: 18'
Instr: 2/2/2/2 - 2/2/0/0 - timp. hp. str.
f.p.   Bath Festival Orchestra/Colin Davis - Bath, 20 May 1960 (Bath
          Festival)
Pub: Belwyn-Mills, 1961; Central Music Library, 1973

Two Carols (1961)
[1. O men from the fields 2. Three Wise Kings]
Dur: 3'
f.rec.   (No. 1) Bangor Grammar School Choir/Ian Hunter - *Abbey CAPS 402(MC)*
Pub: OUP

Wind Quintet (1961)
Commissioned by the BBC
Dur: 13'30"
Instr: Fl. Ob. Cl. Hn. Bsn.
f.p.   BBC Chamber Ensemble - Maida Vale Studios, London, 4 May 1961
          (BBC Thursday Concert)
Pub: Belwyn-Mills

Suite for recorder and piano (1961)
Dur: 9'30"
Pub: Schott

Psalm 96: 'O Sing unto the Lord' - anthem for SATB choir and organ (1961)
Commissioned for the St. Cecilia Day Service in 1961
Dur: 7'30"
Pub: Novello, 1961

Clarinet Quintet (1961-62)
Commissioned by the Lord Mayor of London for the first City of London Festival.
Dur: 15'
Instr: Cl. Vn. Vn. Va. Vc.
f.p.   Gervase de Peyer (Cl.)/Allegri String Quartet - 16 July 1962
            (City of London Festival)
f.broad.p. above artists - 18 January 1963
f.rec.   Thea King (Cl.)/Britten String Quartet - *Hyperion CDA 66428(CD)*
Pub: OUP

Prelude, Intermezzo and Finale for organ (1962)
Dur: 8'30"
Pub: Novello, A-AMP

Sonata for oboe and harpsichord (or piano) (1962)
Written for Evelyn Rothwell and Valda Aveling
Dur: 18'
f.p.   Evelyn Rothwell (Ob.)/Valda Aveling (Hpschd.) - Huddersfield, 1962
f.Eur.p.   above artists - Hamburg Radio broadcast, 1963
f.broad.p. above artists - 26 February 1964
Pub: OUP, 1963

The Lord at first did Adam make - carol for SATB chorus and organ (1963)
Dur: 3'
Pub: Novello, 1963 ('Sing Nowell' album)

Symphony No. 2 in F (1963)
Dur: 32'
Instr: 2/2/2/2 - 4/3/3/1 - timp. perc. hp. 'str.
f.p.   Hallé Orchestra/Lawrence Leonard - Royal Festival Hall, London,
            29 January 1964
Pub: OUP, 1963; A-AMP

Ode on St. Cecilia's Day - cantata for soloists, chorus and orchestra (1964)
Dur: 35'
Instr: 2/2/2/2 - 4/3/3/1 - timp. perc. str. org.
f.p.   Cambridge, 20 February 1968
Pub: A-AMP

Loving Shepherd - anthem for choir and organ (1964)
Dur: 3'
Pub: Banks

Quartet for flute, clarinet, cello and piano (1964)
Commissioned by the Macnaghten Concerts
Dur: 17'
f.p.   Chantry Ensemble - Patricia Lynden (Fl.), Georgina Dobrée (Cl.), Margaret
            Moncrieff (Vc.), Alexander Kelly (Pno.) - Arts Council Drawing Room,
            London, 13 November 1965 (Macnaghten Concert)

Pub: A-AMP

Fantasia for organ (1964)
Commissioned by Peter Marr for the opening of a two-manual organ at St. Mary's
Church, Shinfield, Berkshire
Dur: 5'30"
f.p.   Peter Marr - St. Mary's Church, Shinfield, Berks, 19 September 1964
Pub: Hinrichsen; A-AMP

Quartet-Sonata (1964)
Written at the request of Carl Dolmetsch and dedicated to the Dolmetsch- Schoenfeld
Ensemble
Dur: 12'30"
Instr: Rec. Vn. Vc. Hpschd.
f.p.   Dolmetsch-Schoenfeld Ensemble- Carl Dolmetsch (Rec.), Alice Shoenfeld
          (Vn.), Eleonore Shoenfeld (Vc.), Joseph Saxby (Hpschd.) - Wigmore Hall,
          London, 3 February 1965
f.broad.p. above artists - 19 July 1965
Pub: Schott

Suite for recorder quartet (1965)
Dur: 5'30"
Pub: Moeck Verlag

Piano Sonata No. 2 in B flat (1965)
Dur: 17'
f.p.   Rosemarie Wright - Cheltenham Town Hall, 5 July 1966 (Cheltenham
          Festival)
f.Lon.p. Richard Deering - Purcell Room, 30 May 1975 (at a concert celebrating the
          40th anniversary of the founding of the Composers' Guild)
Pub: A-AMP

Trio in E flat (1965)
Written for the Hilary Robinson Trio
Dur: 21'30"
Instr: Cl. Vc. Pno.
f.p.   Hilary Robinson Trio (Rachel Herbert, Hilary Robinson, Marion Hirst) -
          Wigmore Hall, London, 1966
f.broad.p. above artists - 20 August 1968
Pub: A-AMP

**Kleiner Gedichtkreis - Three Songs for baritone and instrumental
septet (1966)**
[Words: Rainer Maria Rilke
 1. Ueber die Quelle geneigt ach, wie schweigt Narziss.
 2. O wer die Leyer sich trach.
 3. Töpfer nun trüste, treib, treib deine Scheibe Lauf]
Dur: 8'30"
Instr: Fl. Cl. BCl. Hp. Vn. Va. Vc.

Song on May Morning for unaccompanied chorus (1966)
[John Milton]
Dur: 3'
Pub: Novello, 1967 (Musical Times supplement)

Serial Theme and Variations for recorder (1966)
Dur: 7'
Pub: Schott

Variations on a theme of Dufay for orchestra (1966)
Dedicated to the memory of the Indian scientist and artist Dr. Homi Bhabha who was
killed in a plane crash on Mont Blanc in January 1966. The theme is taken from Dufay's
3-part chanson "Ce Moys de May soyons lies et joyeux".
Dur: 18'
Instr: 2/2/2/2 - 4/3/3/1 - timp. perc. hp. cel. str.
f.p.   Royal Liverpool Philharmonic Orchestra/Sir Charles Groves - Royal Albert
          Hall, London, 25 July 1969 (Promenade Concert)
Pub: OUP

Toccata and Aria for organ (1966)
Commissioned by Peter Marr to mark the restoration of the organ at St. Giles, Reading,
and the centenary of the instrument's maintenance by
J.W. Walker Ltd.
Dur: 8'30"
f.p.   Peter Marr - St. Giles Church, Reading, 22 April 1967
Pub: A-AMP

Impromptu for organ (1966)
Dur: 2'30"
Pub: OUP

String Quartet No. 3 (1967)
Dur: 21'30"
f.p.   English String Quartet (Nona Liddell, Marilyn Taylor, Marjorie Lempfert,
          Helen Just) - BBC, 26 June 1968

Fugal Adventures for organ (1967)
Dur: 6'30"
Pub: A-AMP

Symphony No. 3 in D (1967)
Dur: 24'
Instr: 2/2/2/2 - 4/3/3/1 - timp. perc. str.
f.p.   London Philharmonic Orchestra/Nicholas Braithwaite - BBC, 1968
f.rec.   above artists - *Lyrita SRCS 78*
Pub: A-AMP

Six Country Songs for bass and piano (1968 rev. 1975)
[Words: Thomas Hardy

1. The Ballad Singer 2. Let me enjoy 3. The Fiddler
4. At Day-close in November 5. Julie Jane 6. Summer Schemes]
Dur: 12'
f.broad.p. Don Garrard (Bs.)/Geoffrey Parsons (Pno.) - 19 April 1979
Pub: A-AMP

Piano Quintet (1969)
Commissioned by the Faculty of Music of the University College of Wales, Cardiff for
the Cardiff Festival.
Dur: 24'
Instr: Pno. Vn. Vn. Va. Vc.
f.p.   Cardiff University Ensemble - Eric Harrison (Pno.), Alfred Wang (Vn.),
           James Barton (Vn.), Gordon Mutter (Va.), George Isaac (Vc.) - Cardiff
           University, 1970 (Cardiff Festival in conjunction with UCOW Cardiff)
f.Lon.p.   Cardiff University Ensemble - Purcell Room, 14 May 1971
f.broad.p. Iris Loveridge (Pno.)/Alberni String Quartet (Howard Davis, Peter Pople,
           Berian Evans, David Smith) - 5 March 1978

Sonata for solo violin (1969)
Commissioned by the Welsh Arts Council for the Cardiff Festival
Dur: 16'
f.p.   James Barton - Cardiff University, 1970 (Cardiff Festival)
Pub: Peters Edition, 1976

Pavane for flute and piano (1969)
Dur: 3'30"
Pub: OUP

Quartet for recorders (1970)
Dur: 12'30"
Instr: Desc. Treb. Ten. Bs.
Pub: Moeck Verlag

Trio for recorders (1970)
Dur: 11'
Instr: Desc. Treb. Ten.
Pub: Moeck Verlag

Festival Prelude for brass and percussion (1970)
Commissioned by the Cambridge Philharmonic Society
f.p.   Cambridge Philharmonic Society Ensemble/Hugh Macdonald - King's College
           Chapel, Cambridge, July 1970 (Cambridge Festival)

Harmonica Sonata (1970)
Written for Douglas Tate
Dur: 16'
f.broad.p. Douglas Tate (Harm.)/John Constable (Pno.) - 20 July 1975

Organ Sonata (1971)
Commissioned by Cardiff Arts Council for University College, Cardiff
Dur: 16'30"
f.p.   Richard Elfyn Jones - Music Department, University College, Cardiff,
            14 February 1973 (Cardiff Festival)
f.broad.p. William Minay - Radio 3, 31 March 1976
Pub: Peters Edition, 1973

Septet for clarinets (1971)
Commissioned by the London Clarinet Septet
Dur: 16'
f.p.   London Clarinet Septet, 1972
Pub: A-AMP
Alternative version:
Instr: Cl. Hn. Bsn. Vn. Va. Vc. Db.

Suite in C for recorder trio and harpsichord (1971)
Written for the Dolmetsch Consort at the suggestion of Carl Dolmetsch
Dur: 11'
Instr: Desc. Treb. Ten. Hpschd.
f.p.   Carl Dolmetsch Consort, (Jeanne, Marguerite and Carl Dolmetsch, Joseph
            Saxby) - Wigmore Hall, London, 1 March 1973
f.broad.p. Carl Dolmetsch Consort - 30 November 1976
Pub: Moeck Verlag

Intermezzo and Capriccio for harpsichord (1971)
Written for Joseph Saxby
Dur: 5'
f.p.   Joseph Saxby

York Suite for recorders and orchestra (1972)
Written for the Northern Recorder Course at York
Dur: 9'
Instr: timp. perc. str.
f.p.   St. John's College, York, April 1972

Sonatina for recorder trio (1972)
Dur: 6'15"
Instr: Sop. Alt. Ten.
Pub: Moeck Verlag

Cello Concerto (1972-73)
Commissioned by the BBC
Dur: 25'
Instr: 2/2/2/2 - 4/3/3/1 - timp. perc. cel. str.
f.p.   Thomas Igloi/BBC Symphony Orchestra/Sir Charles Groves - Royal Albert
            Hall, London, 6 August 1975 (Promenade Concert)
Pub: Novello

Symphony No. 4 in E flat (1974)
Commissioned by the Royal Philharmonic Society for its 163rd season.
Dur: 31'
Instr: 2/2/2/2 - 4/3/3/1 - timp. perc. str.
f.p.   BBC Symphony Orchestra/John Pritchard - Royal Festival Hall, London,
           15 January 1975 (Royal Philharmonic Society Concert)
Pub: A-AMP

Divertimento (1974)
Written for and dedicated to the Carl Dolmetsch Ensemble
Dur: 18'
Instr: Fl. Ob. Vn. Vc. Pno.
Pub: A-AMP
Alternative version:
Instr: Desc.rec. Treb.rec. Vn. Vc. Hpschd.
f.p.   Carl Dolmetsch (Rec.)/Jeanne Dolmetsch (Rec.)/Bernard Partridge (Vn.)/John
           Stilwell (Vc.)/ Joseph Saxby (Hpschd.) - Wigmore Hall, London, 3 April 1975
Pub: A-AMP

Piano Suite No. 2 (1975)
Dur: 18'
f.p.   Richard Deering - Purcell Room, London, 20 May 1977
Pub: A-AMP

Variations on two Christmas carols for recorder trio (1975)
Dur: 3'30"
Instr: Sop. Alt. Ten.
Pub: Moeck Verlag

The Invisible Duke - comic opera in one Act (1975-76)
Dur: 45'
Instr: 2/2/2/2 - 4/3/3/1 - timp. perc. hp. cel. xyl. str.

A Jacobean Suite for unaccompanied SATB chorus (1976)
[1. A Hymn to the Muses (Robert Herrick) 2. Sweet Content (Thomas Dekker)
 3. Virtue (George Herbert) 4. The Life of Man (Henry King)
 5. False Astronomy (Nicholas Breton) 6. The True Perfection (Ben Jonson)
 7. Winter Nights (Thomas Campion)]
Dur: 18'
f.p.   St. Alban's Chamber Choir - Purcell Room, London, 14 November 1976
           Pub: A-AMP

String Quartet No. 4 (1976)
Dur: 24'
f.p.   Delmé Quartet (Galina Solodchin, David Ogden, John Underwood,   Stephen
           Orton) - BBC Radio 3, 18 July 1978

Quartet for clarinets (1977)
Written for a clarinet group at Huddersfield Polytechnic

Dur: 15'
Pub: Emerson, 1983

Quartet No. 2 for recorders (1977)
Dur: 17'
Instr: Sop. Alt. Ten. Bass
Pub: Moeck Verlag

String Quartet No. 5 (1978)
Commissioned by Ticehurst Music Club for the Bochmann String Quartet with funds
provided by South-East Arts.
Dur: 10'
f.p.   Bochmann String Quartet - Ticehurst, 1980
Pub: A-AMP

Suite for three viols (1978-79)
Written for and dedicated to Carl, Jeanne and Margeurite Dolmetsch
Dur: 12'
f.p.   Dolmetsch Ensemble - Haslemere, 24 July 1981 (Haslemere Festival)
Pub: A-AMP

Symphony No. 5 in G (1978-79)
Dur: 35'
Instr: 2/2/2/2 - 4/3/3/1 - timp. perc. str.
f.p.   BBC Northern Symphony Orchestra/Bernard Keeffe - BBC New Broadcasting
           House, Manchester, 28 January 1981
f.broad.p. above artists - Radio 3, 28 March 1982
Pub: A-AMP

Prelude and Dance for clarinet and piano (1979)
Dur: 3'30"
Pub: Weinberger, 1980 (in `Jack Brymer Clarinet Series')

Invention for treble recorder (1979)
Dur: 10'
Pub: Moeck Verlag

Cello Sonata No. 2 (1979-80)
Dur: 27'30"
Pub: A-AMP

The Seamew for voice and chamber ensemble (1979-80)
[Words: Francis Loring]
Written for the baritone Francis Loring
Dur: 22'
Instr: Fl. Ob. Vn. Vn. Va. Vc.
f.p.   Francis Loring (Bar.) - Mayhurst, Sussex, 1 November 1981
f.rec.   Francis Loring (Bar.)/Roger Garland (Vn.)/Lynn Fletcher (Vn.)/ Andrew
           McGee (Va.)/Roger Smith (Vc.) - *Meridian E 77064*

Pub: A-AMP

Sonata No. 2 for organ (1981)
Dur: 16'
f.p.   William Minay - First Church of Christ Scientist, Edinburgh, September 1981
Pub: A-AMP

Psalms 19 and 100 - anthems for choir and organ (1981)
Dur: 10'
Pub: A-AMP

Clarinet Concerto No. 2 (1981-82)
Commissioned by Stephen Bennett
Dur: 25'
Instr: 2/2/0/2 - 4/2/0/0 - timp. perc. str.
f.p.   Stephen Bennett/BBC Philharmonic Orchestra/George Hurst - BBC
           Manchester, 8 February 1985
Pub: A-AMP

Piano Suite No. 3 (1982)
Dur: 12'
Pub: A-AMP

Symphony No. 6 (1983-84)
Dur: 31'30"
Instr: 2/2/2/2 - 4/3/3/1 - timp. perc. str.
Pub: A-AMP

Trio for oboe, clarinet and bassoon (1984)
Written for the London Wind Trio
Dur: 14'30"
f.p.   London Wind Trio - Neil Black (Ob.), Keith Puddy (Cl.), Roger Birstingl
           (Bsn.) - Oxford, Autumn 1985
f.broad.p. above artists - 18 June 1986
Pub: A-AMP

Repton Fantasia* for orchestra (1984)
Commissioned by the Repton Music Society in celebration of the opening of the new
Music School.
Dur: 14'
Instr: 2/2/2/2 - 4/3/3/1 - timp. perc. str.
f.p.   Repton School Orchestra - Repton, 28 June 1985
Pub: A-AMP
(* a set of variations on The Repton School Song, the hymn tune `Repton' and The
Pilgrim Hymn.)

Capriccio for recorder and piano (or harpsichord) (1985)
Written for William Alwyn's 80th birthday and dedicated to him.
Dur: 3'

f.p.   John Turner (Rec.)/Peter Lawson (Pno.) - BBC Radio 3, 13 October 1985
           (broadcast as a tribute to William Alwyn who had died on 11 September
           1985)
f.conc.p. John Turner (Rec.)/Stephen Reynolds (Pno.) - Woodbridge School,
           Woodbridge, Suffolk, 25 October 1985 (Mercia Music Concert)
Pub: Forsyth Bros. (Manchester)

Sonatina for alto flute and piano (1985)
Written for Mary Benchley
Dur: 14'30"
f.p.   Mary Benchley (AFl.)/Peter Sanders (Pno.) - Little Benslow Hills, Hitchin,
           21 September 1986
Pub: A-AMP

Concerto for orchestra (1986)
[1. Fanfares 2. Elegy 3. Scherzo 4. Finale]
Dur: 25'
Instr: 2/2/2/2 - 4/3/3/1 - timp. perc. str.
f.p.   BBC Philharmonic Orchestra/Bryden Thomson - Free Trade Hall, Manchester,
           8 December 1987
f.broad.p. above artists - 1 February 1988 (rec. 7 December 1987)
Pub: Novello

Arietta for piano (1986)
Dur: 1'20"

Arietta for recorder and piano (1986)
Dur: 1'20"
f.p.   John Turner (Rec.)/Peter Lawson (Pno.) - BBC Radio 3, 4 November 1986
           (in a broadcast celebrating the composer's 80th birthday)
Pub: Forsyth Bros. (Manchester) in `A Birthday Album for the Society of Recorder
           Players', 1986

Little Suite for solo recorder (1987)
[1. Intrada 2. Sarabande 3. Badinerie]
Written for and dedicated to John Turner
Dur: 5'30"
f.p.   John Turner - London College of Music, 3 November 1987
Pub: Forsyth Bros. (Manchester) (in `Pieces for Solo Recorder Vol. 2')

Sonata for bassoon and piano (1987)
Written for and dedicated to Roger Birnstingl
f.p.   Roger Birnstingl - BBC, 1988 (recorded December 1987)
f.conc.p. Roger Birnstingl - Royal Northern College of Music, Manchester,
           15 August 1989
f.rec.   David Baker (Bsn.)/Alan Cuckston (Pno.) - *Swinsty FEW 124 (MC)*
Pub: Emerson, 1988

Five Songs of William Blake for baritone, recorder and piano (1987)
[1. To Spring 2. Spring 3. To the Muses 4. Night 5. The Fly]
Written for John Powell, John Turner and Peter Lawson
Dur: 14'
f.p.   John Powell (Bar.)/John Turner (Rec.)/Peter Lawson (Pno.) - Manchester
           Royal Exchange Theatre, 3 March 1988 (Manchester Midday Concert)
Pub: Novello

Sonata for flute and harp (1987)
Dur: 15'
Pub: Emerson

Three Flower Songs for soprano and treble (sopranino) recorder (1987)
[Words: Robert Herrick 1. To Daffodils 2. To Blossoms 3. To Violets]
f.p.   Claire Daniels (Sop.)/John Turner (Rec.) - Ambleside Parish Church,
           3 August 1987 (Lake District Summer Music Concert)

Suite for organ (1990)
Written for Tudeley Parish Church, to celebrate their new organ.
Dur: 15'
f.p.   Stephen Bennett - Tudeley Parish Church, Five Oak Green, Tonbridge,
           Kent, 1990
Pub: Anglo-American Music Publishers (A-AMP)

Song of Innocence for soprano and recorder (1990s)
[Words: William Blake]
Written for Tracey Chadwell
f.p.   Alison Wells (Sop.)/John Turner (Rec.) - Wilmslow Parish Hall, Cheshire,
           26 October 1996 (Tracey Chadwell Memorial Concert)

Little Suite No. 2 for solo recorder (1993)
Written for John Turner

FILM MUSIC

Colorado Beetle (1948)

INCIDENTAL MUSIC

(a)   Radio

Njal's Saga (1947)
[1. The Death of Gunnar 2. The Burning of Njal]
Instr: 2/2/2/2 - 2/2/0/0 - timp. perc. str.
Music played by: Ensemble/Alan Rawsthorne (recorded 11/12 March 1947)

(b)   **Stage**

Peer Gynt (1932-33)
[Ibsen]
Written for performance at the Cambridge Festival Theatre.

The Merchant of Venice (1932-33)
[Shakespeare]
Written for performance at the Cambridge Festival Theatre.

Percussion accompaniment to a Greek play (1932-33)
Written for performance at the Cambridge Festival Theatre.

Pageant: Music for the People (1939)
Scenario: Randall Swingler
f.p.   People's Festival Wind Band/Alan Bush - Royal Albert Hall,
            London, 1 April 1939
(Cooke's contribution was an Introduction - other composers included
 Lutyens, Maconchy, Rawsthorne and Alan Bush q.v.)

The Masque of Schollers - Overture to a play (1957)
[Words: Eric Maschwitz]
Written for Repton School in celebration of the 400th anniversary of its
foundation*
Dur: 7'
Instr: 2/2/3/1 - 2/2/1/0 - timp. perc. org. str.
f.p.   Repton School Orchestra - Old Reptonian Weekend, Michaelmas
           Term, Repton 1958
(* the other composers were Norman Demuth and Jonathan Harvey - the latter
 was then a pupil at the school)

MS LOCATION

BPL   This Worlde's Joie (1954)
           Three Elizabethan Love Songs (1959)
           A Song of Comparisons (1959)

BIBLIOGRAPHY

Anon   **Arnold Cooke - list of published works.** Novello, 1982 rev. 1987

Arnell, Richard   **Arnold Cooke - a Birthday conversation.** Composer, No. 24,
                        Spring 1967

Clapham, J.   **Arnold Cooke's Symphony.** Music Review, Vol. 7, 1946

Clapham, J.   **Arnold Cooke: the achievement of twenty years.** Music Survey
                     Vol. 3, No. 4, 1951

Cooke, Arnold   **Paul Hindemith.** Music Survey, Vol. 2, 1949

Dawney, Michael   **Senior British Composers - 10, Arnold Cooke.** Composer No.
                     45, Autumn 1972

Loring, Francis   **Dr. Arnold Cooke.** British Music Society Newsletter No. 12,
                     January 1982

Routh, Francis   **Arnold Cooke.** in his 'Contemporary British Music', London:
                     MacDonald, 1972

Wetherell, Eric   **Arnold Cooke.** British Music Society Monograph No. 3, 1996

Title Index

1. JOHN ADDISON

Trio for oboe, clarinet and bassoon 2
Trumpet Concerto 1, 2
Twelfth Night 19
Two Times Two 12
Uncle, The 11
Variations for piano and orchestra 1
Way of the World, The 14
Wellington Suite 4
Workhouse Donkey, The 17

2. WILLIAM ALWYN

A.B.C.A. magazine series 45
Accident Service 46
Ad Infinitum 21
Africa Freed 45
Air Outpost 42
Alliance for Peace 49
An African in London 44
Aphrodite in Aulis 25
Approach to Science 48
April Morn 22
Architects of England 43
Armagh: City set on a Hill 57
Atlantic Trawler 46
Autumn Legend 35
Bach: Siciliano arr. 61
Ballade for viola and piano 23
Bath 42
Battle for Freedom, The 45
Bedevilled 53
Beethoven:Prelude and Fugue for strings
    arr. 61, 62
Behind the Scenes 43
Bhairvi 23
Big City, The 43
Birth of the Year, The 42
Black on White 60
Black Tent, The 54
Blackdown 22
Border Weave 44
Boys of Wexford, The 62
Britain to America 56
Britain's our Doorstep 57
British News 44
By the Farmyard Gate 25
Captain Boycott 50
Card, The 52
Careerist, The 58

Carve her Name with Pride 54
Chaconne for Tom 41
Cherry Tree, The 31
Chimes, The 57
Christmas Journey 59
Citizens of Tomorrow 45
City Speaks, A 48
Clarinet Sonata 38
Colonel March of Scotland Yard 60
Commandos 56
Concerto for flute and wind 41
Concerto for oboe, harp and strings 31
Concerto Grosso No. 1 30
Concerto Grosso No. 2 32
Concerto Grosso No. 3 38
Conquest of the Air 42
Contes Barbares 24
Coronation Day Across the World 59
Country Town 47
Countrywomen, The 44
Crépuscule for harp 35
Cricketty Mill 26
Crimson Pirate, The 34, 52
Crown of the Year, The 44
Cure for Love, The 33, 51
Daybreak in Udi 48
Derby Day 37
Desert Victory 30, 45, 46
Devil's Bait 55
Divertimento for solo flute 29
Down by the Riverside 29
Drawn from Life 60
Each for All 48
Eight Irish Folk Tunes 62
Employment Exchange 47
Empty Sleeve, The 60
English Inn, The 44
English Overture 26
Escape 50
Escape to Danger 49
Ex-Corporal Wilf 57
Fairy Fiddler, The 21
Fallen Idol, The 32, 51
Fancy Free 22
Fanfare for a Joyful Occasion 36
Fanfare of Welcome 38
Fantasy - Waltzes 36
Farewell Companions 35
Festival in London 48

4. RICHARD ARNELL

5. MALCOLM ARNOLD

6. DON BANKS

7. STANLEY BATE

8. ARTHUR BENJAMIN

10. ARTHUR BLISS

11. BENJAMIN BRITTEN

12. ALAN BUSH

13. GEOFFREY BUSH

14. FRANCIS CHAGRIN

15. ARNOLD COOKE